The Forgotten Story
Marnie
Greek Fire

WINSTON GRAHAM

D1324289

CHAPMANS

Chapmans Publishers Ltd
141–143 Drury Lane
London WC2B 5TB

A CIP catalogue record for this book
is available from the British Library

ISBN 1 85592 074 3

This omnibus edition first published by Chapmans 1992

Typeset by Falcon Typographic Art Ltd, Fife, Scotland
Printed and bound in Great Britain by Clays Ltd, St Ives
plc

The Forgotten Story

Prologue

On a stretch of yellow sand on a beach of north Cornwall, just below Sawle cliffs, there lie the remains of a shipwreck.

Every tide submerges it; seas have dashed over it, men have come and gone, but something still survives: a few spars deeply overgrown with seaweed and mussels round which venturesome children sometimes play. Indeed, at dead low tide when a heavy ground swell has sucked away the sand it is possible to make out the way the vessel struck, broadside on, and to see the backbone and the iron ribs lying exposed among pools and dripping a little in the sun.

There are still some who remember the wreck and will tell you the date she came in, a handsome ship, on the ninth of December, 1898. But these have been years of flux in the village of Sawle; successive wars and depressions have seen rapid changes, and few are left to tell the tale. Even those who remain and remember find that no one is interested in something that happened in Victorian times. Their own children could not tell you anything: they are far too deeply involved in today to bother about the past. Although the information is still to be had for the asking, they do not ask and will not listen.

So with the instability of unaired memory, the facts themselves are harder to come by with each year that passes. You may learn the vessel's name – that she was registered at Falmouth, that she was carrying a mixed cargo and bound, some say, for Liverpool, that some of her crew were saved, though whether all or how many it is hard to recollect. Some will nod and draw at their pipes and tell you that there were passengers aboard, but of course they do not remember names or details.

1

For this information you may if you are curious turn up the files of the local paper and find a photograph of the ship and the bare bones of the story, just as the tide will ever and again draw back the sand from the bare bones of the wreck, like a wicked child pulling away a cover and saying with secret gloating: 'See what I did!'

But there is no flesh upon the bones, and for this it is better to rely upon what is still to be gathered in Sawle. There the men who remember will tell you that on the evening of December the eighth, 1898, a strong wind blew up round the coast and that before the night was far advanced the wind had reached the force of a heavy gale. In the morning, almost as the late dawn broke amid the scream of the wind, a farmer called Hoskin, out on the cliffs on business to do with his cattle, glanced out over the grey scud of the sea and saw, only just visible on the low horizon among the shifting mists of the morning, a sailing vessel driving before the gale.

One minute she was there, the next she was invisible again, her sails blown to shreds, her decks swept by the hurrying seas. But Hoskin had seen enough and, dog at heels, hurried across two fields, climbed a stone wall into a lane, and ran down the steep hill to where the sometime mining and fishing village slept in the fold of the hills with the wind roaring among its cottages and ruined chimney stacks.

Rousing the rocket crew was a matter of minutes, but by the time they had struggled up with their apparatus in the teeth of the wind upon the lower cliffs which guarded the entrance to Sawle she had already struck.

A boy named Coad saw her come in. One moment she was leaping and plunging like a horse among terriers, the next she had sharply stopped and was heeling over as if about to capsize. From the extremity of the swing she partly righted herself, and the great waves, unable to move her, began instead to smash into her exposed side, sending up fans of sea and spray.

Hardly able to see or speak for the wind, the rocket crew

dragged their gear to the nearest point on the cliffs, pushed it to the edge and fired their first rocket, carrying its thin lifeline over the broken sea towards the wreck.

Normally the distance would have been amply spanned, but so strong was the wind that the rocket fell into the sea some distance short. The crew wiped the spray from their faces and tried again. By now in the growing light it was possible to see figures clinging to the deck of the ship.

There was little time to spare if the rescuers were to be useful, and they fired two more rockets before deciding to wait upon some slackening of the wind. But the gale, though often rising to new heights, seldom dropped below a constant pitch of fury, and although they chose the best moment of the morning the line again fell short.

Helpless now, while others from the village came on the scene, they watched the ship settle in the water. All around them the rocks were grey with flying scud, and now and then a back-wash from a returning wave would sweep the slanting deck. Almost everything had been carried away – but the tiny figures still clung there mutely appealing for help.

Then one of these figures was seen to crawl away from the poop and work his way towards the bows.

'Thur's a fool thinks he's going to swim ashore,' said the leader of the rocket crew. 'Fire another rocket, Joe; try an' stop 'im; he'll not go to save 'imself that way.'

Another rocket hissed and sputtered away from the cliffs. One or two of the men made gestures at the ship, but before any more could be done the figure in the bows of the ship had slipped over the side. A wave hit the vessel and everything upon it was hidden from view in an explosion of white and green water; the mist and spray from this was blown across to the watchers and some minutes passed before one of them shouted and pointed with a gnarled finger at the sea some distance from the wreck.

A head could be seen bobbing and disappearing on the bubbling crest of a great wave. They caught sight of the swimmer again two minutes later. He was being swept towards Angader Rock, which barred the entrance to Sawle Cove. But he was not seen again. Men do not live in Cornish seas when a gale is calling the tune. The watchers cursed in broken snatches and strained their eyes towards the wreck.

Then one shouted: 'Try Sawle Point. Can't we get the gear down thur; the wind'll be abeam of us.'

With sweat mingling on their foreheads with the spray, they hauled their tackle away from the cliffs, dragged it round the edge of Trelasky Cove and with a clumsy impatient care began to half-haul, half-lower it towards the edge of Sawle Point.

The seas were breaking over this, but as the point lay almost due west of the ship they would no longer be firing into the wind but across it. Slipping and sliding in their haste, hobnailed boots sparking on the rock, they set up their gear and prepared to fire their next rocket.

From here the ship lay pointing north-east with her stern towards them; the angle of her deck was acute, her masts reaching towards a gleam of yellow sunlight among the racing clouds. Her mizzen mast was at a greater angle than the other two.

They fired the first rocket well out to sea and away from the ship, and there was a moment's silence and then a cracked cheer as the line was seen to have been blown full across the poop. All along the cliffs people waved and opened their mouths in sounds which were lost as soon as uttered.

One of the figures on the ship snatched at the line as it passed him and quickly made it fast.

Now began the task of paying out by means of this thin rocket line first the whip, which was an endless rope much thicker than the line and had to be secured to the main mast, then the hawser, and finally the breeches buoy.

You may still hear all this from the lips of a man who saw it. You will be told that just for a moment when the mizzen mast collapsed it looked as if the breeches buoy would be carried away, with only two of the crew rescued.

4

You will be told what happened when the survivors came ashore, of the efforts of the Sawle people to provide them with dry clothing and food, of how some of them were accommodated at the Tavern Inn and others in the cottages near.

But from that point the account becomes vague. Even though he remembers the sensation which shortly followed the rescue, a sensation which set it apart from all other wrecks of the century, the shipwreck is still the main concern of the narrator. This much he saw; the rest he read about. At the time it was a topic on everyone's lips; but lips and ears are not eyes, which take the lasting impressions.

Turn up the newspapers of a few weeks later and you will find that much was written in them on this later sensation. But reading the faded pages, one is struck once again by a sense of inadequacy, of seeing the bare bones of the events and being not quite able to imagine the flesh which hung upon them. This person lived and that person died, this woman made a public statement to the press, that woman left the country quietly and was hardly heard of again. Like palaeontologists trying to reconstruct an extinct animal we patiently fit the pieces into place and from them build up a probable structure which will pass for the real thing. At heart, though, it is artificial, an inverted creation, reaching from the overt acts back to the unstated reasons and not growing, as life grows, from the need to the wish, from the desire to the intention, from the reason to the act.

In Sawle, therefore, the curious will find something at once to excite their interest and to frustrate it. A description of a shipwreck and the shadowy outlines of something more. The spectre of human hopes, defeated or fulfilled and now forgotten, the shadows of human conflict and affection, generosity and greed, must stalk sometimes on December nights over the remains of the wreck.

To this the newspaper, crackling as we turn its pages, can only add a faded epilogue.

But further inquiry is not as fruitless as it might appear. Still living in another part of the world are people who remember these events because they were an intimate part of them, who perhaps cannot tell you the end, for their own lives are not yet ended, but can, if you get them in the right mood, explain exactly how it all began.

Book 1

1

On a sunny afternoon in mid-June 1898, a train drew into Falmouth Station, and among the few passengers who alighted was a boy of eleven.

He was tall for his age, reedy of build, with a shock of fair hair, good open blue eyes and a clean skin. He was dressed in a brown corduroy suit, obviously his best, and a wide new Eton collar with a bow tie. In one hand he carried a cloth cap, in the other a wicker travelling bag secured by clasps at the top and bound by a leather strap.

He stood there irresolute, blinking a moment at the stationmaster, who had taken off his silk hat to mop his damp forehead in the sun, then followed the other passengers to the ticket barrier.

Just outside the barrier, eyeing the outcoming passengers with a purposive gaze, was a tall girl of about nineteen. Occasionally she would put up a hand to steady her wide-brimmed hat against the wind. When the boy passed through the barrier she took one more glance up the platform and then stepped forward.

'Are you Anthony?' she asked.

He stopped in some surprise, changed hands with his bag and then set it down and blushed.

'Are you Cousin Patricia?' It was noticeable that their voices had a resemblance, his low but not yet beginning to break, hers contralto and of the same timbre.

'I am,' she said. 'You look surprised. Did you not expect someone would meet you? Come along. This way. The train was late.'

He followed her down towards the town and presently fell into step beside her on the pavement, darting glances about him, towards the crowded harbour and the noisy docks, and the tall chimney of the sawmill, then sidelong at his companion who now was holding her hat all the time.

'So you're Cousin Anthony,' she said. 'How tall you are! I was looking for a *little* boy.' When he blushed again, 'Are you shy? Haven't you ever been on a journey by yourself before?'

'Yes,' he said stoutly. 'Often.' Which wasn't quite true. He had in fact never been to a seaport of this sort before. Born and bred on Exmoor, he had not even seen the sea for four years – almost a lifetime – and that had been no more than a glimpse from the top of a high cliff and upon a grey day. Today the harbour sparkled and shone. Ships of all sizes mingled bewilderingly in its blueness, and away to the east the lovely line of St Mawes Creek glittered in the sun. But this was not why he blushed.

'I was frightfully sorry to hear of Aunt Charlotte's death,' said the girl soberly – or at least with an attempt at soberness, for all her movements were instinct with the joy and vigour of life. She brightened up. 'What shall you do? Have you come to stay with us long? Joe will tell me nothing.'

'Joe?'

'Dad. Your Uncle Joe. Everyone calls him Joe. He's frightfully close about things.'

'Oh,' said Anthony. 'No. That is, I don't rightly know yet. Father wrote to Uncle Joe. He says it just means me staying here till he can make a home in Canada. Of course, I'd go out straight away, but father says where he is now isn't fit for children.'

'What's he doing?'

'Prospecting. He's been out two years, you know. Mother and me were going out as soon as he could make a home. Now, of course . . . it's all different.'

'Yes,' said Patricia, nodding sympathetically. 'Well, you must stay here and make your home with us.'

They walked on in silence. The memory of his dire misfortune cast a black shadow over Anthony's mind for some moments. Even yet he could not accustom his mind to the change. He still felt that his mother existed in this world, that she had gone away for a few weeks and would soon be back; already his mind was stored up with things he wanted to say to her, little questions he wished to ask, matters which had cropped up since her going and which seemed to need her personal attention. He felt mature and lonely. Nothing would ever be the same.

'Well,' said Patricia, lifting her skirt to step fastidiously across a littering of old cabbage stalks which someone had carelessly tipped, 'there's plenty to do here. Boating and fishing and helping in the house. I suppose you know we run a restaurant?'

Anthony nodded.

'There's always plenty going on at Joe's. Mind you, it's mainly an evening business; but there's always plenty to do during the day. If you can lend a hand you'll never need to feel in the way, even if your father won't have you for another couple of years. There's plenty of fun too. Look down there; that's Johnson's; our chief rival.'

Anthony peered down a narrow, dirty street leading to a quay. In doorways ill-clad urchins sat and played, but he could not make out anything which looked like a restaurant. The glance served to bring his attention back to his present surroundings, and especially to the girl at his side. Youth has the resilience of a young birch tree: you may bend it till its head touches the earth, but in a minute it will spring erect again, head to the sun and no thought of contact with the soil.

Anthony had been startled at the first sight of his cousin. She was wearing a high-necked white lace blouse with a fine white drill skirt and a wide-brimmed hat turned up at the side and trimmed with broad green velvet ribbon. In one green-gloved hand she carried a parasol. She was very pretty, with curly chestnut hair swept up from the ears, large expressive brown eyes and the complexion of an early peach. She was tall and slender and walked with a grace which was curiously interrupted at intervals by a sudden lifting upon the toes like a barely suppressed skip. She talked vivaciously to him – treating him as an equal – and bent her head graciously from time to time in acknowledgment of a greeting from some passing friend.

He noticed that many of the sailors, even those who did not know her, looked at her from across the street or glanced round as they passed. For sailors were prominent in this strange, exciting little town; dark men and lascars, Dutchmen and French. The whole town was different from any he had been in before: it was foreign and smelt of fish and seaweed and strong tobacco. It smelt of all sorts of things he had not smelt before; as they walked along amid the sun and shadow with the dust playing in whorls between the ramshackle houses his nostrils were assailed now with the odour of untended refuse from a squalid courtyard, now with the sudden strong smell of salt air and the sea. That fresh wind was like a purifier pushing through the slits of streets straight from the Channel and distant lands.

'I wonder if you'll ever have a stepmother?' said Patricia. 'I have, you know. Dad married again last year. My mother died two years ago, nearly.'

'I'm sorry,' said Anthony.

'Yes, it's never the same. Good afternoon, Mrs Penrose; breezy, isn't it? She's all right in her way – Aunt Madge, I mean – she looks after Dad, but not like Mother did. Dad doesn't love her: he married her because she was a good cook.'

For the second time Anthony felt faintly shocked. Patricia's outspokenness was something new to him and as fresh as the wind. A large fat seaman with some tattered gold braid round his cuffs stepped off the pavement to make way for them and beamed at the girl. Anthony stared away from the sea up, up a seemingly endless flight of stone steps climbing the hillside, with grey slate cottages running in uneven terraces from them. But Patricia's way was not up the steps. She still went on, along the endless winding main street which skirted the whole western part of the harbour. The wind was less boisterous here and the sun more strong, but she did not raise her parasol. He wondered if it was carried only for ornament, since the handle was so long and the silk cover really so small.

A plump little lady passed them and carefully averted her head.

'Is there anyone else lives with you?' Anthony ventured. 'I mean, I haven't any other cousins, have I?'

'No. There's Joe and Aunt Madge and me. Then there's Joe's brother, Uncle Perry. He came home from America last year. He's made money and is looking round for somewhere to retire; but he hasn't found anywhere yet. Then there's Fanny, the scullery maid . . . oh, and one or two others who're about, but they don't live in. Are you tired? Shall I give you a hand with that case?'

'Thanks, no,' said Anthony, overcome by the thought.

She did not in fact press for the honour. 'Well, we're nearly there. Just up this hill and down the other side.'

They climbed a short rise where the street became so narrow that the two sides seemed about to meet; the crooked bow windows of an antique shop peered fastidiously down upon two conger eels for sale on the marble slab opposite; then the street dropped again, and Patricia turned off down a short and precipitous side-way which stopped abruptly upon the brink of the harbour.

Here, above the door of the last building on the right, there was an old and weather-beaten signboard, sorely in need of a coat of paint. On this signboard was the simple legend: JOE VEAL'S.

2

You entered Smoky Joe's – as the café was universally called by its clientele – through a narrow shop door, and immediately encountered Smoky Joe himself. Indeed it was not physically possible to dine in the café, whether upstairs or down, without first coming into contact with the proprietor; for it was his unvarying custom to sit brandishing a carving knife and fork on the opposite side of the counter as you entered the narrow shop; and so belligerent was his look that no one had ever dared to pass closely by him without first learning what there was to eat and then ordering on the spot the meal he wanted.

Spread on this counter were the viands which made up the choice. At one end there might be a roast turkey or a couple of chickens, with a huge leg of lamb and a piece of sirloin on succeeding dishes. Further down there was a choice of three or four kinds of pudding or tart steaming over an elaborate gas-ring.

The decision made, one could, if one wished, linger to see the portion cut off; one paid up, and the dishes were set aside to be taken into the kitchen where they were piled with vegetables and presently delivered to the customer wherever he had taken his seat.

The system was a good one. Bad debts were never incurred, complaints seldom; and so succulent was the aspect and smell of the dishes on the counter when one entered that scarcely anyone was ever put off by the gruff and grudging manner of the Tyrant with the carving knife.

In appearance Joe was short and thin with a pale slate-grey complexion and eyes like a small black terrier. His heavy black moustache drooped over a mouth which was at once obstinate and astute. In the shop he always wore a dark alpaca coat the length of a frock coat and a high wrap-round collar with scarcely any tie.

Anthony saw nothing of this on the afternoon of his arrival, for he was ushered down some steps and by a back door into a big low kitchen, where a thin red-faced girl not much older than himself was trying half-heartedly to tidy up the disorder, and a big woman with a distasteful expression was making pastry.

Aunt Madge was a disappointment. This lovely creature who had escorted him all the way from the station, talking cheerfully to him as if they were old friends, had warmed

14

and brightened his heart. He had forgotten his tiredness, his loneliness, the fact that he was thirsty and hot. He had been uplifted in her company. Aunt Madge restored his perspective.

'Late,' she said. 'Have you been. Round the sea front, I thought. Pat, you should have . . . Fanny needed help. Take him to his bedroom. A cup of tea presently.'

Anthony found himself following Patricia up the stairs with an impression that he had not yet really met Aunt Madge at all. In the kitchen there had been a large rather over-dressed woman, a fleshy rather than a fat woman in early middle age, with fair hair going grey, with a pince-nez straddling a short nose, and a discontented mouth built upon a pedestal of chins. But he did not think she would recognise him again. Being introduced to her was like making an appointment with somebody who forgot to turn up.

These old black winding stairs with rickety banisters and creaking boards. They climbed half a flight and two full flights to an attic.

'You'll find yourself a bit at sea at first,' said Patricia, on whom her stepmother's welcome had left no impression. 'It's with being altered for the restaurant that has made the house confusing.'

She opened an old door and showed him into a bedroom with a ceiling which sloped three ways from a central part where it was possible to stand upright. There were all sorts of odd crossbeams. A large iron bedstead decorated with brass knobs was the chief article of furniture. The window was on floor level.

'You can see most of the harbour from here,' she said helpfully.

He went to the window and again his spirits began to rise. The view was fine.

'Thanks awfully . . . Patricia,' he said. 'You've been . . . Thanks awfully for meeting me at the station.'

'That's all right,' she said, pulling off her hat and shaking out her curls. She met his frank gaze and smiled. 'You'd do

15

the same for me. Tea in ten minutes. Don't wait for someone to shout, will you?'

She ran off down the stairs humming.

Tea was the one meal at which Joe Veal consented to sit down and partake of food in the bosom of his family. He never ate breakfast, and dinner and supper were served to him on a little table behind the counter of the shop where he could supervise the orderings and preferences of customers. But the café was usually empty about tea time; the trip-bell was set to work over the shop door, and Joe and his pipe came down into the kitchen to tea.

Anthony ate buttered scones and drank several cups of hot tea, and absorbed all the newness about him and glanced diffidently but candidly up at the faces of this family into which fate and unfair bereavement had suddenly thrown him. Two months ago he had been at school at Nuncanton in the Vale of Exmoor; he had taken his home and his existence for granted, accepting it as unthinkingly as he drew breath. Now he was here among this family of strangers – related to him perhaps, for Uncle Joe was his mother's brother-in-law – but still strangers, of a quantity and quality unknown.

Anthony instantly took a liking for Perry, Uncle Joe's brother. Uncle Perry was bigger and younger than the other man and had a jovial, rollicking air. He had strong black hair which he wore rather long, and a lock of it was inclined to fall across his forehead when he laughed. He had a plump fresh-complexioned face and roving black eyes. It was a face which might have belonged to a buccaneer.

Joe made very little of the boy by way of greeting. He took his strange square pipe from a corner of his mouth and said, 'Well, Anthony,' and shook hands with a jerky gesture like someone turning the handle of a door, then put his pipe back in its corner. Anthony thought he looked not unkind but over-busy about his own concerns, which was natural in a man with a restaurant to supervise. Anthony felt that he ought to offer some thanks for the hospitality which was being extended to him, but by the time he could muster a sentence the opportunity had passed.

16

Uncle Perry's greeting was different. He said, '*Houd vast*, now; so we've taken another hand aboard. Greetings, boy! I could do with a second mate.' He laughed as if he had made a joke and thrust back his hair and looked at Aunt Madge and laughed again.

And Aunt Madge, earringed and small-featured and monumental, went on pouring tea.

After the meal Anthony was left to wander about the building and to make himself at home. The building was old and ramshackle and as smoky as Joe himself. From the shop one went down five steps into the lower dining-room or up five steps into the one above. Both were square rooms with windows looking out upon the bay and very low black rafters which made tall men instinctively bend their heads. The one kitchen served both rooms by means of a manually operated dumb waiter. The family lived and fed mainly in this kitchen, but Mr and Mrs Veal had a private drawing-room next to their bedroom on the second floor. Besides these there was an office into which Joe retired from time to time and smoked his curious pipe and counted his gold.

As the evening advanced customers began to come in. Fat brokers from the town who knew where there was a good meal, Chinese dock hands, captains of casual tramp steamers, sailors out with their girls, passing travellers, local clerks and apprentices, Belgian fishermen. They varied from week to week as one ship left the port and another put in.

Anthony watched the rooms fill up in some astonishment. Everyone smoked, and very soon the atmosphere was thick and blue. Everyone talked and argued, and presently a man with one leg came in and sat in a corner and began to play an accordion. He did not play it loudly and the sound only just emerged from among the sea of voices, but there was something in the music which added a touch of colour to the room.

The boy from Exmoor could not get over the fact that he had come to live in such a place, which to him seemed to be

17

the height of the exotic, that *his* relatives owned and ran it. When Aunt Christine died two years ago his mother had come to Falmouth for the funeral. He could not understand why his mother had not come back to Nuncanton full of talk about this place.

Two boys of about seventeen dressed in white coats did the waiting: Patricia superintended and sometimes helped out whichever boy was busiest. Through the fog of smoke Anthony perceived that she was tremendously popular in this company. There was pleasure in merely watching her weave a way among the crowded tables. Anthony did not reason that the charm and piquancy which at a glance had subjugated a boy of eleven would be likely to have the same effect on hardened, weather-beaten men of fifty or sixty; had the thought occurred to him he would have felt it disgusting that old men should have any feelings at all. But he enjoyed her popularity without analysis of its causes.

There was great competition for her attention but no advantage taken of it when gained. Neither did it occur to the boy to see any connection between this good behaviour and the presence of the severe little man sitting in the shop with a carving knife.

Later in the evening, when the smoke in the restaurant was making his eyes prick and water, and when the clamour of dish washing in the scullery was no longer a novelty, Anthony moved hesitatingly towards the shop, found a vantage point, and watched fascinated the procedure by which each customer chose and paid for the food he was to eat.

In a lull Joe Veal saw the boy standing awkwardly in a corner, his rather scared, frank blue eyes taking everything in. He beckoned with a dripping carving fork, and Anthony came and stood by him and stared down at the almost empty dishes.

'Why don't you go to bed, boy? Too excited to be tired, I s'pose.'

'I'll go soon,' said Anthony. 'I thought perhaps you might want me. Do you – do you close soon?'

18

Smoky Joe showed a row of small, yellow, false teeth of which one had been filed away to provide a suitable lodgment for his pipe. It was not so much like a smile as a display of a set of coins.

'Close, boy? Not just yet awhile. In a trade like this you always have to remember you're the servant of the public, see? Can't just close and open when you want. Did Charlotte leave you any money?'

Anthony blinked. 'Mother? I don't rightly know, Uncle. Mr Parks, the solicitor, said something, but I didn't quite catch . . .'

Smoky Joe's pipe had a sudden downward curve an inch from his lip, and the queer, square bowl emitted smoke from opposite the top button of his waistcoat. He took this bent stem from his mouth and wiped his moustache with it.

'Never trust lawyers. Scum of the earth. The law's like a basket, full of holes; and it's the lawyers' job to find the holes and slip through them. Slippery, they are. There was one I knew in Java . . . This Parks, did he give you any money for yourself, eh?'

'Yes,' said Anthony, staring hard at the skeleton of a roast duck. 'Three pounds he gave me before I left. He said that he had come to some arrangement with –'

'Oh, some arrangement. Yes, some arrangement. That's lawyer talk. We want more plates, Fanny! You're slow with the plates! Lawyers are always coming to some arrangement.' Uncle Joe fastened his terrier-like eyes on the boy. 'Where is it?'

'What?'

'The three pounds the lawyer gave you. It isn't safe for a boy of your age to carry sov'rins loose in your pocket. Might lose them. I'll keep them for you.'

Anthony hesitated. 'There's only two now. I had to pay my railway fare.'

'Well, two, then,' said Joe Veal, holding out a dry and scaly hand. All his skin looked dry and mottled as if the natural oil had long perished from it.

19

Anthony felt in his jacket pocket and took out a purse. In it were two sovereigns, a shilling and a florin piece.

'I'll have those as well,' said Uncle Joe, taking all the coins and slipping them into a deep recess of his greasy waistcoat. He puffed at his pipe and stared meditatively at the boy for a moment. 'You're a big fellow for your age. Going to be a big man, I reckon. Is your father big?'

'Yes,' said Anthony.

'But, then, it don't signify. Look at me, I'm small. Your aunt was small. But Pat's shot up like a weed. Maybe we could make use of you in the restaurant, eh? How would you like that?'

'I think I should like it,' said Anthony. He put his empty purse back in his pocket.

'Wait,' said Joe. 'Don't ever let 'em say I was mean.' He put down his carving knife, reluctantly it seemed, and pressed some keys of the automatic till. There was a 'ping' and the drawer shot open. He took out twelve pennies and handed them to Anthony. 'There. That's pocket money. That'll do to buy sweets. You can spend that; different from a sov'rin. Make it last a month; then come to me for more.' His expression changed and his moustache bristled as two smart young seamen came into the shop, and said, 'Evenin', Joe.'

'No lamb,' was his belligerent reply. 'You're too late. There's a bit of beef left,' he admitted reluctantly. 'It's tough.'

Soon afterwards Anthony went to bed. He waved to Pat, who gave him a brief, brilliant, glinting smile which warmed his heart afresh; then he slowly climbed the two creaky flights of stairs and groped a way into the attic.

There was no candle in the room, but darkness had only just fallen, and he could see what was necessary by the loom of light in the west and the glitter of the first stars. From his window he could see the lights of Flushing across the creek and all the winking eyes of the ships, big and small, riding at anchor in the road-stead. The lower window would not open, but through the upper one came the strong smell of seaweed and tidal mud.

For a long time he knelt by the window absorbing the strangeness of the scene. He felt as if he were in a foreign land. But presently tiredness got the better of interest and he slowly undressed and said his prayers and climbed into bed. It was a large double bed, and once in it he was suddenly beset by loneliness and bereavement. Years ago he had slept in a bed like this, but beside him there had been the warmth and softness and all-including guardianship of his mother. Nothing then had been for him to do, to decide, to consider: it had been sufficient for him to *be*, to exist unthinkingly, in the aura of that loving, understanding, comforting protection.

Now he was alone in an alien world.

Much later he woke. He had been dreaming that someone was quarrelling violently, crying wild curses and threatening to come to blows. He had been dreaming too that someone played upon a piano and rough men sang jolly choruses. The sounds still seemed to echo in his ears.

Pitch dark and there was no means of telling the time. A soft summer wind soughed across the estuary.

He turned over and tried to go to sleep. Then a door banged and he sat up.

Silence had fallen again. He lay in bed and wished he was not such a baby, that such a waking in the middle of the night should make his heart beat faster.

Another door banged and there was the clatter of a pail. Then down in the very depths of the house, as if from the inmost recesses of its rickety old soul, someone began to sing:

'They heard the Black Hunter! and dr-read shook each mind;
Hearts sank that had never known fear-r;
They heard the Black Hunter's dr-read voice in the wind . . .'

21

It was a man's voice, quavering and drunken. Another door banged. Then came the sound of feet on the stairs.

The attic was the only room on this floor; it was really built into the roof. But the feet were on the flight of stairs lower down.

All the same Anthony wished there had been some means of locking his door.

All the sounds in this house seemed to echo; due perhaps to the way in which it was built about the well of the staircase. Anthony could hear the over-careful feet stumble against one of the steps and the curse which followed.

'Hearts sank that had never known fear-r. (Rot and blast the thing! Who left it lying about?)

'They heard the Black Hunter's dr-read voice in the wind!
They heard his cursed hell-hounds run yelping behind!
An' his steed thundered loud on the ear . . .'

Presently the drunken voice died away and silence reigned. In the distance the siren of a ship hooted. After a long time Anthony felt his muscles relax, and drowsiness crept quietly over him like an unreliable friend.

Later still he was awakened by hearing someone being violently sick.

3

Daylight brought a more homely aspect to his new domicile. From his window he saw that the tide was out, and many of the little boats loafed on their elbows in the mud. Seagulls crossed and recrossed the sky, flying lonely and remote as a cloud, wings scarcely moving, or suddenly darting down and fighting in a screaming, undignified pack for some morsel which one of their number had found. Two lighted on the flat end of the roof immediately below the attic window and side-stepped warily along to the corner piece. In the distance a small tramp steamer moved lazily out to sea.

Last night he had not put the twelve pennies Uncle Joe had given him into his purse, and this morning when he came to put on his trousers they fell out of his pocket with a clatter and rolled in all directions about the room. One had rolled beneath the bed and he pulled away the strip of carpet to get at it. As he retrieved it he was surprised to see a cork embedded in the floorboards.

Interested, he lifted up the valance and wriggled further under the bed amid the dust and fluff. Then he took out his penknife and with very little difficulty was able to pull the cork out. He put his eye to the hole which resulted and found himself looking down into the room below.

A small room, with a desk and a filing cabinet and an armchair. There was a pile of letters on the desk and newspapers and magazines on a chair. Tacked to the door was a nautical calendar.

He was suddenly afraid of being surprised in this prying position; he felt that someone was just about to enter his bedroom and find him there; he thrust back the cork and replaced the carpet and hurriedly resumed dressing.

When he went downstairs it was still early but he found Aunt Madge up and swatting flies. She seemed to have a particular aversion for them, for there were six flypapers hung about the kitchen. She was dressed in a pink kimono with lace and frills and ruches and long sleeves of which the wide lace cuffs were stained with bacon grease. On her head was a pink lace cap.

She looked at him from above her chins and evidently recognised him.

'Ah,' she said. 'You slept? Fanny's late. You could get . . . sticks for the fire.'

Under directions Anthony went out upon the stone-paved

23

quay, which was directly accessible from the kitchen door, and found a pile of driftwood and an axe. He began to chop up the wood. This was a job to which he could bring some skill, for he had always done it at home, though with good stately logs to work on, not miserable chunks of deal and pine, many of them half rotten with worm. He came on one spar which split into pieces at the first stroke and he found it honeycombed inside like a model of the catacombs. This idea so interested him that he went down on his knees to trace the burrowings more closely; and he was still there when Patricia came out.

'Good morning, Anthony. Did you sleep well? Have you got some sticks? Madge seems to be in one of her moods this morning.'

She was wearing a pretty black and white striped apron drawn in at the waist with a big bow at the back, over a simple high-necked blouse and dark skirt.

'Look at this,' he said. 'Isn't it pretty? What's made it like this?'

'Barnacles. Haven't you ever seen them?'

'No.'

'They're big black worms with heads like mussel-shells and long ferny red tongues. The sort of thing you see in a nightmare. But Madge'll start reading you a sermon if she doesn't get her fire soon.'

Breakfast was a feminine meal. Neither Perry nor Joe put in an appearance. Little Fanny arrived down red-eyed and weary as the meal was about to begin, and Anthony saw what Aunt Madge's sermon was like when directed at someone else.

She did not show any signs of anger. Seated in immobile serenity with a cup of tea steered unerringly from time to time to the plump little opening from which emerged so much sound, she talked on and on at Fanny in a pained rather hoarse voice with majesty and persistence. Sometimes she put an *H* in front of a word to give extra emphasis. Having said what she had to say, she shook her earrings, adjusted her pince-nez, and started anew. Finally

24

Fanny burst into tears and went breakfastless to brush out the upper restaurant.

At this Aunt Madge turned up her eyes as if in surprise at a rebuff, and poured herself another cup of tea. She had a peculiar habit of putting her eyes away under her small lids as if she were withdrawing them for inner consultation.

'Girls,' she said to nobody. 'Difficult. Can't reason with. Hi try to be patient, to *lead* . . .'

Anthony was kept busy all the morning. Uncle Joe appeared, wizened and sallow, about eleven, Uncle Perry, dark-eyed and plump-faced and laughing, an hour later. Before lunch Anthony went shopping with Patricia. When it was done she hired a landau and took the boy along the sea front, past the new houses shining in the sun. The ride was in the best possible style. Pat prudently dismissed the landau a hundred yards or so from JOE VEAL'S and they reached home in time for the midday meal.

Mrs Veal clearly suspected that they had been up to no good; she went round and round the subject while she was dishing out the stew, but they gave her no satisfaction. Finally Uncle Perry diverted her by launching into a long account of what had happened to him once in the Barbados, and Patricia caught her cousin's eye and winked.

The Barbados story went on indefinitely. At least, thought Anthony, Aunt Madge can cook. I shan't starve in this house. 'Yes,' he said to Uncle Perry, with his mouth full. 'No,' he said, taking another piece of home-made bread to wipe up the gravy. And, 'Fancy,' he said, leaning back and wondering if the pudding would be as good.

'Fanny,' said Aunt Madge, and waved an ostentatious hand. 'See if Mr Veal . . .' She smoothed down the geometrical frills of her yellow silk blouse and adjusted her pince-nez to look at Patricia. 'Hubby called this morning.'

For the first time Anthony saw the girl's face lose its soft contours; colour moved across her neck and cheeks.

'What did he want?' Her voice was brittle and calm.

'Wanted to see you, of course. I told him you weren't . . .

25

Pity, I think.' She glanced at the plate Fanny had brought back. 'Mr Veal hasn't eaten . . .'

'Mr Veal says he don't want any pudding, mum. An' he says two Roast Porks have gone upstairs, an' these are the plates.'

'I'll do them,' said Pat, rising. It seemed as if she welcomed the opportunity of movement.

Anthony was served with steaming hot lemon pudding with treacle sauce. For the moment he could not touch it.

Patricia returned to the table. 'If he thinks I'm going back,' she said, still in the same brittle voice, 'he's mistaken.'

Anthony slowly moved his eyes to her left hand. On the third finger there was a gold ring.

'Think you ought,' said Mrs Veal. 'Marriage vows. Taking these things lightly.'

Patricia poured herself some water. 'It's my own life, and I – don't want to live it with him. Why should I always go on paying for one mistake?'

'Hi don't approve.' Anthony suddenly found himself under Mrs Veal's gaze. Her pince-nez had slipped a little and her eyes were looking over the top like unmuzzled guns. 'Not eating pudding. Young boys not saucy.'

He hastened to eat several mouthfuls. Hours he had been in Pat's company and never noticed that ring. It shouldn't have made any difference, but in fact just at the moment it seemed as if nothing would ever be the same again. He was suffering the shock of broken puppy dreams.

'Three weeks,' said Aunt Madge. 'No time. After a good trial . . .'

'What did he say?'

'He said, "Good morning, Mrs Veal," he said, "I want to see Patricia." Into the kitchen quite sudden. The pork. Almost burned. "Marriage vows," I said. "Mr Harris, I don't approve. Made in the sight of God."'

'You'd no business to take his side against me,' Patricia said quietly. 'You shouldn't have given him encouragement.'

26

'There, there,' said Uncle Perry. 'It isn't as if anyone was going to make you go back.'

'I don't see why they should try,' Pat said mutinously.

'More pudding, Perry,' said Aunt Madge. 'Manners at the table . . .' Her chins went up and down as she ate some cheese. 'Those flies. In from the river.'

'Marriage should be like it is in the Pacific Islands,' said Uncle Perry. 'If you fancy someone there you just have a tribal dance.' He laughed infectiously.

'Perry . . . Please.'

Uncle Perry winked at Anthony and pushed his lank black hair away from his brow. It was the second wink Anthony had received that meal, but he no longer felt in a mood to appreciate them. When Patricia pushed the cheese across to him he refused it. He felt terribly uncomfortable and his cheeks were burning. When at last he could get away he went straight out to the woodpile and spent all the afternoon in the hot sun chopping firewood.

Presently Uncle Perry came out and sat on a mooring stone and watched him, and after a while began to talk.

Perry Veal was a good story-teller with an eye for picturesque detail and the slightly suggestive phrase. In spite of himself Anthony at last laid down his axe and sat beside the dark man listening with his ears and blue eyes open wide. More than half the allusions were lost on him, but that made his interest all the more intent. Here before him was a man who knew everything in the world that was worth knowing, and the boy would have given a lot to have understood all the sly nods and oblique references which as often as not made up the point of a story. He felt as some men do when an after-dinner speaker persists in concluding all his bawdy stories in French.

But he learned much, and in the process temporarily forgot the tragedy of this afternoon when the sweet green shoot of his first romantic attachment had been broken off and trampled in the dust. He remembered it again only when Uncle Perry lit his short black 'nose-warmer' and

27

began to tell a story of a friend of his who had married a native queen in Patagonia.

'Four feet six broad she was, boy; handsome arms and shoulders; a fine figure of a woman. Well, there's not much a native queen don't know about marriage, you can take it from me.' He drew at his pipe with a wet sucking noise, then spat over the side.

'Cousin Pat never told me she was married,' Anthony blurted out, committing the impropriety of interrupting his uncle in full spate. 'When was she married? What's her husband? Don't they get on?'

'Eh? What's that?' Perry's winking dark eyes grew vague. He took his pipe from his mouth and stared at it, then knocked out the contents upon the palm of his hand. This black half-burned tobacco he rolled again into a ball between his palms and thrust it back into the bowl of his pipe. Then he blew away the ash, took a little fresh tobacco and pushed it down on top of the old. He struck a match and the wet sucking process began afresh. 'Pat. Oh, Pat.' He laughed. 'She's fickle, boy. A little filly who doesn't know what she really wants, see?' He nodded and sucked and his black hair fell across his brow. 'At that age, boy, they're nervous. Not properly broken in, as you might say; mettlesome. First touch of the bridle and they're up and away. But she's tasted flesh. She'll go back one day. Once they've tasted flesh, they always go back to it. That's what the tiger does, boy. In Madras; when I was in Madras in '91 –'

'Who is he, her husband?' the boy persisted. 'Have you seen him?'

'Seen him? Of course I've seen him. He's a lawyer from Penryn. They were only married in April. Couple of little budgerigars inching up to each other on the same twig. Sweet, they were. Little love birds. Then they were married. She went to live in Penryn. Handsome house, money no object. Eating off silver. Then of a sudden she comes home all of a sweat, nostrils quivering. "Go back?" she say. "Not I!"' Uncle Perry's pipe had gone out again. 'Little filly . . . Wants breaking in, that's all. She'll go back.'

At that moment they heard the subject under discussion calling them to tea. Anthony felt he had that afternoon become an adult. Never before had he been admitted to the confidences of a man. He was tremendously grateful to Uncle Perry for being treated as an equal. The enormous mysteries of life bulked large in the hot June sun. All the same he felt that Perry had gone over the mark in his talk of Patricia. As he sat at tea with the family all his admiration for the charm and prettiness of the girl filled him afresh.

The evening passed much as the previous one had done. Feeling more at home, the boy began to make himself useful, and during the evening rush hour his quick legs were a help. Recovering from the shock of dinner time he set himself whenever possible to help Patricia. The fleeting smiles that she gave him were sufficient reward. She was not so vivacious as the previous evening, and it was evident to the boy that her husband's visit had upset her.

The fact that the unknown man was a lawyer made Anthony think of someone like Mr Parks, who was thin and grey-bearded and dry and talked through his nose. The idea that this beautiful fresh young girl should have tied herself for life to such a creature, covered with the dust of the law, appalled him. For the first time in his life his inquiring mind turned upon the subject of divorce. He resolved to ask Uncle Perry. Uncle Perry would be sure to know not only all about divorce in this country but also in Asia, Africa and the South Sea Islands.

Anthony decided to stay up later tonight to see all that there was to be seen, but by nine o'clock he could hardly keep his eyes open. He had slept badly last night and had been up very early two mornings together. So after a struggle nature had its way; he wished the kitchen staff good night and climbed the stairs to bed even before the old man with the one leg had begun to play his accordion.

Dead tired, he slept much better. Once or twice he was conscious of shouts and music. Then after what seemed a century of sleep he heard again the drunken voice singing as it climbed the stairs to bed.

No song of a ghostly rider tonight. This time it was about a lady called Aluetta.

4

The next day was a Sunday, and even Smoky Joe's was compelled to remain closed. Shortly after breakfast Joe himself appeared in an old frock coat with a grey woollen muffler wound round his throat and a straw hat in his hand. He beckoned to Anthony.

'Can you row?'

Anthony shook his head. 'I rowed on a lake once, that's all.'

'Never mind. You'll soon learn. I want you to row me out to a ship in the roads. It's a nice morning. You'll enjoy it.'

Anthony was of the same opinion. He rushed upstairs for his cap and joined his uncle on the quay. Joe was pulling in a small dinghy by its painter, and Aunt Madge with folded arms was watching.

'Currents,' she observed didactically. 'No experience. Tide is going out. You should send over . . .'

'Fiddlesticks,' said Joe, breathing heavily with the effort. 'Anybody can row. And *I* haven't forgotten how. Here, boy, down this ladder and jump in.'

Swelling with responsibility, Anthony climbed down the iron ladder attached to the quay and got into the boat. After a moment Joe joined him.

'Cold wind on the water,' said Mrs Veal to the doorpost. 'No coat . . .'

This remark was ignored until they drew jerkily away from the land; then Joe said:

'Women. They coddle you. Your aunt wants to make a baby of me. See that she doesn't make one of you.'

30

It occurred to Anthony, struggling with the oars, that his aunt had taken no noticeable step in that direction so far. So he just smiled, showing his good regular teeth, and nodded. When they were about a hundred yards out Uncle Joe pointed over the boy's shoulder.

'See that barquentine. No, there, letting go her heads'ls. That's where you're to row me.'

Anthony caught a crab in his effort to do two things at the same time, and operations were suspended while Joe gave him one or two lessons. Anthony thought how thin and old and dry his uncle looked in the morning light. After each sentence his moustache clamped down like a trap door from which nothing more must be allowed to escape. His small eyes were like gimlets in the sun, glinting as they turned to stare about the bay.

The ship indicated was well out in the roadstead, almost halfway across to St Mawes. She had only recently arrived, and between her and them there were all manner of craft. Anthony was in a fever of concern lest he should run into or be run down by one of these vessels.

'You stick to your rowing, boy; I'll tell you what to do,' said Joe, pulling his hat lower over his eyes. 'Don't pull your guts out; take it slow and steady. He-eave-o-o-o. He-eave-o-o-o. That's it.'

Joe was in a better mood than he had previously seen him, more human and approachable out here than when crouched like a terrier over the till. None of the Veals, except Patricia once, had offered the boy any word of sympathy on the loss of his mother, and barely consciously the boy resented it. Joe at least, who knew her, might have said something. Instead of that he had asked about the money, nothing more. Not even a word on Anthony's prospects of joining his father. The prospects might be discussed, but Anthony was of no account in them, no more than a mere chattel.

'Where did you get that funny pipe, Uncle Joe?' he asked, as Veal took the object from his pocket and began to fill it.

'Funny? There's nothing funny about it except to the ignorant. Many a man smokes a pipe like this out East.'

'Oh,' said Anthony, and was silent for some time. He was already hot and breathless. 'Have you been out East a lot, Uncle Joe?'

'Java. Twenty-two years. Starboard a bit, boy. Right arm. *Right* arm. Me and your aunt were out there twenty-one years and eight months, on and off.'

'Aunt Christine?'

'Yes. Your mother's sister. That's where she got the worm that killed her. Once you've got it, it's hard to be rid of it. Starboard again. Now ship your oar. *Right* oar.'

They glided close beside an old barge which was moored in their path. Anthony expected the sides to grate.

They were well out now in the dancing water and could feel the thrust of the strong breeze. The sun was brilliant this morning without warmth. All about them were the sailing ships which another decade would see abandoned for ever. Four-masted barques with nitrate from America. Grain ships from Australia. Brigs loading with pilchards for the Italian ports. Schooners carrying salt to the Newfoundland cod banks. Away in the distance was the St Anthony lighthouse, white against the grey-green of the cliffs.

'But we always come back, we Veals.' said Uncle Joe suddenly, wiping his moustache this way and that with the stem of his pipe. 'There's been a Veal in Falmouth, boy, ever since there was a Falmouth. An' we're proud of it, see? A Veal was steward to the first Killigrew. Up in that ancient old house by the docks. His daughter had a natural son by William Killigrew. We trace direct back to him.'

Anthony wondered what a natural son was, since hitherto he had thought that all children were natural.

'Straight as a die,' said Uncle Joe. 'Sons of sons all the way. Not many families can say that. And we've outlasted the Killigrews. They're dead and gone. That house and land should all be ours if right was right.'

Across the water in the centre of old Falmouth a church

was ringing its bells. The sound floated to them, gentle and iterative and sweet.

'We're the last Veals,' said Joe. His pipe had gone out and his eyes for a moment were still, because they were focused on nothing. 'Uncle Perry and me. We're the last Veals. And he's not married and I've no male issue. So that's the end of us, too.'

Anthony rowed on. His mind went back to Patricia and her marriage. But he held his tongue. After that for some time there was no conversation between them.

As they at last neared the barquentine a dinghy approached them from the direction of the ship and a tall, well-set young man raised his blue cap very respectfully to Joe and called a courteous greeting as he passed. Joe responded with a brief nod.

'Who's that, Uncle Joe?'

'That's Ned Pawlyn, mate of *The Grey Cat*. No doubt he's off ashore to take Patricia out.'

The boy struggled again with curiosity and this time was defeated.

'Patricia's married, isn't she?' he asked.

Uncle Joe's face went hard and narrow. He stared at a passing barge.

'Nobody's business if she is.'

Anthony's face could not take on any more colour; instead it paled about the mouth.

'No . . . I'm sorry.'

'Nor is she by rights,' said Joe after a moment. 'Not if the law was as it should be. She married wi'out any consent. That should be enough to get it annulled. What did she want, marrying at her age. I'd nought against her having a good time. But her place is at home, as she rightly realises now. Her place is with me, helping me. Who told you, anyhow?'

'It was – just mentioned,' said Anthony, catching a crab.

'Well, it's no business of anybody's except hers and mine.'

33

The dinghy had gone right off its course and he had difficulty in pulling it back. 'I'm sorry if I shouldn't ought to have said anything, Uncle Joe. But why did she marry him if you didn't want her to and she didn't love him?'

Uncle Joe took out his pipe and pointed it at the boy. 'Questions. Questions. Too young to ask so many questions. Perhaps you're going to be a lawyer. Pah!' He spat over the side. 'Scum of the earth are lawyers. Wriggle here and wriggle there. Keep clear of them, I tell you.'

'Yes, Uncle Joe.'

'Why did she marry? you say. Because she's a woman and goes by opposites, that's why. But to you she's your cousin Patricia, nothing more and nothing less. See, boy?'

'Yes, Uncle Joe.'

Veal's little eyes travelled past Anthony to the bulk that was looming ahead. 'Now ship your oars. Gently does it. Don't wet my feet! There, that'll do. Now go up in the bows and ease her off as she touches.'

They spent three hours on board and had a meal before returning. Anthony was surprised to find his uncle treated with extreme deference. Even the captain, a square hard man with mutton-chop whiskers, called him 'sir'.

Anthony played about the deck, pretending himself already at sea. He talked to the crew and watched the ships and tried to find out what every piece of rope was for and leaned over the side seeing what sort of a splash he could make with his spittle in the water below. The time passed like a flash; he had never enjoyed himself more despite the blisters on his hands.

Only for dinner was he invited to the captain's quarters, and the three of them ate together. Much of the conversation was of nautical matters he could not understand. Uncle Joe had quite recovered his good humour and joked with the captain, whose name was Stevens, about getting his nephew a berth in the ship as cabin boy. Joe ate very little indeed but drank a good deal of whisky. Anthony noticed how clumsily he held his knife and fork even before he touched the whisky.

Then before they left wines were brought up and several kinds tasted. The ship had just arrived from Lisbon with a cargo of port and was unloading here. When that was completed, Joe said, she was to take on a general cargo for Liverpool.

Some semblance of the truth was dawning on Anthony. The full significance of the matter was suddenly illuminated by a nautical magazine which lay open on the desk. Written across the top by some newsagent or supplier were the words, *The Grey Cat. J. Veal, Blue Water Line*.

He rowed his uncle home with increasing blisters on his palms and a proportionately increased respect for the old man.

When Anthony, sore and breathless and hot, at last brought the small boat back to its mooring and they had walked precariously over the mud by way of a broken wooden landing jetty, they found Mrs Veal standing with arms folded at the side door, just as if she had not moved since they left.

'We're not drowned, you see,' said Smoky Joe, wiping his eyes, which were watering a good deal.

'Caught a chill, I'll be bound,' she observed from a small mouth above the unmoving mass of her figure. 'And things waiting for you . . . Attention.' She waved a hand.

'What things?' Joe was at once irritable.

'Pat's hubby here again.'

'Don't call him that! Don't you know his name?' Joe walked into the kitchen and pulled off his scarf; he sank into a chair as if he had been doing the rowing. 'Did you send him about his business?'

'In the lower restaurant now.'

'Who let him in?'

'He came by the back. You can't expect me . . .'

'I'll soon get rid of him. Where's Pat?'

'Out with . . . I forget his . . .'

35

'Ned Pawlyn. She's always off with him. What does the man want? Fetch me a glass of whisky, Madge.'

'Milk you should have.'

'Whisky, I said.'

Aunt Madge waved a hand helplessly and moved to a cupboard in the wall.

'More than that. Three fingers. Don't drown it. Hah!'

While Joe drank it Anthony reflected that in a queer way he had become quite fond of his uncle since they set out. The old man's bark was worse than his bite. And the boy warmed towards him because of his hostility for Patricia's husband.

Joe Veal stared at the empty glass, said 'Hah!' again, then rose to go downstairs.

At a discreet distance Anthony followed.

5

Thomas Wilberforce Harris sat tilting a chair and reading *Punch* in the empty café. He was a young man of medium height, smartly dressed in black. On the table beside him was a silk hat and a gold-mounted stick. He was dark, with a strong nose, a strong neck and full brown eyes which gave the impression of seeing more than surface things. He was not good looking but his face had personality. He looked as if he might be both self-confident and self-doubting.

When he saw who it was who had entered he put *Punch* carefully beside his hat, untilted his chair and got up.

Joe strode across to him like an angry dog.

'What do you want?' he demanded.

Harris glanced behind Joe Veal to see if anyone else had followed him in.

'Can you let me have a meal?' he said quietly.

'Restaurant's closed,' snapped Joe. 'It's Sunday and against the law.'

'There's no law against providing food for one's son-in-law.'

This remark was evidently looked upon by Joe as the height of provocation. 'You're no son-in-law of mine!'

'Well, the law, for which you have so much respect, says so.'

'I'm not interested in that. By a trumpery trick you persuaded Pat to go through a marriage ceremony . . .'

The young man's eyes, which had been cool and reserved, flickered with a spark of anger.

'There was no trickery unless Pat practised it in pretending that she loved me. The marriage was entered into of her own free will.'

Joe eyed him up and down with contempt. 'No doubt you know the law. I'll give you credit for that. Well, she's changed her mind. She was too young to know it then, easily influenced. But she knows it now and there's no use your coming here with your patronising airs.'

'I want to see her first,' said Harris.

'Well, you can't because she's out. Nor will she be back until dark. And you can't sit there. We're going to clean the place.'

'Well, I'm not particular. I can wait in the kitchen.'

Joe was about to deny him the right to do this when the sound of voices could be heard coming through the shop. Anthony ducked behind a curtain as Patricia appeared, peeling off her lavender gloves and laughing up at the big young sailor closely following her. There was silence in the restaurant as the voices passed the door and went into the kitchen.

'See here,' said Joe. 'Are you looking for trouble?'

Harris said: 'No. Only for my wife.'

'Because,' said Joe, 'there'll be trouble if you don't get out.'

In the distance Mrs Veal's monotonous voice could be heard talking to the young couple.

'Confound the woman!' said Joe.

37

Harris was looking at the little man with intent eyes. He seemed to be trying to sound the depth of his hostility.

'You gave me some very good turbot one time when I was here,' he said. 'With lobster sauce. There's a body about turbot that I like.'

'You'll get no food out of me today,' Joe said weakly.

There was a footstep outside and Patricia passed the curtain where Anthony was hiding. Following her at a distance came Ned Pawlyn. Patricia's face had completely changed from what it had been three minutes ago. Anthony watched the colour come and go in her cheeks.

Ned Pawlyn was a powerfully made young man with broad shoulders and long legs and a quiet walk, as if he was accustomed to moving along the deck and catching lazy seamen unawares. He had a deep slow voice with an attractive Cornish burr. His black straight eyebrows almost met over a nose nearly as strong as Harris's.

Harris coloured slightly when he saw his wife approaching.

'How are you, Pat?' he said, ignoring Pawlyn.

'Well, Tom,' said Patricia.

'I very much wanted a chat with you,' said her husband.

'What about?'

'I'd prefer to tell you that in privacy.'

'You can say anything you wish to say here.'

Neither of the contesting parties seemed quite as confident or as much at ease in the presence of the other.

'Why?' said Harris. 'Are you afraid of giving me a few minutes?'

Ned Pawlyn bulked close behind the girl. 'Should she have reason to be afraid?'

Harris looked at him for the first time. 'Do I know this gentleman?'

'Mr Pawlyn,' said Patricia. 'Mate of *The Grey Cat*.'

'How d'you do. What was your question?'

'You heard me the first time,' said Ned.

38

'Well, since you ask, I think perhaps Patricia is afraid of having a few minutes' quiet talk with me alone.'

'What're you getting at?' Joe said, looking as if he regretted not having his carving knife.

'As Pat persistently refuses me a private interview,' said Harris, 'it looks to me that she is afraid of being persuaded to return to her gilded cage.'

'So you admit it was a cage?' said Patricia.

Tom Harris looked at her with his brown eyes.

'All people live in cages,' he said. 'Cages of good behaviour and decent manners. A cage is none the worse for being gilded.'

'See,' said Ned Pawlyn, 'you talk too much, mister –'

Pat put a hand on his arm. 'Let me manage this, Ned. Tom, I'm not coming to talk with you – not because I'm afraid, but because there is nothing to discuss. When I left you I told you I was not coming back. I haven't changed my mind and am not likely to. So that's all there is to it.'

'Not quite,' said Harris.

'What have you to say to that?' demanded Smoky Joe, plainly pleased with his daughter's attitude.

'Only that I might petition for a restitution of conjugal rights.'

Anthony saw the girl's bosom begin suddenly to rise and fall.

'What d'you mean?' demanded Ned Pawlyn. 'Talk English. Restitu . . .'

Harris looked at the other man pointedly. There was that flicker in his eyes again.

'I've stood your interference with very great patience, Mr Pawlyn. May I ask what damned business it is of yours?'

'Look,' said Ned, 'if you care to step outside I'll teach you what business it is of mine.' Pat laid her hand on the seaman's arm.

Harris nodded. 'I know. Bare fists. The only argument you understand. But today I did not come here to quarrel.' He picked up his silk hat and slowly began to brush it with

39

his long fingers, for all the world, Anthony thought, as if
he were reassuring the hat that no harm would come to it.
'Tell me,' he said. 'Give me one valid reason among the
three of you why I should not so petition. A wife's place is
with her husband – unless he should be brutal or diseased
or insane. The marriage ceremony was entered into freely
– I might even say eagerly. There's no legal reason why I
should be summarily deserted.'

'No legal reason,' said Pat quietly. 'That's the whole
point. You only deal in legal things. You don't feel
things, I believe, until a seal has been put on them.
Nothing is yours until it's sworn to before witnesses.
Then nothing else matters. Very well, then, go and
petition. See what a laughing stock you'll make of
yourself!'

She raised her eyes and found his fixed upon her. She
turned sharply away with a gesture of impatience.

'I didn't say I was going to – yet. I came here today to
approach the matter in a friendly way, to ask you to return
to me like an honourable wife. It *is* a matter of honour,
you know.'

Pat had gone white. 'You twist everything round to your
own way of thinking.' She added: 'Please go now.'

'May I call again?'

She shook her head.

Harris rose and picked up his stick. There was a
momentary quirk in one eyebrow. 'No wife. No turbot.
A disappointing afternoon.' He went to the door. 'I wish
you all good day. Including the small boy peering through
the curtain.'

He went swiftly out. Mrs Veal had come from the
kitchen at this moment and was standing with short, fat
arms akimbo in the doorway. Although she had several
times openly favoured his suit, he went past her without
a glance. In fact he seemed to withdraw his arm as if to
avoid contact.

Clearly, thought Anthony, he did not consider any of
them good enough for him.

40

6

Two days passed before Anthony had an opportunity of saying anything to his cousin. She had been rather moody since the visit and only brightened each evening when Ned Pawlyn called to take her out.

Patricia was taking some flowers to her mother's grave, as she did every Wednesday, and he offered to accompany her. They set off up the hill, at first through working-class streets, then down a hill past some fine residential houses to the cemetery, which was situated upon the hillside overlooking a lake. The lake was in the hollow of the hills and was surrounded by trees; at one end thick rushes grew and at the other a narrow bar of shingle separated it from the sea.

'What a lovely place!' Anthony exclaimed. 'I shouldn't mind being buried here.'

Patricia laughed. 'I'd rather be alive at Smoky Joe's.'

The grave was just inside the gate. When the old flowers were removed and the new ones arranged she said soberly:

'Let's go down and feed the swans. I always bring something with me.'

So they clambered down to the lake and sat on its edge throwing bread and kitchen scraps to the big white birds, which knew Pat and came over to her at once.

An older and wiser person would not have mentioned the fracas of Sunday afternoon; but Anthony's was a nature which could not rest in peace while there was the possibility of misunderstanding with someone he liked.

'Look, Pat,' he said. 'I'm awfully sorry about – about Sunday. I mean about me peeping through the curtain. I didn't intend – it was . . .' As she did not speak he went on, 'I'd only just come out of the kitchen, and I heard the

41

noise and . . .' He was astonished with himself for telling this lie but was somehow forced into it by her silence and by his desire that she should think well of him. The words had come from him unawares.

She shrugged. 'Oh, it doesn't matter. My affairs are free for all anyway.'

'Oh, no,' he contradicted. 'They shouldn't be.'

'Why?' she said after a moment. 'Do you think I should have seen him alone?'

Thus questioned, he drew back quickly within himself like a snail which has touched something foreign and perhaps dangerous.

'I – I don't know. How can I tell? I don't know anything about it.'

'No,' she agreed moodily. 'How *can* you tell?'

There was silence, while the swans ducked their heads in the water and drank and waited for more food.

'It's funny,' said Anthony. 'I never even *saw* your ring, you know. I just didn't notice it until it was mentioned last Saturday . . .'

'Where d'you think I met him?' she said, taking off her picture hat and letting the wind and the sun play with her curls.

'. . . Don't know,' said the boy.

'In the police court.'

He screwed up his cap. 'In . . .'

'And who do you think introduced us?'

'Don't know.'

'Dad himself.'

Patricia emptied her bag into the lake.

Anthony's mind was struggling in deeper waters than any the pond could offer. 'I thought Uncle didn't like him.'

'Not as a *son-in-law*. Women aren't the only contrary ones, are they?'

The sun went behind a cloud and a breeze ruffled the waters of the pool.

'Of course, I was chiefly to blame,' she went on after a pause, more brightly, as if she found some cause for

42

self-congratulation in being in the wrong. 'You see, it all began like this. There was trouble in our restaurant one Saturday night; there sometimes is; but this was worse than usual; a Dutchman got a knife stuck in him. I've always told Joe; I've told him and told him not to let *anybody* in. On a Friday and Saturday a lot of men spend part of their time in a public house and then come into our restaurant half drunk. I'd refuse them admittance. But Joe says, no, they're all customers and have a right to buy what they can pay for – and *he'll* keep them in order. That's all very well most times, but if bad trouble ever starts it's too far gone before he can stop it. And Uncle Perry shouts a lot of terrible oaths but he doesn't do much. Fridays and Saturdays are usually the nights; you may have noticed the last two evenings have been quieter.'

Anthony nodded. 'Uncle Joe said there was a Greek ship in this afternoon,' he volunteered.

'Well, this night in March a lot of men wanted to come in together, and there were two or three among them who were pretty drunk, and I happened to be standing at the counter and I said to Dad, "Say we're full up," but of course he wouldn't. Joe can't bear to turn away a penny. So in they came. They were a lively lot in the lower restaurant even then. Well, somebody started a quarrel, and before you knew where you were everyone was fighting everyone else – and by the time the police came someone had stuck a table knife into a Dutchman who had nothing to do with it at all. Two or three others had to be treated for broken ribs and things.'

'Did he die?'

'The Dutchman? No. But he accused a man called Fossett of having stabbed him. Mr Fossett was a shipbroker and practically Dad's oldest friend. But sometimes he would drink heavily and he was a bit hot-tempered. Dad didn't like the idea of him being accused: he's funny that way when he makes up his mind about a thing, and he tried to get all the blame put upon the Dutchman himself. Two or three witnesses went into the box and testified that

43

the whole place had been sweetness and light until the Dutchman came in and that it was he who was the only drunk one, and that he'd started an argument about the Transvaal and then things went wrong. But that wasn't true at all.'

'What happened?'

'Mr Fossett got six months in the second division. Of course, I never thought of getting him as much as that when I did it.'

Anthony looked at the girl. 'Did what?'

She pulled down a piece of stick and stirred the lake gently while the swans nosed about it expecting more food.

'You see, I was called as a witness, as I was in the restaurant at the time of the quarrel; but instead of testifying that it was all the Dutchman's fault as Dad expected, I supported the Dutchman's story, because he was telling the truth. He hadn't even been drunk at the time; he'd just come in for a quiet meal and was eating away when the quarrel broke all around him. It was Joe's fault for letting any rag-tag come in and be served; it was Joe's fault for being so grasping for every penny that it hurt him to turn a single one away. You know . . . he wouldn't shut the restaurant the day Mother died. He even begrudged her having a doctor until near the end . . . I thought this would teach him a lesson. At least . . . I didn't reason it out as plainly as that at the time. I went into court feeling a lot and not quite knowing what to say, and then before I properly knew, I was telling the whole truth. I'd just got to.'

Anthony spent some minutes wondering if even at nine-teen he would have the moral courage to speak against his father in a court of law.

'And that was where you met – your . . .'

She shook her head. 'No. That was later. You see, other things happened then that I didn't expect. No sooner was that case settled than the police brought a charge against Joe for keeping a disorderly house. Of course, Joe was *furious*.'

'Yes, I suppose he would be,' agreed the boy.

'He quarrelled with almost everybody at that time. Even Uncle Perry had a job to stay on.' She smiled wryly at this. 'He turned me out of the house the night after I'd given evidence favourable to the Dutchman.'

'What did you do?'

'Slept with Aunt Louisa in Arwenack Street. That was easily arranged because I lived with her during holidays while Mother and Dad were abroad. But it made things worse in a way because Dad can't stand his sister nowadays. Well, he quarrelled with his solicitors too about their conduct of the case, and when the police summons came along he put it in the hands of Harvey & Harris of Penryn.' She was silent a moment, pondering her own strange feminine thoughts. 'Tom . . . Tom Harris did very well for him in that: he was only fined ten guineas and costs. But he wasn't a bit grateful; he quarrelled with Tom because he hadn't got him off altogether.'

The swans had become aware that this stirring of the water was a trumpery deception; one by one with slow imperceptible strokes they moved away, breasting the water square and smooth like a convoy of white East Indiamen.

'We ought to go,' said Patricia rising. 'They'll wonder what has happened to us.' She picked up her hat and parasol. 'Come on: I'll race you to the top of the hill.'

Womanlike, she started off before he could even get to his feet. He rushed after her, but she was half-way up before he overtook her, laughing his triumph. Whereupon with the same curious lack of logic she at once abandoned the race and sat on the hedge careless of her frock and breathless and smiling.

But when they had restarted her mood changed again.

'You know, Anthony, mine was a funny sort of marriage. The way it happened, I mean. When I first saw Tom in court I admired tremendously the way he defended us. I thought him very good looking then. Of course he was in his element; I didn't realise that. But you don't marry a lawyer for the way he behaves in law courts any more

45

than you'd marry a sailor for the way he sails his ship. I was silly; but there you are. He came to me when it was over and asked me to go out with him the next evening. I said yes. Joe started raising steam when he heard of it. I was living at home again when this second case came off, and we were good friends again; but me wanting to go out with the lawyer who, in his view, had just let him down was more than he could endure. So of course we had another quarrel and the more he said I wasn't to go out with Tom the more I went – and so it developed quickly.'

Anthony said nothing, but he could well understand that much. Joe had been trying to govern someone with a bit of himself in her.

'So there you are,' she said moodily. 'That's the way it is, as you'll find when you're older. People never are what they seem. Nice people turn out nasty and nasty people nice. Tom has awfully pretty manners when he likes. I – I thought I was in love with him. In a way for the time I was. A sort of infatuation, I suppose. I was absolutely in earnest, though it may not seem so now. After we were married things seemed to change.'

'How did it change?' he asked, all attention.

'Oh, you – you wouldn't understand,' she said, and again the conversation lapsed.

But now she was like a moth fluttering round a flame; at each remembrance she singed her wings and sheered away, but the flame still burned, attracting her back. She persuaded herself that there was pleasure in explaining to someone who did not matter. In fact she was glad to speak more fully than she had ever done since her return, to justify herself – but whether to him or to herself was a moot point.

'They live in a big house in Penryn, you know.'

'Who do?' he asked, for he had been watching a yawl dipping out to sea.

'The Harrises. There's Tom and his mother and an aunt. He took me there for the first time after we were married. That was the first shock.'

'What was?'

'Well, the house was big and old and full of big old furniture that looked as if it could never be moved. It's the sort of house you'd never expect anyone would ever dare to sneeze or giggle in. That didn't matter much of itself. Surroundings aren't very important, and you can be happy in a public house or a museum if you go the right way about it. But Mrs Harris and Miss Harris and their surroundings were all of a piece. A – a stiff elderly maid let us in and another stiff elderly maid showed us into the drawing-room, and there were two stiff elderly old ladies waiting for us for tea. I hadn't – it had all been such a rush that I hadn't met either of them before, and I think Tom must have had a bit of a quarrel with his mother the morning before he left when he told her he was going to marry me. That didn't make for a good beginning . . .'

'Didn't he tell her till then?'

'It had only been decided the day before. Then we went away for three days and came straight back to the house. I think now that Tom was in a hurry in order to *forestall* criticism. He thought that once we were married they would make the best of a bad job and put a cheerful face on it. But I didn't want anybody to start looking on me as a bad job that had to be made the best of. That isn't the way to start married life. Anyway, they didn't try hard enough to deceive me. You see – you see, when I went there I felt very happy, bubbling over with good spirits. Their reception was a sort of smack in the face. It didn't take me long to see what the position was. They thought I wasn't good enough for Tom.'

She stopped to push some grass through a gate to a pony.

'Of course I could see his mother's point of view. She wanted him to marry well, keep up the tradition, in the same house with the same furniture, be gracious, entertain the right people and live to be seventy-seven. In some ways she was nice, and could have been nicer if she'd tried.' Judicially she repeated: 'I could *see* her point of view, but

47

she couldn't expect *me* to fit into it, could she? Sometimes she made a real attempt to be agreeable, and we got on fairly well then, though I was always thinking "What an effort it must be for her!" and "She doesn't really like me, she's only trying to," and "I wish I didn't mind being patronised, she doesn't really intend it as that."'

They turned and walked slowly on.

'I wonder what it is that makes some people seem so afraid of coming unmelted. Tom has grown up in a house where every feeling and emotion has to be – to be muted and restrained, kept under lock and key because it's bad form to let them go free. Why are some people so scared of their dignity, Anthony?'

Anthony did not know.

'I was really thinking of Aunt Phoebe then,' she said. 'I *might* have got on with his mother if there hadn't been Aunt Phoebe. She . . . I never could make up my mind which was the tightest about Aunt Phoebe, her mouth or her stays. Sorry if you're shocked, I keep forgetting you haven't had a sister. Aunt Phoebe disapproved of me from the start. I was socially inferior and hadn't been educated in the wooden-face school. I was too flighty and unstable. She didn't give me a chance before she started picking holes.' Patricia choked as if the memory were not to be borne. 'Naturally, the more holes she picked the more opportunity I gave her. You may say this isn't anything to do with Tom, but it is. You see, Tom couldn't understand us at all. He didn't seem to try. In his own house he was different, seemed a part of it. It was *fantastic*. You can't be legal in a home, not if it's going to *be* a home. You can't weigh up things as if you were a judge, and then give so much credit to this side and so much credit to that. You may be able to *see* both sides, but you can't *take* both sides. If he'd come down on one side or the other, then I should have known where I was earlier.

'After three weeks it was about as bad as it could be. Then Dad was taken ill and I wanted to rush home and nurse him. Tom didn't want me to do that. He raised all sorts of objections that were just silly. He even offered to pay for a nurse for Dad, but I wouldn't have that. Joe wouldn't either, you may be sure. In the end of course I could see what it was: living with his family had convinced Tom that my manners needed a bit of tightening up – when I met a stranger I didn't say "How d'you do-o" as if there were a nasty taste in my mouth; I went up and shook hands – and I'd committed the terrible sin of being found in the kitchen, talking to the tweenie. Anyway, I think he thought that if I stayed at Mount House long enough I should get like them, but Smoky Joe's was a bad influence for me. As if I'd lived anywhere else since I left school! He thought that if I went backwards and forwards between one house and the other I never would improve. So then I told him that I didn't want to improve by getting like him and his mother and his aunt, and that if he wanted someone like that I didn't know why he'd married me, and anyway the Veals had a longer pedigree than any Harrises he could find, and whether he liked it or not I was going to nurse Dad, and I wouldn't bother to come back and lower his prestige any more . . .'

Towards the end of this statement her breath had been coming as quickly as her speech. They began to go down the other side of the hill. Anthony glanced at his cousin. In talking to him she had relived some of the emotions of that time. Until two days ago she had put all this behind her, tried to shelve it and forget it. Tom Harris's visit had brought it all up anew. She looked neither so young nor so happy as she had done a week ago.

'Was Uncle Joe very ill then?'

'Oh, yes. We thought he was going to die. He's better now. I'm watching his diet so that he takes regular meals.'

'Is that why you're not going back to Tom Harris?'

'Oh, no,' she said. 'That doesn't make any difference. I'm never going back to him. I'm never going back.'

Anthony looked down the hill and saw Ned Pawlyn coming up it to meet them.

7

It became a regular practice for Anthony once or twice each week to row his uncle out to some ship in the harbour. One week it was *The Grey Cat*. Then it was *Lavengro*. Then it was *Pride of Pendennis*. This was followed by *Lady Tregeagle*. Then *The Grey Cat* returned from Liverpool. There were two barquentines, a schooner and a tops'l schooner, all around three hundred tons; tidy little craft busy about their owner's business. And the owner was J. Veal. How many, if any, more there might be trekking across the oceans of the world on the business of J. Veal, Anthony did not know.

Sometimes he sat in the little master's cabin and listened, less than half comprehending, to discussions on freights and port dues and insurance costs. He noticed that whenever the conversation was turned by one of the captains upon what they considered necessary repairs to their ships Smoky Joe had a talent for turning the conversation to something else. If they insisted that the repair or replacement was urgently necessary he always ended the discussion with, 'Well, we'll consider it, mister, we'll consider it.'

He never saw his uncle consult with anyone ashore, though Joe sometimes ventured forth in the morning on his own business with ship's chandlers, Board of Trade authorities and the like. Once Anthony pulled the cork out of the floorboard of his bedroom and saw his uncle in the office below counting a heap of gold into little piles. There were twenty or thirty such piles by the time he replaced the cork.

There is something about a spy-hole which has an irresistible fascination for a young boy, even the most honourable young boy, and Anthony on a number of occasions took out the cork and stared down on the greying head of his uncle as he was writing or sorting out papers or adding up figures in a huge ledger. Once a knock came on the office door, and the boy noted with what care Joe put everything away – this in the safe, that in a drawer – before unlocking the door to admit, as it happened, Uncle Perry. Uncle Perry looked round the room curiously and made some joke and laughed: it was clear that he had not often been in this room before; and Joe answered his questions tightly and disapprovingly as if to make it plain that he did not like to be interrupted.

On another occasion, hearing gruff and unfamiliar voices in the room below, Anthony saw the master and mate of *Lady Tregeagle* being entertained to a glass of rum and milk. This was the first time he had seen anyone invited into that private office. When they had finished their drink Joe brought out a piece of foolscap paper and signed his name on it, and they both signed their names after him. He did not however give them this paper but kept it himself; and when they had gone he sealed it up in an envelope and stood hesitantly in the middle of the floor for some seconds. Eventually he went to a small oil painting of an old lady on the wall and taking it down clicked it open on some sort of a hinge, so that between the painting and the back there was room to slip the paper.

Anthony tried to take a firm hold on himself over this matter of peeping. He seldom yielded to the temptation without feeling mean about it afterwards; also he had no lock on his door and knew that if someone were to come into his room while he was so engaged he would never live down the shame.

No word came to him during these weeks from his father. He had received one letter only since his mother's death, and he anxiously awaited another. He was quite happy in his new life, chiefly because of Patricia; but he longed to see his father. He longed above all to be in the company of someone to whom he personally belonged. He could not quite get over the feeling of not *belonging* here. It was as if he had been in the centre of a circle of friends, and suddenly he had lost that circle, and now he was attached to another circle, but was only at the extreme outer edge.

He did not come to know Aunt Madge any better than the day he first arrived. That small precise face built upon its column of chins seldom carried much expression beyond a certain vague distaste for the vulgarity of the world around it. The large, shapeless body, with its fondness for ornament – overburdened, one felt, as much by clothes as by flesh – seemed to dominate the kitchen without stamping the impress of a personality upon it. The weak, husky voice was what Anthony chiefly remembered when she was not before him, its habit of breaking off before its objective was reached, its capacity when angry of endless reiteration without being raised a semi-tone.

But he sympathised with Uncle Joe for having married her even though she was so unattractive; for she was a real commercial asset. With her to do the cooking, Patricia to charm the clientele with her pretty ways, and Joe himself to drive his hard bargains at the door, the supremacy of the restaurant was secure.

The only times Anthony was really uncomfortable were on the Friday and Saturday evenings. These nights might have improved since the law case, but they were still rowdy enough. The boy had few thoughts on the ethics of the matter, but he didn't like Patricia being in contact with a crowd of singing roisterers and he always felt a sensation of relief when Saturday drew to a close without having given rise to another mêlée.

This business of Friday and Saturday evenings was the only one on which Uncle Perry condescended to compromise his amateur status. When the fun got fast and merry he was usually somewhere in the middle of it with his laughing buccaneer face and Spanish-black hair. Sometimes he would be persuaded to sing, and he had a fine repertoire of comic songs with an occasional bawdy number thrown in. He would stand under the figurehead of the *Mary Lee Melford*, which had sunk off Maenporth, smile his attractive wayward smile, and sing his songs accompanied by the lame accordionist, while the crowded room roared the choruses.

One night by way of a change he chose the 'Song of Tregeagle,' and Anthony knew for certain the identity of the nocturnal carouser who still periodically disturbed his sleep.

'They heard the Black Hunter! and dread shook each mind;
Hearts sank that had never known fear;
They heard the Black Hunter's dread voice in the wind!
They heard his cursed hell-hounds run yelping behind!
And his steed thundered loud on the ear.'

The boy came to know much of Falmouth during these weeks, for he was constantly out and about, rowing Joe to a ship in the bay, accompanying Pat on shopping expeditions among the huddled narrow streets and courtyards, shopping on his own for Aunt Madge, roving round the town with Uncle Perry when Uncle Perry couldn't get his favourite baccy at the usual shop.

He came to appreciate and understand the pulsing life of the port. News would come through that one of the big nitrate ships was becalmed off the Scillies, and at once rival pilot cutters set off to race to meet her. Then one by one over a period of weeks the great grain ships arrived in the bay, standing well out in the calm sea, sails furled at last after a world passage of anything up to half a year's duration. Sometimes there were fifteen to twenty of them at once, awaiting their orders; then one by one as they received them they would slip away in the night, off to Queenstown or Liverpool or Clydebank or the Thames. The crews from these ships did not come ashore, but many of the masters and mates crowded into Smoky Joe's and sat there over their food talking of storm and stress which scarcely seemed believable with the quiet sea lapping the old stone wall outside; of scudding down the roaring forties, of heat and boredom in the doldrums, of rounding Cape Horn in the black of the night and losing men swept from the frozen yards by the giant seas.

Sometimes there were as many as two hundred head of sail in the roadstead and the bay, and among them all almost the only steam belonged to the Irish coastline boats. During busy periods keen-eyed old men sat in Woodhouse Terrace, the highest in the town, and scanned the horizon with powerful telescopes. As soon as a sail was sighted word went secretly down and the competing bum-boats and tailors' cutters tried to slip quietly out of the port without arousing suspicion in the breasts of their rivals. Once the news became public it was a free-for-all race to the incoming ship to reach it first and bespeak it for re-victualling and supplies.

Nothing more was seen of Tom Harris. He had apparently given up his erring wife as a bad job. As for Patricia, she pursued her light-hearted way, being taken out in turn by several good-looking young men, though the perceptive might have detected an element of determination in her gaiety.

The one obvious cloud in her life now was Joe. Joe appeared to be sickening for another bout of his old complaint. He carried on his unfailing routine without break, working in his office in the mornings and sitting the rest of the day behind the counter of his shop, fierce and intractable and dry. But although the spirit remained indomitable the flesh was weak: he could eat practically nothing, and his small terrier eyes had sunk deeper into a face narrow and hollow and grey. His appearance began even to affect the attendance at the restaurant on Friday and Saturday nights. People did not like to be jolly with a sick man serving their food.

Aunt Madge pressed him to take a couple of weeks in bed to see if that would help, and everyone joined her in urging him to see a doctor; but he refused to do either. If he took to his bed who would carry on the supervision of his numerous interests? And a doctor would only prescribe sickly potions which would do him no manner of good.

Besides, doctors were expensive; they were the luxury of a rich man. One did not throw away one's shillings soliciting useless advice.

And doctors, he argued, could not rid him of a fluke-worm. He knew what to take and was taking it. Plenty of purgatives and a starvation diet. When the attack subsided he'd soon pick up again.

In August the town was visited by Poulton's Players, a company of itinerant troupers who toured the south-west with their melodramas. This was an event of popular importance in the life of the community, Ma and Pa Poulton being respected figures and their return visits awaited with pleasure. Not for Poulton's Players the inconvenience of performing in strange halls with makeshift scenery and unpredictable lighting. Snail-like, Poulton's carried their house on their back in the shape of a tent, and this was erected on the Moor and the plays given before a select audience for which suitable seating accommodation was provided – easy chairs and couches for the patrons who came in evening dress from the big houses of the town, grading finely down to hard wooden benches for those who had not the money to afford better.

Patricia went to an early performance with one of her friends and enjoyed it so much that she persuaded her father to let Anthony go with her on the following night. Anthony had never been to a play in his life, and they set out together bubbling over with excitement at the thought of it all.

The Moor was centrally situated and they had only a short distance to walk. Patricia was wearing a blue dress trimmed with velvet which showed up her slender waist, and a feather boa. Her face was pretty and piquant under a small straw hat. They were talking animatedly as they walked, when Pat suddenly gave a little exclamation and was silent. The boy saw that on the other side of the street and plainly bound for the Moor himself was her husband.

At the moment Tom Harris turned his head and saw them; he stopped and crossed the street, hat in hand.

His manner was more friendly than it had been last time.

'I wonder,' he said, 'if you would care to admit to your society a member of the ancient borough of Penryn.'

Patricia, after a moment's embarrassment, evidently decided to meet him on his own ground.

'Well, Tom,' she said. 'So *you're* going to the play too. I thought you would not consider it quite respectable.'

'Oh,' he said. 'It is not so much *where* one goes as the company one keeps.'

Anthony felt rather than saw the girl begin to flush darkly. 'Then,' she said, 'I am sure you would not wish to be admitted to our society. Good night.'

'On the contrary,' he said, quickening his pace with hers. 'I thought you might sit with me in the theatre.'

'Thank you,' said Pat. 'I've promised to take my cousin. We'd prefer to sit alone.'

'So this is your cousin,' said Tom. 'How d'you do?'

'How d'you do, sir,' said Anthony, lifting his cap, not to be outdone in the frigid courtesies.

They climbed the hill towards the tent. From the summit of the 'theatre' a flag fluttered briskly in the breeze.

'I suppose you know,' Harris said, 'that I've resigned my job.'

Patricia looked at him quickly. 'You've –'

He nodded. 'I want a change.'

She seemed to suspect some calculated manoeuvre on his part. 'Why did you do that?'

They had come now to the crowd of people who gathered about the entrance to the tent.

'I said before I should like a word with you in private. Otherwise,' he added, 'I might take the seat next to yours and spoil your evening's enjoyment.'

She hesitated a moment longer, biting her lip.

'Anthony,' she said, 'will you buy our tickets, please. I'll join you when you've got them.'

She passed him the money and he fell in reluctantly at

the back of the queue, already aware that Tom Harris had begun to speak to the girl in a steady undertone.

The queue was slow in moving. There was some dispute at the booking window.

Then a voice in front of him said: 'That's Joe Veal's girl over there.'

Anthony glanced up quickly at the speaker. He knew him by sight, a tall man with a drooping moustache called Treharne, who kept the public house on the corner of the street. Anthony had often seen him standing at the door of his place, and sometimes he had been in to Smoky Joe's for a meal. Treharne belonged to that strange breed of people who always have confidential, advance information upon any subject which crops up for discussion. If the King has gone to Scotland they know why; if there has been unrest in the Welsh coal districts they know where; if a fine ship has run aground in a fog they know how.

'Who's she with?' asked his companion, peering. 'He's a new one to me.'

'Well, not to *her*,' said Treharne. 'That's Tom Harris, her *husband*, from Penryn, that's who that is.'

The other man whistled. 'I thought they was estranged. I thought they was separated.'

Treharne speculated. 'Hm, well, maybe he's trying to make it up. Lawyers usually have an eye on the main chance. She'll have a tidy little packet to her name one of these days soon.'

'Yes, I s'pose.'

'Smoky Joe'll be a very warm man, mark my words. He had a tidy nest egg when he came back here six or seven years ago, and since then he's made big money. Big money. He's never spent a penny, y'know; and that restaurant idea of his was a gold mine. Then there's the shipping and one or two side lines. Young Harris will have to play her pretty careful; she's a 'andsome piece of goods but flighty, and there'll be plenty of other wasps round the jam-pot when she comes in for the money.'

'Well, maybe they'll have to wait a bit yet. Old Joe –'

The man broke off as Treharne emphatically shook his head. Then he went on: 'I didn't know Smoky was as ill as all that . . .'

Treharne shook his head again. 'Same thing as his wife, you know.' He made the observation in a confidential undertone with the air of having received the news direct from the surgeon's lips. 'It's all U.P. when a person gets that.'

'Hm. I'm sorry. Is it . . . ?'

'Well, there we are . . .'

Uneasily: 'It surely isn't catching.'

'Oh, I wouldn't say that. But I've noticed husbands and wives often seem to get it after each other, haven't you? Of course, mind you, mm-mm-mm-mm . . .'

'Poor old Smoky.'

'Yes. Poor luck for him.'

A moment later the men had passed on and Anthony found himself facing Ma Poulton in the box office.

He bought the seats and waited for Patricia to separate from her husband and join him. She did this almost at once and they entered the tent together. But Anthony's excitement and anticipation for the evening had dropped from him. Somehow the pleasure of the present had become submerged in a dread of the future.

8

Whatever the Poulton Players lacked in the finer points of acting as understood by the sophisticated few, they made up in verve and power and conscientious determination to see that nothing was missed by the slower members of the audience. The play was called *The Last of His Line*; a title, the boy thought at first, with some aptness for the grey little tragedy which was taking place behind the drawn curtains of Smoky Joe's. But as the play progressed even the encounters of this evening were driven from his mind by the strange glamour of the footlights. For nearly three hours he lived in a world of Marquises and milkmaids, of mortgages and suicides, of love trysts broken and hearts with them, and of Christmas reconciliations to the sight of snowflakes and the sound of church bells.

He came out with his mind still staggering under the weight of enormous visual impressions. He was thrilled and delighted almost to the core of his being. But at the *very* core was a hard heavy weight which seemed to say: 'This isn't what's happening to you; the part of the evening that's *yours* is what happened before you went in.'

As they were leaving the tent Tom Harris joined them again. He asked if he might see them home, and although the boy felt that this was a usurpation of his own position he could see that Patricia was not unwilling to accept the offer. There were bound to be numerous drunks about at this time of night.

They walked some distance talking of the play. Anthony thought how much more reasonable they seemed in each other's presence now they were alone, except for himself. Then Tom Harris spoiled it by suddenly saying:

'Patricia, I want you to leave Joe's. I want you to come back to Penryn with me tonight.'

She said: 'I thought we'd finished discussing that, Tom.'

'I don't know why it is,' he said. 'I can't give you better reasons than I've already given you. But I've a *feeling*. I don't like the atmosphere of the place. I want you to get out of it.'

'I'm not coming, Tom. I've told you; I'm not coming.'

They walked on.

'In a different way,' he said, 'you're just as obstinate as your father.'

'If knowing my own mind is obstinacy, then I am. But what is obstinacy? Only the determination of another person to do what you don't want them to do.'

59

'You're learning, Pat. You're learning the art of argument. But don't get too theoretical, I beg of you.'

'I thought,' she said, 'you would like me to get all dry and precise and withered up like Aunt Phoebe.'

'Why should I? Why should I compare the lily and the teasel?'

Against her better judgment she uttered a brief murmur of amusement. 'That's just right for Aunt Phoebe. She's hard and dry and – and prickly and rustles when the wind blows.'

'But even teasels have their uses. You're no botanist if you expect all nature to fit into one mould. If –'

'That's what's the matter with Aunt Phoebe,' Pat said quickly. 'She's no botanist.'

He inclined his head. 'A good point. But I'm to blame, not she. Nor you. I thought I was a botanist, yet I expected the lily and the teasel to grow in the same soil. Crabbed age and youth . . . Well . . . I've learned my lesson. Now I'm suggesting that we try again on a different basis.'

A long silence followed. Tom Harris knew how to argue his point. He carried too many big guns for the girl. Anthony felt that he should not have allowed the conversation to begin, that now it had begun he should exert himself to break it off. But he could not. He still laboured under the disadvantages of childhood. These were adults, arguing out their own problems between themselves. They had forgotten him. He could not muster the necessary self-importance to interfere.

'We can't turn life back,' Patricia said in a low voice. 'We can't just go back and start afresh as if nothing had happened, nothing been said.'

'I'm not asking you to go back in the same way. I'm asking you to come back and live with *me*.'

In the distance, through a gap in the houses, the St Anthony light winked at them and disappeared.

'But you see, Tom,' she said very quietly, 'I don't love you.'

They crossed the street. They were nearly home.

60

'Oh,' said Tom.

'I'm sorry. I didn't really want to put it as bluntly as that.'

They reached the steep little street and turned down it.

'How long have you known this?'

'Since – since soon after I came home.'

'Any *particular* reason?'

'No . . .'

They came to a stop just out of range of the lighted windows of JOE VEAL'S.

'Then I think,' said Harris, 'that you might perhaps change your mind again. That I might be able to persuade you to change your mind.'

'Now you're merely being odious,' said Pat.

'I'm sorry,' he said. 'That wasn't my intention.'

She said: 'I must go now. Dad is still far from well. In any case, it's my duty to stay with him.'

He took the hand she had offered. 'Is it also your duty to go out with Ned Pawlyn?'

She quickly took her hand back. She stood very still for a moment. When she spoke again her voice was quite changed.

'I suppose that's the sort of remark I might have expected.'

'Certainly it is; if those are the sort of men you go out with.'

'Good night,' she said. 'Thank you for bringing us home.'

He said, 'Some of them may be good fellows; I don't know. But I took a dislike to Ned Pawlyn. I think I might come to dislike him more. The low forehead shows a lack of intelligence. I'm surprised that you should find him interesting.'

She had left them and entered the shop. Anthony found himself alone with their escort. They looked at each other.

'Good night, Anthony,' said Harris.

'Good night,' said Anthony, raising his cap.

Then he too pushed open the door of the shop.

The light indoors was so bright by comparison with the feeble lighting of the streets that for a few seconds the boy could see very little. All he could make out was that Patricia was not there and that his uncle occupied his usual position behind the counter.

Then to his great astonishment he perceived that it was the wrong uncle.

He rubbed his eyes, but the man opposite him refused to change or disappear.

'Where's Uncle Joe?' he got out at last.

'Upstairs with a pain in his tum,' said Uncle Perry. 'Behold his deputy; as large as life and twice as efficient.'

All the remarks of Mr Treharne came flooding back into his head. He looked round again for Pat.

'Is he bad?' he asked in a voice instinctively pitched in a lower key.

'He'll be all right in an hour or two, me boy. Just one of his "do's".' Uncle Perry seemed in the best of spirits.

'Where's Pat?' the boy asked.

'Gone upstairs to see her Dad.'

'Oh.' Anthony glanced down at the savoury dishes set out on the counter. 'Are there many people inside?'

'Business is a bit slack.' Uncle Perry pushed back his hair and waved a carving fork. 'Now, sir; what can I do for you, sir? What would you like tonight, sir?'

Anthony glanced round, but he was the only person in the shop.

'A little bit off the rump?' said Uncle Perry. 'Guaranteed tasty and never been sat on; just the thing for you, sir.' He picked up a carving knife and prodded each of the dishes in turn. 'Now here we have a fine chicken. Chicken, did I say? Well, an old hen. May I offer you the guts of an old hen? Guaranteed to stretch *and* stretch. Very suitable for violin strings. No? Then a little roast swine? Can't I offer you some swine? The poor thing died last week, we don't know of what, so it *had* to be cured. Ha, ha! Or a duck's gullet? Help yourself, me boy, no waiting. Pay only if pleased. A five per cent discount for quiet eaters!'

Anthony tried to smile; then he tried not to smile.

'Uncle Perry; do you think Uncle Joe is seriously ill?'

'I'll? Belay there. We all get pains in the tum. You must have had pains in the tum. Were you seriously ill? Good grief, no.' Uncle Perry took from under the counter a large mug of beer and drained it. Presently all that was left was a thin white froth upon his lips, which he carefully licked off with a large flat tongue. Then he parted his lips in a smack.

At that moment three customers entered. There were explanations; Perry laughed and joked with them and at last succeeded in selling them three plates of beef. *Ping – crash!* went the till. He sliced off the beef inexpertly, narrowly missing his thumb in the process. With the point of the knife he pressed the bell which summoned little Fanny. She came limping in.

'Three underdone beefs,' said Perry. 'Three beefs full o'blood for three customers short of it. There you are, Fanny, my little pet. Why, what's the matter? Hurt your leg?'

'Twisted my knee,' said Fanny. 'Twisted it on them dark stairs . . .'

'Elliman's Embrocation,' said Perry. 'Elliman's is the stuff. Makes excellent gravy. Rub it well in, my pet. Look, I'll rub it for you. An expert at massage. The Sultan of Kuala would have decorated me for what I did for his fourth wife, but I couldn't stay. Is it swollen? Let me see.'

Fanny blushed and giggled and picked up the three plates and fled.

Uncle Perry opened another bottle of beer.

'They're all the same, me boy. They all like a little bit of fuss. From countess down to scullerymaid; black or white, red or yellow. Stap me if they don't!'

'The play was all about a Marquis tonight,' said Anthony.

'Lor' bless me, yes, if you haven't been off gallivanting to a play tonight like a young lord yourself, while I've been working my fingers to the bone. To the bone.' Uncle Perry scratched the back of his neck with the points of the carving fork and eyed the boy speculatively. 'What did you think of it? Don't tell me. I guess you enjoyed it. Lucky young tinker. Not that this is much in my line, this food business. I wouldn't demean myself by touching it if it wasn't for obliging a brother.'

'It was called *The Last of His Line*,' said Anthony. 'It –'

'Not that I couldn't turn my hand to anything if I chose,' said Perry. 'In 'Frisco in the winter of '89 for two weeks I helped a Chinaman to run his restaurant. Friend of mine, he was; I never believe in this colour bar.'

'The play had a Chinaman in it,' said Anthony. 'At least, I think it was only a white man pretending to be a Chinaman, but –'

'Now there was a man for you,' said Uncle Perry, tilting his chair back and putting his feet on the counter. His head disappeared for a few moments into the beer mug. 'There was a cook. None of these fat, flabby joints sawn straight off a dripping bullock. He used to buy *innards*, me boy, *yards* of 'em, and serve 'em up as anything you asked for: grilled pigeon, lark's breast, noodles, bamboo shoots. And they all tasted different. And if there was fungus growing on what he bought, so much the better; he'd make it into soup. He was a genius. None of this undercooked, *recognisable* stuff that'd turn anyone's stomach. No wonder your Uncle Joe's ill. No wonder he can't eat. Sitting here day after day with his nose bending over slices of sheep and diseased ducks. Poo, how they stink! They almost spoil a man's thirst.'

'Thank you, Perry,' said a voice. 'You will not need to spoil it any longer.'

Smoky Joe stood on the threshold of the little shop holding carefully to the door. He was fully dressed but his face was an ashen grey. His sharp eyes were watery and bloodshot and he spoke with difficulty. Behind him in the darkness of the passage was Patricia.

Uncle Perry put down his mug and put down his feet.

'Well, Joe, me bonny boy! I was just saying to our Anthony it was time you were down again. I knew you'd be down again soon. Welcome back to the old grindstone!'

'It's high time I came,' said Joe.

'Well, I've been doing my best, Joe. Haven't I, boy? Not a dissatisfied customer. Is there, boy? I've sold half your beef and a bit of duck. *And* given the right change. To a penny. Behold Matthew at the seat of custom. Always ready to do my bit when the proprietor's off his food.'

'With a mug of beer and your feet on the counter,' said Joe between tight lips. 'A fine business this would soon be with a drunken man at the till.'

Perry blinked and pushed the hair out of his eyes. 'Come now, Joe; that's a malig – malignancy. If you think I'm drunk you're barking up the wrong tree. Like the little dog Fido in the song.' He laughed. 'Why, if –'

'Let Joe sit down,' said Patricia. 'You don't seem to realise he's very ill. He should never have come down tonight.'

'Well, it's not my doing that he's come,' said Perry, suddenly sulky. 'This isn't my business. God damn it! I might have been doing him an injury instead of a favour.'

'No favour to me,' said Joe, sinking into his chair. 'I manage my own affairs –'

'When you're sick in bed, I suppose.'

'When I am ill Patricia will manage them. She is my daughter.'

'And I suppose you think I'm your brother and can be treated like dirt! Well, you're mistaken! I'm sick of this household and its airs. I'll not stand for it another week. Being treated as if I was a no-account! You can sit on your chair and rot, Brother Joe; you won't get any more help from me!'

Uncle Perry brushed past Anthony and the shop door slammed.

Patricia put her hand on the counter and kept her eyes down. With slow, painful movements Smoky Joe settled

65

himself into his usual position, rearranging the plates and the carving knives, rang the till and stared at the money in the various compartments of the drawer.

'Can I get you anything more, Dad?' Patricia asked.

'No . . . But you'd best stay here with me a while yet. Maybe you'll be able to help.' Smoky Joe slowly raised his head and looked at Anthony. 'Isn't it past your bedtime?'

'Yes. We've been out, you know.'

'That's no reason why you should stay up now, is it? Turning night into day will stop your growth. I'll be responsible to your father if you're pale and weakly when he sees you. Good night, boy.'

'Good night, Uncle. Good night, Pat. Thanks awfully for taking me out tonight.'

Patricia smiled as he passed her.

But he did not immediately go to bed.

9

As he entered the kitchen the heat and the familiar smell of it struck him like something he had known all his life. Here was the big square raftered room lit by gas which flickered uncertainly in the steam. On the left was the dark hole and the four steps which led down to the scullery and pantry. Welsh dressers lined one wall; the great table in the middle of the room was piled with dishes and jars and a pastry board; aprons were piled upon a chair; a cupboard door was open showing cooking utensils. Two cabbages and a bowl of scalded milk occupied another table. From the rafters, where they were not likely to catch in the hair, hung a string of onions, several fly-catchers and a dozen tea-towels. Along the wall opposite the dressers the huge kitchen range roared and hissed.

Among all this confusion, presiding over it as if she were its chosen deity, Aunt Madge stood stirring a giant cooking pot. There was no one else in the room, and she stood there big and slow-moving and withdrawn, thinking her private thoughts, her hair piled, her features snub and insignificant, a boned collar, earrings, and a cameo brooch showing above the anonymous pink apron. She considered it vulgar to have a bare neck even when cooking.

She turned when she heard a footstep and looked over the top of her pince-nez to see who it was. Then she relinquished her spoon and took off the pince-nez to wipe away the steam.

'A carrot,' she said. 'I should like. The scullery. Fanny . . .'

He ran down the dark steps into the scullery and found little Fanny wading through a stack of dirty plates. He got the carrot and returned.

Aunt Madge took it and began to slice it into the pot.

'You're cooking late tonight, Aunt Madge,' the boy said, reluctant to go upstairs, feeling too unsettled to sleep.

'We have an order,' she said. 'Men coming in. A ship. Who was that in the shop? Arguing . . .'

'Uncle Joe's just come down again.'

'Foolhardy. Was he shouting?'

'No. You see, Uncle Joe . . . Uncle Perry was drinking beer behind the counter. Uncle Joe didn't seem to like it. Uncle Perry's gone out.'

'Huff,' said Mrs Veal. 'Too touchy. But Joe was very wrong. He shouldn't . . . So foolhardy. Must persuade him. A doctor.'

Anthony walked round the kitchen. There were no confidences between himself and his aunt; nevertheless all that he had heard this evening seemed to come bubbling to his lips. It worried him and he could no longer contain it.

'I heard Mr Treharne talking tonight,' he said. 'You know, up at the Ship and Sailor. He said – he said that Uncle Joe was very . . . might not recover . . . He said . . .'

Aunt Madge took out her spoon. 'What were you doing . . . Ship and Sailor?'

'Oh, I wasn't there!' Anthony hastened on. 'It was in a queue at the theatre.'

There was silence. Aunt Madge shifted the pot a little off the stove and put on more coal. She opened the oven door and then shut it again without taking anything out. Anthony perceived that something was going on behind the pince-nez.

She took off her glasses and blew her nose. 'People. So unkind . . . Unkind to say such a thing. How does Mr Treharne . . . How does anybody know? Nobody, until he sees a doctor.'

'I'm sorry, Aunt Madge,' Anthony said. 'I just heard him say that.'

Mrs Veal shifted back the pot and began again mechanically to stir it. 'Married a year,' she said. 'I don't want . . . to be alone again. Lonely all my life. Your uncle . . . very kind. Though a little close. If he would take care. Give up drink and take care. I don't believe there's anything serious. That's if he takes care. But look at him. Won't have help. Hi've told him. Your Uncle Perry . . .'

Anthony shifted uncomfortably from one foot to the other and tried to think of something to say.

'Well, perhaps he'll be all right again tomorrow.'

There was a familiar rumble, and the dumb-waiter came up from the restaurant below. On it was a pile of used plates.

'For Fanny,' said Aunt Madge. 'Perhaps . . .'

Anthony hastened to obey this request. Glad to be out of an embarrassing situation, he remained in the scullery for some time helping Fanny to wipe the dishes. When he emerged, hoping that Patricia would be in the kitchen, he was disappointed to find his aunt still alone.

The stew was simmering on the stove, and she had begun to roll out some pastry.

'Bed,' said Mrs Veal. 'I thought you'd gone. High time.'

She was making pasties for the party of men who were expected in an hour. Fascinated he watched her short plump fingers cut out the pieces of pastry and arrange the potatoes, meat and onions upon it, scatter a pinch of salt, then in a

68

trice the pastry had been turned in to contain the meat, and the nimble fingers had made a curious decorative pattern where the pastry joined.

'Aunt Madge,' he said, 'I wonder when I shall hear from Father again.'

She worked silently for some minutes, and the pasties multiplied, ready to go into the oven.

'Bed,' she said. 'He should have stayed in bed. No reasoning . . . Where's Patricia?'

'In the shop, I think.'

'Must go and see when these are done. See if he's . . .'

'Aunt Madge, how long does it take for a letter to come from Canada?'

'Eaten nothing all day. Can't go on like that. Canada? The one we had yesterday. Weeks . . .'

'You had a letter yesterday?' he exclaimed excitedly. 'From Father! I didn't know. What did he say?'

Another pasty grew and came into shape. Her fingers were like machines.

'Schooling,' she said. 'Only about schooling.'

'What did he say? You mean . . .' Excitement suddenly left the boy as air will escape from a pricked balloon. 'Does he mean I'm to go to school here?'

Through her wobbly pince-nez she stared at the pasties as if trying to estimate whether she had made enough. Then she took up a few bits of pastry which were left and began to roll them together.

'One more. One or two more . . .'

'Aunt Madge . . .'

She looked at him. 'Not good enough. Father's duty to his son. *Make* a home. That's what I say.'

'Aren't I to go out to him? Why mustn't I go?'

'Questions. Next spring, he says. School here this winter. We must see what your uncle says.'

'Didn't he put in a message for me?'

'His love. He says conditions . . . no place for a boy in winter. Not quite right. Your uncle isn't fit to see about schooling. Inadequate, besides.'

Anthony watched her for some minutes. All the pasties were put upon a shelf and slipped into the oven.

'Tomorrow,' she said. 'Doctor. Your uncle has too much on his mind. Won't allow others to help.'

'Aunt Madge,' the boy said, 'do you think I could read Father's letter? You see, I haven't had one from him for ages. I wrote to him last week and the week before. If I could see what he said I should know more what to say.'

She waved a hand. 'Your uncle. Personally . . . boy's place is with his father. Should go to school in Canada. Or he should come home. Evading responsibility. Your uncle must see a doctor. That Mr Treharne . . . No right to spread such stories. So unkind. Get back to Joe and then he'd think perhaps it was true. Hi shall speak to Mr Treharne.'

'Has Uncle Joe got the letter?'

Patricia entered the kitchen. Aunt Madge peered at her.

'He seems better,' said the girl. 'What happened, Madge? How long was he like that?'

'Fanny,' said Mrs Veal, shaking her earrings. 'Always dawdling down there. Dawdling over a few things. Everything left to me. Where's your Uncle Perry?'

'He went out in a rage. How was it –'

'*He* saw him. He just said: "Perry, help me upstairs." When I went up he hardly knew me. Just said his limbs were numb.' Aunt Madge took out her handkerchief again. Her short fleshy nose disappeared into it. 'But Mr Treharne has no right. He only needs a few days in bed.'

The girl looked perplexed. 'What has Mr Treharne to do with it? Did he help?'

Mrs Veal went back to stir the stew. 'Must have a doctor. Tomorrow morning. Can't go on. What time are these men coming?'

'Tonight? In half an hour, Joe said.'

'The pasties won't be ready. Have to wait. Persuade him to go to bed. Hi can't.'

'I'll do my best,' said Pat. 'I'm afraid it's a hopeless case, though.'

She went back into the shop.

Aunt Madge tasted the stew.

'Another carrot,' she said. 'In the scullery. And Anthony . . . see what Fanny is doing.'

What pressure was brought to bear upon Joe – unless it was his own feelings – Anthony never knew; but the next day the doctor was summoned. He was a tall, elderly man with muttonchop whiskers and he was upstairs for an hour.

When he came down a cloud had been lifted from the house. He had been not at all discouraging, Pat said. Joe must spend at least a week in bed. Milk food was to be his only diet and he must neither smoke nor drink. Absolute rest and quiet; then perhaps a little change of air. He'd give him some ointment for his eczema and some pills to be taken after meals. There was no reason why there should not be a big improvement before the month was out. Joe lay in bed, looking smaller and more dog-like than ever in his nightshirt, and watched the doctor out of shrewd inimical eyes.

The business of the house was arranged to meet the new situation. To assuage her father's restless spirit, Pat promised to take over his vigil behind the counter; but she found this task even more tedious than she had anticipated, and two or three times each day she risked the Wrath by handing over charge to Perry. Perry was quite undeterred from doing this by any memory of the quarrel he had had with Joe. The morning after the quarrel he had turned up for breakfast at eleven o'clock, laughing his usual laugh and cracking his accustomed jokes as if nothing had happened. The memory of what had occurred had run off him like water off the champion swimmer he claimed to be.

On the fourth day *The Grey Cat* was seen lying in the roads, and Joe sent out his daughter to ask Captain Stevens to call on the morrow.

Anthony always enjoyed these visits to his uncle's ships but today was a special treat. Patricia could in fact row as well as any man, but she had no objection to sitting in the back of the dinghy and trailing a hand over the side if that suited her cousin better.

She was very simply but very charmingly dressed today, and Anthony wondered if the extra care she had taken was on Captain Stevens's account or was directed at his mate.

The effect was certainly more obvious upon the latter. They had been under observation as they approached, for Ned Pawlyn was down the short ladder to meet them, his clean broad face a-beam, the breeze ruffling his black hair.

'I could hardly believe my eyes,' he exclaimed. 'I said to myself, "That can't be the Old Man; is it my eyes that's wrong? Or have I a fairy godmother?" Hold on, son; ship your oar; steady up; make her fast; that's the way. Now take my hand, my dear.'

Patricia laughed at his eagerness. She stepped upon the gunnel of the boat, and then climbed swiftly and easily up the ladder with a flutter of lace petticoats. Anthony fumed a little at the unnecessary instructions which were offered him, but soon was climbing the side after the other two.

'Where's the captain?' said Pat. 'Dad's not well and I have a message for him.'

'In his cabin. When I saw who it was I didn't tell him of your coming. Well, and I'm sorry to hear about the Old Man; but 'tis an ill wind that blows no one any good. Otherwise I'd not have seen you before this evening. I couldn't have got away until then. Don't tell me you're engaged to do something else.'

Patricia turned her face to the breeze and smiled. 'The ill wind does not bring all good. With Joe in bed I must stay in and help. I am deputising for him behind the counter.'

Ned Pawlyn made a face.

'Then I'll help you there. I'll sit behind the counter too! I am sure I can carve a chicken better than you.'

She shook her head, pursing her lips a little. 'Joe wouldn't allow it. The only time you will see me will be when you are ordering your evening meal –'

72

'I'll order everything in the place,' he threatened. 'And eat it. And come back for more. You'll not get rid of me so easily as that –'

She laughed again, enjoying his easy good-tempered banter; but at that moment Captain Stevens came on deck and approached them.

'Mister Pawlyn; ye did not tell me we had a distinguished visitor.'

'Beg your pardon, sir; I was so astonished myself –'

'I hope your father's well, Miss Patricia.'

'Well, no, he isn't. I've brought you a message from him.'

'Will you step down into the saloon, please . . . ?'

Anthony was left alone with the tall, good-looking mate. There was silence for a time, for the boy was taking in all the shipping which lay around him. One of the great wind-jammers on the Australian run had arrived in Falmouth yesterday after the worst passage in her chequered history. Anthony had heard the story in snatches last evening when the master had had a meal at Smoky Joe's. She had limped into Falmouth after a passage of 197 days from Brisbane, having faced consistently adverse weather and having been partly de-sparred off the Portuguese coast near the end of her long ordeal. So instead of riding silently and proudly out in the bay she had accepted a pilot and come into the harbour to lick her wounds.

'Well, son, and how have things been doing at Smoky Joe's while I've been away? I hear that the threepenny gaffs are here again.'

'Yes.'

'You should go to Liverpool, son. They have proper theatres there. 'Tis not many days since I was at a handsome music-hall show.' Ned Pawlyn began to describe it.

'Did you have a good voyage?' Anthony said, still looking at the battered windjammer.

'Eh? Voyage? Oh, it was all right. Head winds off the Carnarvon coast. Has that fellow Tom Harris been round plaguing your cousin's life out since I left?'

Anthony looked up at the mate. 'Not really . . . We've seen him once.'

'Well, let's hope we don't see him while I'm ashore,' said Pawlyn. 'Else I shall be tempted to pull his tall hat down over his ears. I'd dearly like to have him aboard this ship for a voyage or two.'

They chatted for some minutes until Patricia reappeared, escorted by the captain.

Anthony climbed over the side and got into the boat.

'Goodbye, Captain Stevens. Goodbye, Mr Pawlyn.'

'Goodbye, ma'am.'

'I hope I can have the pleasure o' calling upon you tonight,' said Ned.

Patricia smiled. 'I hope you'll be hungry.'

A moment later she had joined Anthony in the dinghy, and he was pulling away.

Ned waved from the side and the girl waved back.

None of them would have been quite so light-hearted had they known all that the evening was to bring.

10

While they were away Dr Penrose had paid his third visit, and he seemed very cheery and much encouraged by Joe's improvement – so much so that when he had gone Joe announced his intention of getting up that evening. This went so far beyond the medical sanction that Aunt Madge and Patricia did their utmost to dissuade him.

But as usual he was adamant. This was Saturday night; there might be a big crowd; the whole place would need his supervision; besides, he felt better, the doctor had said he was better; this staying in bed was no more than the usual physician's fad, instructions designed to increase the doctor's importance so that he could charge an extra two shillings a visit. As it was, three visits in little more than a week was pretty tight going; he should think Penrose thought they were made of money, coming so often and doing so little. Anybody could stand by a bedside and look important at so much a time. They were all the same; Penrose was no better than Dr Barrat Clark with whom he had quarrelled over the bill for his wife's last illness. Had Fanny done enough potatoes for tonight? It was wasteful not to give customers enough potatoes.

He was helped into his alpaca coat and high white collar and assisted downstairs. They brought him a drink of patent milk food which he swallowed with many grunts and grimaces. Then before they were able to stop him his hand was fumbling with his bizarre old pipe and a match trembled and flickered at its bowl. A cloud of blue smoke hid his thin, wasted face, and when it emerged there was a different and more satisfied expression on it. Smoky Joe was himself again.

The restaurant began to fill up. There were many ships in the bay, the summer gales of last week having forced the smaller ones to run for shelter. The crew of the windjammer had also been allowed ashore, but so far only the three mates had arrived at JOE VEAL'S. The rest were celebrating their release in a succession of public houses.

Ned Pawlyn arrived about five-thirty, and when he knew that Joe was about again he pressed Patricia to go out with him for the evening. This she agreed to do, but only for a limited time, and they were back soon after seven. Pawlyn then went with her into the kitchen, anxious to help. Later in the evening nine of the windjammer crew, all Finns or Swedes and all in a merry state, arrived for supper. They ordered a slap-up meal and tramped into the upper restaurant; but finding the three mates there they turned round and tramped, laughing and talking, down to the lower restaurant where they would be free from the oppressive influence of authority.

Shortly after this Anthony had to take another milk drink into Joe and was told to stay while he drank it. All this week he had been anxious to ask his uncle for details of what his

75

father had written, but there had been no opportunity to do so. Now, with some trepidation and spoken apologies for troubling the old man, he brought up the subject.

Joe peered at him with watery eyes over the top of the repulsive glass.

'I've only met your father once,' he said, 'so how can I tell what he means? Of course he's offered to pay for your schooling, for I haven't the money to spare. But I doubt if what he offers will cover the cost. And a young fellow like you eats up a pretty penny in the way of food; then there's clothing and what-not. We'll have to see.'

'Doesn't he want me to go out to Canada at all?'

'I went prospecting once in my young days,' said Joe. 'It isn't a time when you want somebody *attached* to you. You've got to be free. You've got to travel light and travel rough. He says he'll be in Winnipeg in the spring; maybe you'll be able to join him then. But you can't just do nothing here all winter; he sees that. Your aunt'll see about a school, see which we can afford on what your father's sent. 'Tisn't a lot he's sent; we've got to cut our coat according to the cloth. Can't be ambitious on a few pounds.' He put down the empty glass and shuddered. 'Pah! Pobs . . . Babies' food. No stuff for a grown man. That's what this life does for you: when you're young you feed on milk; then when you grow up you grow to know what's good; when you're old you have to go back to milk again . . .' He hastily re-lit his pipe.

Two customers entered. They were the bosun and sailmaker of the windjammer, both Germans. The sailmaker was an inoffensive, pleasant little man; but Todt, the bosun, square-built and fair-haired and mean, although one of the best sailors afloat, was hated in his ship. They parleyed for a few minutes in guttural tones, then paid for their meals and went in. Following almost on their heels came three more men off a Penzance tug which had brought in a damaged brig that afternoon. Two were weather-beaten west-Cornishmen; the third, who had had a little too much to drink, was a red-haired Scottish engineer. While they

76

were discussing what they should have, a single customer entered. It was Tom Harris.

He stood back while the other men were being satisfied. There was not so much of the dandy about him tonight, Anthony thought; he was wearing a cap and a tweed suit.

Joe had bristled at the sight of him, but he said nothing until they were alone. As the other three men disappeared he put down his carving knife and fork and took out his pipe to wipe down his moustache with the mouth-piece.

'What do you want?'

'I'm glad to see you up,' said the younger man in an uncontroversial tone. 'I'd heard you were unwell.'

'Never mind that,' said Joe. 'What do you want?'

'A meal. It's not Sunday today.' Harris glanced along the counter. 'This is a clever way of running things. There's something about an array of cooked meats and fowl and other tasty dishes that appeals to the glutton in us all. The sight of them together –'

'I don't want any of your advice,' Joe said, trembling with weakness and annoyance. 'If you've come to see Patricia you'll be disappointed.'

'I want a meal,' Tom Harris said. 'Nothing more. I'm in Falmouth for the evening and have come to the place where I can get the best meal. It's a matter of business. I think it's against your principles ever to refuse a customer, isn't it?' He took out a sovereign and put it on the counter.

'I can look after my own principles, thank you,' Joe muttered. 'I don't want a legal opinion on them.' But his eyes wandered to the gold coin.

There was silence. Tom looked at Anthony and smiled slightly.

'Are you full?' he asked. 'I can wait.'

'It's just a trick to see Patricia. I know you. It won't do you any good.'

'She's under no compulsion to see me. It's quite outside my control. Is that pheasant you have there? I should like some of that, with a little steamed fish before it.

Come, take the money and give me what change you please.'

'I've my fixed charges,' the old man said aggressively. 'You needn't think I profiteer on anybody. Have you come here to spy?'

Tom Harris looked mildly exasperated.

'My dear sir, your daughter happens to be my wife whether we like it or not. I'm not likely to wish to bring you into disrepute while that's the case.'

Smoky Joe picked up the coin and rang it on the counter. Then he put it into the till and slid a half-sovereign and some smaller change across to the younger man.

'Lower restaurant,' he said. 'You'll get your first course in a few minutes.'

Joe's reason for directing Harris to the lower floor was that he knew Patricia to have been helping on the upper one, which had rapidly filled up. What he did not know was that, with the immediate rush over, Pat had gone down to the lower one to begin her own supper at a table with Ned Pawlyn.

When Tom entered they had just been served at a small corner table near the window. His eyes went as if by a magnet towards them, but his expression did not alter and he walked across to the other side of the room and took an empty table next to that occupied by the nine Finns and Swedes.

When Patricia saw him her colour changed, as it always seemed to do when he appeared unexpectedly, and Pawlyn, following the direction of her gaze, uttered a growl of dislike.

'What's the matter with the fellow?' he said. 'Always skulking around. Don't he know when to take "no" for an answer?'

'He's not here at my invitation,' said Pat. 'I told him last week; I was quite straight about it. He said . . .'

'What did he say?'

'Oh, it was nothing important. Let's forget about him.' She suddenly realised it would have been dangerous to mention her husband's objection to Ned Pawlyn in front of Ned Pawlyn. 'Dad should never have let him in. He must know that it's embarrassing to me to have him calling here.'

'What he needs is a lesson in how to take "no" for an answer. I'd dearly like to give it him. He'd stop skulking if he felt the weight of my boot.'

'Hush, hush. Eat your supper like a good boy and talk of something else.'

The meal progressed. Tom Harris was served and ate his meal very slowly. So did Patricia and Ned, for they were talking and joking between themselves. The girl paid more attention to the sailor than she had ever done before, in order to show Tom her complete freedom and independence. Ned was enchanted to find he was making progress at last.

Tom finished his second course and ordered cheese and coffee. This ordering of more food when the other dishes had been eaten was something 'not done' at Joe's. David, the young lascar waiter, was nonplussed and went into the kitchen to ask for instructions. Presently he returned with a large piece of bread and cheese on a plate, but no coffee. Tom gave him a shilling and lit a cigarette.

All through the meal one of the Swedes at the next table, a big, blond, pasty-faced man, had been giggling at Tom Harris. There was nothing specially funny in the solicitor, but the Swede was in such a state that anything would amuse him. The episode of the coffee and cheese was altogether too much. His laughter shook the room, then he choked and knocked over a glass of beer and all his comrades fell noisily to smacking him on the back and laughing and arguing among themselves. The German bosun, eating an enormous plate of roast pork near the door, put down his knife and fork and shouted at them a command to make less noise.

His voice was as ill-tempered as his look. The air was filled with catcalls in reply.

> *'Falla Båtsman! . . .'*
> *'Inga bra, bawsted! Inga bra!'*
> *'Satan och Satan; kyss me, Satan!'*

When it seemed that there might be a scene, several new-comers entered the room and the worst of the noise died down. But the pasty-faced Swede still went on giggling.

Then the lame accordionist struck up a tune and several people hummed and whistled the chorus. After a few minutes some of Uncle Perry's friends pushed him forward from his corner. With a self-conscious grin he took up his usual position beneath the figurehead of the *Mary Lee Melford*, pushed back his hair with two fingers and began to sing.

> *'There was a youth, a well-loved youth*
> *And he was a squire's son;*
> *He loved the bailiff's daughter dear*
> *That lived in Islington.*
> *Yet she was coy and would not believe*
> *That he did love her so;*
> *No, nor at any time would she*
> *Any favours to him show.'*

Tom Harris finished his cigarette and stubbed it out. He was well aware of the amusement he was giving the Swede, but he ignored the man with good-humoured tolerance. All the same, the consciousness of being laughed at, together with the circumstance of seeing his wife flirting with another man, had frayed the edges of his temper.

There was applause when Perry finished. He grinned again and turned to the accordionist, wiping his good-humoured, feckless, indolent face. Tom Harris got up to go.

Perry began the verse of a popular song of the eighties. Tom took his cap from a convenient hatstand while the Swede went off into a fresh burst of giggling. The solicitor went across the room to the table where his wife was sitting and spoke to her. Ned Pawlyn, in an instant changed like a dog from playful pleasure to prickly dislike, sat and glowered at him but did not speak.

Perry reached the chorus, and all those who had finished eating, and many who had not, joined in the rollicking song.

Explosions of violence in public places usually occur without the least warning to the majority of people indirectly concerned. Ill-temper, enmity, malice, have flourished unawares in their midst. No one has seen or suspected anything. Two, four, half a dozen people may be quietly reaching a point of white-hot anger while all about them others read or eat or are entertained quite unaffected. Only when these emotions reach flash point are they communicated to spectators through the medium of action. Of such insensitive clay are we made.

It is as if gunpowder has been quietly scattering itself about the room. No one notices, no one cares. All tramp where they please, kicking or stumbling with impunity. Then someone drops a lighted match.

The room was noisy but peaceful. Square and low and raftered and full of smoke, with its ancient bow windows looking out upon the winking lights of the river and harbour, there was a faintly Continental air about its decorations as well as its company. Perry, with his bold, lazy, brigand's face, stood under the painted figurehead singing his song while an old man, with a wooden leg and a bald head shining in the gaslight, accompanied him upon his battered accordion and many of the company joined in. Near the service hatch and underneath a picture of Admiral Pellew in action against the Malay pirates, two Germans, with the air of starving men, were rapidly finishing off large plates of pork. In the corner window-seat a respectable, staid-looking young man in a neat respectable tweed suit was conversing with a pretty girl and a dark-haired sailor. In the middle window-seat was a mixed party of six and in the other corner window-seat two hard-bitten Cornishmen were arguing good temperedly with a red-haired engineer. Stretching across the width of the ancient brick fireplace was a long table containing the nine Norsemen from the windjammer. The rest of the tables were all filled. There were model ships on shelves and ships in bottles, and dark smoky oil-paintings of ships hung on the yellow-painted walls.

Into this comfortable cosmopolitan scene a lighted match was dropped. It flashed and flared suddenly at the corner table by the window. The man in the respectable tweeds was speaking to the girl, and the sailor lolling on the opposite side of the table made a remark. That was the match. The man in the respectable tweeds abruptly leaned across the table and smacked the sailor across the face with his open hand, the sound being heard clearly and sharply above all the other noise. In a second the sailor was up, had grasped the other man by the throat, and pulled him across the table regardless of the plates and the cutlery and was trying to force his head down.

11

The singing persisted only for a few moments against this unfair competition. First the diners stopped. Then Perry stopped. Then the cripple stopped; and everyone's attention was on the scuffling couple in their midst.

Ned Pawlyn had never in his life known what it was to be so grossly insulted as by that open-handed smack. A straightforward punch he would have accepted with far less malice.

For a few moments he went berserk, pulling his struggling opponent across the table by sheer muscular strength before Harris could break free. Then, while Patricia shrank back against the wall, he pursued the half-strangled Harris round the table, hitting him almost as he chose until the solicitor staggered back into the table containing the two

Germans and sat on the knee of Todt the bosun. At this there was an unholy shriek of laughter from the drunken Swede.

Todt swore and dragged his pork away from a tweed elbow and thrust Harris to his feet again. Harris stood up and drew breath. There was a look in his eye which Pat had never seen before. He took off his coat and dropped it on the floor. Then he went out to Pawlyn with a will.

It is possible at this stage that had Perry stepped forward with an air of authority and thrust himself between the two the clash would have ended there, or at least been transferred to a more suitable venue out of doors. But Perry was a man concerned in avoiding his own troubles, not one to interfere in other people's. And Patricia, who should have run upstairs for her father, found she could not move. She was like a witch who had been playing with forbidden potions and was now aghast at the spectre she had conjured up.

The next table to suffer was that of the six in the window, and this time it was Pawlyn who was retreating with Tom closely following him. The table went with them and the girl at the end screamed shrilly as she was nearly pushed through the window. The men at this table were all youngsters; one of them put his hands on Pawlyn's shoulder but he was shaken off and brushed aside. The table continued to slide back, and the red-haired Scotsman found himself suddenly hemmed in by strange people who seemed to want to push him off his chair. He got to his feet and shouted and began to push back.

At this moment pressure was relieved by a turn in the nature of the fight. The two men grappled and went reeling back into their own table. David the waiter appeared on the stairs, gazed open-mouthed and fled.

Neither of the two men now seemed to have any advantage. They were both far too angry to remember any boxing they had ever been taught. What Tom Harris lacked in hardness of hand he made up in determination and staying power. There was something about the shape of his neck when his collar came off which suggested he would be a hard man to have done with, for all his respectability.

One of Ned Pawlyn's eyebrows had begun to bleed, and to clear his sight he tried to break away. But Tom was still holding, and in the next scuffle he succeeded in getting two more punches to the same eye. Then Pawlyn butted Tom and sent him staggering. He arrived back once more on top of Todt, and the chair beneath them, which Smoky Joe should have discarded nine months ago, gave way and collapsed on the floor.

A jeer of satisfaction went up this time not only from the drunken Swede but from all his less intoxicated companions.

Todt cursed and rolled over and kicked Tom Harris furiously in the back. He was about to kick him again as he got to his feet, but at that moment a bottle sailed through the air and smashed against the wall above Todt's head. He was showered with beer and broken glass.

His attention diverted from Harris, he rose to his feet and looked where the bottle had come from. As he did this the red-haired Scotsman, irritated by the press about him, cuffed one of the inoffensive youngsters on the ear and in so doing upset his own table.

David the waiter had been up to summon Smoky Joe. Joe, his hands wavering and clumsy, rose from his seat, locked the till, gave a key to the youth to lock the shop door and directed Anthony to run for the police. Then Joe picked up his carving knife and proceeded, supported by David, to the scene of battle.

But before they reached the head of the stairs they were met by a stream of people anxious to get out. With an irritated angry wave of his carving knife Joe directed them towards the kitchen, then went on. Half-way down the stairs he halted.

This was worse than the uproar of six months ago. Stopping it was obviously beyond even his moral powers. Certainly it was beyond the physical power of a single carving knife. Not two were fighting now but eighteen or twenty. In a bedlam of overturned tables and broken crockery men were fighting desperately with each other as if the mortal enmity of a lifetime had bubbled over and was blistering their souls with hatred.

There were four Swedes and five Finns and two Germans and two Cornish sailors and a red-haired Scotsman from Ayr and two young shop assistants who had never been to Smoky Joe's before and would never come again, and a Cornish mate and a Cornish solicitor and three or four odds and ends who had been unwittingly embroiled. The one-legged musician had retired into the most isolated corner of the room. Perry Veal stood by the fireplace shouting horrible curses and threats and eating a piece of cake.

Even now the thing might have ended as suddenly as it had begun. While light persisted reason was not far away. There would be a point when the first impulse to violence had exhausted itself and most of the men would be glad to draw breath.

Unfortunately at this point the three mates of the windjammer, having heard the noise, came hurrying down from the upstairs room. Joe greeted their arrival thankfully; he waved his carving knife towards the struggling figures and shouted quaveringly. A tall young Finn heard the shout and glanced up; he saw the mates and knew well the feel of their hard fists. So as they came down the stairs he reached up and turned off the three gas-taps of the chandelier.

Darkness fell on the room.

Patricia found herself deprived of sight. She wanted to scream; the sound choked in the back of her throat. She stared into a darkness which had not yet even assumed shape; outside there were the winking lights of the harbour shipping; these grew brighter in the corner of her retina; but ahead and around was nothing at all. Only her ears told her that the darkness, far from putting a stop to what she had last seen, had added its own secretive encouragement. The scuffling and grunting of men, the shouts and threats, the crack of dishes and the thud of furniture ebbed and flowed about her. She could press no closer to the wall, could shrink no further into the corner. Once a man thumped into the wall beside her. Then a chair fell against her legs and a bottle rolled off it.

Suddenly a man rose beside her, touched her hand and arm, following it to the shoulder. She drew in her breath.

'That you, Pat?' said the voice. It was Tom.

'Yes,' she said, feeling sick.

'Is there any way out of this place but by the stairs?'

Anger and hostility followed relief. He had begun everything; but for him there would have been no trouble at all.

'Well?' he said, his voice rough and low.

'Ned!' she called. 'Ned! He's over here, by me.'

'He won't answer you just yet,' Harris said grimly. 'What sort of a drop is it from this window?'

She would not answer. Someone, she thought it was one of the shop assistants, had got into a panic and was shouting in a shrill voice: 'Bring a light! There's somebody dead! Bring a light!'

By now shapes and different degrees of darkness were coming to the room. Dim light reached down the stairs from the shop above.

'You little fool,' said Tom. 'Haven't you the sense to come out of your sulks at a time like this?'

He had never spoken to her in that tone before. It made her desperately determined not to help him.

'It's like you to run away,' she said, 'now that you've caused all the trouble.'

He had opened the window and was peering out. He withdrew his head. 'There are knives about,' he said. 'You're just as likely to get one as I am. Come on.'

'Where's Ned?' she demanded

'Under the table. Safe enough, but he banged his head.' He put his hand on her arm.

She shook herself free. 'Let me alone!'

He gripped her elbows with hands which had no time to be respectful. He pulled her to the window.

86

'Will you jump or shall I drop you?'

'Let me go! Ned! Ned!' she shouted.

Someone struck a match in the room behind her, and immediately it was knocked out. 'Bring a light!' screamed the voice. 'Bring a light!'

She found herself sitting on the window-sill. Fear of falling made her cling to it. Then he was beside her and before she had time to say any more they had fallen together.

The ground came up so quickly that it seemed to hurt more than if they had had some way to fall. She bruised her hand and twisted her ankle on the hard cobblestones.

As she sat up the first impression was of peace and coolness and that great emptiness of the open air which, after leaving a room full of people, seems to echo with the faint sounds of a thousand miles of space. The whisper of water came to her ears, reminding her that the tide was in.

He was already up and bent to help her to her feet.

'I can't get up,' she said. 'I've hurt my ankle.'

Only the second of these statements was strictly true.

'I'm sorry,' he said. 'If you'll put your arms round my neck I'll lift you.'

'Leave me alone,' she said. 'I can get back to the house myself.'

'You're better out of it at present. The police will be here any minute.'

'Well, I want to go back. Dad will need me.'

He bent and with a big effort picked her up – for it is no easy task to lift a woman from the ground level when she offers you no help at all.

Once up, the carrying was quite simple.

'Where are you going?' she said. 'I tell you Dad needs me! He'll want my help. He's been ill!'

'I know that well enough.' He walked on, to the edge of the wall and began to go down the stone steps to the water.

She was afraid to struggle lest they should both fall. She could not imagine where he was going. Did he intend to take her out in a rowing-boat at this time of night and argue with her in the middle of the harbour?

At the bottom she found that the tide was not as far in as she had imagined; there was room to walk along the base of the wall among the flotsam of this morning's tide, which was what he now did.

'I don't know what you think you're doing,' she said, finding it hard to think of the dignified protest.

He did not reply, and she stared at his profile in the darkness. His hair was over his forehead like a new Uncle Perry.

'Dad's been seriously ill,' she said. 'If he has a relapse you'll be to blame; it was his first time out of bed; I didn't think you'd ever do what you've done tonight, Tom.'

'It's time we all started thinking afresh,' he said.

About a hundred yards from where they had descended a big square shape loomed up. It was a large boathouse belonging to the Royal Cornwall Yacht Club. Harris was a member of this club and as he reached it, stumbling once or twice over the seaweed and the loose stones, he turned towards the back of the house and found a small door.

'Can you stand a minute?' He put her on her feet, keeping one arm round her waist while he found the key. Then he unlocked the door and carried her inside.

They bumped against a boat, and he set her down upon some sort of a seat against the wall while he stood by the door and lit an oil lamp which stood there. Then he shut the door and the light from the oil lamp spread itself slowly.

Patricia found she was sitting on an old couch which had evidently begun its days in the club room and was ending them here. The house was full of the usual paraphernalia of its kind: oars slung from the ceiling, rowlocks hung on nails, pots of paint and fishing tackle on shelves. There was only one small boat in residence, for the sailing season was not yet over.

88

He came across to her carrying the lamp. He was still in his shirt sleeves, and one sleeve was torn and his waistcoat had lost all but one button. There was blood drying on his forehead and a big black bruise on the left cheek-bone.

'I'll go to the police and make a statement in the morning,' he said; 'but you're keeping out of this, Pat. I'm not having you in the courts again. We can stay here for an hour and then I'll take you back.'

She stared at him again curiously, trying to fathom the change which had come over him tonight.

'I don't care about the courts,' she said. 'It's not fair to keep me here when Dad needs me.'

'He's got a wife. There's nothing you can do except become involved with the police.'

She sat there in mutinous silence.

'Is your ankle painful?'

'Yes,' she said.

'There's a tap somewhere. Perhaps I could bathe it.'

She did not reply. He sat looking at her for a moment, then rose and picked up a bucket and walked over to the double doors, seeking the tap.

She watched him carefully until he was the furthest distance away, then sprang up and ran to the little door. She reached it before he even heard her. She would have been through it before he could move but the door stuck. She pulled at it madly; there was a catch on it somewhere which she could not see; there it was; her fingers fumbled; that was it; the door opened; she was out; but on the very threshold of freedom his hands closed round her waist and pulled her struggling back again.

Patricia was the reverse of an ill-tempered girl, but she was hot-blooded, and tonight's experiences had jagged her nerves. In his arms she was suddenly beside herself with frustration and anger. She twisted and hit him in the face and kicked him with her pointed shoes. It was a bad policy. With a display of faintness she would have disarmed him and taken control of the situation. But such a reaction reawakened the devil in him which had been roused for the first time that night.

He pinned her arms to her sides and began to kiss her. The sting of her kicks were a bitter flavour added to the sweetness of her face.

She wriggled like an eel and fought herself half free. He laughed and exerted all his strength to hold her. She tried to bite him, and he avoided the mouth while it was open and kissed it as soon as it was closed.

'You beast! You beast!'

'This,' he said, '. . . possession – ten points of the law.'

She tried to scream, but every time he squeezed the breath out of her; and presently it began to dawn on her that she was fighting a losing battle. Now she went suddenly limp and helpless. But the trick was played late. He only seemed to take her limpness for deliberate acquiescence.

Scandalised, she began to struggle again, but more weakly, for her strength was partly gone.

So it came to pass that Patricia, who had begun the evening flirting with Ned Pawlyn, ended it in the company of her husband. Had Tom Harris been more of a brute the encounter might have gone further than it did. Patricia, for once in her life, was really frightened, for she did not misread his intention. Love can so change that it becomes instead a fusion of hatred and desire. That was what Tom Harris found.

But unless the change is absolute, it can injure but it cannot wilfully destroy. That and something in the fundamental relationship between civilised man and woman finally stood in his way.

Not, however, before she had paid in good measure for her deceit and resistance.

He turned quite suddenly and left her there on the old couch, bruised and breathless and silent. She had never been so shaken up since she was three.

12

Policemen are not often found when and where they are most needed. Anthony had to run half a mile, as far as the parish church of Charles the Martyr, before he came on two standing defensively in the recess by the steps.

Market Street and Church Street were not pleasant at this time of a Saturday night; the boy was astonished and rather frightened by what he saw. Sailors were sitting on doorsteps singing, women were arguing shrilly outside public houses, and drunks lay about in the gutter waiting for the wheelbarrow men to come along and take them back to their ships or to some convenient doss-house.

By the time he reached the policemen he was so much out of breath that he had difficulty in explaining what was the matter, but rather suspiciously they decided to accept his word and hurried with him back to Smoky Joe's.

When they reached the scene of the trouble they found that order was just being restored. The Chief Mate of the windjammer had succeeded in lighting the gases again, and the fight had been broken off. Casualties were about to be examined for serious injury. Contrary to the statement being shouted in the darkness, nobody was dead, but four were unconscious, and this made an impressive picture. The most seriously injured was Todt, who in addition to a broken arm had been hit over the head with a bottle. Then one of the young shop assistants had been hit by the Scottish engineer and had fainted clean away. The tall Finn who had turned out the gas had been put out of reach of further mischief by the second mate, and the drunken Swede with the giggles had gone under with drink and was snoring peacefully with his head in the fireplace.

The second mate had a knife cut on his cheek and one of the Cornish sailors was bleeding from a similar cut in the forearm. Ned Pawlyn was on his feet, supporting himself against a chair and looking furiously round the room. One of the girls with the shop assistants was in tears. Uncle Perry had finished his piece of cake.

The long process of inquiry stretched out to infinitely tedious lengths. During it Joe Veal sat upright in a chair, his mouth set in a line beneath the grey-black moustache. He did not move and hardly spoke except now and then to shoot out a word at this witness or that. Aunt Madge stood beside him, her pince-nez wobbling with indignation from time to time. In this crisis Joe had gone back to his whisky, and no cajolings could persuade him to renounce it for milk food.

The upshot of all these painstaking inquiries, so far as the testimony went, was that the disturbance had been begun by one Thomas Wilberforce Harris, a solicitor of Penryn. It seemed that this man, under the influence of drink, had forced his way into the restaurant much against the wishes of the Proprietor, Mr Joe Veal, and having seated himself at one table for a time, had then gone across to a table where Edward Pawlyn, mate of *The Grey Cat*, had been peacefully having a meal and had tried to pick a quarrel. Edward Pawlyn had refused to take him seriously until he leaned forward and hit him across the face. Despite all efforts to calm him, Thomas Wilberforce Harris had continued to fight. Failing to rouse his chosen opponent to the proper pitch, he had then set upon the six young people eating in the middle window table, and pushed their table across the room and knocked one of their number unconscious with a foul blow in the stomach. He had then thrown a beer bottle at Heidrich Todt, bosun of the *Listerhude*, rendering him unconscious, and had finally begun to aim any crockery he could lay his hands on at the nine Norsemen eating by the fireplace.

This was about as far as the matter could go at the moment. The only circumstance which troubled Constables Smith and Behenna was that this Thomas Wilberforce Harris, having, as it were, stirred up trouble on every side, had somehow with diabolical ingenuity succeeded in making his escape in the darkness, leaving all these peaceable people fighting furiously among themselves. However, being not without experience in matters of this sort, they made no editorial comment.

And presently, when all the names and addresses had been taken and all the statements had been written down, one by one the witnesses were allowed to go. After that, in their own good time, the policemen also went; and there were left only Smoky Joe and his wife Madge and their nephew Anthony and brother Perry and David the waiter and Ned Pawlyn, standing and sitting in various attitudes amid the dust and the ruins.

The instant they were alone Ned Pawlyn snapped:

'Where's Patricia?'

'That's what I want to know,' said Aunt Madge.

'So we shall,' said Joe, between tight lips. 'So we shall.'

'Do you know where she is?' Pawlyn asked.

'No, I don't. And don't bark at me!'

'They went out through that window,' said Perry. 'I saw them. Blast my eyes, what a mess!'

Anthony went to the window. 'There's no sign of them. It's not a big jump to the ground from here.'

'The bastard may have kidnapped her!' Pawlyn exclaimed. 'I wish I could get my hands on him again.'

'Are you looking for me?' said a voice from the stairs.

Patricia had come from somewhere in the interior of the house. She was neat and tidy and cool – outwardly cool. But somewhere in her appearance there was a difference. Her eyes were too bright, the corners of her lips not quite sure of themselves.

'Where have you been?' Ned demanded. 'We were all worried. The police have only just gone.'

'Are you all right, Dad?' she asked.

'No credit to you if I am,' he snapped.

'I know,' she said quietly. 'I'm more than sorry –'

'What happened?' Pawlyn asked. 'Did he force you to jump through the window? I was out for a minute or two and when –'

93

'Get back to your ship!' said Joe. 'This is a family affair. We don't want outsiders in it. David, get this place cleared up. Perry, make yourself useful.'

'Yes, we went through the window,' the girl said. 'Then . . . he wouldn't let me come back until it was all over. He – he wanted to keep my name out of it.'

'He'll find his own name in it tomorrow, by God!' said Ned Pawlyn. 'The police will be round at his house first thing –'

'Your place was with your father,' said Joe. 'I thought I came first.'

'So you do. But . . . he wouldn't let me . . .'

'D'you mean he held you by force?' Ned asked.

'I've told you,' said Joe, 'to get back to your ship! Otherwise you'll lose your job. I'll not have every Tom, Dick and Harry interfering in my affairs. Good night.'

'Well,' said Ned, 'I –'

'Now I'm going to bed. Madge, give me your arm.'

Patricia came forward quickly to take his other arm. For a moment it seemed that he was about to refuse, but he accepted her help.

'Pat,' Ned said. 'Can –'

She gave him a queer constrained smile.

'Not now. Tomorrow.'

The trio moved slowly up the stairs.

'Well,' said Uncle Perry when the procession was out of hearing. 'A pretty peck of pickles we've stirred up tonight. A good thing one of us kept cool about it. I remember when I was in Jo'burg, much the same sort of thing happened. You need to be able to keep your nerve at a time like that.'

Ned Pawlyn looked at him. 'Oh –' he said, using a vulgar word, and left them.

Midnight was long past before even Anthony found his way to bed. He could not sleep. For some reason he kept thinking of the occasion when Mr Lawson, the master of his school, called him out of the class and said, 'Your mother is ill, Anthony; she would like you to go home at once.' He remembered the way in which he had snatched up his satchel, first making sure that his homework was inside, and then gone bounding off down the lane that led home. Certainly he had been anxious, but he did not expect anything serious, and almost outweighing the anxiety was the pleasure at missing most of an afternoon's school. Then, he remembered, he reached home and through the window he could see three people standing talking gravely in the drawing-room. One was Dr Braid, one was the next-door neighbour, the third person, a woman he had never seen before in his life. At that moment he wondered where his mother was, and it seemed as if a cold hand clutched at his stomach. For minutes he stood on the door-mat and was afraid to go in.

The incidents of that afternoon were a watershed which divided his life. Before that he had been a child; after it he had become half adult, acting for himself, answering for himself: things that happened to him now remained with him, were confided to nobody. There was an end of frankness.

He had been pitchforked abruptly into an adult world. Nobody really troubled about him; they were not concerned what he thought, and therefore they were not concerned with what he learned. *They* did not hide things.

He remembered the foreshortened figure of Uncle Joe counting up his little piles of gold. He saw again Uncle Perry slipping through into the restaurant with a couple of bottles of gin under his coat. Other happenings too; things occurred which he could not quite understand, for the explanation of which he did not yet possess the adult key.

Over and over again he remembered the expression on Patricia's face as she came down the steps into the restaurant, returning from they knew not where. Her face was beautiful then rather than pretty in its strange suppressed wildness; she kept her eyes down so that they should not be seen.

★　★　★

95

He remembered also an incident of two days ago when Patricia had rolled her sleeves up almost to the shoulder to do some washing in the kitchen, and he had seen Uncle Perry looking at her pale, slender arms, and he had glanced away and suddenly perceived that Aunt Madge was watching Uncle Perry. And Aunt Madge had said: 'Joe thinks *The Grey Cat* might be here tomorrow. Nice for you that will be, Pat . . . Ned Pawlyn.'

Once or twice he dozed off to sleep, but woke with a start as if there had been voices in his ears. He seemed to hear his uncle say: 'There's been a Veal in Falmouth ever since there was a Falmouth; an' we're proud of it, see? Straight as a die. Sons of sons all the way.' And he seemed to hear Perry laughing and his words: '*Houd vast,* now, so we've taken another hand aboard. Greetings, boy! I could do with a second mate.' Then there were the stumbling drunken footsteps making their way to bed and that queer haunting song: 'They heard the Black Hunter! and dr-read shook each mind; Hearts sank that had never known fear-r.'

. . . He woke suddenly with the sense of a frightening dream still upon him. He thought he had heard strange unpleasant sounds somewhere below. The noises were still in his ears. The room was pitch dark and he had no idea of the time; he only knew that the dream had struck down the defences of his courage and he was afraid. The menace was the greater for being unseen and unguessable. Everything was at its lowest ebb in this dark hour; he shivered and turned over and tried to bury his head and body under the tangle of the bedclothes.

So he lay while the dream like a slow tide of horror ebbed gradually away. Dank pools of it still lay in his mind. Fear of death, fear of illness, fear of sex, fear of the whole hollow cavern of life, these lay on his struggling reason. A light would have helped, but the matches lay on a table by the window and he could not bring himself to jump out, to leave the semi-security of the bed and venture among the unknown dangers of the room.

Time passed and he felt warm again, and warmth brought a return of drowsiness. He was just dropping back into the comfort of dreamless sleep when he started into wakefulness.

This was no dream. The sound was coming up from the darkness below.

The menace of a dream is usually harder to combat than the reality because its outlines are vague and fearful. But sometimes not even nightmare can stand against the brutal hard clarity of waking fact. A man may dream of the cut of a knife and wake in perspiration. But that is nothing if he feels the knife itself.

No sooner was Anthony kneeling up in bed than he heard footsteps climbing the uncarpeted stairs which led to his room.

Frozen, he waited. They came slowly but with a hidden suggestion of urgency, as if haste were intended but not achieved.

A light showed through the cracks in the door and someone began fumbling with the door handle.

'Yes?' he said, his voice cracking.

The door opened and someone came in. A wavering candle showed up the ambiguous bulk of Aunt Madge.

'Yes?' he said again when she did not speak. He saw that she was trembling.

'Dressed,' she said. 'Get dressed. Your uncle; very ill. We want you . . . go for Dr Penrose.'

13

By the half light of a gibbous moon Anthony picked his way through the deserted streets of the town. He was thankful that this mission led him in a different direction from when he had run for the police. At four o'clock in the morning the main streets were probably as empty and silent as any others, but the earlier memory of them remained.

In white night things and a white dressing-gown Patricia had come down the stairs with him.

'You know the way we always go to Mother's grave? Well above the cemetery a lane leads out towards the sea. There are four houses on it; Dr Penrose's is the last. You can't miss it.'

'Is Uncle Joe . . . Has he –'

'He's ill again, Anthony. I feel so awful about it, as if it was my fault. The doctor said he mustn't have worry or excitement.'

Anthony had overcome his shyness sufficiently to touch her hand. 'It wasn't your fault a bit. I'm sure everything will be all right. And I'll run like anything.'

This promise he was now proceeding to carry out. Up the hill, padding silently in his rubber shoes, his breath coming sharply, he moved among the shadows, one moment slipping through darkness, the next crossing one of the brilliant shafts of moonlight, which lay in bars athwart the narrow street. Soon he had reached Western Terrace and the going became easier. He dropped down towards Swanpool.

In the moonlight the cemetery looked unfamiliar and ghostly. All the white tombstones trailed black cloaks of shadow. They were like an army marching up the hills, an army of invaders fresh landed on the coast and marching to attack the town.

Every few yards along this lane the boy glanced over his shoulder to see if there was anything behind. Once he stopped and sheered to the other side of the road. But the object which barred his path was no more than the shadow cast by a misshapen hawthorn tree.

Once past he was comforted by the thought that on the return journey he would have company. He reached the doctor's house and pulled at the bell. At length his summons was answered, and in about ten minutes he was on his way back, walking and trotting beside the

98

tall physician, whose breath came in grunts and whistles in the cold moonlit morning.

They reached Smoky Joe's almost without conversation; Dr Penrose seemed a little petulant at the inconsiderateness of a man who could take ill at such a time of the night. Anthony led the way upstairs and then was shut out of the lighted bedroom. For a few moments he hung about on the landing listening to the murmur of voices within; then he slowly went down.

Little Fanny, red-eyed and sleepy, sat by the stove on which a kettle and a pan simmered. She looked up at Anthony's entrance and said: ''As 'e come?'

Anthony nodded. 'Have you heard how Uncle is?'

'Miss Pat was down just now. She didn't say much.'

Anthony took a seat on the opposite side of the stove and the conversation lapsed. Fanny began to doze.

'What's that?' Anthony asked suddenly.

She jumped. 'Uh? What? What's what?'

'I thought I heard someone talking downstairs.'

'Oh? Oh, yer-rs. That's Mister Perry. 'E's still clearin' up the mess what was made. 'E's not been to bed at all.'

Silence fell again. Fanny's small tattered shoes were stretched towards the warmth, toes touching. Her mouth fell slowly open.

The boy got up and tip-toed out. Better to help Uncle Perry than sit and do nothing. Sleep was impossible until the doctor had left.

Down in the restaurant a single gas jet cast its anaemic light upon the ruins. For a moment Anthony could not see his uncle and supposed him to be brushing up the floor. But further inspection showed him to be sitting at the little corner window table where all the trouble had begun. He was resting from his labours.

Anthony's rubber soles made no sound until he stepped upon a piece of glass. Uncle Perry jumped a visible inch and glared at the boy.

'Belay there! Damn me, I thought it was a ghost! Never

99

wear rubbers, boy; they're an invention of Old Scratch himself.'

Anthony saw that there were three bottles on the table, and two were empty. Uncle Perry had been resting from his labours almost since they began.

'Sorry; I thought perhaps I could help. I . . . don't feel like sleep.'

Perry was not long in recovering his temper.

'Don't go away; don't go away. Of course, you don't feel like sleep. No loving nephew would at a time like this. Nor do I; no more do I; that's why I'm down here trying to think of something else. I've worked myself to a standstill. Have a taste of rum?'

'No, thanks, Uncle Perry. I'll just wait down here till the doctor goes.'

'So you've been for him? There's a good lad. I said you would. I said, "Young Anthony's got the fastest legs of any of us. Why ask me?" I said, "I'm good for nothing tonight. I'm out of sorts myself. I'm worried about Joe," I said. "It's the anxiety that's getting me down." I'm a – an abstemious man, Anthony; anyone'll tell you that, but the anxiety over Joe is getting me down. I'd got to do something, so I came down here and began clearing up.'

Anthony perceived that he had mistaken the nature of the relationship between the two brothers; evidently the way they barked at each other sometimes only disguised their real affection. He forgave Uncle Perry for getting drunk.

He shivered, having cooled off from his run. 'It's a bit cold down here.'

'Get a glass,' said Perry. 'Ever tasted rum, boy? That'll warm your lights. Go on, there's nothing to be afraid of.'

The boy brought a glass and sipped at the liquid Uncle Perry put in it. He thought he had never tasted anything so vile: sweet and sticky and hot in the throat. When it was gone he shivered worse than ever.

'It's the starting that matters,' said Perry, pushing back his hair. 'It's the first drop that counts. The first teeny drop. Once you've taken a sip there's no turning back, no innocence any more. Life's like that; I tell you, boy, take it from me. You drink a glass of rum or have a bit of lovey-dovey, and where does it lead? Nobody knows; you've started something and 've got to follow it; one thing leads to another; see what I mean? It isn't that a man's bad – nor that he's good – it's just following a lead. Often it's just being good-natured; nothing more than that; no intentions of any sort, and then where are you? They say who rides on a tiger . . . But which of us isn't in that fix? Can I get down? Can you get down? We're all on our own tigers which – which we've fed for a bit of sport or brought up from being a cub; and – and now we wish we hadn't . . .'

The rum was warming the boy. Sleepy in spite of himself, he gazed out across the harbour. There were two lights on the water, that of the setting moon and that of the dawn. The reflection of the moonlight was like tinsel silver, twinkling, without colour, except a suggestion of coffee brown in the water not immediately caught by it. The dawn light was a pure cold blue glimmering on the water like a shield.

'What's that?' asked Uncle Perry, peering towards the shadowy stairs.

'I didn't hear anything,' Anthony said after a moment.

'I thought maybe it was the doctor. I thought it was him or somebody else. I thought it was. But there you are, mistaken again.' He drained his glass and the lock of hair fell back from his forehead. This morning hour seemed to have caught Perry in a strange mood. He was not his usual jovial buccaneering self. Even Perry had his moments of doubt.

'Shall I go up and see?'

Perry tapped the boy on the shoulder. 'I know how you feel. I know what it's like to be young. You think you know everything at that age. But the older you grow the more you see your mistake. The world's a snare, boy, make no mistake of it. *And* everybody in it. Everybody's different. Like – like the trees in a forest. Some's crooked; some's straight. Some's healthy; some's got moss on 'em. Some'll

101

stand any storm; others'll fall at the first puff. Some's got fruit that's good to pick; some hasn't. *And* you can't tell. That's my meaning, boy: you can't tell. Not the cleverest person in the world can tell what's behind a face. They think they can, but they can't. It's been a shock to me . . . Many times it's been a shock to me. It shakes your nerve. You don't know where you are. Then before you can say knife you're riding somebody else's tiger . . .'

Silence fell. Uncle Perry's disjointed allegories were too much for Anthony. Eyes pricking, he watched the shadowy light grow in the east, slowly gaining ascendancy until it penetrated into this room, showing up new outlines of disordered chairs and tables, whitening a pile of broken crockery, driving before it the dismal defeated light of the flickering gas jet. Unnoticed, Uncle Perry's face had also emerged, wan and bloated and strained. When he poured himself a drink the bottle neck went *tat-a-tat* against the side of the glass.

The doctor had been here a long time. He could not have gone for they would have heard his footsteps.

Day was coming. Clouds high in the sky had begun to flush. They reflected a terracotta stain upon the opal blue of the harbour. Seagulls had begun to wheel and cry.

Suddenly there was a footstep behind them. Uncle Perry knocked over his glass. They had both expected to see the doctor, but it was Aunt Madge.

The monumental calm was shaken. 'Very tired,' she said distantly. 'Brandy or something . . .'

'Well?' said Perry, and his mouth twitched.

'About the same. Dr Penrose is doing all he can. Touch and go, he says . . .'

Perry wiped his forehead. 'Poor Joe.'

'Brandy or something,' said Aunt Madge. 'I feel . . . can't stand it.'

Perry put some rum into Anthony's glass. 'This'll do.'

She kept pausing to wipe her eyes while she sipped it.

'What does he say?' said Perry anxiously.

She waved her glass in sudden irritation. 'Joe's right: doctors *pretend* to know. Anthony . . . should be in bed.'

Perry slumped back in his chair. 'I've had an awful night . . .'

'You? You've done nothing. There's . . .'

'It's the waiting. All of you up there and me down here. Me thinking of poor Joe and doing nothing to help. Not able to do anything; you know, Madge, it isn't so easy as you think when a brother goes down like this – stricken down in his fifties; when we were kids; it reminds you of that time; we used to go out in a row-boat together; used to fish for dabs; used to bathe up the river; he was a big boy then, or so he seemed to me; there was six years, you know; that's a difference when you're kids; now it don't seem much; those days I never dreamed there'd come a time when I should sit here while Joe lay upstairs; it shakes you up more than you'd think, more than I thought. Blood will tell, you know; blood's thicker than water; you don't think so till it comes to the test; at a time like this. Honest to God, Madge, I'd – I'd rather . . .'

Aunt Madge had risen to her feet again. She looked down upon Perry from an altitude, remote as a snow-covered peak, frozen and impersonal and secretive. 'How do you think I feel? Ill myself. Husband. Lonely. Got to carry on. Not sit there. Some have got to do. To act. Not sit there over a glass. Where should we be if everyone sat over a glass? Where should we be if I'd done nothing all this night? Anthony . . .'

The boy got up sleepily and stood beside her. 'All right.'

'Let him stay here,' said Perry argumentatively. 'He's company for me. If you're going I'll have no company; it's too late to go to bed now; we can sit here. I'll light a fire. I'll get Fanny to light a fire and we'll sit down here; it'll help to brighten things up; then when it's light we'll go on with clearing away the mess; somebody'll have to clear the mess; if the boy goes to bed now he'll sleep till midday. We might need him before then. You don't want to go to bed, do you, boy?'

'Not if I can help.'

'There's the boy. We'll stay down here together, Madge, if it won't affect you. We'll be anxious to know –'

'Anthony,' Aunt Madge said, as he was about to reseat himself.

He straightened up again.

'Quite light now,' she said. 'You can clear up, Perry. But –'

A voice came from upstairs. It was Patricia calling her.

'Aunt Madge! Aunt Madge!'

Ponderous in her haste, the older woman left them. With a premonitory chill Anthony watched her climbing the stairs. There had been something in Patricia's voice which told its own story. Joe Veal, for all his tenacity, had this time met an opponent who was going to get the better of him. Standing in the battered restaurant with the first full light of day creeping among the final shadows, his nephew knew this as surely as if he already heard the toll of a requiem bell. He knew it, and he was afraid.

From behind him came a *tat-a-tat* as Uncle Perry shook more rum into his glass.

14

The death of Smoky Joe and the other events of that August night had consequences which completely changed the lives of those concerned in them.

Everything came to a standstill. To the boy, who had known only the busy routine of Joe Veal's when it was in full working order, the silence which fell was peculiarly oppressive. It was as if he had been in a railway terminus and there had been an accident out on the line and the station had suddenly emptied. In such a case he would no doubt have wandered at will, through the turnstiles, past the ticket office, through the luggage departments and back upon the deserted platform. So now he found himself at a loose end, sitting in one or other of the empty restaurants, mooning through the kitchen, passing into the larder, where quantities of uncooked food gradually became offensive, standing in the shop behind drawn blinds allowing his fingers to play with the keys of the automatic till.

Not that there was no activity at all on the closed premises, but none of it concerned him. Everyone had more *time*, but no one had any *attention* to spare him, not even Patricia.

There were the endless visits from old customers and friends who came round with suitably grave faces and talked and drank cups of tea in the kitchen. There were the relatives: Aunt Louisa from Arwenack Street, a small tight woman with varicose veins, received with statuesque dignity by Aunt Madge. There was a cousin from Percuil and a second cousin from Mawnan Smith. By virtue of their relationship they stayed much longer than anyone else, sitting back purse-lipped in a corner while others came and went. By tactful stages they steered the conversation round to money matters and Joe's belief in blood ties; but Aunt Madge said Joe was very reserved about his private affairs, Joe's financial arrangements were a closed book to her, she'd left everything to Joe, all that would have to come out later, when the proper time came they'd be told if there was anything for them. With that they had to be content.

Then there were the men in silk hats and black suits with shiny elbows who came and went furtively with a sort of shop-soiled grief. They spent some time in the lonely room with the blinds drawn in the front of the house and later returned with something bulky which was manoeuvred with difficulty up the crooked stairs.

Joe might have been flattered had he been able to see and appreciate the gap his disappearance left in the lives of his relatives and how much they felt his loss. Patricia went about the house with her face full of tears: they were there

105

impending but would not fall; her eyes were like flowers which had cupped the rain. Uncle Perry was hardly seen at all: he was up in his bedroom and only appeared for an occasional meal, puffy and pale, or when he wanted another bottle. Even little Fanny sniffled about her duties.

As for Aunt Madge, she said she could not sleep, and appearances bore her out. During those first three days of gloom and waiting, when the whole house seemed oppressive with what it contained, she sat nearly the whole time listlessly in the one armchair in the kitchen, dozing before the fire and waking suddenly with a jerk to stare about at the familiar scene as if she did not believe it was still there. She seemed to need company and she seemed particularly fond of the kitchen. Even the closest relatives were never invited upstairs.

It was as if the shadow of mortality had brushed close beside her and she needed the reassurance of all the most familiar things of her everyday life. Anthony wondered how, just from a physical point of view, she could stay in one room for such a long time without moving.

On the day of the funeral there was a marked improvement in her bearing. She came down in an impressive dress of fine black silk with great cascades of lace pouring down the front like the Zambesi Falls and began to busy herself making sandwiches for the mourners when they returned. For the first time she seemed conscious of the full dignity of her position as the Widow of the Deceased. The three-day siege was nearly over. The last night was gone.

One of the black-coated gentlemen arrived early, and this time she went upstairs with him. Later she came down with an expression on her plump face of having triumphed over a weakness.

When she came into the kitchen she put on a pair of big black earrings and said: 'Do you wish to see him?'

Anthony waited a moment and then realised that he was the only other person in the room.

'Who?' he said in surprise.

'Uncle. It's the last chance. Hi thought you might.'

'Oh, no,' he said. 'Thank you.' Things moved up and down his spine at the suggestion.

'His nephew . . . I thought you might.'

'No,' he said. 'I'd . . .'

'It's as you like. Haven't you . . . black tie?'

'No, Aunt Madge. This was the nearest.'

'Go and get one.' She felt in her bag. 'Due respect. Round the corner and down the hill. Thought you might have liked to see him. Very peaceful . . .'

He picked up his cap and ran quickly out to buy his tie. The wind and the spattering rain were refreshing to his skin but still more refreshing to his spirit. They seemed to say to him, 'You are young; life for you is here outside; not in there; not in there; life is sweet and wholesome.'

He dawdled about in order to prolong his freedom. He watched a cutter slipping gracefully out of St Mawes Creek. He saw a fisherman returning from a morning's sport and tried to count the fish in his bag. He stopped at the street corner to talk to a boy he had come to know. They talked about wholesome interesting things, about a catapult, a dog which hunted rabbits, a farmer and an apple tree. At length he could stay no longer; people would be arriving in another few minutes; he must go back to the hushed voices and the drawn curtains and the smell of moss and chrysanthemums.

Aunt Madge was sitting in her favourite chair. She glanced up at the clock as he slipped in.

'Been playing,' she said. 'Not nice to be out and about today. Not seemly. Thought you might have liked to see him for the last night. Nephew and all. I thought you might. But it's too late now.'

There was some expression in her eyes which suggested she begrudged him his escape.

That night he had another unpleasant dream.

He dreamt he had been down feeding the swans at Swanpool, and on his way back who should be waiting for him at the cemetery gates but Uncle Joe. They walked home together, Joe smoking his foreign-looking pipe. As they walked along he was trying to persuade Anthony to do something which Anthony was reluctant to do: the boy could not afterwards remember what, but it seemed a matter of urgency to the old man. While they argued they kept meeting people Anthony had never seen before, thin grey people all going in the opposite direction. Many of them seemed to be moving without walking, like figures in a rifle gallery. Uncle Joe said: 'These are all my friends; we're all of a family now.' As they passed one woman Anthony peered under the hood of her cloak and saw that her head was shrivelled to the size of a clenched fist.

They reached the restaurant. The Joe Veal sign had been torn down; the shop door hung on one hinge and the place looked empty and dark as if nothing had moved in it for years.

Uncle Joe put something into his hand. It was a chrysanthemum flower.

'This is where I live,' the boy said. 'Won't you come in?'

'No,' said Uncle Joe. 'I'd best be going Home.'

He left him there and Anthony stood alone with the flower in his hand staring at the dark and empty shop. Then he looked down at the flower and saw that it had crumbled to moss.

He dropped it quickly and put his foot on it, feeling the squelch beneath his heel, then stepped up to the threshold of the ruined shop. He knew that he must go in in order to go to bed; but he knew also that something was waiting there for him among the cobwebs and the darkness.

He entered the shop.

Something moved at the back of it. He turned to flee, but his feet were as if bogged in quicksand and the shop had become enormously big and the door of escape a small oblong of light in the distance. He tried to concentrate his attention on the effort of moving his feet but each step he took carried him no further away.

With his eyes wide open the scene did not change. He sat up in bed and it was still there. He was still in the shop; his bed was in the shop and he had been sleeping there. The thing still moved by the stairs and he could still see the lighter oblong of the door with the hump of the automatic till.

He rubbed his eyes, his mind tearing off the fetters of nightmare even more slowly than it had done four nights earlier. He knew he had been asleep and dreaming, but he was still in the shop, still terrified. He knew that if he went outside he would be able to pick up the piece of moss that Uncle Joe had given him. That had just as much reality as the bedclothes he plucked.

The realisation that the oblong of the shop door was really the oblong of his bedroom window finally brought him to safety. He lay back in bed breathing his relief out slowly from between closed teeth. He should have laughed; anyone as old as he was should have been amused at the perverted vitality of the dream. But you never could see things like that in the dark, however much you might do so in the following day's sunshine. Besides, the stirring and rustling had not stopped.

He raised his head and listened. There it was again. But he was completely mistaken as to its character and direction. This was someone moving about in the office below him.

Determined not to give way to the reasonless fear which had beset him when he heard Aunt Madge coming up the stairs, he listened quietly for a time while the square of light at his window grew and spread into the room. Just daybreak. A few mornings ago he had sat with Uncle Perry while a life ebbed slowly away. Daybreak. No reason why somebody should not be moving about in the office. People could get up at what time they pleased. It was just the

109

sort of noise Uncle Joe made: the shutting of drawers, the occasional scrape of feet, the movement of heavy books. Strange to think that Uncle Joe was no longer interested. But was he not? Who was to say that it could not be so? Supposing he was moving about down there, still attending to his affairs.

Anthony climbed cautiously out of bed. As he did so the sounds beneath him ceased. With the hair prickling upon the back of his neck he slid silently under the bed and pulled out the cork spy-hole.

The early light falling through the narrow window lit up the office greyly. Some books were piled on the desk, and papers lay in disorder on the floor. But the room was empty.

As he replaced the cork the unmistakable smell of Uncle Joe's tobacco came to his nostrils.

The old man had kept the threads of his various business undertakings so jealously within his own hands, had so refused to delegate responsibility, that the unravelling of them was like fumbling with a tangle of string to which one cannot find an end. In his time he had had dealings with every solicitor in town, and Mr Cowdray, whom Aunt Madge called in, knew little more of his affairs than anyone else.

But in a sense, too, Joe's one-man business resembled a clock which has been wound and will run of its own accord for a time although the owner is gone and the key lost. Goods were delivered; letters arrived from ships' chandlers and shipping agencies; a cargo appeared for *The Grey Cat* and she proceeded to take it on board and would shortly depart for Hull. *Lavengro* arrived with a cargo of pit-props from Norway and the purchaser was ready waiting for them; bills and receipts arrived and could be filed or settled. Aunt Madge and Uncle Perry – who had recovered his good spirits – and Mr Cowdray worked hard together to keep the clock still ticking.

A few days after the funeral the relatives of Smoky Joe, together with Mr Cowdray, who was plump and untidy and wore a heavy beard to conceal a birthmark under his chin, assembled in the upstairs parlour to hear what there was to hear about the settlement of the estate. The parlour faced north and was therefore hung with dark red wallpaper which took away most of the light that filtered through the thick lace curtains. On the floor was a red carpet with blue flowers and a blue border showing ridges of wear by the door, and the furniture consisted of an upright rosewood piano which no one had ever used, a red plush music stool, and crimson plush furniture which emitted an ineradicable smell of dust. The mantelpiece carried an ornate overmantel with numerous small shelves and a gilt mirror.

Present were the cousin from Percuil and the cousin from Mawnan Smith, the sister from Arwenack Street and the brother from across the landing, who, incidentally, seemed to want to open the proceedings with a joke and a toss of his black hair. Aunt Madge and Patricia sat side by side on the sofa; and Anthony had slipped in almost unnoticed and pricked the backs of his legs on a horse-hair stool.

Mr Cowdray opened with an explanation of the difficulties which confronted him in clearing up the estate. He talked ponderously and leisurely from behind his beard, and no evidences of impatience on the part of the sister from Arwenack Street or the cousin from Mawnan Smith were sufficient to hurry him by so much as a syllable or cause him to miss out a single rusty clearing of the throat. Nor was he influenced by Perry's good-natured desire to make a party of the occasion. As if he were addressing a jury on a clear case of tort, he went on and on, making each point with the maximum of effect and the minimum of brevity. Perry caught Anthony's eye and winked wickedly, then it roved round for fresh eyes to contact. But all the others were too conscious of the solemnity of the occasion to meet such a challenge. If they were aware of it, as it must have been difficult not to be, they avoided it as the good little

111

boy will avoid the bad little boy thumbing his nose on the way to church.

Aunt Madge was a mountain of unrelieved black, installed with closed eyes on the larger end of the couch. A breath moving from time to time among the darker recesses of her bulk was the only evidence that she lived. Beside her Patricia looked slender to the point of frailty, taut like the stem of a daffodil and as easily snapped.

So far as any final settlement of the estate was concerned, Mr Cowdray went on, the work entailed might stretch over many weeks. But it was felt – he personally felt, and he knew Mr Veal's widow felt – that to give at once a broad outline of the disposition of the bequests would be the fairest to all concerned. He did not propose to read the Will, but would just state the facts, and of course anyone could examine the documents afterwards –

'I think you should read the Will,' said Aunt Louisa sharply. 'What do you say, Peter?'

There was a faint stir. Louisa's harsh voice had disturbed the reverential dust.

Peter from Percuil looked uncomfortable and pulled at one end of a drooping moustache. 'Reckon I don't mind one way or th'other.'

Mr Cowdray glanced at the widow but she did not open her eyes. 'Very well, then, if you wish it – hrrr-hm! – naturally no objection myself.' He opened his bag and took out a sheet of parchment. 'Actually, quite a short document; Mr Veal was not a man to waste words; that is so far as I knew him; he deposited this Will with me, but I had not previously had business transactions . . .'

'When you've been about the world a bit,' said Perry, 'it teaches you not to waste anything. Words, time or money. Joe was a regular one for seeing nothing went to waste. That's Joe all over.' He chuckled. 'Well, read it out; I'll bet old Joe's got a surprise or two up his sleeve.'

'"This is the last Will and Testament,"' read Mr Cowdray stiffly, '"of me, Joseph Killigrew Veal, of Falmouth, in

112

the County of Cornwall. In consideration of the fact that for forty-seven years he has proved unpunctual in all his dealings and appointments, including the day he was born, I give and bequeath unto my brother, Perry Veal, my gold watch and ten pounds for its maintenance. Unto my sister –"'

'Well, I'll be stung!' exclaimed Perry. He threw back his head and laughed in a sort of unmalicious indignation. 'If ever there was an old –'

'Perry . . .' said Aunt Madge, opening her mouth but not her eyes.

'Go on with the Will,' said Louisa.

'Hrr-hm . . . "Unto my sister Louisa . . ." Yes. "Unto my sister Louisa I give and bequeath forty-six pounds ten shillings and eightpence, which is the return of a loan made to me thirty years ago plus compound interest added to the year 1905, a return for which she had persistently pestered me. To my dear sister I also bequeath such records of the family as survive, dating back to 1690, and the family Bible, which I trust she will make more use of than I have.

'"To my cousin Peter Veal, of Percuil, I give my piano, my edition of Chambers' Encyclopaedia, and twelve pounds, one pound for each of his twelve children. If any of his children should predecease me, let him lose proportionately. To my cousin, Polly Emma Higgins, of Mawnan Smith, I bequeath my cottage and two fields situated near that village.

'"To my daughter Patricia, in view of the fact that she has seen fit to marry against my express wishes and against my specific threat to disown her if she did so, I leave five hundred pounds as a free gift and no further interest in my estate. To my wife, Madge, I bequeath the residue of my property absolutely. And I appoint my said wife sole executrix of this my Will, and revoke all previous Wills – mm-mm-mm . . ."' Mr Cowdray's voice descended into the depths of his beard. For some time it stirred and rustled in the undergrowth and then was still. He raised his eyes

113

and his eyebrows as if to say, 'There you are; there it is; I disclaim all responsibility.'

15

Anthony's eyes flew unbidden from face to face. As the only person not directly concerned, he alone had the leisure to appreciate the situation. But appreciate was not the word, for he felt a burning sympathy for the girl on the sofa. While the solicitor had been speaking of her Patricia had gone so pale that it would not have been difficult to imagine her slipping to the floor in a faint.

The boy was furiously indignant with his uncle. Although he was not old enough to put the matter in an ethical frame he felt the bitter injustice of leaving such acrimonious remarks to be read after one was dead and free from query or reproach. No one had the right to make a bitter accusation, to leave a smirch where it could not be answered or removed. That was not playing the game. Especially was it unfair when the accusation was groundless. Patricia had left her husband to nurse him and had been with him to the last. There had seemed no enmity between them. To her alone he had been prepared to delegate little business items during that last fortnight in bed. She –

'When is that Will dated?' Patricia asked.

'April the twelfth of this year.'

'Thank God!' the girl said.

The boy's forehead wrinkled a moment, then he remembered that in April had occurred the estrangement between Smoky Joe and his daughter, first over the court case and then over her marriage. She had –

'I call it perfectly scandalous!' said Aunt Louisa, fiddling suddenly with the bits of fluff on the armchair. 'I do really. I've never heard anything like it. He goes out of his way to insult all his blood relations and then leaves everything

114

to his – wife. 'Tisn't right. 'Tisn't right at all.' She looked up suddenly, her eyes like darts. 'And I don't mind telling you I'm not at all content with it!'

'Now Louisa, now Louisa,' said Perry. After the first brief spurt of indignation he seemed to be taking his own lack of fortune in his usual philosophical manner. Everything with Perry was easy-come, easy-go. 'Put about. It'll do you no good bringing your head up to the wind. We've all of us suspected what Joe thought of us, and now, bigod, we know! Well, it's cleared the air, but it don't alter the Will, do it? I get my gold watch and you get your family Bible. And that's the end of it.'

'I'm not so sure.' Louisa allowed the words to escape from between tight lips. ''Tisn't only for myself that I care, though I care for myself sure enough; but it's Patricia. Look at the way he's treated her!'

'Don't bother about me, Aunt Louisa,' the girl said, her fine eyes dark. 'I wouldn't touch any of his money now if I had it.'

'But something can be done about it surely!' Miss Veal transferred her gaze, which had been fixed for so long upon Aunt Madge, to the bearded solicitor. 'Look, Mister Cowdray. This Will you've been reading . . . it was made in a fit of raging bad temper when Joe, when my brother was estranged from his daughter. In another month they'd made it up again and were as friendly as you like. Can't that be taken into account? What about his earlier Wills?'

Mr Cowdray shook his beard. 'Each Will has a clause revoking previous testaments. Unless he has made a later one this must stand, Miss Veal.'

'Well, what of a later one? What about that? Has any search been made for one? Has the house been searched? Or he may have deposited it with some other solicitor. I refuse to accept this until a full search has been made.'

'I've looked,' said Aunt Madge, speaking for the first time. She closed her eyes again. 'Everywhere . . .'

'That may well be, but –'

'Aunt Louisa,' Pat said quietly. 'If you're saying this for

115

my sake, don't bother. No doubt Dad gave me what he thought I deserved. Well, if he thought that, I am quite content to accept it.'

'Are you indeed!' said Miss Veal, her nose going pale with excitement. 'Well, I'm not. You should be ashamed of yourself, Pat! I thought you had more spirit. Why Joe – your father – must have been worth fifteen or sixteen thousand pounds if he was worth a farthing. It may be much more. That's no right to go out of the family. That's Veal money and should stay Veal money –'

'Mrs Veal,' said Mr Cowdray sombrely, 'happens to be his wife, you know.'

'His wife! Who two years ago was his cook! That's no true wife. His true wife is dead and buried, Patricia's mother. You don't make a wife of your servant. Besides, where did she come from? Nobody knew her in Falmouth till she came as his cook. She's no Veal –'

'*Houd vast*,' said Perry, patting her arm. 'You're working up for a squall, sister. It'll do you no manner of good to spill a lot of bad blood. The law's the law and that's an end of it. Learn to face your disappointments with a smile like me. I can't pretend that I'm pleased with my share but there's nothing to do about it. We're both in the same boat and it's no manner of good standing up and whistling for the wind –'

Aunt Louisa withdrew her arm impatiently. 'Your concerns are your own, Perry. You make your own peace with your conscience and I'll make mine.'

'That's what I'm telling you, sister. Leave Patricia to mend her own affairs. I'm sure she'll not lack for a home, will she, Madge? There, I knew not. And besides, she's married to a rich and handsome young man who'll see that she's well taken care of. Now if I were you –'

'The black sheep,' said Miss Veal distantly. 'You've always been the black sheep, haven't you, Perry? If you must know, I'd trust *you* no further than I could see you. I'm not here to cast insinuations, but maybe you think you'll not come off so badly after all –'

116

Aunt Madge's eyeglasses wobbled at last.

'Hi've tried,' she said. 'Politeness. Manners. How long am I to stand this? My own house . . .'

'Your own house, indeed! It's Patricia's house by every manner of right, and Joe's no licence to disown her. I'll warrant there's a later will than this – if it can be found.'

'Insinuating . . .'

'My dear Miss Veal – hrrr, hm – I beg you to calm yourself. It is not at all unnatural for a man –'

'And what have you to say to this, Peter; and you, Emma? Joe was not in his right senses when he made this Will. Will you help me to contest it?'

Peter pulled at the end of his moustache. 'Well, can't say that I'm altogether satisfied. But if we get mixed up in the law all the money'll go to the lawyers. It was like that when I went to law over that cow. It isn't what they get for you, it's what they take from you . . .'

'We don't want that to happen,' said Polly Emma hastily. 'We certainly don't want that, for sure. As for me, I can't say as I expected much more than I've got. I've seen little of dear Joe for these pretty many years, and husband was saying only last month that I did ought to call. But when he's that ill, I said, it looks like asking. It looks like begging, I said, going round and calling special on my dear cousin after all these years, when he's that ill, I said.'

'Insinuating,' said Aunt Madge, towering over Aunt Louisa. 'Don't like. Own home . . .'

'Nothing but a cook,' said Aunt Louisa, bantam-like. 'A cook from nowhere, to wheedle into his good books. Where *did* you come from? I'll see it doesn't end here!'

'By rights,' said Peter, 'he should have left a little something for my eldest. Eldest was his godson. He'll be eighteen in January month, and a little something might have set him up in something. Never a present has he sent in all these years, though Christine remembered it now and then. A little –'

'Well, I'm sure we never bothered him,' said Polly Emma, 'except that husband would pass the time of day

117

if he saw him in the street. I think well-to-do folk don't like to be bothered. But Albert is that way, you know; proud as proud, and not liking to go licking people's boots.'

'Any action,' said Aunt Madge, quivering. 'Any action you think fit . . .'

'Well, there are other solicitors in the town besides Mr Cowdray, and I don't mind telling you I intend to consult one. I should consider it a sheer neglect of my duty if I did not. And I may tell you that not only me but all the town will be of the same opinion, that – that undue pressure –'

'My dear madam – hrrr, hm – you may take any action you think fit. You are legally within your rights to do so. But I may inform you that your brother has made himself *persona non grata* with every one of my colleagues in this district, and is unlikely to have deposited a Will with them. I may also say –'

'Maybe we're not so partic'lar about these things, Emmie Higgins,' said Peter, 'but when we asked Joe to be Billy's godfather, 'twas intended as a mark of respect, not anything more. Lizzie and me don't go round licking of people's boots – neither his nor yours, see?'

'Oh, dear me, I'm sure I beg your pardon, cousin,' said Polly Emma; 'it was a figure of speech that was intended. It's not for the like of me to criticise other people. But, of course, what I say and what Albert always says is, if the cap fits, wear it, you know. That's what Albert always says. And it seems to me that when people are too quick to take offence –'

'Everybody in this town will feel just the same as I do. Public opinion is something you *can't* ignore –'

'Vain loud voices,' Aunt Madge was heard to say. 'House of mourning . . . Not yet cold . . .'

'If takin' offence is to be mentioned, what about when your Albert was in St Mawes soon after Lizzie had been ill with pneumonia . . .'

Anthony, still withdrawn, again the only spectator, suddenly realised in a flash of inspiration what was missing

at this gathering today. It was the presence of Tom
Harris.

One might say or feel hard things about Tom, but he
would at least have kept the meeting in some sort of order.
He would never have allowed himself to be dragged into
the arena, to be pulled into the thick of the quarrel, as
Mr Cowdray had done. His presence alone would have
prevented this awful squabble. Give him his due, Anthony
thought; give him his due, Pat, he's a cut above all these.
Well might she sit there with her brown eyes down and a
pulse beating in the white curve of her neck.

Strangely enough, it was the boy himself who provided
the first effective check to the wranglers. In boredom he
got up from his prickly stool and walked to the window and
stood looking out. Something in his attitude there by the
window, his hunched shoulders, his hands in his pockets,
seemed to be an unspoken commentary upon the unseemly
arguments going on behind him. One by one the quarrellers
fell silent, stood about in sudden self-consciousness and
constraint.

Miss Veal picked up her bag, felt for a handkerchief and
blew her nose loudly.

'Well, you know my views. I was brought up to be blunt
and I've been blunt all my life. I believe in honest dealing.
That's more than some people do. What I've said to your
face I'll say behind your back. You know what action I'm
going to take. So there's nothing more to be said. I'll bid you
good afternoon. Are you coming down the street, Peter?'

The thin man looked from one to another of his relatives
and hesitated.

'Yes, I reckon so,' he said at last.

'And you, Polly Emma?'

'Thanks, dear, I think I'll wait for the trap. Albert is
calling for me in the trap.'

Aunt Louisa went across and kissed Patricia on the
forehead.

'Don't worry, dear. Don't worry at all,' she said firmly.

'She won't if you don't,' said Perry.

But his sister ignored the remark and walked with dignity from the room.

There were still two hours of daylight left, and Anthony presently escaped from the house and ran down to the derelict wooden jetty which led out into the harbour from the wall of the quay. This jetty was submerged when the tide was in, and was one of Anthony's favourite haunts. He could sit here and watch the water lapping up through the cracks, covering one slippery black board after another, and he could imagine himself stranded on a desert island – or trapped in a cellar under the Thames while the river rose.

Fancy was a pleasant companion after the grim and dusty happenings in the house, and his mind turned to his imaginings as a parched man to water. To be free of the chains of reality, to slip them off and wander at will, to be independent of time or space or hunger or heat, to make life up as you went along, to fashion life as you *wanted* it, romantic and exciting and bright with the obvious colours, no second thoughts, no reservations, no avarice, no frustrations, no hidden complex motives, no adult deceits: a world of good and evil where each was plainly marked for what it was, in which good always triumphed and the ill-fortunes that you suffered, however tragic and toilsome they might be, were edged about with the silver thought that you could change them at will.

Anthony felt that he wanted to re-write the world. It was not right that there should be death for good people, and permanent unchangeable sadness and incurable illness, and strange muffled hatreds which hid themselves for years under a cloak of everyday behaviour. Or, if there had to be death, then it should only come to good people when they were very old and tired and when all their children were grown up and had children and grandchildren of their own. And especially there should be no bitterness which went beyond the grave, no tawdry squabbling over a dead man's goods, no remarks which made insinuations and left a stain.

Tonight the tide was going out so he could not play his favourite game. He had hoped to find his friend Jack Robbins somewhere about the quay.

The harbour itself was unusually empty for this time of day, and there were few big ships in. A solitary oarsman was rowing out from further up the creek and would pass close beside the jetty. A flight of starlings were wheeling and fluttering just above the rippling surface of the water, making dark shadows as they swooped, turning and manoeuvring with military precision, climbing the cloudy sky in a dense flock and then suddenly straggling out like children dismissed from drill. A group of them came to perch upon the roof of the house, arriving in ones and twos with a sudden swift dart and a flutter. One minute there was none, then they were all there like pegs on a line, chattering and arguing, turning their tails to each other and edging up and down. A moment later, as it seemed by a single instinct, they were up and away again, their short wings fluttering the air above the boy's head.

He watched them out of sight beyond the clustered climbing grey roofs of the old town, then turned to see if the tide had gone down sufficiently to allow another step.

As he did so he recognised the solitary man in the boat. It was Tom Harris.

16

He had not been seen, for the rower had his back to him, but before he could make up his mind whether to call out or to make his escape, Tom turned his head and nodded and smiled. He began to pull on his right oar, which would bring him nearer to the jetty.

Presently they were within speaking distance. Tom

glanced up at the tall grey house with the bow windows of the restaurants looking out over the harbour.

'Hullo, Anthony. I'm just going over to Flushing. Like to come?'

'Yes, rather!' said the boy, and then hesitated. 'How long will you be gone?'

'I've only to collect some fishing nets. Should be back in an hour.'

For a second longer Anthony hesitated, wondering if, by continuing to associate with this man, he was being disloyal to Patricia. But during these last days Patricia had hardly spoken to him; she had never once mentioned the night of the fight; she had been preoccupied with her own concerns and had left him to his. Besides, she had never forbidden him to speak to Tom; how was he to know her mind?

With these sophistries he was content, and he stepped eagerly into the boat when Tom paddled it nearer. In a moment he was seated in the stern, enjoying the unusual experience of being a passenger and happy to ripple his fingers through the water and watch his cousin-in-law do the pulling.

Harris did not look as well as usual. There was still a slight swelling over one eye and a piece of plaster on his chin, but it was not these relics of battle which were responsible for the change. His eyes were tired and there was a hint of puffiness about his cheeks as if he had slept badly or been drinking.

Still, he engaged Anthony in conversation brightly enough – conversation which was adroitly steered away from dangerous subjects. The distance to Flushing was short, and there were no awkward silences on the way.

Flushing is a little old town built down to the very edge of its quay, and all day it quietly mirrors its grey slate and sash windows in the blue-grey waters of the harbour. Anthony was left to take stock of it while Tom went in search of his fisherman. Very soon he was back carrying a roll of net and they pushed off on the return journey.

Tom said: 'Have you started school yet?'

The question no doubt was innocently meant, but its answer would entail considerable explanation. However, Anthony could hardly deny him this, having already accepted his companionship. He told the other how he had come to be here in the first place, that he had been expecting to join his father almost any day but that there was now some sort of delay, that just before Uncle Joe died there had been talk of sending him to school in Falmouth but that his death had put a stop to all plans. Soon, he supposed, as soon as everything was settled up, he would be going somewhere, if only for a term or two.

He stopped, aware that he had been getting near a proscribed subject. But Tom did not hesitate.

'Have they read the Will?' he asked.

Anthony crimsoned, trying hard to make up his mind what to say. If he replied as he should he would give offence to a man for whom he had begun to feel a sneaking liking. But if he told . . .

'Don't answer me if you don't want to,' Tom said. 'You're under no obligation to tell me. But of course I shall know all the details in a day or two. They can't withhold information from someone directly concerned.'

The matter hadn't struck Anthony that way.

He said awkwardly: 'They read it this afternoon.'

'Were you present?'

He nodded, still hoping that the subject might be allowed to drop there.

'How was the money left?' Tom said.

Underneath his casual tone there was a note of keenness, of anxiety.

'They . . . It . . . nearly all to Aunt Madge.'

'And Patricia?'

'Five – five hundred pounds. Look, Mr Harris, I –'

'Tom is my name. Were there any other important bequests?'

'No . . . Aunt Louisa was angry; she talked of doing something, fighting the Will . . .'

For some moments Tom had only just been keeping way

123

on the boat. He seemed to have lost interest in his rowing. His brown eyes were fixed on the distant cliff line which had begun to haze over with the setting of the sun. He seemed to see more there than Anthony could.

'It's only what I expected,' he said at length.

The boat began to drift. The boy shivered.

'I ought to be getting back. They'll wonder where I am.'

'Well, I'm glad it's turned out that way anyhow,' said Tom.

The boy stared. He could not make head or tail of that remark. Tom's questions had seemed to suggest only one thing, the obvious thing: that he had hoped all the money would come to Patricia, so that he would stand a chance of getting some of it himself. Tom's eyes had been specially keen when he put the questions, if not with cupidity, then with what? Slowly it began to dawn upon him that if Tom had plenty of money of his own it would suit him better that Patricia should not also be independent. There would be more chance of inducing her to return to him if she was without money or prospects.

Anthony had felt a little disillusioned at Tom's inquiries. Pumping *him* did not seem quite playing the game. At this development he did not know whether to feel relieved or further disillusioned. He wished most earnestly that he had never come. He wished that he had been left alone with his own make-believe.

'Anthony. Will you do something for me?'

The boy looked across at the man. Their eyes met, and then the boy looked down at his finger-nails. Tom Harris had a very direct gaze and, meeting it, one could not believe him capable of the worst forms of trickery. It was the way you looked at a thing, the boy supposed. If *he* was in love with Patricia – well . . . if he was *married* to Patricia – and she had left him, would he not welcome any lever which might persuade her to return? All was supposed to be fair in love and war. Would he want to see her independent?

'First,' said Tom, 'I'd like you to give her this letter.'

124

He stared at the envelope offered him.

'But then she'll know I've been out with you.'

'There's no crime in that. But I might have met you in the street.'

He slowly accepted the letter and put it in his breast pocket.

'Thank you. The second thing is something rather bigger, Anthony. It may come to nothing, but then . . .'

He stared at the glow among the clouds. The sun was already down. Soon it would be dark. The light was moving off the water, moving away as if someone were gently rubbing it out.

'I trust you,' Tom said. 'There's something very frank and honest about you, and I feel that young as you are, you wouldn't willingly let anyone down. Well, I can't come to the house; you know that and the reason for it. Patricia is alone in the world now – except for, except for a stepmother and an uncle who don't really count. I'm anxious about her and about what she'll do. I should like to be by her side to help and – and to advise. As I can't be there, I want to feel that there *is* someone there, someone I can trust. I want you to be that person.'

Anthony murmured something inarticulately. He was warmed and pleased by Tom Harris's words. Everyone is gratified at being paid a compliment, but with Anthony the sensation was something more. Ever since his mother died he had been one apart, and desperately lonely. He had moved among ordinary people and behaved in an ordinary manner, but he had had no sense of belonging. Even Patricia, who had been so kind, had not *needed* him. He had been in her life but not of it.

'It may not be very easy,' said Tom, 'and there may not be much you can do. You're only young and no one can expect you to reach big decisions on your own. But I do feel you can help me just by being there.'

'What do you want me to do?'

'When you get in,' Tom said, 'and think this over you may feel that all I've asked is that you should spy upon

125

people to my advantage. But I don't want you to look at it that way. I don't care anything about my own advantage, I'm only concerned with Patricia's – though I'd like her to come back to me, of course. But she's young and hot-tempered and impulsive, and this is a testing time. I want you to come and see me now and then and talk to me. Come to see me in Penryn. It's only fifteen minutes' walk and we can have a cup of tea together and talk about how things are going at Veal's. Will you do that?'

'Yes,' said Anthony.

'Good man.' Tom slowly resumed his rowing.

'How shall I find where you live?'

Tom gave him instructions. 'If you have any difficulty ask for the Harrises. Everyone knows us.'

Tom Harris seemed only to want a thing and you were prepared to give it him. Perhaps it was in such a mood that he had persuaded Pat to marry him. But the first stirrings of criticism were already awake in Anthony's mind.

'I don't know what Pat will say if she ever gets to know.'

Harris looked up thoughtfully.

'I think I know what she'd say. That you were a traitor to your own family carrying tales to me, wouldn't she?'

Anthony nodded.

'Well,' said Tom, 'it's not a pretty position for any of us. But I don't think in the long run that you will ever regret helping me. And I think you've a fairly good sense of right and wrong. It's entirely up to you what you tell me and what you don't. I have no means of judging whether you are telling me everything or only a part, but I'm prepared to leave that to your good sense. Only remember that I'm trying to help Pat. Even if she wants to free herself from me altogether, I still want to help her.'

'That's what I want,' Anthony said stoutly.

'Then it's a pact?' Tom rested an oar beneath the other elbow and extended his free hand.

They shook hands. Anthony was glad then that it was going dark, for some sort of emotion had brought tears to

126

his eyes. If Tom was appealing to his sentimentality he was not aware of it.

They were almost at the jetty.

'One last word,' the other said. 'I want you to promise me that if anything really important should happen you'll come to me at once. Whether it's day or night doesn't matter. Slip away and come straight to me.'

Anthony felt that he was constantly being asked to concede fresh ground. He had yet to learn the first lesson of all conspirators, that there is no such thing as limited co-operation.

'How do you mean, important?'

The boat grounded gently in the mud.

'I'll leave that to you,' Tom said abruptly. 'Nothing so far as I know is likely to happen. But if anything should, well, you'll easily recognise it as something that I would be anxious to know.'

Now that it was time to go Anthony felt reluctant to leave the intimacy of this newly founded partnership. It seemed to him that he had taken on a good deal with far too little to guide him. The terms of definition were still so vague. That so much should be left to his own initiative and judgment was flattering but a little oppressive. He knew many questions would come to his mind as soon as he got indoors, but now, while there was still time to ask them, he was tongue-tied.

'No second thoughts, Anthony?' Tom's teeth gleamed white for a moment. 'Great men never indulge in them. Remember, I'm relying on you. And again, many thanks.'

The boy climbed out of the boat and smiled back into the dusk. Then he leaned upon the bows of the boat and pushed it gently into the water.

'All right, Tom,' he said, and watched the shadowy figure turn to row away. Then he himself turned and picked a path among the mud and the seaweed towards the dark bulk of the house.

★   ★   ★

Only Fanny was in the kitchen. She was reading *Home Chat*, and her feet, toes together as usual, were on Aunt Madge's favourite footstool.

'Hullo,' she said. 'Where've you been? 'Ad your supper?'

'No . . . Is there anything left?'

'A pasty. 'Tisn't 'ot, but there's plenty of meat in it.'

He picked up the pasty and absently took a bite, his mind still busy. Instinctively he drew nearer to the fire, for his hands and feet were frozen.

'Did they ask for me at supper?'

'No, I didn't 'ear 'em.'

'Where's Miss Patricia now?'

'Gone out. Mr Pawlyn came round.'

The letter was burning a hole in his pocket. The brilliant idea came to him that instead of handing it direct to Pat he would slip it under her bedroom door. Then she might not even think of asking if it was he who had put it there. He couldn't quite understand what had driven him to promise Tom what he had done. Pat would look on it as plain treason. He was torn between two loyalties.

'And Aunt Madge and Uncle Perry?'

'In the parlour.'

'I think I'll take this to bed,' he said. 'I'm tired.'

'Coo, it's early yet. Don't go readin' in bed and leaving your candle burning an' setting the 'ouse afire.'

'Getting bossy, aren't you?'

She pulled a face. 'Well, that's what *she* always says to me.'

He went out into the hall, ducking instinctively to avoid the flypaper, and paused a moment to stare into the darkened shop. All the lower part of the house was unlighted: the shop and both restaurants and the various storerooms. A week or two ago the place had been thronging with people and Uncle Joe had been sharpening his knife behind the counter and bargaining with customers for the various cuts off the joints. Life and bustle. Darkness and decay. Better the light and the heat and the noise. Anything better than darkness. Anthony hated and dreaded it.

The memory of that dream crept into his mind like a

128

thief, and he turned abruptly away from the shop and began to mount the stairs. So vivid had been the dream that even now he could almost hear that furtive rustling in one corner of the shop.

On the first landing a tiny oil lamp burned. A single pearl of light in all this darkness, no larger than a drop of water in a cavern. Beyond, round the corner, another flight of stairs, narrow and gaunt, led to his room.

But first the letter. He took it out and turned it over. There was no writing on it at all. Perhaps Tom had been afraid that if she saw his writing she would destroy it unopened. He crept past the door of the parlour, from under which emerged a thin bar of light, and came to Pat's room. The sound of murmuring voices had reached him for a moment like something warm and cosy as he passed the parlour. He wished so many of the floorboards did not creak; useless to be light-footed and stealthy when the whole house complained at every other step.

Greatly daring, he turned the handle of Pat's door and pushed it a few inches open. He had never been in here before. (Strange how many rooms in this house he had not yet been in.) A faint sweet smell of femininity came to his nostrils. It thrilled him; everything that was dainty and pure and untouchable went with that smell, the essence of womanhood and beauty and grace. Reverently he tiptoed to the dressing-table, put the letter upon it and, suddenly afraid of being surprised, turned and hurried out again.

The door made a noisy click as he closed it, and he stood in the darkness of the passage for some seconds listening to the beating of his own heart. But the two in the parlour had no reason to be suspicious of noise; faintly he heard their voices again. Uncle Perry seemed to be doing all the talking. But then Uncle Perry always did.

He reached the door of the parlour and paused, hesitating whether to go in. He would not really be welcome; he would be in the way; their talk would not interest him. He was about to move on when he heard Aunt Madge's voice raised.

129

'No, Perry; I won't . . . definitely won't allow . . .'

He heard Perry's masterful buccaneering chuckle, then silence fell, to be followed by a little high-pitched laugh. The boy did not know where that laugh came from. It might have been uttered by Aunt Madge, though it didn't sound like any noise he had ever heard her make before. But then he had never heard her laugh. You wouldn't have thought it possible; you wouldn't know what to expect.

'Too soon . . . not decent . . . How dare you? . . .'

Perry's laugh went slower and deeper and subsided to a little throaty chuckle. Then the other laugh broke out again, but short and breathy and sustained upon a giggle. It was as if delight and outraged dignity were fighting for supremacy in it, and dignity was losing ground.

Anthony turned and ran up the stairs to his room. He knew that if he had had the courage he might have opened the door of the sitting-room and walked in.

But he knew he would not have done that for all the jewels of Asia.

Book 2

17

On a mellow day of late September proceedings were
opened at Falmouth police court whereby one Thomas
Wilberforce Harris, solicitor, of Mount House, Penryn,
was charged with assault and battery upon the persons
of Edward Pawlyn, of Mevagissey, and Franz Todt, of
Hamburg. The case had been held up because the beer
bottle which came into contact with Franz Todt's head had
done more damage than was at first supposed. He was,
however, now well enough to come into court with his
head swathed in bandages and an expression of justifiable
resentment on his milestone of a face.

Harris had elected to be dealt with summarily and was
represented by one of his partners, a tall man with a decep-
tively gentle manner. The gravamen of the charge against
Harris was that he had come down into the restaurant
in a quarrelsome drunken mood, had gratuitously picked
a quarrel with Pawlyn and, not content with taking on
one good man, had also contrived to commit a battery
upon Todt.

Harris pleaded guilty to having begun the quarrel with
Pawlyn, but not guilty of having struck Todt. People in the
court felt that history was repeating itself and wondered if
Harris would get six months in the second division like
Mr Fossett in the last case.

There were a large number of witnesses, and although
they had all seen what had happened before someone turned
the gas out, nobody had seen anything at all after. Very soon
it became clear to anyone with a moderate knowledge of
the law that the accused was in little danger of being found
guilty on the second charge. However morally responsible
he might be for making the opening move in the affray,
there was no proof that he had assaulted Bosun Todt in

133

any other way than by accidentally sitting on his knee. Indeed, the weight of evidence suggested that if any blow at all had been exchanged between the two men it had come from the German, who took exception to his supper being interrupted.

The quietus was given to this part of the case by the third mate of the windjammer, who had stayed behind to give evidence. Under cross-examination he admitted that there had been bad feeling during the long and very arduous voyage home, and also that when he arrived on the scene of the quarrel, just before the lights were put out, Bosun Todt was fighting with several of their own men. These men, it was ascertained, were no longer under the jurisdiction of the court, being with their ship, which was now in the Baltic.

At this stage Mr May, Harris's partner, submitted that there was no case to answer in law, and the Stipendiary Magistrate in charge of the court agreed with him and dismissed the charge.

There remained, however, the first charge, to which the accused pleaded guilty; and the magistrate gathered his papers together and prepared to deliver a weighty homily on the folly by which a young man of a highly respected local family, of good education and holding a responsible position in the affairs of a neighbouring town, should find himself in this deplorable position. But just as he was about to begin Mr May rose again and in a quiet voice said that he had one further witness to bring forward, one whom he produced with considerable reluctance, but who insisted upon entering the witness stand and giving testimony in this case. He called Mrs Tom Harris.

There was a stir in the well-filled court, and Patricia was to be seen making her way down the centre aisle. Tom half rose from his seat, then glanced at Mr May in annoyance.

Every person in the court, with the possible exception of the two foreign witnesses, knew something of the history of the whirlwind marriage and the equally sudden separation. There was a general peering and shifting and craning, and

134

a rising murmur of voices was to be heard until the rap of the hammer checked it and brought a return of silence.

'You are Mrs Patricia Harris, wife of the accused?' Mr May said, when the formalities had been gone through.

'I am.' She spoke in a low voice. She was dressed all in black with a small black hat worn rather forward on her head and a veil hiding her expression. But in order to give her evidence she had lifted the veil. In these last few weeks since her father's death she had matured, grown suddenly and quietly adult. Her features had fined off, the chin had lost a little of its roundness. She had done her hair a different way, which emphasised the pale curve of chin and neck.

'You were present in the restaurant on the night in question?'

'I was.'

'Will you tell the court, Mrs Harris, in your own words, what happened?'

Patricia put down her small black muff and looked at the magistrate.

'Your worship, I must first explain that I am the daughter of the late Mr Joe Veal who owned the restaurant at the time. I had – left my husband some weeks before this happened, and he came to see me at the restaurant, where I was living. He was not drunk. I have never seen him in any way under the influence of drink. When he came –'

The magistrate looked over the top of his spectacles.

'Why was this witness not produced before?'

'Your worship,' said Patricia, 'because everyone wished to spare me the pain of appearing in court. There has been that intention from the beginning – my husband, Mr Pawlyn, all of them wished to prevent it becoming known that the – the quarrel was – over me. But . . . I have insisted, because it – it is not fair that all the facts should not be known. Not from any – not from any . . .'

'Take your time, Mrs Harris,' said Mr May gently.

Patricia put her gloved hands together in an effort to steady her nerves. That other time, when she had appeared in court and given testimony damaging her father, had been nothing to this. Then her personal, private life had been in no way involved. She had been in a spirited, reckless mood, not at all enjoying the experience but keyed up to do what she had suddenly, impulsively resolved. But now she hardly knew how to keep her hands or her lips steady.

With a great effort she went on:

'A few months ago, I separated from my husband *permanently*. Once or twice he has visited me, asking me to return, and I have refused. Mr – Mr Pawlyn is an old friend whom I knew before I married and who always calls in when his ship is in port. My husband objected to my associating with him. I claim the right to associate with whom I choose. On the – that night I was having supper in the restaurant with Mr Pawlyn. Tom – my husband – came across and spoke to me. He was absolutely sober and I think had no idea of making trouble. But a few words were exchanged between them and then . . . then Mr Pawlyn called Tom an offensive name – and it was then that the – that my husband hit him.'

'Your worship,' said the prosecuting solicitor, 'I completely fail to see in what way this witness is going to affect the case. The accused has already pleaded guilty to assault and battery.'

'Go on, Mrs Harris,' said the magistrate.

She hesitated. 'I – I think that is all.'

Mr May had no questions to ask, but the prosecutor at once came to his feet again.

'How did you know that your husband was not drunk, Mrs Harris?' he asked.

'. . . He wasn't. He was quite sober.'

'You've just told us that you have never seen your husband drunk. How would you know, then, if you saw him?'

'Well . . . he was not unsteady – or – or . . . I've seen too many drunken men not to be able to tell.'

'Certainly he was not unsteady: look what happened to the restaurant. But a man needs just the right number of

136

drinks to become quarrelsome – or to have been drinking steadily for some time. Since you had not been in his company, how could you tell?'

'. . . I'm quite certain that –'

'Mrs Harris, what was the offensive word Mr Pawlyn used to your husband?'

There was a titter at the back of the court.

Patricia fumbled with her muff. 'I don't wish to repeat it . . .'

'As bad as that? Or have you forgotten?'

'No, I haven't. Your worship, I'll write it down if necessary.'

'She'll write it down, if necessary, Mr Prior.'

Mr Prior did not pursue the subject.

'Do you wish to return to your husband?'

'No.'

The man looked at her with his head on one side.

'Not?'

'Certainly not.'

'Are you sure that your testimony today is not given with a view to effecting a reconciliation?'

'Certainly it is not.'

'Are you still – friendly with Mr Pawlyn?'

'Yes.'

'A little damaging for him, isn't it, to come forward like this?'

'I don't know what you mean.'

'To say nothing of your own reputation?'

'I can only tell you the truth. Your worship, I can only tell the truth. There was never anything at all between myself and Mr Pawlyn. I have no wish to return to my husband. I don't want to at all. But I don't want to see him go to prison for something that was only partly his fault.'

'Quite so,' said the magistrate sympathetically. 'Have you any other questions, Mr Prior?'

'No, your worship. But I submit that this young woman's testimony is entirely useless. She has proved nothing which was not already admitted and disproved nothing that the prosecution alleges. The case surely remains unaffected by it in any way.'

'You may leave the stand now, Mrs Harris,' said the magistrate.

Patricia had promised to meet Ned Pawlyn after the case and spend the rest of the day with him. But when it was at last over she would gladly have made some excuse and gone straight home. Always, it seemed to her, when she became involved in the law her testimony had to be damaging to the people whose interests were closest to her own.

But Ned Pawlyn, whatever his private feelings, was waiting for her when they came out of the court-room, and in a few moments he had led her past the staring bystanders to where a closed landau was waiting.

They got in and drove off.

A long silence fell between them. The day was unusually warm and sunny for the time of year, with the temperature in the sixties. The month might have been August were it not for the angle of the sunshine slanting through the trees and casting the long shadows of houses across the dusty road.

At last Ned could contain himself no longer.

'Bound over to keep the peace for twelve months,' he said explosively. 'That's what comes of being tried local. And the law looks after them that's in the law. If it had been me that had been in the dock I should never have got off with less than twenty-eight days.'

Patricia leant back and looked out at the slow panorama of lane and tree and river.

'It was my fault,' she said.

'I don't care about myself,' he said; 'but it seems to me it was a pity you had to come in as you did. I wondered why you went out of court with that Mr May. I don't know enough about those things to say whether they would have twisted things round to suit him in any case, or whether what you told made all the difference; but you know what they'll say about you now . . .'

'No.'

'About us, then. They'll say that you and me –'

'I know, I know, I know! What does it matter?' she said suddenly, angrily. 'What does it matter what narrow-minded people say?' She was taut beside him. 'I couldn't help it. I'm not good at conspiracies, especially if I benefit. I didn't want to get him off; but it wasn't fair for him to be judged on only one side of the story just because you're all too delicate to let me be involved. Don't you see? *I couldn't let that happen*. I'd have been under an obligation all my life. And an obligation to him. What happened was as much your fault as his – and – and quite as much mine as either. I'd got to tell the truth. Now it's all out and he's free and it's all over. Let's not talk about it. Forget it. Forget it.'

He saw that she was near tears.

'Sorry, Pat,' he said. 'It was what we were both thinking about, wasn't it?'

'I'm sorry too,' she said, suddenly quiet again. 'I'm sorry to have – to have turned on you in court. I always seem to be – up against my friends. I don't want to be. And you're always so very patient and kind . . .'

Silence fell again; but this time it was one from which the electric charge had been dispersed.

'Where are you taking me?' she asked, after they had passed through Penryn.

'Anywhere you like. I thought the drive would do you good. I thought while you were giving evidence, I thought: what she could do with after this is a drive, just sitting back and nothing to do. And I thought I might get you away without meeting *him*. I slipped out before you and got this cab. I thought we could go as far as the Norway Inn and have tea there. I know the man who keeps it.'

They were beginning to climb the overgrown winding hill out of the town. The horse had fallen to a walk.

'You're very kind, Ned,' she said, touched by his solicitude. 'I don't deserve it. I wish I . . .'

139

'What?'

'Oh, nothing.'

Only scraps of conversation passed between them for the rest of the drive, down the other side of the sharp hill, through the valley where the sunlight lay in wasp bars across the road and the trees were showing their first tinges of autumnal yellow. In places the rank vegetation of the hedgerows had grown lushly out to flop across the road and catch at the carriage as it passed. This was the old coaching road, but since the railway came it had fallen into disuse. Ridges of grass grew between the dusty and uneven ruts.

They drew up at the inn, and Ned told the driver to wait and they went inside and ordered tea, which was served in a low, shadowy little private parlour.

Patricia lay back in her chair and drank tea and ate a split with jam and butter on it to please Ned. She was more than grateful to him for his tact and consideration. So pleasant and restful was it to lie back here and say little and feel that for a time you were away from prying eyes. She knew well that Ned was right in his appraisal of the situation, that she would only get notoriety and ill fame for the part she had played this afternoon. She knew that tomorrow *The Falmouth Packet* would be out, and the fullest possible report would be given of the events of today. The paper would probably sell out in no time, for everyone would be anxious to read for himself the exact account of Tom Harris's trial and what Patricia Harris – *née* Veal – had actually got up in the court-room and said about herself and Ned Pawlyn.

Her position in Falmouth had been a little difficult ever since she left Tom. There were some who said she deserved a good whipping for turning her back on a well-to-do young gentleman who had done her the honour of marrying her. This view was strong among those who would have liked to marry him themselves or had eligible daughters. Marriage vows were not to be treated like waste paper; what would the world be coming to if everyone acted in such a fashion?

140

Besides, it was a wicked bad example for all the young folks growing up. Pat Veal, they said, had shown her upbringing and her parentage: the Veals were a queer lot nowadays – all except Miss Veal of Arwenack Street. Young Mrs Harris must be carefully and systematically cut.

Then after the contents of the Will became known she noticed the onset of another change. Young women who had come in for a good deal of ready money, considerable property and a complete shipping line were somehow more entitled to their impulses and foibles. But young women who had been practically disowned and left penniless would be well advised to eat humble pie and go on eating it. If they did not do so, then so much the worse for them.

Now, after this afternoon, the town would be well confirmed in its worst views.

Not that it mattered, she told herself. What did anything matter any more? They would go their way and she would go hers. She did not yet depend on their patronage.

'You know we're leaving by the morning tide, don't you?' said Ned.

She nodded, but the information chilled her afresh. Ned was a good friend who had stood by her in everything. His friendship did not waver with changed circumstances. He was one of the few who were worth knowing.

They were quite alone in the little parlour, and the last sun had left the room. It was dark and quiet and smelt of damp earth from some ferns in the window.

'Why don't you come away with me?' said Ned.

She looked at him startled.

'How do you mean?'

He grunted. 'I don't mean in *The Grey Cat*, of course. I could cut that and stay behind. What I mean is . . . Well, I can't ask you to marry me, because you're already married. But why not come away with me somewhere? Later on Harris will get tired of hanging on and will divorce you. Then we can do things legally. But . . . that may be a year or two. Come away; let's leave the country altogether. You can't stay in Falmouth. Everybody'll talk and talk. You

141

can't live on what you've got. Well, I've not much, but I can earn. I can earn enough for two. We can go to Australia, start a new life. Nobody'll know us there. It'll be dropping all this and starting all over again. What d'you say?'

It is doubtful if Ned Pawlyn had ever before said quite so much without a break. Patricia stared somewhat startled at the sudden vista which opened before her. She had never contemplated such a thing; but she suddenly found the prospect not without its attraction. Two months ago she would have dismissed the idea with scarcely a thought. Then life in Falmouth, for all the break-up of her marriage, was good. She enjoyed the life of the restaurant; besides, she was so young that she looked into the future eagerly and without fear. But now . . . the restaurant was closed and Aunt Madge was making as yet no effort to open it. Even if she did, she, Pat, would not feel the same proprietorial interest in its success. And she had lost her father and the respect of most of her neighbours. If Uncle Perry eventually found somewhere to retire, as he still talked of doing, the household might boil down to no more than herself and Madge; and although she had no special complaints to lodge against Madge as a stepmother, there was no pleasure in looking forward to having her as a sole companion. (Besides, Madge had made no secret of her view that Pat's proper place was in her husband's house; when Pat first returned she had always been going on at her about the sanctity of marriage vows: on and on in her best water-weareth-away-stone manner. Though in fairness, Pat had to admit that she had never suggested it since Joe died.) But what alternative was there now except either to return to Tom or to live with Madge? With only a few hundred pounds she could not set up in a little cottage of her own.

Here was an alternative suddenly before her eyes . . . Australia was a new conception: a big hot land of rolling sheep farms and miles of ripening wheat. Life there with Ned might be adventurous and new. Men had made big fortunes out there in the last few years; why not Ned?

142

She pictured herself as his partner and companion all through life, living in a wooden shack, then later in a big ranch house, sitting on a veranda with a warm, sweet wind blowing in from the miles of grass land, and perhaps two or three children tumbling about at her feet.

'What d'you say, Pat?' Ned repeated.

Slowly her eyes came back to the drab little room and to the dark-browed eager young man opposite. With Ned. That was the point. With Ned. Slowly the vision faded.

'It's sweet of you to ask me,' she began.

In a moment he was kneeling beside her, one arm resting upon her knees.

'I needn't go tomorrow,' he said. 'Stevens can get someone else. There's a ship leaving for Brisbane one day next week. We can make a long honeymoon of it.'

She felt that she wanted to refuse him, but she did not seem to have the strength left. And, although the vision had faded, there remained a thread of self-knowledge in her mind which told her that this was what she was really cut out for: not to be a lawyer's wife, not to live as a grass widow in a narrow circle of relatives and friends, not to live in a provincial, respectable, genteel comfort, but to launch out with the man she loved, risking hardship and overcoming difficulties, finding adventure and frustration and fulfilment.

'I'll think it over,' she said. 'I'll think about it, Ned, truly I will. If –'

But he knew that such a favourable moment was unlikely to return. Tomorrow things might look different to her. But he knew that if he could coax a promise out of her tonight she would stick to it tomorrow and the next day.

And, if nothing happened, he was due to sail on the morning tide. In a few hours he would be gone.

He bent towards her and found her face closer to his than it had ever been before. It delighted him and he kissed her gently on the mouth.

Her lips were yielding; they did not respond but they were not unfriendly. He kissed her again, and the success

143

went to his head. He put his arms about her and drew her towards him and tried to kiss her again.

And then suddenly he found that she was resisting him, unmistakably resisting him. They strained for a moment or two and then he let her free. She rose to her feet quickly and went to the window. He could see her breath coming quickly, misting the pane.

He went and stood beside her, put a hand upon her arm.

She turned. 'Please, Ned,' she said quietly, and her face was white. 'Please, Ned; take me home.'

18

Amid the opal clouds of dawn *The Grey Cat* slipped out quietly into the bay. Anthony was awake and craned his neck from his window to watch her shake out her sails one by one like a white flower unfolding its petals at the touch of the sun. He was sorry to see her go, for he liked the burly mate with his long legs and his quiet, slouching walk and felt sympathy with him in his obvious devotion to Pat. Since his pact with Tom, however, he had experienced a sense of constraint in Ned's presence and had tended to avoid him. He felt as if he were accredited to an unfriendly power and did not want to abuse his diplomatic privileges.

It was a beautiful morning with the early autumn sun dispersing a scarf of mist which clung to the low hills on the other side of the harbour. Anthony was the first stirring in a house which had curiously cut adrift from its old routine since Joe died. In the old days Perry had been the only member of the household to stay late in bed, but with the incentive of business removed Aunt Madge was now not rising until about half-past nine, and little Fanny, a reluctant waker at the best of times, usually succeeded in putting in an appearance a bare ten

144

minutes ahead of her, like a saucy frigate in front of a ship of the line.

Patricia was usually the first about, with Anthony close behind her, but this morning he was down much earlier. When he happened to go outside and saw what someone had written in white on the pavement outside the shop and on the shop window, he felt there was a reasonable hope, if he was very quick, of being able to remove the writing before Patricia came down.

Although he had not been at the police court, Aunt Madge and Uncle Perry had discussed it in front of him later in the evening, and he realised that the inscriptions had some reference to what had passed there. The writing on the window said: 'SAILORS ONLY.' That on the pavement was more explicit, and ran: 'CALL IN ANY TIME YOU ARE IN PORT.'

There was another reason for haste, for it was now full daylight. The street was at present deserted, but people would soon be passing this way.

The shop door was not open, so he had to carry a bucket round from the kitchen door and up the steps at the side. He realised he had brought nothing to work with and ran back for a cloth and a scrubbing brush.

He began on the window, and at once found that the stuff used was not whitewash, as he had first thought, but paint, and it had been dry several hours. The letters would be removable only with great difficulty. He could barely reach the top of the letters, but that did not matter so long as he made them unreadable.

He had been at work about five minutes when Warne's milk cart stopped at the corner. Fred Warne, the big, overgrown son, came down the narrow, sloping street carrying a milk churn. He stopped at the sight of Anthony and set down his can.

Fred Warne was the result of a marriage of first cousins and was not among the brighter intelligences.

'Whar'ee doing that fur?'

Anthony stopped a moment and shrugged his shoulders.

145

'L-O-R-S,' spelt Fred laboriously. 'O-N-L-Y. That don't make sense. Who's been writing on the pavement?'

'Don't know,' said Anthony.

'Out early this morning,' said Fred. 'Don't b'long to see anyone stirring round 'ere s'early as this. Not since the Ole Man died. What are 'ee out s'early fur?'

Anthony began to sweat with the effort of his work. Fred Warne watched him with a slightly open mouth. There was silence while the L O disappeared.

'Call-in-any-time-you-are-in-port,' Fred read out, putting his tongue round his mouth in between words. 'What fur should anyone want fur to write that, eh?'

'Isn't it time you delivered the milk?' the boy suggested.

'Reckon you're opening again,' said Fred, suddenly struck with the idea. 'Reckon that's what 'tis. 'Tis a bit of a joke fur to attrack people. Did Widow Veal ask fur that there notice to be splashed on the pavement, eh?'

'Your horse is straying,' said Anthony, glancing up the road. 'Look . . .'

Fred scratched the fair stubble on his chin.

''E can't do that fur 'e's tethered to the lamppost. Reckon that's another joke, eh?' He burst into hearty but contemptuous laughter.

'You'll waken everybody.'

Fred shifted on to his other foot and leaned a hand on his milk churn. 'Well, 'tis daylight. Didn't people ought to be woke up when 'tis daylight, eh?' His hearty laughter brayed out again. A small child came to the end of the street and stared down with his finger in his mouth.

'Call-in-any-time-you-are-in-port,' said Fred. 'I'll tell fathur 'bout you opening 'gain. Maybe you'll be wanting more milk again, eh?'

A window opened above their heads. With a sinking feeling the boy saw Patricia looking down.

'Anthony! Whatever are you doing?'

'I thought,' said Anthony. 'I thought I'd – I'd clean the windows. They were dirty and I thought it would be –'

146

'What's that writing? Move the bucket, will you? I –'
She broke off and her face went a sudden white.

'Shall I tell fathur you be goin' t'open up again, eh?'
called Fred.

She quickly shut the window.

'Don't seem to like it, eh?' said the milk boy. 'What's
the matter with she?'

'Mind your own business!' Anthony suddenly snapped,
losing his temper. 'Get on with your milk round . . .' He
stared at the shop window. The R S had gone. ONLY did
not convey much. He glanced at his water, which was now
a greasy grey.

'You must be windy 'bout something,' said Fred Warne.
'Getting snappy an' –'

But the water had been suddenly emptied on the pavement, swilling almost over Fred's feet, and Anthony and
the empty bucket were gone.

In the kitchen Anthony came full tilt into the girl. He
swerved past her and hurriedly clanged the bucket under
the kitchen sink and turned the tap on full. She came
and stood beside him without speaking while the bucket
filled; he could see one white sleeve of her dressing-gown
trembling against the table.

The tap was turned off and he grabbed the bucket.

'Leave it, Anthony,' she said, speaking rapidly but with
some difficulty. 'What does it matter? Leave it. Don't –
show that – we care . . .'

'It'll be gone soon,' he gasped, and rushed out up the
steps and round the corner to the front of the shop.

The small boy and a strange man and Mrs Treharne, the
publican's wife from the corner, had joined Fred Warne. An
effort of will was needed to go out and ignore their questions
and their sly looks and get down on your knees and begin
to scrub for dear life. Learning from experience, Anthony
concentrated on the important words: CALL, TIME and
PORT.

Three youths going to work at the docks now joined the
gathering, and then a shrewish little woman from a cottage

next to the public house who, having had the situation explained to her, gave it as her opinion that after all folks generally got what they asked for in this world, but that boy didn't ought to be the one scrubbing it off, the one to do it should be *her* that was in the fault.

All the time he was at work the audience remained, though in the nature of things it was a fluctuating one. Even with such a pleasant and original spectacle to view and discuss, people in the early morning were generally up at that hour to some purpose, and work called the faithful to their several tasks. But others came to take their places.

When the thing was at last done, Anthony took up his bucket and brush and, ignoring the last questions and humorous remarks, slid quietly round to the back of the house, leaving the solitary word ONLY still upon the shop window as a mark of the defamer's hand.

Breakfast that morning was a joyless meal. Patricia had gone upstairs and did not reappear, Perry as usual was still asleep, so Aunt Madge presided in due solemnity with Anthony beside her and Fanny occupying an obscure seat at the end of the table. Without the lightening effect of the two other adults Madge was like a blanket, and conversation ran into blind alleys. The only time Madge was ever talkative was when she had a grievance.

The morning passed, and it was not until lunch time that Patricia came quietly down the stairs and took her seat at the table. She smiled faintly at Perry's humorous sallies, but bent over her meal in silence until little Fanny had carried off her own meal into the scullery.

Then Pat raised her head. 'Madge,' she said, 'don't think I'm not happy here; but I'm going to get a job.'

Her stepmother put up a plump, white hand to pat the pad in her hair.

'While I'm alive . . .'

'Yes, I know, my dear, and thank you. But I can't stop here on your – charity all my life. Besides, forgive me, but I don't want to. I've been trying to make up my mind for days – ever since the Will was read. This morning has decided me –'

'Pah! What's there in that to take on about?' said Perry, patting her knee. 'You've no need to pay attention to a few old gossips. They mean no harm. Everyone gossips. Even me. Even Anthony, don't you, boy? It will die down in no time. Now in China –'

'What,' asked Aunt Madge, turning up her eyes, 'did you think of doing?'

The girl puckered her smooth brow. 'I've hardly got as far as that yet. There's so few things a woman can do. But I'll find something.'

'People will think,' said Aunt Madge, blinking. 'People will blame me. Your Aunt Louisa. They'll say . . .'

'In China,' said Perry, 'there's a sign language, you know. If they draw one little figure under a roof, that means harmony. If they put two little figures that stands for marriage. If they put three little figures that means gossip. It's just the same wherever –'

'I don't see why they should say anything against you,' said Patricia. 'I'll tell Aunt Louisa it's nothing to do with you. I'm a free agent and –'

'Not the solution,' said Aunt Madge; 'not the solution Hi should have . . . A good husband . . .'

Pat's firm young face did not alter. 'I can't, Madge. I don't want to go back to him. I want to live my own life, stand on my own feet . . .'

'Whereas in Japan,' said Perry, 'there isn't the same inducement, as you might say.'

'Not nice,' said Aunt Madge. 'A young girl to go out . . . earning her own . . . Later. This restaurant. We shall open again. Shan't we, Perry?'

'Yes, duck. Anything you say. I remember in Yokohama, there's a geisha palace. I've heard it said that they thrash the girls' bare feet with bamboo canes if they aren't obliging to customers. Which just shows that there's two sides to every story.' He pushed his hair out of his eyes. 'There's one side, and there's the other side. Like young Pat wanting to go out and earn her own living. Some would say it was all right, and others –'

'I shall try in Falmouth first,' said Pat. 'But if nothing turns up here I shall try somewhere else. I'm fairly good with my fingers and there might be an opportunity at somewhere like Martins or Crosbies.'

'No cause to hurry,' said Mrs Veal. 'Your father. Dead only a little while. I don't think . . . would have liked . . .'

But this time she had definitely chosen the wrong appeal. Patricia said: 'I'm not concerned with anything my father would have liked.'

Aunt Madge rose slowly, and her pince-nez wobbled a little on the top of the monument. She took away Perry's plate before he had quite wiped up all the gravy and began to stack the dishes.

'In that case . . . nothing further . . . Nothing Hi can say . . . One goes one's own way . . . regardless. Naturally I . . .' She mumbled on for some moments and her voice mixed itself up with the clack-clack of the plates.

'What's for after?' Perry asked, trying to smooth things over. 'Lemon pud? D'you like lemon pud, boy? Don't tell me, I believe you hate it. It always reminds me of an African native I knew once. His head had been burned in a bush fire and all his hair was gone –'

Pat got up from her chair and went up to Aunt Madge and kissed her soft loose cheek.

'No offence, Mother Madge. Nothing against *you*, you know. Besides . . .' After a pause she went on: 'Besides, it may be weeks and weeks before I'm off your hands in any case. So cheer up.'

The pause had been occasioned by the kiss. As she withdrew her lips Anthony saw a peculiar expression cross the girl's face and disappear. It was as if she had had a sudden twinge of pain or distaste . . . or it might even have been one of presentiment.

★   ★   ★

After dinner, in the privacy of her own bedroom, Pat stared at the reflection of her flushed face. She felt bitterly rebellious and bitterly unhappy. With this morning's tide Ned had gone, perhaps for weeks, perhaps not to return. Now she was alone, desperately alone.

She did not regret her refusal of last evening; she felt she had done right; but that did not comfort her loneliness now; rather did it accentuate it, for a woman does not think the worse of any man for being in love with her and wishing to marry her, and these last few days Ned had been her only companion, the only one she could trust and to some extent confide in. Anthony, of course, remained, and in a way his friendship was the most reliable of all because his devotion was without any thought of personal profit. She would not forget his work this morning when, but for him, the writing might have been there until midday for everyone to see. But you could not talk to an eleven-year-old boy in quite the same way as you could to an adult.

She wondered, as she had wondered several times during the last week or so, what it was in her character which made her rebel against so many of the things which the average person, the average girl, accepted as a matter of course. Was there some perversity in her nature which prevented her from living a normal life? Above all, in all her actions of the last six months, was *she* in the wrong? Pat had a reasonable belief in her own judgment, but she could not help but think of the Irishman who said all the regiment was out of step but himself.

In the first place she supposed she should have put affection for and obedience to her father above an abstract love of justice in the case of the wounded Dutchman. Then again filial piety should have prevented her from going against her father's wishes by marrying Tom. Or, if she had married Tom, she should have accepted such dispositions as he had made for their married life meekly and without criticism. Other women did. When you accepted a man in marriage you did so for better or worse; you automatically transferred your fidelity from one man to another. Henceforward husband came before father. It was like changing situations. In either case the man was not open to criticism.

Or was this a jaundiced view of the matter? Were they truly right and she wrong? Perhaps the rest of the regiment were not entirely mistaken in their views. Between a man and a woman who loved each other there was often a sort of sex loyalty which went beyond mere personal judgment. There was something rather admirable in the type of patriot who in a crisis said, 'My country, right or wrong.' So, in married life or in family relationship, was there not something equally admirable in the woman who . . .

Yes, she thought; in times of crisis, yes. But there was nothing so admirable in the patriot who said, 'My country, right at all times.' The best type of patriot was surely the man who would always stand by his country in a pinch but reserved the right to his own judgment when the pinch was over. Why then could a woman not reserve a similar right?

The point was, of course, to define exactly what was a crisis. She had certainly not seen the incident of the Dutchman as such at the time, but from the immense consequences following it she was prepared to admit her mistake. And the analogy of a crisis did not quite work out in her relations with Tom. A sudden incompatibility had emerged, had hardened, and she had come to see that it was insurmountable. In such circumstances, was the patriot justified in leaving his country?

She unpinned her crisp thick hair and let it fall about her shoulders; then she began to brush it with a measured sweep which she often found soothing. But nothing seemed to have the right effect this afternoon and presently she gave up and sat on the bed.

She supposed that the fate of all rebels was loneliness. In a sense she had felt herself to be a rebel all her life, she had felt always a reluctance to bow heedlessly to the things other people bowed to. Without conceit, she had known there was a difference between herself and most of the people she had met. She moved quicker and thought quicker. Often

152

in conversation she had found herself running on ahead like a child before its grandparents, coming back to pick them up, then running on again. And often she chafed at the delay. But always she had cherished, as a sort of most-prized possession, a sense of personal freedom. That it was a spiritual rather than a material freedom did not seem to matter. It had been there for her to fall back on in the privacy of her own heart.

Not until this year had the material dependence come into conflict with this independence of spirit; but once the struggle was joined it had seemed vitally necessary to her that there should be no compromise.

And so far there had been no compromise. But she felt that she now had arrayed against her all the forces of precedent and public opinion. The struggle would be long and hard, and she was not enjoying it. She wanted only to be happy and free and to live on terms of friendship with everyone. Essentially there was no one less quarrelsome than she was if life was only prepared to concede her a measure of liberty and self-respect.

She got up impatiently, picked up a towel and went to the bathroom, where she bathed her hands and face in cold water. Back in her room, she put on a different frock and put up her hair. In opening one of the drawers to take out a brooch she saw the letter which she had found on her dressing-table a week ago.

She picked it up and unfolded it, stared at it a moment with a queer sense of guilt as if by even regarding it she were being disloyal to herself.

Dear Pat [it ran]:

I have made a number of attempts to begin this letter and each time have torn it up to start afresh, faced with an extraordinary sense of difficulty in trying to express my true feelings about Saturday night.

First, let me make it clear that I'm more sorry than I can say if the disturbance I started in any way hastened your father's death. He did not like me because I was a lawyer and because I wanted to take you away from him. But I could sympathise with him most sincerely in the second particular, and I only felt deep sorrow on hearing he was dead.

But it is not so much of that as of what came afterwards that I want to write – of what passed between us.

Regret – the word springs to one's mind and conveys nothing. Nor would it be true to use that word alone. Oh, yes, regret enters into it. I should regret it for ever if hope for a reconciliation between us had been further squandered by what happened. But if reconciliation was already past, then there was nothing to lose, and some pagan pleasure makes a mockery of all the polite emotions. Shakespeare wrote of taking a woman 'in her heart's extremest hate, with curses in her mouth, tears in her eyes . . .' I know what that means now.

But unfortunately I still love you, and love, I found, is not satisfied with the fruits of conquest – rich though they may be. So even conquest was not for me.

For excuse, if excuses are wanted, remember that you lied to me. There: is that a pretty plea? You had been with another man, giving him your companionship, and I had not seen you for weeks. Then when we were alone for a few minutes you lied to me about your ankle and would have been safely away but for the self-locking door.

Perhaps we should not have married. Love doesn't always go with affinity – sometimes not even with liking, for you certainly seem to dislike me with a will.

As I told you, I'm resigning my partnership in Harvey & Harris. I feel I want a change, and feel I must get away from this district now. If we have to be separated then I want the separation to be a wider one.

I should like you to know that if ever you are in need of help and feel you can accept mine, I shall be more than happy to do anything I can.

Believe me,
Ever your
Tom

For some time after reading the letter Pat stood before the dressing-table playing with a string of pearls which had been her mother's. She had dropped the letter back into the drawer, but now she picked it up again and stared at the envelope, turning it over as if in speculation.

With a sharp, painful impulse, she grasped the letter and ripped it across and across. With the need to destroy it still on her she struggled with the pieces, but her fingers were not strong enough to tear it again.

As sharply as she had begun she dropped the bits back into the drawer and turned to the window, staring blindly out. Tears formed in her eyes and she blinked them away. They formed again and this time overflowed upon her thick eyelashes and presently began to drip upon her cheeks. It was the first time she had cried since her father died.

19

Patricia's attempts to find work for herself did not meet with conspicuous success. She had never realised before what small opportunity there was for an intelligent, energetic girl to earn her own living, to become self-supporting in a decent respectable business-like way. One had to be a nursery governess or a sempstress or a milliner, working endless hours for a starvation wage. It was as if the world had entered into a conspiracy to prevent the independent young woman from breaking away from the herd, so that she found herself hemmed about and compelled to conform. For the first time Patricia found herself becoming a rebel against the whole structure of a society which condoned this state of affairs.

Towards the end of the third week she was surprised to receive a letter from an old school friend in Truro.

Dear Pat [it ran]:

I don't know if Maud Richards is mistaken, but she told

155

me yesterday you were looking for something to do. Perhaps you'll forgive me for being nosy, but do you know that a Miss Gawthorpe, who runs a private school here, is looking for an assistant? I don't know what the qualifications must be; Miss Gawthorpe was telling Mummie the other day that it was not degrees she was particular about – probably she doesn't want to pay for them – but chiefly she needed 'a young lady of good appearance' who could help her manage the younger children and take them in a few elementary subjects.

In case this appeals to you her address is Green Lane, Truro. I don't suppose you could get back to Falmouth at night, but it would be nice having you living near here.

Affectionately,

SYLVIA KENT

In haste Patricia wrote to the address supplied, using her maiden name and glossing over such facts in her life as seemed likely not to appeal to a lady of Miss Gawthorpe's calling. Three weeks ago she would have scorned the idea of sailing under compromise colours, but disappointment rubs off the sharp edges of integrity, and she had seen too often the change which came over a prospective employer's face when she explained the fact that she was married but separated from her husband.

Three days later a reply came asking her to call, and she left for Truro by an early train.

Miss Gawthorpe was large and formidable but not shrewish. She was clearly the sort of person who formed her judgments rapidly and she seemed at once to take a liking to Pat. The salary, although poor, included meals and sleeping accommodation at the house, and Pat saw that she would just be able to manage. In any case she was so delighted at the offer that no thought of quibbling entered her head. She arrived home bursting with the news that on Saturday next by the four o'clock train she was leaving Falmouth to take up her new duties.

Nobody looked very happy at the news. Widow Veal, as she was now generally called, had had a trying day with

Mr Cowdray. So many details of the estate still needed settling, and Aunt Louisa, true to her promise, was doing her best to put all possible obstacles in the way of their being settled. She had some papers connected with the land Joe had owned, land inherited from his father, and these she could not be persuaded to part with until legal action to recover them was actually put in motion. Lengthy letters were still passing almost daily between Aunt Louisa's Mr Crabbe and Aunt Madge's Mr Cowdray.

But despite all efforts to the contrary, the time steadily approached when everything should legally become Aunt Madge's, and Louisa Veal persisted in her efforts in the light of faith rather than reason. About a week after the reading of the Will another Will had been produced by a solicitor at Helston, dated five years earlier and leaving the bulk of the property to Joe's first wife, 'in trust' for his daughter Patricia; and this had encouraged Aunt Louisa in the belief that there must be a later Will as well as an earlier one. No man, she felt, who had so vented his spite at a sudden quarrel could so criminally neglect the decencies as to fail to register the reconciliation in a like manner.

Her latest idea was that she or her representatives should be allowed to search the house for such a document, and this Aunt Madge statuesquely refused to concede. It was against all right, she was heard to mutter. The idea offended her to the core. She would sooner die, she implied, than let that woman come into her house again, picking over her personal belongings like a carrion crow. Mr Cowdray, growing sick of the endless altercation, suggested that he might be able to make some capital out of the concession if she were to permit it as a gesture. He might even wring some promise from Mr Crabbe that, if such permission were granted, he would persuade his client to drop the quarrel.

But so far Aunt Madge would not move an inch. The position was at a deadlock. When Aunt Madge was at a deadlock she looked it. For the last two days life had congealed in her and words emerged from that little pursed mouth reluctantly, like slow drops of wax from a melting figure.

So her reception of Patricia's news was a preoccupied and a grudging one. She seemed to feel first that she was too busy to be bothered with Pat's affairs and later, when the news had sunk in, to feel a grievance against the girl for adding one more trouble to the sum of her burdens.

Aunt Madge was getting fat. She had put on weight noticeably in the weeks since her husband died. One day when she sat down to supper Perry had jocularly remarked: 'Stap me, Madge, but if you go on at this rate you'll be a big woman when you grow up!' But he did not repeat the joke. Sometimes lately one might have thought that the irreverent Perry went slightly in awe of his sister-in-law. He broke out from time to time, but on the whole, especially where the decencies of mournings were concerned, he increasingly took his cue from her. Since the long bout of drinking at the time of Joe's death Anthony had not seen him drunk once, nor had anyone's sleep been disturbed by hearing *The Black Hunter* sung in a wavering voice as its owner stumbled to bed in the small hours.

As for Anthony, Patricia's appointment struck him almost with the force of a second bereavement. As the term was getting on and no more mention had been made of his going to school he had begun to hope that his affairs would be entirely overlooked until after Christmas. From the time of Ned's departure he had had a good deal of Pat's company and in it had found a real compensation for his disappointment in not joining his father. But if Pat went – with Pat gone – his life would be so dreary as to be scarcely supportable. Even school might be preferable to the emptiness of the days which lay ahead. When the time came for her to leave, as it did all too soon, he stood with his uncle on the station platform and tried his hardest to put something of his dejection into words, but found to his own annoyance that he could only stumble and mutter before her and hope that his face expressed what his tongue could not.

Patricia had her own private intentions. She did not feel

158

that Madge or Perry had any real affection for the boy, and if his father still failed to send for him and if she was happy in her new situation, she thought there was a possibility of persuading her stepmother to consent to his being sent to the school at which she taught. Accommodation might be found in the house for him and he might even be able partly to work his passage by doing odd jobs.

But all that lay in the very doubtful future. Any of a dozen obstacles might emerge to prevent it, and she had no intention of raising hopes on such a flimsy foundation.

'You'll hardly notice I'm gone,' she assured him. 'I shall be back at the weekends and it's only a short time to Christmas when I shall have three weeks' holiday. So there's no need at all for you to look despondent.'

'No,' said Anthony. 'It'll be quiet, though.'

'Well, make it noisy, then. Uncle Perry will go on walks with you, won't you, Perry?'

'Ugh,' said Perry. 'I'm past my walking days. Though at his age I could do fifteen or twenty miles without turning a hair. I well remember in the Uganda –'

'It's time I got in. You'll write to me, both of you, won't you? I really don't know why you both need look so glum. I'm the one who ought to look glum, leaving home and . . . Oh, well, this is the time when . . . I shall be glad when this is over!'

There was a slight tremor in her voice. She put a hand on Perry's shoulder and kissed him on the cheek. He kissed her in return twice rather noisily, and pinched her arms and eventually released her. Then he pushed back his hair and laughed to disguise the pleasure he had got out of it.

The guard whistled.

Patricia turned on Anthony. He put out a hand woodenly, but she drew him to her and kissed him, not on the cheek but on the mouth. For about a second the world lit up for the boy. Then she stepped into the carriage and a moment later the train was drawing noisily out of the station.

'Well,' said Perry, 'a rattling good job your aunt didn't see

159

that, eh?' He laughed one of his old infectious laughs as they left the station, but his mouth twitched a little as if he had bitten on something that wasn't there.

'Why?' asked Anthony, still warm inside.

'Oh . . . You wouldn't understand. What it is to be young.' Perry sighed and stared a second at the tall boy by his side. 'Wish I was young again. Innocent as a new-born infant. Clean as a baby's whistle. That's what I like to see.'

'Perhaps I know more than you think,' said the boy.

'Ah. Good luck to you if you do. Then why ask me silly questions?'

'Well, I don't see why Aunt Madge should object to us saying goodbye to Pat.'

'Us? Ha, ha! *You* can do what you like, boy; Auntie won't shed a tear.'

Silence fell as they began the long walk home. It seemed a long time since that first walk through the town on the day of his arrival with Patricia at his side. He wished that she was here now, not chuffering away in the direction of Truro. Then it had been high summer. Now winter was on hand and the sea in the harbour was grey and choppy. He glanced at the man walking beside him. Perhaps it was fancy, but Uncle Perry seemed recently to have lost something of his buccaneering look. Instead of being a hunter, you could fancy that he was now one of the hunted.

If Anthony had ever paused to look back over the weeks which followed Pat's departure he might have seen them as a bridge between two periods. The first was the period of decay, when the restaurant was shut and all life and vitality had gone out of the house and nothing at all seemed to happen; the second was the period of crisis when all that had been festering under the surface since Joe's death came to a head. But Anthony never did look back on this interim period. To him it was a time best forgotten.

To him it was a series of dull, grey, lonely days during which he slept and rose and washed and ate and pottered about the house, staring at the whip of the rain on the windows or going

160

out for a brisk but dismal duty walk under heavy skies with a sharp wind cutting round the corners, or shopping for Aunt Madge with a huge wicker basket which now was never more than half filled while the shopkeepers rubbed their hands and treated him with respect though all the time out of the corners of their eyes they were watching him queerly. A period, he would have said, when nothing worth noting happened.

He would have been wrong. Had he been a little less unobservant, a little more aware of the undercurrents moving around him, he would have marked a number of minor events which showed which way the stream was running.

First there was the dismissal of Fanny. This happened so quickly that he could hardly believe his eyes. One day she was there, the next gone. Nor could he obtain from either of the adults an explanation for her going. When he put his questions Aunt Madge turned up her eyes and Uncle Perry grinned and shook his head behind his sister-in-law's back. Obviously she was not dispensed with for reasons of economy or because she was superfluous to the running of the household, as the two boy waiters had been when the restaurant closed. She had been very useful about the house, and the house was not the same for her absence. Only when he learned that she had been given a week's money in lieu of notice did he begin to suspect that she had been dismissed for some offence. Perhaps she had been caught stealing knives.

Anthony began to feel that the house had too much in common with the story of the Ten Little Black Boys. First Uncle Joe, and then there were seven. Second the two boy waiters, and then there were five. Next Patricia, and then there were four. After this, little Fanny, and now there were three. Anthony wondered when it would be his turn.

It could not come too soon. After Fanny's departure Aunt Madge took to staying in bed still longer in the mornings, and often the boy was the only one stirring before ten o'clock. Breakfast was not until eleven when Perry would join them, jovial but unshaven. Whereas in the old days Mrs Veal was always cooking, the closing of the restaurant appeared to have robbed her of the incentive, and meals were now designed for the least possible trouble.

There did not seem much prospect at present of his becoming another little Black Boy, he thought. His aunt had never been one for going out much, but another phenomenon of these strange weeks was that if she did leave the house Anthony must go with her. Not Perry but Anthony. He spent many a dreary hour in the dusty ante-room of Mr Cowdray's office while she conferred inside, later to walk back through the main street adjusting his pace to her slow, heaven-ordained progress. At first she wanted to take his arm, but he contrived to fall out of step so often that eventually she abandoned the idea.

Twice every Sunday he had to go to church with her. Again the slow parade through the narrow main street, dressed in their Sunday best, people nodding and wishing them good morning or good evening. She always insisted on sitting in one of the front pews and in staying behind to speak to the vicar after the service. Then came the slow walk back with more nodding and an occasional pause to pass a word, usually arriving home to find that Perry had burned the dinner or let the supper potatoes boil dry. Then Perry had to tell exactly what he had been doing while they were out and Aunt Madge would chudder away at her grievances all through dinner.

Anthony often thought of the remark made by Perry after they had seen Pat off, and he came to notice that if they were all three sitting in the parlour together in the evening and Perry rose or shifted his chair, Aunt Madge would at once look up from her knitting and adjust her eye-glasses and never take her gaze from him until he sat down again. Sometimes, too, she quietly watched him from a distance when he was washing up or sitting in his shirt sleeves in the kitchen smoking and reading his paper. Her face was like that of a plump Persian cat which reflected the temporary lights and shades of the outer world but gave away little of what was happening inside.

One evening they sent him out for beer. He ran across to The Ship and Sailor on the corner of the main street

and found the bar crowded. Mr Treharne was behind
the bar and he took the boy's order while talking to
another man. Only when he handed the jug back over
the counter, did he turn upon Anthony an inquisitive,
knowing look.

'Don't see much of your Uncle Perry these days, boy,' he
said. 'He's well, I hope?'

Anthony was getting used to sly glances.

'Yes, thank you.' Politely he passed over the money.

'Used to be one of our best customers,' said Mr Treharne.
'Folks' habits change, I suppose.'

'Can't come out for his own beer now,' said one of the
men at the bar. ''As to send the nipper.'

Another said: 'Reckon he's found a pair of apron strings
lyin' around.'

There was a general laugh at this.

'*And* they ain't his mother's.'

With cheeks burning Anthony waited patiently for his
change.

'Ever 'eard o' the Table of Affinity, eh, boy?' said the
first.

He pretended not to hear.

'Go an' ask your uncle. Maybe he do know . . .'

'Deceased wife's sister or deceased husband's brother,
'tes all the same. A pity for she. They can't call the
banns.'

'Reckon they've done all but.'

Another roar of laughter greeted this.

'What's it like in thur, boy, eh?' said the wag. 'Must be a
cosy nest. Think there's room for me?'

'Let the boy alone,' growled someone. 'Tesen't narthing to
do with him.'

'No' said the wag. ''Oo blames the gooseberry fur 'anging
on the bush?'

With the laughter following in gusts Anthony pushed his
way out through the crowd. In the welcome darkness outside
he stopped a moment and found that he was trembling
all over.

20

Patricia settled into her new work very quickly. She found her occupation, though always making demands on her nervous energy, curiously restful from one point of view. It was impersonal in the sense of having no concern with her private affairs, and after the hurly burly of the two previous months she gladly sank her individuality into that of the tireless Miss Gawthorpe.

She did not go home each weekend. She made the excuse that she could not get away, but this was not the real reason. Having got this post under a mild form of false pretences, and finding the work not unpleasant, she lived in a daily but decreasing terror of being found out. There were, she knew, people in Falmouth who would 'feel it their duty' to write to Miss Gawthorpe if they knew she was employing 'that Patricia Veal'. Her chief hope of escape was to keep out of their sight.

There occurred, however, a half term, and with it no reasonable way of avoiding a two-day holiday. She found the house dingier and more untidy and not so clean and her stepmother larger and more puffy, like a cake with too much yeast in it. Perry's chuckle was as frequent as ever, but was on a furtive note and there had been an increase in that curious nervous twitch about his mouth as if his upper lip were biting upon something which could not be properly secured. Anthony looked thin and self-contained and was less free in his manner, especially towards her. The candid gaze had gone from his blue eyes.

At the first opportunity she brought up the subject of his schooling with Madge.

Madge hedged. Or rather she created vacuums around isolated words, which was her way of being non-committal. Pat asked if she had heard from his father again and Madge

164

said, no. Pat had the impression that she was still hedging. What did they propose to do with him after Christmas? Had they made any inquiries at Falmouth Grammar School? Madge turned up her eyes and said something about Perry having it in hand.

'Oh, Perry,' said Patricia. 'You can't really leave anything to him. Not, I mean, like fixing up a boy's schooling. Isn't there some law nowadays about children *having* to go to school? He's missed one term already.'

Her stepmother said something indistinct about being very well aware of the law. She gave the impression that she would make a move almost any time now. There was clearly no point in spending a lot of money on the boy if he was likely to be moving again. Really just a question of finding a stop-gap.

This seemed the chance the girl had been waiting for. 'If it's only that – and of course you're probably right – why not see about sending him to Miss Gawthorpe's? There are boys of twelve and thirteen there, and we do teach them manners, which is more than some schools do.'

Madge fumbled with her cameo brooch. In the deep lace folds of her dress something rose and fell and a faint breath of a sigh escaped.

'Away from home . . . Oh, no. My responsibility. No mother. I couldn't . . .'

'I should be there to look after him.'

'Oh, no . . . The travelling and . . .'

'I believe Miss Gawthorpe might put him up. There is a bedroom vacant there, and I think she might be glad of someone to help in small ways. I haven't actually asked her –'

'I should think not . . .'

'I haven't actually asked her, but in that case I think she might be content with the ordinary day fee.'

Mrs Veal shook her head. 'Oh, no . . .'

Patricia could always understand and appreciate a reasoned argument, but she still had a small girl's dislike of an unreasoned refusal.

'Why not?'

'Useful . . . he's useful here. Fanny has gone. A great deal to do. Your uncle naturally isn't . . . And I . . . Hi am not too well. Severe headaches. Rheumatism. I sometimes wonder how I carry on. A great help . . . Anthony. Besides . . . my nephew. Responsibility . . . And he's happy here.'

'Why not put the idea to him and see if he likes it?'

Madge's chins shook above her lace collar. 'Children. No idea . . . what is best for them . . . adult matter.'

'I suppose you think I'm still a child,' said Patricia, feeling angry. It was not altogether being frustrated in this way that irritated her. But Aunt Madge seemed to have become so much more pontifical since she went away. This absurd dignity had been growing worse ever since she came in for the money.

'Not at all,' said Madge. 'But the matter. Hi must decide.'

'Well, do for heaven's sake do something,' the girl said, swallowing her annoyance. 'If you won't send him to Miss Gawthorpe's send him somewhere so that he has an interest in life. I don't think he looks as well as he did, and it surely can't be good for him just to mope about the house all day.'

'We will decide. I will decide . . . as I think best. I will think . . . Hasty decisions never . . . Plenty of time. Christmas is . . .'

So Patricia left on the Monday morning without being able to fulfil the promise she had made herself. She felt thwarted and unreasonable, and vowed that if it were not for Anthony, Falmouth and stepmother would see no sight of her during the Christmas holidays. Something of her disappointment showed in her parting with Anthony, and he for his part felt separated from her by far more than a few weeks of idleness and doubt. This time they did not kiss, but shook hands quietly, and very soon he was walking back through the town alone with his own thoughts.

Some time after Patricia went Aunt Madge finally agreed

to allow Louisa's representatives – not Louisa – to make a search of the house for any later Will which Joe might have made. Mr Cowdray put this to Madge as a reasonable way of settling the dispute, but perhaps what weighed most with her was his remark that rumours were going about the town that Miss Veal had been unfairly dispossessed, and this seemed the obvious way of quietening them. Madge for all her dignity was very sensitive to public opinion.

The first Anthony knew of it was a suggestion from Aunt Madge that he should go across the river to St Mawes and take his lunch with him. The idea was such an odd one coming from her that he was too surprised to raise any objection, so the picnic was arranged. As an outing for a warm June day there was a good deal to commend it, but undertaken in November it was a fiasco. Having eaten his sandwiches much too early, he mooned about St Mawes gazing in at the handsome houses and gardens of the retired people who lived there, then took an earlier ferry back than he was expected to take and arrived at his home to find some of the rooms practically dismantled and his uncle and aunt arguing among the debris.

She greeted him very sourly and Perry informed him that his aunt had decided on a day's spring cleaning and that he was lucky to have missed it. This did not look quite like spring cleaning as he understood it. There were no buckets of water or brushes or dusters about, and nothing looked any fresher, but he spent the rest of the afternoon and evening putting things back and was told just before bedtime that on the following day the house was to be gone through by Miss Veal's representatives in case Uncle Joe had made a later Will.

It seemed to him that this would result in all the things he had put back being pulled out again and that they might have saved themselves the trouble. But of course they were such a house-proud pair that they naturally wouldn't want the searchers to find any dust.

It was on the tip of his tongue to remind them to look

167

behind the picture in the office where he had once seen his uncle put a document, but he supposed that would be one of the first places they would have looked as soon as Joe died. Probably Perry was looking there the morning when he had wakened him. By now he had become quite used to the smell of Uncle Joe's tobacco coming from Uncle Perry's pipe.

He still wondered sometimes who had made the hole in the floor and when. The hole had not just happened of its own accord, and the cork was a biggish one which had been cut to fit. He wondered if Perry had ever had the room. Several times he had intended to mention it to Tom Harris, but each time it slipped his memory. Last time he went to Penryn there had been another man there who seemed to know a good deal about his household, and he had not altogether liked that.

Then by chance he met little Fanny. The men had come to make the search: Mr Cowdray, an auctioneer from Penryn and his assistant; and he had gone out for a walk, taking the road through the town and towards the sea front.

He had not seen Fanny since the day she left and, having always associated her with a cap and apron, he scarcely recognised the little figure in brown with the curly feathers round the collar and the prim little muff. She would have passed him by with her eyes down, but he stopped and said, 'Hullo, Fanny,' and asked her how she was getting on. She looked at him aslant, as so many people did nowadays and said, 'Oh, all right.'

'Sorry you left,' he said awkwardly. 'What did you go so quickly for?'

'Well, I ain't one to stay where I'm not wanted.'

'I've got no one to sew my buttons on now,' he said.

She looked less unfriendly.

'I'm home, helping mother. I ain't going out to service again, not just yet. You got anybody in my place?'

'No.'

Anthony put his hands in his pockets and kicked at a

168

stone. 'Often thought of asking you something,' he said. 'Who had my bedroom before I came?'

Fanny looked at him sharply. 'Nobody. Why?'

'Oh, nothing.'

Fanny fumbled with the parcels in her basket.

'Did Uncle Perry ever sleep there?' he asked.

'No, he didn't, and you don't need to mention yer Uncle Perry to me! Anyway, I was only there eleven month, and that was a month too long. After Mr Veal died . . .' Her eyes glinted a moment and she looked suddenly grown up. ''Twas the cook's room. Afore my time. When I went there there wasn't no cook.'

'Did Aunt Madge have it when she was cook, then?'

''Ow should I know? I suppose so. Yes, I should think. A sight better'n the poky little 'ole they gave me. *She'd* see to that. Don't *she* sew your buttons on for you?'

'Um? No. No, I manage myself.'

'I suppose *she's* just the same, eh? Waggin' about like a queen.'

He was surprised at the hostility which had come into the girl's voice.

'Oh, she's all right,' he said defensively. 'Why shouldn't she be?'

'Why shouldn't she be! 'Deed, yes! She's fell on 'er feet 'andsome, 'asn't she?'

'I don't see what you mean.'

She tossed her head. 'Well, you wouldn't, would you? You're 'er nephew. You'd stick up for 'er if she was 'anged for 'igh treason.'

'No, I wouldn't,' he said doggedly.

'You say you wouldn't, but you would. I know. Hoity-toity, off we go to church together!'

The boy felt himself going red. 'It's nothing to do with you, anyway. What's wrong with us going to church? You've only got a grudge against her because she gave you the sack.'

'No, I 'aven't. I wouldn't lower meself.'

'If you haven't, what did she sack you for then?'

169

Fanny's eyes went smaller. Her thin face pinched itself up like the closing of a hand.

'She didn't 'appen to tell you that, I s'pose.'

'No.'

'Well, why don't you ask 'er instead of me? Try it on, Mr Clever, an' see what she says.'

'Afraid to tell me?' he challenged.

'I don't tell things like that to kids. You be careful of your aunt. She's got a dirty mind, she 'as.'

'It must have been something awful you did.'

''Twasn't nothing of the sort. 'Twas 'er dirty mind an' nothing more to it. 'Er and Mr Perry between 'em. Wasn't my asking, I can tell you.'

'Didn't you want to leave?'

'Oh, I should've lef' whether or no! Didn't like it well enough the way it was going.'

'What happened?'

She hesitated and again arranged her parcels. 'I'll be going now. I got to go. Ma's expecting me.'

'Go on,' he said persuasively. 'Tell us. Be a sport. Wasn't it your fault at all?'

This cunning appeal was too much for Fanny.

'Course it wasn't! You know what your uncle is. 'E started tickling me. Same as 'e's done before; same as 'e's done to you; there weren't nothing to it. But she came round the door quiet like, and she was *mad*. Thought she was goin' to 'ave a fit. I'm well out of that 'ouse, I can tell you!' Her eyes, in which there was a trace of embarrassment, searched his thoughtful face for blushes or condemnation, but this time neither came. 'You know now, Mr Clever. But don't say it was my fault, because it weren't. And if Mr Veal'd been alive nothing wouldn't've happened.' She paused again, waiting for his response, seeking it because it did not come. 'You're welcome to your nice big bedroom at that 'ouse. I wouldn't 'ave it as a gift, I can tell you. Never know what's goin' on in that 'ouse, do you?'

With this parting shot, and still unsatisfied, Fanny gave her basket a contemptuous jerk and went on her way.

When he returned home, studiously late this time, the searchers were gone, and he could tell from the faintly self-righteous expression showing over the top of Aunt Madge's boned collar that they had been unsuccessful.

At supper Perry laughed and joked like his old self, but Anthony's responses were slow. He was still thinking about what little Fanny had said. Sometimes he turned his thoughtful blue eyes on the jovial man at the table, and his mind conjured up the scene Fanny had described. That she might have been lying never occurred to him; the incident rang true. It had happened like that.

After a time he began to think of the spy-hole in his bedroom, and his eyes turned on his aunt, whose knife and fork were working up and down like pistons. Her table manners were studiously refined in company but not so select in the bosom of her family, and her plump little cheeks were puffed out with what she was chewing.

Somehow, almost in the last few hours, the matter of the envelope in the picture had become real to Anthony. For a long time he had forgotten the incident, even when there was the wrangle over the Will; or perhaps it would be more true to say that the memory had remained at the bottom of his mind as an unimportant one. Lately it had come to the surface, floating about without serious or connected thought. He had felt that someone besides Uncle Joe was bound to know of the existence of the cache and to have examined its contents. Now he began to think he had taken too much for granted.

He wondered what to do. He might just say at the end of the meal: 'Oh, about this Will; I suppose you've looked behind the oil-painting in the office, haven't you?'

But that put the initiative in their hands. He didn't fancy that. He might leave the issue three weeks until Pat came again. Or he might ask Tom Harris's advice. But Tom, he knew, was away, staying with his sister at Maenporth. He wouldn't be back for a week.

There was of course one other way. He could look for himself.

171

21

Ever since he came to Falmouth there had been nights on which he had been sleepy and others when he could not settle off and tossed and turned for hours. This was one of the latter, so he had no difficulty in keeping awake until half-past eleven, which was about the customary time for the others to retire. From then on, however, began a struggle. The minutes were dragging at his eyelids, and although he felt a bit strung up, yet at the same time he was falling asleep. He had had to lie in the dark all the time, because from the bottom of the stairs you could see a light under his door.

Soon after twelve he found he couldn't wait any longer. He lit the candle and climbed out of bed, putting on his coat and trousers over his nightshirt and taking care to avoid the loose boards as he moved about. Then, just to be on the safe side, he slid under the bed and pulled out the cork. There was no light below.

Opening his door was difficult, for if it was done slowly the creak was enough to wake the dead, and if it was done too quickly the sudden draught made the upper sash of the window rattle violently. But he had practised earlier that evening and he was successful in making no noise. He wedged it open with a spare sock and, shielding the flame of the candle with his hand, began to go down.

With no idea of ever having to make a secret descent he had often played at going up and down without treading on a creaky stair, and he knew by heart the numbers to avoid: one, three, nine and twelve going down; four, seven, thirteen and fifteen coming up.

On the landing below it was necessary to pass Aunt Madge's and Uncle Perry's doors, for these two doors faced each other and the office was between Aunt Madge's room

172

and the drawing-room, from which a door led off into it. As he had only been in the office once there was no means of knowing whether this door creaked; there was no guarantee that it was not locked, but he had seen the adults go in and out freely during the daytime.

With his hand stretched out to grasp the knob he realised that the best means of entry for him was the parlour. This would mean passing two doors instead of one but would keep him further away from Aunt Madge, and he did know that the drawing-room door did not squeak.

He slipped into the sitting-room, and as he did so the French clock under its glass shade on the mantelshelf chimed the half-hour after midnight. The room still had an occupied smell, and some of the ash from Perry's pipe lay in a grey heap upon the top bar of the grate. The embroidered bag with Aunt Madge's sewing in it was slumped upon a chair with something of the shapelessness of its owner. When he put back the bound volume of *The Quiver* this evening he had not turned the key in the bookcase and the door gaped an inch open.

After a pause to gather his courage he turned the knob of the door leading to the office, and the door to his relief opened easily and silently. Feeling uncomfortable about his way of escape, he left this open behind him and set the candle down on the office desk. The picture of the old lady faced him on the opposite wall. It was the head and shoulders of a little grey-haired woman in a lace cap and her small black eyes seemed to be fixed upon something just over Anthony's shoulder, as if there were a person standing behind him. He saw that he would need a chair.

He carried one across. He felt very uncomfortable about the curtains not being drawn, but he could not move them without risking noise and the window looked out over the harbour. No man was tall enough to stand with his feet in the mud and stare in at a second-storey window; nevertheless one could not get over the feeling that someone might.

The chair creaked under his weight and the picture-hook

173

nearly fell off the rail, but at last he was safely down with the old lady between his hands.

He carried her to the table which had once been littered with papers and set her face downwards. There was no obvious catch as he had expected or anything which suggested to the casual gaze that the back was detachable. He tried to remember what he had seen his uncle do. There was no glass in the frame. He unscrewed the two hooks by which the picture was hung but this had no effect. Then he turned the old lady over to face him and the painting and the back fell out of its frame upon the table.

The noise made him sweat, and little pricklings of nervousness ran out to his finger-tips like pins and needles. After a moment he summoned up the courage to continue and as he lifted the picture away from its back he saw the envelope which his uncle had put there.

So his latest idea had been the best. He had been wrong not to think of it before, not to look before. Perhaps he was still going too fast. This was probably something to do with the shipping line; he had seen . . .

He slid the document out of its long envelope and opened it with a crackle of parchment. He read hastily through about half and that was enough. He put his find on the table and picked up the frame to put it back, his mind already leaping ahead to what he should do next.

The point was, whom should he trust? His duty was to hand it to Aunt Madge, his inclination, to keep it until Pat came home. Or again he might take it tomorrow to Aunt Louisa. But he didn't like her well enough, for all that she seemed to be working with Pat's good at heart. And taking it to her was too much like rank treason. Aunt Madge and Uncle Perry looked after him and were not unkind. They might be as peculiar as some people thought, but they were honest in all their dealings and they had been kind to Pat and not wanted her to leave home. Since Pat left, Aunt Madge had made quite a fuss of him; the fact that he could not somehow take to her was surely his fault, not hers. To give this document

174

to the opposite side was a rank betrayal he could not quite face.

He might let Tom see it, or first tell him about it, or better still go straight to Mr Cowdray.

But that was obviously showing a distrust for Aunt Madge. She would see that he had gone behind her back, and it would be horribly uncomfortable facing her afterwards. He could hardly go on living here unless he took the Will to her first thing in the morning.

Anthony began to see that the possession of such a document as he had found was more of a responsibility than he had bargained for. All very well for grown-ups to make decisions, but he was so young and so alone in the world. He didn't know when his father would be able to send for him, whether he even wanted him or not. Tom did not want him; Patricia could not have him; where would he go if he left here? Why turn against the people who gave him shelter? He almost regretted having found the envelope. If he had looked and there had been nothing there, then his conscience would have been clear.

But first get the painting back. This was something over which he had not expected to have any difficulty, and not until he had tried three times to fit the back into the frame did he realise that the frame had 'sprung'. He broke out into a new perspiration as he failed at the fifth attempt. The only way seemed to be to take the picture and hide it and hope that no one would notice that it was missing from the wall.

'Stap me, boy; I thought you were asleep hours ago!' said a voice in his ear.

Anthony jerked his head up, and his heart and throat congealed, so that he could not even cry out. He could only hold the table and stare at Perry and try not to fall. Perry, in a nightshirt and big coat and his black hair all towsled.

'What's the matter, boy; been sleep walking? Don't look so scary; I'm not going to eat you.'

Then he saw or pretended to see for the first time the

175

document Anthony had found in the picture. He picked it up and opened it.

'What's this, eh? Don't say it's what . . . Hm. Where did you find it, in that picture? Glory be. What made you look behind old Granny. How's it work? Show me.'

'I – I don't know. I – it just came to pieces. Er – Uncle Joe showed me once . . . but I forgot how he did it. I –'

'What made you think there was something here? Rot me, what a place to look!'

'I . . . saw Uncle Joe put something one day. It – never occurred to me it would be – anything important – till this search today. Then I thought I'd . . . just look.'

'Um,' said Perry, staring at the paper and twitching his lips. 'Can't say whether it's important or not, not just at a glance. Don't think it's much, you know. Fancy old Granny having a secret for us like that. But if you'd known the old Four-Master you'd know it was quite in keeping. Not that it's likely to be important. I'm pretty sure it's not much; but perhaps it will be as well to let old man Cowdray see it, eh, boy?' He pushed back his hair and met Anthony's gaze. 'Did you read any of it?'

The boy said: 'I only just glanced at the front and then I tried to put the picture back. I . . . can't get it back.' In order to hide his eyes he turned to the table and tried to force the picture into its frame.

'Easy does it.' Perry slipped the document into his pocket and bent to help. But something had gone wrong with the frame when the back fell out. 'Oh, blast that! We'll be waking the old lady. Leave it now, boy; it's time for our beauty sleep. Now if –'

'Did you see my light?' Anthony asked.

'No. You dropped something overboard, boy. Well, well, you never know what's going to turn up in this world, do you, now? Everybody searches the house and finds sweet Fanny Adams, and then you go adrift in your sleep and tickle up old Granny and out comes this. But I think it's a mare's nest, boy. I think it's nothing important. I think it's nothing much. Keep it to yourself for the time being, what?'

'Oh, yes,' said Anthony.

They had come out of the office into the sitting-room. 'Keep it from Aunt Madge, too, shall we?' he said in a conspiratorial whisper and dug Anthony in the ribs. 'Just the two of us in the secret. Then tomorrow I'll lay off to board old Cowdray and we'll see what sort of a signal he runs up.'

His manner was so friendly that Anthony felt ashamed of himself. Ashamed of himself for feeling frustrated in his purposes. He knew now that in his heart, for all his professed loyalty, he had never had the least intention of handing over to his uncle and aunt anything he found in the picture, certainly not if it was a Will. They might give him shelter and food and reasonable consideration but they did not give him confidence. He might defend them before any outsider who presumed to criticise, but he could not defend them to himself.

He did not sleep much that night, and more than once he wondered how Uncle Perry had come to hear the noise he had made with the picture frame, for Uncle Perry's bedroom was on the other side of the passage. He thought he could guess the answer to that.

The next morning *The Grey Cat* was in harbour. She had slipped in some time during the night and was a little nearer the quay than her usual anchorage.

Although he had been sorry to see her go, Anthony was far more pleased at her return. He was lonely, missed Patricia more than ever, and his meetings with Tom were too infrequent to be looked on as more than an isolated adventure. Now for a week or more there would be the gruff Ned Pawlyn to bring a breath of fresh air into the house. Never, he felt, had he so much needed it.

The captain and mate put in an appearance while he was at breakfast, and he at once dropped his knife and fork and rushed out to meet them. But it was not Aunt Madge's rebuke which made him stop and blink. Captain Stevens had as a companion a dark, thick-set man none of them had seen before.

'Morning, ma'am,' said Captain Stevens, removing his cap. 'This is Mr O'Brien. Mr Pawlyn went ashore at Hull. He said he felt the need of a change. Morning, sir,' he added, addressing Perry, who was just making a dishevelled appearance. But it was to Madge that the Captain gave his account of the voyage. Joe's widow not only held the money, she also held the reins of business, and although one or two of the older captains might feel a prejudice against dealing with a woman, there was no question of shifting any of the responsibility upon Perry. Aunt Madge was now the *J. Veal Blue Water Line*, and no one who wished to continue in her employment must make the mistake of thinking otherwise. And, however much she might neglect the re-opening of the restaurant – which entailed a resumption of the old routine of hard work – one had to admit that she seemed perfectly capable of continuing to conduct the *J. Veal Blue Water Line* on the basis that it was bequeathed to her. Captain Stevens had not been in the house ten minutes before she announced that a new cargo was waiting for him as soon as he had discharged his present one.

Four days went by after this disappointment and Perry said nothing to Anthony about the picture. Several times during the week the boy thought he saw his aunt regarding him curiously, and not once during the week did she ask him to go with her. But so far as Perry himself was concerned there was not the smallest indication that the incident had ever occurred. The boy began to wonder whether Perry intended to forget the whole occurrence and rely on his superior age and position to override any questions that were put him. If so, Anthony was determined that Uncle Perry should be mistaken.

But on the fifth day Perry came to him and waved the document in his face.

'Well, boy, we were blown off our course a bit that time. I could see it myself when I read it, but I thought 'twould be fairer not to tell you until old man Cowdray had cast his optics over it, see?'

'What is it?'

'I told your aunt. I thought it for the best after all. I thought it not important, but I thought it for the best. We took it to old Cowdray. It's what I guessed. It's a copy of the Will we already have. Just the same, word for word. See, look for yourself.'

Anthony took the document and unfolded it quietly.

'Folk usually keep a copy for themselves. Solicitor makes it out same time as the original. It's for reference, d'you see?'

Anthony read through the first part of the Will. 'Yes, but . . .' He broke off, keenly aware that his uncle was watching him while pretending not to. 'But if it was just a copy like this, why should he put it behind the picture?' His intended question had been something quite different.

Perry chuckled and lit his pipe. 'Come to that, why put anything there at all, where like as not it would never be found? You didn't know Joe as I did, boy. He'd got the mind of a squirrel. Liked hiding things. Some folk do. There was a man I knew in 'Frisco. When he died they found he'd papered his bedroom with dollar bills and stuck a wallpaper over them. Might never have been discovered but the man who took his room noticed a bit peeling. Friend found him two days later, room full of steam, three kettles going, still busy. When you've seen as much of the world as I have, boy, you'll know it takes all sorts.'

'Yes,' said Anthony.

'How was it you said you came to know of the hiding-place, did you say?'

Anthony tried quickly to remember what he had said. 'Uncle Joe showed me. One day – I was in there, you see, and he showed me how it worked, just for fun.'

'Was there anything in there then?'

'I'm – not sure. I think – He said he sometimes put things in there.'

'Well, 'twas a good thought to try.' Perry chuckled again, but his mouth twitched. 'A bright idea, if you follow me. I wonder you didn't think of it before, though. I suppose you'd have given it to Aunt Madge if I hadn't come up and frightened the wits out of you?'

'Yes . . . I . . . I'd hardly thought. I didn't really expect to find anything, you see.'

Perry seemed satisfied. 'Well, pity it wasn't a deed of gift making over to us a thousand pounds, what?' He dug him in the ribs again where he knew him to be most ticklish. 'A thousand pounds each. Then we'd have gone off on the spree, just the two of us together, boy. How would that suit?'

'Fine,' said Anthony quietly.

'We'd go off to Marseilles and Alexandria; those are the places for a good time cheap. I knew a girl once . . . And then we'd go across the Atlantic to Canada. We wouldn't wait for your old father to send for you; we'd go and find him. That would give him a shock, wouldn't it? We'd turn up at his camp one day, just when he came back from his diggings, and somebody'd say: "Dick, here's a young man called to see you," and he'd say: "I wonder who in tarnation that can be?" And he'd go inside and you'd be standing there waiting for him . . .'

There was a good deal more of this before the conversation ended. Perry was trying to divert the boy's mind and partly succeeding. While something in him rejected the vision as a spurious one, Anthony was yet beguiled by it because it approached so near to many he had had himself. The mood in which he fell in with Uncle Perry's clumsy romancing and laughed at his jokes was therefore only partly assumed; and Perry the deceiver was himself deceived.

Never in his life would Anthony quite regain the frankness and freedom of manner he had lost during his stay with the Veals, that fresh, clear-eyed candour which feared nothing and withheld nothing. Always there would remain as a mark of these days a hint of reserve which would make him a little difficult to know. People would say of him: 'He's charming, but hard to understand'; and they would never know that they were reaching back into an untidy kitchen of Victorian days with Perry manoeuvring and bluffing and pushing back his hair and Aunt Madge's shadow in the doorway, and the water lapping against the old stone quay outside.

22

Further delay, the boy felt, would not help him or anyone else. Already he was greatly to blame for having waited so long. He must move at once.

He did not know where Maenporth was, but he slipped out just before supper and asked Jack Robbins, who told him that it was a few miles beyond Swanpool.

That evening there were visitors to supper: Captain Stevens of *The Grey Cat* and Captain Shaw of *Lavengro*, which had come in a couple of days after the other ship. They were both due to leave again soon, and Aunt Madge had shaken herself out of her sloth and cooked them a supper reminiscent of the restaurant in its best days. But this was even better because it was free and Joe had always charged them full price.

Captain Shaw, a fat man with a trace of Mongol blood in him, grew expansive with the wine and began to pay Aunt Madge extravagant compliments which she lapped up like a dignified tabby offered a bowl of cream. Then, having made himself popular, he began to undo the good work by referring to Joe and the way he had starved his beloved ship; if they ever revictualled in Falmouth they always ran short of provisions and supplies before the voyage was done, and if they victualled at any other port Joe always complained of extravagance and took a percentage off the captain's wages.

Aunt Madge was nothing if not jealous of her late husband's reputation, and she began to look as if the cream had turned sour. Perry grinned and twitched and rumbled in the background like an extinct volcano, content it seemed to let someone else have the limelight and divert Madge's attention from him.

Presently the party adjourned to the sitting-room upstairs, and Anthony went with them and sat and looked through another volume of *The Quiver* while they played whist. At nine-thirty he wished them all good night and went slowly up to bed.

He sat on his bed in the dark for fifteen minutes, and then picked up his shoes and came down again. Never since he had been here had anyone climbed the second flight of stairs to see if he was in bed – the fact that his light was out was deemed good enough – so he felt fairly safe in taking the chance. And if they had gone to bed before he returned, as seemed probable, he knew a way of prising open the scullery window and there shouldn't be much difficulty in wriggling his body through.

As he passed the parlour he heard Captain Shaw's thick voice: 'Aye, aye, Mrs Veal, I grant you that. But how was I to know ye had the ace?'

He slipped out through the back door and was rather upset to find a thin mist lying over the river. There would in any case be no moon tonight, and he had hoped the stars would be out. At present the mist lay on the water more than over the town, but as the night advanced it might spread, and he had never been to Maenporth in his life.

All his cautious, baby instincts told him to give up the project; the thought of creeping upstairs again and sliding between the sheets suddenly became infinitely desirable; he could put the visit off until tomorrow when the weather might be better – or even until Saturday when Tom would be home at Penryn. He might go all the way and be unable to find the house. If the fog came down he might even lose his way and wander through the secret little lanes all night. Then the fat would be in the fire; if Aunt Madge knew he had been out she would take care that he didn't go again. Better to return.

But there was growing up in Anthony already an obstinate dislike of being overborne by his weaker instincts. He quietly shut the door behind him and put on his mackintosh and cap and a scarf. In this life you had to do what you meant to do or else shrivel up in self-contempt.

He set off at a trot. The faster he moved the sooner he would be there, the sooner he was there the less chance there was of Tom's being in bed, the sooner he was back the better prospect he had of slipping in before the door was locked.

Up Killigrew Street and across Western Terrace and down the hill to Swanpool. There were still plenty of lights about and a number of pedestrians. The grey mist began to move around him in waves, increasing when he got near the sea, but it was not a cold mist and he was soon perspiring. By the time he had passed the cemetery and reached the bottom of the hill it was bellows-to-mend, and he fell into a walk. The swans were asleep, hidden somewhere in the rushes, and ahead of him the waves cracked dismally and rattled on the pebbly beach. The sound was sad and old and impersonal, as if it spoke of creation and decay.

From the mouth of the little cove he mounted the next hill and thought he would never get to the top of it. Then by great good fortune he came upon a pony and trap turning out of a side lane.

'Please, sir, is this the way to Maenporth?' he called up into the darkness.

'Ais, sonny. Straight acrost the moor, then down-along the hill and turn . . . Are 'ee going thur? Jump up, I'll give'ee a lift.'

Anthony accepted the invitation, glad not only of the lift but of the company. The farmer was curious to know what a youngster like him was doing out past his bedtime, but he evaded a direct answer until they had gone down another steep hill and through a narrow thickly wooded lane which came out once again within sound of the sea.

'Now, son, this is whar'ee do want to go. Down this yur path: that 'ouse nigh buried 'midst the trees: that's Mrs Lanyon's 'ouse. This old broom of a fog. See it now, do'ee? *Tha's* a boy. Now, Emmie, *ck, ck,* come on, my 'andsome . . .'

Anthony walked down the dark, muddy lane towards where the gables of a sizeable house showed among the fir trees. The sigh of the sea was abruptly cut off by the dripping hedges as he walked up the short shingle drive and pulled the front-door bell.

There were lighted windows in the front of the house and a glimmer in the hall which increased as a uniformed maid turned up the lamp before opening the door.

'Yes?' she said.

'Is Mr Tom Harris staying here, please?'

'Well . . .'

'Could I see him, please? He . . .'

'He's busy now. What do you want?'

'Tell him it's Anthony. He asked me to call.'

The maid hesitated, then opened the door. 'You'd best come in. You'll have to wait, I expect.'

With a sense of timidity the boy entered the hall and the maid turned the lamp up. Hunting trophies and a few shields came to view and peered down at him suspiciously. Then the maid went into a room on the left and he caught sight of a well-lit drawing-room and people sitting round on chairs. At the end of the room was a piano and several people standing up with violins and things.

She reappeared. 'He said for you to wait. He said he'd not be long.'

'Thank you.' When he was alone he stopped twirling his cap and dropped it on a chair and sat on it. Wisps of fog had followed him into the hall. Then someone began to play the piano in the room. It was a pleasant sort of piece to listen to, not with any detectable tune but a lot of nice

184

ripples running up and down, up and down, like the sea coming in on a sunny day.

The music suddenly became louder and was damped again as Tom Harris slid out of the room through the smallest gap he could make in the door. He came towards the boy smiling and handsome and gentlemanly in a black evening dress suit.

'Hullo, Anthony; this is a surprise. Come in here. My sister's having a musical evening. You've some news?'

He led the way into a small library, taking with him the hall lamp. Usually Anthony had seen him in tweeds, and he was suddenly struck by the different worlds in which Tom and Patricia revolved. Patricia had hinted as much to him, but he had never personally realised what she meant until now. Tom was a gentleman. Pat, although he had never known her to be the least bit common or vulgar, was not quite what the world at present understood as a lady. Tom had been brought up to find his pleasures in this sort of an evening: people dressed for dinner and having musical evenings and card parties and the rest. Pat had spent her evenings in the atmosphere of the restaurant. Even though she no longer did so the deeper differences remained. This was another gap between them, perhaps wider and deeper than their lovers' quarrels.

Anthony did not reason all this out, for he hadn't the time or the experience; what he sensed was the outlines of the difference, and, aware of himself as a connection of Pat's, he felt the inferiority for her. Then he told his story, forgetting social complexes as he went on.

In silence Tom heard him out almost to the end.

'Do you think he was lying to you this afternoon? What makes you sure? Did you read the document you found?'

'Yes. It wasn't the same.'

'In what way did it differ?'

'The Will I found seemed to leave the – the property nearly all to Pat. I think it just left the restaurant business

185

to Aunt Madge, but I didn't get a chance of reading it all through.'

'Any other divergence?'

'Di . . .'

'Difference between what you found and what he showed you.'

'Yes. Well . . . what I saw Uncle Joe put behind the picture and what Uncle Perry showed me can't be the same thing. I saw Uncle Joe sign the other, and the captain and mate of the *Lady Tregeagle* witnessed it. The thing Uncle Perry showed me wasn't signed or witnessed.'

'I wish you'd told me this before, Anthony, before investigating yourself.'

'I know . . . I know. Sorry.' He could not quite explain the complex pull of loyalties which had made him reluctant to inform against his aunt in such a way as to make it obvious that he did not trust her.

'You see we've nothing at all to go on. If the Will was as you say, they – well, they may have destroyed it. Then it's only your word against his.'

'But there's the captain and mate of the *Lady Tregeagle*. I don't know –'

'When *Lady Tregeagle* left she was going to Alexandria. She may pick up another cargo there and be months returning. And, of course, their testimony proves very little without a document to back it up.'

'But if they said –'

'Yes, I know.' Tom began to walk up and down the room. 'If the mate and captain of the *Lady Tregeagle* were prepared to swear that they had witnessed on such and such a date a Will made by Joe Veal, and you swore that you had found such a Will, your aunt would be in a very difficult position morally. But legally, without the document we could save our breath. Besides, Joe being so secretive as he was, it's unlikely he told the captain and the mate what it was they were signing. I'm afraid, old boy, that there's nothing to be done.'

Anthony stared up at the young solicitor as he turned

186

from the window. All that day and for three days before, a conviction had burned in him that his actions of the other night had irrevocably destroyed his hopes of helping Pat. Tom's attitude confirmed this. But the odd thing was that he felt Tom did not care. He remembered Tom's attitude once before when he had seemed relieved that Pat had been cut out of her father's Will. If Tom really loved Patricia he should be more concerned for her future than his own gain – even supposing that there would be any gain to him in Pat's loss, which at present seemed unlikely. He personally might have made a complete failure of his attempt to help, but it was wrong to treat the news with indifference. After the excitement of stealing out of the house and the long run and the drive through the mist Anthony felt suddenly let down. He had brought news of vital importance; possibly he was too late with it, but the only chance of not being too late was to take some action at once. He had not stopped to reason what action *could* be taken: Tom would know that; the main thing was to get the information to him. Let Tom turn on him furiously now for his mistakes if he chose, but not treat the information as if it did not matter.

Harris stopped and looked at the boy with his intent brown eyes. 'Does anyone else know of this?'

Anthony shook his head.

'Do you think Perry knows you suspect him of lying?'

'No. I don't think so.'

'Has he any idea that you've come here?'

'Oh, no.'

'Well, then, he mustn't have. You realise that, Anthony. He mustn't have any idea. We must keep this a dead secret between ourselves.'

'What are you going to do?'

Tom shrugged. 'What is there to do? I'll make further inquiries, but it's most essential that Perry shouldn't know we're suspicious. Do understand that. Because – because, you see, if he so much as suspects a thing the new Will, if it still exists, is likely to be burnt. Give him time, Anthony. There's nothing to hurt for a day or two. Give him time.'

Faintly to their ears came the sound of applause as the pianist finished her second piece.

'I'd better be going,' said Anthony.

'Has Patricia been over since I saw you last?'

'No.'

Tom said: 'You can't walk straight back. I'll get you some sandwiches and something to drink.'

He protested that he didn't want anything, but Tom left the room and presently returned with a dish of tongue sandwiches and a cup of steaming coffee.

'If you wait an hour,' he said, 'Mr and Mrs Vellenoweth will be driving back to Falmouth and can give you a lift.'

'I'd rather go, Tom. You see, they might miss me. It's not very far, and . . .'

'Perhaps you're right. It was sporting of you to come here like this. Will you have tea with me at Mount House next Sunday?'

He met Tom's eyes for a moment. 'Oh, I don't suppose there'll be anything fresh by then.'

'Come, anyhow.'

'I'll try. Sometimes Aunt Madge wants me to go out with her.'

As Tom saw him to the door, string instruments could be heard tuning up in the drawing-room. Tom put a hand on his shoulder.

'Don't think I'm unmindful of your help, Anthony. It has been worth a good deal to me, and we shall get over this disappointment. To have known that another Will has existed is a big step forward. Even that much will mean a great deal to Pat, to feel that her father fully forgave her. I'll warrant she'd as soon know that as know that the money was actually hers.'

'Ye-es.'

'One thing I want you to promise me.'

Anthony twirled his cap and peered out into the misty darkness which was soon to receive him.

'If Patricia should by any chance come home this weekend, I want you to promise not to breathe a word of this to her.'

'But –'

'I want you to *promise*.'

Anthony twirled his cap. 'It's her money. I couldn't . . .'

'Nevertheless I want you to.'

In the distance could be heard the faint hush-hush of the sea. Near at hand water was dripping into water.

'We agreed to trust each other, didn't we?' said Tom.

'Ye-es.'

'Well, I want you to trust me on this point. I want you to promise not to tell her anything about this new Will until after you've seen me again.'

'But why?'

'Why? Well, it's for her good that she shouldn't know, I assure you.'

Anthony eventually promised. Unless he wished to quarrel with Tom and accuse him of not playing fair he could hardly do otherwise, and he hadn't the courage to do that to his face. Besides, he had no real facts to go on, only a sense of general disappointment.

But when he promised he did so with his fingers crossed, like they did at school when the speaker was supposed to be absolved from doing what he said. He knew in his heart that this was only a moral quibble which really evaded nothing; he had never used it before in any serious matter. But his new-growing duplicity was finding many outlets.

If the opportunity came he knew he would tell Pat everything.

The night received him like an over-attentive and slightly sinister friend; its damp embrace cloyed, and he pulled off his muffler as soon as he was in the lane. There was no air, only a drifting mist which had to be breathed in wet and breathed out in a finer form as if the moisture had been refined into steam.

The fog was thicker than when he had gone in. Branches dripped high overhead and somewhere near water was running in a ditch. After the lights of the house he was quite blind, and he had to grope his way foot by foot in the direction of the main road. But he was used to darkness from his Exmoor days and as his pupils expanded he began to move more freely. Once the road to Falmouth was reached there were few chances of going wrong; only one sharp-right turn to take at the top of the hill.

For a long time he was too preoccupied with his thoughts to feel any sense of his own isolation. Tom wasn't playing fair. This was not a solemn compact to help Patricia as first planned, but a one-sided flow of confidences with nothing in return. Tom, he felt, was using him to obtain this information, and the information was not being turned to Pat's benefit, but to Tom's own. There had been the incident of his last visit to Mount House when the tall grey-haired man was present, a stranger to whom he was apparently expected to speak as freely as to Tom. Now there was tonight with its impression of divided loyalties, its sense of confidences withheld. However it had begun, he was being treated as a child again, as a pawn in a game considered outside his comprehension.

Midnight was past before he reached Swanpool, and until now perplexity and disappointment had been stronger than any childish fear. Only when he began to walk down the long snaky hill which led to the pool did he realise that in a few minutes he would have to pass the cemetery. Only then did he realise with an extraordinary shock of conviction that this was the occasion he had dreamed about; when he would meet Uncle Joe at the gates and walk home with him, and when they reached the restaurant they would find it in ruins and the ball of moss would be in his hand and something unnameable stirring in the shop.

190

23

For perhaps half a minute he stopped in his stride and considered turning back. Then common-sense reasserted itself, reason gently unclasped those alien fingers; he smiled unconvincingly and went on his way.

Strange that a simple, tree-rimmed reedy pool which one has seen so many times by day can by night become lonely and fogbound and sinister. All the way round its edge he was pursued by the sound of the waves breaking on the steep, pebbly shore. It was like the tipping of bags of small coal: the first heavy fall when the wave broke, then the rattle of the small coal as the bag was pulled away. It was like the loneliness of life, the loneliness of himself.

He began to climb the hill towards the cemetery, thinking hard of his grievances and mistakes, striving hard to regain that armour of preoccupation which had protected him so far; no doubt his own mistakes far outweighed his grievances; Tom was right to look on the matter of the Will as a cause already lost; his own proper course should have been to have waited until Pat returned for Christmas; and – and then . . .

And then there was a light in the cemetery. A white glow like the rising moon below the horizon.

He stopped and told himself that the light came from one of the houses behind. He went on a few paces and stopped again. The light was in the cemetery and near the gate. It was not the light of a lantern or of a torch or of a candle, but just a white glow showing through the fog. An indistinct glow in the swirling mists.

He couldn't understand it. He went on a bit farther, stopped again, biting his finger-nail. Nothing to do with him; run past and don't bother to look. Something perhaps which had no right to be there, but it was not at all his business to inquire what.

On a clear night he would have been able to trust his eyes. The fog had spread its web over the land and even normal things were imbued with enormity and suspicion.

By now he was close beside the cemetery wall. He edged along it until he came near the top corner where Uncle Joe and Aunt Christine were buried side by side. The fog was thicker than it had yet been anywhere. But he was now so near that nothing could hide the exact location of the light. It was beside the gate, about twelve paces inside, and came from behind a wooden or canvas screen which apparently had been erected across the path just there.

A possible explanation suddenly came to him, and his slow breath of relief mingled with the fog. Someone no doubt had died and the sexton, being pressed for time, was working on after dark to prepare the grave. To confirm this view his nearer approach brought the sound of a scraping spade and the thud of heavy earth.

Then he heard the murmur of voices.

There was still no reason why he should have inquired further. He could have walked on up the hill and kept his eyes and his thoughts averted. But a force stronger than fear made him stop at the gate of the cemetery. He felt himself to be in the grip of some compelling attraction. And there was an inevitability about the location of the diggers.

As he went in a figure loomed up, and he ducked down against the first grave-stone with a thumping heart. Tall and dark the figure, with an oddly shaped hat. It was a canvas screen, he saw; there were several figures behind it, and he thought at least six lanterns. The figure which had passed him had taken up its stand by the gate, thus cutting off his retreat. Recklessly he climbed across the stones, striking his boot on one, but there was noise behind the screen and he reached it unheard.

Nightmare-like now, he was gripped with an urgent necessity to know the worst; so inimical did delay seem that he might have taken out his knife and slashed at the

192

canvas to see what was happening within. But there was already an inch-long tear through which he could peer.

There were five lanterns and seven men and a number of grave-stones. So bright were the lanterns that he could see the lettering on two of the grave-stones, words which he had come to know by heart. One of them had only just been put up. Two men in shirt sleeves were in one grave almost up to their shoulders and partly screened from view by the pile of mineral-yellow soil which they had dug up. Another grave was also open, and beside it and beside an even larger mound of rubble was something Anthony had seen before. Two men with masks and aprons were bending over it. A third, in a silk hat, was standing well back from them. Two policemen made up the party.

Anthony turned and ran, ran careless of noise and stumblings towards the outer gate. He ran as if the Devil and all Hell were after him. He ran on wings of fear, while ice-cold sweat stood out on his face and hands. He reached the gate and was through it while a figure turned and grasped at him. He ran along beside the cemetery blindly and wildly, turned away from the other gate and up the hill. No dreams troubled him now, no fear of dreams. He would gladly have gone back to all the bad dreams in the world. What he was running away from was reality. All his life as a result of this experience he would do the same.

He ran up the hill and across the main road and down the hill, with the thick mist closing in behind him and the hand of Fate heavy on his shoulder. Twice he almost fell, and in the wider spaces of the Moor where the landmarks were less easily seen he strayed across and lost his sense of direction.

Had he come to a stop there his instincts and fears might have been brought to a stop as well. Even a short pause might have set him thinking. But he found the next narrow street just in time and fled on towards his home. In no time, though his breath was coming in great gasps, he was before the back-door of the shop. Panting, he stood on the mat and tried the handle. It opened and he saw that the kitchen was lighted. Before he could withdraw Aunt Madge caught sight of him. But he was not sure that he wanted to withdraw. He was too far gone for manoeuvre or temporising.

They were clearing away the remnants of the evening's feast.

'Anthony!' said Aunt Madge. 'I . . . Bed, I thought you. How have you . . . ?'

He sat on the nearest chair and panted for breath; in this warmth there was less air. The perspiration under his cap was still cold, as if it were a part of the mist and not of his own body. He put his head down.

'Disobedience.' Aunt Madge's voice came through walls of fear and nausea. She began to talk, to scold, to chew the cud of her grievance. For a time her words glanced off unheeded, only one or two coming through like solitary survivors of an attacking army. They kept him in touch with his surroundings, they and the grip of his chair. His normal boyish mind kept struggling to revert to its own preoccupations; solid, decent, homely things; the smell of new bread and kicking a ball in a narrow street, the feel of the ball in his fingers; lemon pudding and sleep; rowing across the harbour, Pat's laughter, his mother's voice: thoughts that were his brain's warmth and refuge. But not yet, not yet could he escape. This other thing was too near, it blocked everything else from view. Life it seemed never would be the same again, for how could the ugliness and horror ever grow smaller? His dreary existence of these last weeks seemed golden with health by comparison with what the future must be.

He heard his aunt call something and Perry emerged from the scullery, an apron still about his waist.

A hand touched his cap, lifted it off, and his head was turned up towards the light.

'Hell's hounds! Where've you been, boy? Been swimming? Your hair's as wet –'

Anthony looked up and his voice came back.

'They're taking them away! I saw them. The police it is!
I don't understand!'

'Who are? Taking who away?' said the voice on a
different note.

'Uncle Joe. Aunt . . . Christine. I came past. They were
digging. They'd put a screen round. The . . . *It* . . . was
on top. They'd . . . the lid . . . they'd . . .'

Tears choked further words. Tears streamed down his
cheeks for about a minute. The hand had left his head.
Uncle Perry went away and sat on a chair.

The tears were a safety valve letting out dangerous
accumulations of terror. He constantly smeared his face
with his sleeve and the back of his hands. When the tears
began to stop he groped for his handkerchief and wiped the
last of them away. He saw a drop or two fall beside Perry's
chair and thought that perhaps he too was crying. Then he
saw liquid trickling down the side of his chin and Aunt
Madge withdrawing a glass which she had been trying to
put between Perry's teeth.

'Your uncle,' said Mrs Veal. 'Been took queer. Been
– been drinking too much. This excitement. I never.
What have you been doing, Anthony? Hi wish to know
the truth.'

Even in this crisis he knew that the whole truth would
not do.

'I – I sneaked out, Aunt Madge. I wanted – wanted to
see where the swans slept at night. Jack told me – Jack
told me they didn't nest like other birds –'

'Yes, yes.'

He realised she was not interested in this part of his
story. Her eye-glasses were not quite still; there was a
tremor moving through them, as a newspaper will quiver
when there is machinery beating somewhere below. Her
small eyes seemed to have disappeared behind them, as if
they were hiding themselves in the folds of her puffy face.
Anthony went on to tell what he had seen. While he was
doing so Uncle Perry belched and a thin trickle of saliva
joined the driblet of whisky on his chin.

195

Abruptly Aunt Madge set down the tumbler and took out her own handkerchief.

'Envy, malice, hatred, all uncharitableness,' she said in a high-pitched voice as if it were being squeezed out of her. 'My life . . . All my life. Pursued. Saul, Saul, why persecutest thou me? All my life. People. Evil tongues. My dear mother. My dear sister. Always the same.' She put an uncertain handkerchief waveringly up to her small snub nose. 'People, evil people, whispering. The way they insinuate. All the wickedness of this world. My mother, one of the noblest of women. Never loved any one more, unless it was my dear husband. Persecuted by evil tongues. Always the same. I have been. Bearing my cross of loneliness. And now. Desecration of the hallowed dead. Wicked evil tongues. They know I'm all alone. Poor widow. They think they can do anything. But they can't. I'll see them prosecuted. I'll see them . . . utmost letter of the law. My poor husband. Insinuation . . .'

Perry lifted his head from the side of the chair. His face was the colour of Aunt Madge's pastry before it went in the oven. His skin was the same texture too, thick and soft and slightly pitted; his face was twitching persistently.

'Deliver my soul, O Lord, from lying lips,' said Aunt Madge, hoarsely and rapidly, 'and from a deceitful tongue. Sharp arrows of the mighty, with coals of juniper. Woe is me, that I sojourn in Mesech, that I dwell in the tents of Kedar. Remember, Anthony, when you are grown up. A lesson in the wickedness of the world. Remember your aunt.' She waved her hand. 'Calumny is her lot. She has bore herself with Christian fortitude. When thy enemy smitest thee upon the one cheek . . . Remember a delicate woman broken upon the wheel. Never have pity, Anthony, for Philistines shall put out your eyes. They will stop at nothing, dragging even the bones mouldering to dust.' Her voice quivered higher. '*Dragging* them, I say, out of the . . . The Serpent has them in his power. Wicked evil that they are! Won't even let the dead, the blessed dead, rest in peace. Interfering, *dragging* them out of their sleep.

196

Vile, vile in your sight! The light of the wicked shall be put out!'

Perry's hand closed round the glass and slowly transferred it to his mouth. It clicked against his teeth and the liquid disappeared as down a drain. He tried to get up from his chair, but failed.

'Why should they do it, Aunt Madge?' Anthony asked. 'Why should they do it? And who is it, anyway?'

Perry's next attempt put him upon his feet, and he reached the cupboard in the corner where the whisky bottle was kept. Aunt Madge lowered herself into a chair and took off her pince-nez and wiped them. When next she spoke her voice was lower. Her eyes had reappeared.

'Being unwell does not entitle you . . . Perry, not neat alcohol. We must act. We must take steps . . . restitution of our rights. We must see Mr Cowdray. We must –'

'I said this'd happen!' Perry drained his glass and glanced sidelong at the boy. 'God! I said this'd happen. All along.'

'You should be in bed, Anthony,' said Aunt Madge. 'You must have been . . . Yes, upset, I'm sure. Go to bed. Better in the morning.'

'But what are they doing?' he demanded.

Aunt Madge put on her pince-nez. 'A dispute. Over the . . . your dear uncle. The Veals have a vault in the old church-yard . . . the parish church. That woman, your Aunt Louisa, wished him to be buried there. We did not. They have made a lawsuit of hit. They have acted while we . . . We must do something. Something must be done in the morning.'

'There's nothing we can do now,' said Perry.

Aunt Madge's pince-nez continued to wobble but she did not assent to this view.

Anthony woke very late the following morning. He had gone to bed with little more said, but he had turned and tossed for endless hours in the darkness, sleepless and alone. He knew himself lost and without guidance.

197

Instinctively he felt himself to be in a position which would have puzzled many a grown-up. He was helpless before the drift of events. Could he have become a fatalist to order he might have saved at least some of the anxiety of the night; but no fatalism and no resignation could prevent the fevered living-over-again of what had happened.

Once, after hours of tossing and turning, he crept out of the room to go downstairs to see what the time was; but a light under the door of the drawing-room and another light reflecting up from the ground floor showed that nobody was in bed but himself.

Dawn was late on that misty December morning, and he just remembered hearing the seagulls crying and seeing a greyness encroach upon the bar of night between the curtains; he was about to get up and pull the curtains when he fell asleep.

Perry woke him.

'Show a leg, boy. It'll soon be seven bells in the forenoon watch. Show a leg; we've good news for you.'

He had pulled back the curtains and the window let in a shaft of wintry sun. It also showed up Perry's recently shaven face trying its best to look swashbuckling and doggish. The attempt was not a success. Red-eyed and collarless, he smiled unconvincingly at the boy. The mouth was trying to turn up but the lines turned down.

Anthony slid quickly out of bed.

'News? *Good* news? What about?'

'Never mind, boy. Wait till you get below; your aunt'll tell you.'

Perry went unsteadily out, leaving a strong smell of rum behind him.

Anthony followed with the least possible delay. He found them both in the kitchen. Aunt Madge was reading Malachi. Her little lips were forming the words as she went from line to line. She was wearing the same dress as last night and he suspected it had not been off; its stiff lace collar and heavily brocaded front with flaps and frills over it looked out of place this morning. She

198

had not even taken off her earrings or the four strings of pearls.

'And the day that cometh shall burn them up,' she said. 'News. Your father. A letter this morning.'

Daylight had undermined some of the terrors of the night. This announcement abruptly drove away the rest to a distance at which they could be tolerated.

'What does he say? Does he –?'

'You're to go out. Early boat. He's sent money. Passage paid. And ye shall go forth and grow up as calves of the stall.'

Anthony let out a whoop of delight.

'Did it come this morning? When have I to start?'

Aunt Madge turned over a page. 'That is left . . . Hi thought. Fare is booked from Bristol. No regular service from here. *The Grey Cat*. Leaving on tonight's tide. Calling at Bristol. And he shall turn the heart of the fathers to the children. We thought . . . Your uncle and I. Save the train fare. Bristol the day after tomorrow. Captain Stevens knows you. He would look after you.'

'Yes,' said Anthony. 'Go to Bristol by sea, you mean. I'd like that. That'd be fine. By sailing ship. Yes, thanks, Aunt Madge. Would that be tonight?'

'Tonight.'

'I must pack. I can hardly believe . . . It's nearly twelve now. What time do they leave? Does Captain Stevens know?'

He hurried upstairs again, bursting with excitement. But behind the excitement, like the structure behind an ornamental façade, was relief. Relief to be leaving this house and its shabbiness and hysteria. Relief at the thought of leaving the horrible scene of last night three thousand miles behind. It wasn't explained. Nothing was explained; some instinct told him that there might come a time when these perplexities and unsolved relationships would irk him, when he would blame himself for leaving them without a backward glance. The weakness of this escape might leave a hard core of self-despisal, overgrown but not overthrown,

199

which some day would serve him ill. But at this instant he had no second thought, only a surging happiness at the idea of casting everything away. Somebody else could worry about the policemen in the cemetery. Someone else could argue out the problem of the Will. Somebody else could carry tales to Tom Harris. Not he. Not he.

Only one thing he would have liked to do, and that was to say goodbye to Patricia. That being impossible, he would drop her a short note; he had her address and could get a stamp from the nearby post office.

The day was a bright one and mild, a fresh southerly wind having puffed away the remnants of fog. It seemed in keeping with his mood of relief that the sun should shine and the harbour look as bright and gay as in summer. There was little time to lose, since *The Grey Cat* would be weighing anchor at seven. Even in a few months he had collected all manner of souvenirs which he was anxious to take with him, and these had to be fitted somehow into his one wicker travelling bag.

All the afternoon both Aunt Madge and Uncle Perry were very quiet. No doubt they were worrying about the news he had brought last night. But neither of them seemed anxious to go out and consult Mr Cowdray, unless they had already been out before he woke. They had an odd air of waiting, of sitting still and having nothing to do. Aunt Madge took down a number of flypapers in the kitchen and put them into the stove. Perry had reverted to his rum again. His face had that heavy, studious look which told its own tale. He always looked as if he was going to produce some great thought and never did.

The sun went down that night behind the town glowing red among the clustered black clouds. For half an hour after it had gone all the old town of Falmouth stood out clear-etched in the twilight glow as if impressing itself indelibly upon the boy's brain; the church steeples and the grey houses and the narrow quays and the climbing cottages looking down over the pink flush of the harbour.

He finished such preparations as there were to make

200

and knelt for a moment at the window of his bedroom. Not many minutes' rowing away were the three masts of the barquentine which was to take him on the first part of his long journey. He felt no apprehensions that the journey might be tedious or difficult: his only wish was to be gone.

Perhaps it was only in these last few hours that he had begun to realise how much the happenings in this house had weighed on him. Like a man who had been carrying a burden, he had not felt how much his shoulders were cramped, his breathing restricted, until the weight was eased and he was standing there waiting for it to be finally lifted off. Most burdensome of all perhaps had been the necessity for making judgments of his own; not decisions, but judgments of people. He had been pitchforked from a world of friends and acquaintances, in which he had instinctively drawn his opinions from his mother, into a new circle in which he had to form every judgment upon complete strangers for himself. He had at first seen many things through Pat's eyes, but for the last two months he had found himself forced more and more back upon the bedrock of his own immature sense of values, and these were blown like a leaf in the wind turning one side and then the other up. To be released from all his contacts here, to wipe out all the past mistakes and begin anew, this was almost the greatest relief.

As the brightness faded from the sky there crept over him, without any sort of prompting, the conviction that even now he was not leaving all the problems behind as he had supposed. Somehow, in some manner, they were now a part of him and had to be resolved. Most gladly he would have forgotten the horrible scene of last night. But it would not be forgotten. It was only over-laid for the moment by the happy and exciting news of today. Some time it would return. He had seen something which no manner of excuses from Aunt Madge and Uncle Perry would explain away. Something which was not a final event in itself but which had to be searched and sounded to the depths. He was young but he was not a fool. His judgment of events was often faulty but not always. Aunt Madge's lame explanation did not convince him. The police were in it. That was what frightened him. The police were in it.

As the light of the thin crescent moon began to show up he saw a small dinghy cutting a dark rippling arrow through the silver water. Captain Stevens coming to fetch him.

Not before time. Five o'clock was past and he would be happier away from the house. Once in the ship he would recover his confidence and his good spirits of this afternoon. Once in the ship he would really begin to believe the journey begun. Not until then.

Now there were goodbyes to be said. Must not forget to thank them for their kindness. His father would be sure to ask. (Or at least his mother would have been sure to do so. He suddenly realised that he hardly knew his father.) Anyway, he owed them thanks, Aunt Madge and Uncle Perry: they had given him food and a home; he had barely given them loyalty in return.

He picked up his bag, his cap, his coat, two parcels, looked round the now familiar room, at the sloping raftered ceiling and the pieces of cheap furniture, which had the friendly pull of five months' intimate association. Then he went down the two flights of stairs into the kitchen. He found Aunt Madge and Uncle Perry with hats and coats on and valises packed, waiting to accompany him.

24

By the frail light of the sickle moon following the sun down towards the south-west, *The Grey Cat* slid quietly out of the harbour under a strip or two of canvas. Once past Pendennis Point she shook out the rest of her sails and bent and quivered under the touch of the wind like a horse feeling its master after a long rest. Then she moved off slowly with the wind on her starboard bow, dipping lightly in the choppy sea, her lights winking their farewell to the shorebound castle and the line of darkening cliff.

The barquentine had never been designed to carry passengers, and accommodation was uncomfortably cramped. Captain Stevens had given up his own cabin to Mrs Veal, and Anthony and Perry were to share the store-room which led off from the main saloon on the opposite side and which had been hastily made habitable by the provision of two floor bunks fitted up unpleasantly like two premature coffins by the ship's carpenter.

As Aunt Madge said, addressing nobody, the inconvenience was only for a couple of days. They had important business in Bristol and at the last moment had decided to take this opportunity of settling it. Together with this business matter they could discharge their duty to Anthony's father by accompanying the boy and seeing him safely aboard his ship for Canada. Uncle Perry said it did his old guts good to feel the deck under his feet again, and Aunt Madge said it would be a nice change and a rest for her; she had been feeling thoroughly run down and she wished she had thought of the idea before.

Anthony did not believe a word of it. He didn't know quite what was happening, but he was beginning to have a fair idea. Uncle Perry didn't in the least look as if he was deriving any pleasure from being at sea again, and unless he was very much mistaken Aunt Madge was the last person in the world to accept this sort of discomfort out of a sense of duty to *him* or even in the interests of her own health. She would, one guessed, almost prefer to die in comfort rather than live without it.

But there was very little he could say or do. If he had been powerless to influence events before, he was certainly no less helpless now. He comforted himself with the thought that so long as he was going to meet his father it was not really his business to inquire into the motives of the people who went as far as Bristol with him. So long as he was moving, and moving in the right direction, the entanglements would slip off one by one.

Captain Stevens, although he put a good face on it, did not look pleased at having the owners aboard and had insisted in putting himself right with the Board of Trade by signing them all on as part of his crew at a shilling a day. Anthony wished that Ned Pawlyn had still been a member of the ship's company.

That night he spent in uneasy, sickly slumber, listening to Perry snoring and muttering to himself in the opposite bunk, and when he did close his eyes it was usually to start into wakefulness as last night's detestable scene flashed suddenly before his eyes, or at some unfamiliar sound, the tramp of feet above his head or the clink, clink of glass as Perry poured himself another tot of rum. Perhaps there were others who could not forget what had happened yesterday.

All the night the barquentine was beating into a tenacious headwind, which increased sharply during the dark hour before dawn. Presently he heard Perry being sick, and shortly afterwards he began himself.

After that he lost count of time and sequence, except that at some period of his illness a member of the crew came in and turned out the smoky, swinging oil lamp and let in grey fitful daylight through the port-hole.

Then later, after discovering within himself that he had no further incentive to live, he was sick for the last time and fell asleep.

When he awoke the colour of the daylight had not changed, but he felt that a considerable time had passed. Uncle Perry was no longer in the bunk opposite. Light-headed and painfully weak, he pulled himself gingerly out of his bunk and was at once flung on the floor beside Perry's. He clawed himself slowly upright and looked out of the port-hole.

The first impression was that all was lost. There was no horizon that he could see and nothing that he had ever visualised as a seascape. The port-hole was crushed down among walls and valleys of racing grey water towering at all angles above his vision and from time to time burying the window in total darkness. There was no such thing as a level, no datum line of balance or equilibrium. It was impossible to tell how far the sea engulfed the port-hole, how far the port-hole buried itself deep in the sea. There was no means of knowing the difference between the two or even of knowing that there was a difference. The sky when it was visible was a low, tattered shawl of brown. All the noises of ship and sea were dominated by a high-pitched variable whine like the heart-beat of an infernal dynamo.

Giddy and in danger of more sickness, he felt he could exist no longer without some water to moisten his parched throat; so he pulled himself to the other side of the cabin and opened the door.

Voices greeted him. Perry and Aunt Madge and Captain Stevens were in the dining saloon, which was in a state of chaos and semi-darkness. No one noticed him enter; there was far too much noise to take heed of a little more: rattling doors, straining woodwork, creaking chairs, loose things carrying on a scattered conversation of taps and rattles; above all, the roar of the sea and the scream of the wind.

'Persistent neglect of running gear, ma'am,' the captain was saying. 'We've got to take that into account. I wouldn't mention it only . . . mind you, it's not a question of danger yet – and these 'ere sharp sou'westers often blow themselves out as quick as they get up. But I'd not fancy tackling the Bay in this weather. Not as things are aboard. Mebbe you remember I asked –?'

'Turning back,' said Aunt Madge hoarsely to the table. 'Absurd. Hear no more. Wind'll go down. Face it out in due time. My dear husband always said, *The Grey Cat*, utmost confidence, captain and ship.'

'Thank you, ma'am. It's my wish to please you. But I've got my crew to consider. I put the facts before you just in case. We can ride this out till nightfall. If it don't abate we'll have to turn and run into the nearest port.'

'Think you could make the Scillies?' Perry asked, pushing his hair back.

Captain Stevens tapped the water out of his sou'wester. 'I don't. And shouldn't want to.'

'I don't fancy the Bay meself in this weather,' said Perry. 'Stap me, I've seen the seas flying as high as the royals. It makes a man cautious. But maybe it'll abate before morning.'

'Of course it will.' Mrs Veal put a handkerchief to her mouth and wiped away a hiccup. Apart from the fact that her cheeks seemed looser than ever and to shake with the pitching of the ship, the monument was not yet overthrown. A night of nausea had not prevented her putting on her pearls and her earrings.

'Well, there it is,' said Stevens. 'I trust you're right. The cook'll prepare you some hot cocoa if you've a mind for it. That's the best we shall be able to do just at present.'

By means of various fixtures he pulled himself round to the saloon door and went out. About half a gallon of water came down the companion and slipped about on the floor of the saloon as if seeking a way of returning to its own element.

Anthony let himself go and brought up with a rush against the table. 'I want a drink. Is there any water?'

Both stared at him suspiciously as if they suspected him of eavesdropping. Perry's face was yellow with sea-sickness and rum. 'In there,' he said, jerking his thumb.

The boy entered a little wash-up, and found some water in a carafe fixed to the wall. He drank it too greedily and was sick again. He stayed in the wash-up about half an hour, feeling too ill to move, but at last plucked up the strength to crawl up a hill back into the saloon.

Neither his aunt nor Perry was there; presumably they had gone into her cabin, for the space of movement was very limited. In the din he found a chair and sat on it and leaned his head back and watched the whole saloon at its dizzy acrobatics. After a time he found his eyes accustoming themselves to the changes of position; he was moving in exactly the same relationship and that helped. He began to feel better. The time by the clock above the door was nearly two, so they had been at sea nineteen hours.

There was a clatter of boots and Mr O'Brien, the mate, came into the room. He took no notice of Anthony but, maintaining his balance in a remarkable way, went over to a cupboard, knelt before it and began rummaging inside.

Anthony said: 'This is a bad storm, Mr O'Brien.'

The mate gave him a half glance but did not reply.

'Are we in danger?' the boy asked.

Mr O'Brien thumped something back into the cupboard. 'Not if it was a ship ye was in, me little fellow,' he snapped. 'I wisht I'd never signed on but stayed in Hull with me two feet on dry land. Well, well.'

There was a crack above them and a thud, and water suddenly came down the companion ladder to join up the pools which already existed.

'Are we far from Bristol yet?'

O'Brien rose to his feet. His fat red face under the sou'wester gleamed with water. Salt had whitened the stubble of his beard.

'I wish we was nearer. But, Holy Mary, why Bristol? If I could see the colour of Mount's Bay I should be satisfied.'

'Well, we're going to Bristol, aren't we?'

O'Brien buttoned up his oiler. 'Not this trip, young feller. Oporto we was making for. But where we shall make landfall if this breeze don't drop, God only knows.'

Anthony ran after him as he went to the door.

'I know the ship's going to Portugal. But we're calling at – at Bristol first to pick up more cargo. That's – that's where I'm getting off.'

O'Brien pushed away his detaining arm.

'Och, I've no time to stand here arguing the toss. Ask your mother, or whatever she is. She'll set you right.'

*   *   *

207

Nightfall brought no abatement of the wind but only a slight shifting of direction.

At 8 P.M. Captain Stevens came down and with a steady hand entered the following particulars in the log:

8/12/98. Days on passage, 2. Course SSW. Wind and weather: SW 7–9. Rain squalls; steep seas. Ship taking seas solid over fo'c'sle head, pitching and labouring.

Later came three other entries.

9/12/98. Midnight. Wind and weather: SW 9–10. Running before full gale under foresail and tops'l only. Course now approx. NNE by 1/2 E. Heavy squalls. Two helmsmen. Heavy damage on deck.

2 A.M. Wind and weather: W by S 9. Fore topm'st carried away. Seas breaking over all the time. Ship labouring heavily.

4 A.M. Wind and weather: W by N 9–8. Bare poles. Trying to set up jury rig for'ard. Water gaining on the pumps. In much danger of being pooped.

A superstitious person might have imagined that Joe Veal was taking some part in the situation and exacting his revenge. If nothing more, his parsimony was coming into its own.

But Madge Veal was not a superstitious woman. She was far too self-centred to believe in omens. She was not interested in retribution, divine or astral-human, nor if she had been would she have thought herself a subject likely to incur it. Anything she had done she had done with the best of intentions; indeed, she had never acted but on the highest principles and from the highest possible motive, that of her own welfare.

But Perry . . . Perry, like all sailors, had a strong thread of superstition in his character. Not that he had been a sailor any length of time. Three years of hardship before the mast when a young man had given him a working knowledge of the argot but no further desire to employ it in its proper element. After that when he travelled he travelled as much as possible on dry land. Cab-driver in Cape Town, waiter in Buenos Aires, casual cow-hand in Texas, hobo, soft-drink attendant at a drug-store in San Francisco; these were casual points in the career of a rolling stone who had attracted a record low level in moss. Then a lucky ticket in a sweepstake had put him on top of the world and given him the money to travel home to England first class. It had been the beginning of a run of luck which had brought him a comfortable corner by his brother Joe's fireside and the favour and side glances of his brother's statuesque wife. It wasn't that he'd ever been really attracted by Madge, it was only that he never could resist an implicit challenge of that sort: there was the mischievous temptation to know what the statue was like when it was tipped off its pedestal.

Well, he knew now.

He had thought then that it never would end, that run of luck; there seemed no reason why it should. But imperceptibly the change had come. Not at any single point could he say the vein had given out; nor was he the sort of man who would ordinarily concern himself with regrets that it had done so. Not ordinarily.

But these last few weeks he had begun to wish he had never left San Francisco.

He knew now, although his mind was working in a haze of rum and sea-sickness, that there was only one serious concern in his head: to cut the painter and slip away. To do that he would take any reasonable risk. His was not a conscience which had been unduly exercised in the past; it had accepted shady little episodes and adventures without protest. But the essence of them was that they were *little*. He knew his limitations. And for the last few months he had been playing right out of his class. For the last few weeks he hadn't been able to call his soul his own.

The knowledge was on his lungs. Not so much his conscience as his lungs. The knowledge was a weight; it was a tangible thing. Sometimes he found he could hardly breathe for it. The only palliative was rum.

As the storm grew worse he left Madge and went to lie down in his bunk, aware of the quiet figure of the boy in the other bunk. If he had any beads to tell he would have 'told' them. He could not escape a superstitious twinge at the fury with which the gale had broken upon them, but he still had the gambler's belief that his sudden bad luck was about to change and that the gale might yet turn to his own benefit. Now that they were being forced to run for one of the Bristol Channel ports he might get a chance to slip ashore unobserved.

What disconcerted him in this hope was the manner in which Madge was bearing up. By all the laws this storm should have shaken her nerve. The only sign she gave was that of going into her most withdrawn mood. But she was far from any mood in which she could be easily given the slip.

The boy stirred and sneezed but didn't speak, although he was certainly awake and had seen his uncle come in. Perry had never wanted to bring the boy at all. To him he represented an encumbrance and an added risk. But Madge, with an inside knowledge of the facts, had said that he could not be left behind to bear tales and tell everyone where they had gone, or at least *how* they had gone. During his five months' stay he had seen too much. Little boys had big eyes. Besides, he had done all her shopping for her. If examined by some impudent prying busybody he would give too much away. And, though she did not put it into so many words, Anthony still fulfilled a purpose he had fulfilled for some time: he lent respectability to a *ménage* which without him would be morally suspect. When they reached Portugal, Aunt Madge said, they could put him on a boat to Canada from there; it would be a nice surprise for his father who, even if he hadn't sent for him, would certainly be glad to see him. But Perry was not quite sure if she meant this; he would never be sure of anything Madge said again. He was coming to appreciate Madge's conscience which, if always active, was always malleable; he had known it to make the most acrobatic *volte-faces*. He was not exactly comfortable about the future of the boy.

Anthony would have been much better left behind.

But as the night advanced Perry's fuddled humanitarian

promptings were lost in fear for his own safety. In his few years at sea he had known enough of storms to recognise the dangerous quality of this one, and his experience of ships was at least sufficient to tell him that the barquentine was fighting for her life, and fighting with declining heart.

At five o'clock Captain Stevens was brought down into the water-logged saloon amid the wreckage of the furniture. A wave had brought a broken spar round and knocked him down with it. He was conscious but in considerable pain. Nobody but himself had the least knowledge of medicine, but he said he thought he had broken some ribs. At this stage Perry realised that their chances of survival were becoming slight. In the Atlantic they might have drifted before the storm until it abated. In these narrow seas they were likely to pile up on the rocks which could not be far away.

They took Stevens into his own cabin where Mrs Veal sat stubbornly in a corner and would speak to no one but herself. Perry made an effort to get him comfortable in his bunk and then put on the captain's oilskins and went on deck. At least he succeeded in opening the companion doors and putting out his head as one will put one's head out of a train when it is rushing through a tunnel. (There is only the noise and the pitch blackness and the flying wind.) The doors banged to after him as he retreated into the cabin and more water followed him down.

He wiped water from his face and poured himself out a tot of rum.

He sat there all alone, feeling desolate and trapped and frightened. He would have given a good deal merely for a confidential friend to talk to. But in one cabin there was a sick boy distant and reserved; in the other was an injured man watched over though not tended by a woman who frightened him more than anything else in the world except the things she had done.

So there was nothing for it except to get drunk, and that was something beyond his powers; all he could do was take enough to solace his loneliness and deaden the worst of his fear.

A member of the crew sighted land at 6.35 when dawn had begun to thin the blackness of the flying night. For twelve minutes with O'Brien and another man at the wheel, barely able to cling to it and constantly washed by half seas, they kept their distance from the high desolate coast. More desperate attempts were made to increase the jury rig, not without success, and O'Brien brought her up a little to the north. But then as they plunged on he saw through the slow, fitful daylight that the coast ran out ahead of him across the path of the wind.

He knew then that *The Grey Cat* was on her last voyage.

A wave came over and swept the length of the deck, licking like a hungry animal over a bone which has already been picked clean.

'May!' he shouted at the top of his voice to the carpenter. 'Below! Get 'em up.'

May the carpenter did not hear what was said, but he understood the gesture that went with it. He glanced backwards at the hurrying mountainous seas, then quickly unlooped the rope about his waist and dived towards the hatchway.

Perry was still alone in the saloon, leaning heavily on the table with a glass before him and water swilling about his knees. He had been singing glassily to himself, having almost achieved the end he had not thought possible.

''Elp me to get the cap'n up,' said May. 'We're drivin' in 'pon the land. Stand a chance.'

Perry followed him into the cabin. May had already explained the position to Mrs Veal. She was standing up, steadying herself by holding to a bookshelf which had long since emptied its books into the water at her feet. She had put on her hat and coat, and her pince-nez was awry. She looked highly indignant that this was happening to her and peered at May with hostility for disturbing her.

'On deck,' Perry said thickly. 'All hands. Safest place now. There's rocks ahead. Get the boy. Bring him up. Safest on deck.'

Captain Stevens said: 'Leave me here. Look to yourselves.'

'Come along now,' said May.

Between them the two men lifted the captain from his bunk and staggered with him out of the cabin. For the moment the onset of immediate danger had cleared Perry's brain; he was not so much afraid of the sea. The companion was not sufficiently wide to allow of three abreast, but he brought up the rear without stumbling.

Left behind, Madge took off her pince-nez and carefully stowed them away in an inner pocket of her dress. Without them her face looked curiously bare, bare and plain and commonplace; passing in the street you would not have given it another glance. She drew on her kid gloves, fastened the two buttons of her black astrakhan cloak, took out her hatpin and thrust it back in a different position, picked up her bag. Her mind could not visualise what the scene was likely to be on deck. She could not dissociate herself from the conviction that she would step into a dinghy and be rowed ashore. That was the only fitting way out. Her sense of dignity would not allow it to be otherwise.

She splashed her way across the saloon to the stairs but turned back towards the spare cabin. There was the boy in there. She reached the door of the spare cabin and then saw that there was a key in the lock and that the door was of good teak. She turned her head without haste in the direction of the companion way. The others were already on deck. She put out a gloved hand and turned the key. Then she took out the key and dropped it in the water.

She turned away and crossed the saloon and began to climb the slippery companion ladder towards the deck.

Epilogue

By noon of that day the worst of the gale had spent itself, though the seas were mountainous and puffs of foam still eddied about the streets of Sawle. Before dark the sky cleared and the sun came out.

All day the village had been in a hubbub. Most of the survivors were housed in the Tavern Inn, but one or two had overflowed into the cottages of hospitable neighbours. Altogether it had been a busy time, and when evening came the bar of the Tavern Inn was crowded with men in need of something to wet their parched throats and congenial company with whom to share the experiences of the day. Wrecks were not so frequent as they had once been, and this one had yielded interesting dividends in crew and cargo.

All the members of the life-saving rocket crew were there, except Tom Mitchell, who was a little boy and had been put to bed, and Abraham Jarvis who was a teetotaller, and Mike Smith who had begun celebrating too early and had gone to sleep outside his own front door. There had been one or two reporters down during the day asking questions and taking photographs and generally getting in the way, and tonight two had arrived from Plymouth and had attached themselves to Benjamin Blatchford, the captain of the crew.

Now that all that could be done while daylight lasted had been done, he was not averse from giving them an account of the wreck in return for a measure of free beer. Ben Blatchford had a wholesome dislike for charity; he would not have accepted a free drink from a foreigner in ordinary circumstances; but in this case he was giving the two reporters something in exchange, so that set things to rights in his mind.

The bar was full of smoke and noise and good-humoured banter.

'Mind you,' he said reasonably, ''twas Abe Jarvis's idea to pull the old gun round upon that point. I think 'twould have come to one or another of us soon enough, but he thought on it first. "Try 'er over to Sawle Point," he said. "Run her down right b'low Hoskin's field." And sure 'nough, though 'twas plaguey work gettin' 'er thur, once she was thur, first rocket fell plumb acrost the barque. Handsome bit o' shooting, 'twas, though I say it myself. We'd the wind almost abeam, see? A nice judgment was all that was required.'

'About how long did it take to get them all off, Mr Blatchford?' asked one reporter with gold-rimmed spectacles.

'. . . Once the line was took fast, you mean? I couldn't say that fur certain; we wasn't looking at no clocks. A 'our, p'raps. Thur was no time to waaste, mark you, not a minute to waaste. We was all sweatin' bad when 'twas over, though the wind was as cold as charity. That's what I said at the time. "Thur's no time to waaste, lads," I said. "We must get the line acrost now," I said, "or else . . ."'

The reporter nodded sympathetically. 'Yes, I suppose it was touch and go. Who did you rescue first; the lady passenger, I suppose?'

Ben Blatchford wiped his beard. 'No. They sent the ship's boy over first to test the line. Then the captain –'

'The captain? I thought usually –'

'He was 'urt about the ribs. He was in a bad way when he come over. We thought he was dead, but 'e was only knocked out. They do say he's been took to Truro Infirmary. The lady came third. Then seven of the crew, mate last. That made the lot.'

'Was she the captain's wife?'

'No.'

'Ah,' said the other reporter, scenting romance.

'They do say as she owned the ship.'

'Is she still in Sawle, do you know?'

'In the Tavern Inn when last I heard. They give her the

215

best room over the parlour. So Mrs Nichols says, and I've no cause to think 'er a liar.'

'Another pint, Mr Blatchford? Certainly. Three pints, *if* you please, miss. I wonder if we could see her, George? Might add a feminine interest.'

'I'll have a shot later. Carry on, Mr Blatchford, what were you saying?'

''Lo, Tom,' said Ben Blatchford, putting down his mug. 'Got away from the missus at last? Rare good job she made of getting that barrel ashore this morning. What was in it?'

'Well, I s'pose you 'ad your eye on it yourself, Ben Blatchford?'

A good-tempered wrangle sprang up amid the smoke, and other voices joined in. Mr Nichols, the landlord, leaned his elbows on the bar and argued with a fat man in a tight red jersey. In the corner a blind man nodded his head and grinned and chewed his toothless jaws. Presently Blatchford gave his attention to the reporters.

'Do we understand that a man was drowned, Mr Blatchford? A member of the crew?'

'No, 'twas a passenger. Tried to swim ashore wi' a line when they thought we was not going to get a line aboard. Foolish that, but they say there was no 'olding him. Said 'e'd been a champion swimmer and wouldn't listen. Many a man's done it before. 'Tis a question of keeping your nerve, see? Before now, I've seen 'em try to launch a boat. A pity, for 'tis just throwing away good lives. We always try to signal to 'em to stay where they are, but they won't see.'

'This passenger; was he any relative to the lady, do you know?'

'Brother, I bla'. But you'd best ask her, didn't you?' Ben Blatchford's small grey eyes brooded on nothing as he re-lit his pipe. 'He'd be sucked out, ye see. They always are. They say when he went under they pulled in the line, but it had broke. What else did they expect? 'Twas a pity, too.' Blatchford's eyes transferred themselves to the spectacled reporter. They seemed to mourn the loss of a man.

216

'Those two were the only passengers, I suppose? Sad, as you say, that one of them should have been lost. All the crew were saved, I take it?'

The Cornishman's eyebrows came together in a slow frown.

'Thur was one other passenger.'

'A man? He was saved, I presume?'

'No-o . . . A boy. A lad of eleven or twelve, I s'pose. No . . . He got lef' be'ind.'

The noise in the bar had increased during the last few minutes, and the two reporters pressed forward so as not to miss any word which came from the bearded lips of the man who was speaking to them. But for a moment he did not go on.

'Left on the wreck?' prompted the spectacled reporter. 'Then there were two lives lost. How did that happen?'

'Gracious knows. There was some confusion betwixt the first boy that come over and this one, they do say. An' then wi' the captain being knocked out . . . Mebbe you can imagine what 'tis like on the deck of a ship which is being washed b' the sea. 'Tisn't a time when you always remember to count 'eads. I reckon 'twas the leddy's fault; he was with she, and she ought to have seen he was took off wi' the rest.' Blatchford stroked his beard. 'One thing did seem a straange thing to 'appen. He'd somehow got himself locked up in a cabin in the captain's quarters. Whether he'd locked himself in thur fur safety, or . . .'

The reporter motioned for another refill. 'Has the boy's body been recovered, do you know?'

Blatchford's eyes travelled to the approaching mug. 'Oh, the boy was all right. 'E were as safe as any of 'em. We found him thur still in the cabin when the tide went out. Scared, you know, as any young tacker would be. Scared, but keepin' his end up like a good 'un. Just broke down a bit when we busted the door in. Boys o' that age have plenty o' give an' take, as you might say. Like a sapling, bend but won't break, see? I well remember when I was ten . . . Yes, 'e's upstairs too. They put 'im to bed, and

217

I bla' Landlord Nichols gave 'im a tot o' brandy to keep the chill out . . . But I can't understand 'ow that thur door come to be locked.'

In a cottage on the opposite side of the square from the Tavern Inn two of the crew, Anderson and Mallett, had met again after having been separated by minor injuries and lack of dry clothes. They were both men who had been with Stevens in *The Grey Cat* for some years.

They sat for a time before the fire, glad of safety and a pipe of tobacco and not anxious for speech. The two old people who owned the cottage had left them alone.

'Funny thing,' Anderson said at last. 'Funny thing about old Veal's brother, Perry Veal, or whatever 'e was called. Funny thing about 'im. You was near 'im when 'e says 'e'll swim. I'd got me finger broke an' I'd not much mind for anythink else, like. But I sees 'im wavin' 'is 'ands like a preacher. What was 'e wantin'?'

'A line,' said Mallett.

'Well, wasn't you wantin' to give 'im one?'

'O'Brien wasn't. O'Brien didn't want to. O'Brien thought as they might still get a rocket over. 'E didn't see as Veal'd do it, champion swimmer or no. With the Old Man bein' knocked out . . . Well, it was like this. You mind when we struck? D'you see 'em come up on deck about five minutes before?'

'Yes.'

'Well, it was like this. May come up first, more or less carryin' the Ole Man. Then come Perry Veal staggerin' as if 'e was in two ships an' near gettin' washed overboard first wave. You seen that. Then Mrs V. clawin' 'er way up, 'at goin' one way an' bag the other. Well, two minutes later they was flattened up agin' the after bulwarks along of me and Peter.'

'That was when we struck.'

'Aye. Aye, we struck just then. An' over we went in a 'eap, clingin' for dear life as if we was all goin' over

218

the side. Then the mizzen topm'st cracked right over our 'eads, an' she come up again, drainin' all the sea off of her deck like Niagara Falls. I was next to Perry Veal and the old lady was the other side of 'im. 'E was brimmin' over wi' drink, I could see that. I don't know 'ow you was fixed, but where we was, tilted the way we was, we was sheltered from the worst of the wind. And we looks up and tries to see what the coast looks like before the next wave smacks over the top and washes the guts out of us. An' then, mark you, I 'ears Perry Veal say to Mrs V., Where's the Somethin'-or-other?'

'Where's the what?'

'I don't know what. I don't catch what. And she says: "Follerin' me up. Just be'ind me." Then they lies quiet for a few minutes while O'Brien tries to get the distress flares goin'.'

'They was a wash-out.'

'Like everythin' else. Then, when we was splutterin' and breathin' in a bit of air after a back-wash, I 'ears Perry Veal say again, Where's the Somethin'? Bag, I thought, but 'e talked so thick.'

'Boy, mebbe.'

'Well, I might've guessed that if I'd knowed there was a boy except for Mike aboard. An' she says, high-pitched an' hoarse, "'E was follerin' me up, I tell you!" Then Peter sighted the rocket crew on the cliffs, and for the next ten minutes I was watchin' them too close for to have time to spare for Perry Veal. But when I looks next 'e was still clingin' there, lookin' at 'er like as if 'e'd never moved in ten minutes. Just starin' at 'er till I thought 'e'd got a fit. Not lookin' at the rockets fallin' in the sea. Lookin' at 'er. Then O'Brien crawls over and says: "It's a poor chanct we've got, bhoys. Every man for hisself if she breaks up." Then Perry looks at 'im like 'e was dreamin', an' his face twitches, and then he looks at Mrs V. again, and when O'Brien 'as crawled away he shouts the same question at 'er as before, though she's 'alf drowned with water suckin' about 'er waist. An' when the water goes back she doesn't

219

answer 'im nothin' this time, but just looks at 'im one of 'er hoity-toity looks. Then –'

'I know them. She give me one when she come aboard a couple of months ago.'

'Then that's when 'e breaks out. "God almighty!" he shouts at me, with the sea sprayin' over us like bits of stones. "I ain't in wi' this bitch. See? I ain't. God almighty! I'm gettin' out o' this. God almighty, I ain't in wi' this bitch!" Just like the sort of face Tim Chudleigh got when 'e took the D.T.'s. Then 'e lets go 'is 'old, even though we're just waitin' for another wave, and crawls after O'Brien back to the poop. An' some'ow 'e ain't washed off like a whitebait, and gets to the poop, and that's when you sees 'im arguin' with O'Brien.'

There was silence after Mallett had finished speaking. They both drew meditatively and appreciatively at their borrowed pipes. Anderson had always been a slow thinker. But he usually got somewhere in the end.

'Reckon there was somethin' betwixt those two,' he said at length. 'I shouldn't think 'twas all D.T.'s with Perry Veal.'

Above the bar of the Tavern Inn was a long dusty passage with an elbow bend in the middle; this fed the bedrooms of the inn; and at about the time that the bespectacled reporter was thinking of slipping away from the bar and interviewing Mrs Veal, a tall, slender young woman came out of one of the rooms, closing the door softly as if not to disturb a sleeper. She was dressed in a long grey frock and still wore a grey hat with a veil, but no outdoor coat. She walked along the passage and, lifting up a corner of her skirt, ran quickly down the dark stairs, slipped past the bar and turned into the kitchen.

Mrs Nichols looked up from her crochet-work and was inquiring:

''As 'e woke up yet, miss?'

220

'About five minutes ago. I thought he might like something to eat. I wondered if I might make some gruel. That was what the doctor said, wasn't it?'

''S, I think. But sit you down, dearie; I'll make it for 'ee. No, no, no trouble 'tall. You must be wearied out coming all that way in Jess Parson's wagon. I don't knaw 'ow 'ee kept saw clean. No, no, I'll make it. Sakes, I don't, in ole Jess Parson's wagon all cagged up in mud.'

'I was lucky to have the lift,' said Patricia.

'Well, yes . . . I s'pose 'ee was frightened out of your life when you 'eard 'bout this 'ere shipwreck. But there wasn't no need to worry, you see. They'll be right as ninepence in the morning. Least . . . 'Twas a mortal shame that Mr Watsit was drowned. Relation of yours, wasn't 'e?'

'My uncle.'

'Dear life, now isn't that sad? Well, well, that's a poor job. Well, well, dear soul.'

Conversation continued while the gruel was made. Dazed and uncertain herself, Patricia could only parry the polite little questions put by the polite little woman stirring the pan. She had only been here an hour and most of that time she had spent beside Anthony's bed while he slept. There she was away from prying eyes, which she most wished to avoid. They had told her her stepmother was sleeping too, so she had not seen her yet. In any case she had a strange reluctance to see Madge until she had first talked with Anthony and learned more of this unexpected trip. Queer, her dependence in this crisis on Anthony. She felt that from Anthony she would get the truth as far as he knew it without subtlety and without evasions. That, she felt, she needed more than anything else.

Also they had told her the facts concerned with Anthony's survival, and although a doctor had examined him she wanted to reassure herself that he had come to no serious harm.

The gruel was ready and she took it from the hands of Mrs Nichols and went out into the narrow passage leading to the stairs. As she reached the bend to go up the stairs, two men came in at the private door of the inn talking to Nichols the landlord, who had been called out of the bar. Pat shrank against the banister and started up the stairs. But to one of the men that figure was beyond mistake even in the gloom of the hall. She heard him mutter an excuse and spring up the stairs after her. He caught her at the turn of the landing.

'Pat . . .'

'Well, Tom . . .' She turned half defiantly, half defensively, to face him.

'What are you doing here, Pat; surely you were not on the ship? I . . .'

'I heard of it this afternoon. Anthony had written me a letter. I came over as quickly as I could. They're – my relatives, aren't they?' She spoke quietly, unprovocatively.

'Have you seen Anthony?'

'I'm taking him this gruel.' She took a step to move on.

'Pat, I'd like a word with you. Is there anywhere we can go?'

'I can't stop now. I must take this in.'

'Take it in and come out again, can you? I must have a word with you.' He spoke as quietly and gravely as she. They were not talking like strangers, but like people who had known each other years ago. He had taken off his hat, and his hair gleamed in the dim light.

'I ought to stay with him. Besides . . .' She did not finish the sentence but he understood it.

'You may not have anything to say to me, but . . .'

She hesitated. 'Oh, it isn't that . . .'

'I'll wait for you.'

She entered the bedroom and found that in the interval Anthony had gone to sleep again. She waited five minutes in the hope that he might wake and give her the excuse not to return at once to the passage. When he showed no signs of doing this she put a plate over the gruel and left the room.

She found Tom where she had left him.

'There's a sort of parlour in here,' he said. 'There's nobody else about.'

She followed him into a small room at the end of the passage. In one corner of it a table-lamp showed an ancient yellow light like something which had been burning for centuries. The room smelt of mildew and stale lavender.

She went over to the window and stared nervously down into the square, where various horses were tethered and people moved about and talked in groups in the starlit, windy darkness. He stared at her and tried to think how best he might put what had to be said.

But the sight of her had pushed the carefully formal speeches out of his head. When he had not seen her for some weeks he fancied that the old lure was fading, but as soon as he set eyes on her nothing else mattered.

'It's weeks now,' he said, his thoughts coming to his lips. 'It's weeks now . . . How have you been getting on?'

'Very well,' she said almost inaudibly. 'Thanks to you.'

'To me . . .'

'Yes. Miss Gawthorpe didn't tell me she was your cousin.'

'Oh . . .' He hesitated, not quite sure of the tone of her voice. 'So you know that?'

'I found it out this week. It was kind of you to arrange for my future.'

Now he knew that his 'kindness' was not appreciated.

'How did you know I was looking for a job?' she asked.

'I just heard.' He was not going to let Anthony down.

'I gave in my notice yesterday.'

'You . . . but why? Miss Gawthorpe finds you very satisfactory.'

'I might have known,' she said bitterly, 'that I shouldn't have been engaged without references. Thank you for standing sponsor for me.'

'Oh, nonsense. Miss Gawthorpe wanted someone reliable. It happened that I knew of someone. She wouldn't have taken you or kept you if you had not been suitable. There's no reason at all to give notice. That's absurd.'

223

'I frequently am absurd.'

He said: 'Seeing you now after so long revives . . . all the old hopes and dreams. For me, Pat, there'll never be anyone like you. I've tried – to take a different view, but it's no use.'

'I'm sorry . . .'

He took a step nearer and then stopped. 'This wasn't what I had to talk to you about, but seeing you again . . . Before we drop it, Pat, tell me once more if it has to be all over between us. For my part –'

She said: 'After everything, how can there be anything more? No, Tom, how can there be? We've never – deceived ourselves. Tell me what it is you have to say.'

Silence fell between them, and much more besides, the shadows of old memories. The memories, bitter and sweet, were like puppets, jerked into motion with a pseudo-life of their own but deriving from impulses outside themselves. There was no chance at all of ignoring them; they were a part of their relationship.

She turned and walked towards the door with an instinct for escape. Her movement was hasty and impulsive, thrust on her by inadmissible emotions.

'Where are you going?'

'If you've nothing else to say . . . I must see Madge. I haven't even spoken to her yet.'

He barred her way. He was torn between impulses. The issue was so vital to him that he wanted desperately to pursue it. But he knew that if he did so she would leave him, and it was impossible that he could let her go to see Madge.

'Let me pass,' she said.

'I've got to tell you, Pat. I've got to tell you. Somebody has to. Your – your father's body was exhumed the night before last. His and . . .' He could not get beyond that.

She put a hand on a chair and stood and stared at him as if suspecting some trick to detain her. Then she saw that he was completely in earnest. All the other feelings which had so engaged her a moment ago drained away, were engulfed in a great chasm of surprise and horror.

'Dad? . . . What for?'

'There was a suspicion about the cause of his death. You see . . . I began, the police began to make inquiries. I began . . . and that started . . .'

'What suspicion?'

'Something that wasn't without cause. They've found more than four grains of arsenic in your father's body.'

Madge Veal had been sitting before the fire without stirring for nearly an hour when the knock came on her bedroom door. She had a faculty for remaining perfectly still like a brocaded effigy in a waxworks; at such times her personality was purely negative, it seemed scarcely to exist; her body was like an empty house in which a single night-light burned to show that the owner would be back.

She had asked for the fire as a special favour, saying that she was cold in bed and felt she had caught a chill. But in fact it was not so much the warmth she needed as the encouragement of the brightly flickering flames. All her life she had found comfort in gazing into the fire; it stimulated her thoughts, and this evening her brain was rusty and tired and disjointed like an old railway line which has been long in disuse.

For years her thoughts had known the comfortable tracks to follow; one ran along them for months almost without consideration; strict guidance was unnecessary, conscience and instinct doing all the necessary work. To be jolted on to unfamiliar lines was, she felt, grossly unfair, and subconsciously she was trying to think herself into a state of mind in which she could abjure the necessity of following them to disagreeable conclusions.

When the knock came it was not unwelcome as a diversion; the effigy slowly came to life and put on an extra dressing-grown before calling, 'Come in.'

A thin man with gold-rimmed spectacles gingerly entered, and she at once regretted not having added her pearls. She pulled a scarf up under her various chins and looked down at him from above them.

'Yes?'

'Mrs Veal?'

'That is so.'

'You'll pardon my intruding, ma'am. I could find no one to bring me. I represent the *Western Daily Post*.'

'Yes?' She had become very jealous of her dignity.

'I'm taking down a few personal notes about the shipwreck. I was told the position of your bedroom. I hope I don't intrude.'

'You may come in,' she said coldly. While he moved further into the bedroom she eyed him up and down and the thought came to her that she would have been glad of someone to talk to, if only it could have been someone intelligent and understanding like Perry. Had reporters any intelligence?

He began to make the conventional inquiries about her health and safety, and while she answered him the need to unburden her grievances became steadily more important.

'You were the owner of the ship, ma'am, weren't you? Very sad indeed. Did you often travel in her?'

'Oh . . .' Mrs Veal waved her hand. 'From time to time. Since my dear husband's death, of course, not the inducement.'

'No, no.'

'Bristol,' said Mrs Veal. 'Business there. My poor brother-in-law. A wicked wicked shame. The captain had no right . . . expose to danger. Should have made for port earlier. My poor brother-in-law . . .'

'Mr Perry Veal. A great pity. I understand he was lost trying to swim ashore with a line.'

The reporter discreetly waited as Madge Veal began to fumble among the many folds of three dressing-gowns and presently produced a handkerchief.

'I look upon it – shall always look upon it, gave his life for me. Great gentleman. Said to me: "I must go, Madge.

226

I'll bring you help. Never fear." "Never fear," was what he said.'

The reporter made a note of the words. 'What were your feelings when the ship struck, Mrs Veal?'

'Only man ever understood me. My dear husband, deeply sympathetic, but his brother Perry, finer mind. Great loss. I mourn, Mr – er . . . Many ways, wish I had been taken. I look to the afterlife and reunion.' She dabbed at her nose. 'Many fine spirits. Passed on. One wishes that one were in closer contact. I often think. Very sensitive to such things. Deeply sensitive. Coarse-fibred people.'

The man glanced up. In an appropriately sympathetic voice he said: 'How long had you been at sea when –?'

'Suffered,' said Aunt Madge, turning up her eyes. 'All my life suffered. Persecution, grievous thing, Mr – er . . . When my dear sister died. Eve of her thirtieth birthday. Acute gastritis. With her to the end. People said. But what did I gain who lost a sister. Were devoted. Devoted. My mother and I were all in all to each other after that, but were we not indeed before?'

'Your nephew, I believe, was very fortunately rescued later? If –'

'Been determined,' said Mrs Veal, 'all my life to go on, follow the straight path. The straight and narrow. It invites the scoffer, philistine, scurrilous tongues. Sustained by conscience. An unhappy woman, Mr – er . . . You see before you one. Stung by scorpions.' She waved a hand at him, forgetting for the moment that she despised him, remembering only that he was the audience she must have. The experiences of the last three days had upset her more than she thought. Her cheeks trembled with indignation. 'Your paper. Put that in. Stung by scorpions. We all have our crosses. Hi try . . . Consolation in conviction. The lonely people of the world.'

Through a mist of preoccupation she was aware that he was addressing her.

'Mrs Veal.'

'Yes?' She paused and her small mouth hung open

like a little bag which someone had forgotten to fasten. 'Yes?'

The reporter said in a depressed voice: 'Could you tell me your emotions, just simply and – and simply, when your ship came ashore. It is unusual to have a – a lady aboard and I'm most anxious to get a woman's point of view.'

She looked at him with contempt. 'All my life, fate has deprived me . . . loved ones have fallen by the way. By the way, Mr – er . . . It has been my misfortune. *NOT* my fault. I do not complain. My dear, dear sister in the flower of her youth. My dear mother when her advice, most needed. My good, kind husband. I am. Lonely woman. Stricken with sorrow. My husband's first wife, she often said to me, "Madge, you look bowed with secret grief." It was the truth. Only Perry felt and understood. He alone knew what it was.'

The reporter fidgeted and glanced towards the door. He had not been taking notes.

'That's very, very sad, madam. Naturally we always regret intruding upon –'

'Unusual,' said Mrs Veal doggedly. 'The one who stands out. Always picked at by the herd. An unusual woman. Hi often think. Destined. One does not know. The end is yet to be.'

'Yes, yes,' he said.

'The end is yet to be! Mr – er . . . Put that in your paper. Joan of Arc did not know. Jeanne d'Arc. Envious men may deny me . . . Right of speech is mine. Always remember that, right of speech. Don't go,' she said as he made a movement to rise; and so sharply did she speak that for the moment he accepted her veto. 'Don't go. I have much to tell you. Afterwards. You'll be glad.'

Pat found herself back on the sofa in that musty old parlour of the Tavern Inn. She didn't know how she had got there, and Tom was trying to persuade her to drink something from a glass.

228

She sat up. 'I'm all right. I'm all right. It – just made me sick.'

He sat back upon his heels and waited quietly for her to recover. A sudden gust of wind boomed down the chimney and shook the old building in its depths. He saw now that her colour was returning.

He felt it particularly unfitting that he should have had to strike this final blow. Patricia, for all her slenderness and youth, had always been so inwardly strong and self-sufficient; while he, outwardly confident enough, had never been really confident in her presence. (Or only once, and that had been when his desire for her had outweighed his deference.)

That had been one of the stumbling blocks in their relationship, but the fact that she was down at last brought him no comfort or satisfaction. He raged against the circumstances which had weighted the dice against her. In the space of two years she had lost both her parents; her marriage had come to grief; the standard of life she had grown used to had been overthrown, the money rightly hers had been given to someone else. She had gone out to earn her living among strangers. But now something was upon her less bearable than any of the foregoing. Something crooked and unclean and not to be thought of. But something which would have to be thought of. In the next few days and weeks it would take a larger and larger place in her life until there would be room for nothing else. Then, perhaps it would be in three months, perhaps six, the bubble of talk and trial and publicity would be pricked and she would be left to herself again, empty and neglected and alone. Alone but with a stigma of talk and rumour still clinging to her like cobwebs from a sewer. Wherever she went they would go, casting an unrelenting stain over her cleanness and her youth. 'Oh, do you know who that is staying with you, Mrs So-and-So? Patricia Veal: you remember, the Falmouth poisoning case. No, she was only a step-daughter, but of course they were a peculiar family. I've heard it said-mm-mm-mm-mm . . .'

That was her future unless . . . He realised that this was the very first time since she left him that they were alone together and she not trying to get away. He wished he could somehow heal the wound his words had inflicted, a wound which was going deeper with every minute that her brain worked, here alone with him in the lamplight. They were alone together but that counted for nothing.

He said: 'When this is over . . . It'll take time, Pat, obviously it will take time. When this is over . . . Oh, I know this isn't the time; there couldn't be a worse. But I may not get another opportunity.' He still sat on his heels beside her. She made no response. 'This . . . all this trouble that's coming. We could help each other. It's bound to be hard to get through alone. Life's pretty rotten for you since your father died; it will stay rotten for a time. Afterwards . . . I've had an offer of a partnership in Cape Town. All South Africa's unsettled. Two things it needs are honest politics and honest law. I'm going to take the chance. There we could really start afresh, really afresh. The past could be more easily forgotten. We're both young. We can wipe things out and begin again.'

His voice, which had become eager and moving, tailed off. He looked at her.

'Perry,' she said. 'Was he in it? His own brother. That's the hardest of all . . . to understand.'

He got up, sat on the edge of the couch, leaned his head on his hand. The moment was gone.

Neither of them knew how long passed before she said: 'What made . . . *you* suspect?'

'Oh . . .' He tried to bring back his thoughts to the subject which, until he had seen her, had prominently occupied them. 'Something about your father. His appearance wasn't quite natural. The clumsy way he handled things as if there wasn't much feeling in his fingertips; the look of his skin. Then I'd been reading for an examination in criminal law. Not that I suspected anyone in particular at first. Thought perhaps he took some sort of drug. I . . . didn't see enough of him and there was nobody I could inquire from.'

230

'When was this?'

'I noticed it particularly the first time I saw him after you had gone back.'

Two men were mounting their farm horses outside in the square. You could hear them talking to the horses, shouting to each other, then the lumbering clop-clop of iron hooves on cobbles.

'Go on.'

'I might have done more. I wish now I had, but I was very unsure then. And I'd quarrelled with him and wasn't on speaking terms with you. I dropped one or two hints to you, but you naturally thought I was only trying to scare you into coming back. It was dangerous to start talking outside. I made one or two inquiries about your mother . . .'

'Oh, dear God!' she said. It was a cry of pure distress. He took her hand and held it.

'Oh, Tom!' she said. 'Oh, Tom!'

They sat there for a long time in silence. Presently tears began to run down her cheeks. 'Don't cry, Pat,' he kept whispering. 'Don't cry, Pat.'

He forced himself to go on, trying to pick his way.

'After – after your father's death I began to feel there must be something, some cause. I went to see the doctor concerned, but of course he would tell me nothing. What sealed everything was the Will. I felt there was no doubt then. When your father made that Will he signed his own death warrant – forgive me for being blunt. But I was very relieved when you didn't come in for the money. I had been afraid that you might be next. That's why I hoped no later Will would be found. That's why I plotted and schemed to get you away from the house, out of danger.'

'Thank God I haven't been to see her,' she said through her tears.

'At last I got the police interested. Inquiries were made at likely shops. Nothing led anywhere. Anthony gave us the clue. He said one day that he did a lot of shopping for her. When he went through the list we at last came to – to flypapers. He'd bought them at various shops in the

231

district, twice at Penryn, once even at St Mawes, though none had been bought since late August. Inquiries were made about the type bought and an analysis made of them. Each one contains enough poison to kill a man. That gave the police evidence to take action.'

He still held her hand and she made no attempt to release it. She needed companionship in the dark.

'What are they going to do now?'

'The police? Nothing until tomorrow. They haven't quite finished all . . . all the reports haven't come through yet.'

She said half passionately, half fearfully: 'I wish it was tomorrow. I wish it was tomorrow.'

In the bar Ben Blatchford and the younger reporter were still standing side by side at the counter, although there had not been much conversation between them since the other man left. Two miners had walked in from a neighbouring village and were being regaled not only with beer, but with a lively account of the day's pickings in flotsam. The captain of the rocket crew, while not taking a prominent part in the discussion, was listening with an attentive smile. The reporter was reading through the notes he had made.

He felt a touch behind him and found his colleague had come back.

'Any luck?' he asked.

The other man shook his head and began to polish his glasses. 'Hopeless. Couldn't make head nor tail of her.'

'You got to see her, then?'

'She wouldn't talk sense. You know the sort: you ask a straightforward question and they go off into the story of their lives. Death beds of all her nearest relatives, *with* details of what they died of. She kept on burbling about being misunderstood and nobody loving her. I think she's got a mash on this fellow who was drowned. But as soon as I turned the conversation on that she was up and away about something else. Couldn't pin her down. We'll rig up some sort of a story, but I made my excuses as quick as I could.'

232

'What now, then?'

'We ought to catch the midnight train from Truro. Look, I'm going to have a shot at interviewing the mate, who's been put up at a cottage across the way. You got all you can out of this man?'

'Ye-es. I think so. But there was one thing. These notes –'

'Get a photo of him if you can. It'll fill up. I'll be back in twenty minutes.'

Left to himself again, the younger reporter read his notes again. This was his first assignment and he didn't want to fall down on it. He looked at his watch. Then he touched Blatchford on the sleeve.

The old man turned and regarded him with eyes which had grown more friendly and benevolent as the night advanced.

'Yes, boy?'

'Many thanks, Mr Blatchford, you've been very helpful. Do you happen to have a photograph of yourself, free of copyright, that you could let us have?'

'Well, boy, I've a snap that was took last August month of the whole rocket crew, and I'm thur wi' the rest. 'Ow would that do, eh? I don't know whether 'tis free of what you say, but I'll not charge ye fur it.'

'Thanks. That would do very well. We're leaving soon, so perhaps you could get it for us? The – er – I . . . in looking through these notes it's occurred to me there seems a slight contradiction, so to say, between – er . . .' Under the keen eye which was now turned on him he stammered and hesitated; then he gathered courage and plunged on. 'Look, Mr Blatchford, earlier when we began to talk, I have it down here that you said there wasn't a moment to lose in saving these people from the wreck.'

'Nor was there. Nor was there.'

'No, certainly; very good. But you said – mind you I'm only trying to clear the matter up – in speaking of the boy you say that he was saved later, much later, by a rescue party which boarded the ship, and you spoke as if it was only natural that he should be. I suppose that's all right; but if as you said every minute was precious –'

'So 'twas. So 'twas.' The tough weather-beaten face twisted slightly and the eyes glinted. 'Precious to we. We always get a pound for every life we saave bi' the rocket. They was safe enough where they were if the ship didn't break up. Naturally the ship *might*'ve broke up, but we was anxious to get 'em off whether or no. Tide was goin' out fast. In another hour they'd 'ave been able to walk ashore.' Blatchford exchanged a few words of farewell to a friend leaving the bar. Then he turned back to the reporter. 'Now 'tis real nice to've seen you gentlemen, but you'll be careful not to put that in your papers, won't you. Folks might think it read straange. But I'm an honest man and you ast me an honest question. Sometimes things do work out straange round these shores, and it's no fault of we as've lived 'ereabouts all our lives.'

After the reporter had gone Aunt Madge went back to her seat by the fire, aware that she had been casting pearls before swine. She was sorry she'd wasted her breath in trying to explain as much as she had; the man had no soul above the common herd. You could not expect such a man to be sensitive and understanding when so few people had the quality of brain to appreciate her confidences. Only Perry had fully shared her way of thought. Perry and she had been soul mates. In the maelstrom of the Cornish sea he had been lost, and she would never see him more. The thought was a deep grief to her.

True, there was still a faint, uneasy memory that all had not been quite well between them at the end, that in his courageous effort to save her he had appeared distraught; but her brain was rapidly disposing of this remembrance. Each time she thought of it the lines were less distinct, the occurrence lit by a softer light.

Soon she would forget it altogether, having convinced herself that it was unimportant and did not affect the deep,

234

rich stream of their love and understanding. Only Perry had known all. Or not quite all, but she thought he understood all. One day soon she had been going to tell him everything in a burst of confidence. Now it would never be.

In the cottage opposite the bespectacled reporter was busy taking notes and wondering how to describe Mr O'Brien's accent. Just once or twice while he listened to the mate's ready flow and contrasted its factual pungency with Mrs Veal's windy hesitations there came to him a twinge of uneasiness, such as he sometimes had when he went to a racing meeting and on impulse put his money on another horse from the one he had all along intended backing: a sort of mental dyspepsia of second thoughts.

Not that he was aware of having missed something which would illuminate his story of the wreck, but he felt once or twice that a cleverer man might have been able to turn her peculiar personality to some account. She was a bore, but an unusual bore. He had watched her closely at first, and listened closely, keen to catch the thread of sense which must lie behind it all. Then he had failed and lost interest and become impatient.

So Madge Veal sat by the fire with her secrets still safe and the reporter made up his story with the larger part of the story left out. Later he would bite his nails in fury and regret.

He might have comforted himself when the time came by reflecting that he failed to understand her where cleverer men had failed. Where all men would fail who tried to assess her behaviour by their own.

For her brain was like a dusty room which had had its doors all locked and barred, a room in which the air had grown stale and noxious for lack of contact with the outer air. Her egoism provided the bolts and keys, sealing up the smallest crack whereby there could be any contact between other people's ethics and her own. Within this room her commonplace, rodent, dangerous personality had had its living and being, like a prisoner free within limits, building up its self-deceptions, concocting its own excuses,

235

imagining its own triumphs, plotting its own satisfactions, growing large and fat and white like a slug under a stone.

Only during the last few days – for the first time for years – events, especially the news Anthony brought, had burst open some of the doors and left them wantonly swinging. She had hastened to press them to again, her etiolated mind recoiling at the touch of the cold air. She had fought then like a querulous invalid from whom the bedclothes had been pulled away, fought tooth and nail to cover and protect herself again. She had succeeded, but only by admitting the existence of disturbing facts inside the protective screen. Even now they were still there, and Perry had been insistent that they were of a nature which would not remain sterile but would grow and develop and have a fruition of their own.

It had needed hard thinking to put them in their place.

That was why she had felt lonely and off her balance tonight. That was why she had said so much to the stupid staring reporter, talking in spite of herself, ventilating the stored complaints of a lifetime, justifying herself, pitying herself, inviting his commendation of her behaviour, using him in some degree as her confidant. It didn't matter. No harm was done. He had taken nothing in. The mere fact of having been able to talk to a man and of feeling herself so greatly his mental superior had had a reassuring effect; that and the relief of having talked it all out had brought reassurance. Before the comforting warmth of the fire and the self-supporting glow of these reflections she began to doze.

She was very tired. As she dozed she thought of her sister, a tall, comely girl who had had all the good looks of the family. Half dreaming and half waking, she thought of the strange way in which her sister had lost her good looks before she died; her cheeks had sunk and so much of her beautiful fair hair had come out; the family were renowned for their fair hair; her mother had retained it to the end. She thought of her mother, and how one year she had been essential to her well-being, the next superfluous, the next obnoxious, and the fourth she had not been at all; her death had been quite sudden. One, two, three, four, the years had peeled off like ripe plums falling from a tree; like flies falling from a flypaper.

She began to think of flypapers and of flies dying and dropping off them like the years. And in her sleepy mind she began to confuse people and flies, flies and people, so that each had the same relative importance to herself. Sometimes before she had done this; it was a convenient way out of many a moral impasse; her thoughts often repeated themselves in this way, working their way into grooves and sophistries of their own. The older she grew the more unreal became the affairs of other people, the easier it was to reduce the concerns of all living things outside herself to a common level of triviality and unimportance.

As she dozed her over-clothed, flaccid body dropped into new and more indolent shapes, as if the cold Cornish sea had washed away some of its familiar contours, as if someone had shaken the yeast cake when it was rising. Her pinze-nez sat slightly awry, the lines of her mouth drew themselves out like slackening purse strings. When she awoke the facts would have adjusted themselves more closely to her liking. Until then she would sleep.

In the last few days the rude world had broken into her privacy, upon her complacent day-dream. Doors had been shattered, but her patient, persistent, third-rate mind was already building them up again. They should be built stronger than ever before.

At this moment she lacked Perry, who had never imprisoned himself within such lofty seclusion and had therefore a more ready appreciation of the dangers of the outside world; she lacked Perry to insist that no repairs her egoism could effect were strong enough to stand before the impact of what was to come.

The machinery of the law, however trumpery it may be to anyone concerned, as Madge was concerned, with the higher values of her own life, has an unwelcome appearance of reality while it is in motion – as Perry had never failed to appreciate – and deeper resources even than egoism are needed to reject the impression made by steel about a wrist or rope upon a throat.

Pat woke. She had been sleeping for some time, her head in the crook of his arm. She was not cold for the room was not cold, and he had drawn his overcoat across her. The lamp had almost gone out. A small, dying yellow bead of light barely lifted the heavy darkness away from them.

She was not aware of having accepted this position but had not been forced into taking it. Somehow they both felt the need of companionship, and for tonight at least she could not bear to be left alone. She didn't want to go to bed or in fact to move until daylight came. Daylight would bring its own tests and problems but would, by driving away the darkness, help her to meet them. She felt lonely and sick and afraid and yet temporarily at rest, as if in this one corner of an alien and ugly world lay safety and peace. She was afraid to move lest she should break the thin shell of their isolation. Above all else she felt sick as if everything she had eaten in her life, everything and everyone she had known, had suddenly become unclean.

She raised her eyelids to get a glimpse of him without moving her head. He was dozing, his head inclining to one shoulder. Whatever else, he represented stability and cleanness in a tainted world.

He had said more, avowed more tonight than he had ever done before – except perhaps in his letter. She liked him in this eager mood when he carried conviction without eloquence. That was how they had married. Their marriage had been a mistake, but it did not appear so big a mistake tonight as it had recently done. She wished he was never dry and reserved and hesitant and inclined to look on the legal title to a thing as the be-all and end-all of possession, upon flesh and blood as inferior to pen and ink and a revenue stamp.

Perhaps he had never thought that. But a habit of shyness

238

and reserve had been imposed on him all his life. She had to admit that he had shown very few signs of this side in his recent meetings with her.

It occurred to her for the first time that perhaps her judgment had been coloured by her father's prejudice against all lawyers, by his insistence that the one she had married ran true to his general estimate of them. The influence had been there without her realising it.

Tom stirred and woke, and she found herself looking into his eyes. She was suddenly in contact again with the personality she had been dispassionately considering. The change was drastic. Of all the prospects now open to her the one thing she could no longer do was consider him dispassionately. His eyes, his looks, brought back all the liking and disliking to its original personal equation. There was no avoiding it.

He said: 'I've been dreaming I was on trial again for assault and battery. You came and testified for me.'

She lowered her eyes. 'What time is it?'

'Not late. There are still voices in the bar. Do you want to move?'

It was a question she would have preferred not to answer. Presently she said, 'No.' Bluntly and honestly.

The monosyllable sent the blood coursing through his veins. In self-defence he took the admission at its lowest value to himself. During the last hour all his hopes had been given up.

'What'll happen to her, Tom?' she asked.

'Who?'

'. . . Madge.'

'A clever Q.C. may get her off, but I don't think so. If the – the second analysis confirms the first then there won't be any escape.'

'Perry didn't come back to England until after mother had died,' she said almost inaudibly.

'No. Whatever his part, he came late to the scene. I don't think he was more than an accessory to her.'

'I wish these next weeks were over. I wish . . .'

239

'They'll pass, my dear. It's a question of keeping up until then.'

Silence fell.

'Dear God,' she said suddenly, a twitch of horror going through her. 'My mother . . . It – it doesn't bear thinking of.'

'It's a nightmare,' he said. 'Look on it as that. There'll be an awakening.'

'Yes, but always, always it will have happened.'

He did not reply to that, for he did not know what to say.

Time had passed in the old inn. Almost everyone had retired for the night. The bar at last was empty, except for the smell of stale beer and the tobacco fumes curling like fog about the low ceiling. Mrs Nichols, dozing off to sleep beside Mr Nichols, was aware that she had intended going up to see if the young lady wanted anything, but she had been busy at the last preparing the other two attic rooms for the two men who had come in very late and who her husband said must be accommodated. When she finished that it was so late that she had hesitated to go up and disturb her. Perhaps she was still with the boy. A pity there had not been anything better than an attic room to offer her. It was seven years since they had had such a full house in December, when the *Madrid* ran aground by High Cliff.

In his attic bedroom the detective who had travelled with Tom Harris lit his pipe and wondered what had become of the young solicitor. He had already been to his bedroom, but there was no response. Presently, when he was sure that the house was quiet, he would take a stroll round. It was not his business to sleep tonight.

In the parlour little had changed. The lamp had gone out and the lace curtains let in a glimmer of starlight.

She slept again, fitfully, uneasily, but he was awake. He didn't want to sleep during this time. Her piled chestnut hair had come loose and was straying across

240

his coat. Her breathing was quiet but not quite regular.

His mind wandered lightly, irrelevantly, over his past life, coming back to its present surroundings with a twinge of pleasure and sorrow. He knew that over Falmouth estuary the water would be whitening under the stars. The trees about Penryn, quieter now after all the wind and rain, would stand in groups upon their lonely hills and whisper of man's mortality. Human life was a stirring, a thin fermenting between the breasts of the world, a reaching for the light and a gathering of the dusk. A shifting and temporary interlocking of relationships between light and dark. The worst heartache and the brightest happiness would soon be still. They loomed large as mountains, like clouds they were as large as mountains but dispersed like smoke.

He thought of his schooldays and his mother, and Anthony lying sleeping in another room, and Patricia marrying him, proud and defiant, yet warm and lovable; sweet and kind and forgiving but hasty-tempered and undisciplined and rashly impulsive. Cold and warmth; they were here in his arms now. Anger and love. Waywardness and obedience. Incalculable but loyal. Would he have her any different? Not if he could have her at all. Birth and death, daylight and sunset: they were the impersonal things. Now, now was reality, the few hours in between of youth and understanding.

He thought of his profession and his future. South Africa drew him, accompanied or alone. There, among the great mountains and rivers and forests, small humans were quarrelling as if the world were theirs and theirs not the most temporary lease. He thought of the shipwreck and the baleful wind still moaning from time to time round the inn. He thought of Anthony and *his* future. They owed him much more than a casual thought . . . Affection and a return of loyalty for loyalty.

'Tom,' she said.

He hadn't realised she was awake again. He stared at

her in the darkness, knowing his expression couldn't be seen.

She said: 'Why do you want me to come back to you?'

Trying to keep the feeling out of his voice he said: 'I've already told you why.'

'For you it means giving up so much,' she said indistinctly. 'Your place is here, in Penryn, working in your own firm, doing the work you were meant to do. Why give all that up? You're known in Cornwall, known and respected. It means starting somewhere quite new –'

'I'm going to Cape Town in any case,' he said.

'There's your mother. Why spoil her life? Why should I come between you?'

'You haven't. We're on perfectly good terms and I think you could be. She's become reconciled to the idea of my going abroad in any event.'

She stirred restlessly, but didn't try to move away.

'I'm – I'm not your type, Tom. Honestly. I don't fit in. I felt that always before. Why should it –?'

'One doesn't have to fit in in a new society.'

'I don't even fit in with you. I'm – not worth your career. I'm restless, capricious, changeable . . .'

'I want you as you are. Life can be too safe, too easy. You've made me see that. We're different, but we can each help the other. It's just a question of taking the chance.' He said no more, hardly able to believe that so much progress had been made, afraid to spoil it by a wrong emphasis, the ill-chosen word.

Silence fell in the room. In South Africa the strange stars had moved on two hours ahead in their flight towards a new dawn.

Then he said: 'There's bitter feeling between the British and the Boers. No one can tell how it will turn. That's another chance.'

She did not reply.

'All this unpleasantness that's coming,' he said, 'will pass quickly enough. It's the further future that counts. If we back it for all we're worth it won't let us down.'

'Give me two or three days more,' she said. 'Will you? Then I'll decide.'

He said quickly: 'As long as you like.'

'No. Not as long as I like. Two days more. You see – you see, Tom, I'd like to put a term on it. We got married in such a hurry, on the impulse of the moment almost. Then I left you in the same way. When I married you I thought it was for good. I truly meant it to be. Then when I left you I meant that to be for good as well. Now if I come back to you I want that to be all quite changed. I don't want to come back on impulse like a – a beastly shuttlecock. I want it to be entirely deliberate. And if I *do* come back – it's really going to be for good this time.'

He put his hand on her hair for a moment and thought she did not notice.

'For better or worse,' he said.

'For richer, for poorer, in sickness and in health. Easy to promise and hard to fulfil. I – I've always felt ashamed of leaving the way I did, for the reasons I did. They seemed good enough at the time, Tom. But sometimes I was desperately ashamed. Somehow, it was because I hated myself so much that I tried to hate you. But – I didn't seem to be able to help it. All sorts of things came up, confused the issue. I – I've tried so hard to hate you. Remember that.'

'So long as you failed.'

'I failed.'

There was silence in the room.

'Nothing else matters,' he said. 'Nothing. Nothing. Sleep now.'

Her head settled more comfortably upon him. Her breath for a time continued to have a catch in it that would not quite settle down.

He listened to it and wondered if she could hear the beating of his heart.

★   ★   ★

243

In another room Anthony slept. About him the human comedy had played itself out, swinging him with it from time to time as it gyrated. For the most part he had been uncomprehending, either as spectator or participant. The larger issues had passed him by, happening just beyond his purview, casting shadows upon his life but leaving him out of sight of the main procession.

Lonely and forlorn, he had come to the house of Joe Veal at the crucial moment of its decay. Like a sick plant the outer petals of the family had one by one peeled off, at length revealing the worm in its heart. Now the ruin and disintegration was complete. Torn between conflicting loyalties, having no mature standards by which to judge, he had contrived to steer a middle course of which no adult need have been ashamed. Much that was unpleasant had happened to him and more was yet to follow.

But at present, worn out by sea-sickness and nervous strain, he had forgotten what had happened and was ignorant of what was to come.

He did not know how Pat had contrived to be here so soon. He did not know how the cabin door had come to be locked, nor exactly how, when he should have been drowned, he had yet come to be saved. He did not know that the polite gentleman who had questioned him at Tom Harris's would come to see him again in the morning and take down a statement which he would later be required to confirm before a stern old judge in a court of law. He did not know that his young personality and companionship were yet to prove the final cement which would bind together during the next two difficult years the young couple who, after an initial breakdown, had just resolved to begin again.

Nor did he know that his father was married again, to a widow with two young children, and that they could see no place for him in their household. Nor did he know that he would never see Canada, but would travel to South Africa instead.

Being a normal boy and not a seer, he knew none of these things, and for the present did not care. He had been cold and frightened and sick, and now was warm and safe and comfortable.

Anthony slept.

Marnie

1

"Good night, miss," said the policeman as I came down the steps, and "good night," I answered, wondering if he would sound as friendly if he'd known what was in this attaché case.

But he didn't, and I took a taxi home. Throwing money away, because you could do it easily by bus, but this was a special day and you had to splash sometimes. I paid the taxi off at the end of the street and walked down to my two-roomed flat and let myself in. People might think it lonely living on my own nearly all the time, but I never found it lonely. I always had plenty to think about, and anyway maybe I'm not so good on people.

When I got in I took off my coat and shook out my hair and combed it in front of the mirror; then I poured out a half and half of gin and french as another part of the celebration. While I drank it I went over a few train times and emptied a couple of small drawers. Then I took a bath, my second that day. Somehow it always helped to wash something out of your system.

While I was still in it the telephone rang. I let it go on for a bit and then climbed out of the warm water and draped a towel round myself and padded into the living-room.

"Marion?"

"Yes?"

"This is Ronnie."

I might have guessed it. "Oh, hello."

"Do I detect a lack of enthusiasm in the voice?"

"Well, it's a bit inconvenient, dear. I was just in my bath."

"What a delicious thought. How I regret this isn't television!"

Well, I mean, I might have expected that from Ronnie.

"Are you still set on going away on your own tomorrow?" he asked.

"But, Ronnie, I've said so at least six times."

"You're a queer girl. Are you meeting another man?"

"No, of course not. I've told you. I'm spending the week-end with this school-friend in Swindon."

"Then let me drive you down."

"Ronnie, dear, can't you understand? We don't want a man. We just want to natter together about old times. I don't get much opportunity to see her."

"They work you too hard at that office. I'll come and see old Pringle one of these days. But seriously . . ."

My thumb-nail had got caught on the office door and the varnish had chipped. Needed touching up.

"Seriously what?"

"Won't you give me your phone number?"

"I don't think she has one. But I'll try and ring you."

"Promise. Tomorrow evening."

"I can't *promise*. I'm not sure where the nearest box is. But I'll really promise to try."

"What time? About nine?"

"Ronnie, I'm beginning to shiver. And there's a horrid stain on the carpet all round my feet."

Even then he clung on like a cadger at a fair, taking as long as he could to say good-bye. When I could get the phone back I was nearly dry and the water had gone cold, so I dusted myself with talc and began to dress.

Everything I put on was new: brassiere, panties, shoes, nylons, frock. It wasn't just taking care; it was the way I'd come to like it. I suppose I have a funny mind or something, but everything has to be just as it should be; and I like it to be that way with people too. That was why the tie-up with Ronnie Oliver was something I'd be glad to be out of. Human beings . . . well, they just won't be ticked off, docketed, that's what's wrong with them; they spill over and spoil your plans—not because you are out in your estimates but because they are. Ronnie, of course, thought he was in love with me. Big passion. We'd only met a dozen times because I'd kept on putting him off, saying I'd other dates etc. Anyway it was the old old story.

My cast-offs were in my case, which would only just shut. You always seem to hoard up stuff even in a few months.

I went round the flat. I started in the kitchenette and went over it inch by inch. The only thing I saw in it was a cheap tea towel I'd bought just after Christmas, but I grabbed that and packed it with the rest. Then I went through the bathroom and lastly the bed-sitting-room.

I always reminded myself of the coat I'd left behind in Newcastle last year. Remembering that kept me on the alert; your eyes get to see something as part of the background and then you've left something behind and that's too bad because you can't come back for it.

I took down the calendar and packed that. Then I put on my coat and hat, picked up the suitcase and the attaché case and let myself out.

They were glad to see me at the Old Crown at Cirencester. "Why, Miss Elmer, it's three months since you were here last, isn't it? Are you going to stay long this time? Yes, you can have your usual room. It's not been good hunting weather this month; but of course you don't hunt, do you; I'll have your cases sent up directly. Would you like some tea?"

I always grew an inch staying at the Old Crown. Often enough I got by as a lady nowadays—funny how easy it was—; but this was nearly the only place where I could believe it myself. The chintzy bedroom looking on the court-yard, with this four-poster bed and the same servants, they never changed, they were part of the furniture, and every day out to Garrod's Farm to pick up Forio and ride for hours on end, stopping at some little pub for lunch and coming home in the failing light. It was life; and this time instead of staying two weeks I stayed four.

I didn't read the papers. Sometimes I thought of Crombie & Strutt, but in an idle sort of way as if working for them was something that had been done by another person. That always helped. Now and then I wondered how Mr. Pringle would take it and if Ronnie Oliver was still waiting for his telephone call, but I didn't lose any sleep over it.

At the end of four weeks I went home for a couple of

251

days, but said it was a flying visit and left on the Saturday. I dropped most of my personal things at the Old Crown and spent the night at Bath at the Fernley, signing in as Enid Thompson, last address the Grand Hotel, Swansea. In the morning I bought a new suitcase, a new spring outfit; then I had my hair tinted at one of the stores. When I came out I bought a pair of plain-glass spectacles, but I didn't put them on yet. When I got to the station that afternoon I took out of the left-luggage office the attaché case I'd left there nearly five weeks ago, and there was room for it inside the new suitcase I'd bought that morning. I bought a second-class ticket for Manchester—which seemed as good a place as anywhere, as I had never lived there—and a *Times*, which I thought might help me in picking out a new name.

Names are important. They have to be neither too ordinary nor too queer, just a name, like a face, that'll go along with the crowd. And I'd found from experience that the Christian name had to be like my own, which is Margaret—or usually Marnie—because otherwise I might not answer to it when called, and that can be awkward.

In the end I choose Mollie Jeffrey.

So at the end of March a Miss Jeffrey took rooms in Wilbraham Road and began to look for a job. I suppose you'd have seen her as a quiet girl, quietly dressed, with fair hair cut short round the head and horn-tipped spectacles. She wore frocks that were a bit too big for her and a bit too long. It was the best way she knew of looking slightly dowdy and of making her figure not noticed—because if she dressed properly men looked at her.

She got a job as usherette at the Gaumont Cinema in Oxford Street, and kept it until June. She was friendly enough with the other usherettes, but when they asked her to go places with them she made excuses. She looked after her invalid mother, she said. I expect they said to each other: poor object, she's one of those, and what a pity; you're only young once.

If they only knew it, I couldn't have agreed with them more. We only had different ideas what to do about it. Their idea was fooling around with long-faced pimply men, ice skating or jiving on their days off, two weeks at Blackpool or Rhyl, queueing for the Sales, Pop discs, and maybe hooking a man at the end of it, some clerk in an export office, then babies in a council house and pushing a pram with the other wives among the red-brick shops. Well, all right, I'm not saying they shouldn't, if that's what they want. Only I never did want that.

One day I tried for a job at the Roxy Cinema, close by the Gaumont, where they wanted an assistant in the box office. The manager of the Gaumont gave me a good reference and I got the job.

When I'd been there three months the staff arrangements worked out that I was due for a week's holiday, so for the first day or two I went home.

My mother lived in Lime Avenue, Torquay. It's one of a row of Victorian houses behind Belgrave Road, and it's easy for the shops and the sea front and the Pavilion. We had moved there from Plymouth about two and a half years ago, and we'd been lucky to get a house unfurnished. My mother was a cripple, or at least she got about fairly well but she'd had something wrong with one leg for about sixteen years. She always said she was the widow of a naval officer who was killed in the war, but in fact Dad hadn't ever got further than Leading Seaman when he was torpedoed. She also said she was a clergyman's daughter, and that wasn't true either, but I think Grandfather was a Lay Preacher, which is much the same thing, only you don't lose your amateur status.

Mother was fifty-six at this time, and living with her was a woman called Lucy Nye, a small, moth-eaten, untidy, dog-eared, superstitious, kindly creature with one eye bigger than the other. One thing I'll always say for Mother, you never saw her anything but carefully and properly got up. She always had a sense of what was right and proper and she lived for it. When I got in that day she was sitting in the front window watching, and as soon as I rapped on the door she was there stick and all.

She was an odd person—she really was—I got to realise it more as I grew older—and even though she kissed me and even though I knew I was the apple of her eye—God help me—I could still tell there was a sort of *reserve* in the welcome. She didn't let up, and even while she kissed you she kept you just that bit at a distance. You knew she'd been waiting at that window for hours to see you come down the street, but you wouldn't be popular if you let on.

She was a thin woman; I always remember her as extremely thin. Not like me because although I'm quite slight I'm well covered. I don't think she'd been like that even at twenty-two. She had a really good bone structure, like old pictures of Marlene Dietrich, but she'd never had enough flesh to cover it, and as she got older she got haggard.

That was the hard thing of living away from home. I should never have thought of her as haggard, not that word, if I'd stayed with her; it was going away and coming back that forced you to see things with new eyes. She was in a new black tailormade today.

"Bobby's, seven guineas," she said, as soon as she saw me looking. "I took it off the peg, one advantage of keeping your figure, isn't it? They know me there now. Hard to please, they say, but not hard to fit. Well, Marnie, you're looking a bit peeky, not like you should after being abroad. I hope Mr. Pemberton hasn't been working you too hard."

Mr. Pemberton was my fiction man. I'd made him up three years ago, the year after I left home, and he'd worked like a charm ever since. He was a wealthy business executive who took trips abroad and took his secretary along; it explained me being away and not always able to leave an address; it explained me being flush when I came home. Sometimes I had nightmares that Mother would find out; because there'd be Hell to pay if she ever did.

"And I don't like your hair that colour," she said. "Blonde hair looks as if you're trying to attract the men."

"Well, I'm not."

"No, dear, you're sensible that way. I always said you'd got an old head on young shoulders. I always say so to Lucy."

"How is Lucy?"

"I sent her for some scones. I know how you like scones

for tea. But she's gettin' slower and slower. It tries me beyond human patience sometimes, what with this leg and seeing her *creep* about."

We were in the kitchen by this time. It never changed in here; honestly it didn't; not any of the house really; it always struck me coming home like this; you moved homes and you stayed the same; *everything* moved with us; from Keyham, I suppose, to the bungalow at Sangerford, then back to Plymouth, and now here. The same cups and saucers even, laid out for tea on the plastic tablecloth, the framed colour print of "The Light of the World", the rocking chair with the padded arms, the awful fretwork pipe-rack, the Welsh dresser with the woodworm, that clock. I don't know why I hated the thing. It was oblong, coffin-shaped with a glass front, and the lower half covering the weights and pendulum was painted with pink and green love-birds.

"Cold, dear?" Mother said. "There's a fire laid in the front, but it's a close day and I didn't put a match to it. Of course, this side of the street don't get the sun in the afternoon."

I made tea while she sat there eyeing me up and down like a mother cat licking over its kitten. I'd bought presents for both of them, a fur for Ma and gloves for Lucy, but Mother always had to be got into the right mood first, she had to be talked round so that in the end it was as if she was doing you a favour by taking it. The only risk was getting her suspicious that you had too much money. She went word for word by the framed texts in her bedroom, and God help you if you didn't keep in step too. Yet I loved and thought more of her than anything else in the world because of her guts in the struggle she'd had and the way above everything else she'd kept up *appearances*. Appearances for her were the Holy Bible. I still remembered the terrible rows she gave me when I was ten and had been caught stealing; and I still admired her for acting like she did even though I hadn't enjoyed it at the time and even though I hadn't reformed the way she thought I had—only got smarter so she didn't find out.

She said suddenly, "That's French silk isn't it, Marnie? It must have cost you a pretty bit of money."

"Twelve guineas," I said, when it was thirty. "I got it in a sale. D'you like it?"

She didn't answer but put her stick down and fidgeted round in her chair. I could feel her eyes boring my back.

"Mr. Pemberton all right?" she asked.

"Yes, fine."

"He must be a man to work for. I often tell my friends, I say Marnie's private secretary to a millionaire and he treats her like his daughter. That's right, isn't it?"

I put the cosy on the tea and the caddy back on the mantelpiece. "He hasn't got a daughter. He's generous, if that's what you mean."

"But he's got a wife, hasn't he? I doubt she sees as much of him as you do, eh?"

I said: "We've gone into this before, Mam. There's nothing wrong between us. I'm his secretary, that's all. We don't travel *alone*. I'm quite safe, don't you worry."

"Well, I often think of my daughter knocking about the world the way you do. I worry about you sometimes. Men try to catch you unawares. You've got to be on the lookout, always."

Just then Lucy Nye came in. She squeaked like a bat when she saw me and we kissed, and then I had to go about the business of giving them their presents. By the time this was over the tea was cold and Lucy stirred herself making some more. I knew of course what Mother meant about her; she moved round the scullery emptying the teapot like an engineer in a go-slow strike.

Mother stood in front of the mirror, fidgeting with her new fur. "Do you like it under the chin or loose over the shoulders? Over the shoulders is more the thing, I shouldn't wonder. Marnie, you spend your money."

"That's what it's for, isn't it?"

"Spent proper, spent right, yes. But saved too. You've got to think of that. The Bible says love of money is the root of all evil; I've told you so before."

'Yes, Mam. And it says that money answereth all things."

She looked at me sharply. "Don't scoff, Marnie. I shouldn't want a daughter of mine to scoff at sacred words."

"No, Mam, I'm not scoffing. Look." I moved across

256

and pulled the fur down at the back. "That's the way I've seen them worn in Birmingham. It suits you that way."

After a bit we all sat down to tea again.

"I had a letter from your Uncle Stephen last week. He's in Hong Kong. Some port job he's got, and with a good screw. *I* wouldn't like it among all those yellow people, but he was always one for something different. I'll find his letter for you later on. He sent his love."

Uncle Stephen was Mother's brother. He was the one man I really cared about; and I never saw enough of him.

Mother said: "What with my fur and one thing and another. Your father never give me anything so good."

She did an act with a bit of scone, picking it up in her thumb and first finger as if it was breakable and putting it in her mouth and chewing as if she was afraid to bite. Then I noticed the knuckles of her hands were swollen, so I felt cheap for being critical.

"How's your rheumatism?"

"Not good. It's damp this side of the avenue, Marnie; we never get a gleam of sunshine after twelve; we never thought of that when we took it. Sometimes I feel we ought to move."

"It would be a job to find anything as cheap."

"Yes, well it depends, doesn't it. It depends what you like to see your mother in. There's a lovely little semi in Cuthbert Avenue, just down the hill from here. It's coming empty because the man who lived there has just died of pernicious anaemia. They say he was like paper before he went; he made no blood at all, and his spleen swelled up. It's two reception and a kitchen, three bed and one attic and the usual offices. It would just suit us, wouldn't it, Lucy?"

This bigger eye of Lucy Nye's looked at me over the top of her steaming cup but she didn't say anything.

"What's the rent? Is it to rent?" I asked.

"I b'lieve so, though we could inquire. Of course it would be more than this, but it gets all the sun, and it's the neighbourhood. This has gone down since we came. You remember Keyham, how it went down. But you won't remember. Lucy remembers, don't you Lucy?"

"I 'ad a dream last night," Lucy Nye said. "I dreamed Marnie was in trouble."

It's queer. Being out and about in the world, especially the way I'd lived, was enough to knock the corners off you, to make you grown up. Yet the tone of Lucy's voice gave me a twinge just like I used to have when I used to sleep with her when I was twelve and she'd wake me up in the morning and say, "I've 'ad a bad dream." And something always seemed to happen that day or the next.

"What d'you mean, trouble?" Mother said sharply. She had stopped with a piece of scone half-way to her mouth.

"I don't know; I didn't get that far. But I dreamed she came in that door with her coat all torn and she was crying."

"Probably fell down playing hop-scotch," I said.

"You and your silly dreams," Mother said. "As if you didn't ought to know better by your age. Sixty-six next birthday and you talk like a baby. 'I had a dream last night!' Who wants to hear about your old woman's fancies!"

Lucy's lip quivered. She was always touchy about her age and to say it out loud was like treading on a corn.

"I only just said I'd 'ad a *dream*. You can't help what you see in your sleep. And it isn't always so silly. Remember I dreamt that last time before Frank came home——"

"Hold your tongue," said Mother. "This is a Christian household and——"

"Well," I said, "whatever else I came home for it wasn't to listen to you two rowing. Can I have another scone?"

The kitchen clock struck five. It was a funny note, loud and toneless, that I've never heard from any other clock, and the last note was always flat as if it was running down.

"But while we're talking of old times," I said, "why don't you throw that thing out?"

"What thing, dear?"

"That perishing clock," I said, "it gives me the creeps every time I hear it."

"But why, Marnie, why? It was a wedding present to your grannie. It's got the date on the bottom, 1898. She was real proud of it."

258

"Well, I'm not," I said. "Give it away. I'll buy you another. Then maybe Lucy'll stop dreaming."

The other girl in the box office of the Roxy Cinema was called Anne Wilson. She was about thirty, tall and skinny, and she was writing a play, hoping I suppose to be another Shelagh Delaney. We worked overlapping shifts so that there were always two of us in the box office in the busy hours—except Sunday, that was. Only one could take the money but the one not serving helped behind the scenes.

The box office was a glass and chromium kiosk in the centre of the marble foyer. The manager's office was to the left just past the entrance to one of the tunnels leading to the stalls. It was just out of sight of the box office but Mr. King, the manager, prowled about between his office and the box office during the busy hours. He kept his eye on the staff; usually he would go up to the projection-room at least twice in every performance, and he was always at the doors to say good night to his patrons at the end of the show. Three times every day, at four and at eight and at nine-thirty, he would come to the kiosk, see we were all right for change and take away the money that had come in.

Every morning at ten he came to the cinema, unlocked his Chubb safe and carried last night's takings in a shabby attaché case two doors down the street to the Midland Bank.

Sometimes, of course, in spite of his care we would run short of change at the wrong moment, and then one of us would go across to his office for more. This happened in October soon after I got back, because the syndicate made a change in the price of seats and we found we needed a lot more coppers. One day Mr. King was at a meeting and we ran short of change.

"Hang on," said Anne Wilson, "I'll go and get some."

"You'll have to go upstairs," I said. "Mr. King's in the café with the two directors."

"I don't need to bother him," Anne said. "He keeps a spare key in the top drawer of the filing cabinet."

Christmas came on. I wrote home and said I couldn't get home because Mr. Pemberton would need me all through the holiday. In the second week of December we had the record-breaking *Santa Clara* booked and we were following the new fashion and running it for three weeks. It was my day on on the second Sunday.

On the Friday I told my landlady I was going to see my mother in Southport. On the Saturday after I got home from the Roxy I began my usual turn-out, and while I was doing this a strange thing happened. I was using an old newspaper as an inner wrapping and came across a paragraph about a girl I'd pretty nearly forgotten.

It was an old *Daily Express*, dated as far back as February 21st. "Police in Birmingham are looking for pretty, mysterious Marion Holland who vanished without trace from her work and from her flat last Monday evening. They are also looking for one thousand one hundred pounds in cash which vanished at the same time from the safe of Messsrs Crombie & Strutt, Turf Accountants, of Corporation Street, where Marion was employed as confidential clerk. 'We didn't know much about her,' forty-two year old balding branch manager George Pringle, admitted yesterday, 'but she was a shy retiring girl and always most reliable. She came to us with a good character.' 'A very quiet one,' is landlady Dyson's view. 'Never had no friends but always polite and well spoken. Told me it was only her second job. I think she'd come down in the world.' 'It's like a nightmare to me,' confessed twenty-eight year old Ronnie Oliver of P.O. Telephones, who has been dating Marion. 'I can't help but feel there has been some terrible mistake.'

"The police are not so sure about the mistake. General description and type of job are similar to those of Peggy Nicholson who disappeared from a position as secretary to a Newcastle business man last year with over seven hundred pounds in cash. They would like to interview both ladies and would not be at all surprised if they turned out to be one. General description. Age twenty to twenty-six, height five feet five inches, weight about eight stone, vital statistics to fit and a 'taking' way with her. Susceptible personnel managers please note."

It shook me coming on it like that. It shook me because I hadn't ever seen details like that before. And living my life in sort of separate compartments the way I do, it jolted me seeing it just then. Of course there was nothing connecting Marion Holland of Birmingham with Molly Jeffrey of Manchester, still less with Margaret Elmer who kept a thoroughbred horse at Garrod's Farm near Ciren-cester and had a strict old mother in Torquay. But it was a coincidence. It was a hell of a jarring, nasty little coinci-dence.

The only thing I liked about it was the bit about having 'come down in the world'. It just showed what elocution lessons would do.

For a while after reading the paper I sat on the bed wondering if I should go through with it or if this was a warning that this time I was going to be caught.

In the end I got over that nonsense. Really, once you start thinking, you're done. But I thought I wouldn't try this sort of job again. It was riskier than most.

I left on Sunday at twelve and took my suitcase with me. I took it to London Road Station and put it in the left-luggage office as usual. I had lunch in a cafeteria and was at the Roxy by ten to four.

The doors opened at four and the first film began at four-fifteen. I went with Mr. King into his office and got twenty pounds in silver and five pounds in copper. He was in a good humour and said we'd had the best week's takings since 1956.

"Let me carry those for you," he said as I picked up the bags.

"No, really, thanks. I can manage." I smiled at him and straightened my spectacles. "Thank you, Mr. King."

He followed me out. A small shabby-looking lot of people were waiting at the door of the cinema. It was two minutes to four.

'I said: "Er—have I time to get a glass of water? I want to take an aspirin."

"Yes, of course. Hold them a minute, Martin." This to the commissionaire. "Nothing wrong, I hope?" he said when I got back.

"No, not really, thanks very much." I smiled bravely. "Go ahead. I'm fine now."

By seven the cheaper seats were full, and there was a queue outside for the two and eightpennies. A trickle of people were still coming in and paying four and six so as not to wait. In five minutes the secondary film would be over, sixty or seventy people would come out and a ten-minute break for ice-creams would give the queue outside time to get in and be settled before *Santa Clara* came on for the last time.

I never remember being nervous when it comes to the point. My hands are always steady, my pulse beats like one of those musical things they have for keeping time.

As the last of the stragglers leaving the theatre went out and Martin moved to let in the first of the queue I called quietly to Mr. King.

"What's the matter?" he said when he saw the look on my face.

"I'm—frightfully sorry. I feel awful! I think I'm going to be sick!"

'Oh, dear! Can you . . . Can I help you to——"

"No . . . I—I must see this queue through."

"Can you?" he said. "No, I see you can't."

"No . . . I'm afraid I can't. Can you—hold up the queue for a few minutes?"

"No, I'll take your place. Really. I'll call an usherette."

I grabbed up my handbag and stumbled out of the box. "I think if I lie down for about five minutes . . . You can manage?"

"Of course." He climbed into the box as the first members of the queue came up to the window.

I stumbled off down the right-hand tunnel away from the manager's office. You passed the man who tears your tickets, went down the corridor, and just this side of the doors into the cinema proper, was the Ladies.

But instead of turning in at the Ladies I went through into the cinema. A girl flashed a light at me and then saw who I was.

"Where's Gladys?" I whispered.

"On the other door."

As I went along the back of the cinema a big American face was telling the audience why the film he was appearing in at this cinema for seven days beginning next Sunday week was a unique event in motion picture history.

There was no Gladys at the other door because she was down flashing her light looking for vacant seats, so my excuse wasn't needed. I went out of the door and up the other tunnel until I was almost in the foyer again. Then I turned in at the manager's office.

The light was already on. I shut the door but didn't catch it. Then I pulled a chair forward and kicked off my shoes.

The filing cabinet, top drawer. The key wasn't in the back … I went all down the other five drawers. Nothing … The cabinet was high and I pulled a stool over and stood on it. The top drawer was full of publicity pamphlets, copies of *The Kine Weekly* etc. At the back was a pair of Mr. King's gloves. The key was in one thumb.

Almost two minutes gone. At the safe I slid back the key guard; the key clicked nicely; but it was a real effort to pull the big door open.

There was nothing but papers in the three top compartments, but in the drawer beside the bags of change were piles of stacked notes. Not only today's takings but Saturday's as well.

You can get a lot of money in a medium-sized handbag if it's empty to begin with. I shut the safe, locked it and put the key back. Then I slid my shoes on and went to the door. I could hear the movement of people and the click and rattle of the change machine.

I went out without looking back towards the foyer and turned into the cinema again. This time Gladys was back.

"Full house?" I asked before she could speak.

"There's about two dozen four-and-sixes and some singles, that's all. You off duty now?"

"No, I'm coming back in a minute." I went on down the side aisle.

"It's pretty tough leading the life I lead," said the man on the screen, and he seemed to look at me.

"I don't like it but I can take it," said the girl, "if I'm with you."

That stuff was as real as nothing. I got to the end of the cinema and let myself out by the exit door.

2

It was the year after all this that I wrote for the job at John Rutland & Co. at Barnet.

I don't know; maybe there's such a thing as fate, as luck. If you walk under a ladder or spill the salt or cut your nails on a Friday. Well, I had no feelings before I wrote. I might just as well have picked out some other advertisement or opened another paper.

I'd been working in London since January at a firm called Kendalls who were Insurance Brokers but I'd soon found that the only thing I'd get there was a reference, so I'd worked on just for that and kept my eyes open to see what else was about.

The letter that came back was headed "*John Rutland & Co. Ltd., Printers of Quality, established 1869*" and it said: "Dear Madam, Thank you for your letter replying to our advertisement for an assistant cashier. Would you kindly call to see us next Tuesday morning the 10th inst. at eleven o'clock. S. Ward (Manager)."

When I got there it was quite a big place, and after waiting in an outer office while another girl was interviewed I was shown into a small room with two men sitting behind a desk, and they asked me the usual things.

I said my name was Mary Taylor, and I'd been with Kendalls since January. I hadn't been employed before that. I'd married at twenty and had lived in Cardiff with my husband until he was killed in a motor accident in November last. Since then, although he'd left me a little money, I'd started to work for my living. After leaving school I had done shorthand and typing and also taken courses in book-keeping and accountancy. I was a shorthand typist at Kendalls but was looking for a job with more prospects.

I had a good look at the two men. The manager, Mr. Ward, was in his fifties, a sour dried-up man with gold-rimmed spectacles and a big wart on his cheek. He looked the sort who had worked his way up in forty years and God help anyone who tried to do it in thirty-nine. The other man was young, dark, with very thick hair that looked as if it needed a brush, and face so pale he might have been ill.

"Are you a Cardiff girl, Mrs. Taylor?" the manager asked.

"No. I come from the East Coast. But my husband worked in Cardiff as a draughtsman."

"Where did you go to school?"

"In Norwich, the High School there."

"Are your parents there now?" this young man said. He was twisting a pencil.

"No, sir. They emigrated to Australia after I was married."

Mr. Ward shifted in his seat and put his tongue between his teeth and his cheek. "Can you give us some other references apart from this one from Kendalls?"

"Well . . . no, not really. Of course, there's my bank in Cardiff. Lloyds Bank, Monmouth Street. I've been banking there since I went to live there."

"Do you live in London now?"

"Yes. I have furnished rooms in Swiss Cottage."

The young man said: "I take it you haven't any family of your own—I mean children?"

I looked at him and turned on a smile. "No, sir."

Mr. Ward grunted and began to ask me whether I understood P.A.Y.E. and insurances and whether I'd ever worked an Anson adding machine. I said I had, which was a lie, but I knew I could get any machine taped quickly enough. I noticed that once he called the young man Mr. Rutland, so I guessed he was one of the directors or something. I'd thought so from the minute I saw him, a younger son or something learning the business by starting at the top. I'd seen them before. But this one looked all right.

"Well, thank you, Mrs. Taylor," Mr. Ward said about five minutes later, and something about the way he said it, even though he said it as if it hurt, told me I was in. I mean, it was as if he'd had a hidden sign from the young man.

Later when I went there I looked through the back files and saw they had written to the bank in Cardiff. The bank had said: "We have known Mrs. Mary Taylor only for three years since she first began to bank with us, but her account with us has always been in a satisfactory condition. Our personal contacts have been few, but we have been favourably impressed by her dealings and her personality."

It isn't hard really to get a job these days. Very often you can build a background as you go along if you look far enough ahead. Some firms of course will ask for all sorts of references, and then you have to gracefully back out; but at least fifty per cent will be satisfied quite easily, and a few will even take you on sight, if you look respectable and honest.

Opening a bank account under a wrong name is a real pain in the neck. I'd managed this one as an experiment when I was working in Cardiff three years ago, in the name of Mary Taylor, but it had meant getting known under that name first, and I'd thought I wouldn't bother with another. P.O. Savings Accounts are easier, and they don't ask for any proof of who you are. I'd simply used this bank account to put money in from time to time, and once or twice I'd spoken to the Bank Manager about little things, and so I'd built up this background there. I hadn't used it as a reference before, because you can only do that sort of thing once, and they hadn't asked for it at Kendalls; but I gave it them here because I got the impression that this job might be worth sacrificing a background for.

The other minor problem is insurance cards, but that's not really too difficult to get around. I know a place in Plymouth where you can buy them; then all you do is fill in your name and a nice new National Insurance Number, and buy the stamps up to the date you want and stick them on and cancel them. Insurance cards run for twelve months, and of course nowadays they're 'staggered' so that they don't all have to be in at the same time. The important thing in starting a new job is to start with a nearly new insurance card—it saves you stamps and it gives you perhaps ten months before the card has to be surrendered. The important thing is never to stay in a job until the card has to be surrendered.

I find it all interesting. I like tinkering with figures, and lots of people are such fools with them. I've seen one or two clever boys in my life, and some of them were really clever, but once they've got the money they haven't a notion. They're like children playing in the sand: it just runs through their fingers. You've seen films like *Grisbi* and *Rififi*. Honestly it's just like that.

I started at Rutland's the following Monday week. Nearly as soon as I got there I had an interview with Mr. Christopher Holbrook, the managing director. He was a fattish man of about sixty, with big-business spectacles and a smile that he switched on and off like an electric fire.

"We're a *family* firm, Mrs. Taylor, and I'm pleased to welcome you into it. I am a grandson of the founder and my cousin, Mr. Newton-Smith is another grandson. My son, Mr. Terence Holbrook is a director, as is Mr. Mark Rutland whom you have already met. We have a staff now of ninety-seven and I don't hesitate to say that we do not work merely as individuals but as a *unit*, a family, everyone being concerned for the good of all."

He switched on the smile, which started slowly and warmed up nicely; then just when it began to get really good it switched off and you were left with his face going cold like a two-watt element, and his eyes watching you to see the result.

"We are *expanding*, Mrs. Taylor, and this year, as an experiment, we have opened a retail department which you will see if you look to your right through the window just across the street. This all means the engagement of new *staff*. For the moment, for a week or two, we want you to go over to the retail side, but ultimately we hope to have you here in the main building assisting Miss Clabon whom you have already met."

He picked up the house telephone. "Has Mr. Terence come yet? . . . No? Well, ask him to come in, will you, as soon as he arrives."

I said. "You want me as cashier on the retail side, sir?"

"Temporarily, yes. But if our present plans go forward we shall bring in an assistant for you who will take over when you are transferred here. Miss Clabon is engaged to be married, and she may leave us within a year or two. Have you been in printing before?"

"No, sir."

"I think you will find it interesting. We are high-class jobbing printers, as the saying is. We do all kinds of work from expensive illustrated catalogues to publicity posters for British Railways, from menu cards for City dinners to text-books for schools. Rutland playing cards and diaries, Rutland writing papers, are, I don't hesitate to say, known all over England. I think you will find, Mrs. Taylor, that ours is an *enterprising* firm and one that it will be rewarding to work for."

He paused there, waiting for somebody to say 'hear, hear', so I said, "Thank you, sir."

"Later on this morning I believe Mr. Ward will show you round or he will detail someone else to do so. I always believe that new members of my office staff should be given a general *over all* picture of the firm's activities at the earliest opportunity. I feel one can't afford merely to *employ* people, one must *interest* them."

He switched on his smile as he got up, so I got up too and was going to leave when there was a tap at the door and a young man came in.

"Oh, this is my son, Mr. Terence Holbrook. We have a new member of the staff, Terry, Mrs. Mary Taylor, who is coming to us this morning as assistant cashier."

This one shook hands with me. He looked older than the other young man—probably over thirty—and there was no likeness. He had fair hair, almost yellow and worn long, and a lower lip that stuck out, and beautiful clothes. His look took me in in four seconds flat.

"How d'you do. I hope you'll be very happy with us. You wanted to see me, Dad?"

Later I was shown round; but I didn't get much intake that first morning, except of noise and machinery and new faces and smells of paper and print. The building was on two floors, and the upper floor was where the office staff worked. I liked the look of the cashier's office, which was the last one before the stairs. It was divided off by a frosted-glass partition, and to reach it you had to pass through the next office where there was only the telephone switchboard, with one girl, and some filing cabinets. I mean, it could hardly have been better.

I've got the new-girl approach pretty well laid on by now, and I soon settled in. I thought Sam Ward the manager showed me the sarcastic side of his tongue sometimes, and Susan Clabon, the main girl cashier, took a bit of thawing; but as soon as I went over to the retail side and met Dawn Witherbie I had a friend for life who told me anything I wanted to know.

"Well, dear, it's like this. Mr. George Rutland, Mark's father, was managing director when I came, but when he died Christopher Holbrook became M.D. and Mark Rutland came into the firm. Rex Newton-Smith—that's the fourth director—he's just a passenger, turns up four times a year for directors' meetings. Lives with his mother, even though he's fifty odd. D'you like sugar? One or two?

"Of course Christopher Holbrook, he booms away in his office, but it's the two younger ones and Sam Ward who do most of the work. Terry Holbrook and Mark don't get on— you noticed that yet? Sticks out like a sore thumb. Damn, this spoon's hot!

"Mark's made such a difference since he came—he's turned the place upside down. It's his idea, this retail side, and it's been making money ever since it opened. You coming to the staff dance? It's not until May. We usually have a good time. Didn't get home till five last year. *You* ought to have a good time with your looks. They all turn up, directors and all. Mark didn't come last year because he'd just lost his wife; but absolutely everyone else. Terry's great fun; really lets his hair down. But watch out for him. He's mustard. He talks rather sissy but that means nothing. Phew, only half eleven; how the mornings drag."

"He lost his wife?"

"Who, Terry? No. He's married but they don't live together any more. It's Mark who lost his wife. A year last January. Kidneys or something odd. She was only twenty-six."

"Perhaps that's why he looks so pale."

"No, dear, that's natural. He looked just the same

269

before. It's funny how they don't get on, Mark and Terry. I often consider. Why do two men hate each other? Usually it's a woman. But I don't see how it can be in their case."

It did not worry me how they got on. I didn't expect to stay that long.

But it didn't pay to hurry. I opened an account at Lloyds Bank in Swiss Cottage and transferred to it the balance of my account in Cardiff. Then I told them to sell my few little investments and had the money paid into my Swiss Cottage account. Then I began to draw the money out in cash and pay it into my account under my own name at the National Provincial Bank in Swindon.

I didn't go down to see Mother during this time. She had an eye like a knitting needle, and sometimes being asked questions got on your nerves. It always surprised me she'd swallowed the Pemberton story so easily. Perhaps I'd cooked up so much about him that I almost believed in him myself. It's a great help with people like Mr. Pemberton, to believe in them yourself.

One day when I'd been with Rutlands seven weeks I was called into a sort of summit conference and there they all were: Mr. Ward, and the progress chaser, Mr. Farman, and the sales manager, Mr. Smitheram. Newton-Smith, the fourth director was there too, an enormous great man with a moustache and a thin squeaky voice as if he'd just swallowed his kid brother.

Old Mr. Holbrook did most of the talking, and as usual he made it sound like an election speech, but in the end I realised he was saying they were all pleased with the way I'd helped to rearrange the bookkeeping on the retail side, and now they wanted to ask my advice about re-organising the cash system of the works itself. I was flattered in a way and a bit caught out of step, because the one they should have really asked first was Susan Clabon; and after a minute I suddenly looked up and saw Mark Rutland watching me and knew he was behind this, behind me being invited in like this.

I asked questions and listened, and soon saw there were two opinions about it on the board. Then I gave mine as well as I could, though I sided more than I wanted to

270

with the stick-in-the-muds because on the whole the more machines you have the harder it is to cheat.

In spite of what Dawn Witherbie had said I was quite surprised at the polite nastiness there was under the skin at that board meeting. It seemed to be Mark Rutland against the Holbrooks and Sam Ward, with Rex Newton-Smith acting peace-maker and the other people trying to keep their feet dry.

Just as it was over the bell went for the dinner break and there was the clatter of feet on the stairs coming up to the canteen. I thought as I left I'd walk through the printing shop while it was all stopped. Almost right off Terry Holbrook caught me up.

"Congratulations, Mrs. Taylor."

"What on?"

"Do I need to say, my dear? Not to an intelligent girl like you."

I said: "You should have asked Susan Clabon to come in as well as me. It wasn't really fair to her."

"They did want to," he said. "But I wouldn't hear of it. I said you'd got better legs."

I looked at him quickly then, like you turn and look suddenly at someone who's leaned on you suggestively in a bus.

He said: "In twelve months you'll be chief cashier. Twelve months after that—who knows, my dear. You need sun blinkers to look steadily at your brilliant future with Rutland's."

We walked down between the litho machines. There were several girls and men still lingering. By now I knew most of them by sight and a few by name.

"Hullo, June," Terry said to one of the girls familiarly. "Ready for the dance next week?"

She was one of the girls who worked a folding machine, and the three-sided plywood partition round her high chair was stuck with pictures of Pat Boone and Cliff Richard and Tommy Steele and Elvis Presley.

"You a jive expert?" Terry Holbrook asked me, looking where I was looking.

"I've done it," I said. "But a long time ago."

"Blasé, that's what she is," he said to the girl. "Hullo, Tom. Back any winners on Saturday?"

"Yes, one," said a young man who was wiping some yellow dye off his thumb. "But it was Eagle Star at five to four on, so I didn't clear anythink by the end of the day."

Eagle Star, I thought, as I walked on. I've seen him. A big brown horse with a spot on his nose. He was at Manchester and ran in the November Handicap . . . The way the posters were printed got me. The ink was brilliant and the machines printed one colour at a time, building up the poster until it was complete . . .

"Interested?" Terry Holbrook caught up with me. "It's an Italian machine we bought a few years ago. An Aurelia. Does everything we want slightly better than any other, my dear."

He wasn't really thinking what he was saying: he was eyeing me. The place was nearly empty now. I thought this frock isn't dowdy enough.

"Why Italian?"

"Why not? It was the time of the credit squeeze over here, and the Italians offered us ten different variations of H.P. This next one's a German—pre-war. It'll have to be replaced soon. Mark—the directors are keen on a new idea that's just come out . . . these two are English. Aren't you bored?"

"What with?"

"Looking at machines."

"No, why?"

"It isn't girlish to be interested in machines."

I looked at him out of the corners of my eyes, and noticed for the first time that he'd got a rather bad birthmark on his neck. That was probably why he wore his hair long. He wasn't good looking anyway, with his jutting bottom lip. There was a sort of sly smiling wildness about him, though.

"We're the wrong way round," he said. "This is the typesetting room where all the work begins."

"It doesn't matter," I said. "Anyway I have to get my lunch."

"What do you think of the firm, my dear? I don't mean the work, I mean the people."

We were there by ourselves in this room, and the whole building seemed suddenly quiet. I had a feeling he was going to do something, put his hand on me or something: so I moved away, went over and stared at a Linotype machine.

"One big happy family," he said. "That's Dad's line, isn't it?"

"What I've seen of the people so far I like."

"The important thing is to choose your company. I wonder what sort of company you like, Mary."

That was making his sordid thoughts rather plain.

"Of course," I said, "it's only a few months since I lost my husband."

That held him. His look changed, but I couldn't make out what he was thinking. Then I caught sight again of the mark on his neck and for some reason or other I began to feel sorry for him. Feeling sorry for people is something I've been able to live without in my life. So far as I recollect no one has ever wept over me, so for me there's strictly no traffic either way.

But he was out of the run. I wondered if that mark had always pulled him down, if boys had jeered at him at school and teenage girls had sniggered, and maybe *he* had been let down and was on the wrong side of the fence too.

I went to the door of the composing room. I wondered if that was why he dressed the way he did: yellow waistcoat, chocolate-coloured trousers etc. I wondered what he was like inside and what he thought about me there in that comp room and what he would have said or done if I'd been the easy catch.

I wasn't the easy catch. I said: "I must go and get my bag, Mr. Holbrook."

Every day when the retail department closed, the money taken during the day was carried across the street to the main building and locked away for the night, because there was no proper safe in the shop. This money was never banked because every Friday twelve or thirteen hundred pounds was paid out in wages, and the takings from the retail side went towards this. Takings on the retail side varied a lot; sometimes there was hardly a hundred in cash taken in a week, sometimes four or five, it depended what particular customers we had and how they paid.

On Thursdays before the bank closed the wage cheque was taken to the bank by two men and enough money drawn out to make up—together with what had built up on the retail side—the total wages to be paid on Friday morning. Susan Clabon and another girl then worked making out the pay envelopes. When the change was made I should be one of the two paying out the wages.

The safe was in the cashier's office, but of course the girls didn't have keys. Mr. Ward kept one set and Mark Rutland another. The managing director, Christopher Holbrook, had a third.

One day Mark Rutland came on me in Mr. Holbrook's office sniffing at the roses on his desk. I'd just got round to the right side of the desk in time. I blushed and said I'd brought the cheques for Mr. Holbrook to sign and had got taken by the smell of the roses.

He said: "They're the first of the season. My father was a great rose grower. In fact he was more interested in that than in printing."

I licked my lips. "The only one I ever had was that pink rambler with the white centre. It used to climb all over the gate of our bungalow in—in Norwich. What's this one called?"

"It looks like Etoile de Holland." He put his sallow face down and sniffed it. "Yes. I think it's still the best of the crimsons . . . Have you ever been to the National Rose Show?"

"No."

"It's on next month. It's worth a visit if you're interested."

"Thank you. I'll look out for it."

As I got to the door he said: "Oh, Mrs. Taylor, we're having our annual dinner and dance next Friday. It's the usual thing for everyone to turn up, especially new people. But if you don't feel like it because of having lost your husband let me know, will you. Then I'll explain to my uncle."

"Thank you, Mr. Rutland," I said, butter hardly melting. "I'll let you know."

274

3

I suppose I wasn't the sort of child anyone would ever hold up as an example to others. Ever since I was seven or eight I've found myself sharper than most. If I got in a mess I always managed to slide out of it, and most times I avoided the mess. So by the time I was nineteen I thought pretty well of myself.

The twice I'd been caught stealing, when I was ten, was because the other girl had suddenly gone un-brave and confessed all. It was a lesson about working with other people that I never forgot. And the fearful row Mother kicked up when the police came, and then all that stuff with the probation officer, had taught me a lot too. I don't mean I was a hardened criminal in my teens, or anything like that, but when I did anything I watched out I wasn't caught. And I wasn't either.

The second time I got into trouble when I was ten my mother had beaten me with a stick, and I still have one mark on my thigh where she dug a bit deep. I was scared out of my life, I really was, because I'd never seen her in such a rage before. She kept shouting, "A thief for a daughter, that's what I've got, a thief for a daughter. Surely God have afflicted me enough without *this*." *This* being a real old *wham* on my behind. "What've you lacked, eh? What've you lacked? Fed, dressed, clean, respectable, that's how I've kept you, and now *this*!" Another *wham*. And so it went on. "Disgrace! D'you hear me, child? The meanest, disgracefullest, sacrilege blasphemy! Stealing from the house of God!"

She'd gone on like that for what seemed like about six hours, while every now and then old Lucy had put her head round the door saying: "Stop it, Edie, you'll kill the child!" "Stop it; Edie, you'll have a stroke. Stop it, Edie, give it a rest, you've done enough!"

I suppose, knowing her, I couldn't have done anything to tread on her corns so badly as break open the alms box in the chapel. And with the tears streaming down my face and bits of wet hair sticking to my cheeks, and my voice half plugged with pain—not remorse—I couldn't explain to her then, and never had got round to saying so afterwards, that I had really been doing it all for her.

Of course I wasn't hungry or down-at-heel; Mother saw to that; she went without things herself to do it. And that made it harder for me to take. Try being grateful when you're *expected* to be grateful; it mops you up. Lucy would even rate Mother sometimes. "All on your back it goes," she'd say. "Better in your belly, Edie. It don't do no good to be well dressed in your coffin." "When it's our time to die we'll die for sure," Mother would say. "But not before. God's will be done. Marnie, get on with your homework. And don't call it belly in this house!"

Breaking open those boxes had been the first shots in my own private war, as you might say.

There were all sorts of things at the root of it. When my Dad was killed in 1943 Mother was expecting her second baby. I was nearly six then, and first Mother got the shock of losing her husband, and then within a few weeks of that she was bombed out of her house in Keyham and we went to live in a tiny two-bedroomed bungalow in Sangerford, near Liskeard. I could just remember that.

When it came time for the baby to be born they sent for the doctor, but it was before National Health and he was busy with some more profitable cases, so Mother had the baby without anaesthetic and with only the district nurse to help. Something went wrong, the baby died, and ever afterwards Mother dragged her leg. There was a court case against the doctor, but nothing came of it and he got off scot free.

The year after that we went back to Plymouth, but the other end near the Barbican, and I went to school there till I was 14. When I left the headmistress wrote: 'Margaret is a girl of real ability and it is a great pity that she has to leave school so young. Had she been prepared to work I am certain she would have gone far and even achieved something special in Mathematics and Science. I am equally sure that her abilities are capable of misdirection, and in her last year she has given ample evidence of this. It is vitally important to her welfare that she should keep the right company. I wish her well in her future life and hope she will not fritter away her gifts.'

Well, I'd tried not to fritter away my gifts.

The annual dinner and dance of the firm was held at the Stag Hotel in the High Street. Mark Rutland's suggestion had let me out nicely, but at the last minute I decided I didn't want to be let out. You know how it is sometimes, you get the urge to see for yourself.

Everybody was there, all the printers and binders and setters and all their wives, and all the girls, with their husbands or boy friends. Old Mr. Holbrook had brought his wife. Mr. Newton-Smith was a bachelor, Mark Rutland a widower, and Terry Holbrook a divorcee.

Dawn Witherbie said: "It makes you think, girls."

When the dinner was over old Mr. Holbrook made a speech, giving a review of the year's work; but it was a hot night and the windows had had to be opened on to the High Street, which still carried a lot of traffic.

He said: "Ladies and Gentlemen. It gives me pleasure to rise for the fourth time at this our annual dinner and dance to propose to you . . ." Heavy lorry and four cars. ". . . on the whole a very satisfactory year. I won't hesitate to say that we suffered some uneasiness over the trading disputes of last June but happily . . ." Three motor bikes. ". . . so that we were not ultimately involved." He turned on his smile. "It is, as I have said before, a source of great comfort to me that we in this firm are something of a *family*. We are not so large . . ." Sports car overtaking two buses. ". . . also our order sheet gives rise to some satisfaction though naturally not to complacency. Compared with last year . . ." His smile died away as he compared this year with last year, but he switched it on again at the end to show that the figures pleased him. "During the year we have had three marriages in the firm. Will the happy couples please stand up and take their medicine." The happy couples stood up and were clapped. "Six of our staff have for one reason or another left us, but we have taken on fifteen new members. We say to them . . ." Several cars both ways. ". . . up, please, so that we can see just who they are."

The man next to me was squeezing my elbow. I moved it but he squeezed it again. "You're new, Mrs. Taylor. Stand up."

So I stood up, the last of the few, and smiled vaguely and somehow caught Mark Rutland's eye and then quickly sat down.

After dinner I stayed out for quite a while, but as soon as I came back Terry Holbrook asked me to dance.

He was good, so he made it easy. I hadn't danced much these last few years but that wasn't because I didn't enjoy it. It was because I hadn't had time, and because going to a dance with a boy usually leads to necking. But I often dreamed of having lots of money and lovely clothes and a diamond necklace and going to a Ball where everything would be beautiful and gracious and softly lit and full of colour and music. One of the romantics, me.

Terry Holbrook said: "Has anybody told you before what a pretty girl you are?"

"I don't remember."

"Oh, modesty, my dear! Anyway, let's be impersonal and say that's a ravishing frock."

I'd bought it yesterday, falling for it because it was expensively simple and thinking people here wouldn't realise. But this man knew all about women's clothes . . .

He did a few odd steps, and I thought last time, last time . . . It was in a dive called 'Sheba'; I'd gone in with a girl called Veronica; I couldn't remember her surname; she'd let herself go good and proper, shoes off, hair flying; I never could quite, something short; I'd stand back and look at myself and think, it's crazy to get that way over a dance. That fellow in the shirt striped like a wasp had come over; blue jeans so tight they creased the wrong way, Brando hair cut; hands were clammy and he smelt of sweat . . .

"You dance like a dream, Mary."

"Thank you."

"But a slightly dead-pan dream. Do tell me what you're thinking."

"What a nice family party this is."

"Please! How tactless!"

"Why? Isn't it?"

He looked me over, eyes drooping. "Can you do Latin American?"

"Some."

"Did you know Jive and Rock 'n' Roll were Latin American in origin?"

"No."

"It's all essentially the same style of dance. The man is only the central figure; all the real action is done by the woman. Don't you think that's as it should be?"

Again that feeling he was poking sly fun at me. His face would flare up at the corners of his mouth and eyes when he spoke.

Later we danced again, but half-way through the band started introducing stunt novelties that sent him into a temper.

I said: "Well, if you don't like it, let's sit down."

"My dear, you can if you like but I'm a director, I have to look as if I *enjoy* it."

"Does Mr. Rutland never dance?"

"Why don't you ask him, if you're interested."

"I'm not specially, but you spoke as if the directors *have* to join in."

"He doesn't, my dear, that's why he's unpopular."

"*Is* he unpopular?"

"Ask your friends."

"Hasn't he joined in any of the other dances before?"

"My dear, this is the first annual dinner he's ever condescended to attend since he condescended to join the firm."

We didn't seem to be getting on very well, so for the next hour or so I wasn't surprised that he didn't ask me to dance. Not that I was short of partners. But about one, when a good bit of the top table was making a move, he came across and said:

"It's getting a fearful drag now. I'm asking a few people

279

over to my place to finish off the evening. Care to come?"

"To dance?"

"No. For a few drinks and a chat and a gramophone. Quite *unambitious*."

This was the time to slide out. I'd kept free of everything personal in Manchester, and it always paid off. But you don't always do the clever thing. I said: "Thanks, I'd like to."

"Divine. We'll meet at the door in about ten minutes. I think the MacDonalds will have room for you in their little car."

Well, he only lived about ten minutes away. The Mac-Donalds were two of the firm's guests and were both as tall as cranes—the steam sort—but nice enough in their smart way. They were London smart, which means a bit phoney, but not as phoney as provincial smart. She was a blonde with that sort of urchin cut that makes you look like a drowned cat, and she was wearing a flowered grosgrain frock that showed too much leg and too much bosom. He wore his hair long and a dinner suit with blue velvet lapels. I shared the back seat of their Mark 9 Jaguar with Dawn Witherbie and a funny type called Walden. Alistair Mac-Donald drove like a madman, but Terry somehow got there first, so we all got out and went into his flat, which was three rooms done very modern; you know, bright purple carpet, orange and yellow walls, neon lights shaped like letter Zs, and a cocktail bar in one corner with the front made of padded and buttoned blue leather.

There were twelve of us and everybody talked and drank a lot. Not that *I* drank much because it didn't do to be talkative the way I lived. Somebody shouted, "Put the tape on," and then a sort of round-the-clock dance music started coming out of the radiogram, and two or three couples began to circle in one corner. But on the carpet it was hard work, and after a while Terry dragged a table forward and said, "D'you play poker, Mary?"

"No. Do you mean gambling?" I said. "No."

He laughed. "It's only fun. Not really gambling. I'll soon teach you."

"No, thanks, I'll watch."

"If you're as quick at learning this as you were the cha-cha . . . Two shilling maximum, Alistair?"

"Low limits kill bluffing, old boy, old boy," Alistair MacDonald said. "Anybody will see you if they can do it on the cheap."

"Yes, dear boy, dear boy," Terry said, mimicking him. He lowered his voice and did a little finicking wave towards the dancers. "But we're a mixed bag this evening. I think we have to take a democratic view."

Gail MacDonald pulled the shoulder strap of her frock up. "Darling, don't be a bore," she said to her husband. "We're slumming tonight." She glanced at me. "Darling, I don't mean you. In that divine frock—is it Amies?"—she knew it wasn't—"you look like an early Modigliani, that lovely warm skin . . . Of course we'll play for whatever you say, Terry, poppet." She kissed him.

Some of them got round a low table which had a banquette on two sides. I wouldn't play at first but Terry insisted on teaching me. Somehow in the process one of his hands was always touching me somewhere; one minute it was round my waist, then it was on my shoulder—and always two or three fingers seemed to overlap on to the bare part—or he held my arm or my hand. I didn't like being pawed, and I was glad the MacDonalds had offered to take me home.

I pretended I hadn't any money, so Terry leant me two pounds, but I had no luck and when that was gone I said I was drawing out; this gave me the chance to slide away from him.

I began to watch the game. Terry was right, it was easy to learn—anyone could go through the motions in ten minutes: but it didn't stop there. It looked as if anybody with a bit of time and head exercise would be able to work out what chances of winning you had when you picked up a card and what chances you had of doing better by swapping your cards. For instance if you had four cards of the same suit and hoped to pick up a fifth, for a—what was it?—a flush, the odds against you, because there were four suits in the pack, were roughly four to one. But if you had three cards of the same number—three fives, for instance, and

281

hoped to pick up a fourth, the odds against you must be forty-eight to one because there was only one more in the whole pack. No, twenty-four to one, because you had two chances.

When nobody was looking I grabbed up my bag and found some paper and began figuring.

About three o'clock, the Smitherams and Dawn and another couple went home, and we all had a drink and I thought it was going to break up: but two or three of the others shouted to go on, so they squatted down once more, and this time they made me play again. I took out a pound note of my own and sat down swearing I'd *walk* home when that was gone.

But it didn't go. I won. All the things I was quite good at came in then. For years I'd had to hide what I was thinking however I felt. Ever since I was ten I'd had to do it. Then the liking for mathematics and money. Then the fact that I'd been watching everybody and trying to guess whether they were bluffing.

Not that I got any fun out of it. Gambling has always scared me to death. The only time I ever put a pound on a horse I felt sick like seasick, and it was almost a relief when the race was over and the money was lost. I don't know why it is because I never much mind giving money away.

By five o'clock when it all broke up I had won twenty-two pounds. I felt clammy and awful and glad it was over. I wouldn't pick up the money at first.

"No," I said, "take it back. It's too much."

"Taken in fair fight," said Alistair MacDonald, patting my shoulder. He was the only other one who had won. "But don't ever be ingenuous again or we won't believe you."

"The candles burn their sockets, the blinds let in the day," said his wife with a gaping yawn behind her spread-fingered hand. "It's me instantly for bye-byes. Home, James."

Terry wanted everyone to have farewell drinks, but nobody would, and we began to get coats and things out of the bedroom. I found I'd picked up a stain on the sleeve of my frock, and stayed dabbing at it, but I swear I was

282

only about five seconds longer than the others. When I came out all my winnings were still on the table and Terry was saying good-bye to the man Walden and two others, so I clutched up the notes and stuffed them in my bag.

I went to the door with my coat over my arm as Terry saw the others out. He looked at me half winking, with this odd lower-lipped smile of his, and then when he closed the door on the others I said:

"Thank you very much. It's been lovely. And I'm really awfully sorry about this money."

"It was fair fight, as Alistair said. Stay a few minutes more, do."

"I couldn't. I'm asleep. And the MacDonalds are waiting for me."

"Oh, no, they've gone."

"Gone?" That pressed the bell all right. "D'you mean——"

"Don't look so *alarmed*. I'll run you home in a few minutes."

"But they said they practically passed my door."

"Did they? They must have forgotten." He took my arm and led me back into the living-room. "No, seriously, my dear, I told them you were staying a bit longer and I was going to drive you home. Really, I'd be enchanted."

"And what did they think?" I asked.

"Think?" He snorted with laughter. "Oh, really! Victoria's dead. Don't you know?"

"I'd heard," I said.

He went across to the curtains and pulled them back. "You see. It's half daybreak already. The sun will be up in a few minutes. Your honour's saved."

I didn't answer. He came back and looked closely into my face. "Look, sweetie, I thought it was a delicious idea. It's no *use* trying to go to sleep at this hour. We've got to be back in slavery in less than four hours. Besides, I'm raving hungry, and I expect you are. I thought we could have breakfast together; then I could drive you home, wait while you changed and bring you back to Barnet."

I went across to the table and started gathering up the cards. There's a lot of things I know about, but this was a bit out of my league. I mean, I could handle the Ronnie Olivers of this world and get through without them laying a finger-nail on me. And I could deal with most of the numerous models that prop each other up at street corners and roam in espresso bars. But this one was different. For instance, his language. I wasn't even sure he meant any harm now. And he was my boss. If I wanted to stay with the firm I ought to try to keep in with him.

"What do you want for breakfast?"

He laughed. "I knew you were a girl after my own heart. Bacon and eggs, d'you think?"

"All right. But please, I don't want to be driven home after. When we've had breakfast you can phone for a taxi. After all, I can afford it today."

I went into the kitchen and began to put some bacon and eggs on the grill. He laid the table in the living-room while I cooked and did the toast. Then he came into the kitchen to make the coffee.

"But, my dear, you may spoil your delicious frock. I'll get you an apron." He came back with a blue plastic one with flowers.

"Is it one of yours?" I said.

"Naughty. It belonged to my wife."

"Where is your wife?"

"She lives in Ealing now. We didn't get on. Let me do it."

I tried to take the apron off him but of course he had to put it round my waist and tie it. When he had finished it his arms got back round my waist.

"Did I tell you you were pretty?"

". . . watch the toast."

"Well it isn't true any more. Now you're beautiful."

"Uh-huh." I slid round the side of the stove.

"It's too true. Because now you're pale—and tired. It fines off the *shape* of your face, makes just the difference." He kissed the back of my neck.

"Terry, if you do that I shall go home."

"Why?"

I pulled the toast out, put it on the table and began to cut the crust off. "Have you made the coffee?"

"Why will you go home if I do that?"

"I just feel that way."

He was still standing near by. A lot too near by. "I don't think I'm exactly well acquainted with you yet, Mary. I don't at all know how you tick."

"Just like anyone else. *Tick—tock—tick—tock*."

"No, you're not like anyone else. I've—well, to put it in a genteel way, I've had my adventures. Girls, women, not to exaggerate, my dear, are not exactly a closed book to me. But you're not like them. Your mechanism's different."

"I expect it's the hairspring. Could you turn off the grill, please."

He reached back and switched it off without ever taking his eyes from me. "Bury me deep if I lay claim to too much, my dear, but with most women I know—I'd know what they'd do or say if I made a pass at them—I'd know it before they knew themselves—I'd know if they were willing. Not you."

"Here's your plate—careful, it's hot."

We went back into the living-room and started in on breakfast. He was quite right about one thing; I was hungry. I ate like I was hungry in spite of feeling on a knife edge. He kept looking at me. Opposite me like this, his face was pear shaped. It wasn't a nice face but it was an interesting face. It was wild and sly and very, very alert. I felt scared, and a bit mad at being stared at. I wished I'd never come.

"Mary, can I say something very, very *rude*?"

"I can't stop you."

"Well, you could slap my face." He pushed out his lip. "This is what I'm going to say, if I may. I know your husband has been dead for only a short time but . . . well, you don't look like a married woman."

The light from the window had got brighter while this was going on, and the room with its card-table and its empty glasses and its full ash-trays was a pretty ghastly sight. I got up.

"Well, I think that's a good cue for me to go home."

He got up too and came round the table. "I'm waiting."

"What for?"

"This is the best side to slap. The other side is already well coloured behind the ear."

It was the first time he'd mentioned his mark. I said: "Why should I? It's only your opinion."

"You could prove me so wrong."

"I could but, thank you, I still think of Jim."

His eyes were a sort of gum colour—that gum you get in grip-spreaders for office use. Only it wasn't thinking of offices that made them like that.

"I wish you'd slap my face."

"Why?"

"D'you remember *Through the Looking Glass* and the Queen who cried *before* she pricked her finger?"

"I never read it."

"Women usually slap men—if they feel that way—*after* they've been kissed. I thought you might like to try before. It would be a variation."

My heart was going now. "No, thank you. But will you ring for a taxi."

I made to step away but he got his arms around me very expertly and nearly squeezed the breath out of me. Then as I jerked my face away he began to kiss my neck. I put my hands on his chest and when he felt the pressure he stopped and let me go to arm's length, but still held me round the waist. I nearly forgot my new voice then and let him hear the way I could really talk the Queen's English. But I had to get out of it nicely if I could.

"Consider yourself slapped."

He said: "Sorry, beautiful, but you really are enticing. And you bend like a wand. Like a wand. Shall I say something else?"

"Yes. Good night."

"It's morning. And very early in the morning like this, after not having been in bed all night, is a delicious time to make love. You're tired and relaxed and your skin's cool and slightly damp, and there's nobody, nobody, *nobody* awake. Have you tried it?"

"I will sometime."

"Nothing doing now?"

I tried to smile and shook my head. "Nothing doing."

286

"One kiss ere we part?"

Oh, well . . . he looked clean and healthy. "And then you'll get a taxi?"

"Sure will."

I turned my face up to his and he put his lips against mine. Then instead of it being just a kiss it grew and grew. His lips and tongue were wet and thrusting all over my lips and clenched teeth. I jerked my head away violently, trying not to be sick. I must have caught his nose with my cheek-bone because he let me go suddenly and I nearly fell down on the floor. I clutched hold of a chair and looked at him and he was rubbing his nose and looking at me in a way that put the fear of God into me. It really did. I saw my coat on the chair and grabbed it up and my bag beside it and walked to the door. I fumbled about with the catch, all fingers and thumbs, thinking he was just behind me. The door opened somehow and I was out and had slammed it shut. Then I beat it down the steps at full speed and got out into the cold morning air, rubbing my mouth with the back of my hand.

4

I wondered if I ought to give in my notice and leave. I wondered a lot about it. I expect it would be small change to most women, just a kiss in a flat. But I didn't like it at all. I felt sick every time I thought of it, and I didn't want to meet him again.

He didn't turn up at the firm that Saturday at all. Dawn said: "Where did *you* get to last night; I thought you was coming when we went?"

"No," I said. "The MacDonalds took me home."

"Oh. Very *a la*. I didn't think she was pretty, did you?

My life, didn't his Lordship have an eye for you! Where'd you get that frock?—really, you are a dark horse."

When Terry came on the Monday he didn't look the side I was on, and that suited me fine, if it would just stay like that. All the same I felt pretty unsettled all that week—until the following Monday when I was transferred to the reorganised cash office in the main works. Then the sight of all the money I would be handling soothed me like a tranquilliser.

There was a lot of extra work to do that week. I was technically 'under' Susan Clabon, but in fact I'd had a rise in salary and was on equal terms with her. The same week a holiday list was posted up in the main office. Susan Clabon at once put down for the fortnight beginning Saturday the 10th September, so I wrote my name in for the following fortnight. She would be due back on the 26th. I began to work on these dates.

On the Thursday I was alone in the office when Mark Rutland came in. He went to the safe and put some books in, and as he passed on his way out he dropped a ticket on my desk. I stared at it.

He said: "Just in case you're really interested."

It was a ticket for the National Rose Society's show. I looked up at him in real surprise, nothing pretended.

"Oh, thank you. You shouldn't have bothered, Mr. Rutland."

"No bother."

"Well, thank you."

At the door he said: "First day's the best. But then you can hardly get there, can you. They're still pretty good on Saturday afternoon."

He'd hardly spoken to me except in the way of business since I came. And after all, nothing could be more innocent than being given a ticket for a flower show.

After he'd gone out I took up a compact and powdered my nose. I exchanged a look with myself in the mirror. I was imagining things.

The only rose I had ever had was the dusty rambler that bloomed every year in the back yard at Plymouth; but it always got smothered with green fly and fizzled out. It used to make me wonder about that song, 'Roses of Picardy' and why anyone should bother to go nasal and wet-eyed about a plant as feeble as the rose I knew. I've never had any room for things that gave in without a struggle.

Not that 'Roses of Picardy' didn't mean something special to me. One day I'd been watching some men clearing a bombed site in Union Street when they found an old portable gramophone buried in the rubble. They turned it over and laughed, and one of them said: "Yur, ducky, you 'ave it." I went scuttling home with it and found it still worked, but the only unbroken record in the bottom shelf was 'Roses of Picardy' sung by some Irish tenor with adenoids or something. For three years after that I couldn't afford to buy any others, so I just played that and played it until it was worn out.

I used to come home from school at half past four. Mother and Lucy would be out at work still, and Mother used to leave a paper with the things she wanted, and I'd go shopping. Then I'd get the tea ready, which was usually ham and chips, or kippers, with bread and butter, in time for when they got home about half past six. Always I'd play 'Roses of Picardy' over and over because it was the only tune I had.

Sundays were sombre because they were all church; but Saturdays, with Mother and Lucy at work, I was free most of the day. Of course it was my job to clean the rooms, but I'd fly through this and be ready to join the others by about ten. We'd go mooching around Plymouth and watch the bulldozers and the builders at work; then when they stopped we'd wriggle under a gate and scavenge around on the site seeing what we could pick up. Sometimes we'd lift off the bricks that hadn't set and bury the spades and fill the cement mixer with stones. Later we'd walk round the stores, or go into one of the pin-table arcades or find some boys and stand at a corner giggling, or we'd climb up by the railway and throw stones at the trains.

One Saturday, in the February that I was fourteen, I'd been out all day with a pimply girl called June Tredawl, whose mother was doing three months; there'd been these

289

two other girls with us but we'd split up, and all afternoon June and I had been hanging around looking for trouble.

It was a cold day, I remember, with a frosty look, and when we went on the Hoe the sea was grey as a skating rink. We wandered about for a time, kicking our cheap shoes together to keep our feet warm, and talking about all the things we'd like to do if we had money. When we came to the car park we looked over the low wall at the cars. There was every proprietary brand there, from little Austins made before we were born to smart M.G.'s and Rileys.

June said: "I'll dare you to go in and let down the tyres."

"Go'n do it yourself."

"I'll give you half a dollar to see you do it."

"Shut up."

"I'll give you these stockings as well. I'll dare you. Are you scared to try?"

"Be a dope," I said. "What's the *good* of it? It doesn't help *us*, so I'm not doing it. See?"

We snarled at each other and walked on. Round the corner there was no one in sight, so we got on the wall and looked over the car park.

June said: "Well there, look at that there shoulder bag in the back of that car. I'll dare you to pinch that, and that's something we *both* want!"

This leather shoulder bag was lying on the back seat.

I said: "Go on, the flaming car's locked, and I'm not going to break it open, even for you, you pimply tramp."

We walked home mauling each other, but when she left me it was still only five and still quite light and I reckoned if I walked back to the car park again it would be going dusk by the time I got there. I didn't like being dared, and I thought, if I get the bag I'll show it to her tomorrow.

I walked back and loitered past the car park, and the car hadn't gone. I walked past twice because I wanted to see where the attendant was. He was at the other end and busy. The third time I climbed over the wall. When I was arguing with June I'd seen that one of the triangular front windows for ventilating didn't look as if it was quite closed, and sure enough when I sidled up and touched it with a finger it moved on its swivel. If you've a small hand it's easy

290

then to put your fingers in and flick open the catch of the door. Then you stop to squint round the car park at all the silent cars. Then you open the door and lean over to the back seat and grab the shoulder bag.

I hid the thing under my coat and slithered back over the wall. Then I began to run.

It was the first thing I'd stolen since four years ago when Mam had beaten the fear of God into me, and I was in a panic for a time. It wasn't till I got near home that I really began to feel good. Then I showed the first bit of sense. I remembered that when I was caught before it was because the girl I'd done it with had turned yellow and gave us both away. If June saw the bag I was never really safe any more. I went into a dark alley and looked what was in the bag. There was two pounds eleven and sevenpence and a book of stamps and a cheque book and a handkerchief and a compact.

I took out the money and the stamps and left the rest in and I walked as far as the harbour near the Barbican and dropped the shoulder bag in the sea.

So I went to the Rose Show on that Saturday afternoon. I didn't care whether I saw the flowers or not, but I thought he might ask if I'd been, and it's not easy to pretend if you haven't an idea what a thing looks like.

When I got there I really did get rather a lift out of seeing those masses of banked roses, and I realised my miserable rambler wasn't much of a specimen to judge by.

There were a lot of people about—people of the type I'd only really seen since I came to London. Although I'd like to have put a bomb under them, you had to admit they carried their money well. I stood by and listened to one woman ordering six dozen Peace and four dozen Dusky Maiden and three dozen Opera, and I tried to think what the size of her rose garden was, because she only wanted these as 'replacements.' I heard two men talking of a lunch they had had in New York yesterday. Someone was complaining that her villa in Antibes grew better roses than her house in Surrey and she wanted to know why. It was a far cry from this to the local Labour Exchange with its scruffy staff and its dead-duck unemployables. I wondered if these people knew that they lived on the same planet.

Well, maybe someday I should have my villa at Antibes, wherever that was.

"Ah, so you came, Mrs. Taylor. I hope you're enjoying it."

Mark Rutland. You never knew your luck, did you.

"Yes. I'm awfully glad I did come. I've never *seen* such flowers!"

"They get slightly better every year. I sometimes wonder how successful a thing has to get before it becomes vulgar. Have you seen the new Gold Medal Rose?"

We walked across the hall together. I thought, well, is he *really* another one? I didn't want to end up having a fight with this partner too.

He was better dressed today—usually at the works he wore an old suit—but his hair looked as if it had been combed with his fingers, and he hadn't a trace of colour in his face. Yet he wasn't bad looking.

I didn't want either him or his cousin, I only wanted to be able to rob them in peace.

Just as I was trying to think up an excuse for leaving him he said: "I have to be back in Berkhamsted for six o'clock, but I think there's just time for a cup of tea. Would you like to join me?"

I was caught not thinking and said: "Where?"

He smiled. "Just round the corner. There's a teashop that makes rather good toasted muffins."

In the teashop, which was quite a discreet sort of place, with pink curtains and alcoves—not a bit like the A.B.C. or Lyons—he began to ask me about the firm and whether I liked my job and whether I thought the reorganisation of the cash department was going to be O.K. I thought, well, it's a change, and he's not interested in me after all, thank God.

He said: "We're a family firm, as no doubt you've heard too often; but the trouble with these firms is that they get into a rut. When sons inherit and don't come up the hard way it's very much a toss-up whether they have a talent for the job. My father wasn't temperamentally suited for business. Flowers were his hobby and his life. Nor do I

292

think that some of the present . . ." He stopped, and a quick smile went across his face. "But that's another story."

"You've only been in the firm quite a short time?"

"Yes, until my father died I was in the Navy. I had a brother, six years older, who was going in the business, but he was killed in the war."

"I'm told you've made big changes in the firm."

"Who told you that? But never mind; it's true. Some of the departments hadn't been touched since about 1920. I ran the firm into a handsome loss last year. Considering the state of business generally I think that was rather ingenious."

"I enjoyed the dance last month," I said. "Do you always go?"

"No, it was my first time. The first year I joined, my wife had just been taken ill. Last year she'd just died."

So Terry Holbrook was being bitchy.

"You must find this a big change from the Navy, Mr. Rutland."

"I find it's equally possible to be at sea in either."

Personally I doubted that, though I didn't say so. He looked very much like someone who knew what he wanted and generally got it.

"Why do they dislike each other?" Dawn said. "Well what else could you expect, really? Family jealousy, and him coming into the firm like that, when they were all set to go along at the old jog-trot, drawing their fat salaries. Sam Ward practically ran it. Mark and Terry are *opposites*, if you see what I mean. And opposites in a family are worst of all. Their women were opposites too,"

"Did you know them both?"

"Well not exactly know them. Mrs. Terry was an actress—still is, of course—she played fast and loose with some TV producer, so Terry divorced her. Blonde, she is; tall and wh-huh. Sort of 38–25–38. *Handsome* of course, but going places. I don't think our Terry ever quite caught up."

"And Mrs. Rutland?"

"Mrs. Mark Rutland? I always thought she was a bit

293

queer. Brainy type. Not pretty. *Attractive*, but made nothing of herself. Used to dig up old stones—Arche—what do you call it. They say she was writing a book when she died."

I combed my hair and turned it under at the ends with my fingers. "Does Mark ever do like Terry?"

"What d'you mean, do like him?"

"Take the staff out—makes passes at them."

Dawn laughed. "Not Mark. Not as far as I know. Why, has there been a pull on your line?"

I noticed as the weeks went by that nobody checked the weekly takings on the retail side against the size of the cheque drawn for the wages each Thursday. Of course, it all had to balance up in the books; but if the wages to be paid were £1,200, and the weekly retail takings were £300 no one except the cashier had the responsibility of taking 3 from 12. If she took 3 from 12 and made the answer 11, so that the cheque to be drawn was £1,100, no one would know until at least the following Monday.

Late in June Mark Rutland sprained his ankle playing squash, so nothing was seen of him at the works for two weeks. Terry Holbrook had hardly spoken to me since the night of the dance, but he'd looked at me quite a bit when he thought I wasn't noticing. He made me more uncomfortable than any man I remember.

One day I had to go in to him, and he was standing by the window thumbing over a copy of the *Tatler*. After I'd done what I came to do he said: "And how *is* my *donna intacta*?"

I said: "I'm sorry I don't know what that means."

"Can't you guess, my dear?"

"I can guess."

"Well, I'm sure you're on the right track."

"I didn't have that sort of education."

"No," he said, "that's exactly what I suspected."

He'd turned my meaning round. "I can't stop you thinking what you like. I'm sorry it bothers you." I turned to go.

He put his hand on me. I don't know why but he always

managed to find the place where your sleeve ended and your arm began. "Must we fight?"

"No . . . I don't want to."

"I mean to say, dear, most women don't consider it an *insult* to be thought madly attractive. Why do you?"

"I don't."

He looked at me sidelong but rather seriously, as if he'd been considering it.

"I'm a persistent fellow. Water weareth away stone."

"Not in one lifetime."

Looking back, I suppose that sort of answer wasn't smart, but I felt I had to say something because he was seeing too much, seeing too deeply into what I was, and I wanted to cover up.

He let me go then. He said: "Life's awfully short, Mary, and seven-eighths of it is spent in work and sleep. You should try to enjoy the other twelve per cent. Give out, let your hair down, *spread* yourself, dear. Give some man a run. It's all right while it lasts, but it doesn't last long, nothing lasts. One should try to make hay, even at Rutland's . . . Do I bore you? That's a great mistake. I can't believe you were born to be an accountant. It's contrary to nature."

That same week the holiday season was beginning, and in a small firm like Rutland's people had to double for each other at times. Mr. Christopher Holbrook's secretary was one of the first to go and Mr. Ward told me to do her work in the mornings. The first morning, I went into his office before he came, opened his post and put it out on his desk ready for him to read. About half an hour after he came he rang the bell and I went in with a pencil and pad.

"Oh, Mrs. Taylor, did you open these letters?"

"Yes, Mr. Holbrook."

"Did you not notice that two of them were marked 'Personal'?"

"I believe I did see it on one envelope."

He looked through me. There was no electric fire on this morning. "It was on two envelopes." I saw he had fished them out of the waste paper basket. "It's not customary in this firm, Mrs. Taylor, for a secretary to open such letters—nor is it in any firm I know."

"I'm very sorry. I hardly thought anything of it."

"Well, remember it in future, will you?"

"Yes, sir."

I went out, duly torn apart. I tried to recollect what the letters had said. The first, if I remembered rightly, was from a firm of stockbrokers in the city. It said they had purchased on Mr. Christopher Holbrook's behalf the two hundred and fifty shares held by Mrs. E. E. Thomas in John Rutland & Co. Ltd. They said they had been successful in obtaining them for only three shillings above the latest market quotation. And they remained his faithfully.

The second was from a firm called Jackson & Johnson Solicitors & Commissioners for Oaths, and it was a personal letter from one of the partners telling Mr. Holbrook that they had been making further inquiries following Mr. Terence Holbrook's visit of last Monday and indications were that the Glastonbury Investment Trust was interested. "However," the letter went on, "it is perfectly clear that with so few of your shares in public hands, you cannot be coerced into taking any steps that would be out of accord with the wishes of your present board. Let me know what your feelings are, either as a board or, if you differ from the rest, as an individual. In the latter event I am sure that a private meeting with Mr. Malcolm Leicester can be arranged."

One letter seemed to tie in with the other. If he hadn't made a fuss about me opening them I should have forgotten them.

The whole of June was hot, but the third week was hottest of all. On this Thursday afternoon Mr. Ward sent for me and said: "Can you drive a car, Mrs. Taylor?"

"No." I could, but I had no licence in that name.

"A pity that isn't among your many virtues. I hoped you could have helped us."

"What is it?"

He unhitched his spectacles and looked at them as if he didn't like them. "It's this printing job for the Livery

Company. It's promised for Wednesday next and I'm not certain as to the lay-out. In the ordinary way I should change it as I thought fit, but it is one that Mr. Rutland has taken on personally, and of course it involves the dinner they're giving to the Queen Mother, so we have to have it right. I've been speaking to Mr. Rutland about it."

"Do you mean he wants to see it?"

"Yes. And of course, as you may have observed, he's still laid up."

"I could take a taxi," I said.

He looked at me down his long thin sarcastic nose, and you could see him working out what it would cost. "Yes, I suppose you could. He's at his house at Little Gaddesden. If Thornton was not away I'd send him . . ."

I thought it would be cooler out, but it wasn't. The day had been clouding up and the atmosphere was as heavy as one of Lucy Nye's yeast cakes. The clouds were over London and looked as if someone had exploded the H-bomb. It took the taxi best part of forty-five minutes, and the house was on the edge of a golf course, not big but smart-looking with tall chimneys and long windows and lots of grass all round to give it prestige.

A middle-aged woman in a striped apron let me in. He was in a room with open french windows that looked over one of the lawns towards some pine trees and the golf course. One of his legs was up on the sofa and he was watching a race on TV.

He smiled and said: "How are you? Sorry to bring you over like this. Do sit down."

I smiled back and gave him the programme. "I expect you know what Mr. Ward wanted to know. Is your ankle better, Mr. Rutland?"

"It's doing fine. Now let's see." His thick wad of black hair was as untidy as ever, but in an open-neck shirt and old flannel trousers he looked less pale than in a city suit. It was funny that he looked less delicate when he ought to have looked more.

While he turned over the programme I looked at the TV.

"Yes, Ward was right. I don't like this a bit." He

took a pen up off the table. "Hot, isn't it. Did you come by taxi?"

"By hire car. Yes. He's calling back in fifteen minutes."

"Switch that thing off if it annoys you."

"No . . . it's nearly over. It's Kempton Park, isn't it."

He began to write on the margin of the programme. "Are you interested in racing?"

"I love it."

He looked up as if he'd caught something different in my voice. "D'you often go?"

"Not often. When I can."

"Going to race meetings seems the sort of thing one does in company or not at all. But perhaps you do have company?"

"Not now," I said, remembering in time that I was a widow.

"Your husband was fond of it?"

"Yes."

He went on tinkering with the programme. There was a rumble of thunder again. It began as nothing but came nearer, bumping downstairs like a garden roller. I got up and switched off the TV just before the race finished.

He looked up when I didn't sit down again. "This will probably take me another five minutes. If you like roses go out in the garden. They've been very early this year, but there's a bed of Speke's Yellow round the corner."

"I think it's going to rain."

He nodded. "Perhaps you're right."

The room really was dark now. The sky outside was a ghastly coppery yellow and the leaves of a tree by the window glistened like old spoons. There was a flicker of lightning that made me jump about nine inches, and I did a graceful retreat towards the back of the room.

Old Lucy Nye. You couldn't get away from her, you really couldn't. 'Cover the mirrors, dear,' she'd say. 'If you see the lightning in 'em you'll see the Devil *peering* out at you. 'Tis true. 'Tis God's way of showing you Hell. Cover them knives; let the lightning get in 'em and it'll get in *you* next time you pick 'em up. I seen folk struck by lightning, split like a tree. I seen a man with his clothes

298

cut in ribs, his face black and purple, his poor burned hands twisted up like he was boxing. He was still alive when I got there even though 'is eyes and face had gone . . .' You couldn't beat her at that sort of X-certificate stuff.

It was nearly too dark to see at the back of the room, all shadows—and the furniture was pretty depressing anyhow. There were shelves with old cups and figures and vases on them, some of the vases chipped and broken, and some were so smothered in old dry mud or clay that you wanted to get at them with a scrubbing brush. Just in front of the shelves was a grand piano as big as two coffins, and on the piano was a photograph of a young woman standing at the entrance to what might have been a bit of Stonehenge. Dawn had been quite right; she wasn't pretty; her face was too long; but she'd got nice hair and her eyes were big and bright.

A flash of lightning: the thunder that followed was near and nasty and noisy. 'We're all corrupt,' Lucy'd say, holding me on her knee as if I was going to slip down a nick somewhere. 'We're corrupt an' the worm'll eat us. But better be eaten than *burned*. See that one, ah, ah, nearly got us! Come just inside the window, it did, I seen the tongue flickering. Just didn't reach us. The Devil's out tonight all right, lookin' for 'is own. Keep your 'ead covered, dear, don't *look* at it, guard your eyes!' You couldn't beat Lucy, she really was laughable. I laughed.

He looked up, but I turned the laugh into a cough. "That's about it," he said, looking again at the programme. "Anyway it's decently balanced now. Look, can I explain it to you in case Ward doesn't follow."

I went back to his sofa half a step at a time and he began to explain. But while he was doing it there was a flash that cut right across us, and I gave a yelp and dropped the sheet I was holding.

"Sorry," he said, "did it startle you?"

I began to say something, but it got nowhere in a rattle of thunder that stamped down on the house. The whole room shook and shivered like with an earth tremor. Then there was an awful silence.

I could see he was waiting for me to go back to him by the

window but I didn't. So he said: "Put the lights on if you like. The switch is by the door."

I went over and fumbled around, but I couldn't find it and my fingers were trembling. There was not a sound outside, no rumbles, no rain.

"It's like waiting for the next bomb to drop, isn't it," he said. "Would you like tea? it's nearly time."

"No, thanks. Shall I help you away from the window?"

"No, I can get about with a stick." There was a wait. "I think it's moving away."

"Sorry; I always get in a panic over a thunderstorm," I said.

"That's rather surprising."

"Why?"

"Well, when you ask me, I don't know. Except that perhaps you don't give the impression of being a person who would get in a panic easily over anything."

"Ho . . . you don't know!"

"Quite true. We don't know each other really at all. Look, it's beginning to rain."

I edged diagonally nearer the window. Two spots the size of shillings had fallen on the step and were spreading as they dried.

He put down the proof programme and eased himself out of his chair. Then with a stick he got up.

"You interested in Greek pottery?"

"I don't know anything about it."

"I noticed you looking at it. They were my wife's things. She collected them, mainly before we were married."

"Oh." Another rattle of thunder.

"What about my taxi?" I said.

"Oh, I doubt if he'll be back yet."

"I don't want to go in this, anyway."

"Don't worry, it'll soon be over."

I suppose he saw I was in a state, so he started talking about the Greek things to take my mind off it. I heard him say something about Crete and Delos and so many hundred B.C., and he put a little pot in my hands and told me it was a stirrup cup, but all the time I was waiting for the next explosion.

It came. The room lit up—two mirrors, the tiles of the fireplace, the glass over the photographs, all flickered and winked, then there was darkness. Then there was a sound as if the sky was made of cheap tin and was cracking under the weight. Then the sky split open and the weight fell on the house.

Death and disease and disaster. Thunderstorms and judgment and corruption. The worm dieth not.

"And did she—bring it back—with her?" I asked.

"Yes. I don't know if it does anything to you, but to me, to hold in my hand as my personal property a piece of pottery that has been turned by someone living five hundred years before Christ . . ."

Another flash was followed right on top by a great tearing roar of thunder, all round our ears.

"That was a bit close," he said, looking at me. I wondered if he could see the cold sweat on my forehead. Anyway he hobbled across and switched on the lights. "Sit down, Mrs. Taylor, if it worries you that much. I'll get you something to drink."

"No, thanks." I was irritable as well as scared.

"The chances of being struck by lightning are awfully small."

"I *know* that. I know all the answers."

"And it doesn't help?"

"No."

He said: "In a sense I suppose you and I are in much the same boat."

"I don't follow."

"Well, you have lost your husband recently, haven't you?"

"Oh . . . oh yes. I see how you mean."

He put the cup back and shifted a couple of other things on the shelves. "How did it happen—with you?"

"Well, it was—it was very sudden, Mr. Rutland, Jim—was on a motor bike. I just couldn't *realise* at first, if you know what I mean."

"Yes, I do."

"Then when I did begin to realise I felt I had to get away. I couldn't have stayed. It's much worse, isn't it, like you, to have stayed."

He eased his foot. "I'm not sure. In some ways it's a challenge. In others it's a comfort, to be among the things that she knew . . ." He stopped. "One hears a lot about the way one *should* take these things but when it comes to the point it's a new page, absolutely new. What you write on it is anybody's guess. The only thing certain is that it never runs to rule."

The lull came to an end with a flash and an explosion like a bomb hitting the damned house. The lights went out and there was a crackle and a crash outside. I don't know who moved first but we somehow collided. I was in such a panic that I didn't know it was him until some seconds later. Then he seemed to be holding me while I trembled. I was trying to get my breath.

In the silence there were voices somewhere. It was the woman in the apron.

Then it began to rain. The noise grew until it was a noise like the drums at a firing squad.

I was standing on my own now and he had moved to the door. The woman came in. "Are you all right, sir? It's that maple tree: all down the side; and the lights has fused! Lucky you wasn't by the window: I was afraid for you! All right, miss? There's a car outside. I wonder: oo, look, yes, see it's broken the glass in the dining-room window!"

Mark hobbled back towards the window, but I wouldn't go. By the time I got half-way I could see the lawn already under water and bobbling like with fish, and rose petals had drifted off the trees. A branch of a tree had been split and had fallen across the step.

"It's real dangerous today," said the woman. "Worst I ever remember." She pulled the french windows shut and bolted them. There was water already on the carpet.

"There's some brandy in the dining-room, Mrs. Leonard. I think Mrs. Taylor would like a drink."

I sat down in a chair well back in the room, clutching my hands together to keep them still. He seemed cheerful, more cheerful than he had before, as if the whole foul thing was rather fun.

"The chances of being struck by lightning are very small," he said. "In future I'll keep my big mouth shut."

"That taxi-dr-driver. He'll be get-getting drenched."

"Not if he stays where he is."

"I—really can't go yet—not till this is over."

"I don't expect you to."

"Mr. Ward will be fuming. He wanted the proof back by four."

"Let him wait. It won't do him any harm to wait."

There was another clatter of thunder as Mrs. Leonard brought in the bottle and the glasses, but after that last crack ordinary thunder seemed nothing. He poured me something. "Swallow this down. And you too, Mrs. Leonard."

I swallowed some and coughed. It was as strong as paraffin. But I gulped at it and you could feel it like fire, burning as it went down. Mrs. Leonard went out to see if there was any damage upstairs. I began to let go of my hands.

"Well," I said, "I wonder who won the three-thirty."

"Who was leading when you switched off?"

"North Wind. But Gulley Jimson was the favourite."

After about ten minutes the lights came on again, but by now you hardly wanted them. The rain had begun to ease. Water still dripped from the gutter and gurgled in the pipes. Mrs. Leonard put her head in to say there was no damage upstairs. He rang Mr. Ward to say what had happened.

I got up to go. I was still quivering like a drunk round the knees, but he couldn't tell that. He gave me the proofs and hobbled with me to the door. He was friendly and easy. You'd hardly have known him. When we'd had tea after the rose show he'd been picking his way, not sure of himself or something. Now it was different. But there still didn't seem much risk of him heading the way of his cousin.

When I got in the taxi I began to feel a bit cheap and ashamed of myself, which was something rather new for me. I thought at first I was developing a disease. It took a time to work out what was wrong; and then at last I pinned it to that conversation we had had about me losing my husband and him losing his wife.

5

With Susan Clabon taking her holidays from the 10th
September until the 26th the best date to set my sights on
was Thursday the 22nd.

The staff was paid from eleven o'clock onwards on a
Friday morning. Making out the pay packets was quite a
major operation. In calculating a journeyman's wages—
that is, a printer—you had all sorts of additions and sub-
tractions to make. First you put down his basic wage—
say £11 a week—then to that you added overtime, which
might be £4 in a week. Then there was merit money which
was a sort of bonus bribe to keep everyone happy, which
might be £3. Then in some cases there was an agreed extra
if the work was specially awkward. When all that was added
up you began with deductions. First there was Lost Time—
if anyone was late or absent—then each man had his
P.A.Y.E. number, which of course was usually the same over
a period. Then there was National Health, and finally there
was Voluntary Contributions which were not listed separately but which might be two or three small items for the
annual dinner and the yearly summer outing etc.

Susan Clabon and I operated together, one working the
machine and the other putting the money in the pay envelope along with the slip showing how the wages were made
up. Usually I did the second part, and then Susan would
check the money before sealing the envelope and putting it
in a flat tray against the number of the particular printer or
binder. These were usually finished on Thursday evening
before we left and locked in the safe until the following
day; but sometimes we had to run the work over into
Friday morning.

Luckily in August Susan was away with tonsilitis, and
I told Mr. Ward I could do the job all on my own and did.
The one thing that would wreck everything would be an

'assistant' while she was on holiday; and I thought now with luck I wouldn't get one.

In some ways I would be glad to go when the time came, even though it was far the best and most interesting job I'd ever had.

All the time I was there, more or less, Dawn had been plaguing me to go out with her one night and I'd stalled, not wanting any more complications. She lived in Barnet and I'd been to tea with her and her mother one Sunday, but this didn't satisfy her. So now, feeling it was near the end, I said all right, and we joined up with two young men she knew and went along to a road-house called the Double Six near Aylesbury.

It was only after meeting and speaking to people like Mark Rutland—and even Terry Holbrook and Alistair MacDonald—that you realised what awful drags most young men were. The one I had to deal with was a big clammy pink-faced type with close-set blue eyes and the skin peeling off his nose. He talked all the time about his TR3 and golf and a holiday he'd had in Spain. He never stopped talking and seemed to think it was part of his charm. Also he chain smoked, which isn't particularly lovely for a non-smoker like me. I suppose I pretty well shared his cigarettes.

The road-house was the phoniest place with awful black beams and lampshades made out of old wills and tankards with glass bottoms; but I could see Dawn was enjoying it, so I didn't really mind being there; and we'd had a couple of dances and were sitting talking while more records were put on, when a short man with a red bow-tie came across to me and said:

"Pardon me, now, but aren't you Peggy Nicholson?"

Well, I didn't need to act, you see, because I wasn't Peggy Nicholson, and was certain I never had been, so that my blankness was quite true and I'd shown it before the knife went in.

I looked round first to make sure that he was talking to me, and then I said: "I'm afraid you've made a mistake. My name is Mary Taylor. Mrs. Taylor."

He stared and pressed his spectacles on his nose.

"You're—not . . . Oh, I'm awfully sorry, but I thought a man called Don Weaver introduced us in Newcastle two years ago—I was certain you were . . ."

"I'm not," I said and smiled. "I'm sorry I've never been to Newcastle."

"Not even with coals," said Dawn's partner, and laughed.

The man looked very sheepish. "Then I beg your pardon. It must be just a resemblance. I'm awfully sorry."

"Not at all," I smiled. "I'm sorry I can't oblige."

"*That* was a darn silly thing to say," muttered the young man I was with as the other man turned away. "You don't want to oblige a Cheap Jack like that barging in and pretending he knows you, just to get on speaking terms."

Obviously the man, whose name I honestly couldn't remember, didn't know anything about Peggy Nicholson being wanted by the police. Not that they could prove anything anyway. But it just showed. I saw him looking at me once or twice when I passed him dancing. And I saw Dawn looking at me too.

Later in the evening in the Ladies she said: "You are a dark horse, you know."

"Why, what have I done now?"

"Nothing, only I thought you looked a bit peculiar when that man came up. Honest, you didn't really know him?"

"I've never seen him before in my life."

She shook her head. "Of course I believe you. All the same I think you've got a past, dear."

"So has everybody who's more than one day old."

"Too true." She said no more then while she traced out a new cupid's bow. She didn't draw it very well; she always did it like one of those men marking out a white line over the old one on the dangerous corner. But as we were going to leave I thought perhaps I could learn something about myself if I tackled her, so I said:

"What d'you mean, you think I've got a past?"

"Well," she narrowed her eyes and then laughed. "Don't be mad with me, dear, I don't want to pry, but you don't ever *talk* about yourself, do you. Not like I do. Not like you

306

expect a girl to do. It's only *that*. Anyway I was only joking."

"All right," I said, "joke."

She put her arms round my shoulders. "Now don't be cross. But honest, you've been with Rutland's more than six months, yet I don't feel I *know* you. I don't feel I can get *at* you. I like you, of course, but I don't know what you're thinking at this very moment. You're like somebody behind a glass wall. There, now you can be as mad as you like!"

I laughed. "Look out; one of these days somebody might throw a stone!"

On the 7th September Mark Rutland came into my office while Susan Clabon was out, and his hair was as if he'd been running his hand through it both ways for a change. He said abruptly: "I don't know if you're doing anything on Saturday but I'm going to Newmarket to the races. Would you like to come along?"

I had to think round that one pretty quickly. And a nice girl doesn't ask questions.

"Thank you very much, Mr. Rutland. I'd love to."

"Good." His face had a flush on it for once. "I'll pick you up here at twelve-thirty. Any clothes will do."

"Thank you very much." And that was that. Not another word.

In the last two months, since my visit to his house, we'd eyed each other every day at the firm but we'd hardly said more than the usual things. Of course I could tell there was interest by the way he was nice to me; and every now and then when we were alone in an office he wasn't so much the business man; I noticed this specially when Terry wasn't about, especially when Terry was away for three weeks in August.

But this was the first sign of heading for anything more. It was just cruel luck. I know I've the sort of face and figure that people call fashionable nowadays, but it could easily have happened I could have worked for ten firms with young directors and they would hardly have noticed me. It never rains but it pours, as Mother would have said, coining a phrase.

I'd have done better to have said no. Terry and Mark really were madly jealous of each other and ever willing to fight over anything; I'd be a new excuse; and if Terry knew I was going out with Mark after turning down an invitation from him he'd look on it as the deadliest insult.

However, I felt it was no good caring about that; in three weeks I should be away from it all. The other reason which I just couldn't resist was that, because Rutland's worked Saturday mornings, I had hardly seen a race meeting for three months. Mark had made the one suggestion I couldn't bring myself to sabotage.

Saturday was wet in the morning but it cleared by ten and it looked as if the going would be just right. I had brought things to change at the office, and after I'd changed I hung about for a few minutes to let most of the staff go. I particularly wanted Dawn to go off, and I saw her away before I went down to the car park where Mark was waiting. But of course Mr. Ward happened to be there getting into *his* car, and he raised a sarcastic eyebrow. Mark didn't seem to care, and he handed me a package with some sandwiches in.

"This is your lunch, I'm afraid. If we don't stop on the way we may just make the first race."

We made the first race, and we watched it from the enclosure. I hadn't been in there before. I'd only been twice to Newmarket before, and once I'd watched it from the Silver Ring, and once from the opposite side of the course, where you didn't have to pay.

I found I knew more about the runners than he did. For the three o'clock I told him Telepathy, a grey filly that I'd seen being trained as a one-year-old. I knew she'd come in second twice in the last month over longer distances, and each time she'd been passed near the post. The going wasn't heavy today so over this distance she would surely win.

"All right, I'll put a fiver on her," Mark said good-humouredly. "Shall I put something on for you?"

"Me? No, thank you. I don't bet."

"Why ever not?"

"I'm afraid of losing the money," I said straight out, and he stared at me and then we both laughed.

I said: "I just don't have any cash I want to risk."

"Well, I won't press you if you really feel like that."

By the time he came back the horses were lining up in the distance, and I couldn't have used his binoculars more eagerly if I'd had a hundred pounds at stake. Telepathy won by a head. Mark laughed and went to collect his winnings. He brought back six pounds for me.

"I put a pound on for you for luck. She was second favourite anyhow."

"Well, I can't take it, Mark. It was your money you put on. If you'd lost you'd have paid."

It was the first time I'd used his Christian name. He pressed the notes on me, so I took them.

I had no fancy for the three-thirty. He backed his and lost.

"Tell me something," he said. "I'm not a great gambler myself but if I didn't have a few pounds on each race it would spoil the fun. If you don't bet, why are you so found of race meetings?"

"I like the horses."

"Just the horses?"

"Yes. I love to see them. I think there's nothing more beautiful."

He crumpled up his tote tickets and dropped them in a basket. "Do you ride?"

"A bit."

"Not as much as you would like?"

"Well, I haven't the time. And—it costs money."

We began to look over the runners for the four o'clock. As it happened the favourite was called Glastonbury Thorn.

"By the way," I said. "What is the Glastonbury Investment Trust?"

"What?" He looked at me sharply. "Why do you ask?"

"I can't remember where I saw their name recently."

"You could see it anywhere. They're a big investment trust with plenty of money behind them. They recently bought two publishing firms. Vaughans and Bartlett & Leak."

"Oh," I said, "well I shouldn't back him, then. How about Lemon Curd? He won last week at Kempton Park."

Mark stared at his card. "The small printer could be their target next—like Rutland's. Of course they could swallow us tomorrow and not feel it, but fortunately they can't because eighty per cent of our shares are still in the family."

He backed Lemon Curd, but it was a photo finish and Lemon Curd was placed second.

We were standing by the rails at this time, and quite near to us, but of course in the Silver Ring, were seven or eight semi-Teddy boys of about eighteen.

They were dressed like usual and they were rowing with two fat men of about forty who might have been bookmakers or something. These two fat men were really scared, but it all died down when two policemen showed up. There were a lot of cat-calls and colourful language.

"Unhealthy little rats," Mark said.

"What else d'you expect from sewers?"

He looked at me, surprised, not quite sure how to take it. "D'you like Teddy boys?"

"No . . . but they're not true Teds, for one thing. They're just ordinary rough types following a fashion."

He rubbed his hand through his hair and looked at his race card.

I said: "It's just a fashion, that's all, the things they wear, just as it's the fashion for you to wear a jacket with—with slanting pockets or for me to cut six inches off my skirt."

"But we don't gang together and become offensive nuisances in the street and the pub."

"No," I said, "and if you did you ought to be ashamed of yourself because you've been brought up in a decent home to know better. You should see some of *their* homes."

"Have you?"

"Yes," I said, and stopped there. I was going too far.

His eyes followed the eight boys. "It may be something rotten in the state of Denmark that breeds them, I agree. But they don't all turn out like that . . . that sort, they've no brains and their physique is terrible. They couldn't stand up to any decent man so they gang together and be-

310

come bullies. Whether it's all their fault or not, I still don't like them."

"I don't like bullies," I said.

When I didn't go on he said: "And you think they're not?"

"Oh, the real Teds, yes. These are just fringe Teds. Pretty dumb characters, maybe, and not lovable. But nothing terribly *wrong* with them. Most are just—restless. You don't understand. They've nearly all got jobs that bring them in good money, but they're caught on a sort of treadmill and they'll not earn much more over the next forty years. They've brains enough to know that. You try it out and see if it wouldn't make you restless. Maybe if they were all in the Navy they'd be better. But you can't expect them to see that."

"Oh, the Navy," he said; "I'm not holding that up as a solution."

"Then what is the solution?"

He looked at me and suddenly smiled. "To put my shirt on Ballet Girl for the four-thirty."

After the races we had dinner together in Cambridge. On the way he said: "You know, I know absolutely nothing about you, Mary. Every now and then you seem just about to catch fire. And then suddenly you withdraw yourself again."

"There's nothing to know," I said. I think that was the moment when I realised I had really stayed on this job too long. He was the third character who had said I was a mystery, who had got interested enough to want to know more. It was nearly always the flaw in my schemes. In seven weeks you could up and away without anybody wanting to get to know. Seven months was too long.

"Well," he said, "I know you're twenty-three, that you were married at nineteen and are now a widow. Your father and mother are in Australia and you went to school in Norwich. That's about all, isn't it? Apart from that, I know you've a head for business and figures. Since you came to us you've never put a foot wrong. You're terrified of thunderstorms, and you go to race meetings but don't back horses. You know how to dress well—as now—but you don't in office hours apparently care. You have generally good manners but now and then you don't seem to understand simple bits of etiquette that most people take for granted."

"Such as?" I said quickly.

"Never mind. You say you went to a High School, and your accent's right, but sometimes you seem to let it out that your childhood has been very tough. You're never lacking in initiative so far as your work is concerned, but you seem to be in your play. I've never heard of you saying a catty thing about anyone, but you're awfully tough about something inside and ready to fight the world. What's the secret, Mary? Tell me."

I said: "What are those simple bits of etiquette?"

Over dinner I thought it looked as if it might be getting serious. He didn't paw like his cousin, but the light was on. Oh, Lord, I thought, and to keep his mind off it I asked him about himself.

His mother was still living, and had a flat in Hans Place.

"Why did you leave the Navy?"

"You might say, why did I *go* in the Navy. When I was thirteen my brother, who was to have come into the business had already been killed, but by then my father had made up his mind that I was going to be saved the unpleasantness of working in a family firm, so I was sent off to Dartmouth. And from there, of course, it was straight on."

"The unpleasantness?" I said gently.

"Yes. My father and Christopher Holbrook never hit it off. Christopher's one ambition has always been to squeeze out the other members of the family in favour of his own son, and when Tim was killed it looked as if he was going to succeed. Then when my father died I wrecked everything by leaving the Navy and coming in in his place."

"Did you mind leaving the Navy?"

"No, I wanted to get out. In my opinion it's a dead end now—sadly enough. In peace it has a sort of skeleton usefulness, but in war, which after all is what it is designed for, it will become about as serviceable as mounted cavalry.

312

I couldn't see it as a proposition at all, so I was glad to go."

"So you came to fight at Rutland's?"

"I'm not all that combative. I haven't looked for trouble. But I think the worst is over now."

For a moment I thought of two letters marked PERSONAL lying on Christopher Holbrook's desk.

"I've wondered sometimes," he said, "if my cousin Terry Holbrook has ever made things difficult for you."

"Difficult? How?"

"I thought that might have been clear. I'm glad if it isn't."

"Oh . . . well. There hasn't been anything serious."

"Sometimes I wonder . . .'

"Wonder what?"

"As you know, Terry's wife let him down. I sometimes wonder if he gets all that much fun out of his present philandering or whether half the time he isn't trying to prove something to himself."

I said: "Perhaps your father was right, and it was a mistake to come back. You should have become an arch-aeologist."

It was always a surprise when this smile came. It softened up all the rather off-key determination in his face. "You're dead right, I should. But I've done quite a bit of digging up of old bones at Rutland's."

He drove me home about eleven-thirty. The street where I had my rooms was a cul-de-sac and there was no one about, only five or six parked cars and a street lamp and a stray cat sitting near by licking its back foot.

"Thank you awfully," I said, trying to talk even more the way his sort of girls talked. "It's been a gorgeous day. I have enjoyed it all."

"We must do it again," he said. "Let's see, next Saturday, I don't think there's anything near enough."

"I can't next Saturday," I said too quickly.

"Another engagement?"

"Well, sort of."

"There's something the Saturday after at Newbury. What about it?"

"Thank you. That would be lovely." By Saturday the 24th I should be out of his reach.

I put my hand on the door of the car to open it.

"Mary."

"Yes?"

He put a hand on my shoulder and drew me to him and kissed me. There was nothing particularly passionate about it, but you certainly couldn't say he was inefficient. His hand moved over my head.

"You've such lovely hair."

"D'you think so?"

"It's so strong and yet so soft . . . are you cold?"

"No."

"I thought you shivered."

"No!"

"It's been good today—for you?"

"Yes, Mark, it has."

"So far as I'm concerned," he said, "to say it's been good is quite an understatement."

"I must go. Thank you again. Thank you, Mark. I'll—see you on Monday. Good night."

That night I woke up in the middle of the night dreaming I was crying, but it wasn't feeling sentimental about Mark Rutland. It was a dream I sometimes had, although often I didn't get it for twelve or eighteen months. In fact it wasn't so much a dream as a sort of dream memory.

I sat up in bed and looked at my watch and cursed; it was only half past three.

Lovely hair he'd said I'd got. Maybe that was what had started it off, him saying that. I wondered if he would have thought the same ten years ago.

It didn't really start with the hair; it started when Shirley Jameson said something insulting in the playground about my mother. I can't even remember what it was she said but I know at thirteen years old it seemed frightful and I flew at her with waving fists and there was a fight there on the paved yard. In the end I was dragged off and there was a row and we were both kept in, and then we had to go and say sorry to each other in front of the headmistress.

314

At this time I was sleeping with old Lucy, and old Lucy wasn't clean, especially her hair, and I got lice in mine. Mother used to comb my hair out over a newspaper with a small-tooth comb and you could hear the little tat-tat as the lice fell on the paper. Then she would empty the newspaper into the fire and the lice would slide off and *crick-crack* as they went in. After that she would rub in ointment, but I don't think she ever told me that it might be helpful to use soap and water. Anyway, one day soon after that first row, I was coming home from school when Shirley Jameson and two other girls she was friendly with caught me up, and Shirley Jameson said she'd seen something crawling in my hair that afternoon in school. If it had only been her I should have told her to go jump in the sea, but with the other two there I couldn't do that, so I just told her she was a bloody liar. Then she said if she was a liar I could prove it by letting her look through my hair then. We were in an entry, and there didn't seem any way out, so I had to let her. All the time she was doing it I was grinding my teeth and praying to God she wouldn't find anything. At first I thought I was going to be lucky, and then suddenly she squealed with delight and came away with a thing between her thumb and forefinger.

I lost my head then because I screamed at her that she'd never found it in my hair at all and that she had taken it out of her own hair and had it in her fingers all the time. I was going to lay into her but the other two girls grabbed my arms and twisted them behind me and Shirley said, take that back or I'll slap your face. So I said I wouldn't take it back, because it was God's truth, so she gave me a good swinging slap that I think surprised her as much as it surprised me because she stopped and stared at me. Then she said, will you take it back now, so I said no, and then a queer look came into her eyes as she suddenly realised she was going to enjoy this.

So she gave me a slap on the other side of my face that made my head ring, and one of the other girls said, go on Shirley, go on and make her cry. So Shirley went on, first one side and then the other. But of course I wasn't nice to hold, and eventually I kicked myself free and butted her in the stomach and knocked her against the wall and ran up the alley. And they came baying after me. I ran like mad all the way and they never let up till I got to my street.

When I got there I didn't dare go in because I knew I'd get half-murdered coming in like that. My nose was bleeding and I'd lost my school bag and they'd pulled all the buttons off my blouse and torn the strap of my vest.

In the dream I was always crying at this point, and I always woke myself up, because if I didn't it would begin all over again. But when I really woke I never was crying, my eyes were always hard and dry. I've never cried, except for effect, since I was twelve.

In fact—though I never dreamt this part—things went on quite differently that day from what I expected. After I'd sat on the back step for a bit I went in with a story that I had been coming round the corner of Prayer Street and had gone to cross the road and had been knocked down by a bicycle. But when I got in my Uncle Stephen was there, he'd come in on his ship that day and they were making him supper. I told my story, and Mother and Lucy swallowed it hook, line etc., especially as they were busy all the while with their guest and hadn't much time for me.

But I noticed while I told it *his* eyes were on me in a rather queer way, and that made me uncomfortable because I always admired him and thought him the person I should have wanted to be like if I had been a man. He was a good bit younger than Mother and tall and good looking but he had gone grey early, because at the time of this visit he would only have been forty, and he was certainly grey then.

I remember, besides looking at me in that rather sceptical way, he also looked me up and down with a certain amount of surprise because by now I was just on my fourteenth birthday and I was growing up. I remember holding my torn blouse up at my neck when he looked at me because although I knew Uncle Stephen could have nothing but decent thoughts about me, yet I knew he was seeing me as other men would see me and was thinking I was nearly a woman.

After supper he said he would walk with me to the place where I had been knocked down and perhaps we should find the lost school bag, so I could hardly say no. So we went, and on the way he talked about South America, where he had just come from, and I asked him about the horses there. Then I found the corner where I was knocked down and we cast about for the school bag and I casually went down the entry and found it lying under the shadow of the brick wall, so we were able to take it home. But half-way home he said, "What really happened, Marnie?"

I was so angry at being disbelieved, and by him of all people, that I went into the whole story again, describing the bicycle and the boy on it and the woman who picked me up and what she was wearing and what I said and what they said; because by now I almost believed it myself.

So in the end he said: "All right, my dear, I only wondered." But I could tell from the tone of his voice he still didn't believe me and that made me madder still, because I cared what he thought.

We went the rest of the way home, with me in a sulky silence, until at the door he said: "Have you thought about what you want to do when you leave school? What would you like to do?"

So I said: "I'd like to do something with animals, chiefly with horses."

"A lot of girls do. If you couldn't do that?"

"I don't know."

"What are you good at at school?"

"Not much, really."

"Isn't that over-modest? Your mother says you've a head for figures."

"I can add up."

"Only that? Well, Marnie, in another year we'll see. I'd like to be able to help in some way, to send you perhaps to a secretarial college, to give you a chance of getting out in the world. There's more to life than this, Marnie. I'd like to get you away."

On Thursday the 15th I did all the pay packets myself. They offered me Jennifer Smith from the progress department but I said I wouldn't have her, so they didn't press. At two o'clock on the Thursday I made out a cheque for £1,150 payable to Cash and took it to Mr. Holbrook to sign. I then gave it to Howard, the caretaker, who went across to the bank with it, accompanied by Stetson, the foreman. They came back with the money in two blue bags and left it with me. To the £1,150 I added £250 takings from the retail side and began to make out the pay packets. I was left undisturbed and I worked, never stopping. By five o'clock I'd done more than three-quarters of the job, and when Mr. Ward came in to lock the money and the pay packets away he asked sarcastically if I was trying to do Miss Clabon out of a job.

So another week went past. I got a postcard from Susan, whom I'd softened up quite a lot by this time. "Glorious weather. Went Shanklin yesterday. Have just bathed. See you soon. S. C." Like Hell she would.

During the previous weeks I had loitered through the works several times and fingered some of the papers that were stacked in the storeroom and about the works. On the Tuesday I went up to one of the young men, called Oswald, who was on a cutting machine and said to him: "D'you think you could do me a terrific favour? I'm organising a Church social on Saturday afternoon and we're going to play games. I want a lot of small pieces of paper for them to write on. Do you think you could possibly cut me some?"

"Of course. Just let me know the size. What sort of paper do you want?"

"Well any plain paper—no lines—so long as it isn't too thick. And I want the pieces about postcard size or a little longer, about an inch longer. I wonder, could I go and choose from those stacks over there?"

"Sure. Go right ahead."

So I went and chose my paper and he cut it up into the required size just like I asked.

Thursday the 22nd was a windy day, and the dust and leaves blew along the street outside the works. Autumn was coming early, and I felt sorry for types who were going to take their holidays by the sea, skulking behind walls and walking up draughty dismal piers. But it would be all right for riding. It would be just right for riding. In my handbag today I brought 1,200 slips of paper ready cut to size and rubber-banded in packages of fifty. Oswald had done them for me.

Mark made things easier by leaving straight after lunch. One of the girls told me he was going to a sale at Sotheby's. I wondered if there was going to be another Greek stirrup cup in Little Gaddesden.

The amount taken on the retail side during the week was about £350, but Mr. Holbrook wasn't to know this. I made out the cheque for £1,190 and he didn't query it. Afterwards I wished I'd risked more. I took the cheque to Howard, and he and Stetson got the money. They were back by two-thirty and I began work at once with Adcock, J. A., No. 5, whose basic wage as a journeyman printer was £10. 15s. 3d.

When everything had been added and deducted the total amount to go into his pay packet was £18 2s. 6d. I took up the first envelope and opened my bag and took out eighteen slips of paper from the first rubber-banded package and put the slips in the pay envelope. The eighteen pounds went into the other pocket of my bag. I had tried the slips against a similar number of one-pound notes in envelopes at home, and it just wasn't possible after shuffling them to tell which was which.

I went at it flat-out today. As I've said, the next office had only the telephone switchboard and some filing cabinets in it, and the one girl, Miss Harry, at the switchboard. The frosted-glass partition between us didn't quite reach to the ceiling, but there wasn't any real communication; we could hear the low buzz of the calls and she could hear our Anson machine and probably the chink of money. The door beyond her office had to open and about six steps be taken before anyone opened my door, so I had several seconds if necessary to shut my bag and look innocent. In fact, except for the little alteration at the end of each calculation, I was working as usual.

I was only interrupted three times all afternoon.

When Mr. Ward came in at five I only had £260 left.

"Hm," he said, rubbing his mole. "Better even than last week. We'll give Miss Clabon notice."

319

I smiled. "It wouldn't work. She's really very good. Let me just finish this one, will you?"

He stood picking at his finger-nail while I finished off Stevens, F., journeyman apprentice, £8 4s. and put the money in an envelope and sealed it. Then I arched my aching back while he picked up the tray with its neatly stacked and named and numbered envelopes and carried it to the safe. While he was putting this in I got together the rest of the silver and notes and clipped the notes with rubber bands and put them in the cash-box. I carried the cash-box and the ledgers to the safe and held the door while he put them in. He locked the door and put the key in his pocket and took out a packet of cigarettes. He looked as if he was going to help himself, but he thought better of it and offered me one.

The generous impulse must have nearly killed him. I smiled and shook my head.

He said: "No vices?"

"Well, not that one."

"Quite *the* paragon, eh?"

"No." I smiled again. "Do you dislike me, Mr. Ward?" I felt like challenging him tonight.

He was frightfully occupied shaking out a match and looking at the watch-spring of black smoke that came from it. "It's not my business to like or dislike employees of this firm, Mrs. Taylor. My business is to see that they do their work."

"But you must have your own opinions."

"Oh, yes." He squinted down at his cigarette. "But those opinions *are* my own, aren't they."

This obviously wasn't his day for confessions. "I'm glad you have nothing against me."

"What could I have? You're so efficient. Everyone agrees."

I picked up my bag, which suddenly seemed to me to look fatter than it should have done. I looked at my watch, Five-twenty. They weren't working overtime today, and most of the printers would be on their way out. It'd be murder if one came to the hatch now and asked for his wages tonight. It had happened once in April.

I went to the door. "You'll be here tomorrow, Mr. Ward?"

"No, I'm going up to a meeting of paper wholesalers. Why?"

"Mr. Rutland will be back?"

"Oh, yes, he'll be here; and both Mr. Holbrooks."

I went out of the office and walked slowly, pretending to fumble with my shoe, until I heard Mr. Ward lock the door. Linda Harry was putting on her jersey and she followed me out. We went along together to the cloakroom, where there were still two or three girls powdering their noses. I stayed there talking to them until I saw Sam Ward leave the building.

As I was just going to go out Linda Harry asked me if I had a light. I darned nearly opened my bag to see. But I said, no, I was sorry I hadn't.

We were about the last. You wouldn't believe how quickly the place emptied. I said good night to Howard and went down towards the High Street tube.

When I got home I locked the door of the flat and took the money out and counted it. I had over £1,270. In fact £1,272 10s. It was my best haul.

6

So from then on it was the same old routine.

A gin and french first. It always tasted specially nice. Then I combed my hair out quite loose until it fell nearly to my shoulders. While I was finishing my drink I went over the train times.

Then I took everything off, throwing it in a heap on the floor, and went naked into the bathroom. I never would if I could help it take a flat without a private bathroom because as I've said soaking in warm water seemed to wash something away; not guilt because I never felt guilty, but the sort of old contacts with things and people. You skinned them off and left them in the water. When you stepped out you were being born again. Or *reborn* again as Marnie Elmer. I was a real person again, Marnie Elmer, not someone I'd made up and dressed up for half a year. Mary Taylor the pathetic widow, had gone and left her old clothes on the floor.

She really had been a bit of a fool, Mary Taylor, getting so involved. Mollie Jeffrey had had much more sense. When that man Ronnie Oliver had rung up Marion Holland just after she'd helped herself to a large sum of money from the office of Crombie & Strutt, right under the nose of Mr. Pringle, the manager—when Ronnie Oliver had rung her up when she was in her bath just before she left Birmingham for ever, I'd said never again. Don't be a fool, getting entangled. So Mollie Jeffrey had taken that advice to heart. But Mary Taylor had forgotten it. Mary Taylor had let herself be pawed about in private flats and she'd been taken to the races by a director. This was the worst and most incautious ever.

I packed all my old things in my case and dressed again in new clothes, all not to be noticed and not dear. Then began my usual round of the flat. Everything, magazines, newspapers, hand tissues from the waste paper basket, they were all gathered up, and this time it was easy to burn them because the flat had an open grate. I picked up my suitcase and packed the money in a corner of it, then I slung my coat over my arm and went to the door of the flat, stopped for a last look.

It was funny. There was nothing. Mary Taylor was as real as nothing. She left behind her a bank account containing seven pounds in Lloyds Bank, Swiss Cottage, and a few ashes in the grate. In a way, I thought, I was a bit like that man Haigh, was it, who dissolved his victims in an acid bath. I was dissolving Mary Taylor. She was going, going, gone.

I left and took the tube to Paddington, changing at Baker Street. At Paddington I caught the eight-thirty-five for Wolverhampton and got a meal on the train. At Wolverhampton I took a late bus for Walsall and I spent the night there. The next morning I was up early doing some more shopping, and then I went to a hairdressing salon and had a new hair-do.

But sitting there in the chair I began to think to myself that Mary Taylor had lived too long. I should have killed her sooner. It wasn't as easy as usual to get out of her skin.

By now—it was twenty past eleven—they'd know the worst. Who would be the first to find out? Probably, when she didn't turn up, someone else would take over the rest of the pay envelopes—but there really seemed no reason why anyone should find out until the first of her envelopes was opened.

In a way it was rather sad that Mary Taylor wouldn't ever see Mark Rutland again. Whatever else, you had to admit he was different. I mean, if you like to be heavy, he had class. And then there was Terry too—and Dawn. They'd all somehow got themselves into three-dimensional figures, not just cut-outs any more; and they stuck in your memory.

I left Walsall in the afternoon and went by bus and train to Nottingham. It took me eight hours to do fifty miles, but doing it I covered four times that distance. I did this sort of looping the loop every time after leaving a job. You just couldn't be too careful. I also lost my old suitcase, deposited at a left-luggage office to rot for ever, and went on with my new one. I stayed at Nottingham at the Talbot as Miss Maureen Thurston. On Saturday night I stayed at Swindon.

On the Sunday morning I left Swindon and made for the Old Crown, Cirencester.

It was like going back to old friends now, it really was; it was like a second home, and in some ways more homey than the first, because when I went back to Torquay it was sort of going back to being a kid again. The old Crown was a new life I was making for myself, and this wasn't a sham either, it was real.

I stopped only long enough for a couple of sandwiches in the bar and to change, and then I jumped on a bus that passed Garrod's Farm. I had dropped a postcard saying I was coming so they were expecting me, and you'd have thought Forio was too.

He knew it was me before I even got into the yard. He whinnied and stamped his foot and made noises that I've never heard another horse make.

When I went to him and rubbed my face against his muzzle he kept putting his soft mouth over the knuckles of my hand to find the piece of apple that I had for him. Always when I was away a long time I was scared he'd have forgotten me; but I never broke my rule not to visit on a job.

When he was saddled and we clattered out of the yard John Garrod followed me saying to take it easy because he hadn't been able to give Forio enough exercise, but I was too crazy to care, and as soon as we got going Forio nearly ran away with me; if it hadn't been for the heavy going and a slope he would have.

But of course it didn't matter. Nothing mattered; it was a lovely day and the heavy showers didn't count, and I was full of something though it couldn't be food as I'd only had the two sandwiches since breakfast. This was all I wanted, to hell with people; they cloyed and stuck and twisted you up inside and everything went wrong; this was simple, clean, easy, no complications; a woman and a horse. No more. Nothing to be fought out or explained. You just rode together. That's the way I wanted it always.

It rained heavily twice while I was out, the first time I sheltered in a copse, but the second time I galloped through it, Forio at full stretch, the rain pelting into my face. When we stopped, both with no breath, at the edge of the common, we were dripping all over and the last of the shower was leaving us, and the sun threw a rainbow over the woods towards Swindon.

I turned for home, and thought about Forio and the way I'd bought him.

It was after the second job I'd done, the one at Newcastle, and I'd seen Mother all right and still had money in my pocket and had gone to the races at Cheltenham. Not that I was going to bet, but there I was, enjoying myself all by myself.

324

One of the races was a selling plate, and after it was over I heard a man on the rails next to me say: "Let's see how much the winner makes," and walked off, so I followed him and the winning horse was being led into the ring with a few bored-looking people leaning against the rails, and a man suddenly started putting the horse up for auction.

Well, it never occurred to me to be interested until I saw that the horse had hurt its leg in the last few yards of the race and was limping badly and I thought, I suppose no one will bid for him now. And he was a *lovely* horse, with plenty of bone, and *big*, a bit big for me, but it was a good fault. He was almost black, with a lighter patch on his nose and his chest. Something wasn't quite right about his ears but that might not matter. Of course I knew nothing *really* about horses, except riding a few hacks and what I'd read in books, but he seemed such a wonderful bargain, and you know how it is, before you know where you are you've started bidding. And suddenly I had nodded once too often and the auctioneer said: "Going for the last time—*Sold* to the lady in the corner, for two hundred and forty-five guineas."

After that it was a sick panic to make all the arrangements, to leave a deposit with the owner and swear I'd be back with the rest of the money in the morning. Two weeks later I found myself the owner of a horse, boarded at Garrod's Farm at an *awful* cost per week, no job, and less than forty pounds left.

So I had to get work quickly, and I'd been lucky to get a promising job almost right off with Crombie & Strutt, the Turf Accountants. But it had been a bad grind for some months, living myself and paying for Forio out of eight pounds a week.

Not that I'd ever regretted it, not for a second. From the first ride he was wonderful; he'd got a great heart, always good tempered, and such an *eye*. His mouth was the softest thing; you couldn't feel his teeth. And I learned to jump with him and he was such a fine jumper. And when we galloped he'd a lovely long swinging stride. I hadn't had him six months when a man wanted him as a hunter and offered me five hundred pounds for him.

The sun had set before I got back to the stables and I stayed a long time with Forio, rubbing him down and brushing and combing his mane and tail. He loved this sort of thing and almost talked while I did it.

Being Sunday there were people about, and a crowd of half a dozen schoolgirls were in the yard chattering in fluting voices that weren't at all like the voices I used to hear in Plymouth. A dog barked in the farmhouse.

I was hungry now, fairly ravenous. I went through into the farmhouse and looked at the bus time-table. The next one passed the house at seven-thirty. That would get into Cirencester at seven-fifty-three. Time for a bath and a change before dinner. Then an early bed.

Mr. Garrod came out as I passed. "Oh, by the way, Miss Elmer, there was a gentleman asking for you about an hour ago."

"For me?" My heart's all right; it keeps steady most times, but it gave a bit of a lurch now. "What did he want?"

"He didn't say. He asked if you was here and I said you was out riding. I don't know if he'll be back."

"Thanks, Mr. Garrod."

I soon calmed down. I suppose I might have asked what he was like, but I thought, I expect it's that stable-boy from Mr. Hinchley again, wanting to see if I've changed my mind about selling Forio. Well, I haven't. Nor ever will.

But when I stepped out of the farm I just took the precaution of looking about carefully. It was now half dark and there was no one about. I walked down the muddy path and along the short lane to the main road. The bus was due in five minutes.

In the main road there were the sidelights of a car parked about twenty yards away. Just to be on the safe side I turned and walked the opposite way, and as I did so I bumped into a man who had stepped out from the hedge.

"Miss Elmer?"

It was Mark Rutland.

I don't know what they felt like when they dropped the first atomic bomb, but a sort of Hiroshima happened to me then. He took my arm to stop me from falling.

"Where are you staying? I'll drive you home."

7

We got to the car. Somehow I sat myself in the passenger's
seat. He slammed the door on me, and it was like the clang
of a prison cell. My heart was using something thicker than
blood and it was clogging up my brain like dying. I thought
it's not happening, you're making this up to scare yourself;
this man doesn't know Marnie Elmer, he only knows Mary
Taylor. Let him stay there. Let him bloody stay there.

He stuck the key in the ignition and switched on and
started the engine.

"Which way?"

God help me, it was the same car as the one Mary Taylor
had been to the races in. There was the same scratch on the
dashboard and the same indirect yellow lighting. Supplied
by Berkeley Garages Ltd., Hendon.

"Which way?"

I wet my lips and tried to speak but there wasn't any
sound.

"Cirencester?" he said.

I nodded.

He started the car and we went off just ahead of the bus
which was stopping to put someone down and which should
have picked me up to take me back to the Old Crown. You
know, that was the point where the two lines crossed. That
was the point where I wasn't separate any longer from the
girl I'd left yesterday. It was like dreaming a knife-stab
and finding it was real.

We drove on, saying nothing.

As we got to the outskirts of the town he said:

"Where do you live?"

"The—Old Crown."

"Under what name?"

". . . Elmer."

"Is that your real name?"

I tried to say something but my tongue stuck. He said: "It'll save time if you tell me the truth."

I looked at his face in the light of a street lamp. He was wearing an old mack and his hair was damped down as if it had been wet. I wondered how long he'd stood there waiting.

"Is Elmer your real name?"

"Yes."

"Where do you come from?"

"Cardiff."

"Where is the money you stole?"

"Some of it is here—in Cirencester."

"The rest?"

"It's safe enough."

"Not lost on the races yet, then?"

"I don't bet."

"Ha!"

"It's true!"

He didn't speak then until we came into the square by the church. "Which is your hotel?"

"On the corner over there."

He drove across and stopped at the door. "I'll come in with you while you get your things."

"Where are we going?"

"You'll see."

He got out and opened the door of the car for me. I slid out. God, my knees were weak.

Mark went to the desk. "I'm sorry, Miss Elmer is my secretary and she has to cut her holiday short because of illness. Could you make out her bill, please? She'll be leaving right away."

"Certainly, sir. Well, she's only just arrived so there's really nothing to pay."

"I'll come upstairs with you, Miss Elmer," he said as I started to move.

The receptionist raised her eyebrows, but nobody tried to stop him. I hated him for coming into my room because this was the one place where I'd been really myself. This was at the centre of my *own* life, not anybody else's. I didn't see why he had to force his way in here.

He'd gone across to the window and was staring at the thirty-foot drop.

"Where's the money?"

"In there."

He picked up the attaché case, opened it to look inside, snapped it shut. "I'll take this and wait in the corridor. I'll give you ten minutes."

I could have done it in five but I took fifteen. I was like someone coming round after being thrown on their head. I had to take my time.

I was in the completest hole ever. I had always thought, if I'm caught as Mary Taylor or Mollie Jeffrey, that's not me. Even if I go to prison for it, that's not me. With luck I could keep them from ever knowing who I really was. I might have been able to write a note to Mother saying I was going abroad or something, keep up a sham until I came out. But there was no sham here. By some foul swivel-eyed piece of bad luck Mark Rutland had found me out as Marnie Elmer. And while, so far as I knew there had been no link between Mary Taylor and Marnie Elmer, there certainly was a dead straight line linking Marnie with Plymouth and Torquay.

If he checked everything I told him, then I just had to tell him the truth—or part of it. It all depended on whether he was taking me to the police. You'd think it the obvious thing.

He was waiting for me, smoking, at the head of the stairs. The dismal light made his face look darker and more delicate. But I knew it wasn't now. I knew it was as tough as rock and for almost the first time in my life I was afraid of someone.

"Got everything?" he said, and led the way out to the waiting car.

"Where are you going to take me?"

He put my case in the boot. "Get in."

I looked round once, thinking of even running for it because if there's one thing I know it's how to run, but there was a policeman on the other side of the square.

We drove off. He didn't speak while we left the town. I saw a signpost on the road marked *Fairford. Oxford.*

"Now," he said. "Just tell me why you did this."

"Did what?"

"Took the money."

"What are you going to do? Where are we going?"

"If you don't mind I'll ask the questions."

I kept my mouth shut for a long time. I had drawn away from him as far as I could. He glanced at me and then leaned across and locked the catch on the door. I wondered if there was any hope of softening him up.

I said: "Mr. Rutland, I'm—terribly sorry."

"Let's skip the emotional content. Just tell me why you did it."

"How did you find me?"

"I'm asking the questions."

I put my hands up to my face, not needing to act the misery I really felt. "If you turn me over to the police I'll tell them *nothing*; I'll not say a *word*; they can send me to prison and you'll not get the rest of your money back; I don't care!"

"Oh, yes, you do."

"But if you promise you won't, I'll tell you everything you want to know."

"Good God, girl, you're not in a position to strike bargains! I could turn you over to the nearest police station and drive away and have nothing more to do with it! And will quick enough if you try those tactics."

"They're not *tactics*, Mark . . ."

I looked at him to see how he took the Christian name. His hands were fairly tight on the steering wheel. "All right, I'll begin. Where do you want me to begin?"

"What's your real name?"

"Margaret Elmer."

"Where do you come from?"

"Plymouth."

"Oh-ho, so you were lying again."

"I can't help it——"

"No, it seems not."

"I don't mean *that* . . ."

"Well, go on."

"I—I was born in Devonport but lived most of my

330

life in Plymouth itself. I went to the North Road Secondary Modern School for girls, from seven to nearly fifteen. Is— is that what you want to know?"

"Are your mother and father in Australia?"

"No. My father was killed in the war. In the Navy, Mark."

"And your mother?"

"She died soon after . . . I was brought up by an old friend of mother's called Lucy Nye."

"And when you left school?"

"My uncle—my mother's brother—he's at sea too, an engineer—he paid for me to go on to another school, St. Andrew's Technical College, where I learned shorthand and typing and bookkeeping and accountancy."

I looked at him again. He had dipped his lights, and the light from another car reflected off the road on to his thin angry face.

"I suppose this really is true, is it?"

"You can check it if you want."

"Don't worry, I will. I was only reminding you to keep your imagination under control."

I was wild at that. "Have you never done anything wrong, never broken any law? It's different for you, of course, with always as much money as you needed——"

"Get on with your story."

I struggled for a minute trying to swallow my breathing. "When I left I got a job in Plymouth. But I was hardly settled before Lucy Nye was taken ill so I gave it up to— to nurse her. I nursed her for eighteen months, until she died. When she died I found she'd left me the house we were living in and—and two hundred pounds in cash. I spent some of the cash on—on elocution lessons and some more on accountancy, and then I got a job with Deloitte, Plender & Griffiths in Bristol. While I was there I first saw horses— horses as I know them now, not old broken-down things pulling vans but long-legged thoroughbreds, jumpers and— and——"

"All right, I've got that. You saw horses."

"And I fell in love with them. Does that mean anything to you? . . . After a bit the house in Devonport sold for a thousand pounds. It was all mine. I reckoned I could live for two years or more, live like a lady, on what I'd got and what I'd saved, buy a horse, ride it. I bought Forio and——"

"Forio?"

"My horse at the Garrods. So I gave up my job and lived like that. I lived like a lady as cheap as I could, but all day free. I wonder if freedom like that means anything to you. I used to ride nearly every day—then sometimes I'd get a temporary job round Christmas time to get a bit of extra money. But I just spent my capital most of the time. Then last year, about November, it was all gone ... So I came to London and looked for work. I got a job at Kendalls but looked out for something better."

"And you found Rutland's."

"Yes ..."

"That was quite a bit better, wasn't it, with a clear profit apart from wages of some twelve hundred pounds."

I burst into tears. "I'm s-sorry, Mark, it was a sudden temptation. I hated to do it but it was a sudden thought of being able to afford perhaps two more years like those I had had before I came t-to London. I shouldn't ever have taken a cashier's job, I-I suppose. It was handling so much money at—at one time. Oh, Mark, I'm so very sorry ..."

The tears were turned on, of course. But if it had been possible for me to cry naturally I really could have cried—for disappointment, and for being found out, and because I was so scared of what was going to happen.

We were through Faringdon by now and on the main Swindon-Oxford road. I dabbed at my eyes with a handkerchief that was too small. But he didn't offer me his.

After a time he said: "And Mr. Taylor? Where does he come in?"

"Mr. Taylor?"

"Is he a little more of your imagination or does he exist?"

"Oh, no. There ... was nobody. She had never—I've never been married."

"You've been somebody's mistress?"

"*No* ... Good Heavens no! Why should you think I had?"

332

"I don't think anything. I'm asking. Why did you call yourself Mrs. Taylor?"

I paused to blow my nose. Why the hell did I call myself Mrs. Taylor? But I hadn't really. I had just made Mary Taylor a married woman three years ago when I thought her up.

"Mrs. Taylor was an old friend of my father's. He's been dead for years but the name came to my mind."

"Why did it have to come to your mind at all? Why did you open an account in Cardiff in that name three years ago?"

I had been expecting that one. "Mrs. Nye has—has a nephew. He's abroad most of the time but he's not much good. I was afraid of—if he knew Lucy Nye had left me all that money he'd want a share."

"Are you sure he isn't working with you in this?"

"Nobody's working with me! You speak as if it was all cut and dried, planned weeks ago, in cold blood!"

"And wasn't it?"

"No!"

"It was all so impulsive and child-like that you changed your name to Taylor when you came to London nine months ago? That is if you haven't been Mrs. Taylor for three years."

"I didn't change it for that. I changed it because I thought it would be like a *fresh start*! I didn't want Mrs. Nye's nephew looking me up while I was in London! I—I thought I'd stick to the new name, make it something better than the old!"

"Well, you're not really trying to tell me that this theft just happened on the spur of the moment are you? Susan Clabon away on her holidays; a cheque made out deliberately for two hundred and twenty pounds more than we needed to draw; a supply of our own paper cut correctly to size and brought into the office that morning. What do you call cold blood?"

"No, but it was only the last few days that I really thought of it! Then when the chance came I just hadn't the strength of will to resist. I hadn't Mark, really. I know I'm weak. I should never have done it but . . . You see, it

333

was the week before, when Susan was away, that I realised it would be possible, but even then I never seriously thought ... It wasn't really till Wednesday. And then I couldn't rest, couldn't sleep because of it."

Another shower came and he put on the screen-wipers. Through the Japanese fans they made on the screen you could see the suburbs of Oxford squeezing up round the car.

"Have you stolen before?"

I hesitated. "Twice in Plymouth when I was ten—and got beaten for it."

"Not that sort of thing," he said impatiently. "Since then."

I thought it was risky to be too pure. "Yes ... once in Bristol."

"When?"

"About three years ago. I was in a ship and ..."

"How much did you take?"

"Oh, only a scarf. It wasn't worth much."

"How much?"

"About two pounds ..."

"And since then?"

"Not since then."

In Oxford the rain had cleared the streets, and only buses and cars splashed through them. Out in the country again we drove past a signpost I couldn't read.

"Where are you taking me?"

He said: "What proof have you of what you've told me?"

"Proof? Nothing on me."

"What can you get?"

"How do you mean?"

"Is there someone from Plymouth who knows you?"

"Well, I ..."

"Well, is there?"

"... Yes, I suppose so; but if you aren't going to hand me over to the police I'd rather——"

"I didn't say I wasn't."

"I can find my birth certificate—a—a bookkeeping and accountancy certificate—a character from the North Road School ... I haven't kept much."

"Where are those?"

334

"I could get them."

"Where are they?"

"Well, various places . . . I expect I could get a letter from the South Western Electricity Board saying I worked for them. That was my first job. And Deloitte, Plender & Griffiths would say the same—though I was only with them six months . . . I think I've still got the receipt for Forio when I bought him . . . It's—it's hard to think of things. What do you want me to prove?"

"Prove? I want you to prove that you——" He stopped. He sounded choked—with irritation or something. "Never mind."

"That I'm not just a common sneak-thief?"

"If you like."

"But I *am* . . . What else can you call me after this?"

"Never mind. I'm not sitting as a judge on you; I'm only trying to understand."

I sighed shakily. "I think perhaps that's impossible. When I'd done it, stole that money, I could hardly believe it or understand it myself."

"I didn't notice you rushing back."

"No . . . And I shouldn't have done."

"Well, that's honest anyway."

"For one thing I should have been too afraid."

We didn't say anything more for a while.

"It isn't always so easy to know the truth about yourself," I said. "Or is it with you? You've lived a different, easier life."

He said nothing.

I said: "Maybe you don't have two thoughts at the same time. I often have two thoughts—one belongs to the person I'm trying to be now, the other belongs to the kid from Devonport. And she's still a back-street urchin. I mean, you don't *suddenly* grow out of knowing what it's like to be hungry and knocked around and treated like dirt. You don't honestly. I mean, you may think you have, but then when you find yourself holding a thousand pounds in pound notes, well, you suddenly discover you want to bolt down the next dark alley. It's all mixed up with that. I can't explain to you, Mark."

335

"In fact," he said, "that's the most convincing answer you've given me tonight."

We had passed through Thame and seemed to be making for Aylesbury. I knew in the last minute or two I'd gained a bit—I wasn't any longer lying flat with him kneeling on my chest—I'd made the first move for wriggling out from under him. But it was chancy work—I had to move fast, but not too fast.

"The reasons for what I did—they were more mixed up even than that, even than you think."

"How?"

"I can't tell you."

"You'd better."

"Oh . . . there were other things besides the need for money behind it. There was the need to get away."

"To get away?"

"From you."

"Thanks."

I hesitated then, wondering if he was really taking it.

"Well, don't you *see* . . . Or don't you? We were getting—friendly."

"Was that any reason why you should run away?"

"*Yes*. Or I thought so. Maybe I began to take it a bit too seriously. I expect it was fine for you but it began not to be fun for me, and I thought it was time I opted out."

"Go on."

"Well, don't you see?"

"I'd like to hear."

"Look, Mark, I can't help it, I felt that way. And I thought, what crazy chance is there of anything worth while coming of it?"

"So?"

"I thought, he's pretty well out of the top drawer. I'm not out of any drawer at all. I'm just something sucked up in the vacuum cleaner. Well, so well, what was going to happen? Nothing that I could see that wasn't going to be a nasty mess for me."

"So you thought? . . ."

"So I thought I'll get out, and get out in a way that will finish it good and proper: so I did. The back-street urchin made a pretty fine haul, didn't she? Only she never thought —I never thought you'd find me again—so quickly— like magic . . . I don't want to start again—hand me over to the police and have done!"

He took his hand off the wheel and I thought he was going to touch me. But he didn't.

After a minute he said: "Don't worry, you're not in jail yet."

As we got to Aylesbury there was more traffic again because it was closing time.

He said: "I suppose I've got to start calling you Margaret instead of Mary."

"I've always been called Marnie."

"Marnie . . . Marnie . . . Marnie; all right."

"Where are you taking me? Won't you tell me that?"

"Home."

"Where?"

"To my home. You'll have to spend the night there now. It's too late to do anything else with you."

"I—what will your housekeeper say?"

"What should she say?"

I wondered now if I *had* been going too fast. "She won't think it odd?"

"Are you worried about your reputation?"

"What's going to happen in the morning?"

"You're going back to John Rutland and Co."

I sat up. "What? Oh, don't joke about it."

"I'm not joking."

"But how can I?"

"You're going back as if nothing had happened—for a few weeks anyhow. If you want to give in your notice then you can do; but I'm having no unnecessary scandal."

I put my fingers on his arm. "Don't you understand, Mark? You must have been there yesterday. Everyone will know. Even if you don't turn me over to the police Mr. Ward or one of the others will!"

He said: "When you didn't turn up on Friday we tried to get in touch with your flat but there was no reply. So I decided, as Miss Clabon was away and as Dawn Witherbie was busy on the retail side, I'd finish the wage packets

337

myself. I did about half a dozen before I noticed that there wouldn't be enough money to finish off the wages. Then I checked up how much you had drawn out on Thursday and how much there should have been in cash from the retail side. So it didn't take me long to open one of the envelopes you had done and find what was inside."

"Well, then, you see——"

"Oh, yes, I saw. I saw perfectly well."

I sat and watched him.

He switched on the screen-wipers again.

"I thought all round it. I checked up one or two of the pay slips and they were perfectly correct. Odd you should have gone to that trouble when it wasn't going to matter."

"I——"

"The careful worker coming out, I suppose. All that was missing was the money. So I went across to the bank and drew out another thousand pounds in notes. Then I came back and started reopening your envelopes and typing new ones."

I stared hard at him in the dark to see if he was just trying to be plain funny.

"Of course if Ward had been there I couldn't very well have put it over; but there was no one else to interfere. When it came to eleven o'clock I called Miss Smith over and got her to distribute those I'd done. Those I hadn't done had to wait. I sent word round that Miss Clabon was away and Mrs. Taylor had been taken ill. I finished the last by half past twelve. Apparently I only made two mistakes in my haste, and those I had to put right yesterday."

We were nearly in Berkhamsted. My mind was working like a jet now, but it kept flying around one solid fact that just didn't fit with the rest at all.

"Why did you *do* it?"

"Ward always said you were too good to be true."

"He was right."

"Yes. And I was wrong. I'd hate to hear Ward say 'I told you so!'"

I waited. He was being funny. He seemed to have finished.

"It can't be just that."

"Near enough."

"You wouldn't go to that trouble just for that. You wouldn't, Mark. No one would."

"Don't you think it's a good enough explanation?"

"No, I don't."

"Well, I suppose I had my own ideas."

"What were they?"

"Never mind."

When he got to his house Mrs. Leonard had gone home. There was a note and some cold supper in the dining-room. He got some more cutlery out of a cupboard and we had tongue and salad and a bottle of beer. I was nearly out for food, and I tried not to eat like a wolf in front of him. I was still on a knife-edge, I knew. I still had one foot in jail. But it was on its way out. I could see that. Because he was still sweet on me. That was really what it added up to. It was a miracle of luck. But it was still a knife-edge.

And it was different here from being in the car. Then we'd been in semi-darkness, side by side, nothing but voices. Here we sat opposite each other, over a table, like the dinner in Cambridge. I was seen as well as heard, so I'd got to look just right all the time as well as sound it. I'd snatched a look at myself in the mirror in the hall and been able to powder the tears off my face, to comb my hair. But it wouldn't do to look too tidy, too composed. I was surprised how flushed my face was. But it didn't look bad.

He was white like a sheet, looked very tired. And his dark eyes kept staring into me as if they would skewer into my soul.

He said: "How much money is there in that case?"

"Six hundred pounds."

"The rest?"

"In a bank in Swindon, and a post office account in Sheffield. And the Lost Property Office at Nottingham."

"You were spreading your risk."

"I couldn't pay too much into one place."

"You thought of everything, didn't you."

I fumbled with a piece of bread. "Apparently not; you found me."

339

"I found you."

"How?"

Perhaps that wasn't too clever. I saw his face tighten again.

"I'll keep that under my hat for the time being. Just to make sure you won't run away again."

"Mark, I *can't* go back tomorrow as if nothing had happened! Really I can't. Somebody must have suspected something."

"They can't suspect much if there's no money missing."

"Where was Terry? Did you tell him?"

"I told nobody. Anyway he was interviewing clients all morning."

". . . How will I get the rest of the money—from Swindon and Sheffield, I mean and—— It would take me all day tomorrow."

"Come back first. When you go to these places I'm coming with you. In the meantime I can pay six hundred into the firm's account out of my personal account to make up the balance. That will keep the books all right if Ward or one of the Holbrooks should ask during the week. But the chances are very much that they won't anyway."

A good deal of the bite had gone out of his voice. He'd sounded so angry at me at the beginning but now he was cooling off. In a way we might have been working together for something. If I didn't make another bloomer like that 'How?' you never knew your luck. This wasn't a threat any more, it was negotiation. But what was it a negotiation *about*? Even when you're sweet on someone you're not all Christian forgiveness. What did he want? Well, he wanted me; that was it, wasn't it? My skin crawled.

He was watching me now and I had to be careful.

"You're a strange creature. The strangest I've ever met."

I lowered my eyes. "Suppose I am?"

"According to what you've told me, if it's true, you don't have much contact with other people. You say you ride a horse—good exercise, but what about the rest of the twenty-four hours? You say you've spent over two years this way. Didn't you have friends?"

"I didn't have boy-friends. I got to know a few people. There was always something to do. I wasn't lonely."

"But living that way is only half living. You're too withdrawn."

"I enjoyed it."

"Perhaps it all helps you to make up these exciting stories, does it? I'm thinking of what you told me about your husband. You were so upset after the motor accident that if you'd stayed on in Cardiff you'd have become a nerve case. But it was easier for you than for me because you'd been able to move and take a job."

"Don't remind me please. I was—very ashamed of that."

"You were? That's something anyhow. And about your mother and father in Sydney, and how they found it too hot in the summer months. And your father watching the Davis Cup matches. It was quite an effort on your part, wasn't it?"

"I'm *sorry*. I'm desperately sorry."

"I wonder how much of what you've told me tonight is out of the same book."

I raised my head again.

"I'm not lying *now*! They're two different *things*! I was a fool, but it didn't occur to me that I should get to know anyone well in my job. I've told you, I like to be solitary! When I found I was getting to know people I found I had to go on adding to my—to what I'd said at first. It's like a snowball. It piles up and up."

"It's a common consequence, Marnie. But why send your parents to Australia in the first place, when they were both dead? How did that help?"

It was the first time he had used my name. "It *didn't* help. I somehow wanted to make up a—a life quite different from my own."

"There's such a thing as a pathological liar. Are you one?"

"I don't know. Anyway you're going to check everything I've told you tonight, so you can see for yourself."

He was still looking at me sort of funny, half-way between a doctor and a lover. "I can't check everything. I can't

341

check what to me is the most important thing you've said tonight."

"What's that?"

"That one of the reasons you committed this theft was because you wanted to get away from me, because you were afraid of getting entangled and getting hurt."

"It's true!"

"I wish I could be certain."

"Mark, it's true! D'you think I have no feelings at all?"

"I'm certain you have some but I want to be sure what they are."

It was getting a strain, sitting there looking at him all the time, and I knew I was running into a packet of trouble of another kind. But there was no way out.

He said: "I wonder, if you're such a smart girl, that it never occurred to you to play this the other way round."

"What way?"

"I don't know whether to be pleased or insulted that you didn't."

"Didn't what? I don't know what you mean."

Thank God he pulled abruptly away from the table, his chair creaking, moved across the room with a queer energy. His collar had got untidy as he talked.

"Next time you stand opposite a glass look at yourself. Have you never had men interested in you?"

"Yes. Oh yes. But I——"

"Did it never occur to you that I had lost my wife less than two years ago and, in some ways at least, was a fairly eligible person to become friendly with?"

"People in the office made remarks."

"Did they. Well, putting aside for the moment the fact that you may not have thought much of me as a—as a proposition, didn't you ever think that if you hooked me you hooked quite a bit more than twelve hundred pounds?"

"It depends what you mean by hooked."

"Married."

The clock in the hall was striking midnight. It took a

342

long time to strike. Well, it wasn't like that clock in Mother's kitchen but it seemed to strike into my spine just the same.

"That wasn't possible," I said in a panic, in a suddenly stifling smothering panic.

"Why not?"

"We come from different worlds."

"You've got rather old-fashioned notions, melodramatic notions about class, haven't you?"

"Maybe I have. Maybe I'm a fool. Anyway it seems less dishonest to me to take money the way I did than to trade myself for money like that!"

"You dislike me?"

"No, of course not. That's not it at all!"

"Then what is it?"

"If I——"

"You said you wanted to get away from me because you were afraid of getting hurt. That sounds as if you were not exactly indifferent. Then in what way would you have been trading yourself for money by marrying me?"

I was cornered—like a rat in a coal bunker. It was a completely new experience for me, because I've never been at a loss for an excuse or an explanation or a way out. For the second time that night he seemed to be cleverer than I was, and did I hate it.

To give myself a breather I put my hands up to my face. You've only got to think long enough about anything to find a way out. After a minute he came over and put his hand on my shoulder; it was the first time he'd touched me all evening.

"Tell me, Marnie."

I said in a desolate voice: "How can I tell you what I don't know? I thought it wasn't possible. Anyway it's too late now."

Even while I took that line I was afraid of what he was going to say, and my God he said it.

"Doesn't that rather remain to be seen?"

"How?"

"You tell me."

I knew I had to look at him. I knew that this might

343

be about the last moment to bale out. Yet there wasn't really any place to go. If I told him no, it was as clear as gin what would come next—the police. It was a ghastly moment. His hand tightened slightly on my shoulder. I looked up, hoping my eyes didn't show what I was thinking.

"Mark, I'm a *thief*. Don't deceive yourself. There's no getting away from it. Just—forgive me if you can and let me go."

"Is that what you want?"

"I'm sure it's for the best."

"For whose best? Yours? Mine?"

"Yes. Yes, I think so."

"I differ from that. D'you know, I happen to love you. I suppose you've guessed it, have you?"

"No."

"No? Well, that's really the nigger in the woodpile. I love you, Marnie."

"Mark. You're . . . you're *crazy*."

"It's a symptom of the complaint."

I said desperately: "Look . . . be *sensible* . . . I've robbed you and lied to you. That's no—no basis to build a sparrow's nest on, let alone a marriage . . . Do you trust me?"

He half laughed. "No. Not yet."

"You see. How can anything begin like that? Love's got to be built on trust."

"Nonsense. Love grows where it grows. What it builds on is anybody's guess."

I didn't answer. He had me in the corner and I wasn't even like that rat—I couldn't bite him.

He said: "After following you half-way across England do you think I'm going to let you go?"

8

So the impossible happened and I went back to work on the Monday as if nothing was different. Nobody said a thing except that one or two asked me if I was better, and Sam Ward looked down his nose a bit more than usual. Susan Clabon was full of the Isle of Wight, and that helped to pass the day. I found in the waste basket all my pieces of paper that Mark had snatched out of the pay envelopes and thrown away.

On the Thursday he drove me to Swindon and the other places where I had left the money, and I drew it out. On the Saturday he asked me to marry him.

It had been coming at me of course ever since Sunday night like a railway train, and me on a level-crossing. But I was tied there and there was no way of dodging it.

There was just no way.

He wouldn't say how he'd traced me, so I didn't know what mistake I had made. All I knew was that if he looked too hard the way led from Cirencester, clang, right back to Mother like one of those old-fashioned cash systems they used to have in ships. I had to go on lying to him about my mother being dead because if he once knew she was alive it was all up. If Mother knew I was a thief and had been keeping her on stolen money she'd froth at the mouth. In fact I knew it would kill her: she'd never be able to swallow the disgrace. If he ever met her the whole story of Mr. Pemberton and his millions came crashing down, and then in no time they'd both discover I had been taking money for three years. Then as well as Mother having a stroke or something I would go to prison quick. Even marrying him was better than that.

So I had to stop him probing too hard, and the only way I knew was to let him think I loved him. Many of the things I'd told him were true—except that I'd left gaps—so I went painstakingly about getting him the proof he wanted. If I could get him proofs of what was true—birth certificate and the rest—he might not dig into what was not true. In fact he took a lot on trust. Perhaps he thought he ought to if he loved me, even though he'd said he would not.

He seemed pretty crazy about me. So I didn't say no to him, though by turns I fumed and shivered at the thought of it. But I kept thinking, there's months yet—something'll turn up. If I shut my eyes and think and wait something'll turn up.

He said not to tell at the firm for the time being, and that suited me. But he wouldn't let me take my holidays, so I went on working right through October. He said he wanted to keep me under his eye. The way he said it was like an officer putting an Able Seaman on probation. He ought to have stayed in the Navy, I thought, that suited him, and I wished to Heaven he had.

Yet sometimes in fairness you had to admit he did his best to be nice. There weren't many men who would have done what he did, have found out about a woman what he had found out, and then said marry me. The most the average man would have suggested was a flat in London somewhere to visit when he wanted, and me installed there terrified to shift in case he set the police on me. I wondered why he hadn't suggested it. Terry would have, first go. He was a fool not to have tried that first anyhow and fallen back on marriage if he found there was nothing doing.

But every now and then, just when you thought he was being rather stupid about something, he'd say something that suddenly showed he was still a jump ahead of you, and that was what I liked least of all. I could have managed a man who was *really* dumb. But Mark I could never be sure of. I hated that. It was a nasty trick not telling me how he had found out. I wondered what he was going to spring on me next.

In October he said he wanted me to meet his mother, so I said all right, because what else was there to say; and he picked me up and we drove into London on a Sunday

346

afternoon. While we were driving through Regent's Park he told me he thought we should be married in November.

I got heartburn at that. "Oh, Mark, that's crazy! We're not officially engaged yet!"

"There's no such thing," he said in his quiet down-right way. "My mother knows. Who else is there?"

"I—have to get some clothes."

"All right, get them. Give in your notice next week, leave at the end of the month, that will give you two weeks to get ready."

"Are you really satisfied?" I said. "Satisfied that you really want to to marry a thief and a liar?"

"I'm satisfied I love you. Anyway, who hasn't been a thief and a liar to some extent at some time of their lives? It's only a question of degree."

"Yes, but . . . be reasonable. We've only known each other a month or two. It's too soon."

"We've known each other seven months. Do you mean you're not sure yourself yet?"

"Oh, it isn't that," I said, uneasily.

"Well I've been in love with you pretty well since the day you came about the interview, so I don't see there's any need to wait."

"Not since the *interview*."

"Yes. Sam Ward and I had already agreed to engage the girl we'd just interviewed, when you came in. He was going to tell you that but I stopped him. He didn't want to change his mind, but I persuaded him."

"As you—persuade most people."

"I also persuaded him to send you that day with the programme when there was the thunderstorm. I suppose you guessed that."

"No, why should I?"

"Well, we don't usually employ cashiers as messenger boys even when we're short staffed."

I swallowed my spittle. "So I suppose that meeting in the rose show wasn't accidental then?"

"No."

"It must have been a double shock that morning, when you found I'd gone."

347

"It was."

"What did you do—I mean when you had finished the pay packets?"

He wrinkled his forehead at me teasingly. "I set about finding you."

"Did you know where to look?"

"No."

"Then? . . ."

"I'll tell you on our honeymoon."

I'd thought of Mrs. Rutland as tall and dignified and grey-haired—like one of those illustrations in the fairy-tale women's magazines—but she was a short stout twinkling woman with spectacles and beautiful small hands and feet. I didn't think she'd ever been particularly good looking but you could see that she had had a slight figure that had thickened as she got older. Her colouring was the same as Mark's, olive skin, dark brown eyes, thick dark hair.

I don't know what she felt like but I know what I felt like at the meeting: like a caged cat pretending to be a blushing timid canary. I wonder what she would have thought as I shook her hand and smiled at her if she had known that I was no more in love with her son than I was with a jailer.

I must say, though, that we both got through it fairly well; she was neither patronising nor too anxious to please, and in a way I liked her better than Mark. Or perhaps it was just because battle and strife didn't come into it. She talked to me as if she'd known me half her life, and I answered and smiled and looked at her and looked round the flat, which was simply beautiful. You didn't have to know about furniture to admire the colour of the mahogany and the curve of the chair backs and the tapering legs and the oval table and the Regency sofas.

We stayed to tea and talked about her family and she carefully didn't ask about mine—so I suppose Mark had primed her a bit—and it was pleasant enough in its way. I think if I had come into these surroundings differently I should have enjoyed them; they were what I should have got for myself if I had ever had the money. It was right in the

348

centre of London but very quiet, and the rooms were high and the windows tall and looked over a small square where the leaves were just falling, and we drank out of cups that showed the shadow of your fingers through them, and Mark watched us while pretending not to. After tea he wandered round the room while we talked, and once I glanced up at his face as he bent to light his mother a cigarette and I thought, my God, he's happy. And just for a moment then I nearly got up and ran.

But in this life it's Number One that counts most, and after all it was his own fault for pinning me here, and if he got hurt, well, so should I, but not as much as by going to prison; so I stuck it out.

And anyway there was still three weeks.

I thought of Forio, eating his gentle beautiful proud head off at Garrod's and waiting for the touch of my hands. Whenever I was in a spot I thought of him.

When we left I went out to the car first and sat in it while Mark had a word with his mother. Presently he came down and we drove away.

I said: "She's not as terrifying as I expected."

"She's not terrifying at all. I was watching you both and I think you'll get on together."

"I think we shall, Mark." I meant that I thought we should have if we had met any other way.

"What does she do with her time?"

"When my father died she sold up his house in the country because she said she wanted the minimum of personal possessions. She does a lot of welfare work and sits on various committees."

"I thought she had *lots* of personal possessions. Far more than my mother ever had."

"Oh, in a small space, yes. My father was a great collector and she kept the best."

"Don't you think you're cheating her taking me like that and passing me off as a—as a normal person?"

"Aren't you a normal person?"

"No."

"Marnie, you're awfully anxious to keep on beating yourself. Give your conscience a rest."

349

"I think you should tell her about me before we marry."

"Well, that's my problem, isn't it."

I wondered if I should go to see Mrs. Rutland in private and confess what I was, in the hope that she would stop the marriage. But it was too risky. She might have a social conscience.

"What are you thinking?" he asked.

"I'm thinking what it must be like for her, welcoming another girl as a daughter-in-law so soon."

"It's the crowning tragedy for every widow that she can't be her son's wife."

I looked at him, and I knew suddenly again that he'd gone deeper than I could go. In some way what he said seemed to strike at me specially.

I said: "You've never told me anything about Estelle."

". . . What is there you want to know?"

"She must have been very different from me."

"She was."

"Did you love her?"

"Yes."

"If you loved her, don't you still love her? If so, then why me? How can you change?"

"I haven't changed."

"Can you love two women at the same time?"

"Yes. Differently. However hard you try you can't love a memory in the same way you love a living person. I tried . . ." He stopped.

"Yes?"

"You were the first person I'd looked at in that way for eighteen months. I knew that, living the way I had been living, one can get dangerously myopic——"

"What does that mean?"

"In this case ready to fall for the first pretty face . . ." His fingers moved on the wheel. "I sometimes think one's feelings and motives are like a succession of Chinese boxes, one within the other, and Lord knows which is the innermost. Anyway, they are with me. So I tried to be dispassionate about you."

"And did it work?"

"No, I'm afraid it didn't. I soon couldn't get away

from the fact that you were the woman I wanted—and no other."

He said this in such a quiet voice that for a moment I felt touched and pleased. Perhaps this idea about the Chinese boxes was a good one for me to think of, because God knows a third of the time I was a bit flattered because he was so gone on me and a third of the time I hated him deeply, and a third of the time I was sorry for him, and all I could be sure of was that if I married him it would be the biggest mess alive for both of us and that I couldn't *stand* the thought of it.

By now he was feeling much more sure of me, and when I said I had to go to Plymouth to see the lawyer who had settled up Lucy Nye's estate he said all right. I'd mocked up a gorgeously detailed story to tell him, proving why I must go, but it wasn't needed and I was slightly disappointed at the waste. I got the feeling that now I'd given him some proofs, he was making a point of not asking for more. You know, a sort of love-and-trust gesture.

All the same I did not go straight to Torquay. I went first to Plymouth, then back to Newton Abbot, then to Kingswear. By the time I walked up Cuthbert Avenue I was sure I wasn't being followed.

It was the first time I'd been home since they moved, and Lucy Nye, my dead auntie, was waiting on the doorstep for me so that I shouldn't mistake the house.

In the last two weeks I'd had this awful worry over what to tell Mother. I mean, I could say nothing to her at all—or I could give her a sort of Revised Version, I mean the Gospel of Mark according to Marnie—if that isn't a bad joke. Or of course I could tell her everything—but that was out from the start.

I didn't think I wanted to go through the rest of my life tied to the secretarial strings of Mr. Pemberton. In any case he was getting to be a nuisance. If I broke it to her now that I was getting married to somebody I had just met, a Mr. Rutland, a wealthy printer, though not so wealthy as Mr. Pemberton, she might not take it too hard.

Or she might. You never knew with Mother. And that

way there was the frightful danger that she might demand to meet Mark. That could never be, because if once they got together, however careful Mark might be not to mention me stealing from his firm, Mam was dead certain to tell him what a good daughter I was and all the money I'd given her in the last three years, and that would start him asking questions again, and in no time he would have found out about Manchester and Birmingham and Newcastle etc.

I wondered if I could take the risk of telling her and still be *certain* of keeping them apart.

When I got in Mother was dozing in the front sitting-room and I thought she looked younger asleep. When she woke she seemed to take a minute or so to remember where she was.

Then she said: "Why, Marnie, I told Lucy to look for you; we didn't wait tea but there's a tasty bit of ham cooking, I always believe in bay leaves, it adds just that to it; Lucy shut the door, this house is colder than the other, more outside walls."

One thing about Mother: even if she hadn't seen you for six months she took up the conversation as if you had just dropped in from across the way. First I had to be shown the house. It was miles better than the other, with a sitting-room in the back, and a sun porch and a kitchen, and three cream-painted bedrooms with new fawn curtains and a toilet separate from the bathroom, and an attic with a view of Torbay between the chimney-pots.

It really was nice, only all the time I couldn't help but see how different it was from Mrs. Rutland's flat with its lamps and its pictures and its arched recesses and its damned good taste. The two places weren't really in the same world. Neither were the two women. My mother had been the better looking of the two, but it was like comparing Forio with a horse that has been used to pull a dust cart all its life. It wasn't fair. It just wasn't fair. But there was nothing more I could do about it than I had done or than I was doing.

Mam said: "How do you like this black marocain? Got it in the summer sales, model, reduced to four guineas, just my fit, isn't it. You're thinner, Marnie; been going easy on potatoes? I like that way you done your hair; more classy than last time."

"I'm all right," I said. "I'm fine."

We talked for quite a while, and then suddenly without being asked she answered nearly all my questions.

"Your cousin Doreen was here last week—first time for two years—I said to her she might not have an aunt; what with her own mother being dead and her father in Hong Kong, you'd think she might have some thought for me. But no. She's a Sister or something now; gets a better screw, but d'you know what she came down to tell me; she's getting married. And to a doctor of all people. I had to pretend, of course, say yes, yes, fancy, but at the end I couldn't help but put in my spoke; I said, Marnie never thinks of marriage—or of men; I said Marnie's a model daughter to me, and I said she makes more in a month than most people make in a year. And d'you know what she said? She said, well, I hope it's honest. I could have slapped her. I said, in one of my sudden tempers, don't go raking up that filth that happened thirteen years ago; I said Marnie's as honest as the day. I said God took much from me but he gave me one jewel and that's my daughter!"

"Jewel," I said. "Woolworth's best."

"No, Marnie; the very best there is. A real jewel if ever there was one." She dabbed one corner of her right eye with a bit of lace. I'd never known Mother cry anywhere else but just out of the corner of her right eye.

"How's your rheumatism?" I said to change the subject.

"Well, not but what it couldn't be better. Mrs. Beardmore in No. 12 recommended sour milk. Dear Heavens, I said, if it's that or knobs I'd rather have my knobs. This weather doesn't suit it, of course, and what with the chimney smoking. How's Mr. Pemberton?"

"All right. Mother . . ."

Mother's eyes had been looking absent-minded but they sharpened up like pencil-points at something in my voice.

"What is it?"

"You said I never thought of getting married. Well, maybe I don't. But what would you say if I changed my mind ever?"

353

We were at the top of the stairs from the attic. Down below Lucy Nye was clattering about trying to hurry on the supper. Mother buttoned her cardigan.

"Have you got to?"

"Got to what?"

"Get married."

"No, of course not! What ever makes you say that?"

"Tell me if you have. Now tell me."

"Look," I said. "*No!*"

"Women often go like you, go thinner when it begins. I did. It's what I've often been afraid of with you. You're too lovely looking. A lot of men must have wanted after you."

"Well, they've got nothing for their trouble," I said, angry with her now. "I was only asking you a straight question and I thought I might get a straight answer. Women do get married sometimes, you know. Surprising, but there it is. Even you did. Remember?"

She looked shocked. "Marnie! We'll not go into that."

"Why not?" I said. "You talk as if getting married was a disgrace! If you felt like that I wonder how you ever came to have me!"

She didn't speak while we got down the stairs. But at the bottom I saw her hand was trembling on her stick.

"I went into it not knowing," she said. "It was my duty to submit."

There was a ghastly silence as we went down the next flight. The sizzling noise of chips came from the kitchen. Mother led the way into the sitting-room.

"That new Telly is giving trouble," she said in a queer voice, and I could see she was trembling all over. "Keeps snowing. When I twiddle the knob the picture goes round like Ernie stirring the Premium Bonds. There was a wedding on it last night in one of those plays. It's all a sham. I said to Lucy, all that giggling and screaming and laughing; marriage isn't like that, marriage is what happens under the sheets, pawing and grunting, you don't giggle then. Marnie, you won't let me down?"

"Let you *down*?" I said, really angry, but holding her

354

drumstick arm. "What're you talking about? Who's talking about letting you down?"

"You were. You were. Even in a joke it don't do. I bank on you, Marnie, you're all I've got. You're all I've ever had."

"All right, all right, don't get so *excited*. I was only asking a simple question. Can't I ask a question without you going off the deep end?"

"If you ask the questions it shows you've been thinking of it."

"Get away, don't be silly!" I patted her face. "You live alone here with Lucy and fancy too much." I went across and switched on the TV and waited for it to warm up. "Sit down here till supper's ready. And if I ever think of getting married I'll pick a millionaire and then he'll be able to keep us both!"

Mother lowered herself into her favourite chair. She looked better now. As the picture came on she said: "Don't joke about it, Marnie. I'd rather have you as you are. I can't picture my little girl—that way."

On the train back to London next day I worried about it. It would have been an awful lot easier if I could have just faced them both out with the truth, like it or leave it. I suppose I might even have looked better to Mark as the only support of a widowed mother, stealing for her.

And in a way all my life I *had* stolen for her, though it was too easy just to leave it at that. I'd taken money for myself too. It was all mixed up.

On the train I thought of my Uncle Stephen paying for my lessons in elocution and accountancy, and about my first few jobs—where I'd been honest enough—after all it's hardly worth being anything else behind the counter of an electricity shop, our home didn't even get any free bulbs. And then the job in Bristol—two pounds a week more and prospects—but I'd hardly settled there before Mother got this varicose ulcer, and the first I heard was a dirty bit of paper from Lucy saying she was in hospital and probably had to have an op. I hung on then waiting for news, but after a week I couldn't wait any longer and got two days off to visit her.

She was in the South Western General, and a flu epidemic was on, and she was in a ward as long as a railway platform and she was just by the door and had just caught flu herself and she looked like death. I'd only the one day really to see her, and I wanted to know what was wrong and nobody had any time for me *at all*. Mother said they'd done nothing for her in nearly three weeks and that she was getting worse and that she was in a perishing draught and the door beside her bed slammed a hundred and twenty times a day, beginning at five o'clock in the morning, and she thought for all the nurses cared she could very well die there before they did anything for her.

Well, I had words with a sour-faced sister and then a short interview with the matron who acted as if she'd just come from the presence of God; so then I really lost my temper and demanded to see the surgeon and there was a row because he was busy on some other case, but in the end I got to see him.

I told him just what I thought of his hospital and the way they were treating my mother, and he listened with a sort of tired patience that really got me raging. Looking back now, of course, I can see just what I must have looked like to him. I hadn't learned how to dress at all, and my new accent was too new to stick with me when I was mad. I remember I was wearing a print frock that was a bit too short and nylons that were cheaper because they only just reached above the knee and unsuitable white shoes, and my hair had been permed and I was carrying a big plastic hand-bag. I expect he thought I came from a snack bar or an amusement arcade or something—if I wasn't actually a tart.

Anyway when I stopped for breath he said: "I quite see that you are feeling anxious, Miss—er—Elton, but I can promise you your mother is in no danger of dying just yet. Perhaps you don't realise that a varicose ulcer is caused by overwork, too much standing and by general neglect. The skin gets into poor condition, it breaks down and an ulcer forms. We can't operate on the vein until we've cleaned the ulcer up. The time your mother has been in hospital, when you wrongly suppose we have been neglecting her, has been necessary to give her rest and to help the ulcer to heal by seeing she gets proper food."

I said: "Is it much rest when she can't sleep for the slamming of the door behind her? And she says the food is terrible."

At least that took the look of strained patience off his face.

"Young lady," he said, "I don't know if you are aware that an influenza epidemic is raging in this city. We can't find beds for all the urgent cases of one sort and another that exist, and most of the staff of this hospital is run off its feet. In an ideal community your mother would have a private ward, but it doesn't run to that; nor will it in my lifetime or yours. So we do the best we can with the present material and in the present circumstances. I'll try to get your mother moved from the door. I shall hope to operate on her next week. The sooner you have her home the happier we shall be. But—she's in a shop, isn't she?— I'd warn you that in future she'll have to take sedentary work of some sort. She'll just have to keep off her feet or she'll be back here in three months with the same trouble or worse. And although she's in no danger of dying she's certainly in danger of becoming permanently crippled. Now I'll have to ask you to excuse me."

I went back to Mother, feeling I'd done what I could but still boiling.

"Don't worry," I said to Mother. "They're going to move you soon from this door. I seen to that . . . I have seen to that. They've got to keep you here for a bit to get your leg healed, but it'll be all right, I promise you."

I sat on her bed thinking over what the surgeon had said at the end. Just then the nurse came along.

"You'll have to go now," she said. "This isn't a proper visiting day, you know. You've only been allowed in as a special favour."

"Thanks," I said, and added "for nothing" under my breath. "Don't worry," I said to Mother. "We'll soon have you out of here. Did I tell you, I've got the promise of a marvellous job?"

"You have? Where?"

"Swansea. I don't know the details yet. I only heard of it last week but I think I'll get it. If I do . . ."

"Is it respectable?"

"Of course it is. What do you take me for? But as a secretary. I may get paid quite a lot. Anyway it may mean you won't have to go to work right away when you come home."

When I got back to Bristol I gave in my notice at Deloitte, Plender and went to live in Swansea. I took a job in a store in the name of Maud Green. Three months later I slid out with three hundred and ninety pounds. That was my first haul and I was pretty nervous about it then.

At the time I was dead sure I was doing it all on account of Mother. Now it seems to me I was doing it mainly to satisfy myself.

9

"Well, really, I always said you were a deep one," Dawn said, picking at a tiny mole on her cheek. "Well, really, and how long has it been going on? Don't tell me. I really believe it was love at first sight, wasn't it? I thought one time it was Terry: you remember after the dinner; and I am sure he was interested in you; but of course you've done better. Mark—Mr. Rutland I'd better start calling him to you, I suppose—oh, very well, dear, thank you, just between ourselves—Mark is a different kettle of fish. More *serious*, if you know what I mean. With Terry you put it on the slate and it washes off again. Where are you going to live, Little Gaddesden? We shall miss you, you know . . . Tell me, do these things grow? I'm sure it's bigger than it was last year. Of course some men call them beauty spots . . . Are we all coming to the wedding? Oh, very private. Well,

I know how you must *feel*. And I expect with you both having been married before. You *are* lucky, you know, two men before you're twenty-four; some girls have to slog it enough getting one."

Sam Ward said: "Well, Mrs. Taylor, so we have to—hm—congratulate you, I suppose. Such efficiency—business efficiency—should make you a very successful housewife, shouldn't it. Naturally I hope you'll be very happy. But then I'm sure you will be. Would you get me the costing report on the Kromecote. We want to see what the danger is of killing the gloss."

"My dear," Terry said brushing a hand over his suède waistcoat. "My dear, you *have* done it this time."
"What have I done?"
"Well, my dear, Mark of all people. Not really your *style*, I should have thought."
"What is my style?"
"A rather tortuous type. A man with a few wrinkles in his soul. Mark's too downright."
"Have you told him?"
"He knows what I think, I'm sure. It would be unfair of me to dot the i's and cross the t's."
He was breathing through his nose, the way he did at poker sometimes. And he was at his most cissyish—which was queer, because sometimes he wasn't that way at all. I thought he doesn't really care all that much for me, but he cares that Mark is getting what *he* hasn't had.
"Apart from that," he said, "you're a *mystery*, Mary, and mystery women are always a challenge. Dawn was talking about you to me the other evening."
"What was she saying?"
"Never mind, my dear; nothing to your detriment in *my* eyes, I assure you. You've got a past, I'd guess, but what sort I just wouldn't know. Not the *understood* sort, I'm sure."
"Honestly, Terry," I said, "this talking in riddles doesn't amuse me at all. I doubt if it amuses anyone. If you think something, why not say it?"
"No, no, dear. I wouldn't want to offend you. In fact

359

I hope we shall be bosom friends. On behalf of the Holbrooks I have pleasure in welcoming you into the family."

"On behalf of the Rutlands, thank you."

"Is it to be a *lavish* wedding?"

"No. Very quiet."

Very quiet. So quiet as to be almost secret. Just his
mother and two witnesses. But it was happening and there
was no escape. It had crept up on me like a cat on a mouse;
while it was ten days away it hadn't quite mattered so much;
then it was seven, then four, then tomorrow. I should have
gone off the night before, risked everything and run. But
I didn't. I stayed and went to the registry office and a red-
haired square-jawed man in a shiny blue suit said some
words to us and we said some words back and something was
written on a piece of paper and we signed our names. My
true name, that was what gave me the horrors. I wouldn't
have minded so much if it had been happening to Mary
Taylor or Molly Jeffrey. My sham life didn't include
Marnie Elmer.

And now for the first time I really had changed my
name. I was called Margaret Rutland, and Mark kissed me
on the mouth in front of his mother and the red-haired
registrar and the two witnesses, and I flushed because, although maybe he saw it as a promise, I saw it as a threat.

Afterwards we went back to his mother's and had champagne cocktails which I didn't like, but we hadn't long to
spend because we were catching the three o'clock plane
for Majorca. While we were standing about talking and
trying to be natural I thought of Forio, just to keep myself
sane.

Before we left his mother took me on one side and said:
"Marnie, I won't say, make him happy, but I will say,
be happy yourself. I think you're capable of much more
than you think."

I looked at her and half smiled.

She said: "It will be twenty-eight years ago next month
since he was born to me. I felt then I had everything—and
I had! A husband, a son of eight, a mother and father still
alive—and a baby son. I felt as if I were the centre of the

universe. Since then they've all gone—except Mark. I expect it will seem a long stretch of time to you, but it doesn't look very long to me, looking back. Life slips so easily through your fingers."

I didn't know what to say, so I said nothing.

"Life slips so easily through your fingers. So make the most of it while you can. Grasp it and savour it, my dear. Now, good-bye . . ."

We stayed at a hotel in Cas Catala about four miles out of Palma. Over the evening meal I asked Mark how he had traced me.

"Must we talk of that tonight?"

"You promised."

"Well sometime on our honeymoon, I said. Are you itching to know?"

"Not *itching*. But curious. I—thought I had been clever."

"So you had." He rubbed his cheek. He was quite good-looking tonight because as usual holiday clothes suited him. Except that the shape of his cheek-bones wasn't right you could have taken him for a Spaniard. "There was nothing ever more premeditated than that theft, was there?"

"I told you how it was. But I want to know how you found me."

He looked me over. That was truly what he did. "Can you imagine how I felt that Friday morning? I was in love with you, and I suddenly found I'd been made a complete fool of. I was so upset I could hardly think—and very, very angry. I could have strangled you."

"You looked as if you could when you found me."

"I might have done earlier but you were out of reach. The one important thing in my life from that moment was to catch you. I decided to cover up the theft and at the same time follow you and find you, wherever you'd gone and however long it took."

"You weren't sure, then?"

"I hadn't an idea where you were. But all the time I was working, putting the money in the envelopes, I was really thinking about finding you. That's what surprises me, that I only made two mistakes with the pay envelopes; it shows one's mind can work in separate compartments——"

"Yes. Go on."

He half grinned. "I think perhaps I'll keep the secret for a day or two more. Why can't you sit and enjoy the view?"

"*No*. I want to know, Mark! I'll enjoy the view afterwards."

"But it might spoil it for you. It was largely luck the way I found you."

He poured out the last of the wine and sipped a⁺ his glass. "Odd how much better this Rioja tastes here th. ɪ in England."

"It was largely luck?"

"Well, I thought to myself, what did she show herself *really* interested in? Not me, certainly. But wasn't she genuinely interested in horses? Was that a sham too, all that enthusiasm and knowledge? It couldn't be. So I thought of horse racing."

"Yes, I see."

"I thought, what will she do with the money? Go to race meetings, probably, and bet. What race meetings are on next week and the week after and the week after? If I follow them every Saturday I'm bound to catch her out eventually even if it takes a year."

"But it only took a day."

"Two." He offered me a cigarette. I shook my head.

He said: "I went carefully over everything we'd said to each other at all our meetings—piece by piece. And when you feel about a girl the way I felt about you it isn't difficult to remember because—well because you think a lot about it in any case and that fixes it in your mind. And presently I came across something you had said at Newmarket. You advised me to back a grey filly called Telepathy and you said you'd seen her training as a one-year-old."

"Oh!" I said. "Oh!"

"Yes . . . Anyway, it was the only trail I had. I looked up Telepathy in *Ruff's Guide* and saw she belonged to a Major Marston of Newbury, but that she had been bred by a Mr. Arthur Fitzgibbon at Melton Magna, near Cirencester. On the Sunday morning I phoned Marston and got details from him and then went down to Melton Magna. Unfortunately Fitzgibbon had left, and it took me most of the morning tracing him to Bath. Even then he couldn't help me; he knew no one who answered to your description. So I went back to Melton Magna, and just got in the Oak Leaf before closing time at two. Saunders, the innkeeper, didn't known anyone of your description either, so then I asked him if—apart from the ex-Fitzgibbon place, which was private—there were any riding stables around where it was possible to hire a horse. He gave me the names of three. Garrod's was the third I tried."

"Oh," I said again, dismally.

"I almost gave it up just before getting to Garrod's. The sun was setting and I was very tired and feeling very played out."

I looked at him. "It was just as if you had come out of the ground."

"Like your conscience."

"Like the devil."

He laughed. I stared out at the view now, thinking over my mistake. We were on a closed veranda looking over a small cove. A quarter moon was going down, and the small boats anchored in the bay cut the moon's track like into a glimmering jigsaw. I suppose it was beautiful. But I only thought of my mistake. How I could have done it. If I hadn't been such a fool none of this need have happened and I should have been free and happy.

I looked down at the gold band on my finger. I had been feeling sick and frightened but now I felt sick and angry.

"You might not have found me," I said. "You might never have found me again. What would have happened to your money then?"

"I should have had to make it good out of my own pocket and written it down to experience."

"You have so much money?"

"No. But I thought you were worth the risk."

"I'm not."

"I think you are."

"I'm not. I know I'm not. You should just have taken your money back and then let me go."

.   .   .   .   .

363

"Darling, what's the matter?" he said later that night. "Are you afraid?"

"Yes. I can't stand it, Mark. I'll die."

"It seems improbable. Tell me what's the matter. Do you hate me?"

"I hate the thought of *this*. I screw up. I feel—*sick*."

He put his hand on my bare leg just above the knee, and I moved quickly to cover it. He said: "Why do you shrink from me like that?"

"I don't shrink from you. It's just the contact."

"Isn't that the same thing?"

"Not quite."

"Marnie, do you love me?"

"I don't love this."

"Aren't you fighting against something in yourself?"

"Not in myself."

"Yes. The physical act of love is a normal outcome of the emotional state of being in love. Surely."

"Maybe. For some people".

"Of course without emotion there is only sex. But without sex there is only sentimentality. Between a man and a woman the two elements of love become one. Don't they?"

I stared up at the curved stone ceiling which was quite low in the alcove over the bed. "To me it's so degrading."

"Why?"

"I don't know."

"Give me one reason why you think that."

"It's . . . animal."

He made a first little movement of annoyance. "We *are* animal—in part. We can't take our feet out of the mud. If we try we fall slap on our faces. It's only by accepting our humanity that we can make the most of it."

"But——"

"We can degrade anything, of course—that's the price we pay for our brains and our ingenuity—but if we do, it's our own silly fault. We can just as easily exalt it. Whoever made us gave us the whole pack."

In the café on the quay outside someone was playing a guitar. It sounded twenty miles away from me just then. I was trying not to tremble because I knew if I started he

364

would know at once, and I'd really have hated to give my-self so much away. It wasn't exactly a trembling of fear but of sheer nerves. All those nice nerves that kept so steady when I was stealing money had gone back on me just now. And my mixed feelings for him weren't mixed any longer; I didn't like anything he stood for, male body, male superiority, male aggressiveness disguised as politeness. I hated him for having humiliated me, for having come into the room when I had practically no clothes on and put his hands up and down my body so that I was sick and hot and ashamed of myself and him.

Of course it was what was expected. I knew that. You don't live the way I'd lived without knowing it all. But it doesn't mean you have to want it all. Right through the evening I'd been trying to set myself to see it sensibly, like not happening to me, like it might have been if Mollie Jeffrey had got sent to prison, something you could keep at a distance. But you can't always do what you set yourself to do.

He said gently: "I'd give a lot to know how your mind works."

"My mind? Why?"

"It turns too many corners. It never goes the straight way to anything. It ties itself up in little knots and sees things inside out."

"Why d'you say that?"

"These quaint ideas you have about sex. If they were nothing else they'd be desperately old-fashioned."

"I can't help it."

"You're a very pretty girl—made for love. It's like a bud saying it won't open, or a butterfly that won't come out of its chrysalis."

I looked at him. I'd thought when it came to this, when there wasn't any escape, I'd be able to pretend that I liked it. But I knew now I couldn't, not for all the tea in China. But I daren't risk yet being outspoken about it—not any more than I had been. I wasn't sure enough of him.

I sighed and said: "I'm really most awfully sorry, Mark. Perhaps I've got it all wrong tonight. But I promise you, it

365

isn't just something wrong with my reasoning. It's something I feel afraid of and have got to—to overcome. Give me time."

He was really too easy to cheat. "That's a very different matter. Perhaps you're tired and over-excited. Perhaps too much has happened in one day."

He was even giving me excuses. I said: "The plane upset me a bit. Don't forget it was my first flight. And don't forget either that this is my first wedding. It would have been better for you if I really had been a widow."

"Well, we'll carry that over for consideration tomorrow."

The next day the weather was bright but showery. We hired a car to take us across the island to see the stalactite caves and a pearl factory. I bought some ear-rings and two or three brooches. In the evening we went to a night club and watched Spanish dancers. When we'd seen the best I was taken ill with pains in my stomach and we had to get back to the hotel by taxi. That took care of that night, but I didn't think it was going to be a good excuse for long. The day after we spent in Palma. We bought a decanter and wine glasses in the glass works, and a handbag for me and a wallet and some shoes for him. I quite enjoyed it, just as I'd found it all right being with him at the races. That part was all right—though I should have been just as content on my own. When night came I was all tensed up for another argument and with a new set of excuses, but to my surprise he was quite matter-of-fact and didn't try to touch me. We had twin beds, and except for the embarrassment of sharing the room I'd nothing to complain about. The same the next night *and* the next. I mean, it was surprising.

During the day I could tell he was watching me sometimes, and now and then I caught a look on his face as if I was a puzzle that wouldn't come out. But all round he was considerate enough, except that we did so much in so short a time.

Now I'm as strong as a horse, but even I felt tired with all we did. He might be thin and pale, but I realised he was about as delicate as a four-minute miler. Perhaps he was trying to tire me out.

On the fifth day we flew to Ibiza and took a car to watch a Saint's Day fiesta in one of the tiny villages. It was queer and strange, with the sun reflecting off the blank white wall of the church, and the mass of black-clothed peasants seething in the square like a lot of beetles that have just hatched out. The only colour was the procession of sacred images bobbing through the crowd, and the young girls who wore bright fiesta costumes with lace and silk and coloured underskirts.

I saw one of them who was specially pretty standing next to Mark. She had long plaited black hair with a great satin bow and she was chattering to a crowd of these older women who were all in black, and wrinkled and weather-beaten as if they'd spent forty years in the sun and the rain. He caught my look and smiled, and I think he saw what I was thinking because when we moved off he said:

"Youth doesn't last long here, does it? A year or so, and then she'll marry a farmhand and it'll be all child-bearing and work in the fields."

"It's so unfair," I said. "She's trapped—no escape."

"Oh, yes, I agree. Though if you weep for her you weep for all the world. We're all trapped the instant we're born—and we stay so until we die."

I felt he was blunting the point; by making it general he was taking the edge off what I felt for that girl; but I could not find the right words to say so.

Afterwards we sat in a café and drank cognac at fourpence a glass and watched the Spaniards crushing to the bar trying to get served. Quite a lot of the young men were already pretty well on and we could hardly hear ourselves speak for all the noise. Three young men at the door of the café were trying to get three girls to talk to them. The girls were giggling behind their hands and acting like the young men weren't there.

I said: "Men only want one thing from a woman really, don't they? Something that's over in five minutes, and then they can pass on. It doesn't seem to me it matters what woman it is as long as it's a woman."

Mark drank his brandy. I knew as soon as I saw his face that I'd said the wrong thing, and afterwards I wondered why I'd said it, knowing it would really sting him.

"We're all caught up in systems bigger than ourselves, Marnie. This isn't a very good one: most of the girls here will be elderly drudges by the time they're thirty. But it doesn't follow that their standards are lower than ours. In fact what you've just said comes from a lower view of life than theirs, not a higher. Most of them would despise you for it."

"Like you do?" I said gently.

He took a slow breath. "Darling, you're a big girl now. If someone gave you a new system of bookkeeping to learn, you'd learn it. Quicker than I could. Well then, try to keep an open mind, be ready to learn about other things."

"Such as this, I suppose."

"Such as trying not to have set ideas—other people's ideas—about love."

There was an awful wild cackle of laughter from the men at the bar. It reminded me of Keyham. If that was love I thought . . .

Mark said: "Everybody's experience is something new—absolutely new to themselves—unique. Right?"

"I suppose so."

"Well, have you ever been to a Spanish fiesta before?"

"No."

"Would anybody telling you about it be the same thing?"

"No."

"Then don't let yourself be told about sex. It's a nasty trivial little indulgence only if you make it that."

"It isn't what I've been told, it's what I feel!"

"You can't feel about what you haven't known."

I moved my glass into one of the damp rings on the table that other glasses had left.

He said: "If you study some of the Eastern religions you'll find that the act of love is closely linked with the act of worship. Not necessarily in the way of orgies, but because they think that on the rare occasions when there is great love beween a man and a woman, it copies on a lower

368

level the love of man for God and the ultimate union of man with God." He stopped. "All right, that's high-flying stuff you may think. But it's better to keep that in mind than dragging it all down to the level of the lavatory and the gutter and the brothel. You pays your money and you takes your choice."

There was a sort of scuffle at the bar, and three men began to sing through their noses. Others began to stamp and clap their hands.

Mark said: "Darling, if you have memories of some sort, can't you try to forget them?"

"I haven't any memories—of that sort."

He put his hand over mine. "Then I wish you'd help me to make some."

That night we spent at a hotel at San Antonio. He ordered champagne before our dinner and some sort of red wine with it, and then we had three big liqueurs afterwards. This with the brandy I'd swallowed at the fiesta should have knocked me silly, but I just haven't that sort of head. At the end of the dinner I caught sight of myself in a mirror, and although the holiday had browned my skin the drink had only had a sort of paling effect around my mouth and nose.

I was wearing a crimson taffeta frock, off the shoulders with three-quarter-length sleeves. It looked all right. I suppose I looked all right too, which was crazy on my part because this was the time if ever to look a frump.

After dinner we went for a walk, but there wasn't much to see and we came back fairly soon, and when we got into the bedroom I knew this was it. And it was too late to develop an illness. Even he would have seen through it tonight.

He came across and tried to kiss me. "Darling, d'you remember that you made promises when you married me?" He was very gentle and half teasing.

"Oh, yes."

"And are you willing to honour them?"

"Sometime maybe."

"I think it should be now."

"No."

"I think it should be now," he said again.

I could feel the panic growing up in me. "You knew what you were marrying."

"What?"

"A liar and a thief."

"Even in this?"

"Yes, even in this."

"In what particular way have you lied to me this time?"

I looked past him at the room, at the amphora in the corner, at the beaten copper plate on the wall, at my coat carefully hung and his coat thrown anyhow over a chair.

"I don't love you," I said.

He pulled a bit away from me and tried to look in my eyes. But he could only see my face, and that was empty, I should think. "Marnie, look at me. D'you know what you're saying? Do you know what love means?"

"You've tried very hard to tell me."

"Perhaps it's time I stopped talking."

"It won't make any difference."

He didn't let me go. "Why did you marry me?"

The amphora thing had come out of the sea, they said, and was centuries old. Mark had been very interested.

"Because I knew if I didn't marry you you'd turn me over to the police."

"You—really believed that?"

"Well, it was true, wasn't it?"

"Honestly, Marnie, dealing with you I'm in quicksands. Where does your reasoning lead you? How could I have turned you over to the police? Once I'd covered up for you it was only my word against yours."

I couldn't explain anything more, so I shrugged.

He kissed me. He took me by surprise and he made no mistake about it this time.

"Don't you hate me?" I said when I could get a breath.

"No."

I tried to tug away from him, getting in a worse panic every minute. "You're not listening to what I'm saying! Don't you understand plain English! I haven't any feelings for you at all. It was all a lie, right from the beginning,

370

first because I wanted to steal the money and then afterwards when you caught me, I had to say *something*, I had to pretend, so that you wouldn't hand me over to the police. But all the time I was playing up to you, *nothing* else, *nothing*! I don't love you. I didn't want to marry you but you left me no way out! Now let me go!"

Perhaps after all the drink was in me. I know I sounded pretty shrill even to myself. Anyway I hope it was that. I hadn't intended to blurt it out then, and when I did I'd wanted to make it sound decenter than that. He still looked at me, and now I was looking at him. The pupils of his eyes were big and the whites were slightly bloodshot. He said: "I've been thinking something of the sort for the last two or three days. But even that doesn't answer all the questions."

"What questions?"

"Never mind. When I married you I didn't do so with my eyes shut. Love isn't always blind."

"Let me alone."

"Nor is it always patient. Nor is it always gentle." I suppose the drink wasn't lying quite silent in him either.

I tried to swallow the panic. I'd never felt really scared since I was thirteen; I'd never been really scared of anyone, not even the police, never in my life. But I knew now I'd not gone the right away about this at all. I couldn't tell whether he believed me, but even if he did it had worked the contrary way. Now when it was too late I said: "Mark, we're both talking rubbish. We really are. We've both had too much to drink. I'm feeling a bit muzzy in the head. Let's talk about this in the morning."

"All right," he said quietly, and then as quietly as doom began to undo the buttons at the back of my frock.

After a minute I wrenched away and got clear of him and went towards the window; but the window was high up, miles above the rocks, and there was no other way out of the room. As I came round the corner he caught my arm.

"Marnie!"

"Let me *alone*!" I snarled. "Don't you know what I mean when I say, *no*? Leave me go!"

He grabbed my other arm, and my frock slipped down.

I felt an awful feeling of something that seemed to be half embarrassment and half disgust. I was fairly shivering with rage. One minute I felt I'd let him get on with his love-making and be like a cold statue dead to every feeling except hate, and just see what he made of that. But the next I was ready to fight him, to claw his face and spit like a she-cat that's got a tom prowling round her that she doesn't want.

He took me to the bed and slipped the rest of my clothes off. When I just hadn't anything on at all he turned off the light above us, and there was only the small pilot light shining in from the bathroom. Perhaps that prevented him from seeing the tears starting from my eyes. In the half dark he tried to show me what love was, but I was stiff with repulsion and horror, and when at last he took me there seemed to come from my lips a cry of defeat that was nothing to do with physical pain.

Hours later light was coming in from the window, and I got my eyes open to see him sitting in a chair beside the bed. He must have been watching me because he saw right off I was awake.

"Are you all right?"

I made a sort of movement with my head.

"That can't have been very pleasant for you," he said. "I'm sorry."

I looked up at the pattern that the grey light was making on the ceiling.

He said: "Nor was it for me. No man every really wants it that way, however much he may imagine he does."

I moistened my lips.

He said: "You don't realise perhaps what you said before this began—how much it goaded me. You threw all my love back in my face. It didn't mean a damn to you, did it? Not a bloody damn. At least that's what you said."

He waited then 'but I didn't speak, didn't deny it.

He said, "Are you surprised I didn't like it? I still don't like it. I'm still trying to swallow it. If it's true it's a real poison pill."

I wet my lips again and there was a very long silence, perhaps ten minutes.

"Cigarette?" he said at last.

I shook my head.

"A drink?"

"No."

He moved to pull the quilt over me, but I wouldn't have it.

"It's six o'clock," he said presently. "Try to go to sleep again."

I went on staring up at the ceiling. For a bit my mind was all blank, as if everything that had happened before that night had been rubbed out. I hardly saw Mark, except the arm of his pyjamas on the edge of the bed. I was watching the play of light on the ceiling, which must have been caused by some reflection from the water outside. But I watched it as if it had some sort of extra meaning for me.

It must have been an hour before I dozed off again, and when I woke the next time it was full daylight and Mark had fallen asleep in the chair beside the bed.

I shifted my head and looked at him. He looked very young with his head forward on his chest, and still as slight as ever. I looked at his wrist and forearm and there was nothing there to show the strength there was in it. I thought over his brutality to me last night. There was something—well, feline about him, because his strength, like a cat's strength, didn't show. I thought again of what had happened, at first not caring much, like someone still under dope; and then all of a sudden I was awake, and in a second my mind was full up with every second of recollection as if suddenly an empty cage was full of flapping vultures.

Horror and rage came up in my throat, like something I'd swallowed, and chiefly it was rage. Before this I'd more or less felt for Mark the sort of dumb hostility you feel for someone who's generally out-smarted you, a feeling of frustration and irritation. But nothing above that: in some ways, given a chance, I could have liked him. But now it was quite different, all that much more. It was like being infected with something that made your blood run hotter. It was like being stabbed and seeing your blood run.

It was a hazy mix-up of hatred and blood. If I could have done it at that minute I would have killed him.

We flew back to Palma and the following day went out as far as Camp de Mar. It was the warmest day of the holiday, though by now a blight had settled on us like Alaska in December. The sea in the sandy cove looked like fluid green bottles, and he said should we bathe? I said I didn't care, so he said well, then, let's; but when I was ready I stood for a long time on the edge hugging my elbows and afraid to take the plunge. In the end he took my hand, and I went in.

The water was lovely after all, not really cold, and after a while we climbed on to this bathing pier and lay in the sun. I lay with my head over the edge and looked down at the water and at all the sea urchins growing like mussels on the supports of the pier. I didn't want him to break in on my mood by talking, and in fact he didn't try to, but sat hugging one knee with his eyes narrowed against the sun.

Well, presently I slipped off the pier to swim back to the sand. It was so lovely that, although I'm just an ordinary swimmer and not strong in the water, I didn't head back at once but swam parallel with the shore towards the rocks at the side of the bay.

After I'd been going for a few minutes I lay on my back and floated and saw that Mark was still sitting where I'd left him. The slanting sun made his body dark like a spade's, and I thought squatting there he might have been a pearl diver or something in the South Seas. And I thought how two nights ago his body had done what it wanted with mine.

Lying in the water like this a sort of tiredness came over me. I felt as if I didn't have the energy to hate him any longer; I just knew there wasn't any point in me living at all. I never had added up to much, perhaps, but at least for a while I'd been some help to Mother and old Lucy. I'd counted for something the way any protest counts for something. But now my life had run bang into this blind alley of marriage, and there was nothing more to it. I was trapped for good, pinned down like a moth on a paper. If I ended now I would simply help to tidy up a thoroughly nasty mess.

But I knew I wouldn't have the guts just to let myself go bobble, bobble under the water. As soon as you start breathing sea you start fighting to live. It doesn't make sense but there it is. So the important thing was to get so far out that I couldn't get back if I wanted to. I turned over and began to swim easily as anything towards the mouth of the bay.

As soon as I'd decided I knew I'd decided right. It just drew a simple neat little line under everything. Mark would be a widower for a second time at twenty-eight—good going that—and could look out for a female of his own type who could make something of his slushy ideas about sex. Mother could manage, would *have* to manage somehow. It would all be sad—and satisfactory.

I don't really know how long it was before I saw he was swimming after me. First I noticed he wasn't any longer on the pier. Then I saw something on the water, a whiteness of broken water a long long way behind me. Well, he'd be too late with his help this time.

I swam on a bit quicker, fixing on a special point at the edge of the bay. I certainly couldn't reach it. I was getting very tired.

When the first wave slopped in my mouth it was a nasty shock. Sea water tastes nasty and when you swallow it it makes you want to fetch up. It wasn't going to be a bed of roses, this end, but it would soon be over. I just dreaded the first breath. All that gasping and retching. It would soon be over, though.

And then I heard him shouting at me not far away.

Right off all the fear went. I just stopped swimming and sank.

Yet even though I tried not to, I found I was holding my breath the way I'd done jumping off the pier by the Hoe when I was a kid. I tried to force myself to let go of life, but I came up again like a cork choking and coughing. As I came up he got me.

"You fool!" he said. "You'll drown yourself!" He was clutching my arm.

I shook him off. "Let me *go*!"

I tried to dive, but it's hard to go down when you're

375

already in the water, and as I thrashed away he caught me by the leg and then round the waist. We struggled for a few seconds and then I almost got free again. At that he gave me such a slap on the side of the face that he made me taste blood. I screamed and scratched his arm with my nails; then he closed his fist and hit me on the jaw. I remember my teeth clicking together with a sound like lift gates shutting; and that was all.

When I came out of it I was lying on my back in the water. He'd got my head between his hands and was lying on his back too swimming with his legs, towards the shore. I tried to get my head free, but he held me tighter as soon as I tried, and that way we came back to the sand.

We lay there together, absolutely dead-beat both of us, but luckily there were no other bathers today, and the only people in sight, two Spanish women shovelling seaweed into baskets at the other end, had seen nothing and looked as if they couldn't care less if they had.

As soon as he got some breath back he began to go for me. He used most of the words you hear around a dockyard and a few more besides. It looked as if nothing I'd done before had got under his skin like this. I suppose it was the final insult.

I stood it for a bit and then one of the words he used made me giggle hysterically.

He stopped and said: "What is it?"

"There isn't a female of that."

I giggled again and then turned my head away and was sick.

After I was better he said: "I didn't know there was a female like you, but I'm learning."

"It makes a change, doesn't it? I don't suppose Estelle was ever like this."

"No, you blasted bloody little fool. She wanted so much to live and couldn't."

"Whereas I want to die and can't."

"Than that," he said, "there are few uglier remarks a woman of twenty-three can make."

We lay quiet, getting our strength back. Then he said:

"If we stay here any longer we'll both begin to shiver. Come on, I'll help you back to the hotel."

"Thanks, I can manage," I said, and got to my feet. So we walked back a few paces apart, with him a step or two behind me, like a warder whose prisoner has nearly got away.

10

The gardener at Little Gaddesden was called Richards. He came three days a week, Mondays, Wednesdays and Fridays. He was a quiet little man with an ailing wife and three pale-looking children under teen-age. He'd a funny sort of enthusiasm about the garden that I couldn't quite understand, because it wasn't his. He seemed to like me and he always called me 'madam' as if I was royalty or something. "We've got some *lovely* tulips over here, madam; they'll be showing in another week or two, I shouldn't wonder." "I'm going to tidy up these paths this morning, madam; then they'll be nice and clear until the spring." He obviously got a sort of joy out of it. I shouldn't have thought there was much joy in his life, with his wife bent up with bronchitis and him often going home wet and soaking and having to look after the children. Sometimes the eldest, a girl called Ailsa, would call in on her way home from school. She didn't remind me of myself at eleven. I think I must have been fairly hard bitten by the time I was eleven; anyway I'd knocked about plenty. Ailsa was soft and gentle like her Dad. The chances were in this world that sooner or later she'd get trampled underfoot. Richards said she'd asked for a Bible for Christmas, an illustrated one, and Mr. Mark was getting him one through the trade at cost price. I thought why doesn't Mark *give* him half a dozen, but when I said something about it Mark said: "That would never do; he'd hate charity." I suppose I didn't understand.

The garden at Little Gaddesden was about one acre. At the end away from the golf course was an old shed and an old garage and a small paddock. Leading to this was a path bordered by a thing I thought was a yew hedge, but Richards politely corrected me. "It's Lonicera, madam. I grow it in my own garden, you can train it just the same way. I've got a *beautiful* bush shaped like a church. I hope sometime, madam, you'll come and see it."

I went and saw it. I met Mrs. Richards and the two youngest. I didn't know what to do about the charity side of it, but I risked buying some sweets and I baked some buns and took those along. It didn't seem to offend them.

The trouble with Richards, I soon saw, was that he was too conscientious. What's the good of a conscience if it makes you stay out in the rain when you can potter around and pretend to do things in the greenhouse. Mrs. Leonard and I began to work out schemes for him to do jobs in the house on the bad days.

I was somehow managing to live with Mark. When we got home he'd given me a separate bedroom, and although the rooms had connecting doors, he hardly ever came in and never without knocking. He never *touched* me. I suppose I'd frozen him up, at least for the time being. We were quite polite to each other, the way we had been during the last ghastly days of the honeymoon. When he came home at night he told me things that happened at the firm. Once or twice we went into London to the theatre, but he didn't suggest a race meeting and I didn't ask. I could never be quite sure what he was thinking.

Luckily I got on well with Mrs. Leonard. I told her right at the start that I had never run a house before and could only cook the simplest things, and she seemed quite pleased to carry on as she had before Mark married me. Of course I could talk her language, and I knew how she looked at things. Perhaps I should have pretended, but I didn't, and soon she was calling me dear, instead of Mrs. Rutland.

The house was peculiar to live in because I kept coming on things belonging to Estelle. A pair of slippers in a cupboard, two old blouses, a pair of nylons still in their cellophane—they were too short for me—books, a note-book, an engagement diary. And of course the photographs in the drawing-room and in Mark's bedroom. I could see how a second wife could be made jealous. Not that I was. I only wished she could come back and claim her man. I mean I never for a second felt *married* to Mark. Perhaps married isn't a thing any one feels, it's something that grows on you. Well, it didn't grow on me.

One thing I found in the garage was an oldish two-seater car. It had belonged to her—she'd used it going to her excavations, and the boot looked like it—; but Mark said I could drive it if I wanted, so I did go off one or two afternoons exploring round about, though I hadn't anywhere special to go.

After a few weeks, when he still kept his distance, I began to let go, to relax, to feel easier in the house. There was no way of leaving him yet, except the way I'd tried at Camp de Mar—and I knew I'd never try that again—so for the present it was a case of making the best of it.

One night after supper I'd opened up a bit about myself and he said suddenly:

"Marnie, why don't you do this more often?"

"Do what?"

"Talk about yourself. It might help."

"Help what?"

"It might help you to get free of—of things that at present get in your way. It even might help us to understand each other better."

"I don't see how."

"Well, at its lowest it interests me. It's important to talk. Otherwise one gets ingrown. Any psychiatrist would tell you that. So would a Catholic priest."

"I'm not a talker."

"I know. That's what I'm saying. Tell me about losing your brother, for instance."

"What about it?" I said sharply.

"Well, you did lose one, didn't you? Wasn't it through neglect?"

I told him. He said: "If it went as far as a court case the

doctor was lucky to get away with it. I suppose it was war-time. Is that why you hate doctors?"

"I don't think it happened because it was war-time. I think it happened because we were poor."

"Well, that shouldn't apply now, should it?"

"Oh, but it could. You don't realise; you've never been poor, Mark. When my——" I stopped.

He was watching me. "When your what?"

"When my aunt had a varicose ulcer," I said carefully. "You know, the one who brought me up. She was in hospital and I went to see her; I had that job with the accountants in Bristol and I came back to see her and she wasn't being well looked after at all. I made a fuss and it helped a bit, but I could see she was being treated badly because they knew she was poor and couldn't stand up for herself."

"From what I've seen of the Health Service I shouldn't have thought that was often so. It may be pretty rough and ready, especially if you're not too seriously ill, I grant that, but I shouldn't have thought it made much difference, once you were in, whether you were rich or poor. Of course, if you can stand up for yourself, that's a help. But the important thing in hospital these days is to have a rare and interesting disease. If you have, then you're treated like royalty. If you haven't, then you take your chance."

"What's the use of asking me to tell you these things if, when I tell you, you don't believe them?"

"It isn't that I don't believe them. But I try to see it through your eyes and then I wonder if I should see it the same through my own . . ."

"Well, of course, not. I——"

"But never mind. Go on."

"You think I've a chip on my shoulder about poverty and being poor. Well, perhaps I have. But no one's entitled to criticise me who hasn't tried it."

"You've a chip of some sort on your shoulder, Marnie, as big as an Admiral's epaulette, but I doubt if it's just poverty that's caused it. I can't tell you what it is. I wish I knew. Maybe a psychiatrist could tell. But you wouldn't let him try, would you."

"Try what?"

380

"To find out if there was something wrong."

"No."

"Would you be afraid?"

"What of?"

"Of going to see one."

"A psychiatrist? Why should I be afraid? It would only be a waste of time."

"Perhaps yes. Perhaps no."

"Do you go to a doctor when there's nothing wrong with you?"

"Do you think he would find nothing wrong with you?"

"Oh, they always make up something to earn their money."

He was quiet for a bit. Then he got up and went over to one of the bookcases and began to leaf through a book. But he wasn't looking at it.

"Marnie, tell me something . . . Perhaps you don't know but . . . since we were married you've shown pretty clearly that you hate the physical side of love. What I want to know is, do you hate love as such or do you merely hate me?"

I picked up one of the Christmas cards on the table and read the name inside. It didn't mean a thing.

He said: "Try to tell me exactly the truth if you can. Could you imagine finding pleasure in love with another man?"

"No."

"Then I think a psychiatrist might help."

"Thanks. I'm all right as I am."

"Are you?"

"*Yes.* Everyone isn't made alike! Some people love music. Others hate it. It would be a poor world if we all wanted the same thing."

"Ah, but——"

"The only mistake you made, Mark, was forcing me to marry you. The mistake I made was being caught."

It was the nearest we had ever come to the horrible things we'd said to each other on our honeymoon. He seemed to swallow it now and push on.

"That's all right as far as it goes. But it doesn't go far enough."

"Because you think I should be like Estelle?"

"Because sex is a fundamental instinct that you can't compare to love of music. If it isn't there in some form something is wrong."

"I'm not the only woman who's ever disliked it."

"God, no. Some people put the number as high as thirty per cent of the female population. But there are degrees—and yours is an extreme degree. And you haven't the face or figure of a frigid woman——"

"Is there such a thing?"

"I think so."

"Well, I'm sorry. I'm sorry if you've been deceived."

The next morning, Sunday, was wet, so he spent it mostly rearranging his wife's Greek pottery. But over lunch he said:

"I've been thinking about what we said last night. There's a man I know called Charles Roman. I wish you'd meet him."

"Who is he?"

"A psychiatrist. But a very practical one. The sort of person one can talk to."

"Oh, no."

"I thought I might get him over to dinner one evening. He's about fifty, and very wise, and very simple. No frills."

"Ask him to dinner one evening when I'm out."

Mark ate for a few minutes in silence.

"Perhaps we could do a deal."

"A deal?"

"Yes. You oblige me and I oblige you . . . Supposing I promised to have Forio brought here. It wouldn't cost much to turn the old garage at the end into a stable, and the paddock beyond is empty. Then he could be here permanently, and you could ride him whenever you wanted."

I crumbled bread in my two hands, waiting for the catch. "Yes? What do I do in return?"

"You agree to go to Roman for one hour, say, twice a week to see if he can help you."

"I don't want help," I said, but my thoughts were

jumping like fleas. I'd expected Mark was going to make the one condition I couldn't consider. But this . . . Well, it had to be thought of.

"You want Forio?" he said.

"Well, of course."

"It might make you happier?"

"Yes, of course it would."

"Well, there's the proposition. Think it over."

I said: "I'd—think much better of you if you let me have him without conditions, Mark."

"I expect so. But I'm afraid they have to come into it."

At lunch I said to him: "You mean I could keep Forio for good? You mean I could ride him any time I liked? You would pay for his keep?"

"Of course."

"And how long would I have to see this man?"

"It would depend on what he said. Perhaps he wouldn't feel he could help you at all. But if he did try, it's only fair to say it might be a long treatment. These things are usually very slow."

"What would he do?"

"Chiefly encourage you to talk."

"I'm not a talker. I've told you."

"I know. That would be his problem."

I didn't say any more then, but all through Monday my mind was working hard. If I couldn't escape from Mark altogether—yet, I might escape in a way by having a horse to ride. And just to have Forio here, with me, would be like having a friend to turn to.

I thought highly of the idea. The more I thought of it the more I liked it. But to get it I took a risk; Mark would see to that. People like this man Roman had a way of inching into your thoughts so that in the end you gave something away. I couldn't afford to give anything away.

But only two hours a week. Couldn't I hold my own with any doctor for two hours a week? The fact that I hated them all would make it that much easier. It would be a battle of wits, a question of keeping on the alert. Was it worth the risk to have Forio?

I said nothing until the Tuesday morning, and then I

said: "Mark, I've been thinking over what you suggested."

"Oh?" It was too casual, trying to hide the look in his eyes.

"Yes. I—haven't decided yet. But if you like to ask this Dr. Roman to dinner I'll look him over and see if I think I can bear him. But, mind, I haven't agreed to anything."

"No doubt he'll want to see what you look like too. He's pretty choosey."

"What would you tell him about me?"

"I hadn't thought of it. Principally, I think, that you would like treatment. The rest is up to him."

"I mean," I said. "I mean, if you're going to begin by telling him about me stealing the money, then it's off right away."

"My dear, it's up to you, what you tell him. I shan't. Anyway—as you should know—that's not what worries me."

"So you say."

I could tell Mark was pleased, and it didn't give me any satisfaction to please him. But I'd agreed now. Did he really think something helpful to him would really come out of it? Did he really think a few talks with a psychiatrist would turn me into a sweet and loving wife? How hopeful, I wondered, could one really get?

Although living with Mark might mean I'd no special need to worry about money for myself, it did not mean all my money troubles were over. For the last three years I'd never given Mother less than four hundred pounds in any one year; and it was usually more. She and Lucy lived the way they did only because of what I gave them. I'd taken on the responsibility when I bullied Mother into giving up that awful shop job in Plymouth and got her the first home in Torquay. She'd been miles better in every way since she'd given up work. So there it was. If I'd been able to pull off this Rutland job I should have been easy for eighteen months or more. As it was I only had dribs and drabs of money scattered about the country. Two hundred and ninety-one pounds ten shillings.

On the Thursday Terry called. I happened just then to be sitting at the desk working all this out on a piece of paper, so I stuffed the paper away and asked Mrs. Leonard to show him in.

He was wearing a tweed hacking jacket with a yellow silk scarf and pale brown cavalry twill trousers. It was funny how, after not seeing him for a time, it was his dandyism again that hit you first. He didn't look particularly sharp, like he really was; and he didn't look sly; and he looked sure of himself, which he wasn't. Not nearly as sure of himself as Mark, I thought, who *looked* so modest.

We talked for a minute or two, and he made a few silly remarks, but I knew he hadn't come just to be silly. After a time he got up and walked round the room, stopping to finger one of the Greek vases.

"What does it feel like, being married to Mark?"

"All right."

"Compare favourably with your first? You know it *shouldn't* work."

"What shouldn't?"

"Your marriage to Mark, my dear. I've said so before. You're far too *submarine*. We can't all be dashing naval craft like him, churning up a hell of a froth on the surface. Anyway, where does it get you?"

"Do you expect me to answer that?"

"No, I will. It gets you one of the fashionable stress diseases before you're fifty—and a *lot* of money which you've no time to spend."

"I shouldn't have thought Mark was like that."

"Ah, that's newly-wed loyalty. Wait till you've been yawning your head off here for a couple of years. Life's a gilded *cage*, my dear, for girls like you. What do women really want in life? I'll tell you. Lots of new clothes, lots of leisure, lots of admiration, lots of sex. But you can't trade the first two for the last two—as you'll find. Woman's no more monogamous by instinct than man."

"Well, thank you for telling me."

He smiled in a crooked way. "Anyway, I'm sorry you won't come to my party next Saturday."

"What party?"

"Didn't Mark tell you? I invited you both after dinner

385

for drinks and maybe a little gamey. All friendly like, but he said he couldn't make it."

I tucked my legs under me on the sofa, and then, seeing Terry's look, pulled my skirt down.

"I expect he was speaking for himself," I said.

"Mean to say you'd come without him?"

"No, I didn't say that."

"Pity. You did so well last time."

"So well?"

"At poker. The MacDonalds are coming and three or four others. You're a natural, you know. A natural player. Alistair was saying so *only* last week."

Neither of us said anything for a minute. Terry was staring at a piece of broken pottery. "Can't think what people see in this sort of thing," he said presently. "You can get as good on Hampstead Heath any Sunday."

Last time, me a beginner, I'd won twenty-two pounds.

"I don't get it," he said again. "The whole thing's bogus. If anyone was ever shi-shi it was Estelle, the way she used to go around excavating bronze-age barrows. What conceivable use is that to a girl?"

"Tell me about Estelle," I said.

"I'm telling you. She slouched about in slacks, and only put on lipstick at sundown. I should think even Mark was absolutely distraught with her. What's the good of being bronze-age in bed."

"You men have only got one idea, haven't you?"

"Well, it's rather a good one, isn't it?"

Of course twenty-two pounds was nothing much. It wouldn't really solve anything.

"Isn't it?"

"Isn't what?" I said.

"Never mind, darling, don't *listen* to what I'm saying. Just tell me if you're coming to my party on Saturday."

But I hated gambling. It made my heart thump.

"I don't know. I'll see. I'll see how things go."

"Well, it's nine o'clock for drinks if you can."

He left soon after. I went to the door with him. He said: "If you love me, don't tell Mark I've called. I'm on firm's business, and I don't think he'd *approve* of my

386

spending time with you. He doesn't approve of me at all, you know."

As I watched him go I thought, I don't approve of you either; somewhere you've got a streak. But it isn't my streak; you're wrong there.

It seemed to me that he felt for sex what I felt for money. At least it was never lonely in his company.

That evening Mark said: "I telephoned Roman and he's coming to dinner on Friday."

"Oh . . . So soon? What did he say?"

"Not very much. At first he didn't want to meet you socially."

"Why not?"

"He seemed to think it better to see a patient *as* a patient without other meetings."

"What did you say about me?"

"The least possible. But I said I thought you'd come more willingly if you had met here first."

Now that the thing was on top of me, right on my head, the idea of it got me worried. I think he must have cottoned on to this because he said: "I've also telephoned the local builder to come in tomorrow morning and you can tell him what alterations you want to the old garage. You should have Forio here by this time next week."

Forio. I don't think I even liked Mark talking about him that way. Because Forio was a *personal* possession, a personal companion and friend. I wanted him here but I wanted him still to myself.

I said: "Is he coming alone? This man, I mean, to dinner."

"I thought we'd get Mother over. She hasn't been since we came back, and it will make it more of a social evening."

"Very social for me, feeling like a maggot under a miscroscope."

"He isn't that sort of man."

"I wish I hadn't promised even to see him."

"Well, if you hate the sight of him we can always try someone else."

387

I looked at him thinking should I try to persuade him out of it, say, you don't want me brooding all day over my *symptoms*, people like Roman always do more harm than good. But I knew this was a bargain he'd hold me to.

"Mark, I want to go out myself on Saturday night. I'm going out with Dawn Witherbie. We were friends before I married you. I can't suddenly drop her."

"There's no reason why you should. Where are you thinking of going?"

"We haven't decided. Probably only to her house. It's after dinner. But I may be late."

"I turned down an invitation for Saturday. From Terry. He asked us over to his flat."

"Why? Didn't you want to go?"

". . . There aren't a lot of people who get under my skin, but Terry's one of them. Don't you feel it—or does he appeal to you? Honestly I can't bear the sight of him, and I have far too much sight of him in and out of the office every day—anyway too much to want to prolong it into the evening."

He went across to pour himself a drink. "It might be a good idea to ask Rex and his mother for Friday as well, if you can bear it. We need their moral support in the firm, so it would be politic as well as polite."

"In the firm?"

"Yes. The Newton-Smiths have a big minority holding, but with their help I have enough of a hand usually to do what I want. Only about eighteen per cent of the capital is owned by the public, and usually the public never turns up at meetings or uses its votes. The rest, about thirty-five per cent, is in the hands of the Holbrooks."

"Well, then, you're safe enough," I said.

"It's not cast-iron. There's been a good deal of traffic in the public shares recently and the price has rocketed. I know the Newton-Smiths have had an offer from a merchant bank for part of their holding, and they're tempted to cash in. I'm trying to persuade them not to. A merchant bank sounds innocent enough, but they may be acting as nominees for some other firm or person."

"Do the Holbrooks know about this?"

"Well, of course; they're part of the board and part of the family, even though I sometimes wish they weren't."

All Friday I was in a flap. I suppose I wasn't geared right for social life after the way I'd grown up. I got more butterflies in my tummy over a meal for a few elderly people than over taking seven hundred and forty-six pounds from the Roxy Cinema, Manchester.

One you could do in secret, nobody knowing a thing till it wasn't your business any longer. But this. I mean, did you go to the door when they came or wait till they took their coats off; what did you talk about, the weather wouldn't last for ever; who offered drinks and when; and when you got to the table did I have to start eating first or did I wait for Mrs. Rutland?

In the end I got through it somehow. Mrs. Leonard as usual did most of the work. At the last minute the zip of my frock stuck when someone was already ringing the doorbell, and I *wouldn't* ask Mark for help, so I had to wriggle out of the frock again and half zip it up and then wriggle back. And then the soup was salt and the drawing-room fire smoked.

It wouldn't have been so bad if you had just been having Mark's family for the evening. But Roman on top of it was too much. I'd got to be hostess for the first time to three high-grade relatives and at the same time keep a wary eye on him.

In fact when it came down to rock, Dr. Roman wasn't so frightening. I expected somebody like Dracula, so it was a kind of a relief when this tired-looking baldish man came in in a brown suit that needed cleaning and long pants that showed when his trouser-leg worked up. He talked about his two children who were at a co-ed school, and about his holiday abroad and about the diet he was on, not as if these were a front for his secret microscopes but as if they were what chiefly interested him. We talked a half-dozen times during the evening, but he didn't seem the least bit curious about me. You got the feeling he was just out for a good dinner and nothing more, and he certainly ate it.

If I'd wanted a sympathetic, all-understanding, father-confessor figure I should have thought, well I can write off

Roman. But as a person to go to only to fix my end of the bargain with Mark, he looked just the right answer.

I couldn't help liking Mrs. Rutland in spite of her disadvantage of being Mark's mother. She was just that much helpful to me without ever being patronising, and though you'd never mistake her for anything but a lady, she wasn't stiff-backed and *awful* like many old women of her class. They really are awful, so many of them: about nine feet tall and big-busted and thin-ankled, and they never mix with any but their own kind, and they talk about their shopping at Fortnums and Harrods, and they're always frightfully poor, which means they can't afford caviare, and they have voices like the high notes of a Welsh tenor. Old Mrs. Newton-Smith was a bit like that, and it was an ordeal when I had to take the two women upstairs and help them to powder their noses. God, I was glad I had had those elocution lessons, even though perhaps that made me the most counterfeit of the three.

When we got downstairs again things were helped because Mark told them about my horse, and it turned out Rex was mad about horses, and right off he wanted to know all about Forio. Of course it sounded wonderful me having bought him in a sale and keeping him on a farm in Gloucestershire; it put me right alongside them among the landed gentry. Anyway, it turned out that Rex hunted regularly with the Thorn—heaven knew what size horse he would need to get him over the gates—but, as that was only about eighteen miles from Little Gaddesden, he said would Mark and I go over one day for a Meet. I said yes out of politeness, but thought I could probably slink out of it later as I'd never hunted and didn't like the notion.

When it was all over and the last of them had gone Mark said: "That was pretty good, Marnie."

"Good?" I said, looking for sarcasm or something.

"Yes, I thought it could hardly have gone off better. Didn't you?"

"I was nervous as a nit."

"You didn't show it."

"We must have this chimney swept," I said, jabbing at the remnants of the fire.

"You know," he said, "dinner parties were one of the things Estelle could never manage. I'm so very glad you can."

I straightened up, and for a minute thought he was going to touch me. So I edged round out of his reach and asked: "Did Dr. Roman say anything?"

As usual he was too sharp not to notice the move, and his face cooled off. "He made an appointment for Tuesday at two."

"Just that?"

"Not much more. You'll go?"

"I haven't decided."

"He suggested you might go first for five or six weeks as a preliminary period. By then he should know whether he can help you."

I straightened the photo of Estelle on the grand piano. I might not want her husband, but it was nice to know she hadn't been perfection in everything.

"And the shares?" I said. "Did you persuade Rex and his mother not to sell?"

"I've persuaded them to hold on for the time being. I think if they really make up their minds about it I may have to buy them myself. But I'd have to borrow heavily from the bank to take the lot at the present inflated price."

"You say the shares have been going up. Why, if you made a loss last year?"

"We made a loss the year before. There's quite a big profit in the new accounts that have recently come out. But all our premises and stock are much undervalued, that's really the answer. People are buying the few shares there are on the market as a long-term speculation."

I thought, maybe not so long term, thinking of those letters I had read.

When I got to Terry's about nine on the Saturday night the same round-the-clock top-of-the-pops were playing, but I didn't know any of the people there except the Macdonalds. Gail said vaguely, "Why darling, *such* a long time," and patted her urchin cut. Alistair raised his eyebrows across a lot of bottles and sandwiches and nattering

391

people. Terry introduced the others. There were six of them, and they were an odd lot. One was a Jewish film director with a disillusioned expression as if he'd gone right through the alphabet and there wasn't anything more; two were hard-bitten women in their forties, with thin silly lines for eyebrows and the sort of faces that look ancient because they're trying to look young. The other three were all men and they'd all got plenty of money. You could see that right off.

As soon as we got playing, which we did about ten, I saw this was a different game from the last. Last time it had been ordinary middle-class folk having fun and a gamble. This time it was serious. And there weren't any beginners, except me.

And the maximum raise was one pound. I had brought five pounds with me, but I saw from the stuff the others were handling that this wasn't going to count for much if I lost. So I began very cautiously, dropping out every time when I didn't have much and not bluffing at all. I watched the others and tried to learn from them. And I tried to work out the odds, the way I'd done before. But it was all nerve jarring, and if the cards hadn't come slightly my way I should have lost. I was mad when I got out on a limb playing against the film director, and knew in my bones that I had a better hand than he had but didn't dare to call his bluff.

By one o'clock I was two pounds to the good, and by three I'd made nearly nine. Then I had two nasty jolts, and in the second, when I was sure the film director was bluffing again, I found he wasn't and went down eleven pounds on one hand. I played safe as hell after that, and when we stopped at four I was only thirty shillings out of pocket. But I felt sick to the stomach, and even thirty shillings seemed a fortune.

I'd forgotten completely about the time and about Mark, and when I looked at my watch I jumped and said I must go at once.

Terry gave me one of his smooth lop-sided glances. "The old man likely to cut up rough? Well, I hope it's been worth it."

"Yes, I've enjoyed it ever so. Thank you, Terry."

"Come again. I have a party once a week. No needy person ever turned away."

I thought, no, but sometimes they'll be needy when they leave.

I drove home in Estelle's car trying to tell myself I didn't mind being a loser.

11

"Do sit down, Mrs. Rutland," said Dr. Roman. "Over here, if you don't mind. Can I take your coat? That's better. Not a very pleasant day. Did you come by car?"

He lived in one of those tall narrow houses looking on Regent's Part. Everybody raves about them and it just beats me why.

"I want you to look on this first meeting not so much in the light of a consultation as of a friendly chat. Indeed, as I expect you know, much of our time together will be very informal."

Roman was different now you met him on his beat. I suppose he had a 'manner' that he lifted off a nail and wriggled into before the patient came. From the plate outside it seemed he shared the house with another doctor, a consulting surgeon. A manservant had let me in, and I wondered how much all this was costing Mark.

"What has my husband told you?"

"Very little, Mrs. Rutland. Except that you agreed together that you should consult me."

"I'm only coming because he wants me to."

"Well, yes, I gathered that the idea was his. But I assume that you're not unwilling to see me?"

We'd been for Forio over the week-end. "No . . ."

"Of course it's necessary to make that clear at the beginning. I can do very little to help you without your willing co-operation."

I tucked my blouse in at the waistband.

"I shall sit here just behind you," he said. "I don't make notes, so nothing you say will be recorded. What I would like you to do today, if you will, is just give me the general factual background of your life, i.e. where you were born and that sort of thing. That will give me a chance of getting the broad picture."

I thought he was sure to want to be put in the picture sometime or other. Nobody ever talks any other way nowadays. I was sitting on the usual black leather couch. But it was fairly wide and there were two green cushions on it to give it the glamour treatment.

"What, now?" I said.

"When you're ready. No hurry."

Naturally no hurry, I thought, at X guineas a visit.

I thought of Forio. We had driven down to Garrod's Farm on Sunday morning, almost before my eyes were open. (Mark must have guessed I was late back but he didn't mention it.). It had been a lovely drive because the sun was shining, and for miles and miles at every church we passed the bells were ringing. Sort of royal procession.

"I'm twenty-three," I said. "I was born in Devonport. My father was a draughtsman in the dockyard. When war broke out he joined the Navy and he was drowned at sea. The same year my mother was killed in the Plymouth blitz and I was brought up by a sort of aunt called Lucy Nye. I went to the North Road Secondary Modern School for Girls. Then my Uncle Stephen paid for me to go to St. Andrew's Technical College, where I learned shorthand and typing and bookkeeping and accountancy."

I didn't much like the idea of him being behind me. I was telling him exactly the same mixture of truth and make-up that I'd given Mark, but I couldn't see how he was taking it all. When I stopped he didn't speak, so I waited. I waited while a clock somewhere chimed the quarter hour and I thought, well, that's fifteen minutes of the first visit gone already.

That cheered me up, so I went on with the rest of the stuff, about going to work and Lucy Nye dying and leaving me a house, and me getting a job in Bristol. Then I said I'd used all my money and taken work in London. Then I moved to Rutlands and met Mark and we got married. It all sounded so straightforward that I believed it myself.

When it was over he said: "That's excellent. That's exactly what I wanted—a brief biographical sketch. Now, what I would like you to do for the next few minutes is to tell me about some of the personalities involved in your life."

"How do you mean?"

"Well, starting with your mother and father. Do you remember much about them? What they looked like, for instance."

"My father was a tall man, with greyish hair and a quiet voice. He had very strong hands with the nails cut short and keen grey eyes that seemed to know what you were thinking before you said it. He was the one who first called me Marnie, and it has stuck ever since."

"And your mother?"

It was pretty well only as I stopped speaking that I realised I hadn't described my father at all, but Mother's brother, Stephen.

There was a long pause. "I don't remember my mother so well."

"Anything at all?"

"A bit. She was smallish, with high cheek-bones, rather strict. She worked very hard, *always*; when we were poor she did without things to give to me. Everything was for me. I always had to be *respectable*. That was the *most* important thing. She took me to chapel, three times every Sunday."

After a wait. "Anything more?"

"No."

"You've already told me far more about your mother than your father."

Another wait. He said: "I don't quite understand one thing. Why were you poor?"

"Why not? We hadn't any money. That's the way you are poor."

395

"But your father was in work?"

"As far as I remember. I was too young to remember much."

"You'd get a pension, of course, as the orphan of a sailor killed in the war?"

"I don't remember. I expect Lucy Nye drew it for me."

"After your father died, how long was it before your mother was killed?"

"About nine months."

"And then this aunt, this Mrs. Nye, took you in?"

"Miss Nye. Yes."

"Can you tell me about her?"

I told him about her.

It really wasn't bad, talking like this. Three-quarters of the time you could tell the truth, and the other quarter was already fixed in your mind and you could play around with it as you pleased.

If he asked you a question you didn't want to answer, you simply said you didn't remember.

If I stopped he didn't hurry me on, and once or twice I was able to go off into pleasant little day-dreams about Sunday. When we got to Garrod's, a loose-box Mark had ordered was already waiting. I'd gone running through the yard and out into the field to find Forio, and he had come galloping across at the first sound of my voice. Mark had really done his best to be nice all the time, and I could see the Garrods liked him. He seemed to know a bit about horses and he didn't hurry me to start back. In the end we left about three, driving slowly behind the horse-box; and just before dark we got home and let Forio loose in the paddock, and I rode him round bareback half a dozen times just for the sheer pleasure and just to let him know we were going to be together again.

"Were you not an only child, then?"

I dragged myself back and heard a clock striking. It was all over for this afternoon anyway, and I could forget it till Friday.

"I had a brother but he died at birth."

"How old were you then?"

"I'm not sure."

"You don't remember anything about it?"

"No."

"Do you remember anything about when your father died? Do you remember the news being brought?"

I had to think about that. My father hadn't really been killed until I was turned six. That is, I knew he was killed after we'd been blitzed out of Keyham and gone to live at Sangerford, because he died in June 1943, and my brother was born in the September, but for the life of me I couldn't remember coming home from school and being told, or seeing Mother get a telegram and collapse, or even hearing of it second hand from Lucy Nye.

"No," I said, still thinking.

"It's not unnatural. Your memory is remarkably good. It's most exceptional in that you have hardly had to hesitate over a date or anything."

"No?" I said. So I was being too pat.

"And do you remember anything of your mother's death?"

"I remember being told. But I wasn't there. I'd been evacuated to this bungalow in Sangerford, near Liskeard where my aunt Lucy lived. Mother was—was going to join us but she left it too late . . ."

"Well," he said, rising. "I think that's a very good preliminary talk. On Friday perhaps we shall be able to go into a little more detail."

He helped me on with my coat and saw me out. It was still raining, but I walked to the tube instead of spending money on a taxi.

I played poker again on the following Saturday. It was much the same crowd. I won six pounds. I was coming along fast. Except for the film director and Alistair MacDonald, they weren't all that good. They weren't mathematical about it. They went by 'hunches' and by watching how many cards their neighbours drew. They'd never get any *better*. All the same I didn't really enjoy playing. It was too nerve-racking.

The Friday visit to Dr. Roman had run on the same track as the first. I did the talking, he asked the questions.

They were the sort of questions I'd have asked anybody for nothing, not expecting to be *paid*. It was such a bogus business; we could have worked it all out over a cup of coffee in an espresso bar for eightpence each. This man put his name on a brass plate and people paid him *pounds* just to sit on his couch and talk. It made you think. Maybe I had been an honest citizen, just taking money out of tills.

When it was over for the day he had offered me a cigarette and said: "You've done well so far, Mrs. Rutland. It always heartens me to be trying to help someone of your calibre."

"My—er——"

"Well, for a patient to benefit from psychiatric treatment at all, he or she must be intelligent. It's simply a waste of time working on dullards."

"Thanks."

"Please don't think me patronising. But I do feel you have a quick and clear brain. It stimulates an analyst, to work with you."

I gave him a quick and clear smile. "Next Tuesday?"

"Next Tuesday. Mind you . . ." He had stopped and scratched his chin, which hadn't been shaved too closely that morning. "The intelligence in our work can be both a springboard and stumbling block. There is a point at which you will have to decide which yours is to be . . ."

"I'll think of that," I said, but I hadn't thought of it or had time to think of it until I happened to remember it at this poker party. Now I did remember it I got a slightly uneasy feeling as if there was more in the saying than met the ear. There'd been something in the way he'd said it. It wouldn't do to underrate Roman and imagine you were doing awfully well with him if you weren't doing awfully well at all. It was never clever to be too sure. I'd learned that early in life.

After Christmas things were better between Mark and me, even though it didn't last. I think he'd probably had a word from Roman that I was playing fair; so he was hoping I might be cured of whatever he thought I needed to be cured of. And also he was very quick to notice when I was brighter.

I felt better than I'd done since when he caught me in Gloucestershire. I could ride every day, and if that wasn't being free it was a fair copy.

Also Mark still kept his distance. I suppose if I'd been as bright as some people thought, I should have guessed how much this was costing him. But the longer he left me alone the less I thought of it.

Money for Mother still nagged. At Christmas I'd sent her twenty pounds and explained I was frightfully sorry I couldn't get home; but I thought, in the New Year I'll look for a part-time job afternoons, say, in some shop or something. It would be easy to get there in my car and Mark need know nothing about it. I could work under another name; but it seemed doubtful if I could do anything worth while. Of course you could lay a false scent, but it wouldn't really *ever* be satisfactory or safe to be anything but honest so long as I had to come home every evening as Mrs. Rutland.

I thought around the idea of a begging letter in the Personal Colum of *The Times* and even went so far as writing out an advertisement. "Will a few kind and generous people help Reverend Father, working in great poverty in East End, to purchase a small second-hand car for use about his parish? All gifts personally acknowledged. Write Box etc."

You could easily fix an address for *The Times* to post the letters on to, where you could pick them up, and you could easily get notepaper printed 'St. Saviour's Vicarage' for your letters of thanks. But I thought somebody in *The Times* office would see the forwarding address wasn't a clerical one and might start asking questions. It would need more going into before I did anything.

On Twelfth night we had Mrs. Rutland coming for dinner. I'd had a busy morning. I'm no cook, not really; but cakes I do well and I'd been baking a big birthday cake for Ailsa Richards. Mrs. Leonard had been helping me to ice it. It's pathetic, I know, but sometimes you get more fun out of doing things for other people than doing them for yourself, and even missing a ride didn't matter compared with taking the cake down to the Richards's cottage and seeing their pleasure.

I felt fine. When I got back Mark was just in from a round of golf. He kept wanting me to try, as the eighth tee was practically at the bottom of our garden, but I kept putting it off and saying I'd be awful. We laughed about this. We didn't often laugh together, it was quite a change. Mark had a funny side that I'd hardly had a chance of seeing. Just for a few minutes it was as if that horrible night at San Antonio had never happened.

Somehow at the end of lunch talk of the firm came up, and I thought, I'm not playing fair with him, not telling him about those two letters I'd read; it's up to me to tell him and then he can think what he likes. So I told him.

He heard it all through without saying anything. Then he gave an uneasy shrug as if his coat was uncomfortable, and looked at me. "The Glastonbury Investment Trust. That's Malcolm Leicester. I wonder what Chris is *playing* at. Is he trying to get control of the firm entirely out of my hands? Or is he trying to sell? If he's selling on the one hand, why buy on the other?"

"That's all I know. Terry's never mentioned it to me."

"D'you mean before we were married?"

"Yes, of course." I covered up.

"In any event they should have brought the whole thing, whatever it is, to the attention of the board. It'll have to come out now."

"Don't say how you got to know."

He wrinkled his forehead. "No . . . On second thoughts it hadn't better come out—yet. But I'll make inquiries . . . I'm enormously grateful to you for telling me."

"Not at all," I said, copying his politeness, and that made it sound more off-track than ever.

He lifted his head and half smiled. "D'you feel married to me, Marnie?"

"No."

"Nor I to you. Perhaps it will grow . . . Have you ever been to a concert?"

"What sort?"

"Orchestral music. Festival Hall stuff."

400

"No."

"We'll go next week. Like to?"

I said: "I suppose it's the sort of thing you hear on the radio."

"Very much. But it sounds different not coming out of a box."

"All right . . . You're very patient, aren't you, Mark?"

"Have you only just realised that?"

"Patient," I said, "but you keep on. There's no let-up."

"I'm playing for high stakes."

"You want a nice cosy wife, who'll be here every evening to warm your slippers and—all the rest. I could pick six for you."

"Thanks, I do my own picking."

"Yes," I said, and got up. "But it doesn't always work out. What are you taking me to hear?"

I suppose that talk was about the high spot. After that we went down.

12

It was that next week that Roman began different tactics.

As soon as I sat down he said: "Now, Mrs. Rutland, I think we've been making enough progress these last two weeks to pass on to the next stage. It's very simple really, and really very much the same. But I shall stop asking you to tell me about your life and instead I just want you to talk. In the course of the hour I shall put one or two questions to you—or perhaps even just one or two words—and I shall ask you to talk about whatever ideas come into your head as a result of that question or that word. I don't want you to *reason* anything out, I just want you to say the first thing that comes to you, even if it's nonsense—more than ever perhaps if it is nonsense. Do you understand?"

"Yes, I think so."

We sat in silence for a minute or two and then he said: "Are you happy coming here?"

"Oh, yes . . . Yes, quite."

"Do you come by tube?"

"Yes, usually."

"Rain. What does rain suggest?"

"It's always raining when I come here. Every time so far. My umbrella leaks a pool in your hatstand. The buses make noises with their tyres like kettles boiling Hiss, hiss." I thought that was quite clever really on the spur of the moment.

"Water," he said.

"Isn't that the same thing? Not quite, I suppose." I looked down at my ankle. That woman *had* caught my stocking in the tube with her crazy stick. Some women ought to be locked up, not looking where they were standing, and all the time telling this friend about Charles's gallstones.

I thought I'd give Roman a run for his money. "Water? It rains a lot in Plymouth where I was born. And there's water all round there. Why do they call it Plymouth Sound? The sound of kettles boiling. I love tea, don't you? It's the cosiest drink. They were always drinking tea at home. Come in, dear, and have a cup, it's not five minutes since we made it. Sugar? No, I gave it up during the war. Wasn't rationing awful?"

He waited a bit but I didn't go on.

"Baths."

"Baths?"

"Yes."

I didn't speak for a long time but leaned back and shut my eyes. I thought, this isn't bad. He just waits as long as I wait, and the hour ticks by.

"Baths," I said. "Do you take baths, Dr. Roman?"

He didn't answer. I said: "Sometimes when I'm in the mood I have two and three a day. Not often, but sometimes. Mark says what do I waste my time for, but I say well isn't it better to take too many than not enough. People who don't wash smell. You wouldn't want me to smell, would you?"

He said: "What do you associate with baths? What are the first things that come into your mind?"

"Soap, plugs, water, rain water, Boers, Baptists, blood, tears, toil . . ." I stopped, because my tongue really was getting ahead of me. What was I talking about?

"Baptists," he said.

"Blood of the Lamb," I said. "Made pure for me. And his tears shall wash away thy sins and make thee over again." I stopped and giggled slightly. "My mother used to take me to chapel three times every Sunday, and I suppose it's coming out now."

"Did you learn that so young?"

"And Lucy Nye too," I said in a hurry. "Lucy was just as bad after Mother died."

The hour went on like this. Most of the time he seemed to keep on dodging around the same dreary subject of water. I don't know what was biting him, but after a bit I didn't enjoy it so much and thought, let him go and run after himself. Why should I work so hard? He was getting paid, not me.

So we stuck there for a long time, until he mentioned thunderstorms, and I thought, oh, well, this'll colour his life, so I told him all about Lucy Nye and how she'd made me afraid of them. And even then I had this funny instinct that he wasn't believing a word of it.

Anyway, when it was all over I came away with a feeling that for a non-talker I'd talked a lot too much . . .

So on the Friday I went all set to say nothing at all.

But it wasn't so easy because almost the first thing he said was: "Tell me about your husband. Do you love him?"

I said: "But of course," in one of those light brittle voices, because keeping quiet here might tell more than talking.

"What does the word love mean to you?"

I didn't answer. About five minutes later I said: "Oh— affection, kissing . . . warmth, friendly arms . . . a kitchen with a fire burning, come in out of the rain, m'dear . . . God so loved the World that he gave His only Begotten Son . . . Forio knowing my step. Mother cat carrying her kitten away. Uncle Stephen walking down the street to meet me. That do?"

"And sex?"

I yawned. ". . . Masculine and feminine. Adjectives end in euse, instead of eux. Male and female . . . Adam and Eve. And Pinch-me. Dirty boys. I'll slap your bloody face if you come near me again . . ." I stopped.

There was another long wait. O.K. I thought, I can wait.

It must have been another five minutes. "Does sex suggest anything else?" he asked.

"Only dirty psychiatrists wanting to know," I said.

"What does marriage suggest to you?"

"Oh, what's the good of all this?" I said, getting hot. "I'm *bored*. See? *Bored*."

It was so quiet I could hear my wrist-watch ticking away.

"What does marriage suggest to you?"

"Wedding bells. Champagne. Old boots. Smelly old boots. Something borrowed, something blue. Bridesmaids. Confetti."

"Isn't that the wedding you're thinking of, not marriage?"

"You told me to say what came into my head!" I was suddenly angry. "Well, I've flaming well said it! What else d'you expect! If that isn't enough I—I . . ."

"Don't upset yourself. If it upsets you we can pass on to something else."

So it went on. On the following Tuesday we had a real set-to. Then I clammed up and said practically nil for a complete half-hour. I pretended to go to sleep but he didn't believe it. Then I started counting to myself. I counted up to one thousand seven hundred.

"What does the word woman suggest to you?"

"Woman? Well . . . just woman."

I relaxed and dreamed about jumping a hurdle.

"Woman," he said much later. "Doesn't it suggest anything?"

"Yes . . . Venus de Milo. Bitch. Cow. I once saw a dog run over in the street. I was the first one to get to

404

it because it was still yelping and it bit through the arm of my winter's coat and there was blood on the pavement, and the boy driving the baker's van said it wasn't his fault and I shouted at him yes it was, yes it was, you should take more bloody care, and the poor little perisher died in my arms and it was awful it suddenly going limp, just limp, like a heavy old rag; I didn't know what to do so I left it there behind the dustbins meaning to go back for it, but when I got home I got in a screaming row for getting my arm and coat bitten . . . Queer I'd forgotten all about that. Queer how you dig things up."

He didn't say anything. Each time I came he said less.

"You want to know about sex," I said. "All this beating about the bush really comes down to that, don't it? It's the only thing any of your trade are interested in. Well, all I can tell you is *I'm not*. Mark wanted me to come to see you because I won't sleep with him! That's what he told you, isn't it? Well, it's the truth! But I don't aim to be put in a glass case or stared at through a microscope—a sort of—of freak at a side-show—simply because I have my own likes and dislikes and choose to stick to them! See? Everything I've said you've tried to twist round to one meaning, haven't you? I know your sort. Most men have pretty dirty minds, but psycho-analysts are in a class by themselves! God, I wouldn't like to be your wife! Have you a wife?"

After a while he said: "Go on, say exactly what you think. But try to relax while you're saying it. Don't tense up. Remember you won't shock me."

Oh, won't I, I thought. I could if I really got going. All those filthy rhymes that Louise taught me. Your kind don't know the half.

He said: "Tell me one thing, Mrs. Rutland. Apart from this question of—not wanting your husband, are you happy generally speaking, in other ways?"

I kept my mouth shut this time.

"What I mean," he said, "is, do you feel you're experiencing and enjoying life to the full?"

"Why shouldn't I be?"

"Well, I'd be surprised if you do."

"That's your opinion, isn't it?"

"I suspect that for a good deal of the time you live in a sort of glass case, not knowing real enthusiasm or genuine emotion; or feeling them perhaps at second hand, feeling them sometimes because you think you ought to, not because you really do."

"Thanks, I'm sure."

"Try not to be offended. I want to help. Don't you sometimes slightly pride yourself on being withdrawn from life? Don't you sometimes feel rather superior about people whose feelings get the better of them?—or ashamed when you give way to them yourself?"

I shrugged and looked at my watch.

"And isn't that pity or feeling of superiority an attempt to rationalise a deeper sensation, an over-reaction if you like against a feeling of envy?"

"D'you like hysterical people? I don't."

"I wasn't talking of hysteria but of genuine natural emotion, which is essential in a balanced liberated human being."

I pulled up my shoulder strap, which hadn't slipped after all.

He said: "But even hysteria is much easier to set right than your condition. You've grown a protective skin to defend yourself against feelings. Unless you try to come out of it the skin will harden until the real *you* inside shrivels and dies."

"And d'you think all this talking is going to help?"

"It will, I promise you; but only on certain conditions. That's why I'm breaking my general rule and trying to interpret your problems far too soon. So far, Mrs. Rutland, except for one or two rare outbursts like today, you have been watching your step all the time. Whenever anything has seemed to come to your lips that represented the true Free Association I'm seeking you have bitten it off sharp. Well, that's not uncommon at the beginning, especially in a woman of perception like yourself—but I have to differenti- ate between involuntary suppression and deliberate suppres- sion. An analyst can only help a patient who tries to help herself."

"What d'you expect me to do?" I said sulkily.

"I want you to stop being frightened of what you're going to say."

It was that night we went to the concert at the Festival Hall. I went in the wrong mood to sit still for two hours while a lot of sad-looking men and women played prim classical music. The only thing that could have done me any good at all was perhaps jazz, which did at least set your blood moving, your arms and feet twinkling.

I yawned all through the first part of the concert— or at least half the time I struggled not to. The lights and the noise and the dressed-up audience made me sleepy and yet at the same time restless. The second half I thought I was never going to get through, except for the last piece. By then I'd soaked in some of the right mood, or perhaps it was the music. It was something by Brahms. I think it was his fourth symphony. But it might have been any of them.

Anyway, Mark saying it was different from when it was canned, I could see there was this difference. The horns and things showed you what 'brassy' meant, and the strings had a sort of reedy sound, like wind blowing through grass, like wheat stalks shivering, like the crying of trees. In the end it got me; it was like it had slid under my skin and was playing on exposed nerves. I forgot all the sad-looking people and Mark next to me and the gangway on the other side and the lights and the antique faces in the orchestra, and I felt as if I was alone on a peak of a mountain and what I'd done with my life so far was pretty much of a dream and only these few seconds were real.

But you couldn't stay up there, it was too cold or the light was too bright or something, and suddenly the music had stopped and people were getting up and moving out. I wiped the sweat off my forehead and nodded to Mark and we followed the others down to the January wind and the waiting cars.

Afterwards we went to a night club. It was his idea not mine, but by then the want to jive had left me because something else had been there and taken its place. But the something else had gone and left an emptiness, and nothing much mattered any more. We got home about one. I don't

407

know if he thought the evening a success, but for me it had been too up and down; somehow except for just those few minutes I'd never been in step—and even those minutes I hadn't so much been walking as flying.

When we got home I said I was tired and went quickly to bed and put the light out. I watched his light for a time, afraid because of something about him that evening. I thought up two or three different excuses, including of course the most obvious one. I'd never used it even on the honeymoon because I was shy of speaking about it to a man. But I thought I might keep it as a sort of last resort tonight.

I heard him moving about for a long time. It must have been three before he put his light out. But he didn't come in.

I'd missed two Saturdays at poker, but the next one I went again, and this time I gambled heavily. It was quite unlike me. I was losing my judgment. But I won twenty pounds. That's the way it is sometimes; you get the luck when you don't deserve it. That week I'd sent Mother a hundred pounds in two Money Orders, so I was within scraping distance of rock bottom.

On the Sunday morning Mark said: "These Saturday nights with Dawn Witherbie get later and later. What do you do, go dancing?"

"No, we went to the pictures and then I went home with her, and her mother wasn't well, so I stayed on until the doctor came . . . How did you know I was late?"

"I thought I heard the car about two, so I waited and then went and looked in your bedroom and it obviously wasn't."

"No, it must have been later than that."

"It was nearly four. I didn't get to sleep again until after I *had* heard the car."

I rubbed a small stain on my riding breeches.

He said: "Anyway you seem to come up bright and fresh every Sunday . . . How are you going on with Roman?"

"Doesn't he tell you?"

"No, he hasn't said anything yet."

"I'd like to give it up. It's upsetting me."

"I'm sorry."

"I've done weeks and weeks now. It's far beyond what I promised. I don't *want* to go on. I come away feeling tired and depressed."

"Shall I ring him next week, and ask him what he thinks?"

"Oh, I know what he'll *say*. It's only the beginning for him. He's making a good thing out of it."

"He's far too honest to go on only for that reason."

I could see Mark wasn't giving way, so I turned and went out into the garden.

For once Forio wouldn't come to me. It was so out of character I could hardly believe it. He'd let me get nearly to touching distance and then he'd toss his head and trot off. It had been wet practically all week, so I suppose he hadn't had enough exercise. After four or five times I gave up and walked back to the house. A piece of apple would fetch him.

As I got in I heard Mrs. Leonard call out: "I don't know where they are, Mr. Rutland, not this week. I was out, and Mrs. Rutland must have put them away."

"What is it?" I said.

"My new shirts," Mark said.

"Oh, I put them in your wardrobe. Wait a minute." I ran upstairs and into his room. He was standing there in front of the mirror with a handkerchief in his hand. He was wearing a pair of old grey flannel trousers but he hadn't anything on above that.

He said: "Sorry, I thought you'd gone."

"I had but I came back. I took the shirts out of the box and put them with your others." I went to the wardrobe. "Here they are."

"Thanks. I thought I'd just try one."

I lifted the top one out and pulled the various clips and things out. On the table were his keys and his pocket-book and a diary and some loose change. He always put them there each night when he undressed. "I never knew before people ever did buy six shirts at a time."

He laughed. "It's not a sign of extravagance. They wear longer."

When you saw him without his clothes you could see he wasn't delicate, or even thin. His skin was pale and smooth, but the muscles lay under it; there when need be.

I said: "Forio's being tiresome. I came in for some bait."

He took the handkerchief away from his face. "As you're here, d'you think you could get this eyelash out of my eye? I think I shoved it in with the towel."

I went to him and he bent his head. I honestly believe this was the nearest we'd been to each other since we came home. And taking an eyelash out is very much of a close-up project. Your own eyes stare into the other eyes at nearer than love-making range. You see the pinkness under the lid and the tiny blood vessels; but even that doesn't matter so much as the pupil, because that seems to stand for about the closest you can ever expect to get to the personality. It was harder still for me this time because I had to put my other hand somewhere when now and then it wasn't wanted, so I had to put it on his warm shoulder, and of course my body was touching his.

I saw the eyelash and edged it towards the corner. Then with me standing there like this against him it was just as if my own body hadn't any clothes on either. I got the feeling just like it was really happening.

Just about in time I got the eyelash out and shifted away, feeling sick and short of breath.

"There you are. No charge at all."

He took the handkerchief from me. "Oh, heaven, that there were but a mote in yours."

"What?"

"Nothing. Only a quotation."

I went to the door.

"Marnie."

"Yes?"

He smiled at me. "Thanks."

I went out and ran downstairs and went into the kitchen for a minute or two to try and get the thing out of my system. When I went to fetch Forio I realised I'd come out without his bit of apple. But it didn't matter because this time he came to me like a lamb.

I rode till lunch-time and was late back for lunch, but I felt frightful all day. I felt so depressed I could have howled. I was becoming a melancholic. That'd be something fresh for Roman to unscramble.

I was depressed all week, and had dreams enough to keep all the psychiatrists in London on time and a half.

On the Wednesday I went down to see Mother. I found I could do it well enough in a day, so I made the excuse I had to settle up something with the Garrods.

Mother was looking much better. She was mixing in nicer company here, she said, and the house quite suited her. For once she jarred; I suppose because I was still feeling depressed. I thought, here she is having a good time on my money and not really caring where it comes from. Then I remembered how she'd been four years ago and what a difference the money had made.

She went into a sulk when I said I couldn't even stay one night, but she only asked casually about Mr. Pemberton and seemed to take it for granted things were going on as usual. Just after tea, while Lucy was washing up, I said: "Mam, when did Dad die?"

"Die? He was killed, drowned. Nineteen-forty-three. Why?"

"I was only wondering. I was thinking of it the other day. I don't remember it. I mean I don't remember who told me or what they said to break the news."

"Why should you indeed? You were only six at the time. Why should you remember anything about it?"

"Well, I remember other things. After all six isn't all that young. I remember Uncle Stephen coming when I was five and bringing me a pair of fur-lined gloves. I remember the girl next door——"

"All right, you remember one thing and forget another. That's the way of it. If you want the truth, I didn't tell you for months after. I thought it'd upset you, like. I thought, Marnie mustn't know. So in the end it just didn't make an impression on you at all."

I edged around on my seat. "What part of nineteen-forty-three was it? We were at Sangerford then, weren't

411

we? Did he visit us in Sangerford? I mean earlier. I mean one Christmas. I seem to remember he did. Didn't he bring me a present of a box of chocolates? And some sugared almonds. I remember the sugared almonds . . ."

She said: "Wait," and got up with her stick and limped to this old stool we've had since the year one and lifted the top and took out her black bag. "I'll show you," she said, and began to fumble among some papers. "I keep it here. I keep everything here." She passed me a yellow news-clipping.

It was from the *Western Morning News*, 14th June, 1943, under "Deaths on Active Service": "Frank William Elmer, H.M.S. *Cranbrook*, on June 10th: Aged 41, late of 12, Mulberry Street, Keyham. Beloved husband of Edith and father of Margaret."

I gave it back. "I don't remember seeing it before. Thanks."

Mother dabbed her nose. "It was Whit Monday that came out. It was a lovely day. People was on holiday, even in the wartime. I cut it out to keep. That's all I had left."

"It's years since I saw a photo of him," I said. "There used to be one in Plymouth on the mantelpiece. You know."

"There's one here. Same one but not framed."

I looked at that face. I'd come from that face. A stranger he was, because I only knew the photograph. Somehow I'd come from him. He wasn't a bit like what I'd told Roman. His hair was fair and thick and cut short, his face was round, his eyes blue or light grey, small, and I should think twinkling. The oddest thing was he looked *young*. Mother had got older and he'd stayed young.

"How old was he here?"

"About thirty."

"Can I have this or is it the only one?"

"You can have it if you take care of it."

Old Lucy came in with some dishes then, so I put the photo in my bag before she saw. But later when she went out again I said: "Mam, what was the name of the doctor—you know, the one that let you down with the baby?"

412

"Why?" she said. "What's it all about? Gascoigne was his name—may God have mercy upon him, for I can't."

"Was I all right?" I said. "I mean when I was born. No trouble then?"

"Of course not! But that was before the war. You—why, you never gave me a minute's worry. Not till you were ten, that was. And that was all because of the common company you had to mix with. What's the matter with you today, Marnie? All these *questions*."

"I don't know. I sometimes think I'm a bit queer."

"*Queer*. Well, be thankful you're not like other girls. Trollops and flying after men. Painting their toe-nails. You're worth three of any ordinary girl, Marnie, and don't let anyone tell you different. You're so clever—and so good."

"Were you a bit out of the ordinary when you were young?"

"I was always one to want to get on—a wee bit proud perhaps—kept myself to myself. Your father used to say I was too good for him. But I was never as clever as you, dear."

"I'm not sure it's wise to be too clever," I said. "Sometimes you overreach yourself."

That Sunday at breakfast Mark said: "Are you never going to tire of your poker parties?"

I swallowed something that wasn't food and said:

"My what?"

"The poker parties you go to at Terry's."

"Have you been having me—followed?"

"Not really. No."

"Then how did you . . ."

"A few weeks ago I asked Dawn Witherbie how her mother was and she told me she hadn't been ill. After that it wasn't hard to find out the rest."

I broke a piece of toast. "Why shouldn't I go if I want to?"

"Is that the point? Surely the main question is, why lie to me in the first place?"

413

"Because I thought you'd disapprove."

"So I do. But only because it's Terry. Otherwise I try to let you live your own life."

I was feeling scared. Supposing he'd had me followed to Torquay!

"Well, it's Terry. Why shouldn't I go out with Terry if I want to?"

"Two reasons. Perhaps they're both personal and you won't think they affect you. I think Terry is one of the misfits of this life. I spend one-third of the time feeling sorry for him and two-thirds hating his guts. I feel he's utterly misplaced and out of his true element as a printer. But there's no job on earth that I can think of that would *be* his true element. Can you? He's—to me a jumble of ambitions and frustrations that don't quite add up to a real person. He wants to be a first-rate business man, but he never will be. He wants to be a great lover, and is always trying to be, but I don't think he is. He teeters around on the edge of things, dressing beautifully, picking up the latest fads and phrases, running his little poker parties and his jam sessions. You see, Marnie, if he was a really tough bad character, perhaps I could make something of that, but he isn't even big enough to be really bad. And what's worse, along with his failures—perhaps as a result of them—there's a sort of slyness that gets under my skin. He has the sort of ingenuity that turns sour everything that it touches."

"Perhaps it's because he's a misfit that I—get along with him."

"Don't underrate yourself. Look at this business of the Glastonbury Investment Trust—and it's you I've to thank for putting me on to it. I haven't tackled him yet, but it seems to me perfectly typical of the man. I don't resent his enmity but I resent his back-door way of showing it."

"What are you going to do?"

"I don't know. That's reason number two for your not going to these parties. Just at the moment I don't think you, as my wife, can possibly, decently have a foot in both camps. It would be less impossible if the blood-letting were above ground. But it isn't yet."

414

I began to put one or two of the things together on the table.

He said: "I hate unpleasantness. And the feeling that all this is going on underneath all the time poisons every day as soon as I get to the works. I told Rex about the Glastonbury Trust, and he has some weird idea of having the Holbrooks and ourselves over to dinner one night to see if they'll make the friendly move and come out in the open. I've told him he's crazy, but he says it's a pity if an old family firm is going to have to come to a split for lack of an effort on his part."

"When does he want us to go?"

"I don't know. I think the week after next. Anyway you see how it is. You see how impossible it is for you to be out until all hours with Terry, don't you?"

I piled the dirty plates on the dinner wagon. If something was put to me rationally I nearly always saw the point. But I was feeling mulish. I expect I looked mulish, because after watching me he said:

"Ours is about the oddest sort of life anyone could live, isn't it. That's if it can be called a life at all."

"I didn't suggest it."

"No, but to some extent you acquiesced."

"You know the reason for that."

He came over and stood beside me. His eyes were very dark. "I've done what I can to leave you alone, Marnie. It hasn't been much fun, I can tell you. Sometimes it gets me down. That's another form of unpleasantness, to feel that you're being treated as a jailer by your own wife. That, and all the other pressures involved . . . It puts me off balance at my job, it comes between me and my sleep. I'm irritable and short-tempered with things. Sometimes I feel I could kill you. But I don't. I leave you alone. Except for Roman, you do whatever you want. You go your own way. I hope for better things. I keep on hoping. It's the only thing that makes the present set-up tolerable at all. But if you start playing fast and loose with Terry I shall have to think again."

"I don't play fast and loose with him! I can't bear him to touch me!"

"I know he wouldn't be Terry if he didn't try."

"I really believe you're jealous of him."

He took me by the shoulders and tried to bring me round to face him. I wouldn't move. He pulled me round.

"You're hurting me, Mark."

He didn't let go. "So I'm jealous, Marnie. I'm jealous of the men you speak to, of the people you go out with, of the hours you spend here alone while I'm at the works. I even have to be jealous of my miserable back-door sham-smart wise-cracking cousin. More than ever jealous of him because he seems to be the only man you favour. The whole damned feeling is something I've never felt before and never need to have felt, because with any sort of proper relationship between us it wouldn't have arisen."

"You're hurting me."

He let me go, shrugged. "I don't want to start getting melodramatic . . . I've made my own present—and yours too. And for the time being at any rate we've got to live in it. I'm trying to let you go your own way and at your own pace. That's fine—we've agreed to it, and if it's wearing on me that's my funeral. But the bargain doesn't include your going out and staying out with Terry. I'm sorry if you thought it did, but it doesn't. It just doesn't, Marnie."

I pulled my arm away and left him there at the door.

13

My mind sometimes went to Mark's keys which he took out of his pocket in his bedroom each night, but so long as I stayed with him there wasn't a thing I could do about them.

At this time I had my chief pleasure out of being friendly with the Richards and their neighbours. In the cottage next to them were two old men. One was blind and the other half blind and they used to go for walks arm in arm—one eye did for two of them, they said—it was startling how happy they seemed; but their cottage was in a mess, and I couldn't bear to see it like that, so one day I went down with Mrs. Leonard and we had a gorgeous spring-clean. I also found some old curtains which were sixty times better than the cast-off nappies or whatever they'd had over the windows till then. The two old men were puzzled but grateful. Then I found *they* liked my cakes too.

That week Dr. Roman said: "We're almost at the beginning of our third month, Mrs. Rutland. We made quite substantial progress in January, but at the moment we seem to have struck another bad patch. I have been wondering whether you would submit to hypnosis."

"D'you mean—— Who by?"

"By me. But I have to tell you at once that unless you willingly allow it, the attempt is useless. Nobody can be hypnotised against their will."

"Well," I said. "Why d'you think we're not going on all right as we are?"

"I think we might get over the present difficulty. We've made no progress now for five meetings."

It sounded safe enough. "When, do you mean?"

"Now, if you like."

"All right. Do I close my eyes?"

"No. In a moment I'll ask you to watch this silver ring that I shall hold up. But first I'll lower the shades a little."

Twenty minutes later he said in a dry voice: "Yes, I suppose I might have expected it."

"Expected what?"

"Well, you may be giving the appearance of submitting but in fact you're resisting with all your might."

"I'm not! I've done everything you told me to do!"

I liked it better when I'd got him face to face like this. He was polishing his glasses, and he looked tired. Without his glasses you could see the bags under his eyes.

"You *always* do everything I tell you, Mrs. Rutland,

but always with great inner resistance. Had you been a less interesting personality I should have given you up weeks ago."

"I'm sorry."

"Are you?"

He said that as if he was going to make something out of it.

"If you're sorry, may I put another suggestion? I can produce the effect of hypnosis artificially with a simple injection. You will have heard of pentothal. It has no unpleasant after-effects and will, I think, do a certain amount to help us both."

I looked down at my nails. "I think I ought to ask Mark first."

He sighed, "Very well, Mrs. Rutland. Tell me on Friday."

On Friday I said: "I'm awfully sorry but Mark doesn't fancy the idea of me being drugged. He's funny that way, but he has a prejudice against any form of injection."

"I see."

"But let me carry on, will you, just as we are for a week or two yet? I've had some extraordinary dreams since I saw you last . . ."

"I think you yourself would never agree to pentothal, would you? Isn't that really the truth?"

I said: "Mark won't let me anyway."

"And you won't let yourself."

"Well . . . why *should* I? It isn't fair to—to get people like that. It's like bullying them—it's like getting them down in the street and holding them there. I won't give my —myself—away to anybody on earth. It's like giving away your soul."

Later he said: "Tell me this, what more do you want in life, beyond what you already have?"

"Why?"

"Well, tell me. What's your ambition for the future? You're twenty-three. Most women of your age want marriage. You have it but cannot accept it."

"I don't mind being with a man so long as he leaves me alone."

"Do you want children?"

"No!"

"Why not? It's a natural instinct, isn't it?"

"Not for everyone."

"Why don't you want them?"

"I don't think it's any sort of a world to bring them into."

"That could be why you don't *have* them. It would not be why you don't want them."

"I don't see the difference."

"You're trying to find a rational explanation for something you feel emotionally."

"Maybe."

"Do you love your own mother?"

"Yes . . . I did," I added just in time. "I love her memory."

"Don't you think it right and reasonable that someone should come into the world who feels for you what you feel for her?"

"Could be." God, I felt queer just then; he might have *given* me his drug; I was sweating all down my back and in the roots of my hair; might have been in a Turkish bath.

"If a child could be got by an injection, without having any intercourse with a man at all, would you object then?"

"What the flaming hell does it matter what I would object to!" I shouted. "I don't *want* children or anything to do with 'em! See? Now d'you understand?"

"I understand you're angry with me because I'm asking you questions you don't want to answer."

"All right, you are! Well, you said you never pressed a patient, so now you can change the subject!"

It must have been ten minutes with neither of us saying a word. Trouble is, though, you can't hide your breathing. I watched the brooch on my frock going up and down. Reminded me somehow of old Lucy. Not that she had much to go up and down, but she always snorted when she was mad. If I——

419

"Does the thought of childbirth frighten you?"

"What?"

"Does the idea of giving birth to a child frighten you?"

"I've *told* you! I'm not *interested*!"

"Will you give me your free association of thought with the word childbirth."

"Twilight sleep. I wish my analyst would take an overdose. I wonder why *he* was ever born. I wonder why I was. Better if all the doctors in the world were killed off. Maybe better if all the world was. Not long now perhaps. Strontium 90. Deformed babies then. Monsters. That blasted clock's striking eleven. If you——" I stopped.

"What clock?"

"The one in mother's kitchen. I hate its guts. Like a bloody little coffin. It's got a glass front. The top half is the face and the bottom half has love-birds painted on it. It was Grannie's . . ."

"Tell me more about it."

"About what?"

"The clock."

"Kettle on stove. Boiling water. Nearly out of coal. Lucy Nye. Cold weather. We need more blankets. Maybe newspapers will do." I gave a sort of strangled cry that I turned into a cough.

"Were you very cold?" he asked after a wait.

"Cold? Who said anything about cold?"

"You said you needed more blankets."

"I didn't. I was warm as warm . . . Always till that tapping at the window." The sweat down my back had suddenly gone different and I shivered; I really *was* cold then. For a minute I thought I wasn't going to be able to stop shivering.

I said: "Why does Daddy tap at the window? Why doesn't he come the ordinary way? Why do I have to be turned out?" And I began to cry; believe it or not I began to cry like a kid. It really was like a kid in a funny way; not like me making grown-up noises. I darned near frightened myself. So I tried to stop. But all I did was choke and cough and start again.

420

I cried on, and in a mixed muzzy sort of way I was back as a kid being lifted out of a warm bed and put in a cold one; and just before that there'd been tapping; sometimes it was like with a nail and sometimes it was like with a knuckle, but it always meant the same thing. And it was always mixed up with that clock striking away. And I was standing with my back against the wall, the other side of the bed the light was on and the door was shut but they'd been groaning in there, and I know in a minute the door would open and those who'd been torturing in there would come and do it to me. And God help me, just at that minute the door did begin to open, and I stood in my art-silk nightie pressed against the wall watching it. And the door came wide open, and who should be there but Mam.

But it didn't mean the end of anything; it didn't mean the end of the horror but just the beginning, because there she was coming in, and it wasn't Mam at all but somebody just like her, somebody who looked like her but older and torn about, in a nightdress with her hair trailing like a witch; and she looked at me as if she knew me, and she was carrying something that she was going to give me, something that I couldn't *bear* to have . . .

Roman got hold of me as I was half-way across the room. "Mrs. Rutland, please. Do sit down."

"There's a clock striking now!" I said. "That's the end of my hour!"

"Yes, but please don't hurry. I have a few minutes in hand."

"I've got to go! I'm sorry but Mark's meeting me at the station."

"Then stop a moment and rest. Would you like to wash your face?"

"No, we're going out this evening. I've got to meet him now."

"Wait five minutes."

"*No!* I've got to go."

I shook myself free of him, but he followed me out into the hall. There I calmed down and sat down for a minute and rubbed my face with my hankie and powdered most of the stains away; so when at last I got out in the air I looked just as normal as any other woman. It was the first time I'd cried properly since I was twelve.

Of course I wasn't going out, and I was home ahead of Mark by best part of an hour. I went out to Forio who was grazing in a corner of the field by the golf course. We'd had to have the fence raised there because once he'd got out and we'd only just rounded him up before he invaded the seventh green. It was nearly dark but not cold and I went over and gave him a bit of apple, and he took it without ever letting me feel he had teeth at all. He was restless tonight and kept putting back his ears and stamping his feet and snorting. I'd ridden him yesterday, but it was a week since I'd given him a real work-out. I wondered sometimes about hunting. Two or three of our neighbours round here hunted, and I knew the excitement would be lovely and the jumping and the galloping.

One day last week Mark had hired a hack and ridden with me. We'd been out half the day and had stopped for lunch at a little public house, and for a while it was as if all the rows and the coldness between us had taken time off. I don't mean that I felt loving towards him but just more natural. You could forget for a bit and act as if he was a casual friend.

I led Forio back to the stable, and switched on the light and lifted up his left forefoot. Yesterday he'd picked up a stone which in a dozen paces had wedged in tight enough to be a job to get out. He'd limped on the way home and I wondered if there would be any swelling today, but there wasn't. I began to brush his long mane, which had grown more than it should have, but I liked it that way. It was as fine and silky as a woman's hair. Horses don't purr but they make noises that mean the same.

While I was doing it I kept thinking about that little bungalow we'd lived in at Sangerford near Liskeard. I suddenly remembered toddling out to the dustbin in the back yard with some old cabbage leaves Mother had told me to throw away. The smell of the cabbage leaves was as distinct as if they were still in my hands. I remembered the lavatory pan was cracked and the cheap tiles had been so badly laid that you could turn your ankle on them. And the table in the kitchen would never stand firm because the floorboards sloped. Jerry-building. Mother often said so.

After a while I tired of grooming Forio and went into the house and the telephone was ringing. It was Terry.

14

So there was this dinner party at the Newton-Smiths the following week. The night it was fixed for, Mark came home early and we had our usual drink together—that was about the easiest thing in our married life—but I could see tonight he was thoughtful about something and wondered if it was because he didn't want to go. He never had wanted to go because he thought if there was a deal being planned by the Holbrooks behind his back, a social evening wouldn't affect them one way or the other, and it was naïve of Rex to think they could do more over dinner with women present than round the boardroom table.

But over his second drink Mark said: "Roman rang me today. He says you haven't been near him since a week last Tuesday."

"No . . . that's right."

"Any special reason?"

"I don't think I'm getting anywhere at all."

"Roman seemed worried about you, asked if you were all right."

"Why shouldn't I be?"

"He said you were upset when you left him last."

"Upset? No . . . I was sick of being third-degreed all the time."

I accepted a drink from him. He said: "I hope you don't mean this is the end."

"I—think it has to be."

He sipped his drink. When I looked at him now, I saw how much this business had meant to him, what a lot he'd banked on it.

"Terribly sorry, Mark. I've *tried*."

"Roman is certain you have a deep-seated psychoneurosis which only long and patient treatment will cure. But he thinks he could do a lot for you if you went back to him."

"It's making me so unhappy, Mark. You don't want me to be unhappy, do you?"

"He doesn't at all want to give you up. He asks me to *ask* you to go back. But . . . he stresses that if you return to him you must do so of your own free will."

"Oh."

"So I suppose I mustn't bribe or blackmail you into anything. I can only ask you—as he asks you—not to throw everything away now."

I didn't feel I could say anything useful, so I didn't reply.

He said: "All this is a terrible disappointment to me, Marnie. It's like groping along in hope of finding some way out and suddenly coming up against a brick wall. If you don't go back to him there isn't any hope any more."

We went up to change and went out for the evening in very much this mood. We didn't speak to each other all the way there. I looked at his face sometimes and thought, he's a sticker, he's a fighter, but he's got to give in now.

The Newton-Smiths lived in a big house in the country, and when we got there we were surprised to find that there were going to be twelve to dinner. I thought, well, this is a funny idea, having us here for an evening with the Holbrooks apparently to talk about the firm, and then they invite outsiders. But perhaps that was true to intention; that was what they'd said, just a social evening. They were a well-meaning couple but not awfully bright. Terry was there before us looking just shaved and yellow-haired, but a bit furtive and hot as if something hadn't turned out the way he expected it. The MacDonalds were there too and a Mr. and Mrs. Malcolm Leicester were introduced to me, and I couldn't make out where I'd heard the name before. But all that was suddenly swallowed up because through the

424

open drawing-room door I saw another couple arriving, and he was somebody I *did* know, a man called Arthur Strutt.

He was a partner in a firm of Turf Accountants called Crombie & Strutt who had a branch office in Birmingham. It was at the branch office in Birmingham that a Miss Marion Holland had once been employed as a confidential clerk.

Well, there it was, suddenly staring me in the face like the muzzle of a gun. At first it didn't really knock me out at all because as usual I had the feeling that the gun was pointing at Marion Holland, not me. We were different people.

But it was going to be quite embarrassing if it turned out we both had the same face.

Mr. Strutt had travelled up from London once a month while Marion Holland worked there. That meant he'd seen a lot of her. He usually spent a whole day in the office going through things with the branch manager, Mr. Pringle. Twice he spent more than an hour at a time with Marion Holland.

When I could get my tongue away from the roof of my mouth I clutched Mark's arm. He'd been talking to Mrs. Holbrook and he looked surprised.

I said: "Could I—have a word with you. I've just remembered something." When he'd excused himself I went on, "I've just remembered I've left the oven on."

"What oven? At home?"

"Yes." I laughed weakly. "I put it on about five and quite forgot it. I think I'd better go back and——"

"Oh, it'll be all right, surely."

"No, it won't, Mark. I put something in the oven and wrapped it in grease-proof paper. I was cooking a cake, experimenting. If it gets too hot it might catch fire. It might set the house on fire."

"If you're that worried, ring Mrs. Leonard and ask her to come up from the village. It'll only take her ten minutes."

"She can't get in."

"Yes, she can. You know she always has a spare key."

"She told me yesterday she'd lost it. I—really, Mark, I think I'd better go."

425

"My dear, you *can't*. It would take you an hour and a half to get back here. It's impossible. Why if——"

"Mark, I have to get *out*."

"Why——"

"At once. In five minutes it'll be too late. I'll explain later. Please, please trust me."

Terry came up. "Hello, my dear, you're looking quite ravishing. But pale, I think. Pale. Is Mark treating you badly?"

"No. Very well," I said, and took two steps and then saw it was too late. Mr. and Mrs. Strutt had come into the room.

Rex was making the introductions. I saw Arthur Strutt smiling at Gail MacDonald, and I thought, perhaps I *have* changed myself enough. You can never tell. Colour of my hair's different, of course, and the style quite; I was wearing my hair behind my ears in those days. And it was two years. Maybe he never really looked at me. He was a fat little man, and his wife was thin and faded, and——

He saw me and his face changed.

Rex said: "And this is my cousin and his wife, Mr. and Mrs. Mark Rutland."

We said the usual things. I didn't look at him much but I could see Strutt blinking behind his library spectacles the way he did when he was excited.

After what seemed about an hour he cleared his throat and said: "I think we have met before, haven't we?"

I stared at him in surprise and then smiled. "I don't think so. At least I don't remember. Where was it?"

"In Birmingham. With Mr. Pringle?"

I shook my head. "I'm awfully sorry. I haven't often been up there. How long ago?"

"Two years. Rather less."

His wife was looking at him suspiciously.

"No," I said, "I lived in Cardiff two years ago. I'm sorry."

"*I'm* sorry," he said, but he moved on. He had to be introduced to this Malcom Leicester and his wife.

I took a gulp of the drink the maid had just given me. It was strong gin but I needed it. My hand was shaking so

426

much I had to put the glass down before anyone noticed me.

Then someone was holding my arm. "Bear up," Mark said under his breath. "He's gone. Can I help now?"

I think if anything could have warmed me to him it was that. It did me more good than the gin to know he was like that about it. I smiled at him and shook my head.

But Strutt wasn't satisfied yet. I saw him talking to his wife, but he didn't come over again because Mrs. Leicester started talking to him, and by the time she'd got through it was time to go in to dinner.

It was one of those good dinners, with plenty of the right food cooked the right way. You could see how the Newton-Smiths kept their strength up. Mark might think it was all a waste of time, but I saw now that the Newton-Smiths weren't so simple after all, because of Malcolm Leicester. Somehow by inviting him as well as Mark and as well as the Holbrooks, Rex was calling the Holbrooks' bluff. It was a new sort of game of poker, and afterwards I wasn't so sure I'd have liked to play poker with fat Rex.

I had Terry on one side and a man whose name I forget on the other. Although it was all so good, everything I ate sat like an iron lump on my stomach.

Half-way through dinner I heard them talking about Rutland's at the other end of the table. Leicester leaned across and said something to Mark and Mark said something back that made them all laugh; but I could see Mark had taken the point all the same.

I looked across sidelong and saw Mr. Strutt watching me. I lowered my eyes just as quick as he looked away. His wife was on the other side of Terry, and she wasn't exactly being showered with attention by Terry.

Terry said: "D'you mean it's true—you can never come again to one of my little parties, my dear, my dear?"

"I didn't say so."

"We're having a special one next Saturday. No holds barred. Think you can make it?"

"Terry, is that Malcolm Leicester of the Glastonbury Investment Trust?"

An uneasy smile went across his face. "Yes. How d'you know? Did Mark tell you?"

"No. I do it with tea-leaves."

"Or with reading letters? I remember my father saying once that you read personal letters when you were in the firm."

It was the only bit of talk I recollect over that dinner, and I waited for the meal to finish. Afterwards all the women went upstairs. I knew I was in for more trouble yet, but I wasn't expecting Mrs. Strutt to start it. She came over to me when the others were all chattering and said:

"I understand you knew my husband some years ago?"

"No," I said. "I'm sorry but he's confusing me with someone else."

She looked at me in the mirror while I made up my lips. I mean, it wasn't easy to concentrate. She was a drawn sort of woman, not too old, but she'd lost her looks.

"Arthur never forgets a face."

"I don't suppose he's forgotten it, Mrs.—er—Stott. I think he's just mistaken it. Anyway, does it matter?"

She looked over her shoulder at the others. "I knew he was infatuated with a woman all through 1958," she said in a low voice.

"I'm sorry."

"I could never find out her name. He used to go off on these *business* trips . . . Did you *leave* him or something?"

I screwed the lipstick back in its thing and put it in my bag. "Honestly, Mrs. Stott——"

"Strutt, as you well know. He tells me some story now about you being in the Birmingham office; but I know he would *never* have blurted it out if you hadn't taken him by surprise. He's always so *careful* . . ."

There was a whole burst of giggles from the other women.

"I sometimes look in his suitcases, his pockets . . . Only once in 1953, I really caught him. And even then . . ."

Well, I looked at her again in the mirror, and her eyes were brimming up with angry tears. And I suddenly felt awfully sorry for her, so I said: "Look, Mrs. Strutt, honestly, your husband's never been in love with me. Really, dear.

428

He's making a mistake and so are you. We've never even *met* before. Won't you believe me?"

Mrs. Newton-Smith had come up to the table. "Are you girls ready to go down?"

"Yes," said Mrs. Strutt, and she turned away, but I didn't know which one of us she was answering.

I knew of course he was going to have another stab at me. In a maddening sort of way his poor suspicious wife made it all the more necessary for him to prove himself right. Apart from that, he wasn't the type of man who'd easily part with money. I expect Mr. Pringle had got it hot at the time for not making more sure of my references.

I kept near Mark all the time. It looks silly when you come to think of it, but I felt he was a protection. I felt he was on my side. I'd never felt him on my side before.

We stayed on and on talking and drinking and chatting. Then Rex came over to me and started talking about hunting. But I've really no idea what he said. Ten-thirty came and eleven. At half past eleven the MacDonalds got up to go, and then there was a general stirring around. Like a dog off the lead Arthur Strutt came over to me, with his wife just behind.

He blinked and said: "I'm sorry to keep on about this, Mrs. Rutland, but you were Miss Marion Holland before you married, weren't you."

It wasn't a question at all. It was just him stating what he knew to be true.

"No," I said, not politely. "I wasn't."

Strutt blinked up at Mark, then glanced at his wife. "The Marion Holland I mean was employed by my firm as a confidential clerk between September 1958 and February 1959. In Birmingham that was, under my manager there, George Pringle."

I sighed. After all, I'd every reason to be getting impatient by now. "Is it necessary to say it again? My maiden name was Elmer. But in 1958 and 1959 I was living with my then husband in Cardiff. He died late in 1959. His name was Jim Taylor. I've only been to Birmingham twice and that was five years ago."

He stared at me, as if any minute he was going to call me a liar. Then Mark suddenly said: "I can confirm that, Mr. Strutt, if it will give you any satisfaction. Though I don't know what all the excitement's about. I knew my wife before we were married." I was staggered by him coming in like this.

"When?" said Strutt. "In 1958?"

"Yes. I met her first in Cardiff in June 1958. I've known her ever since. I don't know what's worrying you about the resemblance, but I can assure you it can only be a resemblance."

That really upset him. You could see the conviction, the absolute certainty, dying away, and in its place for the first time, real doubt. "Well I'm jiggered . . . I've never seen such a resemblance, honestly. I admit, Marion Holland was a blonde, but you know how women change their hair . . ."

Someone behind us laughed. It was Terry.

Mr. Strutt looked at me. "I beg your pardon, Mrs. Rutland. I'd—you see, I'd a special reason for wanting to meet Miss Holland again. She—well, there it is, I think I've made rather a fool of myself. You haven't a twin sister, I suppose?"

"No sisters at all," I said, smiling now that he was backing down.

The suspicion crept around in his eyes, like quicksilver in a saucer. "You even smile like her . . . Well, I promise you I'll never disbelieve one of those *Prisoner of Zenda* stories again."

They left soon afterwards, and we were not long behind them.

Terry came down the steps with us, and instead of going over to his own car walked with us to ours. He talked away about this and that; but one thing I was certain, he wasn't thinking what he was talking about. He kept darting little glances first at me and then at Mark.

He said: "I didn't know Leicester was a friend of Rex's before, did you, Mark?"

"No."

"I never met him before," Terry said, "but he seems

430

a nice chap. Powerful in his own way, too. By the by, I didn't know either that you two knew each other as early as 1958. You weren't ragging, were you?"

Mark said: "'Fraid not. You remember I was in Wales in June 1958 on that dispute with Verekers. I met Marnie then,"

"While Estelle was alive?"

Mark hesitated. "I didn't know Marnie well. We wrote once or twice."

Terry laughed. "Deceitful, wasn't it, my dears. All this business of her coming and asking for a job. Why so round-about, eh?"

Mark hesitated again. "People talk, Terry. Even you. I didn't want some silly scandal to get around."

"Ha, ha. Well, you see how your misdeeds find you out." He slammed my door and we drove off.

We drove off in one of those silences. I waited for Mark, but he said nothing at all. And his face had really nothing you could read on it.

It was freezing in the car and I leaned down to switch on the heater. It began to whirr but the engine was so cold that only cold air came in to begin with. The air swirled round my ankles and I shivered. I pulled the collar of my coat up. There was another car on ahead that had come from the house but I couldn't remember who had left before us. There were one or two icy patches under the trees and once the car in front skidded. But it kept ahead of us almost half-way home. The moon was rising and some-times it looked like a headlight coming the other way. A slight warmth began to come through the heater.

I said: "Mark, I want to thank you for what you've done tonight. You've been a real friend tonight, sticking up for me the way you did—I shall never forget it."

"No?"

"No. I—it was wonderful and reassuring to feel that you wouldn't let me down. I really am most awfully grateful."

He said: "Well, d'you think in that case it's time to start being most awfully truthful?"

"About—tonight?"

He said patiently: "What else?"

"Are you angry with me?"

He glanced at me. "Angry isn't quite the word. Rocking on my heels, you might say—and anxious."

"It was marvellous the way you backed me up."

"So you've said. But let's not make too much of that. Just put it down to the fact that I still don't like the idea of your going to prison."

I sighed. "Well, thank Heaven for that."

"I honestly think, Marnie, that it's time you stopped thanking Heaven, or me, or anyone else, and faced up to the facts of life."

"Which are?"

"That you're going to have to tell me about all the other money you've stolen in the past."

"What d'you mean? Who said it was anything to do with money?"

"I asked Strutt."

"You *what*!"

"I asked him. I was entitled to know why he was so worked up at the thought of meeting Marion Holland. Eleven hundred pounds is enough to work any man up."

"But he'll think——"

"He's suspicious anyway; but no more so than he was before. I think we've pretty well choked him off, at the expense of making Terry believe I was trailing round after you while I was married to Estelle. Oddly, it's just the sort of explanation Terry would most easily swallow."

"Well, I'm sorry about that——"

"You needn't be."

The other car had gone. We went miles in silence. He said: "I must know, here and now, I've just got to know what the real score is. Helping you at all may be unprofitable, but helping you blindfold is a fool's game."

"I suppose it looks as if I've cheated you. But you see, I never wanted you to know——"

"I can believe that."

"Let me finish. I never wanted you to know because I felt you had faith in me, and if I told you any more, that would destroy it. You may think I care nothing about you but . . ." My voice broke.

"Whatever else happens tonight," he said gently, "for Pete's sake let's not get the issues blurred with crocodile tears."

We turned in at our drive and he drove into the garage.

"D'you remember," I said, "when you caught me before, when you brought me back here and we were having supper, I said I was a thief and a liar. I told you so plainly then. I said forgive me and let me go. And I said it later too. You wouldn't let me go."

"So what's followed is really my fault?"

"I didn't say that——"

"But I have to bear a share of the responsibility? Is that it? Well, quite right too."

He cut the engine and we sat a minute in the dark. I wriggled my handkerchief out and blew my nose. In the garden you could hear the wind sighing through the bare branches of the trees.

"Quite right too," he said. "I *wanted* to believe what you told me before we were married. I checked some of it and took the rest on trust. After all, I was in love with you, and trust must begin somewhere. To tell the truth, I was afraid even then of going too deep, just in case there *was* something wrong with your story. I thought, what's over is over. We love each other. Surely we can begin from here. If you deluded me, I was a willing victim. So in a sense you're absolutely right."

"Mark——"

"But it was pretty bad reasoning all the same. What's over isn't over. I've got to go into your past life, Marnie."

"I'll tell you everything I can——"

"You mean you'll tell me everything you can't avoid. I'm afraid that won't do this time. We've really got to go a bit deeper."

I opened the door of the car and moved my legs to get out.

He said: "*Marnie.*"

"All right."

"No, it's got to be more than all right this time. I'm no

longer the man you married. With your willing aid I've
become cynical and disillusioned. So, though I still want
to help you, I swear to God that if I find you out in any
lies tonight I'll go to Mr. Arthur Strutt and tell him of the
mistake I made. After that nothing can save you from the
police. So bear it in mind, will you?"

We didn't go to bed that night until five. Except that
he was so polite about it he'd have made a good man for the
Inquisition. His face got whiter and whiter as the night
went on. He looked like the Devil. Sometimes I cried,
sometimes I screamed at him; but he just went on.

In the end I told him all about the Birmingham affair,
all about the one in Manchester, all about Newcastle. In
the end I was so exhausted I couldn't stand. And I hated
him more than ever. All the good he'd done by sticking up
for me at the Newton-Smiths was lost.

Even then I didn't tell him about Mother, and I didn't
tell him about Swansea. He thought he'd squeezed me dry
but he hadn't quite. I clung on.

But three was bad enough. I'd never have thought
anyone could have made me tell so much. I've heard about
prisoners being questioned in the war, how once they *started*
talking they went on.

At five o'clock he made a cup of tea and we drank it
together. We'd been in the kitchen all the time because it
was warmest at that time of night. The windows were
steamed as if it was with all the hot air.

After we'd been sipping for a time he said: "I still don't
know why you did it, why you began."

"If you ask me anything more now I shall faint."

"Not with that warm tea inside you, you won't . . .
But anyway I think we may be getting to the end of our
tether tonight. You're sure you've not forgotten anything?"

I just shook my head.

He helped himself to more sugar. "The thing now is
what we're going to do about it."

I shrugged.

He said: "Well, my love, it's just not possible to leave it
as it is."

434

"Why not?" He didn't answer. I said: "Why did you lie for me if you didn't want to leave it as it is?"

"I lied for you to save you temporarily, and to gain time. But it can't be a permanent thing. You can't live a normal life when you're wanted by the police of three separate cities."

"*I'm* not wanted——"

"Not as Marnie Elmer, not as Mrs. Rutland. But you're at the mercy of every wind that blows. Next time I might not be there. Next time you might not be so lucky."

I shivered as if I'd caught cold. "Let me go to bed, please."

"There may be some way out of this, but if so I don't know it. You just can't live all your life as a wanted criminal."

"Let's think of it in the morning."

He put down his cup and looked at me. "I wonder if that's one way you live, by saying when anything difficult turns up—let's think of it in the morning. Or else you've cohabited with this idea so long that the danger doesn't look so big. Well, it looks big to me. Not to mention the fact that I don't think one ought to live with that sort of thing permanently in one's personality."

I watched him walk across the kitchen and back. His tie was round the side and his hair was sticking up. "Every time we went into a room together—think of it—meeting new people, keyed up for the chance accident; then denials, hasty lies, all the rest . . . until one day it doesn't work and you're caught . . ."

"There's nothing else for it," I said.

"And apart from you—though you're the chief problem— I carry not only the moral but the legal load, as accessory after the fact. I don't want to go to jail, Marnie."

"Just let me go," I said. "There's nothing else for it."

"To jail, you mean?"

"No, just let me leave you. I'll quietly disappear. People will soon forget."

"I doubt it. Anyway, that really solves nothing." He came back. "Perhaps that was good advice of yours after all. We'll see it clearer in the morning."

15

It wasn't clearer in the morning, nor the day after that, nor the day after. We stopped talking about it, but I could see he hadn't stopped thinking about it. But each day when he said nothing and did nothing I felt that much safer.

Well, what was there to do, honestly? He either gave me up to the police or he didn't give me up. I didn't believe he would ever really get to the point of betraying me—and every day he left it he was more implicated himself. Anyway, he was still in love with me, or whatever it was he did feel—that hadn't changed—and the way he'd stuck up for me at the Newton-Smiths had been an eye-opener.

But I knew that for the next few weeks, while it hung in the balance, I depended an awful lot on his goodwill, and I was sorry I'd thrown so much of it away. I had to get on the right side of him again, or at any rate not give him cause for complaint. Of course if I'd been able to make up to him like other women it would have been easy.

Then one day, about a week later, he mentioned that Roman had rung him, and had I really decided to drop all that for good? I saw at once that if I could do it, this was the way to please him, so I said I'd try going for another few weeks. I didn't *want* to start again, I said, because it always made me so miserable, but I'd do it because he wished me to.

So he agreed, and I went back to Roman, and I felt that Mark had accepted this as the only way out.

About this time one of the two old blind men—the less blind one, the one called Riley—took ill and was in bed for two weeks with his heart. This was the bad time of the year for Mrs. Richards's bronchitis too, and she couldn't help much, so I went down every morning after Mark had left and did for the blind men. I'd sometimes spend three hours a day down there, what with one family and the other. It was queer, the way those two men worked together. Even with Mr. Riley in bed he would *talk* to Mr. Davis, telling him where things were, so that Mr. Davis had a sort of eye after all. They were closer than twins.

Mr. Davis had a wonderful Welsh voice, and listening to him answering Mr. Riley's instructions was like listening to someone singing responses in church. "Over a little more to your left, David," Mr. Riley would say, and "Over a little more to my left, John," Mr. Davis would answer. "Mind that stool by your left ankle, David." "The stool has been minded, John." By the end of the third week Mr. Riley was up again and they were able to start their walks. I was afraid some motorist would run them down.

What with one thing and another I hardly had time to wonder whether there'd been any other outcome of that awful dinner party, whether Mark was any more on terms with the Holbrooks, or whether the Glastonbury Trust was persuading Rex to sell any of his shares; but I did notice Mark looking very preoccupied, and he was back later than usual. I could always tell if he was thinking something about me or when he was thinking about other things. In a way I was glad he had something else to worry about; he'd have less time for me on his conscience.

Then the second week-end he said he had to be away. He was spending Saturday night and part of Sunday with his mother at the house of some man whose name I can't remember; he said he was a second cousin or something, and did I mind if I didn't go because they had to beat out some family matter?

I said no, of course I didn't mind. And of course I went to Terry's.

Perhaps I asked for it, going like that, but I was getting pretty short of money.

When I got there I found only five of them besides myself, and it was a no-holds-barred evening, as Terry called it, meaning that the limit was off the raise. I did all right for a time and then I began to lose. It was easy to lose big money tonight, and I twice borrowed from Terry. Then I got in an awful hand with Alistair MacDonald, when everyone else dropped out early, and I had a full house. I thought from his discards he had threes and we bet against each other until he 'saw' me, and when he put his hand down he had four sevens.

I lost forty-seven pounds that night. This is the last time, I thought. Never again, this has finished me. When we broke off the Jewish film director came across and said:

"D'you know, Mary, you're the best woman poker player I have ever met."

"Are you being funny?" I said.

"No. There's only one thing wrong."

"What's that?"

"It isn't card sense you lack. It's a sense of knowing when your luck is in. When I'm playing, I know. It is almost like being aware of a gentle breeze. If it blows for me I know that with reasonable cards I shall make money, with good cards I may make quite a lot of money. If it blows against me I have to cut my coat accordingly. I know that if I pick up a good hand, someone else, against the run of the distribution, will probably have a better."

"Well, anyway," said Terry, coming up, "she ought to be lucky in love."

"I'll pay you next week, Terry," I said. "Or I'll send you a cheque."

"Take it out of the housekeeping. That's if Mark gives you any."

"He's generous enough that way."

"Interesting evening at Rex's, wasn't it?" Terry said, when the film director had gone to pick up his winnings.

"Yes?" I said cautiously.

"Well, yes, I thought so anyway. All that business of a man out of your past. What did Mark really think?"

"Darling," I said, "he wasn't out of *my* past. I thought that was clear at the time."

"Well, yes and no, my dear. It was clear that you'd *had* a man in your past. The point that didn't emerge was, had it been Strutt or Mark? They both seemed to be claiming the privilege."

"Really, Terry, how silly you are——"

"And Strutt's wife looking daggers. I've never seen

such a *diverting* situation. And where did your first husband come in? I honestly think you should tell me all about it."

"There's nothing to tell. I met Mark. We were just friends. When the job at Rutland's came vacant he knew I was a widow and wrote to tell me."

"Night, Tommy! Night, John!" Terry called, but when I was going to move for my coat he put those fingers of his on my arm. His eyes were that gum colour again. "Why d'you come here, Marnie?" he said, quite roughly for him.

I looked down at his fingers but didn't answer.

"I know Mark wouldn't want you to come. Things are pretty taut between us just now. Shall I tell you why you come? It's because you're much more like me than like Mark. You breathe freely here. You're not restricted by trying to behave as you think he *wants* you to behave. There's no naval discipline.' You're not put on a charge for whispering when the admiral goes past. Why pretend to yourself? Snap out of it, my dear."

The others had all gone, all except the MacDonalds who were still in the bedroom. I was surprised at the feeling in Terry's voice; there was no shrug-off about this.

He said: "I know you're bogus, my dear. What sort and how much I haven't troubled to find out, even if I could. Why *should* I? It doesn't *worry* me what you've been and what you've done. You could have poisoned your first husband for all I care. In fact, to me it would make you more interesting. Get that in your *head*."

He pulled me towards him before I could stop him; but if I'd wanted to I could have stopped him kissing me. But I let him. Perhaps I saw it as advance interest on the money I'd had to borrow. But chiefly I wanted to know if I'd changed at all. An awful lot had happened to me in the last few months, and I wondered if it made any difference to the way I felt about him. Or about men generally.

It hadn't. I got away.

He was smiling now. "Don't come here again if you don't want to; but don't stay away just because Mark tells you. Understand, there's no right or wrong so far as I'm concerned; there's only survival. You've survived. That's what I like about you."

Since I went back to Roman, I had been trying to play fair with him. Because of me depending on Mark's goodwill to do nothing about Mr. Strutt etc. I had to make some effort. I felt Roman would let Mark know if I did nothing to help. It was like being a schoolgirl who'd had one bad report and couldn't afford another until after her birthday.

So we had a sort of honeymoon two weeks, with me trying to be helpful and him not trying to probe too hard. I even went so far as to tell him I'd once stolen money and it worried me I couldn't pay it back, but he didn't seem very excited or impressed by that.

Somehow, though, as time went on, even though he didn't probe, I began to talk. More things began to leak out, not only in my talk but in my memory. I remembered odd bits of events that didn't seem to link together. I remembered looking out of the kitchen window at Sangerford at the rain splashing down the drainpipe; there was a break in the drainpipe and the water gurgled and splashed against the sill. The taste of brandy-snaps was in my mouth, so I suppose I must have been chewing them. And the heavy jangle of trucks was in my ears (we overlooked a railway siding but it wasn't used more than twice a day). There was a man in the kitchen talking to Mother and Mother was at her most frigid. The man was trying to persuade her to do something, to sign something that she didn't want to, and Mam kept saying: "Part with her? Not if it's the last thing I do!' I could hear her voice so clearly, but I couldn't remember who or what she was being asked to part with.

And another time there was somebody fighting; I don't think I was actually in it, but I remembered the heavy clump of fists and the grunting of men's breath. And there was a woman of about forty I remembered very clearly now. She was probably a nurse from what I could recollect of her clothes, but I was *scared* of her. She'd got braided fair hair that had lost its colour, and a tight upper lip, and she always smelled of stale starch.

One day when things had been dragging rather, Dr.

Roman said: "Let's see, have you one parent alive or both?"

I stopped then. "What d'you mean? You know they've been dead seventeen years, both of them."

"I beg your pardon."

"You're thinking of your next patient, not me."

"No," he said, "I was thinking of you."

"So you don't believe anything I've told you at all?"

"Yes, I believe a great deal . . ." He paused.

"Well, go on!"

"No, you go on, Mrs. Rutland."

"I've told you over and over! Dad died when I was six. I remember he used to carry me round in his arms. No one's ever carried me round since. Coh! I wish I was back at that age now, and none of this palaver. Then maybe *you* could carry me around instead of leaving me floundering on this couch like a landed seal!"

"You'd like that?"

"I might like it if I really was six and if I knew you better. I don't know a thing about *you*, while all the time you're prying into my life. You just sit there behind me like a— like a father who's no good. What good are you, to me or to anyone?"

"Why was your father no good?"

"I didn't say that! I said *you* were no good. You never advise me! You never tell me anything. You never suggest what I ought to do."

"As a real father should?"

"Well, yes."

"But yours did not?"

"Who said not? Now you're putting words in my mouth! When he died I had a picture book with an elephant on and I didn't say anything but just put my head down on the book and let the tears run on to the elephant. It was a cheap book because there was a sun behind the elephant and my tears made the colour run until it looked as if I'd been crying blood."

"Who told you, Margaret?"

"Lucy Nye. Mother wasn't there and Lucy told me. I'd been playing with the kitten next door—there was an

441

old wash-tub in the garden and a broken pram—and she called me in and I didn't want to come and I sulked and at first she didn't tell me why she called me in and I sat and read the book."

Tears were running down my face and I grabbed my bag and took out a handkerchief. This was the second time now I'd cried at these sessions—really, I mean, not for effect. I felt such a fool crying there because I'd remembered something I'd forgotten and because I felt again the twist of the grief inside me, remembering that day and how I knew I'd never have complete protection or shelter or love again.

Mark had invited this Mr. Westerman to dinner. Mark said he was a very old friend of his father's, and I rather got the idea that he had something to do with the underground squabble that was going on around Rutlands. He was a lean man of about sixty with a sharp nose and grey hair slicked back. I suppose I ought to have guessed something by the way he buttoned his jacket.

After dinner Mark said: "I've some business to talk over with Humphry, so I'm going to take him into the study for a time. You'll be all right on your own, Marnie?"

I said I would, and after powdering my nose I helped Mrs. Leonard to clear off. As I passed the study I could hear the murmur of voices, Waterman's booming over the top of Mark's.

When I dried the dishes for Mrs. Leonard she said: "The first Mrs. Rutland was awfully nice—a real sweetie—but she never did help like you do and it makes a difference, don't it, just that little bit extra. She was one on her own as you might say. Often you would talk to her and all the time she was thinking of something else, you could see. Mr. Rutland used to laugh at her—really laugh. You don't often hear him like that now. They used to laugh together. You'd hear them sometimes in the mornings when I was getting the breakfast. It was lovely . . . But by midday every day she was deep in it. Books on the table in the study piled half-way to the ceiling. Then she'd be away three or four days—didn't care how she looked—he used to join her at the week-ends. They used to dig up things called barrows, or some such. Funny what interests some folks have."

I put away the wine glasses. Funny? I wondered what sort of companionship Mark had expected from me. I mean, we laughed sometimes, and of course there was the day-to-day business of living in the same house. But there hadn't been any *real* companionship, not the sort I suppose there might have been. Often he made some move and then froze off short.

Mrs. Leonard said: "Was the lamb *really* all right?"

"Yes. Lovely."

"I said to Mr. Rogers we don't want anything but the best tonight. It's important, because we've got a bigwig coming, and one that'll be on your trail fast enough if you sell us mutton dressed as lamb." Mrs. Leonard tittered at her own wit.

"D'you mean Mr. Westerman?"

"Well yes. Chief Constable and all that. I mean to say."

"Chief . . . Mr. Westerman is the Chief Constable? Of—of Hertfordshire?"

"That's right. I think he retired last year, didn't he? I ain't sure, but I think he did. But once one of those always one of those, I say. Not but what I haven't always been law-abiding myself. And what with that great Telly aerial you have to put up, you just have to pay your licence these days."

She went on talking. I went on drying knives and forks. Mark and this Humphry Westerman were in the study.

I felt as if someone had clamped an iron band round the top of my head and was slowly tightening it. I went on drying the things until they were all finished. I looked at the clock and saw that they had been in the study now for fifteen minutes. I thought, I can go in and ask them if they want more coffee, but if I do they'll stop talking and wait for me to leave. And if I don't leave, if I won't take any of the hints, it will only delay whatever they're discussing until another time.

Because if Mark wants to betray me, nothing will stop him sooner or later.

Mrs. Leonard said: "I'd dearly love to have been there. Of course Mrs. Bond, who used to work for the Heatons, swore that he used to come home drunk practically every night, and they . . ."

If I went out and stood in the passage I might hear part of the conversation. But Mrs. Leonard would be certain to come out of the kitchen and catch me.

There would be enough lamb left for tomorrow's lunch. We could make a casserole. We were nearly out of coffee, that sort you had fresh ground. It was twenty minutes to ten. The study had french windows that looked out on the lawn.

I said: "I'll just go and look at Forio. He was restless this afternoon."

"Well, put your coat on, dear. It's damp outside."

I could hear everything if I crouched down and put my ear against the glass.

Mark was talking. I don't think he'd been talking long —about this—but it was long enough. When it came to the point it was hard to believe. Even in spite of everything I'd thought I must be mistaken. It's hard to believe when you listen and hear your husband betraying you.

". . . I had no idea, of course, when we were married. But all the same I'm absolutely convinced of one thing— that at the time she committed these thefts she was mentally distraught, temporarily unstable. And she no longer is that. You can see for yourself."

"She certainly seems a very attractive young woman, but——"

"That was one reason why I asked you here, so that you could see her for yourself. Already there's been a big change since I married her; and I'm absolutely certain that as time goes on, if she hasn't to face criminal charges, she'll become absolutely normal—even more normal than she is tonight."

"Has there been any——"

"Wait a minute before you say anything. Let me finish. My wife is probably wanted under three different names by the police. There are pretty certainly warrants out for her

444

arrest. But the police have *no clue at all* which can connect the women they want with Marnie. So if she went in and made a full and frank confession to the police of all that she had done, it would be entirely voluntary. That's the first point. Unless she surrenders I'm convinced they haven't a *hope* of tracing her. The second point is that I'd be perfectly willing to repay out of my own pocket all the money that she stole, to the persons or firms from whom she stole it. The third point is that she is already receiving psychiatric treatment, as I told you. But if she were so ordered I know she'd willingly accept any sort of additional treatment that the police or the police doctor—who must have had cases like this before—would prescribe."

There was a pause and I crouched down as someone's shadow fell across the window, but it was only one of them moving his position.

Mark said: "The one thing I'm certain of at this stage is that any sort of public charge or trial would be disastrous. Naturally *I'd* hate it like hell, but that's not the important point. She's the one who has to be considered, and at the moment she's very delicately poised. If she goes on living the sort of life she's living now I'm certain she'll become—and remain—a perfectly normal, completely honest woman. But if she's charged and sent to prison you'll be creating a criminal."

The blood was thumping in my ears as if there was an express train somewhere. I thought, Mark's stretching the case, for his own ends; he's told at least two lies so far.

Westerman said: "No, thanks, just water please . . . I must say it is a pretty problem, Mark."

"I'm sorry to let you in for it. I could, of course, have gone to a good criminal lawyer; that would have been the smart thing to do. But it happened I knew you and have known you pretty well all my life, and I thought this was an occasion to come straight to the fountain-head. Nobody can know better than you what the official attitude would be."

"On that point at least we agree, Mark."

"But on no other?"

"Oh, I'm not saying that. But I don't think I'm quite clear enough yet on all the facts. There's a lot more I should

445

want to know about your wife before making any comment at all."

"Such as?"

"You see . . . No, have one of mine this time; they're ordinary gaspers . . . You see—well you obviously want me to reflect the official attitude, don't you. Supposing you had come into my office last year, before I'd retired; suppose that; then there'd be certain questions I'd want to ask right away."

"Well, ask them now."

"In the fifteen years I was Chief Constable I often came up against problems in which the human element conflicted with the official attitude; and often there was no completely satisfactory solution. A police official is a very decent human being, but he inevitably becomes a little case-hardened to the hard luck story. You see, he knows, we all know, that there are generally speaking three main classes of thief. The first type, who are the great majority, are very silly and careless. Their thefts are unpremeditated and often quite motiveless. You find them in our prisons, unhappy men and women who have to be locked up in defence of the laws of property and common sense, people who can't keep their fingers to themselves, kleptomaniacs in varying degrees of addiction. Then there is the second class, the people who steal—or more often embezzle—only once or twice in their lives. They are the people who find themselves in a job where money comes through their hands or where the books can be cooked, and they perhaps experiment once or twice and get away with it, so they yield to the terrible temptation and disappear with the staff funds or with money they have manipulated at the bank. Their thefts are not as senseless or as unpremeditated as the first class, but often, indeed usually, they act on impulse, or at least with lack of real preparation and foresight."

I waited, knowing now what was coming.

"The third group are the clever, the intelligent ones. They are genuinely immoral—that is, they recognise right at the outset just what sort of life they intend to lead, and they proceed to lead it. They usually work out one particular line as their own and they usually go on repeating it, in general design. That's how they get caught. But sometimes they are too clever for us and they go on and on. Now the first thing a police officer would ask himself is, into which category does the present history seem to fall?"

Mark said: "Yes, I recognise all that. It's very natural and necessary to want to classify criminals. But I think if you try to fit Marnie into any hard and fast group you'd be making a tragic mistake."

"That may be so. I'm prepared to accept it. But you spoke of psychiatric treatment. Now, I've seen psychiatry and analysis do fine things for the kleptomaniac, the sort of women who will go into a shop and steal twenty-three bottles of tomato sauce or twelve egg-whisks or something equally unprofitable. Such a woman is sick, she's mentally unstable. She may not be curable but it's certainly worth a try. Where does—where does Mrs. Rutland come in such a picture? What, for instance, persuaded you she needed treatment before you heard of these thefts?"

It was raining again now, and a cold wind blew the drops in a fine mist over me.

Mark said: "After our marriage she was awfully—I suppose distressed is the best word I can find for it. She seemed to feel an overbearing sense of guilt and horror. Sometimes in her confusion she almost turned against me. All this must have been very much on her mind, because she repeatedly told me I should never have married her. I think her confession to me the other night is a direct consequence of her visits to the analyst."

Well, I thought, he's clever. But this man isn't going to swallow any of it . . .

"How much do you know of her background, Mark? Is she quite open about it?"

"She's become more so. Both her parents were killed in the war and she was pretty well dragged up. If she——"

"Any convictions?"

"Not that I know of. And I've been into it pretty thoroughly with her."

"Well, of course, that would be the first thing we should check. She doesn't know you're telling me tonight?"

447

"Not yet."

The shadow passed the window again. Westerman was walking up and down. "You see, what really troubles me about your story, and what I know will trouble my successor if you put it to him, is that all these embezzlements, all three of them, were undertaken with the utmost premeditation. This isn't a case of a girl cashier who can't resist the notes crackling in her fingers. In each of these cases she *took* the job under a false name. In other words she took the job with only one end in view."

"I tell you, she was mentally disturbed at the time. If she——"

"About what? Had she some reason to be mentally disturbed?"

"That I don't know yet. The psychiatrist should be able to tell us in due course."

"What's worrying me, Mark, is how far you have deceived yourself in this——"

"It's one of the risks I have to take."

"But it's not one that others—especially the police—will readily take."

"I know that, but I'm talking to you as an old friend tonight."

"I agree, but as your friend I have to try to help you to see this straight."

"And you think I'm not?"

"I can't answer that. I think there's a risk that you may not be doing so."

Nobody spoke; it was as if they were stopping to cool off.

"Look, Humphry, tell me this. Suppose you were in my position and were convinced of the facts as I've told you them. What would you do?"

"There are only about two things you can do . . . Of course embezzlement is not the most serious of crimes. But it's a felony. You know, I wish she hadn't done it three times; that's really your biggest snag."

"I know."

"Well, as I say, there are really only two courses open to you. The simplest and straightest is to go with your wife to our headquarters in Hertford. Ask for Inspector Breward—

he's a very reasonable and civilised man—and get your wife to make a full and complete confession. At the same time make it clear that you intend to return all the money. She will be charged in the normal way and will come before a magistrate, who may deal with her summarily or, if the prosecution ask for it, will commit her for trial at the next quarter sessions. In any event get a first-rate man to take your case, and when she comes up he can go all out for the many redeeming features. Free and voluntary confession and surrender to the police, eagerness to return all the stolen money, the prisoner's deep and heartfelt regret, newly married woman, first offender etc. It will sound very well. If you get a decent judge—and most of them are only too glad of an opportunity to show they're human beings—your wife, having pleaded guilty to the Indictment, will be bound over to keep the peace—and at once released."

"What would the chances be?"

"Oh . . . better than fifty-fifty. But if by then you could arrange for her to be with child, I should say at least four to one against any sentence."

I was cramped and stiff with cold.

Mark said: "That makes the whole thing completely public. And it puts her to all the mental stress of going through the normal processes of the law. What's the alternative? Is there one?"

"Well . . . off the record, yes, though it's altogether more complicated. Go with her and make private calls upon each of the three firms who have lost money, express your deep sorrow at the trouble she has caused them and her earnest contrition etc., and while you are saying this show them your cheque for the amount stolen, press it into their hands and ask them as a special favour to an anxious husband if they will withdraw the charge."

"That sounds *less* complicated."

"Perhaps. But it's more tricky. If you follow the first course you are at the most subject to the decision and the outlook of one man, the judge who will try her. I agree it's a risk, he might be a man who feels compelled to make an example of her; but I think it's the risk I personally would take. In the second course you are subject to the

449

views of three lots of people—perhaps three boards of directors. If they are decent people they will take the money back and let the whole matter drop—though there's a snag attached to that—but if there is *one* vindictive one among the three, there is nothing to stop him saying, 'Thanks, I'll take the money back but I'll still proceed with the charge. We've been put to a great deal of trouble and expense, and it's necessary for the sake of other people, our customers, the rest of our staff, to make an example of this woman.' There are plenty of self-righteous people in the world. And once that has happened, if she comes to trial then, she can never stand as well with us, or with the judge."

". . . and the other snag?"

"Warrants for the arrest of the thief will have been issued. It would be necessary for the firms concerned to communicate with the police and ask for the warrants to be withdrawn. It would then depend whether the police were in fact willing to withdraw them."

"Would they not be?"

"Well, they too have been put to trouble and expense. They have their duty to do, their duty to the public as a whole, don't forget. They might at first refuse to get the warrants withdrawn by the Justices concerned . . . Though I suppose in the end, yes, after a period they would agree."

I was wet through and shivering.

Mark said: "Well, thank you, Humphry. I've got to mull this over for a bit; then I have to consult her. Whatever I do has obviously got to be with her willing co-operation."

". . . Perhaps this psychiatrist fellow might be able to advise you and her. There's only one thing, of course."

"I think I know what you're going to say."

"Well, I'm sure you do appreciate that by the act of telling me about your wife you have made me a party to the concealment. The fact that I no longer have an official position doesn't affect that. If I do nothing about what you have told me I'm guilty of misprision of felony—as indeed you will be too."

"What do you suggest?"

"Obviously there's no immediate hurry, and I shall naturally treat this talk in the strictest confidence. But if you could give me the assurance that you will do something within a reasonable period of weeks . . ."

"I intend to," Mark said.

I got in and Mrs. Leonard exclaimed and said whatever had I been doing getting soaked to the skin like that, and my lovely frock; and I said Forio wasn't well and I thought I'd have the vet in the morning, but anyway don't say anything to Mr. Rutland about me being wet, just apologise to them for me and say I have a headache and am going to bed.

I stumbled upstairs and stripped off my things and ran the bath and lay in it for a few minutes trying to take a hold of my nerves and push my brain around. But for once even lying in the water wouldn't do anything. I mean, I was really up against it this time. I got out of the bath and wrapped a towel around me and went into my bedroom. I caught sight of myself in the mirror, a draped half-naked figure with damp hair and eyes too big for her face. My face had shrunk. I dropped the towel and dusted my arms and back with talcum powder. My legs were still damp and I rubbed them. Voices downstairs. Mr. Westerman was going.

I went across and fiddled with the portable radio. It came on to Radio Luxembourg and a sudden voice said I ought to turn to the Lord; but instead I turned to some Latin American music on the Light. But I didn't listen to it. Not properly. It was as if I'd overheard I'd got an incurable disease.

I tried to get into my nightdress, but my back must still have been damp because it stuck and I tore the shoulder strap. As I wrestled my way into it I saw my suitcase on top of the wardrobe.

I'd have to go. That was the answer. There wasn't any other now.

I stood on a stool and got the case down; it was nearly empty but there was a bathing cap and some sun-tan oil that I hadn't taken out since Majorca.

I heard a car start. So he was off. Suppose he didn't trust us and rang one of his inspectors tonight.

I went to sort out some things in the dressing-table and drop them in the case. Then I stopped. It wouldn't work. I couldn't leave tonight. More haste etc. I shut the case and clicked the catches and pushed it under the bed.

There was a knock on the door.

"Who is it?"

"Mark."

"Just a minute." I shut the drawers and pulled on my dressing-gown. "Come in."

He came in. "Westerman's just gone. Are you all right?"

"Yes . . . I had a headache."

"What's the matter?"

"Nothing's the matter."

"You look so pale."

"I feel pale."

He stood hesitating. His eyes went round the room and he saw my frock.

"Is your frock wet?"

"I went out to see to Forio."

"Without a mackintosh?"

"Yes."

After a minute he said: "You know what we were talking about?"

"Yes." I sat on the bed. It creaked as if I was double weight.

He shut the door behind him. "Did you listen?"

"What does it feel like to behave like Judas?"

"Is that the way you see it?"

"How d'you expect me to see it?"

He dragged over a bedroom chair and sat on it, quite close to me, quietly facing me. I pulled the dressing-gown across my knees.

"Marnie, it isn't a thing I could talk over with you any more. I had to make the choice myself, after weighing up the risks and the probabilities."

"You did that, I'm sure. Sneaking to the highest policeman you could——"

452

"I'm not being moral or superior or righteous, I'm just trying to use my common sense. I wish you'd use yours."

"Perhaps I could if it was your liberty that was at stake."

"If it was my liberty that was at stake I'd do exactly the same. Don't you see, you can't just go on living in a dream world until something else happens? I'm by no means sure that Strutt is satisfied by what we've told him. What's to stop him making some further inquiries? It's no good appealing to the judge then, or offering to pay the money back. *We* have to make the first move. Otherwise you'll get three years as certainly as you are sitting here looking so hurt and so beautiful. You wouldn't have the luxury of three baths a day, and daily rides, and poker with Terry; and maybe that lovely fresh skin would react badly to three years indoors——"

"D'you think I don't know all that!" I shouted, getting up. "Don't you see what you're doing—what you've flaming-well done! If I go to prison it'll be your bleeding fault and no one else's! You've ratted on me—like a dirty rat—like a dirty crawling rat—a dirty filthy crawling——"

He got me by the shoulders and shook me. He shook me till my teeth clicked.

"You're terrified, you fool. I know that! So would I be. But can't you use your head at all! This way, you stand a good chance of coming out of it with *no harm whatever*. If we act now, but *only* if we do, *only* if we spike their guns by following up what I've begun tonight, you may be absolutely free."

I tried to wrench myself away. I haven't lived delicate and I know how to fight and I tried to get away. So while we ranted at each other we scrapped too.

So when he'd got my arms behind my back I gave up and just stood there and he said: "D'you know I understand you better when you go back to being a street urchin. . . ."

"You filthy——," I said.

He kissed me. I could have spat at him but I didn't.

"Listen again," he said. "I agree with Westerman that open confession is the safest way. But I know you won't stand for that. And I don't want it either. The way to get you free without stigma is by approaching these people

453

privately. *I'll* approach them to begin, not you. I'm
certain— Are you listening?"

"Westerman'll go straight to his own kind tonight."

"No, he won't. He won't act even in a month—I know
that. But *we* must. Aren't you convinced?"

"Why should I be? It's just a dirty . . ."

"Won't you try to trust me?"

"No!"

In this fight we'd had, my dressing-gown had slipped
off one shoulder, and my shoulder was bare because the
strap of my nightdress had given way before.

He put his hand on my shoulder and then to my disgust
suddenly brushed the nylon down and put his hand right
over my breast. He put his hand right round it. It was just
as if he held something that belonged to him.

"Let me go," I said.

He let me go. I dragged my dressing-gown up to my
throat. He looked at me with a sort of grief, as if the steeli-
ness had gone out of him.

At the door he stopped and turned the handle a couple
of times, looking down at it. "Marnie, you said just now,
would I have done the same if my liberty had been at stake?
Well it is. Or if not my liberty, my happiness. I'm gambling
with that just as much as I am with yours. You see, I can't
disentangle myself from you—even though I've tried."

I sat on the bed again. He said: "It's my future as
well. If you fail I fail. Try to remember that, can you?"

When I didn't answer he said: "Try hard. I don't like
fighting you. I still think of myself as on your side. I
want to fight for you. In fact I will whether you want me to
or not. We're in this together."

I thought when he'd gone how crazy it all was that
even while he betrayed me he still wanted me. *He* wanted
me, Terry wanted me, the police wanted me, Mother wanted
me, all in their several different ways. I'd nothing to
give him back; not Terry, nor the police, nor maybe even
Mother any longer. It was best to go.

16

On my way to see Roman on Tuesday I called at Cooks and asked them what was the easiest way to get from Torquay to the Continent? Well, the young man said, how did I want to go and where? I said, somewhere in France. Mid-France, maybe, or Paris. I wasn't particular. He thumbed through some booklets and said, well the easiest way was to come back to London, but if I *wanted* to start from Torquay, then the best route was from Exeter airport to Jersey. I would have to spend a night in Jersey and then I could fly on the next day to various places in France and Spain.

"Nothing from Plymouth?"

"By sea? Well, possibly. There's the French Line."

"What's that?"

"Atlantic liners call at Plymouth about twice weekly and pick up passengers for Le Havre. We can book you right through to Paris. You leave Plymouth midday, spend a night on board and get to Paris next day in time for lunch."

"What days do they leave?"

"Well there's one next Tuesday and one on Saturday."

"Is there ever one on a Friday?"

"Yes, the following Friday, the eighteenth. The *Flandre*. That's in ten days' time. Shall we book you that?"

"I don't know the language," I said. "I suppose I shall be able to get along."

He smiled. "Oh, yes, miss—madam. You can get along with English anywhere in Paris. But would you like our courier to meet you at the station?"

"No, thanks."

Then there was the business of foreign money and a passport. He gave me the address of the chief passport office, and I went out of Cooks and straight into one of those quick places in Oxford Street where you can have your photo done in a few hours. I said I'd call back later. But the question that worried me a bit was, what Justice of the Peace, or Solicitor or Bank Manager or Doctor was going to testify that they had known me X years and that the details I was going to fill in about myself were correct?

I was ten minutes late at Dr. Roman's, but when I got there I gave him good value. I was inspired that day. I Free Associated like a junkie. I tried to think of all the dirty stories that had ever been whispered to me in the gutters, the attic bedrooms and the waste plots of Plymouth. And I told him a lot of invented dreams full of gorgeous symbolism. I told him I'd dreamt I was the third largest salmon in the world and that I was swimming round in an enormous glass bowl, and that outside the bowl were a whole lot of men trying to reach in and catch me, but I kept slipping through their fingers. (And while I was telling this I thought, what does it matter about getting somebody to testify to the truth of my statements for my passport? I can testify myself. Who's to know my writing?)

I told him I dreamt I was walking down a street, well dressed but I knew I had no underwear on, and I must buy some in case I was knocked down by a car. I turned in at a shop, but when I got in I found all the shoppers were rats. I could feel them running backwards and forwards over my bare feet. (And while I told him that I thought, Mark's keys, the keys of the printing works and the safe, those he leaves on his dressing-table every night. There's two yale keys and a big ordinary key and two small ones like those for suitcases and a brass key.)

I told him I dreamt I was in a condemned cell waiting to be hanged for something I hadn't done, and I think I'm going to get a reprieve; and there's a knock on the door and the wardress comes in and she says, 'I think I'd better finish this off now,' and she snatches up a long knife and comes at me, and I've nothing to defend myself with and I struggle with her and get hold of the blade of the knife in my hands and feel it cut deep into my hands and I feel the blade grating on the bones of my fingers. (And while I tell him this I think, I'm going hunting with Mark and Rex next week. I'll have to get the keys copied by then. The Thursday night I can leave and the day after that see

456

Mother and then cross to France. That's the way it's got to be.)

When the session was nearly over Dr. Roman said: "Last week we were making real progress. What's the matter today?"

"Nothing. I feel rather happy."

"I think you ought to distinguish between being happy and being what the Americans call trigger-happy. Has something happened to upset you?"

"Heavens, no, I'm going hunting for the first time next week and I'm rather excited about it, that's all. Do you know the Thorn Hunt? One of the most popular, they say. I'm riding my horse over there the day before, and Mark's being lent one by the M.F.H. Mark's cousin, Rex Newton-Smith, has invited us. It's really quite an occasion for me. Isn't that what well-bred people call it—an occasion?"

He got up and prowled across the room. His black suit was shiny at the elbows. "When you oppose me so implacably, you're really only opposing your own cure. It delays your progress. But of course it is only another form of protest from that part of you that doesn't want to be cured."

"What part's that?"

He looked at me. "Such protests are not altogether discouraging because they show that the core of the resistance is becoming sensitive to pressure. Next time perhaps we shall be able to recover the lost ground."

"At five guineas a visit I suppose there's no hurry."

"None at all. But I have a long waiting list. You need only come just as long as you want to."

I went to Petty France and saw one of the passport officers. He said if I got the form filled in and signed there should be no delay. I went to a big ironmongery shop in the city and asked to see some keys. They had a big choice. The yales were easy, as any yale looks much the same as any other. I bought two or three brass ones and two or three key-rings because I couldn't remember just what Mark's was like. I told them I wanted the keys for amateur theatricals.

That night I argued with Mark. I asked him please not to do anything about going to see those people and paying the money back, not for a week or two. I said it had taken me by surprise and I had to get it straight in my own mind. I said two weeks wouldn't make any difference—not all that difference. I said perhaps in two weeks I could make up my mind to come with him. If I went to these people *myself* and they saw how sorry I really was . . .

He wasn't easy to persuade but in the end he agreed to hold everything for the time being . . .

My biggest problem of all was Forio. I couldn't take him with me, that was what hurt most. He was my oldest friend, in a way my only friend. I mean we seemed to understand each other just like that. Our moods were the same. I could have ridden him anywhere almost without a bridle. When he put his head against mine it was the gesture of a friend who asked nothing but my friendship in return.

I couldn't even sell him to someone I would be sure would care for him, because I couldn't let anyone know I was going. The best I could do was write to the Garrods the day before I left enclosing money and asking them to have him back. If I *gave* him to them it might be the best thing, but I couldn't bear the thought of him being used as a hack.

I went into Mark's bedroom a couple of times that week when he was dressing and got a better look at the keys and the ring. On the Tuesday I skipped Roman altogether but went into the city again and bought some more keys. All I had to do was get keys and a ring that he would see on his dressing-table without noticing the difference. It wasn't hard. I collected my passport. The vicar of Berkhamsted was called Pearson. Nobody at the passport office queried his signature. I got my ticket from Cooks and picked up some French money. I was scared of the whole thing, of being in a foreign country with only a few hundred pounds, of not knowing the language, of coming to a bad end.

I wondered what Mother would say when I went down and told her she'd been living on stolen money for the last four years.

She was tougher than she looked. Anyway, I'd got to

do it. It was better she should hear it from me first than from the police.

On the Monday Terry rang me from the office.

"Doing anything this afternoon?"

"Why?"

"I want to talk to you."

"What's the matter?"

"Can we meet for tea? Neutral ground."

"If you like . . . St. Albans? There's a café, The Lyonesse."

"Right. Let's meet at four."

When I got there he was waiting for me. His eyes had that funny angry look they'd had when we talked about Mark. I'd been afraid he might want the money I owed him but he never mentioned it. When he'd ordered tea he said: "How much d'you know about what's happening at Rutland's? Are you behind it?"

"Behind what?"

"Well, those *clever* visits of yours to my poker parties which are supposed to be against Mark's wishes. Was it all a *glorious* little sham so that you could spy on me on his behalf?"

"Spy on you? How could I?"

"Mean to say you don't know Mark has sold out of Rutland's?"

"Sold out? What are you *talking* about? He'd never do that!"

"Oh, yes, he has—or next door to it. He told us at the board meeting this morning. He and Rex have sold out to the Glastonbury Trust."

I stared at him. "But I thought that was what you wanted."

He laughed. "Well, it wasn't. You've played us quite *the* dirtiest trick, haven't you?"

Tea came. I poured him a cup. He said: "You read some letters of father's once. He told me. I suppose you told Mark what was in them, my dear."

"I still don't understand."

"Always the Rutlands have had control of the firm, *effective* control, with Rex's co-operation. It isn't a good

459

thing for any company. But when Tim Rutland was killed, the old man, Mark's father, more or less let the reins slip, and for *years*, for *years*, my father kept things going. I helped him. They still had ultimate control but they never exercised it. I grew up to feel that we were building something worth while, that *all* our efforts meant something. But than along came this superannuated naval lieutenant who immediately tried to take all control in his *own* hands and turned the business into a glorified retail shop and threw his weight about as if he was fighting *the* battle of Trafalgar. It was particularly intolerable for my father, who's had thirty years' experience of printing and knows more about it in his little finger than all the tribe of Rutlands put together."

I was quite startled at the venom in his voice. "But I thought it was you who got this Malcolm Leicester interested in the business in the first place?"

"So we did. We knew the Newton-Smiths would not sell to us but we thought they would sell to an outsider. We thought that the Glastonbury Trust would be an enormous asset as a big minority holder. With a nominee of theirs on the board, we could between us slightly overweigh the Rutland interest and preserve a proper balance of control."

With what had happened this last week and what I'd been doing yesterday and today, this thing he was talking about hardly seemed to concern me. I mean it was remote, like a happening in the life of one of the Mollie Jeffreys. In my mind I'd already run away.

"And what's wrong with Mark selling out?—though I can't believe he's done it."

"He's going to do it. The Glastonbury Trust, instead of being a big minority holder who could act in co-operation with us or not at all, becomes virtually *owner*, and I and my father will be reduced to ciphers."

My tea was too sweet. I added some water.

"But isn't that just what you've been trying to do to Mark?"

Terry fiddled with his tie. "So you are on his side, my dear. I just wanted to *know*."

"I'm on nobody's side. It doesn't concern me. Why

460

should it? It's Mark's money. He does what he wants with it . . . Anyway, why are you telling me all this?"

"What sort of influence have you got with him?"

I stared. "Over this? None at all."

"I'm not so sure. Look, Mary, it's this way. The Glastonbury Trust has made an offer of seventy-two shillings for all our shares. Mark told us this morning. A circular's being printed to send to our outside shareholders, recommending acceptance. It will go out next Monday. There's still time to draw *back*, my dear."

My mind was wandering again; I wasn't really interested. Who was he talking about?

"You think I could stop him? You're crazy. Why should I want to?"

Terry leaned back and watched a girl leaving the shop. His eyes started on her legs and worked up.

"*Why* did you marry Mark?"

I shrugged.

"You're not his type. I've told you before. You're more my type. Up against it. Know what they called me at school? Turkey. Because I'd got a red neck. That sets you off on the wrong *foot*, doesn't it?"

"Maybe."

"Somehow *you* got off on the wrong foot too. I don't know how but it hasn't left you feeling too good about life. Not *sure* of yourself. I'm never sure of myself, even though I act that way. D'you know the first girl I ever *had*, all the time I was thinking, she's really bored and disgusted. It puts one off, the knowledge that one is—different in a *disgusting* way. It's like getting out of step early on in the march."

"You're making a lot out of nothing."

"That's what you think. Oddly enough, I get on well with Dad. I'm sorry for him and even sometimes admire him. He held the firm together when it would otherwise have gone to pieces. But the rest of mankind . . . you've got to despise 'em before they despise you."

He went on talking for a bit, off and around the point. He hadn't much to say, but again I felt a sort of link that he was trying to make stronger. But it wasn't anything he

461

actually said, because I hardly listened. If I *had* listened I should have thought him a fool for supposing I couldn't see the truth, which was that in some way Mark had turned the tables on him. How he'd done it I didn't quite understand and I didn't care. I didn't care for Terry's problems at all, nor for Mark's. The firm of Rutland & Co. meant less to me than last week's laundry bill.

Maybe I should have paid more attention to the fact that he was talking to me at all. Asking my help and sympathy really was grasping at a straw, and the proverb says drowning men etc. That didn't register. All I knew was that he was plugging at something that went deeper than what you might call logic. We were like two houses on opposite sides of the street connected by a land-line.

I didn't mention it to Mark that evening or the next day. Most of the time I was busy with my own thoughts. And part of Tuesday I was riding Forio over to the Newton-Smiths for the Wednesday meet. That was a horrible ride because I knew it was the last time I should ever be alone with him. Wednesday, riding in a crowd, wouldn't be the same.

I found when it came to the point there were other things I should miss. There was the Richards family and the blind men. Even in a short while I'd got friendlier with them than anyone I ever remembered before. And it wasn't unpleasant being your own mistress, having your own house, and a nice house at that.

. . . Mark was talkative at breakfast. We were driving over and the meet was to be at ten. Seeing Mark like this, I realised how quiet and moody he'd been these last weeks. And this was next to the last breakfast I should ever have with him. Tomorrow night I was going to go into his bedroom when he was undressing and while he wasn't looking change over the keys and . . .

I said : "Is it true you've sold Rutland's, Mark?"

He looked up and smiled. "More or less anyway. An offer has been made. We're recommending all shareholders to accept it."

"But why? I thought you would never do that."

"So did I a few months ago. And then I thought, however long I work there and whatever I do, we shall never be free from the friction that poisoned half my father's life. And I thought, what's in a name? Let it go."

"But what will you do?"

"Probably go into partnership with someone else. There are one or two printers I'm interested in who do some of their own publishing. That's more attractive to me. I was going to tell you, but I waited till the whole thing was settled."

"And what will the others do?"

"Rex? He's drawing out as I am. Anyway he has plenty of money. The Holbrooks? If they want to stay in I'm sure they can keep their seats on the board."

"Do they feel badly about it?"

"This move? Yes. But I honestly don't see what they have to complain of; they first interested Malcolm Leicester. Of course Rex has been the organiser of this coup."

"He's smarter than he looks."

"Except for the first two meetings with Leicester I've tried to do everything openly. The choice is put fairly before the shareholders now."

"Yes. Yes. I see."

He got up. "It's time we were off . . . It's been a big wrench, but now I've decided, it's like throwing off a hair shirt. It's pretty unpleasant, Marnie, to have this to contend with month after month. And I honestly think that the Holbrooks, once they've swallowed the first pill, will find it better too. Jealousy's a nasty thing: it's bad to suffer under and it's bad to feel oneself."

I got up slowly. He said: "Marnie, I hope you'll let me start approaching Strutt and the other two firms pretty soon. I want to go and see them on my own. I think I could bargain."

"How?"

"Well, it's something Westerman couldn't suggest because it's illegal. But I could put it that I would return the money stolen from them *provided* they agreed not to prosecute."

I shook my head. "It isn't much to bargain with. They'll have been insured."

"Probably. But not certainly. Everyone doesn't do everything he should. Anyway it's worth trying."

The sun was breaking through thick misty clouds as we drove down. Just before we got there he said: "How did you know about Rutland's?"

"Dawn told me."

"She doesn't know. None of the staff has any inkling yet."

I sat in silence.

He said: "When you tell a silly lie like that I get depressed all over again."

We were following a horse-box now which was evidently going to the same place as ourselves.

He said: "If you'll only *trust* me there's no limit to what we can do, how far we can go together. If you don't trust me then we've no solid ground under our feet at all. We're still struggling in the same dreary morass where we began."

He overtook a farmer on a big strong bay which looked as if it might not be very fast but would last for ever.

"Was it Terry who told you?"

"Yes."

"So you still see him?"

"No. He telephoned and suggested it. We had tea at a café in St. Albans."

"Why did he want to see you?"

"He seemed to think I might be able to persuade you to back out of this deal."

"And are you going to try?"

"No. I know it's no use."

"But you might if you thought it would be? Whose side are you on, Marnie?"

I stared out of the window. Once again I didn't seem to care. It wasn't my concern. "Isn't this where we turn left?"

"If you are on the other side, say so."

"No," I said. "I'm on your side, Mark, in this."

But I suppose I didn't have enough feeling in my voice, because he looked at me as if he knew it wasn't true.

.   .   .   .   .   .

The meet was in the grounds of a big house called Thornhill. It was a Victorian place, I should think, built of brown brick with a lot of ivy climbing up it and chimneys as tall as rows of pencils. At the side was this large conservatory with a glass roof the shape of the covers you see in cafés to keep the flies off the cakes.

There were quite a lot of people already about when we rode up with Rex Newton-Smith. There were ten cars and four horse-boxes and two trailers and about a dozen people mounted or dismounted and a farmer or two, hands in corduroys. Before I agreed to come I'd asked Mark to find out if Arthur Strutt was a hunting man but it turned out he wasn't, so I was safe from that risk.

Mark was on a big brown horse that was pretty restive so I steered Forio away from him because Forio, although the sweetest-tempered thing, easily caught nerves. Then a man came along in a velvet cap and a scarlet coat, and Rex introduced him as one of the Masters. We all got down and talked for a bit, but I didn't listen much to what was being said because this was all new to me and, although I was still thinking more about tomorrow than today, I was glad in a way to experience it all once before I bolted. I'd seen horses and dogs streaming over the Gloustershire countryside but somehow had never come full-tilt into them and certainly had never been one. of them before.

Just then the hounds came, bobbling and making strange noises and waving their tails all ways. Then suddenly there seemed to be more people everywhere, people talking, people tightening girths, people mounting, a huntsman talking to the dogs, three men in bowler hats and yellow breeches, horses pawing the soft turf, a girl in a blue habit—I'd like one like that—on a horse with white stockinged forefeet, an old man with a crab-apple face; Forio was excited now, he'd never been in so much company; I checked him as well as I could with one hand; just in time we moved off.

Everybody moved off talking, chattering to each other like a Sunday picnic, waiting their turn at the gates, then off down a rutted muddy lane. They were a queer-looking lot, a good many of them ugly, even the women, and hard in a way; I mean tough. I'd swear none of them had ever been short of anything important all their lives. "Good crowd," Rex said to me in his squeaky voice. "More than usual for a Wednesday. It's the weather I suppose." The sun was still trying to shine, weakly, like one of those poached eggs that come pale. Mark was just behind me but his horse was straining; it was one of those animals that always must lead; like some men; it's a question of temperament. Forio was still lively, kept trying to rear. "Hullo, Mark," somebody said. "It's a long time."

We got to the end of the lane, just by a coppice. Somebody in the front had stopped and everybody was jostling each other. "They've found!" a man in front said, and it was like an electric current going through everyone. A man next to me was biting his bottom lip and trying to edge forward even though there was no room. Then there was a movement up front and people were turning off through a gate and up the hill beside the coppice.

Suddenly there was this horn. I'd heard it before in the distance, but it's different when you're part of it. The hounds must have gone up the hill because everyone was following, but it was hard to get a move on; it was like driving a car in Oxford Street; I thought I'd sooner have a good clean canter any day.

Mark caught up with me, still checking this big brown horse of his. "All right?" he asked, but his eyes were still cloudy with what had been said in the car. I nodded.

Suddenly we were through and galloping up the field. It was only a couple of hundred yards or so before we came up with the leaders who had checked, or whatever it's called, but it did us good to go full out, the wind whipping at my face; and I got a bit of nasty satisfaction out of the fact that Forio left Mark's mount behind.

"I'm thinking the fox has swung left-handed into Cox Wood," said a man in a bowler, looking me up and down as if he liked the look of me. "If so we shall lose him. Scent's always poor in Cox Wood."

For about half an hour we jogged about, up and down fields and lanes, squelching and splashing, and waiting our turn and getting in each other's way, and I thought, there

466

are too damned many of us altogether, and I thought, well done fox, you've had the laugh of us, stay in your hole, don't be a fool and give those hounds a chance to show how smart they are.

But at twelve they found another fox and this time it seemed the crazy thing hadn't been so careful. The horn began to blow like mad, and I followed Mark over a fence, noticing that his horse took it easily, and suddenly the field seemed to spread out and we were racing along level open ground beside a railway embankment. In the distance you could see the hounds and the man called the whip, I think, and the huntsman and about three other riders; then there was the Master and two more, then about a hundred yards behind came Mark and me, but I was leaving him again, and a cluster of about ten others. The rest had been unlucky and had got in a tangle at a bridge.

We had to slow at another gate and then the ploughed field that came next was too heavy for anything but a trot. I was sweating, and I was enjoying myself now. The difference from just riding was that someone else told you what you were going to do, and it was exciting, and just for the minute you didn't think about what was being chased.

We went downhill then full-pelt and almost caught the hounds, which were scrambling and wriggling through a wire fence. Some of the riders in front of me were making a detour to get through a gate, but I saw the M.F.H. take the wire fence and come to no harm so I set Forio at it and we went over. He never as much as stumbled and I'd gained on the rest of the field. I heard a crash and rumble behind me but it wasn't Mark, it was the man in the bowler; Mark had got over all right and was only twenty yards behind.

I'd turned at the wrong moment because a low branch nearly had my hat off, and a bit of it scratched my ear and neck. There were only three ahead of me now, and I was out of breath with excitement. The hounds had checked but only for half a minute and they were swinging in a sort of wide arc, past a farmhouse with a small boy leaning over a gate, across a tarred road and down a narrow lane past three cyclists who shouted and waved, over a thick fence of

467

blackthorn and through a wood where pigeons were fluttering and a dog barked. Then out in the open again.

My eyes were watering with the speed, and Forio was white-flecked and his flanks were heaving, and we came to another bigger fence and this time just cleared it. The three men were still ahead of me but I'd gained on them. And then I saw the hounds. And then I saw the fox.

The ground was rising again, and I saw the fox black against the green of the short grass, and I could see he was nearly done. I saw him turn his head and I saw him sink once and then go on running. There must have been getting on for four dozen hounds. All the time they'd been baying, that odd sound; but now it changed somehow. They could see the fox and they'd got him, so it was a sort of different cry, and their hackles were up and their tails seemed to stiffen. And I thought, he can't get away from them. Whichever way he goes, it's open country. He's run well but now he's tired and done up and there's nothing for him left but a horrible death. Perhaps he's got young at home but he'll never see them again. And I thought no one will help him. No one.

I gave Forio the whip, trying to hurry him forward, with some sort of dim mad idea that I could stop what was going to happen. But all that happened of course was that Forio put on an extra spurt so that I was nearer and could see it all better. The hounds were only a few yards behind the fox now, and he'd no more cunning or strength left in him and he turned snarling for his last stand; and it was fifty to one. Just one minute he was there, a single lonely animal against all the rest, and then suddenly he was swamped in a mass of hounds snarling and fighting and bloodily tearing his life out of him.

Somehow I'd come to a stop, or Forio had stopped for me. The huntsman had gone in with his whip, beating the hounds off the dying fox, so that he could save the brush. That was all he cared about. And then the other three horsemen came up with them and hid the scene so I couldn't see it any longer. And then others came up, Mark with them, and the afternoon was full of blowing panting horses and people talking and people laughing, and somebody waved the fox's brush in the air and there was a cheer, and everybody was saying what a good run it had been. And the afternoon was full of laughter and satisfaction and cruelty and death.

"My God, you made a fine run of it, ma'am," a man said to me. "If you ever want to sell that horse, ma'am, do let me know. You quite outdistanced me."

I didn't answer. Mark said smiling: "You rode beautifully."

I turned away because my throat was choked and I really wanted to cry although I couldn't quite. Because all these people were happy because an animal had been chased over miles and miles and ᵗhen cruelly torn to pieces with no chance of escape. I looked at them all, the way I'd looked at them just as we were starting; they were all well fed, well turned out, just the way I'd seen them before. But now I seemed to be able to see something more in their expressions. They were the sort of people who would have sat in an arena and seen men tortured or horses gored or any other show of cruelty without being personally touched at all. They hadn't any real feelings at all. All they wanted was their own pleasure.

Mark was talking to Rex who had just come up. Rex's face was a lot redder than the sun, and he kept mopping the sweat off his forehead and neck.

Perhaps there was something wrong with me just then; I'd like to think so because it all got out of proportion. I think I was *feeling* more just then than I'd ever felt before in my life. Instead of being able to stand aside from things, as I always used to be able to, this was right in my stomach like a knife. It was happening terribly to me.

And now these people, not satisfied with one kill, were getting ready to move off again. Another fox was going to be hunted to its death. And I fancied that, if they knew the truth, that I'd preyed on them, just the way a fox'll prey on chickens, stealing a few pounds from their banks and their offices, they'd just as quickly turn and hunt me. That fat wrinkled little man with his brass-buttoned coat and white stock and peaked velvet cap, that man looking after the hounds with his whip and his horn, could just as easily set them on me. And once the chase began, once the hounds had started baying, I could gallop and gallop and twist and turn, but I could never get away from them until I too was spent and they came at me with their tearing mouths. But the human beings, so called, would stop that. They'd step in and take me carefully away and very soberly bring me before a judge, and someone would pretend to put my case, although really he'd have his tongue in his cheek all the time, and then someone else would speak for the police, and I would be called to answer questions; but it would all be according to the so-called rules of evidence and I would never be given a chance to explain as I could explain in private and given proper time; and then the judge would speak a few words summing up and he would say, 'Margaret Elmer, you stand convicted on three charges of embezzlement and fraudulent conversion, it is my duty to sentence you to three years imprisonment', and I would be led carefully and firmly away.

It was all part of society—what was allowed and what was not allowed. Prison was allowed but they didn't consult me. Hunting was allowed but they didn't consult the fox.

So they were all moving off again, and I couldn't look at the blood of the fox staining the short grass. But Forio more or less turned on his own and went with the rest. I don't know how long we jogged on, but instead of it getting better inside me it got worse. The thing was boiling up in me like water inside a pan with its lid tied on. The jostling and the neighing and the creak of leather, and the high brittle voices of the women, and the squashing noise of mud and the yelping of the hounds, it all made it worse. 'You ought to distinguish between being happy and being trigger-happy,' Roman said. 'At five guineas a visit,' said the jailer, 'I have a long waiting list.' "All right, damn you, have it your own way," said a man near me, wheeling his horse. Forio whinnied and nearly had me off. "They've found again!" a girl squeaked. "What super luck!" 'How much do you know of her background, Mark?' Westerman asked. 'Well, she was pretty well dragged up.' Was a fox dragged up? Was it any more dragged up or I any more dragged up than a hound; was its mother less loving?

Was my mother less loving than Mark's? To Hell with their damned patronising beastliness. All of them. Hard-mouthed, cruel hunters. What had I done half as bad as kill a fox?

We were off again. The whole damned herd of us, off at a yelling gallop, the horn twanging, people thrusting their heels in, mud flying, faces alight with the blood-lust. We came to a fence and Forio checked and then took it perfectly; I suppose I helped, I don't know. Across another field full pelt and over a ditch and landing among some broken branches: nearly down. The whole hunt had swung right, up rising ground towards a wood. I jerked Forio's head left. He didn't like it. I dug my heels in and we galloped off and away from the rest. I heard Mark's voice: "Marnie! This way!"

I went on. Forio gathered speed, fairly thundering down the slope. I didn't think I could ever stop him; I didn't want to. We breasted a blackthorn hedge, fairly flying.

"Marnie!" There was the beat of hooves·behind me; Mark was following.

I gave Forio his head. He'd been winded when he got to the fox but in half an hour he'd recovered, and he was strung up with all the excitement. He'd never gone so fast. But Mark wasn't far behind. He was coaxing or whipping some extra speed out of his brown horse.

We were still going downhill. There was a lane on ahead with an open gate this side with a line of willows behind. Somehow I slid or slithered through the gate, hooves striking sparks, there was no gate on the other side but the hedge was low; anyway I couldn't have stopped Forio there. We took it and over into the next field. Mark followed and had somehow gained. I heard him shout: "*Marnie!*" again.

I let Forio go across the next field. It was as if not just Mark but all the things he stood for were after me, as I'd fancied they could be.

The next hedge was higher than any so far; and in the sort of flickering way these things come to you I saw that the willows were alongside a river or stream. I couldn't see whether there was room to land in between, but I knew

Forio was going to try and I knew I was going to let him. Mark shouted behind me again and then we took off.

Half over I knew we were for it. The other side was a good four feet lower on to stones and sand, with a twist bringing the river almost up to the wall. Forio saw his danger and seemed to try to check; he'd have landed square but the height did it; he came down on his forelegs and went right over; I went up, and while I was falling I saw Mark somersaulting after me.

I just missed the river, crumped backwards into the low willow branches, came head down on the ground but gently, breaking and bending branches, and my hat took the worst. I just hadn't any breath. That was the only bad thing at first. You had to gasp and strain to stay alive. Then I heard something or someone screaming. I tried to claw myself round and sit up. Mark nowhere. Mark's horse in the river up to its hocks, shaking itself, unhurt. Forio was still down. The noise, that unbearable noise was coming from Forio.

He was trying to get up but he couldn't. He was wriggling and fighting to get up but he couldn't. I pulled myself up and fell down again, got up again, staggered towards him. Then I saw Mark. He was lying very still. I ran towards Forio. He was lying there and rolling his eyes like a mad horse and the foam was flecking out of his mouth; and as I got to him I saw one of his front legs. Something white was sticking out through the skin.

I went up to him and knelt beside him and tried to unfasten his bridle. His mouth bit at me in a sort of agony, and I thought of that dog that had been run over in Plymouth, that mongrel that had bitten right through my sleeve. I got his bridle off somehow; someone else was making a noise and it was me; I was crying out loud as if I was hurt; I looked back and saw Mark hadn't moved. His head was down, almost flat in the mud. I got to my feet again and stared, and it was like being pulled both ways by ropes, like that torture they'd had in the Middle Ages, being pulled apart; but it wasn't my *body* that had to suffer. If only Forio would stop that terrible whinnying scream; and he kept trying to get up. Mark was dead perhaps; and Forio was alive and needed me. If I could hold his

472

head, comfort him somehow, hold him till help came; Mark didn't need me, Mark was dead; Oh Jesus help me; help me to comfort my old friend. I was on my knees and I was crawling towards Mark.

He wasn't dead. The mud was plastered all down one side of his face and in his mouth. I tore his scarf or stock or whatever it's called and began to wipe the mud away from his mouth. He could only just breathe; in fact he was suffocating because the mud had got up his nose too.

"Gawd, you're 'urt!" said a voice. "I thought you'd took a almighty tumble!"

A man, a farmer or something. "Get help!" I screamed.

"Let me see," he said. He slithered down the wall, looked at Forio. "Gawd what a mess, whatever made you come that way?"

"Stop him screaming!" I said. "For Christ's sake stop him screaming. Go and get an ambulance! Telephone!"

Pointing to Mark: "Is 'e all right. 'E looks pretty bad. Something broken?"

"I don't know; I can't *leave* him. Look after my *horse*! Go for help! Don't ask questions."

He scratched his head and then went scrambling up to the hedge again. I began to drag Mark out of the mud. He was right out, and as pale as paper, and perhaps he was going to die after all; and I knew what was going to happen to Forio; I knew, and if I thought of it I should die too, and for some reason until they came it was important to stay alive.

I dragged Mark as far as the stones, and I was panting and groaning myself, and I didn't look round, but thank Christ Forio had gone a bit quieter. I unfastened Mark's collar and dragged my torn coat off and put it under his head; and then there was a noise I thought I'd never want to hear again, the thud of hooves. I left Mark there and stood up and hung on to a branch of a tree and was sick, and then I looked at Forio again, being quieter as if he knew he'd never walk again; and Rex said over the wall: "My God, what a mess. Jack, go for a doctor!"

"Somebody's gone," I said, and wanted to faint and couldn't. Now that 'they' were here I did so badly, badly,

want to faint over and lose myself, faint and be just another
body for them to look after; but I wasn't helped that way.
I stood there and saw it and watched it all, to the bitter
and terrible inevitable end. After all it was my fault so
perhaps it was right that I should.

17

I watched Forio being shot, and I went in the ambulance
with Mark to the hospital and I was treated for bruises and
shock and then sent home. It was easy really. Everybody
said, poor girl, her horse bolted, she's terribly brave, I do
hope Mark will be all right; darling, the best thing for you is
to go straight to bed. You have someone at home? Don't
worry about Mark, he's in the best possible hands, I'm sure
he'll be better in the morning. The surgeon said: "We
really can't tell you yet, Mrs. Rutland; it's severe concussion.
His arm has been set, but he hasn't broken anything else.
By tomorrow morning we shall be much better able to
judge."

So I went home. And nobody blamed me at all.

I went home, and bubbles of pain and grief and sheer
hurt kept rising and bursting in my heart. And Mrs. Leonard
who'd been sent for from the village came up and fussed, and
then Mrs. Rutland rang up. Mrs. Rutland behaved exactly
the way all the mothers must have done in all the wars
England has ever fought, when they hear their son has been
wounded and want to comfort an anxious daughter-in-law,
even though they are really much more anxious themselves.
She did it just right, and you couldn't fault her. And you
couldn't fault me either. After all, how could I possibly be
to blame? My horse too, she said, as an afterthought. It
really was an appalling piece of misfortune. And I thought

474

of those men, how brutal and cruel they'd been to a fox and how gentle and kind they were over a horse.

That night I wondered where I could hang myself. But Mrs. Leonard stayed with me all night and never gave me a chance.

Next morning the reaction set in. I was black and blue all down one side and could hardly move my shoulder or my hip. And I slept. I slept as if I'd been short of sleep for a year. The doctor came once but I'll swear he gave me nothing. Maybe it was the shock.

Sometimes I'd wake out of a black cloud of sleep, and there'd be pain waiting for me somewhere like a sort of illness just round the corner of my mind. But it wasn't the pains of my wrenched shoulder and bruised back; it went much, much deeper than that. It was like the part of your heart that beat, the part of your brain that reasoned, as if there was something wrong at the hinge. I'd wake sometimes and feel this awful hurt and look at the clock and see it was five past three, and then I'd sink off gratefully into a long deep sleep. Then after it I'd wake with a start and see it was only ten past three, and the hinge would still be creaking and I'd look down a long dark corridor of empty echoing horror to the end of my life.

I drank something every now and then when Mrs. Leonard brought it, and just about dusk I looked up and saw Mrs. Rutland was there and I said like asking the time: "How's Mark?" And she said: "He's holding his own."

I ought to have asked more but I drifted off again and had an insane jumble of dreams about Mother and Forio and how Mother said he had to be shot because it wasn't respectable to keep a horse in Cuthbert Avenue. Then I was suddenly in court and seemed to be both judge and prisoner in one, defending and condemning myself. Dr. Roman was there testifying that I was unfit to plead. Once or twice during the day I tried to get out of bed, but each time the pain in my body woke me up, and I lay back panting and staring.

Outside the window were two trees—just skeletons, no leaves; all through the bright afternoon they nodded and leered at me. Then I saw the river again where we fell, and

475

the water was a snake crawling slimy over the sheets of the bed. It wasn't till the Friday about noon, pretty well forty-eight hours after the accident, that I woke up with my mind really clear, absolutely clear, just like a glass that's been emptied and polished, and knew there was an appointment I'd missed today. The *Flandre* had sailed without me.

From then on a few things began to move normally. I couldn't sleep then for the pain in my shoulder and back, and I couldn't even close my eyes because of Forio. The minute I closed my eyes I saw him again. Perhaps it isn't any good describing everything as it happened, the way my thoughts went; but some time later there was Mrs. Rutland in the room again, and I said again: "How's Mark?"

"About the same. He isn't conscious yet."

"What do they say?"

"They say we can only wait." She came into the room; her hair was untidy. "And you?"

"Oh, yes. I'm better now."

"Can you eat a little lunch?"

"No. No thanks. I'm better without."

That evening Mark came round and Mrs. Rutland got back from the hospital more hopeful. The doctors said he wasn't out of danger yet, but they thought it was going to be all right.

"The first thing he said was, where were you, Marnie, and it seemed to help him a lot when I told him you weren't badly hurt."

The next day I got up while Mrs. Rutland was out, and managed to dress and hobble round the house. My back and hip were like somebody'd painted thunderclouds on them, but a lot of the pain was going. The pain in my body, that is. Mrs. Leonard found me out in the stable and tried to get me back to bed, but I wasn't going. I stayed in the stable all morning, just sitting there, until Mrs. Rutland came back, and then I limped in and had lunch with her. Mrs. Rutland said she'd promised to drive me in to see Mark as soon as I was well. I said I'd go the following day. I couldn't very well say anything else. Before dinner that evening I had to go into his bedroom for something, and his keys were there in the corner of the top drawer of his dressing-table . . .

At dinner Mrs. Rutland said: "These flowers are from the gardener, Richards. He brought them for you and he seemed specially anxious to make it clear that they were out of his own garden."

Two daffodils, some wallflowers, a few violets.

"And a blind man came yesterday with a bunch of grapes. He said they were with love. Do you know a blind man?"

"Yes."

We ate nothing much for a long while. Any other time I'd have felt screwed up inside at the thought of having a meal alone with her, but now there wasn't room for any of that. What had happened sat square in my middle like a stone ju-ju; you just didn't see round.

After a time she said: "This reminds me of a meal I once had with Estelle. D'you mind my talking of Estelle?"

"No . . ."

"Mark was away, in Wales on business for the firm. Mark's father had been dead about eighteen months. I'd just sold our house, the family house, and most of the furniture, and was moving to the flat in London. And suddenly I got this terrible conviction that I couldn't go on. I suddenly felt as if I'd wrenched up my last roots; and *that*, on top of George's death and my other son being lost in the war, was more than I could bear. I couldn't live in London, I couldn't go on living *anywhere*. All I wanted was some warm and comfortable place to die. I asked myself to dinner with Estelle because I had to have company at any price, and some sort of sympathy and understanding if I could get it."

It was too dark in the room; I wished I'd switched on the table lamps. That curtain ring needed fixing; Mrs. Leonard never remembered. Mrs. Rutland's fingers were small and pointed; not at all like Mark's; she moved them along the edge of the table.

"Did Estelle give it you?"

"I never asked for it in so many words. When I got here I realised there are some pits of the soul that have to be climbed out of by oneself or not at all. This was one of them. You can't ask for understanding at twenty-five of the awful loneliness that can strike you thirty years later."

She went on talking, and I watched and listened, thinking perhaps Estelle never had that loneliness, yet she must have had when she knew she was going to die.

"It isn't a question of age," I said.

"What?" She'd gone on to something else.

"It isn't just a question of age. Weren't you ever lonely as a child?"

She thought. "Yes. But it's different then, isn't it? When you're young you have something to feed on, an inner iron-ration that keeps your strength up. When you're older, when your life is past, that's used up, there's only the hollow place where the nourishment has been."

I didn't think to ask her why tonight reminded her of that time. She changed the subject right away, as if afraid I'd think her morbid.

Presently I said: "Does Mark ever talk about me?"

"You mean, do we discuss you? No, I don't think so."

"Hasn't he ever said we don't get on well?"

"No . . . Don't you?"

"Not very."

She turned her wine glass round but didn't look at me.

I said: "It's chiefly my fault."

"That sounds half-way to a reconciliation."

"Oh, it isn't just a quarrel. I'm afraid it goes far deeper than that."

Mrs. Leonard came in. When she had gone Mrs. Rutland said: "I hope you'll be able to make this up with him, Marnie, whether you feel it is your fault or his. I think it would bring him down altogether if he had another failure."

"Failure?"

"Well, yes, in a sense. Isn't death at twenty-six a failure? It's contrary to nature anyway. It's a failure of life and vitality, and I think Mark looked on it to some extent as a failure of love . . ."

Her eyes were on me, and I didn't like it now; it was just coming through; they'd a liquid look, but shallow, like holding back at the last.

"Perhaps it's natural for me to think him an unusual man, being his mother. But I try to keep my understanding

478

this side of idolatry; and I do see that he's a man who all his life will be bent on taking risks—risks with the usual things perhaps, but most of all with people. He's tremendously self-willed but also tremendously vulnerable. Estelle's death hit him hard. To fall in love again so soon . . . It doesn't often happen."

I said uncomfortably: "Did Mark tell you he was—what he was doing about the printing works?"

She still turned her wine glass. "About accepting the Glastonbury offer? Yes. I persuaded him to take it."

"You did? Why? Didn't the name matter?"

"The name matters very little if you put it alongside the other things. Mark will never get on with the Holbrooks; he hasn't the flexibility of his father. It's much better for everybody that they should separate now."

"The Holbrooks won't like it."

"Not the way it's turned out, no. But only because of that. Mark didn't want to do it; he said he felt responsible for the staff. But that's what he's been negotiating about, writing in some safeguards. As far as we can tell, no one will suffer."

No one will suffer. I thought, it's a sort of epitaph. No one will suffer except me, and Forio, and Mark, and my mother, and, at the next stage, his.

On the Tuesday Mrs. Rutland drove me down to the hospital. I tell you, I didn't want to go. I'd nothing to say to Mark. Except the things that couldn't be said. Such as, I'm sorry. And, I'm going soon. Good-bye.

He was in a room to himself—private patient I suppose—with a long window, and the sun was falling on a corner of the bed. Thank God she let me go in alone. I was surprised his head wasn't even bandaged, but that frail look that had foxed me when I first met him, it was more so than ever, he looked a stone lighter.

I didn't know *what* sort of way I should be greeted, but he smiled and said: "Hullo, Marnie."

"Hullo, Mark." I tried not to limp on the way to the chair by the bed, and then just as I was going to sit down I remembered the nurse still standing by the door so I bent and kissed him.

"How're you feeling?" He got it out first.

"Me? Oh, I'm all right. *Stiff*. But you?"

"A headache and this arm, that's all. I want to come home."

"Will they let you?"

"Not for a few days. I'm awfully sorry about Forio . . ."

"I'm sorry about it all."

"But I know how much he meant to you."

"It's my own fault anyway."

"Or mine. I shouldn't have chased you."

There was a pause. "Anyway," he said, "thanks for dragging me out of the mud."

"Who told you?"

"I was just that much conscious. I remember you wiping the mud out of my eyes and ears."

"I can hardly remember what I did myself."

"I seem to remember it pretty well."

That's all. We hadn't any more to say. The nurse hadn't shaved him well and his skin would be dark in another hour or so.

He said: "Have you let Roman know about the accident?"

"No."

"Ring him, will you? Otherwise he may think you're deliberately dropping off again."

I said: "What happens to a horse when it's shot, Mark? Do they—bury it, or what?"

"I don't know."

"I couldn't bear to think of anything else, of it being sold . . ."

"I don't think there's much likelihood."

There were some flowers and grapes by the bed, and some magazines and two or three books. I suppose I should have remembered to bring him something.

He said: "It's early days yet, of course, but . . there are other horses. We can go round in the spring, pick up a good one."

"I don't think I'd want one."

"We'll see." He patted my hand.

I must say it was awfully queer. Sometimes since I

married him he'd looked at me as if he hated me. Because I was friendly with Terry or because I drew away sometimes when he touched me he could fairly go white and angry. But after this, after I'd led him a wild chase over impossible country and landed him with something near a fractured skull, well, he didn't seem to hold that against me at all.

Mrs. Rutland went home on the Wednesday. I went to see Mark each day, and they said he could come home on the following Monday.

On the Wednesday night just as I was going to bed Terry rang. He said he was sorry about the accident and he hoped Mark was going on all right and that he'd inquired a couple of times about me through the Newton-Smiths and it was all too bad, wasn't it?

I said yes, it was.

He talked for a minute or two and then said: "I suppose you know the take-over of Rutland's is going through?"

"I—haven't had time to think of it."

"No, I suppose not. Or me."

"Or you. I'm sorry."

"Well, I suppose it's no good gnawing over an old *bone*. We've got to live as we've got to live. When's Mark coming home?"

"Monday, I think."

"Come out with me Friday?"

"Oh, Terry, I couldn't."

"Feel ill?"

"Just miserable."

"All the more reason to get away for a bit."

"No, thanks, I can't. I couldn't." By Friday I should be gone away.

"Tell you what," he said, "I'll ring you again tomorrow when I get back from the works, see if you'll change your mind."

"All right." I wouldn't be here tomorrow evening either.

"That's my girl. By the way, did you hear the six o'clock news tonight?"

"No, why?"

"Warning of hurricane force gales in the south-east. Close your *windows* and hold tight. Is Mrs. Leonard with you?"

"Yes, she's sleeping here till Mark gets home."

"Good . . . Look, I'm relying on you Friday evening, dear. Heaven knows, with all this take-over on our plate I shall need bucking up myself; and only you can do it. Shall we call it a date?"

"Ring me tomorrow evening," I said. "I'll tell you definitely then."

I saw Mark again on the Thursday morning, and he was sitting up in a chair although he still looked shaky. It was just an ordinary meeting, and I couldn't quite believe it was the last.

I said he seemed cheerful and he said: "I've got a hunch this may be the beginning of a new start for us both." When I looked up he went on: "No special reason, no logical reason . . . I feel I'm making a fresh start where my job's concerned, and it may be—once certain formalities are out of the way—that I can make a fresh start where my wife's concerned."

"You'd still be willing to try?"

"I am, yes, if you are."

I liked him better when he was like this—or perhaps it was just the old funny human thing of liking more what you're going to leave behind Anyway just for a second or so there was this twinge of regret in me for all the life there might have been between us. It was like seeing something through a door, suddenly. It was like being in a foreign land and looking through a door at a life you don't know anything about and have never led. You look in and then you sigh and move along. Perhaps for a minute you almost wish you could be a part of it. But really it's a sort of sentimental cramp, because it can't ever be your life at all.

When I got home I tried to write him some sort of note, just a line saying good-bye. But although I started six times nothing worth putting down would come at all, so I burned the lot. Maybe silence was best. That way he'd think the worst, and the worst was right.

I told Mrs. Leonard I was going to stay with friends who lived near the hospital and would travel back with Mark on Monday. That way I could carry my bag out to the car without any hole in corner business, and she watched me go.

Just before I left I went into the stable and looked round for the last time. It still smelled of Forio. I seemed to remember reading somewhere that men often killed the thing they loved. That had happened to me.

It wasn't Richards's day in the garden, so I couldn't say anything to him; but driving away I passed the two blind men out on one of their walks. Usually I stopped the car or at least blew my horn and they waved, but this time I sneaked past. I felt awful. I felt like a thief. I felt like a thief again.

It would take an hour from here to Barnet, half an hour to get into the works and open the safe and get out again, and about four or five hours to drive to Torquay. That would mean Mother's before midnight. They were always late to bed and late up, so with luck I'd be there before they locked up. I'd sleep there and tell Mam everything in the morning, God help me. By noon or earlier I'd be away. I was going to take my chance at Exeter Airport.

I drove to Barnet.

As I drove I began to feel more and more queer. Not queer in the body but queer in the feelings. It was as if the death of Forio, the way he'd died, the fact that I'd *killed* him, was soaking into me all over again. Two or three times during the drive I had to wipe my eyes with my gloves, and once I nearly hit a cyclist. I wished my eyes had got screen-wipers.

It was a nasty evening with a thin fog every time you got away from the streets into a bit of open country, even if it was only a couple of fields. I missed my way once, and it took me more than an hour to get to Barnet.

I didn't drive up to the works, but there was a narrow street running beside the retail shop so I parked there.

Now of course the mist was a help, and I wished it was thicker. The hardest part was going to be to get into the building without being seen, and I wasn't sure which of three keys was the one that fitted the outer door. If you fiddle about there's always the chance of the stray policeman; but there was no way but to risk it.

The front door of the works was on the corner, and there was a lamp on the opposite side. Whoever went in would be seen by anyone passing.

I went right across and up the two steps without looking either way. After all I was the wife of the managing director. The first key went in but wouldn't turn, and then it stuck and wouldn't pull out. I wriggled and fiddled while two cars went past. I got the key out and tried the second. It worked. I let myself in.

It was all dark inside, and the only light was from the fanlight over the door. At two paces was a second door, and when I had unlocked this I didn't shut it behind me because of the bit of extra light that would come through. The passage beyond was dark, but I knew every inch of it. You walked down, turned right, and then there were the stairs.

At the foot of the stairs was the door leading to the printing shop. Usually it was shut at night but tonight it was open. I stopped in the doorway looking into the works.

There were a few shafts of light coming in through windows here and there, falling on the big machines and the bales of paper; but what got me most was the silence. I'd never been in the works before when it was shut, and somehow the quietness was twice as much because you expected and remembered all the noise.

Then in the absolute dead silence I heard a rustling. I stood there not moving and listened to it. It came from over by the paper. I found I was clutching the keys so they hurt. I let my hand relax. I went up the stairs.

I'd brought a torch but still didn't use it, and groped my way along the corridor. I jarred against a bucket that one of the cleaners had left.

I got a nasty feeling any moment that instead of my hands groping along hard things like walls and filing cabinets and doors they'd come up against a warm arm or a body or a face. I suppose it was the dark giving me the jitters. That and me still being under the weather from shock. I thought if I stopped I'd hear breathing near to me.

I got to the office where the switchboard was and pawed my way across it. This time a chair got in the way; but a bit of noise didn't matter, no one would hear noise, it was light that might show in the street outside.

The door of my old office, the cashier's office was locked, but I found the key to fit and went in. A Miss Pritchett was doing my job now. Mark said she was middle-aged and efficient but slow. I wondered how many of the pay packets she and Susan Clabon would have done.

There were two windows in here but no proper blinds so it meant still working partly in the dark.

I went to the safe and put in the key. It slid in easily and the lock turned as if it was in Vaseline. I tugged the door open and switched on my torch.

Anyway none of the routine had been changed. The envelopes were stacked in their tray, the rest of the money was in the drawer underneath. I took out this money and emptied it into my bag. I took the notes, of course, and all the silver but left the copper. Then I pulled out the tray and began to flip the pay envelopes together.

I thought, so it's nearly all the same as it would have been six months ago. I'm taking the same sort of money from the same safe. Mark interfering has only made half a year's difference. Except that Mark interfering meant I was now known under my own name and would be wanted under my own name and would have to get out of the country to be safe. And Mark interfering meant I was married, not single, and Forio was dead, and Mark was in hospital, and tomorrow or the next day was in for a shock when he found I was gone.

I shovelled some of the envelopes into my bag and then stopped again. Just at that second for some forsaken reason all my grief about Forio was coming up more and more and I began to shake. God knows why I shook but I did. I felt mad with myself because I felt so weak. I felt so weak I could hardly walk out of here with this money and drive off to Torquay. But it wasn't just muscle-weak, it was will-weak, that was what made me so mad.

I looked at the money and I looked at my bag and I dropped them both on the floor and sat down and tried to

485

work it out. It's awful when you get so turned up that you don't know where you are.

D'you know, I thought to myself, this is the second or third time you've felt like this. It's Forio's death, that's mainly what's done it. But also there was one time before. It means something, but Lord knows what.

So I picked up the money and put it into the bag and scooped up the next lot of envelopes. And then I thought, something really has got into you because you can't take this money.

I must have sat there half an hour in the dark fighting with myself. At the end of that time I'd worked it out that I didn't in the least mind taking the money—I hadn't suddenly gone all that soft—but there are just some things you can't do. You can *leave* your husband—and the thought of leaving Mark was still a glorious one—but to rob him, to pinch his keys while he's in the hospital, to take maybe a thousand pounds and leave him to do all the explaining, well, believe it or not, it wasn't on.

Sometimes you can plan everything in your mind, and it looks perfect, and then when it happens it all happens differently and you're in a jam. That wasn't so now, and that was what made it all the more crazy. Everything had gone according to plan except me—and I had just gone all to Hell. Or maybe it was that I'd really made all my plans a week ago, and now, a week later, I'd been following them more or less blindfold and in between time something had changed. I sat there with all that money around me, in the safe, in my bag, on the floor, and wished I'd never been born, wished the sea had taken me at Camp de Mar. I tried to think of all the bad things I could about Mark and our marriage—I thought of quite a few—and once I got as far as shutting my bag. But I couldn't even cheat myself now.

I opened my bag and started putting the money back, and every bundle hurt just as much as taking teeth out. I cursed and cursed. Even while I put it back I couldn't help but reckon it up. The notes were in bundles of fifty pounds and the pay packets, well, I could guess what they were worth within a pound or so each. I thought, every bundle I put back, that's taken from Mother (because I'd intended to try to persuade her to take this lot and sit on it; it would have kept her for three years). But even that didn't wash. Because like as not she'd have winced away in scalded horror from accepting a penny more of my money once she knew it was stolen.

So after all if I went to her empty-handed I don't suppose it would make much difference. But it would make a difference to me.

All I had in the world now was about two hundred pounds. I had to keep that myself until I got some sort of a job in France, or wherever I ended up.

When all the money was back I began to swing the great safe door to, and then I had to stand there for several minutes again before I could work up the will to shut it. I was breathing so heavy I might have run a mile. I sounded to myself like an old woman I'd heard dying once. I felt so awful.

When it was done I turned the key and then groped my way out of the office. Somehow I got downstairs, and there I was looking through this open door again into the printing shop and listening for the sound of rustling among the paper like half an hour ago.

This time there was just silence.

I let myself out and drove away.

I was in Newton Abbot by eleven-thirty. The fog hadn't got any worse. I never stopped all the way. Luckily there was enough petrol.

The only thing I was sure of was that the nearer I got to Cuthbert Avenue the less I liked the idea of telling Mother. I could just see her look. I was the apple of her eye, all she had. But if I didn't tell her, the police soon would. If I told her at least I could try to explain.

Explain what? How I came to steal instead of being content to stay a wage slave in the same office all my life? How I came to know I was smarter than most people and could use my smartness? How I found out it was easy to lead a double life and go on multiplying lives so long as you took certain precautions? How I got married and never told her?

Well, I thought, all that's going to take a lot of explaining between now and tomorrow morning. Explain it to yourself before you start on her.

It was raining in Torquay. I parked the old car on a municipal car park and took a taxi up.

There were no lights in the front of the house when I paid off the taxi, but there was a glimmer in the hall coming through from the back. I carried my suitcase up the three steps and rang the bell. There was a long wait and then footsteps. Lucy opened the door. Her face was all red and lumpy.

She gave a little scream and flung her arms round my neck. "Oh, Marnie! Oh, Marnie! 'Ere at last! We was looking for you everywhere! We didn't know where you could've got to. It wasn't right, leaving no address. They said to me, but she must have *some* address. Look in the telephone book, they said——"

"Here, what's this all about, Lucy? What's the matter? What's to do?"

"Oh," she wailed, looking at me, and suddenly she spouted tears. Then behind her came Doreen, Uncle Stephen's daughter.

"Marnie," Doreen said. "Your Mam died yesterday."

18

There was a long stain down the kitchen wall. It looked like a map of the River Nile. I had to draw a map of the River Nile once and I remember it well. There was a nail in the wall just about the place for Cairo. "It was that

storm," said Lucy. "You remember. It blew a slate off
and the rain came in. First week in Jan. We sent down to
Marley's but they never came." One of the padded arms of
the rocking chair had been recovered; it didn't quite
match the other, and somebody, it must have been Doreen,
had hung a tea towel to dry on the fretwork pipe-rack. "She
was took ill on Monday night," said Lucy. "A stroke, the
doctor said. Down her side. She never spoke again, Marnie.
But you know how she was about you. I thought, well, I *got*
to find her; but I looked through your letters. No address.
I found Doreen, that's all. Doreen phoned Manchester and
Birmingham, didn't you, Doreen."

"Dad's coming tomorrow for the funeral," said Doreen.
"He's in Liverpool, luckily. Why didn't you leave an
address, Marnie? We tried half a dozen Pembertons, but
none of them was your man." "Yesterday morning the
doctor says she can't last long," said Lucy. "So we went to
the police. They says they can't help us to find you, why not
put an SOS on the B.B.C.? So we done that. But she
passed away peaceful yesterday five o'clock in the afternoon.
Breathing heavy she'd been ever since Tuesday night, like she
couldn't catch 'er breath. I sat with 'er, and Doreen too."

"Funeral's tomorrow at two," said Doreen. "I've
got to go back right after because I've left my husband and
he's rushed off his feet. It's the time of year, all this bronchitis. I hope I did right but somebody had to make
the arrangements. There's a policy. With the United
Insurance. It was only a few pence a week but it'll cover
the cost. I didn't know whether you'd be here or not."

"I thought you'd *'eard*," said Lucy. "You coming like
that I thought you'd 'eard. She was right as ninepence till
Monday dinner-time; then she said she'd got a 'eadache so
she'd lie down. She got up for tea again and baked. She
was always one for saffron cake. She said to me, 'Lucy,
I've a feeling Marnie'll be down this month. Next thing
you know she was on the floor, just where Doreen's standing
now. I tried to get 'er in the chair but she was a dead
weight, so I ran for Mr. Warner."

Doreen said: "Aunt Edie had a cousin Polly, didn't
she? D'you know where she lives? I wired to the address

489

in Tavistock, but they said she moved soon after the war. Ooh, I'm tired; I was up at six this morning."

Mother's stick was in the corner, propped up against the dresser, and a pair of her going-out shoes; very narrow and pointed: she'd always had narrow feet and wore pointed shoes long before they were the fashion.

"Y'know, tis 'ard to credit," said Lucy. "I still think I shall 'ear 'er coming down the stairs. Would you like to see 'er now, Marnie? We done a nice job, the nurse and me. You'll think she's just asleep."

But she didn't look asleep to me. She looked very faded and very, very small. She didn't look like my mother really at all. I went up to her, and the more I looked at her the more she looked like something that's been left behind. She looked just as much like my mother as the shoes downstairs and the stick looked like her, and the dressing-gown behind the door. Whatever I cared for was gone and this could all be dumped. Maybe it sounds callous but it wasn't, it was how I felt.

I slept with Doreen, or anyway, I shared the bed and lay awake looking at the curtains, the way they went darker and then lighter through the night as the moon set and then the dawn came. I got up at six and made tea, but I didn't wake them. I felt like someone in the boxing ring who's had first a jab on the solar plexus and then a right hook. I'd been to boxing once or twice at Plymouth, and I'd seen that happen to a man. He came out for the sixth round, out of his corner quite normal, but I was close and I could see by his eyes that he didn't really know what he was doing at all. He went on making the motions of fighting, but it was just a question of time before the third blow landed and stretched him out.

I got my third blow about a quarter to seven.

I'd been sitting with Mother for half an hour, but as I say not really thinking of anything or thinking she was there. I mean I'd been sitting by the bed not far away from her as the sun struck in through a slit in the curtains, and I thought how crazy it was I couldn't get her a cup of tea, and there was a fly buzzing somewhere, and I knew how mother hated flies. She used to squash them against the window panes with her fingers sometimes; I hated her doing that. And then I saw that old black imitation crocodile bag of hers that she'd carried everywhere. It was on top of the wardrobe. I could see the corner of it and I thought, I wonder if there's that other photo of Dad in it, because I think she might like to have it with her in the coffin.

I mean you can be punch drunk one minute and as weepy and sentimental and silly as anything the next; so I got the bag down and clipped open the long tarnished clasp. The first thing I found was a photo of me at eighteen, and I thought perhaps that could go as well; and then there were some old newspaper clippings. The first one I saw was out of the *Western Morning News* again, announcing a birth. Frank and Edith Elmer had had a daughter. That was me too.

There was a bottle of the charcoal pills she took for her rheumatism, and then, Heaven help me, my baptism card. Then there was the newspaper cutting about Dad's death, the one she'd shown me. A wedding card, her wedding card, made my throat close up, and clipped to it was an old dance programme that made me feel worse.

Then I picked out another cutting. It was dated November 1943 but it hadn't a newspaper heading. The top of the column said; 'Plymouth Woman Bound Over on Murder Charge.'

I thought this must be someone Mother knew, until I saw the words Mrs. Edith Elmer. Then I took that column in so fast I still can't remember which order the words came in.

"At Bodmin Assizes today Mrs. Edith Elizabeth Elmer, aged 41, of Kersey Bungalow, Sangerford, Liskeard, was charged with the murder of her new-born child . . . Opening for the Prosecution, Counsel said that Mrs. Elmer, an evacuee divorced woman living alone with her five-year-old daughter . . . Her neighbour, Miss Nye, helped to deliver the child, but there seemed some doubt as to the exact sequence of events before the district nurse was summoned . . . Nurse Vannion would tell how she came to the house and found Mrs. Elmer in a state of prostration. Mrs. Elmer informed Nurse Vannion that she had had a miscarriage but the nurse's suspicions were aroused, and going into the next bedroom she found the body of a perfectly formed child wrapped in newspaper under the bed. The child was dead and evidence would be brought to prove that it died of strangulation . . ."

I dropped the cutting and it fluttered to the floor like one of those paper streamers. I bent down for it and dropped the bag. Bits and pieces fell out of the bag and rolled under the bed. A cotton reel, a two-shilling piece, a thimble, a box of matches. I went down on my knees scrabbling for them in the curtained half-light, but I couldn't hold anything, my fingers were shaking so much.

I got hold of the cutting and sat up on my heels, and there a few inches away from my face on the edge of the bed was a hand. It was a thin knobbly hand, and as I looked at it it slid an inch down the slope of the bed.

Somehow I managed to straighten up. I hadn't any feet or knees. I sat balanced on cold water. I looked at my mother's dead face. I looked and looked. I'd sat there for half an hour and never had a qualm. But now I was like in some sort of frozen terror. And then it seemed to me she sighed. Any minute now, I thought, that old face is going to move, those lids will flutter and show grey blobs of evil staring at me, as they'd stared at me that time in Dr. Roman's when I'd been a child again with my back pressed cold against the wall.

I made a move to the door but it was backwards, I couldn't get my eyes off her. Another step and I was there, the knob in my thigh. I got round, my hands were too sweaty and weak to turn the knob. I had to use the other hand and the news cutting got screwed up. I got the door open and backed out. I backed into Lucy Nye.

"Look, dear," Lucy Nye said, "don't 'ee take it like that. Listen, you was never meant to *know*. All these years we kept it to ourselves. I used to say to Edie 'twould be better to tell the girl, you never can be sure someone else won't. But she wouldn't. Oh, no, she was a strong one, was Edie, an' stubborn as a mule. I never dreamed she'd kept that newspaper, dear. I wonder why she done that? Now it's all come out on account of 'er own foolishness."

492

Lucy poured me tea like liquid boot polish. She kept looking at me with her one big eye and her one small one. They squinted at me like marbles that had fallen into wrinkles in the sand. They didn't tell me anything. Only the voice went on.

"Drink this, dear, it'll do you good. Doreen isn't stirring yet. I'll take 'er up a cup in a——"

"Does she know?"

"About your Mam? I don't think so. She's only same age as you. That's unless her Dad's told 'er."

"He knows?"

"Yes, dear. 'E was on convoy work but 'e was in Devonport refitting at the time."

"I don't get it. I don't get anything at all."

"No, dear. Well if you know s'much I'd better tell you. Drink your tea." Lucy scratched in the parting of her grey hair. I remembered when that hair was a faded fair, and I remembered she'd scratched just the same way then, with her three middle fingers. "I knew your Mam when she was a girl, dear. A 'andsome girl she was too. Not so pretty as you but striking, like. I used to live across the street. She was always with boys, always a different one, but always kept 'erself nice like. She was brought up strict. 'Er Dad was *strict* with 'er, make no mistake. An' she kept the boys in their place. I used t' watch 'er. She'd always make 'em leave 'er on the corner of Wardle Street and walk down alone, case the old man was watching. My mother used to say, she'll pick and choose once too often, all that dressing up, all that money on 'er back. Your Mam worked in Marks & Spencers then."

Old Lucy rubbed the back of her hand across the tip of her nose. "Then I moved Liskeard way, and I only saw 'er off'n on. I knew she'd married your Dad, and I seen you once when you was a mite of two. But I never seen much of 'er until the war. Then she was evacuated to the bungalow next to me. Your Dad was in the Navy. She come along with you, an' you was, I s'pose, three and a half or four. Lovely little thing, you was. No trouble at all. I used to push you out. We got more friendly, like. She used to say she was lonely, your Mam did. She missed 'er friends an' the shops an' one thing and another. But she 'adn't changed, always dressed well, kep' herself to herself; *you* know 'ow she was. Well, I say she 'adn't changed . . ."

I turned the newspaper cutting over and over. There was an advert for Mumford's Garage on the back, and a paragraph saying "Enemy Plane Shot Down". The paper was yellow and had been folded a lot. How often had she read it? How often had she read it through?

". . . It was just then she got friendly with soldiers, dear. I don't like to 'ave to say it but she did. Your Dad was at sea and she was lonely, I s'pose. There was a lot of soldiers round about Liskeard just then. *You* know, time on their 'ands. Mind you, you never *seen* her with one, that was the rum thing, but everybody knew it just the same. The soldiers knew it too. I s'pose they told each other. T'was the strangest thing you ever seen; there she was living in that tiny bungalow along with you, *respectable*, you couldn't find no fault with 'er, well dressed, always partic'lar 'ow she spoke and who she spoke to; out walking in the afternoon, never in a pub nor nothing, but everyone *knew*. If a soldier came along after dark, all he'd got to do was tap on the window and——"

I said: "I used to be sleeping with her, and the tap would come and she'd lift me out and put me in the spare bedroom. The bed was always cold. She'd lock me in . . . D'you mean *any* soldier?"

"That I don't rightly know, dear," Lucy said carefully. "She'd never say. I didn't dare ask 'er then, and afterwards she'd never say, never talk of it, word never crossed 'er lips. I reckon soldiers was always being moved here and there. Maybe she 'ad only a few favourites, but of course idle tongues wagged and made it more and more."

"Did Dad get to know?"

"Not for a year or longer, dear. When 'e came 'ome word 'ad gone round and no soldier came near the place. But I think 'e 'ad 'is suspicions. Because one night in the winter of '42, January or February, 'twould be, he come back unexpected."

"So it's true, what it says here, 'evacuee divorced woman . . .'"

494

"Yes, dear, 'e took it bad and divorced 'er. That's how she didn't 'ave no pension. She *denied* it, y'know, said 'twas all a pack of lies, even though he came back unexpected and found what 'e did find. So then she was on her own, as you might say."

"Except for me."

"Yes, dear, and you was coming along beautiful. I never seen a handsomer little girl. Five you was then. I used to take you out every afternoon. Your Mam wasn't strong. She'd go out shopping in the morning. 'Member her walk before she got that bad leg? No, you wouldn't. Rum walk she always 'ad—not like a . . . well, not like a woman who did what she was doing—partic'lar, respectable, feet in a straight line, you know, one knee ever so nearly touching the other. Never too much powder or paint. 'Twas just the same after the divorce as before. Vicar's wife she might have been. But she kept on with 'er games. I was nearest to 'er, y'know.

"I used t'run little errands for 'er; we was close, our bungalows was semis. I could see everything, but she never let on even to me. Once I says something to 'er and she says, 'Lucy, there's evil tongues and evil thoughts; it is for you to choose your company.' I shut up after that. Another time I know she says, 'These poor boys, away from their hearths an' homes, 'tis the least one can do to give them companionship, to offer them the quiet fireside of a Christian home.'" Lucy shivered. "An' then she got caught."

The clock struck half past seven. The paint was coming off one of those damned pink and green love-birds, and there was a crack in the face.

"She got caught, but she didn't let on. It wasn't long before the neighbours began to talk. It was Mrs. Waters that spoke to me first, behind 'er 'and. I said, *oh, no, I don't think so,* but as soon as she spoke I knew 'twas true. We none of us said nothing for months and then Mrs. Waters tackled 'er. She said, 'Oh, Mrs. Elmer, 'ave I to congratulate you?' Your Mam says, 'I don't know what you mean.' Mrs. Waters says, 'You're expecting a certain event, aren't you, Mrs. Elmer?' and your Mam says—'How dare you be so downright insulting!' and goes off with 'er 'ead in the air. Well, after that——"

"Listen," I said. "What's that?"

"What's what?" said Lucy.

"I thought I heard footsteps on the stairs."

We sat there like mice at the tread of a cat; it was a sunny morning but this window faced west and the curtains were drawn, so it was half dark; Lucy's cup began to rattle so she put it down.

So I said: "I'd better go and see."

"Nay, leave it be, Marnie."

I thought of my mother and wondered if she was still upstairs or if she was standing outside listening with that thin knobbled hand of hers on the kitchen door. I couldn't move. I couldn't go and see. There was cold sweat on my face.

I got to the door somehow and wrenched it open. There was nothing there.

But it was darker than ever out in the lobby, and maybe there were things I couldn't see.

I shut the door and stood with my back to it. "She said she wasn't going to have a baby."

"No . . . that's what she said. She wouldn't admit it to no one. Not a soul. I was always in an' out, though she was never afraid to tell me to be off when I wasn't welcome or when she 'ad 'a friend' coming. The last month, of course 'twas clear and plain to everyone, but if I so much as dropped a 'int she choked me off. You know 'ow she could. There was never sight nor sign to the very end of anything made ready, no baby clothes, no linen, no knitting, no nothing. Then on the night it 'appened she come to me . . . Sit down, dear."

"Let me stand."

"The night it 'appened she come to me and says, 'Lucy, I'm very unwell. I think there's something the matter with me. Come in a minute.' When I went in, there was you sitting in front of the kitchen fire crying your eyes out, and she fair collapsing on the bed in 'er bedroom as she followed in after me . . ." Lucy's face twitched. "Well, I done what I could but I seen what was wrong and I was for going for the doctor, but she says, 'No. I won't allow it, Lucy. Get the child out of the way. We can manage. It will all be over very very soon.' Well . . . well, there 'twas, I should've gone, no doubt, but 'twas almost too late anyhow. 'Ow long it'd been going on before she sent for me I haven't the least notion. So I put you in the next bedroom and locked you in, poor mite you was trembling and trembling, and I came back to your Mam, and in an hour a fine baby boy was born. Cor, I was in a terror, I reely was. But when 'twas over, my dear soul, I felt a changed woman! I says to her, ''Tis what you deserve, Edie, for being so obstinate and stubborn, but God be thanked, all has been for the best and you have a lovely little boy!' And she looks at me and says, 'Lucy, don't tell anyone yet. Leave me now for an hour or two to rest.' And I says, I'll do no such thing, the baby wants washing and binding. You've got nothing 'ere, so I'll nip in my place and fetch what I can lay me 'ands on.' So I went . . .''

Lucy poured herself another cup of tea. She slopped a good bit in the saucer too, and sat there all hunched up, licking her fingers. Then she tipped the tea out of the saucer into the cup, and the rattle of the crockery in her shaky hands was like a morse code.

"So I went and—and when I came back in twenty minutes the baby was gone. God 'elp me, Marnie, that's how 'twas! She was there in bed, in a muck sweat, and looking white as paper and she stared at me with all 'er eyes. I never seen the like, God 'elp me, I never. I says to 'er : '*Edie*, where's the baby? Edie!' And she answers me in two words. 'What baby?' Just like that : 'What baby?' as if I'd dreamed it all?''

The milkman was coming round with his bottles. He rattled down a couple outside and then his footsteps went thudding off.

Lucy said : "Maybe she was crazy mad, Marnie. Maybe I was too. 'Twas like looking at someone you loved and seeing 'er for the first time. But you see, I was never so strong-minded as 'er and if there was no baby 'twas my word against 'ers. You was screaming to be let out, and she just lay there with 'er great eyes and said, 'What baby?' as if I dreamed it all . . . Gracious knows what I'd've done in the end. My life and soul, I b'lieve I'd've let it go, but soon after she started a 'aemorrhage and it went on and nothing would stop it, an' I knew then I couldn't just stand there and let 'er die,—though she said I must; she said: 'Let me die, Lucy; no matter, you can look after Marnie, let me die.' But Marnie, 'twas too much for me and I fled from the bungalow and sent for the district nurse. And when she come she found the baby, just as it say in that there paper, under—under the bed in the next room . . ."

I went away from the door and went through the kitchen to the scullery and I vomited there, as if I'd taken poison, and I ran the water and tried to run it over my face and arms. Lucy came out.

"Marnie, dear, I'm sorry. 'Tis all past and done with and long since forgotten. 'Tis no fault of yours and she suffered for it and no one'd have been the wiser but for her silly foolishness keeping that paper, and there's no call to take on so. Lie down and let me see for your breakfast."

I shook my head and got away from the sink and took up a towel. My hair was hanging in wet streaks like seaweed. I dried my face and hands and I stood by the flickering fire and my fingers touched something on the mantelpiece. It was Mother's gloves. I pulled my hand away like I'd touched something hot. I started shaking my head to try to clear it.

"Marnie, dear . . ."

"What got her off?"

"Well, 'twas the doctor really. Dr. Gascoigne. And then——"

"She told me it was all his fault for not coming when he was sent for!"

"Yes, well, dear, that was only 'er way of seeing it later on. It done him no 'arm because 'e was dead. It just made it seem better to 'er to tell it to you that way. If I——"

"Why should he try to get her off?"

"Well, 'twasn't quite like that, but he said in the box she was suffering from something—something like purple——"

"Puerperal."

"Yes, puerperal. Puerperal insanity, caused by worry and distress and what not. It was true more'n iikely . . . Women do get that way sometimes after childbirth. They go off their 'eads temporary like. A few days or so and they're good as new. 'Tis a sort of fever that takes 'em."

I finished wiping my hands. I put the towel on the table. I put my fingers through my wet hair, threading it back from my face and eyes. I said: "I still don't know why she did it. You've told me nothing. And I don't know why she fed me those lies. Why all that story, all that lying story about the doctor not coming and . . . Why did *you* let her lie?"

Lucy's eye was watering. "You was all we got, Marnie."

"That doesn't answer anything."

"Well, dear, you was all we got."

I said: "I mean, if she didn't want to tell me the truth, couldn't she at least have just kept her mouth shut? Couldn't she? Why couldn't she?"

"I believe 'twas comforting to her to feel you was on her side . . ."

There were real footsteps on the stairs this time and Doreen came in. She said: "I had nasty dreams. My, Marnie you look as white as a sheet!"

19

The funeral was at two. Uncle Stephen came about half past twelve. We hadn't seen each other for four years. He didn't look as good looking as I remembered him, but he still had the same smile and the same grey eyes that saw through you. I went through that funeral like a sleep-walker, I really did.

There were seven of us and six wreaths. Doreen had

499

ordered one for me. In fact she'd fixed everything. The only thing she hadn't fixed was the narrow turn out of the stairs into the hall. They had to get the coffin down by sliding it through the kitchen door but then, it wouldn't turn, so they took it up two steps and tried the other way. But it still wouldn't go so they had to stand the coffin on its end like a mummy-case and get it round that way. I wondered if the tiny thin corpse inside had slipped down and was going to be buried in a heap for all eternity.

I thought I ought to be buried too. Or I thought I'll go on the streets to celebrate. But I wouldn't be as discreet as mother. What the hell. No soldiers tapping on my window. The door would be open wide.

Just before we left the house I was sick again, but after that I was all right. I nearly burst out laughing in church, but it's just as well I didn't as I should never have been able to stop. And it wasn't at anything funny either. It was the church on the hill. I forget the name, but from the churchyard you could see over the roofs of the houses to Torbay. The sea was like a blue plate with bits chipped out of the edges. Over to the west I fancied I could see the roofs of the new Plymouth, the Guildhall and the shopping centre, where the buildings had grown up out of the rubble and dust that I remembered as a kid.

It was bright but perishing cold; the wind whistled through the trees from the north and made my coat feel like rice paper.

I thought, I wonder what Mark's doing. It was the first time I'd thought of him since I came last night. I thought, well, no one will be after me in all that much of a hurry now because I didn't steal anything yesterday. I shan't be missed till tomorrow probably or the next day. By then I can still be in France.

But was it any longer all that urgent to run to France? For the first time now with this death I was really, truly free.

Uncle Stephen's hair was blowing in the wind. He'd gone quite white, though he was a good bit younger than Mam, five or six years. He wasn't like Mother at all, except that maybe they'd both got a good shape to the bones of the face. Christ, I thought, I've been living—what have I been living? Why didn't *he* tell me?

I remembered now that girl at school, Shirley Jameson, what she'd said. That had begun the fight; I'd gone at her with waving fists. She'd said: "Garn, putting on airs! Your mother done a murder!"

Well, so Shirley was right after all. Come to think of it, that often does happen—that the thing somebody tells you when you're a kid that makes you the most indignant at the time—sooner or later you find it's true. It's one of the things you learn . . . And me afraid to tell Mother I'd pinched a few pounds to keep her comfortable! I did laugh then, but somehow it must have sounded like a cough because no one turned round.

"Ashes to ashes," said the vicar, "dust to dust. If God won't take her the devil must."

No, he couldn't have said that, I must have misheard him, I was going crazy. But of course I *was* crazy. That was obviously what had been wrong with Edie Elmer. I was her daughter, I took after her. Except that instead of going with soldiers I ran away from them. I couldn't stand them touching me. Perhaps that was just the other side of the penny.

All her life had been a lie. How much of mine had been? Bloody near all of it. I'd started from scratch and built up a beautiful life of lies—three or four beautiful lives all as phoney and untrue as Mother's. I wasn't even content with one.

I felt I wanted to break the top of my head off. What a fool she'd made of me! What a fool I'd made of myself.

The others were moving away now but I didn't move. The shiny brown box with the brass plate and the brass handles had gone into the red earth, the sexton or whatever he was was leaning on his spade. I didn't feel any grief. In a few weeks I'd changed from feeling too little to feeling too much—like a skin rubbed raw—but now I'd passed out of that into numbness again. I just stood and stared at the hole in the ground. It was like a slit trench. The wind blew a cloud over the sun. There was an oak tree about my height standing beside the next grave; it was covered with brown withered leaves that rustled in the wind; the leaves should have fallen long ago. They were like lies that had long since forgotten what they were told for but lingered on and on. You told a child about Father Christmas until he was ten and then you told him the truth. But some people fixed their children up in such a paper chain of make believe and sham that they never got free.

Well, now I was free, free as I hadn't ever been before. Free of Mark and free of mother and free of Forio. They were all gone and as good as dead. I ruled a line under them. Now I started afresh.

Uncle Stephen touched my elbow. "Marnie..."

"Go to hell," I said.

"The others have left. I've sent them on. Anyway Doreen has a train to catch. Lucy can fend for herself..."

"So can I."

"Presently yes. You'll have to. But before we do any more I want a talk with you. Lucy tells me you know about your mother."

"Go to hell," I said.

"Marnie, dear, we have to talk. I've a taxi here. Let's drive somewhere."

"I'll walk, thanks."

"Come on." He got hold of my arm.

Suddenly I hadn't any more fight left in me. I turned away from him and went down to the waiting taxi.

We drove down and had tea somewhere; it was one of the posh hotels, and I thought afterwards he took me into a public place because there I couldn't give way or blow off altogether—that's while I still had some feeling for appearances. He was taking a hell of a risk. I felt like kicking the table over. But it wasn't temper, I swear it wasn't that, it was just the most awful despairing deathly empty desolation, which was more than any human being could stand.

He said: "Marnie, take a hold of yourself."

"What bloody right have you got to say what I shall do?"

"Marnie, stop swearing and try to see this thing straight. I know it's been a terrible shock, losing your mother and then learning all this about her so suddenly just afterwards.

502

But see it in its proper proportion. If you'll let me talk about her—perhaps it'll help."

"If you'd talked about her ten years ago you might have some right to talk now."

"What, told you this when you were thirteen? In any case I hadn't any right to: you were her child, not mine. But if I had, are you saying you would have understood what I'm going to tell you now?"

I stared across six white tableclothes at a bowl of flowers; narcissus, iris, tulips. I realised for the first time that his voice had a west-country burr.

"Edie was older than me," he said, "but I was always very fond of her and I think in a way I understood her. It's all the rage now to blame one's failings on one's mother and father; but if you blame any of yours on her, then you ought to blame some of hers on *our* father. Your grandfather was a local preacher; you knew that, I suppose?"

"She said so."

"He was a local preacher but he was a plasterer by trade, and in the twenties he was out of work for more than eight years. It turned him sour, narrowed him in a funny way. He got more religious but it was religion gone wrong. When your grandmother, my mother, died Dad went more and more into his shell, and Edie took the brunt. Did you ever think of your mother, Marnie, as a woman? I mean apart from her being your mother. She was what you might call a highly sexed woman."

"So I should think!"

"Yes, but don't get it wrong. She was always attractive to men—she always had a boy friend but she was too strictly brought up to kick over the traces with them. I was her kid brother; I know. She stuck with Dad till he died. She was thirty-three then. Thirty-three. Does that mean anything to you? Heaven knows what sort of struggle went on in her. She took the brunt with Dad; he was terrible at times; he'd got tremendous authority too, like an Old Testament prophet. She got to be a bit like him these last few years, only not half as bad. I used to duck out. As soon as I could I went to sea."

He offered me tea but I shook my head. He said: "Two

months after he died she married your Dad. I think they were happy. As far as I could tell they were happy. I think for the first time she began to lead a normal life. I think she—well, let's be blunt, I think she discovered what she'd been missing. I think Frank found he'd wakened something in his wife he'd hardly expected. Not that it mattered so long as he was at home . . ."

This hotel had a veranda overlooking the sea. The only people sitting on it were three tottering old ladies. They were like mother sitting there, like flies in the last sun.

Uncle Stephen said: "When you were evacuated to Sangerford, she was alone, far more alone than she'd ever been before she married. Life had wakened her up—and wakened her late. Now it told her to go to sleep again. That's not so easy. She began to see soldiers."

"Yes, it was plural, wasn't it?"

"I'm not defending what she did. I'm only trying to explain it, to try to see why it happened. With another woman, differently brought up, differently made, it might never have happened. The end, the business of the child, that certainly wouldn't have happened."

"Are you trying to tell me that the way she was brought up made her murder her own son?"

He stopped at that and began to light his pipe. "Marnie, your mother was a strange woman, I'm not pretending anything else. She was capable, especially in later years, of enormous self-deception. The way she swallowed your story of this wealthy employer—Pemberton who showered money on you——"

"You didn't believe it?"

He took the pipe out of his mouth to shake his head. "I don't know how you came by your money and I'm not going to ask, but I don't believe in Pemberton. Neither would she if she hadn't wanted to and been capable of willing herself to. Well, somehow during that fantastic period in Sangerford she succeeded in living in a world of make-believe. I know why she slept with soldiers—because she wanted to and had a consuming desire for love—but I don't know how she got it past her conscience. Have you ever thought what it's like to lead a double life?"

504

I winced. "Well?"

"Perhaps she thought—and I don't mean this as a dirty crack—perhaps she thought she was helping the war effort by giving the soldiers her love. Somehow she went on through each day as if the nights never happened. She was still Abel Treville's respectable, carefully dressed, good-mannered daughter. She was still Frank Elmer's faithful wife. She was still your devoted mother."

I made some noise, but it wasn't words he could answer.

He looked at me with his grey eyes. "When the new child started coming it must have blown her make-believe world to shreds. God knows what she thought or how she reasoned then. But somehow she got herself into a frame of mind in which she could deny the child's existence even to herself. Of course the doctor was right. At the end her mind was temporarily deranged and she did what she did . . ."

We sat there then for a very long time. The waiter came and Stephen paid the bill and we sat there. And the old ladies began to feel chilly in the veranda and moved out into the lounge. A page-boy came past with the evening papers from London. Nobody bought one.

I said: "If I'd been the judge and they told me a woman like that was mad I should have said, why did she make no preparation for the baby? Was she mad for nine months before?"

We got up and started to walk back to Cuthbert Avenue. We walked, and the cold wind was still blowing through the town. By the harbour a few boats bobbed and lurched, and over beyond it the palm trees rustled like raffia skirts.

I said: "Did you know I was married?"

"Married? No. I'm very glad to hear it. Who is he?"

"Glad," I said, and laughed.

"Shouldn't I be? Aren't you happy? Where are you living?"

I said: "It never had a chance. It was queer from the beginning. I was queer. I don't like men. I can't bear them touching me. It disgusts me and turns me cold. I got pushed into it—into getting married. I didn't want to. The man—Mark's his name—tries to love me but it's hopeless.

505

He means well but he hasn't a clue what's wrong with me. I went to a doctor, a psychiatrist. He began to pry around. But he hadn't unearthed in three months a quarter of what I've dug up in a night by finding that newspaper cutting. I remember it all now. But it doesn't help."

"It must help. Any psychiatrist would say so, Marnie. The business of remembering is half the battle."

"It depends what you remember. I'm queer—out of the ordinary, see—I've been different from other people ever since I was ten . . . I'm queer and I'll stay queer. These last months I've learned about psychiatry. This doctor—Roman—has told me——"

"My dear Marnie, I can imagine the sort of shock you got that night—that by itself is enough to explain anything that has happened to you since——"

"But it's too easy," I said. "You don't explain people as X and Y. It doesn't work out. Maybe I had a shock. Maybe I've had another shock now. But it isn't all. Ever heard of heredity? What goes on when people are born? You take after your parents. You've just told me that mother was getting like *her* father. Well, I'm like my mother. What was she, I ask you? She was one of two things. She was either a murderess or a lunatic. You don't need psycho doctors to tot up what's wrong with me. I take after my mother, that's all. I've had proof of it more than ever these last weeks."

His pipe had gone out. He stopped to knock it against a stone post on the promenade. I waited impatiently. He put the pipe in his pocket.

"There's always two to a marriage, Marnie. Frank, your father, was as normal as I am. And I'm her brother; is there anything specially wrong with me? You don't have to take after her. But even if you did, you wouldn't necessarily act as she did. You still don't understand her."

"I don't want to understand her! What's there to understand anyway? Let's change the subject."

"No. You're forcing me to defend your mother, so I will. You see—you see, my dear, she was a very passionate woman and a very inhibited woman—and also rather an innocent woman. Oh, I know you think that's fanciful, but imagine what an experienced woman would have done in her case. First she'd have taken good care not to have a child. Then, if that had gone wrong, she would have quickly seen to it that she lost it. My dear, anyone can if they know the ropes. She didn't. Perhaps she tried a few old wives' brews, I don't know. But nothing more. She went to her full time under the pressure of ignorance, her fantastic conscience ground into her by her father, and her own desperate make-believe. Under these pressures she became temporarily insane. There's no reason on God's earth why she should have passed on to you a character that would act in the same way even given those circumstances. Quarrel with your peculiarities if you like, but don't think they have to be incurable!"

We walked on. I wanted to be rid of him then; I just wanted to be on my own, to walk away somewhere completely solitary and think.

I said: "Have you ever heard her talk about sex, about love? All her life she's tried to poison me against it. Can you beat that? Can you beat it really?"

"People come to hate the things they suppress. The man who loathes cruelty is often the man who's suppressed the streak of cruelty in himself. When your mother recovered from her illness and found sex was no longer for her—as she did—wasn't it natural, with her upbringing, to look on sex as the cause of all the evil that had come to her and want to warn you about it?"

"Well, it was the cause of all the evil, wasn't it?"

"Only because it was at first wrongly denied and then later wrongly used."

"You argue like Mark."

"Your husband?"

"My husband."

"Tell me about him."

"He's no longer important."

"Sometimes, Marnie, I feel very guilty, going off to sea the way I did, first letting Edie take the brunt of Dad and then letting you take the brunt of Edie. Somehow I've got to stay now and help you—try to help you—to see things right."

We turned up Belgrave Road. I said: "I know you helped years ago. I think in a way you've helped now. But there isn't any carry on from here—between us, I mean. Tomorrow or the next day you'll go back to Liverpool, and I shall go—wherever I decide to go. If we talked this over to the end of our lives there wouldn't be an easy answer, because an easy answer—or an answer of any sort—I mean, it probably doesn't exist. You've told me your side of the story. Lucy's told me hers. But the one who could really tell me everything, from the inside, can't any longer. All my life she fed me with lies and she's gone to the grave never saying a word. That's a fact. There's no getting round it, and I have to live with it—if I want to live at all. And the only way I can live with it is fighting it out myself alone. So will you leave me now? I'll come home later. I can't face that house yet. I expect I'll be back some time tonight."

He put his hand on my arm, and we stopped. "Marnie, will you promise to come back?"

"Yes. I promise."

"I'd rather stay with you."

"I'd rather be alone."

20

When he had gone, I turned back down Belgrave Road and began to walk back along the promenade. The wind was behind me now and it kept whipping at my skirt and thumping me in the back as if I ought to hurry.

The sun had just set, and there was a smear like a bloodstain in the sky over to the west, and the sea kept tumbling against the wall and then sucking itself away again. Two nuns were coming along the promenade and the wind was making ugly wings of their habits. They struggled past me, not looking up, their heads bent against the wind.

Well, I suppose I could go and be a nun. That would be one solution, getting rid of my sickness on God. If I took the veil I was at least out of harm's way. Or I could go to the opposite end of the seesaw and try some top-pressure whoring. I wondered if there were any professional whores in Torquay. I wondered how you went about it.

Or were the stones the best way out? Over these railings, and the sea would soon take away all the remains. That was easiest. In order to live, there had to be a reason for living, even if that reason was only staying alive. I hadn't any. The can was empty.

Funny, I thought, I'm free. Free for the first time in my life. I've told myself this twice before today, and it should have given me a thrill. Well, it hasn't.

What was the difference? Mother was dead, and she'd left a poisonous smear behind like a snail that's gone underground. But my sickness lay deep, deep, deeper than that.

I stood by the rails and got hold of them hard, and then I went one by one over the things that had made life pleasant enough during those long months working in Birmingham and in Manchester and in Barnet. I counted them and not one of them helped me. I'd a mainspring gone. My life had been turned inside out like some gigantic awful conjuring trick, and I was like an animal turned physically, disgustingly inside out, walking the wrong way, looking cross-eyed, split down the middle of my soul.

I got moving again. I went past the Pavilion and then turned away from the sea towards the town. It was quieter and less blustery here, and there were quite a lot of people about. But it wasn't like Plymouth.

I walked up the main street. I turned into the pub on the corner and ordered a brandy. Although it wasn't long after opening time the place was nearly full. The man next to me had a mouth like the back of a lorry that falls down to let the gravel out. He was talking about the football match he'd been to last week. "We was playing twelve men," he kept saying. "Twelve men. The ref. ought to've been strung up. Little runt. Twelve men we was playing.

If it's the same tomorrow I'll do for him." The man next to him started eyeing me. He was a little type in a check cap, and his eyes were all over. You could see what he was thinking; I didn't need to be Edie's daughter for that.

It was getting as smoky as an opium den in here already. The bar was wet and the barmaid, a fat black-haired girl, wiped it over with a cloth. I only had to smile at check-cap, just the one smile. He'd do the rest. I thought, what are you scared of? Coming to have a child and murdering it and living with that all the rest of your life? Wanting sex and telling yourself you hate it and it's dirty? Is that what you'll come to?

Well, what was stealing but lies? Why did I blame mother more than myself?

I turned away from check-cap and took my drink to a table. There was this one woman sitting at it. She was about forty and she was floppy, with big eyes and big lips and big comfortable breasts. She was wearing the sort of dress and coat I'd have worn five years ago before I began to learn. She said: "Hullo, dear. Hot, ain't it?" One of those brown ale voices.

As I sat down, there was a mirror advertising Teacher's Highland Cream that reflected us. I saw her, and sitting down next to her was this girl in the short brown coat and the curling hair, and the fringe, with the yellow blouse with the stiff-pointed collars. She didn't look much different from usual. She didn't look like that crazy animal pulled inside out.

"Feeling queer, dear?" said the woman. "All this smoke . . ."

Four new people pushed their way past. A fat man with check trousers and slits in his jacket bumped the table and nearly upset it.

"Clumsy clot," said the woman. There were three empty glasses by her and a fourth half full of Guinness.

I thought, but it isn't only the lies that matter, is it? It isn't just mother sleeping with soldiers, it isn't even her strangling her kid. It isn't just all those things. It's everything that's happened to me on top of it. You get a bad foundation and then you build crookedly on that . . .

"Try a Guinness, dear," said the woman. "Them short nips are no good. What is it, brandy?"

Yes, I said to myself, but not to her. It was the first brandy I'd drunk since that evening in that other pub in Ibiza, when all the crowds had been revelling and I'd argued with Mark. And suddenly I found there were tears squeezing out of my eyes. God knows what they meant, but they came.

"What's the matter, dear? Quarrelled with your boy-friend?"

That girl in the mirror was fumbling about, and then she got a handkerchief out and dabbed at her face, but it took a time to stop. I thought, Teacher's Highland Cream? Rat poison for you.

"I had a boy-friend once," said the woman. "Here swallow that down and let me buy you a Guinness. It's settling, is Guinness. Here, you, two Guinness. See?"

She said this to a barman in a white coat that was spotty and unbuttoned. She leaned her breasts on the table-top. "He was a sailor, this boy, this partic'lar boy . . ."

I thought, Mark didn't know what he was taking on. Neither did Roman. Some hopes they'd got, either of them, of making a normal woman of me. Oh, Mark, I thought, I did make a mess of it for you, didn't I . . ."

". . . I said, Bert, you've got a kind heart, and kind hearts are more than what's-its; but it ain't enough. You got to be loyal. I thought afterwards 'twas a funny word to use. Of course I meant faithful . . ."

Loyal, I thought. Well who'd been loyal to who in all this? There wasn't any loyalty except maybe Mark's for me. It wasn't a thing human beings dealt in much. Keep that for the 'lesser' animals, horses and dogs.

I drank some of the Guinness this woman had bought. Had I even spoken to her yet? I couldn't remember. Supposing I told her everything? What would she say? All her experience was with the normal things gone awry. Mine was with the abnormal ones. Supposing I began: "I'm a thief and my mother's a whore . . ."

After a minute I looked in this mirror again and I saw to my surprise that the girl was talking. And the blowsy

511

woman had stopped. I mean, she'd stopped talking and she'd got her big comfortable mouth open listening. And she looked startled and uncomfortable, like somebody who's picked up a blind worm and found it's a rattle-snake.

I think I told her everything. I'm not sure. I told her enough to make her wonder if she's been getting acquainted with an escapee from the local mental home. Which I suppose was near enough to be true to make no matter.

While I talked I looked in the mirror and thought there goes Marnie Elmer, the old Marnie Elmer. She wasn't a bad-looking girl, and although she was hard-boiled, she didn't really want to do anyone any *harm*. She was just a certain dead loss from the day she was born. Better if her mother had done for her as well.

Well, she was done for now anyhow—this was the end of her, in this pub. When she finished telling this woman all her sad, sad troubles she'd walk right out and disappear for ever. Was there anyone going to be born in her place? Was there anything worth saving? Not Molly Jeffrey, not any of those people. It had to be somebody utterly fresh.

Perhaps I was a fool to take it the way I did. While I talked I unburdened some of the horror and the shock At least I was free. It was the fourth time I'd told myself that. I kept saying it, expecting a reaction, because all the time was married to Mark I'd so desperately wanted to be free

I could go out of here and say, maybe I am a bit mad like my mother, but what about it? I'd got by so far, and no one could call me a fool. I could live off my wits ... Muriel Whitstone ... that was a nice name. ...

I said: "So that's about all. You wanted to know what was wrong with me. Well, now you know. Thanks for the Guinness. Can I buy you one?"

She fairly gaped at me. I said: "I'm not batty—or not very. It's all true, what I've told you. Funny what happens to some people, isn't it?"

I ordered a Guinness for her and a brandy for me. Some more people had come in and that man with the mouth started his same old story: "We was playing twelve men. I tell you. That blasted ref."

The woman said: "You're having me on, dear."

"God's truth, I'm not."

I suddenly needed the brandy. I realised for the first time why some people take to drink. It's to drown the pain in their guts that being alive has put there.

The waiter came and I paid him and I splashed a bit of soda in and had gulped the glassful down while the woman was wiping a moustache of froth off her upper lip after her first swallow.

She said: "But why did you leave your hubby, dear? Didn't you hit it off?"

"Well," I said, "it was more than that." But I looked at her big easy breasts and broad gentle face and thought, it's no good, I can't explain *that* to her—or I could explain it but no amount of talking would ever clue her up. Because for her sex was like a comfy chair, a warm fire, a glass of Guinness. It didn't mean more and it didn't mean less. How could she ever understand what it had been like to be screwed up, horrified, disgusted; how would she have a notion if I explained that the replusion, the dislike had been something more than I could deal with? Had been? Still was? I didn't know.

I said: "I'd better be going."

"Well, dear, you sure give me a fright. You look so young and innocent. Reely . . . But I shouldn't worry if I was you. Life's all right if you don't weaken. You can't help what your Mam did, can you? I mean, it's not sense. How do I know what my mother did when she was twenty? She was a dear old soul when she was seventy, but that's different. Dear life, I'd not want to tell my kids everything!"

As I left the pub check-cap was there. "Like a lift, miss? Which way you going?"

"Not your way," I said.

"Oh, come on, be a sport. I got a nice little Sprite round the corner. I'll give you a run round in it first."

"I bet you would," I said, stepping off the pavement.

He stepped off beside me. "It's over there. See? The red one. New last year. Ever been in one? It's an education."

"Being in yours would be," I said, and shook his arm off and walked away. He followed for a few steps and then gave up.

I walked right up to the top of the street to where there was a church at the top. It was quite dark now. Muriel Whitstone, I thought, blowing out a breath with brandy on it, Muriel Whitstone is being born. I'll go and spend the night in Cuthbert Avenue and tomorrow I'll pick up my few things and push off. I'll go first to Southampton, and then I'll take a bus for Bournemouth. There I'll have my hair done a different way and my eyebrows plucked and maybe some other things done, and on Tuesday I'll leave for Leeds. It's all exciting really, just the way it used to be, building up a new history, making a new person. And this time the money I get I'll spend entirely on myself. To hell with the world.

At the iron gate by the church there was a kid crying.

I said: "What's up with you?"

He said: "I lost me Mum." He was about eight.

"Where d'you live?"

"Davidge Street. Number ten. Over there."

I thought, crazy, leaving a kid of his age to wander about after dark. "Is it far?"

He shook his spiky head. "Dad's there."

It was nearly on my way. "I'll take you if you like."

"Don't wanna go."

"Why not? Your Mum might be home before you."

That started him crying again and then coughing. He'd got a lousy cough, like a shovelful of wet coal. I got hold of his hand, and began to walk with him. Under the light of the lamp he looked thin and hot. Dressed all right but thin and hot.

I thought, maybe if I was a nun I could care for sick children; maybe that would make up for the one that was put under my bed . . . This kid's hand was in mine, as trusting as if I was his maiden aunt.

"How did you come to lose your mother this evening?"

"Didn't," he said.

"Didn't what?"

"Didn't lose Mum tonight."

514

"What d'you mean?"

"Lost 'er Wednesday."

We went on a bit. We came to Davidge Street and went down it. I hadn't got a toffee for him or anything. I thought suddenly, I don't care a *damn* for Muriel Whitstone. I don't *care* if she never comes to life at all! I'm not interested in her and her lousy secretarial jobs and her thieving. I don't know what's going to happen to Muriel Whitstone, but Marnie Elmer has *had* it. She can't invent other people any more. And she can't go on living herself.

"What d'you mean?" I said. "Your Mum went away on Wednesday? What's she coming back?"

"She ain't never coming back," this kid said. "They told me she'd gone visiting but I knew better. I seen her. They carried her out in a box. She's dead."

He began to cry again, and I put my hands round his head and held him to me. I thought that's right, be a mother for a change. Bite on somebody else's grief instead of your own. Stop being so heart-broken for yourself and take a look round. Because maybe everybody's griefs aren't that much different after all.

I thought, there's only one loneliness, and that's the loneliness of all the world.

21

I don't know what time I got back to Cuthbert Avenue. I suppose it couldn't have been all that long. I saw the boy in and saw his father and then walked home. It may have been seven or half past.

The kid's father was a thin weedy type with sandy hair. "We come here from Stoke because of them saying the weather was better. Not so hard for Shirley. I changed me job. Three pound a week less. But so soon as she come here she started spitting blood. They wanted her to go to hospital, but no. 'Never again,' she says. 'I'll die in me own home,' she says. Bobby slipped out when I'd me back turned. He knew. Tried to keep it from 'em but they all knew."

If he'd asked me I'd have stayed. There were three other children and he looked very down. But he didn't ask and I couldn't offer. Afterwards I wished I had. It might have given me something to do instead of just thinking.

If I could have something to do that took up sixteen hours of every day.

When I got to Cuthbert Avenue there was a car stopped outside No. 9, and I thought I'd seen it before, and I suddenly had a funny feeling that it might be Mark.

Of course it wasn't Mark; he didn't know where I was, and anyway he didn't get out of hospital till Monday. But seeing the lights of the car reminded me of that time coming out of Garrod's Farm where he'd traced me and been waiting for me, and I thought, well, he wouldn't be as unwelcome now as he was then. I mean, in a way, I could have told him everything the way I'd told it to that woman in the pub, and perhaps in his case he might have partly understood. He'd always made a great effort to understand. You could hate him and yet have to admit that he did his best to understand.

Perhaps I didn't hate him any more. I was too tired and beaten up to hate anyone, least of all him.

And as I walked up the avenue I knew I would have been glad to talk to him. That was quite a shock but I had to admit it. Compare what the rest of my life had been, and the time I spent married to him had been comfort and sanity and decency and order. Oh, there'd been the big stumbling block, and perhaps it was still there and perhaps it would always be there, but the rest was all right.

And you *could* talk to him.

There was one personality I hadn't thought about when I was writing off all the Mollie Jeffreys and the Muriel Whitstones. That one was Margaret Rutland. What about her?

516

But anyway it was all too late. She'd gone out of the gun with the rest.

I was thirsty again and I stopped at the door wondering if there'd be any drink in the house. Not likely. Mother would see to that. Had she secretly wanted to be a drunkard too?

I hadn't a key and knocked on the door. Old Lucy opened it, just like last night, except that her face wasn't so swollen. She said: "Oh, Marnie, we was hoping you'd come. There's a gent to see you."

I went in and into the front room. Uncle Stephen was sitting there talking to Terry.

22

The room was badly lit. This bowl thing hanging from the ceiling was supposed to spread the light, but in fact it threw most of it up so that your face was in a sort of half shadow. Terry's face was in half shadow.

He said: "Oh, good, my dear. I've only just come. I went to Cranbook Avenue first. I wasn't sure."

He was wearing a yellow tie with a green sports jacket and a maroon waistcoat. I said: "How did you know where I was at all?"

"I heard the SOS message. I never thought it was you until I rang you a second time today and there was no reply. Then it suddenly occurred to me, my dear. I thought, that was her mother."

They were drinking beer. I suppose Uncle Stephen had got it from somewhere. I sat down in a chair. "What have you come for?"

"I thought I might be able to help. I didn't know how you were fixed." He was smiling sympathetically. There was still something not quite clear about it but I was too beaten up to bother. It was like a dream—going on with one I'd begun somewhere else on my own.

Uncle Stephen said: "Mr. Holbrook was telling me your husband had been seriously injured in a riding accident. I'd no idea. You should have told us, Marnie."

I was still looking at Terry. "He's not worse?"

"No."

Lucy came in. "I got supper ready, dear. 'Twill do us all good. Mr. 'Oldbrook? I laid four places."

"Thanks, I'd like to," said Terry. "Though I mustn't be late starting back."

We had the meal in the dining-room which had all new furniture I'd bought for this house, so it didn't remind me so much as the other rooms. I wished I could remember why I hated that clock in the kitchen. I never could. But while I sat there pecking at some cold ham and pickles I remembered the rough feel of khaki on the back of my legs when I was lifted up and put on a man's knee. And I remembered a terrible thing like a battle, like a war, bursting suddenly over my head. It was Dad and another man who were fighting . . .

"Eat your 'am, dear," said Old Lucy. "If I'd known we was 'aving company I'd have baked."

Nobody was talking much at the table. I suppose nobody knew how much anybody else was supposed to know, and they were afraid of saying the wrong thing. Terry and Uncle Stephen began to talk about underwater fishing.

"Marnie." It was Terry.

"Yes?"

"Why don't you drive back with me?"

"Where?"

"Why don't you let me run you home?"

I dug my fork in a piece of ham but didn't lift it off the plate.

"Why don't you?" said Uncle Stephen.

"Why don't I what?"

"Let Mr. Holbrook drive you home. It's been a hard day for you, and if your husband's not well you should be with him, otherwise he might worry. Lucy and I can tidy things up here. Can't we, Lucy?"

"'S I reckon," said Lucy, and looked at me with her big eye.

"I couldn't," I said, "go home."

"You could come down again in a few days. Really, it's much the best way."

"Mark's still in hospital," I said. "I can't help him that way."

But even while I was speaking there was a sudden flush of feeling inside me that said, why don't you. Even though I knew it was mad I listened to it. You see, more than anybody else I suddenly found I wanted to talk to Mark. More than anyone else he'd forced me to talk when I didn't want to, so he really knew more about part of my life than anyone. I wanted to go back to him and fill up the gaps. I wanted to go and tell him and say, this is the sort of female I am, this is what happened to me, this is the rotten stock I came from: can you wonder I didn't fit in with your fancy notions of a wife?

You see, there was no one else I *could* talk to like that. No one at all, not even Roman. I felt if I could see Mark and talk to him and *explain* a bit, it would help me—and also it would help him to understand. I'd say to him, d'you realise who you've been living with, d'you realise who you wanted to be the mother of your children? And if I said that to him I think he would have some sort of a view of it that would make me better able to live with myself.

That was all. I just wanted to explain. It wasn't a great ambition.

I didn't want to go back to him permanently—I just wanted to talk.

Uncle Stephen said: "If you'll leave tonight I'll promise to see personally to everything here. I can stay several days . . ." He rubbed his nose and looked at Terry and then said carefully: "You see, Marnie, this isn't your life down here any more."

Lucy was breathing on her cup of tea to cool it; the steam went across the table nearly to where Terry was cutting the bread on his plate into squares.

I said to Terry: "Why have you come?"

Everybody looked at me. Terry said: "My dear, I thought I might be able to lend a helping hand."

"D'you mean that?"

"Why not? You don't think I came to this Queen of Watering places for *pleasure*, do you? I thought, Marnie's in difficulties and Mark's ill, so perhaps I can help." His mud-coloured eyes flickered up at the other two and he grinned. "Oh, I admit I feel no personal love for Mark. Would you, my dear? But I don't believe in carrying my grudges around on my back."

"You'd—drive me home?"

"Of course. Or if you don't want I'll leave you here. It's all the *same* to me. I'm only offering to be neighbourly."

I was still too tired to think quite straight. I got a feeling that I had missed something, but for once my brain didn't tick. It was still half-way through that dream.

He said: "Or maybe you'd like me to do something else to help. What do you think, Mr. Treville? Is there anything I can do here?"

"Take Marnie home. That's really the only thing. I'd be very grateful if you would—and I'm sure she will be too."

Wishing is like water caught in a dam. You let a little trickle of it escape and you don't think it's much, but in no time the trickle has worn a channel and the edges fall in and the water's doubled and then you get a flood carrying everything away. That's the way it was with me then. Obviously I'd be crazy to even think of seeing Mark again; but I wasn't answering to reason any more. I *wanted* to see him. I'd got to *tell* him.

All the same I didn't let on right away. I just let myself drift along to the end of supper, and then after supper I went up into Mother's bedroom and stood there for a few minutes, and I looked at the clothes in the wardrobe and the old blue dressing-gown with the silk buttons behind the door, and the high-heeled shoes—three pairs, very small, all black; and suddenly instead of being evil she became just pathetic. All she'd done, except perhaps one thing, was pathetic, and her lies and her build up and her crazy pride . . . I thought of her for one last time as the person I'd loved most in all the world, and the person since early this morning that I'd hated most—and the twelve hours since this morning seemed as long as all the rest of life. And now I didn't seem to have any feeling for her any longer except pity.

And I thought, perhaps if you pity her enough you won't have any left for yourself.

The room was empty and cold, and there was the faint stale stink of hyacinths and corruption.

And I went downstairs and told Terry I would go back with him.

It was a cold night but the wind had dropped and I kissed Uncle Stephen and old Lucy and told them I'd come again in a few days, not perhaps ever really intending to.

I didn't imagine, I carefully didn't think it out yet beyond a certain point. I didn't face up to all that going back might mean.

We drove fast through the night. We went through Newton Abbot and skirted Exeter and took the A 30 and the A 303 through Honiton and Ilminister and Ilchester towards Wincanton. I thought, life's like being in an insane asylum. Everybody goes about with their own delusions hugging them close for no one else to see. So you plough through the wards among all the milling figures towards what looks like one sane man. That's what I was doing now.

Terry said: "Queer, you know, I rang up on Wednesday, asking you to come for a drive round with me on Friday evening—and here we are, my dear, having that drive. You never know your luck, do you. You never know which way the dice is going to roll."

That clicked something into place. "But how did you know my name was Elmer?"

"My dear, I'd always felt your first marriage was a fake, you *know* that. I didn't care a cuss, but it irks me to have a feeling that way and not to *know*. So I went to the registry office and looked up the entry of your marriage to Mark, and found that he'd married a Margaret Elmer, spinster, of the parish of St. James's, Plymouth."

"I see."

"Care to tell me about it?"

"Not now, I wouldn't, Terry."

"Did Mark know all along?"

"Fairly early on."

Terry whistled a little flat tune. "He's a queer character, Mark. He's like a weather cock; you never know which way he's going to blow."

"It isn't the weather cock that blows, it's the wind."

"Defending him for a change? It's so much more stimulating when a wife has a healthy antagonism for her husband. Why did you ever marry him, my dear?"

Why did I marry him? I might know that, but did I really know why I was going back to him? Did you go back to a man simply to explain? And after I'd explained, how was I going to leave again?

Terry said: "Pardon me for sounding melodramatic, but did he have a 'hold' on you or something? After all, it was plain as a wall that he was mad about you—and pretty soon it was nearly as plain that, behind that lovely give-away-nothing expression, you hated the sight of him. I mean, it was enough to make any fair-minded cousin curious."

"Yes, I suppose it was, Terry." If I hated the sight of Mark, why did I want the sight of him now? Had I changed? Had something happened? Had a lot of neat little gadgets inside me all suddenly gone into reverse just because I knew a bit more about them? No, it wasn't that, it couldn't be that. Even in a madhouse life didn't make that much sense.

Anyway, if anything had happened to me, I mean had happened to me to make any sort of difference in the way I thought or felt about Mark, it wasn't just this or that, it wasn't just the discovery about Mother or such-like, it was an add-up of everything that had been going on for weeks. It was Roman and Forio and living at that house and mixing with those people and finding out about Mother and being with Mark all in one, all tied up in one great unravellable mess, like a ball of string a cat's been playing with.

"You haven't answered," said Terry.

"Answered what?"

"Are you in love with him?"

"Who?"

"Well, Mark, dear, who else?"

522

"I don't know . . ." My God, didn't I? Of course I wasn't, but it didn't do to tell Terry everything.

"And does he still love you?"

"I think so." Does he? What have you done to keep it alive since you were married? Lived like a sulky prisoner, refused him love, thwarted his intentions whenever you could, played his psychiatrist up, tried to drown yourself and then to break your neck and his as well. Why should he love you? Now you've got stomach cramp. What the hell's that for?

We went through Andover and turned off on the Newbury road. There was more traffic here and Terry had to pick his way.

Terry said: "It's rather important to me to know if he still loves you."

"Why?"

"Well, unless he does, there's not much point in my taking you back, is there?"

". . . You're very kind."

"We all have to do our deed for the day."

What had Mark said once? "I want to fight for you. We're in this together." The stomach cramp didn't go away. Of course I knew what I was going back to. If I found Mark as I'd left him, still anxious to do something about our marriage, even with all this knowledge in front of him, and if I decided to stop and try too, then it meant facing one of the two choices about the stolen money. Even if he could, I knew he'd never settle for any other way, and I knew if I stayed with him I'd have to agree to let him go ahead with the attempt to buy people off, probably.

But was there any sense in even thinking of staying with him, seeing I knew now what I did about myself? Would he want me to? It was pretty lunatic ever to have let myself be talked into coming back at all.

I must have made some move because Terry said: "Getting stiff?"

"No."

"Why don't you go to sleep?"

If I went back now nobody would know I'd been away—that was odd. Except Terry nobody *need* know.

"Terry . . ."

"Yes?"

But that was the old way again. Lies and more lies clogging up the pores. I couldn't ever get straight with Mark or with myself on that platform.

"Yes?" Terry said.

"Nothing . . ."

We had to stop at a garage near High Wycombe for petrol. I thought of Estelle's little car I had left behind in Torquay, and wondered what would happen to it. In spite of myself I was feeling sleepy, and soon after we started again I must have dozed off for a bit. I woke up with the lights dazzling across the windscreen from an oncoming car, but I still felt drowsy and in one of those moods when you haven't got quite all your hard-boiled skin tightly buttoned on. I mean I suddenly thought, what if you do love Mark? You crazy cretinous ape, what if you think you love him now; is it any surer than the hate you felt at Ibiza? And I suddenly realised that I couldn't *reason* any longer, that my brain wasn't going to direct me what to feel any more; I was suddenly emotional and female and hopeless, and if Mark was there at that second I should have gone blubbering into his arms wanting love and comfort and protection. Hell, how feeble-minded can you get. I was glad he wasn't there; but who was to know that I shouldn't act like that when we did meet?

Anyway tonight I should be alone in the house in Little Gaddesden and a night's sleep might give me a chance to get things ironed out and put on the line.

Dirty washing. I was a mass of dirty washing—why should I expect Mark to do the laundry for me? I ought never to have come back. There he was standing at the door and there was a thin woman in black standing next to him and as we got nearer I could see it was Mother. 'Come in, dear,' she said, 'I've explained it all to Mark and he quite understands about the baby. He says he'd have done the same in my place.' And she opened her mouth to smile but in place of her teeth . . .

I reared up in the car and blinked ahead at a twisting road. We were following a lorry, and the red light kept winking in and out as we turned the corners.

"All right?" said Terry.

"All right." After a minute I said: "I'm sorry about you and Mark, Terry. You know I've always liked you. I'm sorry we can't all be friends."

"Think nothing of it. There's a lot of life left. In twenty years we shall have forgiven each other for the dirty tricks we played on each other, and we shall have forgiven each other for not having forgiven each other earlier."

That red eye of that lorry was like Dr. Roman's eye when he tried to hypnotise me—only it worked better. It had a nasty dirty wink about it. Roman said: 'It's no good coming to me, my dear. I can't help you now, my dear, it's not psychological, it's in the blood. Child murder, it carries on from generation to generation; if you had one of your own you'd do it in, my dear. You're for it, my dear, didn't you know?'

Suddenly the red eye got bigger and bigger and came up to my side of the car and peered in like an evil face, and then before I could scream we'd overtaken the lorry and it was gone.

"Not long now," Terry said. I thought even he sounded tired and strung up.

Mark was there waiting at the door again, only this time Mother wasn't with him. He came out, down the path past the stable to the small gate. And he said: 'It's all nonsense, Marnie, all these barriers you're putting up. *Nothing's* in the blood, *nothing's* in the upbringing, *nothing* happened at Sangerford that we can't throw away for ever if you want to *try*, if you've got courage and some *love*. Because they're so much stronger than all these shabby ghosts. If you once find your way through the first thickets, there's nothing then that we can't do together.'

I jerked my head up as the car began to slow. I said: "There's nobody here, because I sent Mrs. Leonard home. But I'll be all right tonight."

"O.K."

I said: "I think I'm pretty well all in, Terry. I'd ask you in for a drink but I'm pretty well all in."

"That's O.K."

I said: "I'll try somehow to make it up between you and Mark, Terry. It may not be too late."

"It'll be impossible."

"Why?"

"Well, my dear, I tell you it'll be impossible."

The car turned in at the drive, but the gravel crackled in a different way. The house—there was a light in the house.

Terry blew his horn.

It wasn't Mark's house. I said: "Where are we? This isn't our house."

"No. I had to call here. I promised. It won't take a minute."

I looked at him. His face had got a shiny look as if it was damp. It was shiny like a fish, with rain or with sweat. It looked green. He was whistling but there wasn't any sound.

The door of the house opened. A man stood at the door, and there was another one behind him.

Terry said: "You see, my dear, I'd arranged to take you for a run this evening. You promised to come so I arranged to call in and see these people—for a drink. It's about four hours later than I arranged but that can't be helped, can it?"

"What are you talking about?"

The man came down the steps. The other man followed him. There was a woman at the door now.

The man who was first down the steps was Mr. Strutt.

Terry said: "In a way I'm sorry to do this to you. At the last minute it seems pretty hard to—to carry through. In a way I'd rather it hadn't to be you, my dear. One makes promises to oneself. One pays one's debts, if you see what I mean. But I doubt if you'd understand."

"I don't understand."

Even his eyes looked green in the light coming from the house. "Just work it out. You don't need to look very far. I'm sorry, but really, you know, Mark had it coming to him, didn't he?" He was still talking half to me, half to himself—talking to keep his own thoughts off himself, I think—when Mr. Strutt opened the door.

"Good evening, Miss Holland. We'd almost given you up."

"I telephoned," Terry said.

"Yes, but it *is* rather late. Do get out, Miss Holland, we want to ask you a few questions. Let me see, you know our Birmingham manager, don't you? Mr. George Pringle."

When that sort of thing happens to you you don't faint. Not if you're my type, you don't. You get slowly out of the car and look at Mr. Pringle for the first time for two years, and you're suddenly back in that office and you remember every pimple and blemish and blotch of his face.

And behind you you hear the other car door slam and you know that Terry has got out, and for a moment that swallows everything else, how you've been such a fool as to think he was willing to be a friend to the wife of the man he hated most in the world. Half of your mind thinks that and the other half thinks but maybe it was better that you never suspected he would stoop this low. If you have to live in the world, then you have to have some view of the world that doesn't drip with slime.

And they've not exactly caught you, but they stand one on either side of you and slowly you begin to walk up the steps to the top where Mrs. Strutt is waiting. And you think, well, this is the end of everything now, it's out of your hands. This is the end. For a second you think, maybe you could fight, you could still fight; deny everything, how can they force you to admit what you won't admit; just go on stalling till Mark comes. But when the second is gone you know somehow that that isn't the answer any more, that is, if you really are going to make a break with things as they used to be.

And you think—because it's true what people say, that a drowning man lives all his back life in a few seconds, and so a drowning woman has plenty of time to think between steps—and you think anyway whatever happens you can still wait till Mark comes. Everything rests on him.

But by the time you are at the top of the steps—and Mrs. Strutt, looking embarrassed and rather sorry for you, has stepped aside to let you go in—I mean you know that really deep down at root it isn't Mark it depends on but you yourself. Because he can only help you to help yourself. If you can't stand him touching you and you still only want to get away from him and you want to go on living a solitary life and codding up a make-believe world with a different name and personality every nine months and rustling bank notes stuffed surreptitiously in your handbag—then he can't help at all. He can only help if all that is over and instead you want at any rate to try to love him and to trust him and to be loved.

And the only way to love and trust now was through this door, among enemies, with a police-sergeant any minute being called at the end of the phone.

I stopped there and looked back, but not at any of the three men. I looked across the garden. The high wind was still blowing here, and a ragged cloud like a broken fish and chip bag drifted just over the trees. The trees were rustling and waving and they smelled of pines. All the garden looked dark and foreign and strange.

Mark had said: 'I want to fight *for* you. We're in this together'; that was something I'd have to hold on to.

I thought, the way to love is through suffering. Who had said that? Did it mean anything or was it just the usual talk?

You know, I thought, this isn't going to be the hardest part, this is the easiest part, going through this door.

I took a deep breath and turned and went in.

Greek Fire

1

The Little Jockey was not much more than a converted cellar. Vanbrugh found it at the second attempt, down an alley just out of reach of the seedy lights of Ommonia Square. But here twenty yards was enough to pace out a thousand years—from hissing trolley-buses and neon lights and chattering crowds, past two doorways, a Greek and a Turkish, past a garbage can with its lid aslant like a mandarin's hat, across a gutter half choked by the mud of yesterday's rain, to an arched entrance and twelve stone steps cut before Charlemagne, rubbed smooth and treacherous and leading down into the dark. At the bottom an attendant dressed like an Evzone took his coat and pulled aside a curtain to see him down a second flight to the main room.

The place was about two-thirds full, but they found him a table in a good position in a sort of upper cellar which formed a terrace on a higher level. Eight or ten tables up here led to six break-ankle steps and a larger domed cellar where there were more tables and room for dancing. The walls were of rough stone and inclined to sweat; curtained arches led to service quarters; and lights from candles in old glass lamp-holders lit up the statuary which stood defensively in recesses: two tired Byzantine madonnas, a stray apostle lacking an ear, St. Francis with a lamb.

The newcomer waved away a couple of the house girls who drifted across to help him with the bottle in the bucket, but when a tall Lithuanian Jewess stopped by and said, "Amerikani?" and slipped into the seat opposite, he raised no objection, and a waiter hovering near quickly put another glass on the table.

Vanbrugh was the sort of man you wouldn't notice in the street: he could have been twenty-five or forty, and his tight rather craggy face, his deep-set, pale-eyed inner containment made no substantial first impression. He didn't talk to the girl, but she re-filled his glass once or twice, and her own with it, and when she stretched forward a hand for his package of cigarettes he absent-mindedly shook one out for her and lit a match with his thumb-nail.

At a table in a corner was a middle-aged stout man in a black alpaca suit, with a fluff of untidy beard worn like a bonnet string under his chin. Vanbrugh frowned as at an uneasy memory. The fat man was eating; he was the only person so occupied; he paused now and then to brush crumbs from his shiny shabby suit, and with a sort of sham gentility he raised the back of his hand to hide a belch; once a piece of shell fish slid out of his mouth and hung like mucus from his beard; his companion, a tall youth with a narrow nose and a girlish mouth, watched him with bright malicious eyes.

The orchestra of four were perched in an odd wire balcony to the left of the steps like canaries in a cage. They were playing a western dance rhythm, and half a dozen couples moved like sleepwalkers about the dance floor. Beside the band was a fair copy in bronze of the third century B.C. Little Jockey which gave the club its name.

"Who is that man, d'you know?" Vanbrugh said to the girl opposite him. "The fat man eating at the table in the corner."

"Who? That one? No. I have never seen him before."

"I have. But it doesn't matter."

"You know Greece, honey?" she said.

"A little."

"I am quite new here. You must tell me."

"Where are you from?"

"Memel."

"It's a long way to come."

"I travel light. And you?"

He said: "I'm far from home too."

The band had stopped and the dancers were dispersing. Two couples climbed the steps and took seats at a table

534

nearby—wealthy young Greeks, both men handsome but running to fat, one girl ordinary, the other a beauty.

Vanbrugh eyed her through his smoke-screen. Her raven black hair was caught together with a diamond clasp at the back; ivory profile with a slender, almost too slender, nose, eyes lit with exceptional brilliance; the classic conception of beauty—by Byron out of Polyclitus —but all on a twentieth century basis, from the peach finger-nails holding the long amber cigarette-holder to the brilliant worldly-wise smile.

With that sixth sense that women have, she soon knew she was being looked at, and her gaze moved to Vanbrugh's table, took in the thin undernourished-looking American, the cheap girl, the waiter changing the bottle in the bucket. A glimmer of amused civilised contempt showed in her eyes before she turned away.

"How long have you been here?" Vanbrugh said to his companion.

"Eight weeks, honey."

"What's this new cabaret you have?"

"The three Tolosas? They are Spaniards. They dance like all Spaniards."

"This their first week?"

"Last week was their first week. They come from Paris. They have been good for business. Before that we had singers from Macedonia. It was very awful."

"When does the cabaret come on?"

"Almost any time now. Like to dance, honey, before it begins?"

"Thanks no, if you'll excuse me."

"You are not very bright, are you?"

"Maybe there's someone else who'd dance with you."

"Does that mean you want to get rid of me?"

The fat Greek had stopped eating to draw breath, and he took his handkerchief from the corner of his collar and wiped it across his mouth. His heavy glance seemed to linger on Vanbrugh's table. Vanbrugh said: "No, stay if you'd like to."

"The floor show's just beginning."

One by one the candles were blown out, and shadows fell on the company like a secret retinue of waiters. Towering wine barrels and weather-born statuettes were sucked up into the darkness, and light played on the circular dance floor.

Vanbrugh said: "D'you happen to know—maybe you won't—but d'you happen to know the name of the girl on the next table but one—the girl with her hair in that diamond clasp?"

"I tell you, honey, I know no one. We do not see the same faces often. Ah, but that one ... Stonaris, isn't that her name? Anya Stonaris. I have seen her photo in the weekly papers."

Her voice was drowned by the clash of cymbals. Four girls in traditional Spanish costume came out and performed a Flamenco, to the clicking of castanets and the vehement stamping of their feet, while in the back-ground a thin lithe man dressed like a matador crouched before a harp and touched it in a casual way from time to time with his hands. The first thing Gene Vanbrugh noticed about him was that he was in a sweat of fear.

When the girls went off, dragging perfunctory applause after them, the thin Spaniard stayed where he was, his short nervous fingers barely touching the strings. Once he raised his bloodshot eyes to sweep them in a quick semi-circle, meeting the darkness and the waiting faces.

"Who is she?" said Vanbrugh. "What does she do?"

"Who?"

"This—Anya Stonaris."

His companion shrugged. "Who knows? That one with her—that man—is called Manos. He is a politician. He has been here often before, but then he has come alone. . . ."

A woman stepped through the curtains on to the dance floor. She was young, about twenty-two, and fat, twelve stone or more, and short, not over five feet. The broad nose and thick flattened lips weren't negroid, not even Moorish. She was pure Spanish. Hands on hips, in perfect ease and confidence, she sang a comic song in a harsh broken power-ful voice.

Nearly everyone in the cellars knew French, and those who did not were jollied along. Her eyes, small as diamonds and as bright, and the good-tempered shock of her white teeth, made you ready to laugh before the joke was out. She was all fat, healthy young fat, mainly in the breasts and behind. Her black crêpe dress fitted her like a sausage skin. And when she began to dance she used her fat as a comedian uses a false nose: with it she laughed at you and then at herself.

At the table where the Greeks were the girl, Anya Stonaris, put out her cigarette. The politician Manos, defer-ential and attentive, offered her another; she took it, twisted it slowly with pointed nails into the holder, thoughtful lashes black on cheeks, glinted a smile across the lighted flame at her escort, flickered her glance back across the American before turning again to watch the show.

Down below the harpist, who, after the end of the applause and while the fat girl stood aside, had been hinting at the sad nostalgias of Seville and Castile, suddenly set fire to his harp with great chords and discords of a new kind. In the sudden silence which followed, El Toro himself stepped into the ring.

Welcoming applause was discreetly led by the waiters, schooled in the dangers of anti-climax, for El Toro, dressed though he was in all the magnificence of a toreador, was tiny, no taller than his girl partner, fine featured, dapper, the perfect lady killer—and perhaps bull killer—but in minus-cule.

The man and the woman began to dance. It was the dance of the bull-ring, hot and bloodstained, to the shrill pulse of the harp. They swirled and twisted to the shouted rhythm, she charging, he adroitly avoiding her with his muleta, sword point to ground, enticing and evading, side-stepping and body swaying. For *she* was the bull, not he. She looked like a bull, heavy shouldered, broad nosed, dark curled, she breathed and snorted and charged like a bull, at his delicate, precise almost feminine evasions, his perfect slender body leaning this way and that. Here was some inner truth from Spain stated in terms of the dance, an allegorical picture of the relationship of the sexes, spiritual more than physical but partly both, a statement of a racial anomaly which had existed for two thousand years.

As the dance reached its climax, the harpist in a sort of frenzy produced unheard of sounds. If a harp was the instrument of angels, then this was a fallen angel, perverting his gifts to the expression of the noise and cruelty of a blinding Andalusian afternoon.

Vanbrugh sipped the indifferent champagne. The bull was tiring, faltering now and stamping in hesitation, watching the toreador who flicked his muleta with small poised formal movements. She lowered her head to charge, El Toro drew back his sword. As she ran at him he turned slightly aside and plunged the sword between her arm and shoulder. She sank slowly, her attitude the conventional posture of the slain bull. In a moment he had drawn away and she was on the floor before him; his foot rested lightly on her shoulder.

There was loud applause at the end of this dance, and the partners, toreador and slain bull, stood bowing side by side.

"You see," said the Lithuanian, "it is not bad after all. Of course, that fat woman, Maria Tolosa, she is the best."

Vanbrugh looked at the harpist as he went off. He was still sweating. The band came back to their cage and a few dancers drifted on to the floor. Manos asked Anya Stonaris for a dance, but she said something smilingly and they did not get up.

Vanbrugh nodded or answered in monosyllables as his companion chattered away. He was debating in his mind one or two things, the least of which was how he might most easily get rid of this girl and go. The most important was whether he should attempt to see Juan Tolosa tonight. He had only landed at Hellenikon three hours ago. Rushing one's fences. Also he thought he had been recognised tonight by the fat man, whose name he thought was Mandraki, and if that were so it was a disadvantage to any move now.

So he made no move now.

He didn't realise then the importance of the decision, because he did not then know that by tomorrow it would be too late.

2

George Lascou was taking his mid-morning coffee when Anya rang him.

"Good morning, darling," she said. "I suppose you have been up hours."

"Since six. But, that's no reason why you should be. Four weeks and it will all be over."

"Or all beginning. I can't imagine in either case that you will learn to relax."

"I relax when I'm with you. That's why you're so good for me."

"It must explain why you have been seeing so much of me lately!"

"Darling, I'm *sorry*. I hate it as much as you do. I wish I could do something about it, but you know what it is at present. This morning we have a press conference at twelve. At five there's a meeting of the party executive. Then this evening there is the manifesto to consider in full session. It will be easier when the campaign is in full swing. What will you do today?"

"I have a press conference with my hair-dresser at twelve. At five I shall buy a hat. This will pass the time until seven when I'm to take cocktails with Maurice Taksim."

"And what did you do last night?"

"Had dinner with Jon Manos and two of his friends. Afterwards we went to the Little Jockey and danced for a while. It wasn't much fun without you."

"You went where?"

"To the Little Jockey."

"Did Manos take you there?"

"Yes. There's a new cabaret. Quite good. I got home about two. My sweet, it's a perfectly *respectable* night-club. One is in far more danger of being bored than corrupted. We must go together sometime."

"Yes. Yes, of course. I know it." As he poured himself a second cup of coffee, the morning light glinted on the heavy silver coffee-pot and on the big emerald-cut diamond in the ring on his left hand.

"But are you being disapproving just the same?"

"Nothing of the sort." He dabbed at a spot of coffee which had fallen on the tray-cloth and sucked the damp tip of his fingers.

"Then what? . . ."

He said in slight irritation: "Perhaps one has to be specially careful at a time like this. The opposition press are always out for snippets of scandal, and they know of our connection. A photograph. A chance of involving me——"

"You can always disown me."

"That I may do in my coffin but not before."

"Darling, a gallant speech before midday."

He laughed politely. "One has to keep up with the Taksims of this world. What did you think of the cabaret?"

"It was Spanish."

". . . Is that all?"

"No. I hate their singing but love their dancing."

"I prefer Greek. What was it, all women?"

"No. A man. Two men. One danced and one played a harp as if he'd sold his soul to the devil. Then there was a woman. They're known as The Three Tolosas."

"Good. Good. I'm glad you enjoyed it. But I must talk to Jon Manos."

"You quite astonish me. I'll go into purdah for the next four weeks."

"Nonsense, darling, you exaggerate. Tell me when you are next going down to Sounion. . . ." He began to talk easily, smoothing over what he had said.

When they had rung off George Lascou sipped his coffee.

From where he sat two reflections of George Lascou aped his movements and were a constant reassurance that he was still personable and still in the early forties. All the same, he was angry with himself now for having allowed himself to be surprised into an emotion which she had detected.

His secretary came in.

"Where had I got to, Otho?"

"Shall I read the last piece? 'It was Aristotle who said that Virtue consists in loving and hating in the proper proportions. The danger of a too-civilised approach is that we become afraid of the positive emotions. If this election——' "

"Leave it now." He made an impatient gesture. "Before we go on I'd like you to get Mr. Manos on the phone."

Otho put away his notebook, but as he was about to go out Lascou said: "And also Major Kolono."

"Sir?"

"Major Kolono. You'll find him at police headquarters. Tell him I'd like him to call round here about four-thirty this afternoon on a personal matter."

"Very good, sir."

While he waited, George Lascou re-read a report he had received that morning from a man whom he occasionally and reluctantly employed. Having done that, he put it in his wallet and began to slit open with a bronze dagger some letters that Otho had brought in. The blade of the dagger was three thousand years old and a lion hunt was inlaid on it. The handle had long since rotted away and been replaced with a modern ivory one. He read the letters, made an emphatic note in the margin of one, got up, lit a cigarette, and went to one of the windows which looked out over Constitution Square. He was high enough here to be un-disturbed by the bustle and noise and all the clamour of the morning traffic below, high enough too to see over the new-budding trees to the Tomb of the Unknown Soldier and to the Old Palace, where Parliament had recently been prorogued. Beyond were the trees of the National Garden. Along the further rim of the square three trolley-buses were

541

crawling like centipedes surprised by the lifting of a stone. A handsome man, with that shadowed pallor that comes to some Greeks; the pince-nez he wore softened the strong cheekbones and the strong skull, gave an uncertain studious look to a face otherwise purposeful. As Otho came in again he let the scarlet-and-white-striped satin curtain fall.

"Sir, I phoned Mr. Manos at his office but he was in court. I left a message for them to ring when he came back."

Lascou put the end of his cigarette in an ash-tray.

"Then get him *out* of court. I want to speak to him."

It was then nearly 11 a.m.

3

At three o'clock that afternoon a short stout young woman was walking through Zappeion Park. Her mane of hair was dragged back and fastened under a scarlet head-scarf. Her cheeks were puffy with crying but she was not crying now; her face was set like iron; it was a good-tempered face riven by lightning, hardened by storm. She walked any way, not looking where she was going and not caring; but after a while she came opposite a statue and hesitated staring at it, not really seeing it but uncertain whether to go on or turn back. As she stopped, a man who had been following the same path stopped also and looked at the statue. After a moment he glanced at her and said in English:

"He died here too."

"What? Who?" She stared at him with blind, angry eyes. "What do you say?"

"Byron. That statue. He loved Greece more even than his own land."

She focused the speaker properly for the first time, saw his slight figure and down-pulled hat. "If you are from the police I will spit in your face."

"If I were from the police that would land you in trouble."

"And you are not?"

"I am not."

"Then get out of my way!"

She turned her back on him and walked off. There were not many people about and he followed her a few paces behind with his easy cat-like walk.

"Tell me one thing," he said, catching her up. "How did the accident happen? I was coming to see him about midday when I heard."

She strode out of the park but at the entrance stopped, breathing again like a bull, formidable for all her shortness, quite capable of knocking him down in the street.

"Who are you?"

"A friend. My name is Gene Vanbrugh."

"What is your business?"

"I was at the Little Jockey last night. This morning I had a certain business proposition to put to your husband, but I was too late."

"So you were too late! Well, I am sorry. But that's the end of it, isn't it."

"Not necessarily."

"Why not?"

"I might put the proposition to you, Mme Tolosa."

"Do I look or feel in a condition to listen to business propositions? Get out of my way."

"How did the accident happen? He was run over, wasn't he? What did the driver say?"

"Clear off or I will call the police. See, that one."

"Your husband perhaps took to many risks."

That stopped her. "What are you talking about?"

"Take a coffee with me and I'll tell you."

She hesitated, fingered an ear-ring, glanced up at him again, looked him over, taking in the lean slant of his jaw, the bony hands he kept thrusting in and out of his pockets, the old suit.

"How do you know I have English?"

"Most cabaret dancers do."

She looked behind her. "I do not want for coffee. But if you have something to say I will sit down."

He nodded, his mouth still tight, but with a gleam of approval in his eyes. "I've something to say."

They sat at a table part protected from draught by a glass screen. It was a chilly day. There were very few people about at this time of day, and a waiter, yawning, came and swept the table-top with a perfunctory cloth. Gene Vanbrugh ordered coffee for himself and a brandy for her.

She said: "Well?"

He looked at her. It might be she was easy-going most times, but once roused she was a fighter. He was a fighter himself and felt drawn towards her.

"How did the accident happen?"

"Accident nothing."

"Tell me."

"He had a phone call at nine this morning. I do not know who it was from, he did not tell me. But as he left the house he was run down by a waiting car. I saw it all because I went to the window to call after him. The car came from up the street, not very fast. You know. There was a lorry turning up the street blocking it to other cars, and the street was empty. It went on the pavement behind Juan. He turned at the last minute and tried to jump out of the way, but it caught him against a wall—crushed him. I . . . I saw his face. . . ."

There was silence. "I'm very sorry. . . . There was no chance of its being an accident?"

She thrust the tears off her face. "The police pretend to believe it was. But they are fools or liars."

"What happened to the car?"

"It was—damaged at the front. It turned quickly round and went off the way it had come."

"Did you see the driver?"

She shook her head. "Now what have you to say?"

He offered her a cigarette but she shook her head again, impatiently. He struck a match and lit his own cigarette.

She watched him suspiciously. He looked like a man who lived on his nerves, but his hands were steady with the match.

He said: "I was coming to see your husband because I think he had something to sell."

"I don't know what you are talking about." —

"Have the police searched his belongings?"

"No. I don't think so. I am not sure. You know. I have been so distracted since it happened. I came out, I had to come out, just to walk, to breathe, to think."

The waiter came with the brandy and the coffee, clacking the glasses and saucers. Gene stirred his glass, but she put out one of her small fat pointed hands and pushed hers contemptuously away.

The coffee was thick and sweet. He frowned as he sipped it. "Two weeks ago you and your company were in Paris. Right?"

"Well?"

"At Katalan's. I live in Paris."

"You saw us dance?"

"No. I have to tell you I don't go much for night-clubs as a normal thing. Maybe I've grown out of them—or through them—I don't know. But a friend of mine met Juan Tolosa. El Toro played a lot of poker, didn't he?"

"So?"

"They met in a poker game more than once. Your husband lost. Once he drank too much and got talkative. He dropped a hint of something he was going to do when he came to Athens. He mentioned a name. My friend knew I was interested in that name. When he saw me a week or so later he passed the information on. By then you'd left. I work in Paris, and it took me a couple of days to put my things in order. I got to Athens yesterday."

She picked up her glass now, frowned at it, contorting her flat lips, then abruptly she drank the brandy at a gulp.

"Give me the name of the man who killed Juan. That's all I want to know."

"I have no proof that would satisfy the police."

She said: "Tell me the name and I will not go to the police."

He studied her. "I believe you. But it wouldn't help. You'd only be putting your hand into the same snake's nest——"

He stopped. A pale shadow had fallen over the table. In the flood of Castilian that followed he could only pick out a word here and there. He got up.

"Join us. I was hoping you'd come."

Philip Tolosa said in English: "I have no wish to talk with reporters. Maria, come."

Gene said: "You play the harp superbly."

The Spaniard's sallow face was drawn and dirty, and there was cigarette ash and stains on his coat. He was a good lot taller than his brother, being about Gene's height. Maria got up and there was another sharp explosion in their own tongue. He had been looking for her everywhere, he said, couldn't think why she had gone out; she was explaining about this man. Tolosa looked at Gene, eyes cagey and bloodshot. He couldn't keep his fingers steady.

Vanbrugh said: "Are you sure you're going to get out of the country? Are you sure they'll let you go?"

The girl pushed her chair aside, nearly upsetting it. "What is this you are threatening us with?"

"I'm threatening you with nothing. Perhaps your brother-in-law knows what I mean."

"I know nothing except that we have no word to say to anyone. Come, Maria."

"This man tells me——"

"Come, Maria."

She shrugged and glanced again at Gene, hesitating between them.

"If you want me any time," Gene said, "I am at the Astoria. Ring me or call round."

There was nothing more he could do now and he watched them go, Philip Tolosa holding the girl's arm. After a few paces she jerked her arm free. But she did not look back.

Gene sat down again to finish his coffee. Then he took out a couple of notes and put them beside the printed bill.

546

4

As a clock was striking five Vanbrugh crossed Kolonaki Square and made his way up one of the avenues running off it towards the slopes of Lycabettus. This was a good neighbourhood, the houses individual and distinguished, some set back from the road with wrought-iron gates and balconies.

It was raining now, a fine drizzle falling like nylon across the city; but towards the sea, towards Piraeus, the grey day was illuminated with broken blue. He walked with the collar of his jacket turned up, hands in pockets, easy slouch, as if the iron pavements were not his natural home at all. He looked like a hobo or a trapper, and had never been either.

At the house where he called the half-coloured maid was new to him and seemed doubtful whether Mme Lindos would see him. He gave his name and waited at the door.

When he went in he was shown in to a small morning-room where a handsome old woman sat before an open fire fingering a book of photographs. There are certain architectures of forehead and nose and cheek-bone which defy the erosions of age. She had them.

He kissed her hand and then her cheek, while her gentle sophisticated gaze went slowly over him, noting that he had lost weight and carried like a monogram his familiar air of strain.

"So. We cannot keep you away, Gene. Have you no home?"

He smiled. "No home. Are you well?"

"When one is as old as I am one is modestly grateful for being alive at all. Let me see, have you ever met M. Vyro?"

Gene turned to the short elderly man with the grey imperial who had been standing by the window.

"M. Vyro is the proprietor of *Aegis*, one of our oldest morning papers——"

"And one of the most distinguished," said Gene.

M. Vyro bowed. "That is too kind. You are English, sir, or American?"

"American."

"Am I up to date with your occupation, Gene?" Mme Lindos asked. "The last time you wrote you were——"

"Yes, still in publishing."

"——M. Vanbrugh is European representative of Muirhead and Lewis, the New York publishers."

"Then we should have much in common," said M. Vyro. "You are here on business?"

"Partly, yes. We have two Greek authors on our list, Michaelis and Paleocastra——"

"Ah, Michaelis, the poet. Yes, yes. His is the true voice of Greece——"

"And partly I come to see old friends—among them Mme Lindos, who always knows so much about all the things I want to know."

"If that was ever true, Gene, it is far less true now. Fewer people come to see me."

"Except the most important ones," said Gene.

"Ah, only my oldest friends. I have known M. Vyro for nearly fifty years. What brings you at this particular time, Gene?"

"Your elections interest me. I wanted to ask you who is going to win this one?"

"There is an astrologer round the corner. My maid will give you an introduction to him."

Gene's face changed when he smiled—the narrowness, thinness, tightness eased and broke up. Lines crinkled across it in a peculiar and original way. "Maybe M. Vyro will hazard a guess. I imagine *Aegis* will support the Government?"

"Yes—but tending to move right of the Government. It is not a tendency I approve, but two years ago I handed over direction of the paper to my eldest son. He must go his own way."

"What of this grouping of all the opposition parties against Karamanlis?" Gene said. "And this new party of the centre, EMO, led by George Lascou?"

"I see you are up to date in some things," Mme Lindos said dryly.

"What sort of a man is Lascou?"

The question was addressed generally, but for a minute neither answered. The question appeared to have been dropped into an empty room. Then Vyro said:

"Intelligent, cultured. His money makes him influential. But I doubt personally if he's dynamic enough for a popular leader. There's something of the dilettante about him."

"You'll stay to tea, Angelos?" Mme Lindos said.

"No, thank you, I must go. You will be here some time, M. Vanbrugh?"

"A week or so. I haven't decided."

"Next week—a week today—is the fiftieth anniversary of the founding of my paper. I am proud to have begun it in a back street of the town when I was twenty-three. Next week we are celebrating the anniversary by setting in motion two new printing presses. I came to see Mme Lindos today about the reception which she is holding here first. It would be very fitting—and a pleasure to us—if you could come, having regard to your profession."

"I shall be glad to. Thank you."

"My very oldest surviving friend," said Mme Lindos when Vyro had left. "My husband's friend too. A man of such integrity. His sons are poor copies."

"Talk Greek to me, will you, Sophia?" Gene said. "One gets out of practice."

"Are you likely to need practice?"

"Sometimes it's convenient."

Mme Lindos got up. Arthritis made her moving ungainly, but once up she was as erect as he was. "You must come into the drawing-room for tea, and then I want to know what you are here for."

"I believe you don't trust me."

"Not very far."

549

The maid came in and opened double doors into a very large airy drawing-room. The old crimson wallpaper had faded rectangles on it of varying shapes and sizes. One handsome mirror still hung over the Louis Seize fireplace. Tea was set on a small table, a fine tea-pot in a silver cradle, cups as thin as egg-shells, spoons with the Lindos crest.

She said: "And do you really love your publishing now?"

"It enables me to live in Paris."

"It's the longest you have ever stayed anywhere, isn't it? Always before you have been wandering, restless—homeless, perhaps? It's the faculty of your type. You moved too much, saw too much when you were young."

"I still get around, but on my job—to Germany, England, Italy . . ."

"And sometimes to Greece. Does anybody here know you have come?"

"Who is there to know or care? Tell me, Sophia, what do you know about a woman called Anya Stonaris?"

"George Lascou's mistress?"

Gene stirred his tea. "Is that what she is?"

"You have met her?"

"What's her history?"

"I know very little. She is still very young but they have been together a long time. She gets photographed often because she is beautiful and smart. A hard brilliant person, and a thoroughly bad influence on him, I'm told. He of course has a wife and two children, and he poses to the electorate as a family man. But most people in Athens know of the connection."

Gene said: "I've heard of Lascou for a good many years, but until he entered politics I wasn't interested in him."

"And now?"

Their voices, though not raised, had been echoing in the sparsely furnished room. The maid came in with hot buttered toast, and the conversation lapsed till she left them.

Gene said: "One gets different opinions. Some say he'll soon be the most powerful figure in Greece."

While they talked the clouds had broken, and the room

brightened and darkened as the sun intermittently came through. The Venetian blinds had not been lowered, and Mme Lindos looked at her visitor whose face was lit with a reflection from the mirror on the wall. She thought again how young he looked in spite of his hollow cheeks: his was the youth which sometimes comes to people with singleness of mind. She remembered her first meeting with him twelve years ago, in the middle of the civil war; he had appeared on her doorstep in rags speaking Greek then with an accent she had thought Anatolian, had warned her to go into the cellar and stay there: the fighting was coming up this street. Sten gun under arm he had said this apologetically, like someone calling about the gas, and then, as it seemed summing her up in a glance, had asked her if she could care for a woman who was dying and needed attention and water. After that she had not seen him for nearly two weeks, when, during the worst famines and the worst massacres, he had come suddenly again with a few tins of food he had stolen from somewhere and left them in her hall.

Gene said: "Things are still bad here?"

"You do not need to listen to the politicians to discover the problems of Greece, Gene. Under the surface prosperity we have a food shortage, except for the rich, and the old, old bogy of inflation—and unemployment, or under-employment, everywhere. Many of our people—perhaps two million, perhaps more than a quarter of us all—have to live on less than two thousand drachmae a year. What is that in your currency? Seventy dollars? That is what we have to face and have to cure."

Silence fell for a while. "How do you plan to spend your time here?" she asked.

"I have to see Michael Michaelis. And I shall wander round meeting some old friends."

"Go carefully. Don't get into trouble like last time."

"I was of use."

Her grey worldly-wise eyes flickered up to him for a moment. "I *know* you were of use. I know that, Gene. But you made enemies in high places as well as friends."

551

"It's an occupational risk."

"That's just what it's not. If you are here on publishing business I'm sure no one will interfere with you. But if you start dabbling in our politics again . . . Besides, it is perhaps not altogether a pretty scene but it could be worse."

"Do you have friends who know Anya Stonaris?"

She made a gesture disavowing responsibility. " . . . I have some."

"I want to meet her. Could it be arranged in some casual way?"

"I suppose it is human nature that if you tell a man a woman is bad it makes him more eager to meet her."

He said: "I've met a lot of so-called bad women. They bore me to death. This one probably will. But I've other reasons for wanting to get to know her."

"Well, make no mistake. She is George Lascou's woman without question."

"That too," said Gene, "is something I'll be interested to discover for myself."

5

The day ended well. Towards evening the last of the clouds split and a vivid sun fell on the scene like an arc light on a film set. The temples clustering at the foot of the Acropolis were like things drawn out of themselves by a stereoscope, and above them the great Parthenon stood crowned against the sky in four-dimensioned light.

Below it the modern city pullulated, a city of no visible connection except that of locality with the marble ruins of Cimon and Pericles, a city separated from the Hellenic age by two thousand years of neglect and non-inhabitation, a mushroom town grown in a hundred years from 5000 people to 1,250,000, spawning, sprawling, raucous and decentralised over all the great plain, ringed by mountains and stretching to the sea. Handsome boulevards and nineteenth century squares stood between the escarpments of the Acropolis and the Lycabettus; and around this central conglomerate a thousand featureless streets segmented to a German design stretched away until they deteriorated into rows of drab concrete boxes on the fringe of the plain.

It was in this sudden brilliance that Gene Vanbrugh walked back to his hotel. The Astoria in spite of its name was small and in a dark side street and rated B class. Gene had known the proprietor for years. As he entered the proprietor's wife said in an undertone: "Oh, M. Vanbrugh, there is someone waiting for you upstairs."

"Name?"

"She wouldn't give a name. But she said you had asked her to call."

"Where is she?"

"In the writing-room."

Gene took his key and turned away.

"And M. Vanbrugh, Paul told me to tell you . . ."

"Yes?"

The woman glanced round. "The police came while you were out, checking over our register. They said it was a routine call . . ."

"Yes?"

"But they asked for a description of foreign visitors. You are the only one. It is unusual for them to come like this. Paul said you should know."

"Thank you. How long have they been gone?"

"About an hour."

Thoughtfully Gene went up the stairs and into the writing-room. After the brightness outside there was nothing at first in the semi-darkness but dusty rexine furniture and the smell of mildew and moths. Then a foot scraped on the bare floor and a voice said in English:

"I have come to call on you, M. Vanbrugh."

"I'm glad you've been so prompt." He went to the window.

"Leave the shutters for just the present."

He could see her now, braceleted, head-scarved, sitting at the table in the centre of the room, her hand moving among the tattered dog-eared magazines like someone reading braille. "Well?"

"You have here the name of the man who killed my husband?"

"I didn't say that. I think I know the name of the man who drove the car."

"Tell me that."

Gene said: "What's the good of trying to revenge yourself on a paid nobody? I'm interested in the man your husband was interested in. Do you know who that was?"

She got up. "Gene Vanbrugh—is that your name?—let me tell you that today I am not a happy woman. I loved Juan. Does that mean anything to you? Yesterday I was—in amity, do you say?—a married woman, a successful dancer, known all over Europe, happy. You know. Today I am a widow. In losing Juan everything is lost. Tonight I have no wish whether I live or die. It is so or it is so—well, who cares? For only one thing do I want to live—d'you understand?"

"Yes, I understand. But there are more ways——"

"Wait. You have understood that. Now understand this. You came upon me this morning saying you know much of this affair, *knowing* much, and saying you have the name of the murderer. What am I to think? Either you tell me that name or perhaps you are the murderer yourself."

In the narrow street outside, some children were playing, and their shrill excited voices echoed in the room.

Gene said: "Juan Tolosa must have known what he was doing. You're his wife. Why don't you?

"Well, I do not."

"Perhaps you know what he had to sell."

She hesitated. "He did not have it here. Was he such a fool? He left it safe in Spain."

He took out a cigarette and offered the packet to her. She shook her black-maned head and watched him break a match head and carry the flame to his own cigarette.

He said: "Does Philip Tolosa know you have come here tonight?"

"No."

"He didn't want you to have any contact with me."

"He thought you were a reporter."

"Perhaps he knows more than you do."

"Perhaps."

One of the children outside had hurt himself and was crying. Maria went across and wrenched open a shutter. Sunlight came in like a rich visitor slumming, falling on dusty leather and unfamiliar floor.

She said: "I will go, since you have nothing to tell me."

He said: "The man driving the car was probably a silversmith called Mandraki. There are only one or two such in Athens, since in the main Greeks like to fight their own battles. But he was there at the Little Jockey last night with a younger man I didn't know. He is not the night-club type. I thought it strange at the time."

"So?"

"But he's just a hired man, a go-between. Can you remember what sort of contacts your husband has had since you came?"

"He was out a lot."

"And Philip Tolosa?"

"Philip knows *nothing*. I have asked him."

"You say this thing you were trying to sell is still in Spain?"

She turned, hands thrust deep into the pockets of her scarlet mackintosh. "Juan was not born yesterday. What was the name you heard in Paris?"

"Avra."

She shook her head. "It means nothing. Who is he?"

"A man I have met. . . . What are you going to do now?"

She said: "I don't know how it is that you are interested in this. Even if you are—what is the word?—level, what have you to gain?"

"It's a personal matter. But I want to help you. Shall you stay in Greece for some time?"

"I—don't know. The funeral is tomorrow. It will depend on Philip and the others. You know. Soon I shall go back to Spain."

"It would be better."

"Why?"

Gene put out his cigarette, screwing it slowly round. "I've already told you, Señora Tolosa, I think you may be in considerable danger yourself—and your brother-in-law."

"Ha!"

"If one accident can happen, another may do. Tell me, is it letters you have in Spain? Or a diary? Or photographs? What will you do with them when you get home—burn them?"

"Why should I trust you? You may be for the people who killed Juan."

"I don't think you believe that or you wouldn't have come here."

She stared at him, her face like a rock. "No, I don't think I believe that."

"Will you trust me?"

"I can't do that."

"Then will you come and see me again tomorrow? I think I can help you more than anyone else."

"There is only one thing I want, and that is the life of the man who killed Juan."

"First you have to be sure of his identity."

She said: "This man Mal—Mandraki should know."

"I doubt it. One like that only knows the next step above him."

She was silent, but even her silences were combative. The more he saw of her the more formidable he realised she was. She was hardwood: hammer a nail into her and the nail would bend.

As she went to the door he said: "You haven't told me what you came to tell me, have you?"

"I came to tell you nothing. I came to ask you what you don't know."

"If you want my help during the next few days, don't

come here again. Go to the first newspaper kiosk in Constitution Square, in the north-east corner. Ask for Papa André. He will tell you where I am staying."

That appealed to her, not because she was a romantic and welcomed conspiracy but because it somehow convinced her that he was not on safe ground himself.

"Philip will wonder where I am."

"Don't trust him too far."

"Why do you say that?"

"A hunch."

After a moment she said: "I can trust only myself."

It was still daylight when she left. Through the blinds in his bedroom he watched her go off down the street. So far as he could tell nobody followed her.

He packed his grip and when dusk fell, paid his bill and left the hotel. He turned due south and was soon in the huddle of mean streets and tumbledown houses which mark the old Turkish quarter at the foot of the Acropolis. Unerring as a dog making for a buried bone, he pushed his way through the lanes of antique dealers, shoemakers, junk sellers, food stalls and second-hand clothes merchants; as the lights came on all this bazaar district was coming to life, people thronged, chattering, arguing, fingering the goods, elbowing each other out of the way. He got through the busiest part and turned into a narrow unpaved way with a gutter down the middle and wooden balconies nodding overhead. At the end of it he stopped and rapped at a door.

Somewhere near, hens were cackling sleepily. He knocked again. While he waited the floodlights were switched on for the Parthenon, and the great temple suddenly stood out like a prophecy above the noisy city.

A light came on and the door was opened by a middle-aged dark-skinned woman who frowned at him and pushed back her lank hair with nails as black-rimmed as a mourning envelope.

"You have accommodation?" he asked in Greek.

The woman made no reply but stepped aside to allow him in.

6

The next morning Gene telephoned Mme Lindos.

"I've changed my address, Sophia. The Astoria couldn't keep me. My present place isn't on the phone, but I'll put a call through to you from time to time in case you are able to do anything in that matter we were talking about yesterday."

She said: "You are not in trouble already?"

"No, no, of course not."

"Angelos Vyro rang this morning. He seemed very taken with you and wanted me to be sure to confirm his invitation to you to the fiftieth anniversary of his paper next Tuesday."

"That's very kind of him. I hope I shall still be here."

Mme Lindos said: "I'm glad you have rung because by chance I have been able to arrange that meeting you desired."

"*Already?* But that's a miracle."

"No, just good fortune. Do you know the Comte de Trieste?"

"An Italian?"

"No. A Corfiote. Certain of the old families there cling to the Italian titles conferred on them long ago. He is taking a party to the gala performance of *Electra* tomorrow evening. Mlle Stonaris will be one of the party."

"And? . . ."

"You also will be one of the party."

"But dear Sophia, how have you fixed it?"

"De Trieste was once under an obligation to my husband. And one of his party is sick. You will go to his house at seven-thirty. He knows all that it is necessary to know."

"It is exactly what I wanted. Tell me one thing—is George Lascou to be one of the party?"

"No. It is a formal occasion. The King and Queen will be

there. George Lascou will take his wife and sit with certain other members of the party."

"I can't thank you enough."

"Let me warn you that this may be no occasion for thanks. Promise me you will go carefully."

"I'll go carefully," said Gene.

7

I'll go carefully, he thought, until he saw her again. He noticed first her bare arm and hand as she put her glass down, and wondered in a detached way why he instantly knew it was hers. Something in the colour of the skin. Then he followed his host and saw again the eyes he had seen before, the lips like painted petals, the elegant fastidious nose. The diamonds round her throat weren't worth more than ten thousand pounds.

The Comte de Trieste said, speaking English for his benefit: "Allow me to introduce M. Vanbrugh to you. Mlle Stonaris. M. Taksim. General Telechos. Mr. Vanbrugh is visiting us from Paris."

M. Taksim was a cotton millionaire from Istanbul, big and middle-aged and fair. General Telechos was older with a face pitted like a map of the moon. Gene remembered he had served under Metaxas.

Telechos said: "This is your first visit to Athens, sir?"

"No, I've been here before," said Gene, using more accent than normal, "but it's all quite a while ago, shortly after the war."

"Ah, yes, you would be here like many of your countrymen. Helping us to our feet again. Rehabilitate. is it; your American Mission. You like Athens, then, to return?"

"The air suits me. It has a kind of harsh clarity. There are no illusions in Greece, are there?" He turned to the girl. "Are there, mademoiselle?"

Her expression as she looked across the room was polite but uninterested. "I should have thought many."

"Maybe a foreigner is entitled to sentimentalise."

"It's a common mistake."

"But excusable?"

"If you're looking for excuses." She opened her bag. He said: "Please smoke one of mine."

"Thank you, no. I don't very much like the tobacco from Virginia."

"Or the people either?"

"Are you from Virginia?"

"Quite near—as those kind of distances go."

"Then it would be polite to say only the tobacco."

"But not polite after that question."

She looked at him then with her great dark eyes before lowering them to fit her cigarette into its amber holder. After a few moments, as she was about to move off, he spoke to her again.

"We've met somewhere before, surely?"

"I don't think so. What was your name?"

"Vanbrugh."

"Oh. No. Have you been in Athens long?"

"This time a few days only. It's quite something to be back again."

"Quite something," said M. Taksim. "Quite something? Is that English? It's also many years since I am in London."

"They don't say that in London," said Anya Stonaris. "It is what they say in Virginia."

"We grow phrases with the tobacco," said Gene. "Rotation crop."

"I am afraid," said the Turk, "this is an argot, is it not? I was in London three years and it is there also. The Cockerney. Very difficult."

"You understand the language well," Gene told the girl.

"I learned it in a hard school. Maurice, don't you think——"

"What school was that?"

"For a year I helped at a canteen, after the liberation."

560

"You must have been very young."

"Well," she said, "not old enough to know better."

The party was getting ready to move off. There were ten of them—all the women superbly dressed. Gene might have felt conspicuous in his hired suit if it had been his nature to care. He had heard of one or two of the others before: a Yugo-Slav ballerina called Gallanova; a French marquis visiting the city; a Greek tobacco king.

Gene found himself sharing a car with Anya and the Turk and the wife of the tobacco king. While he was making casual conversation with the girl, while he was taking in everything about her, her cool challenging indifference towards him, he was also listening to the conversation in Greek between the other two in the car.

"If the Government had resigned in a normal way without attempting to change its colours . . ."

"But why did Karamanlis dissolve the Greek Rally? It is playing into the hands of the extremists."

"Or the new Centre. EMO prospers. Ask Anya."

"Some say the Army is restive. General Telechos no doubt could say if he would."

"Is he back in favour?"

"Oh, very much so. Anya, Telechos is very much in favour with the Army again, isn't he? It is spoken of everywhere."

"My dear Maurice, I only know he is very much in favour with me, because he sent me orchids yesterday."

The Turk laughed. "Your innocence deceives no one. What does George think of it all?"

"You'd be shocked to know how little he confides in me."

They were approaching the theatre. As they drew into the queue of cars waiting to give off their occupants, they could see the crowds of sightseers at the entrance to the theatre.

Taksim said to Gene: "I think, monsieur, you will be bored tonight. A Greek tragedy, in the language of Greece—could anything be duller for you?"

"I've a kind of family interest in it," he said. "My grandmother's name was Electra."

Anya glanced at him then. "Was she Greek?"

"Yes. Electra Theroudakis. She went to the States when she was twenty-two."

"And never came back?"

"No."

"What a calamity."

They drew up at the door of the theatre. "Perhaps you speak Greek, then?"

He shrugged deprecatingly. "Just a smattering."

They went in. The Comte de Trieste had followed his briefing admirably, and Gene found himself between Mlle Stonaris and Mrs. Tobacco King. They were in the eighth row of the stalls and the theatre was blooming with the flower of Athenian society. Programmes fluttered, arms and shoulders gleamed, jewels and orders winked. There was a hum like bees on a lazy afternoon. Most of the ex-Government and the diplomatic corps was there. He saw the girl glint a smile across at one of the boxes, where a dark very pale man sat beside a plump woman whose attention just then was on the two young children behind her. George Lascou in his role of family man and representative of the people.

Then everyone stood and the National Anthem was played as Royalty came into the opposite box. After it was over there was some applause before the audience rippled back into its seats and the lights were lowered for the play to begin.

In the first entr'acte Gene said to the girl: "She's a fine actress but I've seen others I've liked better. For one thing, she's too old for the part."

"Electra has to be at least fifteen years older than Orestes. Would you prefer Marilyn Monroe?"

At least he'd got his reaction. "Have you been to the scene of the crime?"

"Mycenae? Of course."

"The most impressive thing in all Greece."

"After Delphi."

"I've not been there. But I shall be going next week. You know of Michael Michaelis."

"Who doesn't?"

"My firm publishes him in America. He lives near Delphi, and I have to see him there."

"I envy you the experience."

"You're interested in archaeology, aren't you?"

They moved through the crowd of people. "Who told you that?"

"There was a paragraph in the paper a couple of days ago."

"I know nothing whatever about archaeology; but through a friend I'm able to take an interest in some diggings at Sounion. That was what you read of?"

"Yes."

"In a *Greek* newspaper?"

"Well, I guess I can pick out the words if I go slow."

"I guess you can follow everything that's been said on the stage tonight."

"Tell me, do you know everyone in this foyer?"

"No. They're always changing the door-keeper."

A brief smile broke across his deeply preoccupied face. "Who is the man talking over there?"

"The Mayor of Athens. He is leading a party at the election. Were you in the Army during the war?"

"Kind of. You would be too young to remember it."

"I was nine when the Germans invaded us. I have the most vivid recollections of it all."

"You were in Athens right through?"

"Yes. Where did your grandmother come from?"

"Kifissia."

"She was rich?"

"No. Nor was my grandfather when he came over here and met her and married her."

"Could she have been happy in America?"

"It's not impossible, you know."

"I suppose not quite."

"Anyway, she left me a legacy."

"A legacy?"

"Not of money but of blood. Who is that going up the steps now?"

"George Lascou. He leads the EMO party at the election."

"Anyone here who isn't leading a party?"

"Personalities count in Greece. Perhaps you don't understand our politics."

"I'm always glad to learn."

"It is time we were going back."

At the second entr'acte she said: "Thank you, no, I'll sit here."

"Then I'll stay too—if I'm not in your light."

General Telechos on the other side had not gone out either, and for a while he took her attention. It left Gene free to watch her quietly and to collect his thoughts. She was as hard as nails, he could see that. Her brain was as sharp and as cutting as the diamonds round her beautiful throat. And it *was* beautiful. She might be a *femme fatale* but at least if you were fool enough not to care about the danger it would come awfully easy being one of her fatalities. Her eyes weren't black, they were brown but made darker by their lashes, they had a sort of fronded brilliance which was quite devastating.

As he thought this she turned her head suddenly and met his look. They stared at each other then for several seconds.

She said: "Why are you looking at me like that?"

"I remember where I've seen you before."

"That must be very gratifying for you."

"At the Little Jockey on Monday."

"You were there?"

"I was there."

"Now I remember you. You were sitting two tables away from us. Do you like cheap night-club women?"

"They're terrific."

Her eyes didn't move for a second longer, they seemed to deepen with an expression they did not or could not hold,

564

then a flicker of the lashes and they had moved beyond him.

But it was as if they had looked at each other just too long. Some inner content of the look—though it was over—superimposed itself on what they were saying.

"Well, if you do not like cheap night-club women, why do you sit with them?"

"You know how it is when a man goes to a place like that alone—all the girls run away."

"Then why go alone?"

"To see the show."

"You are interested in dancing?"

"I'm interested in dancers. Did you know that the Spaniard, Juan Tolosa, was killed in an accident the following day?"

"I read it in the papers."

The others were coming back. General Telechos spoke to Anya again. George Lascou was re-entering his box. He stared down at the stalls before he took his seat. Gene stood up to let some of the party past. The whole glittering company was moving and murmuring about them.

He said: "Does it strike you—being Greek—as much as it does an outsider, that the first night of this play—first day of this play—when it was first performed two and a half thousand years ago, was on a site probably not a mile from where we're sitting? Or is it left for the foreigner to get sentimental and excited about it for the wrong reasons?—as you implied when we first met."

"Some Greeks think about it."

"It's hard to imagine what that first performance ever would be like—probably connected with some Dionysian festival—people squatting round with their baskets, seeing it on a dais against a plain backcloth. The author would be here, even though he was getting up in years; but what would his critical audience be? Euripides probably, come to see this new work by his great rival. Aristophanes too? Socrates would be here. Pericles, maybe, if he could spare the time from questions of high policy. No, I think Pericles would just have died by then. Plato may have been brought by his mother and father. And Democritus, who first put forward the atomic theory. . . . And that at a time when my ancestors—or most of them—were crouching over smoky fires in damp northern caves."

She looked at him. "We have gone down the hill ourselves since then."

"I shouldn't let that depress you."

"It doesn't. Go on."

He said:"My speculations haven't run any further. Except to wonder if you'll lunch with me one day this week?"

Her expression suggested she'd had fifty such invitations before, all put in just that way.

"Thank you, but I think I shall be busy at present. How long will you be staying in Athens?"

"Not as long as that."

She opened her programme again. "Tomorrow afternoon I shall be driving to Sounion. If you have not seen it . . ."

"I have not seen it."

"Then perhaps you would care to come." It was a statement, not a question.

"Thank you. I'd very much care to come."

8

She was in bed when the phone rang.

"Anya?" Lascou said.

"Yes, darling. Did you enjoy the performance?"

"Good enough in its way. The evening was a social success."

She said: "Did you get to talk to him?"

"To them both for three or four minutes. It was a good *occasion*, before the fight begins. And you?"

"The usual crowd, as you saw. I think Solaris stole the play."

"Otho told me you rang me about twenty minutes ago."

"Yes. You weren't back. I have a little news that may entertain you."

"Oh?"

"Oh, I mustn't forget. General Telechos paid you one or two agreeable compliments. I think he is ready to make a deal."

Lascou listened to the compliments. "Good. And your news?"

"Did you see the man sitting beside me?"

"On your other side? Yes. I didn't know him."

"Klaus was ill, Leon de Trieste invited this man in his place. An American called Vanbrugh."

"Ah. . . ."

"Did you say something?"

"Just ah."

"That's what I thought you said. A coincidence after your telling me about him the other day."

"If it was a coincidence."

"I was wondering; but I should think so . . . I asked Leon about him afterwards and he said he met him first some years ago."

"What is he like?"

"So-so. More grown up than one expects. You haven't told me exactly what you've got against him."

"I tried to."

"Oh, pooh, some fracas in Piraeus five years ago. That's an old wives' tale."

"Not altogether."

"But you were not involved in some fracas in Piraeus five years ago."

"Of course not. He's really nothing to me. As you gather, I never saw him until tonight."

"But you are interested in him."

"So are the police."

"What do they want him for?"

"Some irregularity over his passport, I expect."

567

She laughed gently. "Couldn't we be more original than that?"

"No, seriously. . . . He's a trouble-maker and always will be. To get rid of him is a simple insurance at a time like this."

"Well, if you won't tell me you won't. Perhaps I shall discover for myself tomorrow."

"You're seeing him again? It might be of use."

"That's why I made the arrangement."

"Find out where he is staying, for one thing."

"Apparently he's a publisher or represents a publisher. Did you know that? He also speaks Greek and reads Greek; I'm not sure how well. He has lived in Paris for the last three years. His firm publishes Michael Michaelis. He knows quite a lot of people here; but he doesn't seem anxious to be recognised. Two or three times in the foyer tonight he changed his direction to avoid people, including his own ambassador."

"It shows he's up to no good."

"Even that doesn't make him attractive."

"Go on."

"By the way, did you know the chief dancer at the Little Jockey had been killed in a street accident?"

"No. One of those you saw?"

"The chief male dancer. I wonder why this Gene Vanbrugh was at the club the same night as I was."

"When was the fellow killed?"

"The following day."

"Find out as much as possible when you meet Vanbrugh."

"I'll listen carefully to everything he has to say."

"And of course," added Lascou, "he will say so much more to you."

9

They met as arranged outside the King George at three. There was still no great heat although the sun was brilliant. It fell on a square strangely silent after the abounding life of two hours ago.

She was sitting in a grey Silver Phantom Rolls. A chauffeur was standing beside the car, but when Gene came up he stepped respectfully back and opened the door. As Gene got in she looked at him thoughtfully but did not smile. She'd done her hair in a different way and was wearing Chinese jade ear-rings and a frock of grey jersey.

He said: "You should have warned me."

"What of?"

"If I'd known we were travelling the hard way I'd have put on battle dress."

She lifted a half-ironical eyebrow and started the engine. The chauffeur stood back and saluted as the car turned off into Venizelou Street. It was not until they had gone some way that Gene spoke again.

"You must be very rich."

"Why don't you talk Greek?"

"You must be very rich," he said in Greek.

"Scarcely any accent. It is as if——"

"As if I came from one of the neighbouring νομοι. Never from the one I'm in."

"How do you speak so well? You have relatives still here?"

"Nobody here."

"You are staying with friends in Athens?"

"No, I have rooms."

She waited but he said no more. They left the suburbs of Athens and skirted the barren eminences of Hymettus, travelling fast through olive groves and vineyards. Once they were out of the town there was practically no traffic except for the occasional farm cart piled high and drawn by donkey or mule moving ponderously on businesses known only to the black-dressed, black-scarved peasant woman between the shafts. An occasional village street saw them by, inevitable café, inevitable yellow mongrels, tiny Byzantine church, eucalyptus trees, tattered buildings, black-clad idlers staring.

He said: "Tell me about these excavations."

"You will see them for yourself."

"The paper said you were closely superintending the work."

"That's because it was a paper which favours the people I am friendly with. I act in this for my friend, who is too busy to come down."

"Tell me what you have found."

She said: "Tell me why you went to the Little Jockey on Monday."

He stared out at the road with his grave, craggy, withdrawn face. "Why not?"

"Why did you say at the play that Juan Tolosa had been killed in an accident the following day?—putting on an emphasis as if you didn't believe it was any such thing."

"Did I? No. . . . But it's a little strange, isn't it, that the car which killed him was badly damaged but hasn't yet been found."

"Who told you that?"

"I went along to the police inquiry this morning."

"It was interesting?"

"His widow said the car mounted the side-walk and deliberately crushed him against a house."

"She must have been hysterical."

"Quite hysterical."

She glanced at him. "You don't think so?"

"The police did. That's all that matters, isn't it?"

As they came near Lavrion the green fields and vineyards gave place to old mine machinery, grey heaps of slag and rusty iron derricks. Then they were through the area of the silver mines and the brilliant sun lit up the low cliffs and ultramarine sea of Cape Sounion, with the white temple of

Poseidon like a tall nun brooding on a hill. The girl drove up to the Acropolis and stopped the engine. They got out.

He said: "When I was a student we used to come here at the week-ends to bathe."

"You said last night you had not been before."

"I've not been before with you."

He stood by the car for a while looking about him, and she glanced once or twice at his face.

He said: "Fruitful study of aesthetics as well as of ancient history."

"Why?"

"Where does the impact come from? Thirteen pillars. Half a dozen rectangles of fluted marble with the sea as a drop curtain. If you analyse it, it's nothing."

She said: "A rag and a bone and a hank of hair."

He turned. "*Exactly*." Then his eyes focused on her. "Except that there's a physical as well as an aesthetic element in a woman's beauty."

She didn't seem put out by his stare. "What is physical?" she said. "Where does it become only emotional? And what is emotional? Where does it become only aesthetic? I don't think you can separate them."

"Well," he said, "let's say the difference with marble pillars is that there's no wish for personal possession."

A sea breeze was stirring her hair and she put up a hand to it. "Personal possession is always unwise. What you grasp you destroy. Taste your pleasures and let them go."

He said: "I'm glad you agree with tasting them."

"I'm glad you are glad."

After a few moments he said: "Where are your excavations?"

"Down there, down nearer the sea. Last year a great statue was found here, of a warrior. They think it is of the seventh century B.C. and they think there is more yet to be found. There was of course a temple here long before this one was built."

"Can we go down?"

"The siesta will not be over."

The promontory of Cape Colonna slopes down on its western side into a sandy bay, and they walked to it through pine trees where the ground was littered with the shells of hard-boiled eggs left behind by week-end picnickers. Near the sea just where rock and soil and sand met, there was the usual paraphernalia of archaeology: trenches, rubble, and beside it a disused 'tourist pavilion' in the shade of which a dozen Greek labourers crouched and slept.

"Here we began, you see, and here the statue was found. The head with its great helmet was broken from the body and the body was naked. But they fitted together. It couldn't have been broken naturally or they would not have been so far apart."

He said: "You must be rich to have financed these diggings."

"I didn't finance them—I told you. I have rich friends. It is the way we live in Greece."

An elderly man came forward, hastily fastening his tie, and was introduced to Gene. He and the girl talked for some time on the progress of the operations. They stayed about half an hour. When they were alone again Gene said: "Have you any of the things that have been found here?"

"The big things, like the statue, are in the National Museum, but I have a few of the smaller articles in my flat."

"I'd like to see them sometime."

They stopped, looking out to sea. The rocks showed copper and purple and green through the glass-clear water. A lip of white, inches wide, nibbled at the edge. Gene lingered on when she would have moved.

She said: "Is it true that you really have some affection for Greece?"

"Yes . . ."

"I mean true affection, not just empty sentiment."

"Yes . . . But I don't think I like your politicians."

"Do you like your own?"

"Maybe they're not the most admirable people in any country."

"Well, they are no worse here."

"This morning I was hearing about that man you pointed out to me last night. Lascou, was it? Someone I met this morning said that Lascou was the most dangerous man in Greece today."

She opened her green lizard hand-bag. "Have you a light, please? I haven't smoked this afternoon."

"A match. We'd have to get in the shelter of the trees. . ."

They walked across to the pines. He flicked a match alight and held it to her cigarette. When he got close to her—a few inches from her face, he thought, yes, there really is danger. Her skin at close quarters had a faint luminosity. Nonsense, of course; so one's senses played one false. A rag and a bone and a hank of hair. A rag and a bone. . . . It was her own estimate.

She said contemptuously: "When an election is due one man will say anything about another in the hope that it will win him a vote."

"And this is untrue?"

"You have told me nothing; how can I say what is true or untrue?"

"My friend, who is I think an intelligent man, said that there are plenty of hypocrites in the world who try to deceive others. George Lascou, he says, is that much more dangerous type, a hypocrite with visions of greatness who begins by deceiving himself."

She looked down at her cigarette. "Your friend no doubt is of an opposing party. Did he not also tell you I was George Lascou's mistress? You surely must know that too."

Four or five ragged boys had been staring at the car, hanging on the handles, feeling the polished wings; at the sound of footsteps they scattered and ran off down the cindery track.

Gene said: "I knew he was a man of infinite taste."

She opened the door of the car. "It is time we started back."

"Whenever you say."

She got in and flicked the steering wheel once or twice with her green velvet gloves while he shut the door and walked round and slid into the seat beside her. She started the engine and drove off the way they had come. Behind them the sun was getting lower and the delicate tapering pillars of the temple seemed to support the sky.

He said in Greek: "I owe you an apology."

"That must have needed a lot of hard reasoning on your part, Mr. Vanbrugh."

"I wonder if you could bring yourself to call me Gene?"

"I thought that it was a girl's name."

"Not the way I spell it."

They drove on.

She said: "Perhaps sometime you would be interested to meet this hypocrite, this shady politician."

"I'd be delighted."

"Write down your address. I can arrange it."

"Could I call you? I'm changing rooms and haven't yet decided where to stay."

"Well, where will you be tonight?"

"Out on my ear, I expect, if I don't get back. I promised to vacate my room by five, and have forgotten to pack my case."

She didn't press any more, and silence fell again. He thought; a rag and a bone, a rag and a bone; stick to that; hold on to it for dear life. Plenty of women before but only two like this and both brought shipwreck. How often does the sailor put to sea? Not now; for Pete's sake certainly not now, knowing who she is and already something of what she's like, and who her friends. You don't have to be an optimist, you have to be a lunatic to set sail when all the storm cones are hoisted.

She said: "What have Greek politics to do with you?"

"If I explained that it would take a time."

"I could listen."

"You can't avoid it, can you? Sharing a car with a bore is one of the worst things. There's no escape except the end of the journey."

"Well, you could try not to be boring."

After a minute he said: "It isn't all that easy to explain.

574

You asked me if I was fond of Greece. But it isn't really a question of liking or disliking the country; it's a question of having it in my *blood*. I told you last night, but I don't know if you understood."

"No, I don't think I did."

"When people are born in a place they normally accept it as part of their inheritance; they take it for granted; they're all of a piece. I'm sure you are—in that respect anyway. You're Greek, and Greece comes first and the rest nowhere."

"Maybe."

"I'm American. Many Americans are 'all of a piece'. But some are not. America's a young country—its roots go often into other people's soil. Mine do ... Make no mistake, America's my native country and I wouldn't change it for any other on earth. Just the smell of it the minute you get in takes and holds you like a new experience, however often you return. I enjoy going there. My family and my friends are there." He paused. "Do you mind if I stop talking Greek?"

"No. I don't mind."

"But when I'm in the States, however hard I try, I feel myself there as a *visitor*. I'm a soldier on leave, a commuter, a dog on a chain. And the stake the chain's attached to is right here in Athens. Maybe I'm some sort of a throw-back, who knows, it can't always work the other way. For every hundred Europeans who go to America, maybe three or four—of them or their children or their children's children—travel the other way. I never thought I'd be one."

"And are you?"

"I'm trying to explain. You asked me why I care about Greece and what is happening here. I'm trying to explain because I want you to know."

He glanced at her. She was listening with a vigorous intelligence that went much deeper than good looks. It might be hostile but it was not sham.

"But don't think I have any glamorised view of your country, Anya. In spite of its history and in spite of all the glitter of Athens that makes it look like a carbon copy of Manhattan, I know the other side all too well. I know it's badly governed, poverty-stricken, unenterprising; part East, part West with a dash of the Balkans shaken in to make it more difficult."

"You're too kind."

"But that may be one one reason why I can't get it out of my system. I want to do things about it, just as I would for a lame child that's always falling in the mud. I'm never as content as when I'm here, never as much at home, never as conscious of a *root*. I tell myself it's nonsense, this pre-occupation, a sort of blinkered self-hypnotism; I've got to stop it. At most I'm only one-quarter rooted here. My life's to do with the new world, not with the old. But it doesn't wash. I'm still the dog on the chain."

There was silence for a time. He said: "Maybe even that isn't quite the truth. One's got to be honest sometimes in one's life, and if I'm honest now I have to say I don't really *want* to change. I only tell myself I should. Deep down in my guts—or whatever intestinal part knows best—I *welcome* the chain."

She stubbed her cigarette in an ash-tray and frowned at the road ahead. "You have thought a lot about this?"

"Yes. I've thought a lot about it."

"And this explains why you are interested in the private lives of politicians?"

"It explains why I bother to come here at all."

They were getting nearer home. She said; "Are you married?"

"Not now."

"In America it is always 'yes, just' or 'not now'."

"And you?" he said quietly.

"No. I've told you."

"I didn't know it necessarily followed."

"In my case it does."

"Tell me more about it."

"There's nothing to tell."

After waiting a few seconds Gene said: "Talking of my

business, I shall be going to see Michael Michaelis on Sunday. Would you be interested to come?"

"Where—to Delphi?"

"Yes. I shall not be more than an hour with Michaelis and there'll be nothing private to discuss. I'd like to see the place afterwards in the company of a kindred spirit."

"What makes you think I'm a kindred spirit?"

"I think you could be."

She said: "You must have plucked that impression out of the air."

"I'm assuming only that the experience of visiting one of the great Greek monuments for the first time would be enlarged if it was shared with somebody who feels the way you do about it."

She took her attention off the road for rather longer than was safe to look at him with her great dark eyes.

"I shall be engaged on Sunday," she said.

"A pity. I can't change the day now."

10

After dropping Gene she did not drive to her flat but went straight on to Constitution Square and left the car to be picked up by the chauffeur. Then she walked across to George Lascou's flat, which was in the penthouse or seventh floor of Heracles House, a large block put up since the war by a Greek syndicate of which Lascou was the chairman.

As it happened his secretary saw Anya come into the building, so she was met at the door and brought at once into the huge salon, which was decorated and furnished in French style with fleur-de-lis wallpaper and handsome statuary set in rounded alcoves indirectly lit from below.

She found George saying good-bye to General Telechos. George looked moody and pale as if virtue had gone out of him, his black brilliantined hair veeing up at the temples rather untidily, though still showing the lines of the comb. Telechos breathed raki and garlic over her as he explained rather unnecessarily that he had called on business to do with the National Museum.

When Otho had shown the soldier out George took her face between his fingers like a goblet to be admired before it was drunk from. Then he kissed her with all the appreciation of a connoisseur.

"So?"

"Darling, I need a drink."

"Of course." He released her quietly and went to a side table. "A martini?"

She nodded and walked to the window, pulling off her gloves and looked out on the crowds below.

She said: "Receiving compliments from General Telechos is like being caressed by a steam shovel. Does he think I am quite ignorant of all the negotiations that are going on between you?"

"Telechos thinks women have no part in these things."

"Does it go well?"

"It goes well. But he has all the cunning of the slightly stupid man, and all the obstinacy."

"Is that why your hair is ruffled?"

"Is it?" He smoothed it down. "It dislikes opposition. And Vanbrugh?"

"I didn't discover his address."

George carefully measured out the gin, touching the lip of the bottle with a napkin so that it would not drip.

She said: "He asked to be put down at the corner of Hirodou Atticou. I don't know if he thought he was likely to be followed."

"Does he know of your connection with me?"

"I told him because I saw he knew." She took her glass and sipped. "Um. Good. . . . He said he would like to meet you."

"That might be worth while." Lascou guided her towards a chair, but at the last moment she slipped away from him

578

and went across to an almost life-size statue of Hermes, looked at it, her eyebrows contracted.

He said: "Are you seeing him again?"

"Who? Vanbrugh? I hope not. He is dull, if probably harmless."

"He may be the first, but his record doesn't suggest the second."

"His record?"

"Oh, I mean his history in a general sense. He's been in and out of trouble a good deal."

"Well, tell me."

"It's not important." George felt in his pocket and took out a typewritten card with a small photograph clipped to the corner. "This comes partly from Major Kolono's own police files and partly from a contact he has at the American Embassy. But it's incomplete yet."

Anya took the card and after staring at the photograph began to read aloud. "'Gene Vanbrugh. About thirty-five. Comes of old New York family but educated in Europe. At University of Athens when the Germans invaded Greece—fought against them. Probably was in British Intelligence for some years. In any event was in Athens, underground, until liberation.' Mm—mm." She went on reading to herself; after a moment she spoke again. "'Concerned in both civil wars against ELAS. In '47 badly wounded and invalided home. In States gave evidence to Senate Committee on Foreign Aid.'"

She paused to sip her drink and to turn the card over. "'Married in Washington but marriage broke up.' Yes, he told me that today. . . . Oh, this is what you were talking about. 'In Greece in '51 . . .'"

"Yes."

"'involved in death of Spyros Eliopolis, ship's chandler, of Piraeus. This hushed up.' Why was it hushed up? It doesn't say. Kolono ought to know."

"It didn't come under Kolono's department. Anyway, outside influences were at work. Vanbrugh has friends."

She turned back to the card and read in silence. Then:

579

" 'In trouble in U.S. in '53 ... cited for contempt of Congress for refusing to give information on Communists to the House Committee on un-American Activities.' I don't know what that means. I thought he was anti-Communist."

George put his arm round her shoulders. "I think it simply means, my sweet, that he is a man who prides himself on taking the unpopular line and because of that is always rather an embarrassment to his friends as well as to his enemies. If his own embassy knew he was here, which they probably don't unless Kolono has told them, they wouldn't be sorry to see him go."

She handed him back the card. "Tell me, why were you so angry when you knew Jon Manos had taken me to the Little Jockey last Monday?"

"I wasn't *angry*. . . . Did Vanbrugh mention it?"

"He mentioned the inquiry on the Spanish dancer's death. He had been to it this morning. The wife thought the accident wasn't an accident."

"Does that concern us?"

"You are the one who knows."

"Or Gene Vanbrugh."

"I didn't say so."

"How are the diggings?"

"We're between strata." She stared at the statue. "I don't think this Hermes is very good, George. His legs are too short for the length of his body. I distrust men with short thigh bones. . . ."

"I'm sorry you've had a boring afternoon."

She said: "Do you *want* me to see him again?"

He fitted his pince-nez. "Have you made any arrangement at all?"

"No. I said he might phone me."

"I hope he hasn't made an impresssion on you."

She had finished her drink and held the stem of the glass in both hands. He put his fingers on the nape of her neck under her hair and quietly stroked it. She said: "Of course he has made an impression on me. So does a headache. So does a pinching shoe. Otherwise one would be as dead as Hermes here. Why is sincerity always so tedious?"

He smiled. "It isn't. But it's a plant that needs careful treatment. You have to bring it out regularly and air it alongside other men's so that it doesn't become bigoted and ingrown."

There was the sound of running feet and a small boy of eight burst in.

"Papa, Nina has not been playing fair with me! She says if I—oh, Anya, Papa didn't tell me you were coming—Papa, Nina says——"

"He didn't know." Anya kissed the boy. "Where's Nina? What have you been playing?"

Michael explained to them both in a breathless voice.

Lascou said: " Fair play, Michael, like sincerity, is a matter of proportion. Anya and I were talking of it when you came in."

Michael stared at them with round black eyes, eyes very different in colour and shape from his father's.

"And you were quarrelling?"

George laughed. "No."

"Ah," said Michael.

"Well, what do you expect us to do, pursue Nina and beat her? Where is she, by the way?"

"Gone to find Mama. But I happen to know Mama's out."

Helen Lascou occupied a suite of rooms on the other side of the seventh floor; the children lived with her but unlike the adults trafficked freely between the two flats. Michael was pacified and went off chewing a piece of Turkish delight.

George said: "I find it difficult not to spoil him."

"Should you try?"

"Well, in some ways it's a disadvantage to be a million-aire's son."

"My heart bleeds for him."

"Oh, yes, you can use your tongue, but there *are* dis-advantages. Everyone treats Michael with consideration and respect—already. He'll grow up accustomed to it."

"So he should, a son of yours."

"Oh, no doubt. And that's good as far as it goes. But he'll never know what it is to be cold and hungry and in rags, to be disregarded, to be left to struggle, to know himself to be *nothing,* rubbish that could die off and no one would care." He paused. "It's unpleasant at the time, of course, but it develops the *will* to struggle as nothing else can. It becomes a load upon the ego, an obligation that must be discharged. . . ."

"An obligation to whom?"

He shrugged. "To oneself, I suppose. One goes through phases." He moved the ring on his finger as if it chafed him. "At first one wants to *belong,* one's greatest need is to be accepted as part of a larger part, a necessary unit within a community or an army or a party, a cog serving a greater end than oneself. Then, as one develops and succeeds, one's desire is for the opposite, for non-attachment again, for a withdrawal, away from and above the mass of people. It's a passing through, as it were—from the stage of being disregarded by the crowd to a stage when the crowd is disregarded."

She nodded but did not speak.

"Oh!" He swept the thought away with a hand. "It's not important. Except that no one who has not felt poverty, extreme poverty, can ever understand the inexpressible luxury of luxury. No one who has not grown up in a wind-swept, arid, treeless, soil-less village in the hills, sun-baked in summer, snow-smothered in winter—no one who has not had to apportion his last fifty drachmae between goat's cheese and maize bread and the corner of a draughty shed to lie in . . ."

She said: "You show so little, it might never have happened to you."

"I don't show it but I have it here." He touched his body. "It's what I was saying, it's the thing Michael will lack. I wouldn't be without it now. It's the dynamo powering everything—it's the source of self-control, caution, courage, perseverance, obstinacy—any creative efforts I may make;

582

it's the source of all the things I do to supply an inescapable need!"

She said quietly: "And will you ever satisfy it?"

"No. . . . But in a few weeks I may be nearer that end. Another drink?"

"No, Helen may be coming in."

"Little fear of that."

"I still must go. To tell the truth, George, the only time I'm ever embarrassed is when Nina or Michael come when I'm here "

"No need to be. They both like you."

"Perhaps soon they'll grow up."

"Nonsense. You're full of strange fancies today. It must be this naïve company you've been keeping."

They walked slowly towards the door. She said: "Has it occurred to you, though, that Helen has played fair with me over the children? It would have been easy to have turned them against me."

"I've never denied to you that she's an estimable woman."

"So many women contrive to be estimable without being kind."

"Darling, when is he phoning you again?"

"Who? Gene Vanbrugh?"

"Yes."

"Tomorrow morning."

"What will you say?"

"I shall say nothing. I shall be out."

"Don't do that. Invite him here."

11

When he rang her she said: "I'm sorry. The roads to Delphi are not good and it is 170 kilometres. Too far for one day—if you are to see your poet and also all that is there—and certainly I cannot spare two."

He said: "You were very kind yesterday."

"That's another of those illusions you suffer from."

"I thought you said you would like to meet Michaelis."

"On the whole I've decided it is better just to know him through his poems."

"Then when could I call and see you today?"

"I shall be out all day."

"With George Lascou?"

"Does it matter?"

"How could it?"

She passed the tip of her tongue over her lips. "My friend, if you would be advised by me, I think you would be a happier man if you confined you interests to your publishing."

"I've always found happiness rather an abstract thing to worry about."

She picked up her cigarette-case and opened it and took out a cigarette, but then she put it down without lighting it and snapped the case shut. On the back of the case were some words George had had engraved when he gave it to her. Ἐκ τοῦ ὁρᾶν γίγνεται τὸ ἐρᾶν.

"Hullo," he said.

"Hullo."

"I thought for a moment you had hung up."

"No."

"I would like to see you again."

"Perhaps sometime we can arrange it."

"There are some things I'd like to say to you."

"Well, I am listening."

"Don't be impossible, please."

Her Italian maid, Edda, came into the room with some red roses in a bowl and put them on the piano. She was going to say something but Anya nodded and dismissed her.

Gene said: "I shall be here probably for another week, and . . ."

"And there are some things you would like to say to me."

"As you remark."

She said: "You still want to meet George Lascou?"

584

There was a brief pause. "Yes, I do."

"Then come there tonight. He is giving a small dinner-party—eight or ten. I can arrange it."

"You can arrange it. . . ."

"Does that surprise you?"

"No. . . ."

"Then you will come?"

"Thank you. I'll come.'"

"At nine. Heracles House, the seventh floor."

"What will George Lascou say?"

"He'll do what I ask."

"I don't wonder."

"Then will you do what I ask?"

"What do you ask?"

"Stop sending me red roses."

"It's just a simple whim I have."

"If you wish to be a fool I cannot be responsible for that."

"Why should you be?"

"No. I should not be."

"Or why should you care?"

"I don't."

"Neither do I," he agreed.

When she had put back the receiver she got up from her chair and walked across to the window. Sunshine fell diagonally through it and warmed her arm and side. She turned away, frowning, and moved to the bookshelf, putting back two books she had taken out, went to the chair, picked up the daily newspaper. Edda was in the bathroom running her bath water. She lit a cigarette and stood for a few moments motionless with the cigarette case in her hand. George's inscription made a roughness under her thumb. *"From seeing comes loving."*

12

The Tower of the Winds, an octagonal building put up in the first century B.C. by Cyrrhestes, was losing its sharp outlines in the quick Athenian twilight when Gene came to it, walking like a mean-natured cat expecting trouble. He was about to make a cautious circuit of the place when a woman broke away from one of the ruined Doric pillars and came to him. A vivid scarf over her hair was like a badge of identity.

"Ah," he said, taking off his hat. "You're alone?"

"Yes. This morning I left the message."

"All this week I've been hoping you'd send word."

She said: "I saw you at the police inquiry. Also Philip tells me you have been trying twice to make his acquaintance."

"He wouldn't play."

"He thinks you are a reporter."

"I doubt if he ever did believe that."

Maria looked at him. "You suspect him of not being fair with me?"

"What have you came to tell me?"

"Something it may be very necessary to tell you if that is true."

"Will you come back to my lodgings?"

"No. It is safe here. I—I don't know how it is to begin." Her thick lips, made for laughter, were pouting and strained. "You know that Juan was trying to—make money?"

"Yes."

"I am not quite so ignorant of it as I pretended. You know. If a man and a woman are in love, as we were, they do not have complete secrets. But it is true that I do not know much. He said it is better that I did not know much. I do not know what Juan had to sell. But I know of the—arrangements. He was crazy to paint; he didn't wish for the life of a cabaret artist; he loved Spain and wished to settle in comfort in a small fishing village in Andalusia and spend the rest of his life there. You know. That was why he did this thing. I told him often in the last weeks, go carefully; it is better to work for one's living in honour than to go to prison for a dishonourable thing. But he would not listen. He would say, this is my one chance; if I miss this one chance I shall be dancing until I am old."

"So you came to Greece?"

Maria Tolosa untied the knot of her scarf and pulled it off. Then she shook out her hair, scowling at the sculptured reliefs below the cornice of the tower, which were becoming harder to distinguish against the whitening evening sky. "He had made arrangements. These papers he had deposited in the Banca d'Espagna in Madrid. In the bank he has a cousin. Juan was to ask from this person in Greece that a large sum of money shall be paid into his account in Madrid. As soon as that was paid in, his cousin had agreed to send these documents to him here."

"Your husband was expecting the other side to trust him?"

"I don't know. It is that he may have had some surety which he could give them. You know. I told him; I warned him; I said, you are playing a risk."

"Was Philip Tolosa in this?"

"He knows the attempt to get this money is to be made. He does not know who is the man or what it is that Juan has to sell."

"Has something else happened now?"

"Yes."

Her bracelets jangled as she sat down on a piece of fallen masonry, and after a minute he squatted beside her. The noise and glitter of the city was not far away but seemed as remote as the sea on a frosty day.

"On Wednesday I have talked this over with Philip. We have agreed that now no question of money comes in. We are no longer wanting to sell the papers, we wish to *use* them. You know. That way we can get some revenge. We are

587

agreed on that. And the only way to use them is while we are here."

"So what have you done?"

"I have sent for the papers."

"To be posted here?"

"Yes."

Gene bit his lip. She was watching him closely. "Was this your idea or your brother-inlaw's?"

"Philip's."

"And why have you come to me now?"

"Because, now I have done it, I am not happy about it."

"You think Philip wants the papers to sell himself?"

"I am not sure if my suspicion of him is my own or whether you have planted it. But there is something very wrong with him. He is—going to pieces while I watch. Always he has been the high-strung kind; but now . . . While he was persuading me to do this I thought he was upset because he was burning for revenge. Now I do not know what to think. He lies on his bed smoking all day. He has fits of trembling, trying to keep still. You know. He will not even touch his harp. At night I hear him walking about."

"And so?"

"It may be grief for his brother that is destroying him, but if so it is not the sort of grief that is mine. What use will he be when the letter comes, if such is his condition? I am worried and don't know how to turn. That is why I have come to you."

"You think I'm worth trusting now?"

"You have sad eyes, M. Vanbrugh—as if they have seen many things they would like to forget. But I think you are a man of honour."

Darkness had come like a curtain drawn. Bats were circling over the tower.

"When do you expect the papers?"

"Not until early next week. I cannot cable for them, for it is certain our cousin will not send them without a signature in writing which he can recognise. But in my letter I ask him to cable back. I have that cable tonight." She clasped and unclasped her fat strong hands; they seemed to need something to take hold of. "The cable says he receives my letter yesterday afternoon, that is Friday. The cable says sending today."

"Saturday. . . . They might be here Monday. No, that's barely possible. Tuesday at the earliest."

"That is what I thought."

"Philip knows of the cable?"

"Yes."

"But the letter will come addressed to you—if it is not tampered with."

"Yes."

"Can you be sure of getting it first?"

"The letters are usually put just inside the front door of the house where we live. I can do my best to be about in the hall when the postman comes."

"Do that."

"And then?"

"Can you bring them straight to me?"

She hesitated. In a two-storeyed house nearby someone had switched on a light in an un-shuttered upper room, and Gene's face showed clearly. This time it had no expression.

"And you?"

"If they are what I suppose they may be, then I can help you to make use of them in the most effective way."

"What do you suppose they may be?"

"There's no point in guessing when we shall be sure so soon."

The light went out and they were left in a greater darkness.

'*What* was the name of the man my husband mentioned in Paris?"

"Avra."

"Why are you interested in him?"

"I think when you get these papers it may explain that to."

"I *have* to trust you," she said. "If you let me down . . ."

"I'll not let you down."

589

13

It was just on nine when he got to Heracles House. He knew he was taking a risk in going, but a 'must' within himself made the risk necessary.

There was no one about when he stepped into the self-operating lift and pressed the button for the seventh floor; lights winked and the lift sighed and took him up with a carefully graded acceleration; after a very few seconds it sighed again and let him out. The lobby upstairs was empty and he pressed the bell at the door at the end and a manservant showed him into a small ante-room where half a dozen people were talking.

Some he already knew; Maurice Taksim, the Turk; General Telechos; Gallanova, the Yugo-Slav ballerina; others he knew by sight, like Jon Manos. George Lascou came towards him, grey waistcoated, gold glinting like a welcoming smile from the bridge of the pince-nez. For a short moment their hands touched and eyes met; conventional gestures of welcome and the empty words—good-of-you-to-come, kind-of-you-to-have-me. Almost at once Anya appeared through another door, in a dress that glittered as she walked across the room.

It was a small dinner-party, candle-lit at table, in a handsome high-windowed dining-room; two menservants, black-clad and silent, hovered like benevolent ghosts. On Gene's right was Mme Telechos; on his left was Gallanova, a fine-boned Slav with an imperious chin, in a Molyneux gown of slashed crimson. Beyond her was a stout moustached little man called Major Kolono whom Gene felt he had seen somewhere before and who stared fixedly at him. Mme Lascou was not present. Anya sat on George's right, some distance from Gene. They had only spoken a few words in private, when Gene had said: "I've hired a car for tomorrow."

"What to do?"

"To take you to Delphi, if you will come."

"Thank you, no."

. . . They fed on caviare, coq au vin, fresh woodland strawberries flown in from Corfu; and the conversation was as cultured as the meal. There were three or four very good talkers present; but Gene, speaking Greek now, rose to the mood and held his own. Perhaps only Anya, withdrawn tonight and communing more with herself than other people, perceived the paradox, saw the off-hand wit stemming from the eastern seaboard of the New World, expressing itself in the tongue of Aristophanes.

And George watched them both. George watched everyone with his soft fluid movements and sharp astigmatic eyes. No one could ignore that he was master of the evening: he led the talk, fed it, conducted it down safe and popular avenues, the perfect chairman you'd say, perhaps that was how he had come to lead his party, and then perhaps not, the velvet glove was not empty.

The number was small for splinter groups; when Maurice Taksim asked Gallanova about her early years as a ballerina, everyone listened to her story of the Yugo-Slav ballet after the war. She spoke of her own poverty and early struggles, and Mme Telechos said: "Ah, d'you remember the inflation here? When I sent my son to school he went with his pockets crammed with bank-notes to pay his tram fare. Do you remember when a newspaper cost ten thousand million drachmae?"

"That time must never come again," said Jon Manos, but conventionally as if he didn't believe it ever could, for him.

"We had our troubles in Istanbul," said Taksim, "but of course they do not compare. Were you here, George?"

"It is always interesting to hear how a rich man became rich," said Gallanova, turning her much photographed profile to the candle-light. "Would it bore you to tell us how it happened to you, M. Lascou? Or have you always been wealthy?"

"Happened is the correct word. It happened to me. After

the war I borrowed money and invested it in real estate. Regrettable though it may seem, the successive inflations helped me, and I built more and more flats and offices. Then I was able to buy factories in Piraeus and Salonika. It was all very easy once the start was made."

Everyone murmured in polite disbelief.

"I don't ever quite understand," said Taksim, "why you have bothered to enter politics. Why grub in the gutter now you have money to live on the heights?"

George shrugged. "After a while, when you have enough of it, money becomes unimportant. Then you seek something else—an outlet possibly for idealism."

"And you find it—you find idealism in politics? You must sift the dregs closely."

"I don't find idealism in politicians, but I can find it in political thought. I find scope for it in the situation in Greece today. We do not lack brains in the *Vouli* but we lack reflective brains. Not one in twenty of my fellow deputies attempts to understand Greece outside Athens or the mission of Greece in the world today."

A man at the end of the table said: "I don't see what you personally hope to do."

George sipped his claret. "It is not what one personally hopes to do, it is what one must attempt if one has any vision of the future at all. A nation is not divisible. We share the common lot."

"We need another Metaxas," said General Telechos. "There was a man."

Everyone looked at him. Lascou said: "Metaxas tried to do too much too quickly. No one knows now whether the end would have justified his means."

"The end appears to be justifying Tito's means," said Gallanova.

George smiled gently. "The trouble I see with all these leaders up to now is that ruthlessness and reflectiveness seldom grow on the same stem. Whether a dictator is wholly bad, like Hitler, or partly good, like Metaxas, he is always too much a man of action to be also a man of thought. He has no background of ideas deep enough to maintain him on his way. Plato pointed the solution, but no one has yet followed it."

George was at his most effective in small groups. His persuasive voice did not have to be raised to betray its lack of tone.

"Do men like to be autocratically governed?" cried Mme Telechos. "They are all too fond of equality these days."

"I am all for equality," said Lascou, "but equality on different levels. There can't be complete equality of reward where there isn't equality of service. The intellectuals, the philosophers, the governing élite—they are the brains of a nation and should have equality among themselves; so should the black-coated workers, the heart and the viscera; so should the manual workers, the limbs of the state. But these classes are not the equal of each other. Let each man be equal with his *neighbour* and let every man be judged according to his service to the community."

"Mankind has always been rather unoriginal in his forms of government," said Gallanova yawning. "Perhaps that's because womankind has had so little to do with it."

Everyone laughed. George said: "The finest example of the art of government was in this city as it existed two thousand five hundred years ago. The reward of energy, resource, intellect, reached its highest peak. I think you found there love of life, admiration for strength and beauty, the constant exercise of reason, the acceptance of responsibility . . . and with it went a self-governing genius never since equalled in the world."

There was a murmur of approval.

"I'm not at all sure," said Gene, "that it was quite as good as that."

Silence fell. Servants moved dishes discreetly in the background.

"Oh," said Jon Manos, "what did your night school say?"

"No one," said Gene ignoring him and addressing Lascou, "is a greater admirer than I am of the city state as it existed in Athens in those days. But I think in honesty you have to admit that distance lends a certain glamour to the view. Surely the whole thing, good as it was, was rather a contradiction within itself. Wasn't it? It was a state where one man in four lived the ideal life—at the expense of the other three. It was therefore at most 25 per cent of ideal. Then it was a military state constantly at war with one of its neighbouring states, and I've seen enough fighting to feel that that was not ideal. Thirdly, for all its excellence it was in a continual state of revolution within itself, and that too isn't a particular recommendation. Given those provisos, I'd agree it was a thousand times better than anything that had gone before and a hundred times better than what came after. I'm only trying to see it in its perspective."

"Perfection of course isn't possible," said George. "I wasn't claiming perfection for the system but giving it as an example to be admired and studied. It's not impossible that it could be improved upon."

"As Plato suggested it could be improved upon?" said Gene.

"Athens was the practical state, in operation. Plato's was the contemplative ideal, never properly attempted. I believe that Greece is the one country, right as to size, malleability and temperament, where it might be possible, given the right men at the top, to fuse the ideal and the practical and set up an example of government for the world to copy."

Somebody spoke at the end of the table and talk broke out here and there for a moment or two, but Lascou kept his eyes on Gene and when the talk died again he said: "Isn't that to your liking, Vanbrugh?"

Gene made a face of slight embarrassment and sipped his own wine. "Expressed as you express it, it sounds wonderful. I only have one uncomfortable thought. If you put Plato's idealism into practice, with its all-important duties to the state, its sharing of all property below a certain level, its small élite governing class, its belief that no one should be left alone to live as they choose, that children belong primarily to the state, etc—if you have all that and amend it to meet modern conditions, you're going to produce something that will be hard to distinguish from Communism."

Into another silence Gallanova said: "That word does not terrify me as it used to."

"It does most of us in Greece," observed the man at the end of the table.

"Plato in a sense was the first Communist," Gene said. "I should have thought that was generally accepted."

"Communism as Plato conceived it has very little relationship with the world of Marx and Lenin," said George quickly. "The whole conception has changed. As soon as one harks back one finds a purer doctrine."

The talk went on for a while. But as it went on so it became more and more a duologue, a sort of intellectual clash of arms between Gene and Lascou. Others joined in now and then but their interventions were temporary. They didn't measure up. And Anya said nothing at all. She sat quite still, for the most part looking down at her hand on the table.

At last a move was made. Coffee and brandy were served in the main salon. After his talk Gene was preoccupied, as if he hadn't yet got it out of his system, and Lascou seemed to be gathering about himself the robes of the Greek classic past. Very little was said until the ladies rejoined them.

Presently Gene found himself beside Anya. "Who is Major Kolono?" he asked.

"He's—a business acquaintance of George's. I have not seen him at dinner before."

"I know his face but can't place him. What is his job?"

Before she could reply General Telechos came up and began to pay her compliments. Ignored, Gene stood his ground. Telechos looked a man hardened out of ordinary feeling by fifty years of service in arid mountains; the sap had dried in him. One fancied that he no longer saw people primarily as people but as cadres, units, platoons, to be moved, commended, defeated, deployed on the chess-board of a political and military ethos. He was the exact opposite of Lascou, who was all flexibility, all finesse, who would never

595

neglect the human angle in anything, and who would be far more dangerous either in victory or defeat.

Lascou and Major Kolono were quietly conferring together, their brandy glasses like great soap bubbles nodding at each other as they talked. Then Kolono left the room and Lascou joined the trio by the window.

He said to Gene: "I congratulate you, Mr. Vanbrugh, on your knowledge of our language and of ancient Greece. It is quite unusual."

"In the happy seclusion of my night school," Gene said, "I have long been a Graecophile."

Jon Manos, who was near, turned quickly and took a couple of little side-steps: "Of course I can understand your opposition as an American to the word Communism. In the States nowadays I understand it ranks as an obscenity to use the word at all."

Although the room was large, the party was at present clustered round the coffee-table and within earshot. Nobody seemed to want to move away.

"I would have said we were inclined to use it too often," Gene replied. "I'm dead against raising anything as a bogy, however much I may personally dislike it."

Lascou said: "You know, monsieur, you say the old city states of Greece were contradictions within themselves. I wonder sometimes about the new United States of America."

"You do right to wonder," said Gene, "but I wouldn't lose any sleep about it."

"Surely the equality of opportunity that you boast of is really equality of opportunism—isn't that so?—a chance to get rich quick at the expense of your neighbour? And what is this freedom of religion? Freedom to worship money as the only criterion of success? And freedom from fear? I have never yet met an American who is not afraid—afraid of not making enough money, afraid of being cheated, afraid of not being thought superior, afraid of being down-graded in a social scale as rigid as any that has ever existed in the world before. And freedom from want. No race has ever 'wanted' more."

596

Gene said: "Man always falls far short of his ideal. It happens everywhere. No state has ever existed on earth which has not laid itself wide open to being shot at from one quarter or another. I think if you read Thucydides you'll find descriptions of the Athenian city state that make your criticisms of America read like the Garden of Eden before the snake got in. I might even quote you some. But why bother? One tries to see the best and not judge by the worst. One likes a country or one doesn't like it for better reasons, I hope, than the existence of a few scabs on the surface. The only proviso is that, if one loves a country sufficiently, one may make efforts and even sacrifices to remove a few of the scabs."

The room became suddenly very quiet indeed. Not a coffee-spoon clinked. People's expressions had become frozen. It was clear that the last remark had been taken in its most personal way, as a deliberate and ugly affront. Anya stretched out a hand to tap the ash off her cigarette, but she did it quietly and she did not raise her eyes. Then in the silence Major Kolono came across the room.

"You are Mr. Eugene Robert Vanbrugh?"

"I am."

"The police have been trying to trace you. They called at the address you gave, the Hotel Astoria, but you were not there."

"I was invited to stay with friends."

"They are anxious to ask you some questions about an accident that took place in Galatea Street last Tuesday morning in which a man, a Spaniard, was run over and killed."

Gene looked at him. It was as if the whole room was ranged against him now. "A Spaniard?"

"Yes, a man called Tolosa. We understand that you were seen driving a car away from Galatea Street shortly afterwards."

"Then you understand wrong. I have not driven a car in Athens at all."

Kolono raised his stubby eyebrows in disbelief. "Where are you staying now?"

597

"In Benaki Street. Number six."

"Perhaps if I called to see you tomorrow morning at nine?"

"You're connected with the police?"

"I am."

"You don't know yet who ran this man down?"

"I think we have a very good idea."

"Have you questioned Mandraki?"

Kolono stopped rubbing his moustache. "Who?"

"A gunman. You must know him."

"I know a man of that name. A silversmith. He has not a very good record, but he has nothing to do with this. He was in his shop at the time."

"He always is in his shop at the time. One wonders what protection he has."

"That doesn't happen in Greece," said Manos. "You're thinking of America."

"Shady politicians are not peculiar to any one country."

"Who was talking of politicians?" said George Lascou. "It was an association of ideas."

Kolono said: "May I ask you, Vanbrugh, what you were doing in a hired car on Tuesday morning last?"

Gene glanced at the hostile faces of the men around him. "Your dinner-party, M. Lascou, seems to be turning into a court of inquiry."

"I assure you it is none of my seeking. Perhaps——"

"May I ask—" Kolono began but Gene cut him short. There was a sudden glint in his uneven grey eyes.

"We're meeting tomorrow. I suggest you keep the muzzle on till then. The world won't end if you wait a few hours." He turned his back on Kolono and Manos and said to Lascou: "I'm sorry if I've said anything to give you offence. I was talking in general terms as I imagined you were. However, I think probably your dinner-party will be a greater success without me."

Lascou's pince-nez gave off equivocal glints as he looked at Anya. But she was sipping her coffee and made no sign.

"The matter's of absolutely no importance to me, M. Vanbrugh, and I'm sure my friends will be willing to accept your assurances if I am. But one thing I would certainly advise—and that is, get in touch with your embassy tomorrow morning. It's a common-sense precaution if you have charges to answer."

"I didn't know I had any charges to answer, but no doubt Major Kolono has an inventive brain."

Lascou shrugged. "I only wished to advise you, to help you. I think it would be your advice to me if our positions were reversed. Wouldn't it? But no matter; let's forget it; let's change the subject; it is all very boring anyway. . . ."

Anya stayed behind after the others had left. Gene had gone early, and the rest went away in ones and twos during the next hour. A certain constraint had remained till the end; impoliteness from whatever source is not popular with the cultured Greek.

Last to go were General and Mme. Telechos, and while George walked with them to the door Anya strolled back into the great salon and took a cigarette from an ebony box. She found a lighter and stood a moment, head forward until the smoke came. Then she walked across to a big gilt mirror and began to smooth one of her eyebrows with a middle finger. She heard George come into the room but she didn't turn.

He said: "I shall not see Telechos again publicly before the election. It would not take long for some scurrilous sheet to link our names and smell out a plot."

"And privately?"

"Privately I must. He's not an old campaigner for nothing."

She said: "George, why did you ask me to ask Gene Vanbrugh here tonight?"

He paused to pour himself a brandy. "I wanted to look at him for myself and see what there was about him. One has heard enough."

"And now you have seen him, what do you think of him?"

He warmed the brandy glass with his hands, gently swilling the liquid round. "He has a brain."

"It amused me that you had invited Kolono here so that Gene Vanbrugh could be practically arrested in your own drawing-room."

He considered her. "That was an afterthought. Kolono, the fool, had been looking for Vanbrugh for four days. He traced him to a house in the Plaka and then lost him again. It amused *me* to face him up with his man tonight."

"Sometimes, George, it is as if you were two people. One minute you argue with Gene Vanbrugh as a guest and an intellectual equal—that is a raising of the level of life. Then the next you show you have planned to trick him and cheat him because he is a political opponent—that is where one comes down to earth with a bump."

He caught an unfamiliar inflexion in her voice. He said: "The conflict between theory and expediency can't be a new one even to you."

She began to touch her hair here and there with a comb, but he could not see her eyes in the mirror. "How seriously do you intend to try to involve him in this street accident?"

"That's Kolono's business. It's nothing to do with me."

"Oh, come. Kolono, like John Manos, jumps when you pull the string."

"Well, then, I imagine we shall all be guided by the amount of difficulty Vanbrugh gives. The chief thing is to make him feel when he leaves Greece that he was lucky to get out."

She turned now, but her eyes were not to be fathomed. They smiled at him without apparent emotion.

He said: "You're not seriously interested in him?"

"Interested? My dear, what do you think?"

He shrugged. "One never knows. Men like that with their rather hungry looks and modest-arrogant manners—they can have their peculiar appeal."

"You underrrate yourself."

"Anyway," he said, "you'll not be troubled again. Kolono will see to that."

"If he finds him. I very much doubt if Gene Vanbrugh will be waiting for him when he calls in the morning."

"Oh, we attended to that," said Lascou. "After dinner Kolono telephoned across the square for a couple of his men. They would be waiting for Vanbrugh when he left."

14

Soon after seven the next morning Anya was wakened by the telephone at the side of her bed. The blinds were drawn and she stretched out a sleepy arm for the receiver in the sun-shot darkness.

"Hullo?"

"Mlle Stonaris?"

"Yes?"

"This is Gene Vanbrugh."

She fumbled the receiver into a better position. "Where are you speaking from?"

"A call box. I want to know if you've decided to come with me."

"Come with you?"

"Don't you remember?"

"Of course I remember."

"Perhaps you didn't expect to hear from me again."

"No, I didn't expect it. Certainly not this early. You have wakened me."

"Sorry."

She said: "Perhaps it is I who should apologise for last night. I didn't know that that was going to happen."

"I'm sure you didn't. But it was partly my own fault."

"We are not all so ill-mannered."

There was a moment's hesitation at both ends.

He said: "If you did come today I'd have to ask a favour. For reasons you may be able to guess I'd prefer not to come round to your flat. But I shall be outside the Kotopouli in Ommonia Square at eight."

After a moment she said: "I couldn't be ready by eight."

"Name your time." There was a new note in his voice.

She looked at her watch and then at the mouthpiece. "Eight-thirty?"

"Eight-thirty it is. And thank you."

"Don't thank me," she said. "I have always had a sympathy for the stray dog."

He was waiting for her at the cinema, standing beside an old Buick, looking casual and unemployed like a car salesman not too interested in his job. She was wearing flat-heeled shoes and almost got to the door of the car before he heard her. Then she was sorry she hadn't spoken earlier when she saw the suddenly tensed muscles before he turned.

They looked at each other, and his eyes gave him away before he dropped them.

"Welcome to the kennels," he said.

She got in and he took the driving-seat beside her, and there was silence. His banter had rather quickly run out. They had reached the end of a phase. A new one that they both understood was about to begin. But it was like coming to the banks of a deep-flowing river.

She put her bag carefully into the pocket of the car. "What happened after you left last night?"

"I went home."

"You were not stopped?"

"Did you suppose I would be?"

"From something that was said after you left—yes."

"It occurred to me I might be."

"So?"

"I took the lift to the first floor and looked out of the passage window above the front door. There were two men standing there who looked as if they were waiting for somebody, so I thought I'd let them wait. It's always easy to get out of a big business block."

602

She said after a moment: "And how did you know I wouldn't bring the police with me this morning?"

"Just a rash belief."

"Someone may even have followed me."

"Oh, I'm safe enough while I'm with you. George won't run the risk of having your name mixed up in a police matter, however trivial."

She stared out at the city as it slid past, but didn't comment.

"I'd given you up," he said.

"I didn't know you ever gave up."

"One cuts one's losses."

"And now?"

"One counts one's gains."

"There is no gain. My coming today is only from a wish to stand aside from last night and say, 'I was not a party to it'.

"Commendable sympathy for the stray dog."

"But since I am here, perhaps you can explain one or two things for me. I have not led a sheltered life. I am a grown person. I now have a vote. My intelligence is normal. But I live in a fog of ignorance."

"I wish I could believe that."

"There is no one to compel you to believe it."

"What is it you want to know?"

"First can you tell me a single thing: why it is that a respectable publisher should come to Greece and stay at a third-rate hotel like the Astoria, and then, if he has nothing to hide, that he should move on from one dingy apartment to another so fast that the police cannot catch up with him?"

"The same respectable publisher came to Athens a couple of years ago and stayed at the Grande Bretagne. From the second day he was a marked man. Obstacles were even put in the way of his meeting some of his old friends. So this time he thought he would be less conspicuous and keep out of the public eye. That's all."

"Because he was up to no good?"

"It depends whose good you're thinking of."

603

She made a little gesture. "Just good. The public good if you like."

"At any rate, he isn't here to make trouble that doesn't already exist."

"And what sort of trouble do you suppose already exists?"

He let out a slow breath. "We've got all day. Maybe during the day I'll tell you everything I can. But first . . ."

"Ah, I thought there would be a first."

". . . First I wish you'd tell me more about yourself."

They had left the town now. She slipped out of her short coat and leaned back in the seat. She had never looked so young to him as she did today in her yellow turtle-necked jumper and wide-belted skirt. A different person from last night; she wore that brittle sophistication with her clothes. Indeed, looking at her, one could see her entirely afresh, cut free from all association, untouched, beautiful as a renaissance angel. (Or maybe, he thought, this new innocence is something I'm creating with my own eyes; the astigmatism of desire.)

He said: "I came to Athens with certain purposes in mind. It may seem odd to you, but although I knew a lot about some of your friends I'd never heard of Anya Stonaris. Well, now I have—and getting to know more has already come to mean as much to me as doing what I came to Greece to do. That may not surprise you, but I assure you it surprises me."

She said: "Isn't it quite usual for a stray dog to start looking for a new mistress?"

After a minute he laughed and said: "Yes, I was wrong."

"About what?"

"Just now I thought you looked young and innocent."

"I think it is you who are young and innocent."

"Give me time."

He had to brake as two mule carts laden with vegetables came out of a field in front of them.

Anya said: "And what do you know about my friends?"

"Oh. . . . I know that General Telechos owes the bank of Greece a million drachmae and I know why the bank hasn't yet put the screw on him. Maurice Taksim's wife is divorcing him and he is fixing up a crooked deal in oil. Jon Manos has a big reputation in law—of the wrong sort—and is trying to needle Stavrides out of second place in EMO. I know about George Lascou, his finances and his plans, but nothing about you. . . . Turn right here?"

"Yes. We follow the sea and fork off at Eleusis."

The sun had not quite soaked up the night mists, but the water of the gulf was a rich cobalt with coppery rocks at its brim. In the distance and behind rose the ghosts of the Peloponnesian mountains.

She said: "My father and mother came from Smyrna. Is that what you want to know?"

"It's a beginning."

"But already you know so much. You know that I am—what is it?—innocent-looking but hard-boiled. What more is there necessary to understand about any woman?"

He said: "Isn't it the Greeks of Smyrna who consider their blood purer than the Greeks of the mother country?"

". . . My father's family had been there for over four hundred years, if that is what you mean."

"When did he come to Greece?"

"In 1922."

"The exchange of populations?"

"Yes."

He waited. "Go on."

"Oh, you will know the background."

"I can hear it again."

"My father and mother were of that number of hundreds of thousands forcibly transferred after the defeat of Greece by Turkey. My father had not then finished his training as a doctor, but with what he was able to save from the catastrophe he finished his studies here, and in 1929 he married my mother. I was born three years later. My father was foolish enough to practise for many years among the refugees and dispossessed, his countrymen; and so we too were quite poor. When the Germans came he continued his work in Athens. Twice he was in prison for short periods for helping the Resistance, but the Germans soon let him go because they had need of doctors. Then when the Germans left, the Communists occupied our part of the city."

He waited. "Is that the end?"

"Yes, so far as they were concerned, it is. Because my father had influence in all his district ELAS told him he must publicly join the party. When he said he had no party, but only disease to fight, they shot him and stigmatised him as a collaborator. My mother they took away a month later as a hostage and I never saw her again. She is buried in the north. A priest hid me at that time, in the altar of his church—you know in Greece there are doors to the altar—and he kept me there and fed me for three weeks."

". . . I'm very sorry."

"It is stale history now. All it has left me with is a dislike of the smell of incense."

They passed Eleusis and took the main road to the north, crossing the great plain with its ancient distorted olive trees and red-brown earth.

He said: "I was in Greece all that time, and in Athens too."

"What time? During the occupation?"

"Yes. The war against the Germans became my war very early."

"Because of Greece?"

"In the main, yes. I was here when the Germans came but got out in time. Then I came back and stayed around."

"Doing what?"

"I just stayed around. And noted how the various resistance groups were trending."

"ELAS?"

"Well, there were dozens of different groups to begin with. But after a time ELAS became much the biggest and it was soon pretty clear that they were more interested in making an eventual Communist state in Greece than in wasting their ammunition on the Germans. At least it was clear to a few people but not to those outside. . . . Perhaps you know all this as well as I do?"

606

"I was ten or eleven at the time. It is not always easy to remember."

"ELAS tactics were unvarying. By 1943 they were far the best equipped force in the field. They were the only one with any outside propaganda system, the only one with a proper organisation, because it had been in existence before the war. In addition to doing a little sparring with the Germans to satisfy the British and the Americans, they took on one by one the other resistance movements and wiped them out. It was the same technique as they applied to your father. Each resistance group, each leader of a resistance group was given the alternative—be absorbed by us, toe the party line, or else. The 'else' was to be denounced as collaborating with the Germans and then liquidated. I can give you the names of eight or ten such groups—with their leaders—who went that way. Not three or four killed but hundreds massacred. Some of them were my oldest friends. Only Zervas with EDES survived because he was too big and tough to be destroyed."

"You were in Athens at the end?"

"Yes, and I didn't like that either."

She shrugged. "Perhaps my father was lucky to be shot by a firing squad. At least he was luckier than my mother and some of the others."

For a while they had met on neutral ground. He had tried deliberately to slacken the tautness between them and had succeded better than he'd hoped. They reached Levadia soon after eleven and here swung off the main road on to the loose and uneven surface of the mountain road. A few clouds had blown up, but through them the snow-headed peaks watched them as they passed.

"That's Parnassus," Anya said.

Gene stared ahead.

"I used not to think it existed in fact. I thought it was part of a legend, like Zeus and Aphrodite."

"Nobody knows now what is legend and what is history," she said. "Perhaps there is not all that difference."

"Have you ever been to the summit?"

"No. August is the time."

"It doesn't look difficult. How high?"

"Oh—three thousand metres perhaps. The snow's treacherous of course."

"Next time we come, let's arrange to go."

"Are you very sure of yourself? Or very unsure? Deep down. I'd like to know."

"Physically I'm sure," he said. "The way a rat's sure. Once you've lived in holes, you come to know your own muscles, your own teeth, your own sense of smell. Being wanted by a few tired policemen doesn't worry me. But about you I was never more unsure in my life. Anything you detect to the contrary is purely coincidental."

"It's bad to be on the run," she said, after the minute she had taken to digest what he said. "Even from a few—tired policemen. Bad for something inside oneself. It is like driving on one's brakes too much. I know—though I had it for only a few weeks."

They began to climb by hairpin bends. At one point three ragged children stood by the way offering to sell them bunches of anemones. When Gene did not stop they leapt across the rough moorland like goats and were waiting patiently at the next corner above. When he still went on they got to the third corner before the car, and here Anya made him stop and buy the flowers. Afterwards they went on again between walls of rock and skirting dark and tangled forests. Arakhova was reached clinging uncertainly to the side of the gorge. Then the mountains drew right in upon the pass, they skirted the face of the precipice and began to fall gently into Delphi, which came in view with the clustered tiles and huddled streets of the modern village standing athwart the road and the white skeletal remains of the sacred shrines climbing in tiers to the foot of the great Phocian wall.

Gene found Michael Michaelis's house just short of the village, and the poet, white moustache gleaming like a scar on his old brown face, limped down the steps to meet them.

They had lunch out of doors on the terrace behind the house, while eagles swooped and circled overhead. Everything here was dwarfed by the great precipice behind them, which both protected and threatened from three sides. But on the fourth the ground fell away in an avalanche of forest and olive groves stretching five miles and dropping two thousand feet to the shining rim of the sea.

Over luncheon Michaelis was talkative, Gene as conversational as was necessary, Anya silent. But it was not a bored or a disdainful silence. For all her assumptions of arrogance Gene saw perfectly well that she would look with the same contempt upon herself as upon anyone else who pretended to knowledge they didn't have. The old man wore an embroidered smock like an artist's coat, with buttons to the neck and a white linen collar. On his head was a little black cap shaped like a beret and worn on the slant. He had no family and his wife had been dead some years, but the three small children of his housekeeper kept popping on and off the verandah like puppies for tit-bits that he took from his own plate to give them.

He said: "I never go down into Athens. The skies of the mind so quickly become overcast. Here in Delphi I think perhaps we can still see. . . .

"Of course I am not a poet. I write songs. They are songs which I hope people sing, and some day may even dance to. Because they deal with elemental things it does not make them great; only truth is great—and for that one digs for ever in one's own soul. Perhaps enlightenment comes in death—the supreme moment of all-knowing—or is there just a blank end and candles burning and the thud of a spade? More grapes, Aristide! Man's mind works always to conceive a unity, and enlightenment would complete it, but that alas does not prove the epiphenomenalists wrong. . . .

"How beautiful you are, Miss Stonaris. Beauty I think is so much more than skin deep: on that most poets are wrong, deriving from a puritan tradition which fortunately never rooted deep in Greece; beauty's an outward expression of an inner grace. I think of Apuleius's description of Isis: 'her nod governs the shining heights of Heaven, the wholesome sea-breezes, the lamentable silences of the world below.' It is

609

pleasant to be an old man because one can express oneself without fear of misunderstanding. . . .

"Yes, from 600 B.C. and before, the pilgrims used to come here, by sea chiefly, disembarking down there in Itea and making the long climb up to the Oracle. The people of Delphi had a bad reputation in those days—they lived off the pilgrims and often robbed them. They murdered Aesop, you know."

"I didn't know," said Gene. "More names."

"Well, yes, we are full of them. Croesus sent money for rebuilding the temple when it was destroyed by an earthquake. Nero robbed it. Domitian restored it. Plutarch was a priest here. So it goes on."

"So it no longer goes on."

"No. . . . Nowadays our temporary Hitlers call and stare but learn nothing from their visits."

After lunch Gene had a few minutes' business talk with Michaelis and then they took their leave and walked up to explore the ruins.

"Well?" Gene said.

She stopped to finger a stone out of the side of her shoe. "I think he understands women."

They were climbing towards the temple of Apollo, and for a few steps they went on in silence. He said: "If I can believe my own eyes, you were as impressed by him as I was."

"Well, so if I was impressed by him? What then?"

"Oh, nothing."

She said: "Perhaps I would rather marry Michaelis than any man I have ever met. Does that satisfy you?"

"At sixty-nine?"

She shrugged. "It would solve some problems. Life would be less complex."

"If one could live and think like Michaelis, life might be less complex any way up."

They climbed into the temple.

She said: "All right. Most of us are children fumbling with the keys of a piano and producing only discords—talking with Michaelis is suddenly finding a harmony. But what

610

of it? As soon as Michaelis is gone the child fumbles again. Bang, bang go the discords. So what of it? What good will it do to burst into tears because we cannot play?"

He put a hand on one of the great ruined pillars and looked down over the torrent of rocks and ruins and trees.

He said: "Whatever else, the old men had a superb sense of fitness for the places they chose to live their epics. Nowhere could be better than Mycenae for Agamemnon to ride out of with his chariots of war to the sack of Troy. Here it's as if they have climbed half-way to heaven to build their holy place."

She came to stand beside him, but she didn't speak.

He added: "I wasn't brought up credulous but I could believe one or two things here. Maybe it's the influence of that man, maybe of the place."

Her great dark eyes slid over him coolly, assessingly, and then went past him to stare again at the scene. "These gods didn't ask much. 'Know Thyself.' 'Do Nothing in Excess.' You saw the inscriptions."

"I saw them."

"That's about all."

"It's too much for today," he said. "Most people would prefer: 'Know Excess' and 'Do Nothing for Thyself.' "

She burst out suddenly laughing.

"What's so funny?" he asked.

"I don't know. It just seems to me very witty."

He hadn't seen her laugh like this before. After a while they went on up to the theatre, and then higher still to the flower-grown stadium where the Pythic Games had been held. They sat on one of the moss-grown stone benches and smoked a reflective cigarette and stared out again over the gulf.

He said: "D'you know what I'd like to do now?"

"No?"

"Climb Parnassus."

Her lips parted as if to smile, and then she didn't.

"When do we start?"

"Any time you say."

"Why not now?"

"Better to stop at one of the hotels and go off first thing in the morning."

She raised an eyebrow. "You're not serious?"

"Why not?"

"How do you suggest we should go—by air?"

"No, the normal way."

"Wonderful."

"Well, it can't be more than five or six thousand feet from here and I don't suppose there's snow below the top thousand."

"I've always wanted to climb a mountain in suede shoes."

"That's a difficulty, I admit. But maybe we could hire some."

"In Delphi? But of course. One of the big departmental stores."

"Well, it was an idea."

"You stay on and go up tomorrow."

They sat for a while in silence. The air was like wine, sun glinted on the grass and on all bright things: her wristwatch, the clasp in her hair.

He said: "I suppose it *is* too much to ask of you. When one lives all one's life in a city, in a constant round of cocktail-parties and fashion shows . . . Aside from anything else, it's a question of not having the stamina."

She said quietly: "I will climb as far as you when I please; but only when I please. Let us go back to Delphi."

They picked their way over the boulder-strewn path and began to descend. As they got down a guide was moving with two other people across the theatre; Anya went across to him. He knew her and greeted her effusively and they talked for a couple of minutes while Gene walked slowly round the amphitheatre. When she came back to Gene it was with a flicker in her eyes.

"A friend?" he said.

"A friend. He has a brother called Menelaus. Menelaus is a good climber. If you are staying tomorrow he would know the practical difficulties."

"And what are they?"

"He advised against it, said the snow was treacherous at this time of year. But for your future information the best place to start from is Arakhova. From there it takes about seven hours. But he said never to go alone because of the dogs."

"The dogs?"

"The sheep-dogs. They are very fierce."

They went on down. Gene said: "Menelaus would be a good guide?"

"The best."

"I'll engage him next time I come."

"You'll not stay?"

"No, I may have business in Athens tomorrow too."

"To do with your publishing firm?"

"To do with something that might be published."

"Isn't that the same thing?"

"Not quite."

They skirted the temple ruins and began to come in sight of the road.

Gene said: "Can it be done in one day?"

"Not really at this time of the year." She stopped and peered down at a piece of inscribed stone. "The best way is to spend a night in a hut about fifteen hundred feet from the summit. Then you start out the next morning before daybreak and watch the dawn from the summit."

"My God," he said.

"So it will be something to look forward to if you are here in the summer."

He stopped, and after a couple of paces she stopped and turned and looked up at him from a lower step. "Anya."

She shook her head. "Oh, no."

"There must be women in this village. Some may have suitable boots."

"Women here don't climb. They toil in the fields all day."

"Are you afraid of trying it?"

"I've told you. I could climb just as far as you—and as fast——"

613

"It would be a new experience."

Her eyes were fronded as they looked into the sun. "I don't care to be away from Athens two nights."

"Nor do I. But you don't need to be. It could be done tonight. The new moon's up. We could be back in Athens by noon tomorrow."

"If we have not fallen into a crevasse or been eaten by dogs or caught pneumonia sitting in the hut or altogether worn our feet away in other men's shoes. Yes, that way we should be in Athens tomorrow. But I prefer to be in Athens tonight."

He said: "What were those lines Michaelis quoted? 'Her nod governs the shining heights of Heaven . . . The lamentable silences of the world below.' Why Athens tonight? An appointment for a manicure?"

She thought about that for a munute. "I am waiting to see how offensive you can really be."

"I'm sorry. . . . You know the old saying. All's fair in war."

Her expression was hidden from him now; he didn't know if he was gaining ground or losing it.

He said: "I'll make a bargain with you. If you come up the mountain I'll tell you why I came to Greece and why George Lascou considers me his enemy—that's if you don't know already. I'll tell you why the Spaniard came to be killed. And also perhaps what he came here to do."

"First it was sarcasm and now it is bribery. And all so very unsubtle: that's the most depressing thing. Have you no threats?"

He said: "I only want you to come. I think it is important, for us both. It seems to me that it's more than the summit of a mountain."

She said: "Ah, symbolism, I hadn't thought of that. I'm always a little allergic to symbolism. It is like false money at the best of times."

"Come, Anya," he said. "You must come."

15

They took the car back as far as Arakhova. With them went Menelaus, a man in early middle age, gaunt and bearded and one-eyed, the blind eye slanting across his nose in a treacherous squint. It gave him a look of sneering brutality. With them also went blankets, ropes, two thermoses of coffee and some sandwiches that one of the small hotels had made up. Anya had borrowed the climbing boots of Menelaus's thirteen-year-old brother. In these and her yellow jumper and a pair of shabby ski-ing trousers she said she was ludicrous; in fact they had that provocative effect which ungainly clothing can sometimes have on a beautiful woman.

They left Arakhova at half past four, and there was nothing in the climb while daylight lasted. The sun was still very hot and they made their way without haste up the wooded slopes. After about two hours the going became harder because it was largely over loose stones. Menelaus had needed some pressing to undertake the climb, it being, he said, a bad time of year both because of the treacherous snow and because of the risk of sudden storms. Parnassus, he said, was noted for them; the old mountain was temperamental; like God; you never knew who or where he was going to strike next. He talked almost without a break on the way up, and with the going hard and steep the other two were content to let him.

Once they heard dogs baying in the distance and he said: "Be not afraid: they know me; but they are as fierce as wolves."

As they climbed level with the other mountains snow began to appear—earlier than Gene had calculated, at first only in patches where the sun did not reach, then in long ridges like zebra stripes. They sat on a high mound of stones to watch the sun wink his red eye over the side of the world. The ravine beside them looked like a great hairy armpit which, as the sun sank, perceptibly darkened and seemed to quicken as if the arm had stirred. The breeze had dropped, and all about them was a great silence. But far away in the distance, far below them, a shepherd was playing his pipe to his sheep. The thin sweet notes came up to them out of the darkening void like the last sounds of a drowning world.

She said in English: "I am waiting."

"What for?"

"For you to tell me why you came to Greece."

"Oh, that."

"Yes, that."

"Can Menelaus speak English?"

"No."

Gene said: "I've first got to ask you one question. Only one, I promise. What's your feeling about Communists?"

"I like them like poverty, like disease, like pain, like dirt under the nails."

In the brief over-coloured after-glow the eccentric planes of his face moved in fleeting symmetries of determination and disillusion.

"I think I started life without political prejudices. I came back to Greece during the war with only one idea, which was getting the Germans out. ELAS has made me feel the way I do. Even now I'm dead against witch-hunts—all the paraphernalia of persecuting people because they have liberal ideas and carried a red flag at a meeting. In western countries Communists haven't a hope. Here it's different. Twice they've nearly made it: first in 1944 when the British stopped them, second in 1947 when the Greeks themselves, with American aid, stopped them. But it's never been a knock-out. Remember the spy ring of a few years ago?"

"Which?"

"The Vavoudis thing."

"Oh, yes. Secret radios and the rest. Very boring."

"Not for Vavoudis. He committed suicide. But there were others who stood trial. Twenty-nine."

"I remember."

"Secret radios, as you say; tentacles everywhere covering labour troubles, military espionage, penetration of the political parties, spreading unrest at crucial times, smuggling in of gold to pay and bribe. I got involved in it some months before it broke."

"You did? How?"

"Military counter espionage had been trying to uncover the ring for eighteen months or more; but they couldn't. Quite by chance, I happened on a sensitive spot. There was a sharp reaction and I ran into trouble and a man was killed. There was a police inquiry, and from that—what came out not in court but in private—a new scent started. From there on it led to the uncovering of the Vavoudis spy ring."

"And what happened to you?"

Menelaus was fidgeting. "Let us go, please. We have less than twenty minutes of the day left."

They made the two stone huts about ten-thirty. The quarter moon, following the sun down, had been very bright except for the last fifteen minutes when they had walked into a cloud. Menelaus lit a fire of sticks in one of the huts and filled the lamp with paraffin, and they had their coffee and sandwiches on the bare woooden table in the centre of the hut. Menelaus ate *keftedes* with maize bread and drank a whole bottle of *retsina*.

Gene said: "How are your boots?"

"Wonderful. Only they were not made for my feet." She sat sideways on a bench in her stockinged feet, her knees drawn up and her hands around them.

"Are you blistered?"

"So far there is very little blood."

"Let me see."

"No, I'm unhurt."

He said in Greek: "It's going to be cold here tonight. I think we should make up the fire."

"Don't worry. I will see to that," said Menelaus. "There is some chopped wood in the next hut. We have always kept chopped wood and paraffin here, even during the war."

"You were here during the war?"

"Around and about. Twice I made journeys to Athens, but I don't like Athens. It's unhealthy. All those people crowded together and toilets indoors. I prefer the open fields, like the animals. One becomes half animal up here." He touched his thick goatskin cape and squinted hideously. "So one cares little for heat or cold."

Gene said: "It was ELAS country?"

Menelaus nodded. "It was. But Greek country before and after."

"That's what we should all have remembered."

"Oh, some were in ELAS but many wished to work alone. That first winter in '41, I was a boy of twenty and I had romantic notions. There were six English soldiers hiding up here, in this hut, and we fed them. One was from Adelaide, two from Christhouse, New Zealand, and three from Manchester. That is England? We sent them off to Cairo. And later we got a message back. I have the message . . . No, it's in my drawer at home."

"How did you get them out?" Anya asked.

"We took them by night down to a cave near Kirphi. Then the next night there was a rowing-boat made ready for them on the sea-shore near Itea. All that winter we did that, because stray ones kept coming in. Twice instead I guided men to Athens; but that was in '43; and the second time the Germans caught me and beat me and something went wrong with my eye. But I had the laugh of them in the end because I helped to blow up a bridge across a road when they were retreating and many of them were on it. That was very comical. I will get you some wood."

He heaved himself up, and a great shadow flung itself round the hut as he went to the door and out.

Anya swung her legs down and put her hands in her pockets.

"There are nine children in the family, all living off the same farm and what they can pick up from casual earnings. Yet you would insult this man tomorrow if you gave him more than his agreed fee."

618

Gene said: "This is the Greece that I care about—that I sometimes care about so much that it hurts—not the shoddy-smart, phoney glitter of fashionable Athens."

"My world."

"By choice?"

"By choice."

"It isn't the only one there is."

She shrugged and there was silence. He studied her two profiles, the lamp-lit one and the shadow on the wall behind it. It was like the other self, the *ka* as the Egyptians called it. Which was the one he was addressing himself to, and what were the risks he was running?

Rather sulkily she said: "You were telling me on the way up about the spy ring and how you were expelled from Greece."

"Not expelled, invited to leave. Trouble was my own embassy thought the same and I couldn't rely on their backing. So I left just as the Vavoudis thing was coming to the boil. I think I could still have been useful, but somebody had pulled strings. The next time I visited Greece all sorts of road blocks were put in my way, as I've told you, almost as soon as I landed. I even had difficulty in getting to talk with the chief army intelligence officer who'd handled the case. When I asked him why, he shrugged and said the Vavoudis arrests had only taken the froth off the barrel: the fermenting was still going on deeper down."

"And why are you here now?"

"Just before an election is a likely time for the froth to begin to rise again. And this time one might see deeper into the barrel."

"And what has all this to do with the Little Jockey or the accident to the Spaniard or your feud with George Lascou?"

He gave her a long considering stare. Up to now he had been taking a reasonable risk; at this point the risk became unreasonable.

"Ever hear of Anton Avra?"

"No."

"He was half Roumanian, half Macedonian, trained in

Russia. He was Vavoudis's chief, the organising brain. But he saw the red light and got out of the country just in time. Nobody knew what had happened to him, but it was generally thought he'd gone back behind the Iron Curtain. Then a few months ago it was announced that he'd died in Spain."

"In Spain . . ."

"I suppose he was sent there to improve the organisation of the party. He was brilliant at that sort of thing, especially in places where the party was underground. D'you remember the details of Vavoudis's suicide?"

"Wasn't he surrounded?"

"Yes, in a house in Lycurgus Street. They'd built a big cellar under the washhouse that you could only get into by a sliding concrete door hidden under the sink. Although the military knew there was a transmitter in the house when they surrounded it, it took them a day and a half to find it, and Vavoudis was down there all the time. In addition to the transmitter were all the party papers and records, which he couldn't burn before he was discovered because the smoke would betray him. When he *was* discovered he set fire to them but there wasn't enough draught in the cellar for the stuff to burn quickly. So most of it was saved. Only a few of the most important books and letters were gone. It was generally assumed that Avra had taken them with him when he left."

"So?"

She was sitting now with her back against the wall, her hands round one knee which was drawn up, her lips resting on it; the other leg was stretched out and showed through the thick material the rounded movement of her thigh as her grey-stockinged foot gently tapped the end of the table.

"So these things were lost. But something I believe has recently been found. Did you know that Juan Tolosa was —or used to be—a Communist?"

"How could I?"

"I thought he had brought something back with him to Greece."

620

"And hadn't he?"

"He didn't have it with him. Otherwise the police would have found it."

"How do you know what they have found?"

"I know that."

"So you are agreeing with his wife—that the accident was no accident?"

"I think he was putting pressure on someone here—for private gain; and they didn't like it."

After a minute she said: "What are you saying?"

"That's all I have to say."

"You've said too little or too much."

"Too much, maybe."

Menelaus came back beaming hideously, his arms piled with small faggots. "We have four hours to rest. I will make the fire up and then it will last a time. There is an old straw bed in the other hut and I will sleep there."

Gene looked up. "But the fire's here."

"And only two places to lie." His smile vanished. "That is how you would wish it? I will lie on the floor here if you prefer."

Gene looked at the girl inquiringly.

"It's of indifference to me," she said. "We shall not undress, I suppose? Do whatever you wish, Menelaus."

"I'll go with him if you like," said Gene.

"No, I do not like."

Menelaus said: "Don't be afraid, I shall not oversleep. I'll wake you at half past three."

There was silence while he went about the hut, building up the fire, putting away the remains of the meal. Anya got up and walked across to the window. Gene's eyes followed her as she rubbed the window clear with on old rag and then leaned with her hand against the wall, bending to peer out. She turned suddenly and found him watching her; her eyes glinted and then moved on as if he were part of the furniture.

"Good night, sir. Good night, Miss Stonaris."

When they were alone Gene got up and took a few faggots

621

off the fire. "I think it will get too hot if we have such a blaze. I'll put more on in an hour."

"How lovely the snow looks."

"Have the clouds gone?"

"Yes."

He unfastened his own boots. "Do you want to lie down?"

She came back slowly from the window. "When I first met you, dear Gene, I thought you were foolish. Then I thought you were very clever in disguise. Now I know that you are really a fool after all."

"Thank you at least for the dear Gene. It makes one's demolition more cosy."

She sat on the edge of the table. "From what you have told me so far about this Spaniard, and this Anton Avra, you are suggesting that George is in some way involved in it."

"I'm not saying anything."

"But you are. You're implying that."

"Anya, you wanted to know what I was doing here. I've told you what I'm doing here. Often I grope in the dark myself. I've only told you what has happened."

"And left me to make my own conclusions."

"It's all anyone can do, yet."

"I can tell you that your conclusions are utterly wrong."

"Perhaps you don't know what my conclusions are."

"Apart altogether from George, I know all the chief leaders of EMO. I meet them and mix with them more closely than any other woman does."

"Yes, I believe you."

"Well, I know that none of them could have any connection with this thing."

"How can you be sure?"

"Well, are you suggesting that I don't even know George Lascou?"

"I've said, I'm suggesting nothing. I don't know how much George Lascou confides in you or how much you confide in him. But I know that he's a clever, subtle and complex man."

"Perhaps that is why you do not understand him."

"It could be."

She slid off the table to re-fix the clasp that bound her hair. "The trouble with you is you have too literal a mind. George puts forward some philisophical argument and you think he's talking practical politics. You're too ingenuous to understand the mind of a Greek."

"Even yours?"

"Mine you do not even begin to know at all."

16

There had been silence in the hut for some time. The first blaze of the fire had gone down but there was still some heat from it. She had been sitting quite still on her bunk staring at the fire. He squatted on the floor on the opposite side of the fireplace. About half an hour had passed.

He said at length: "How did you first meet George Lascou? Won't you tell me that?"

"Oh, there's nothing more to say."

"Well, say it."

She stretched. "He saw me first at a concert given for Greek and English troops. Because I was young and knew both languages they asked me to sing. The next day he called to see me and asked where were my parents. I said *kaput,* so he went to see the priest who had sheltered me. Soon after that I was sent back to school, and then on to the university. He paid for everything. I was nearly fifteen when it began. When I was nineteen he came to see me one day and asked me to be his mistress."

"Just like that."

"Why not? We had seen a lot of each other during the previous two years. We'd read and walked together and knew each other well."

"Was he married then?"

"Yes."

"So you said yes."

She yawned. "I don't know why I talk to you."

"Go to sleep then."

"No, I will tell you because it may help you to understand him better. He was married but not happy with his wife, but with young children to think of. He said he'd watched me grow, ever since that first night. He said he'd watched and waited patiently. Which is true. It *had* been four years. Since you will wish to know all about it, he put it to me that there was nothing cheap or sordid about the classic women of Ancient Greece—like Phryne, who modelled for Praxiteles, or Aspasia, the mistress of Pericles: they were highly educated, intelligent women living a fuller and more balanced life than any married woman, moving in true society, which was not the society of aristocracy but the society of brains and art."

"I can hear him saying that."

"Well, it was true!"

"Yes, certainly. And has it been true for you?"

"Dear Gene, even you could not expect me to come up to the standard of women like those, or expect the people I've associated with to have the quality of the people they knew. That is a fault of the times, not of the arrangement. I am very happy."

"And you love George Lascou?"

She laughed. "Of course. I've told you."

He leaned forward to put another couple of branches on the fire. One of them left a circle of damp in the hearth where the snow had melted. "I've been through all the conventional motions myself, on all the usual occasions. So as a generalisation I'm all for the ha-ha-don't-tell-me-fairy-tales attitude."

She said: "Love's like gambling. People always play for too high stakes. They overbid their luck and never know when to cut their losses."

He watched her lips as she spoke. "True enough."

"But?" she said, noting the inflexion in his voice.

"But once in a while, you have to admit, the bank is beaten. There's evidence for it."

"In books?"

"Sometimes in books but not only there. Trouble is, as you say, every man thinks his chick is a swan, every man believes in gambler's luck. It isn't till you're broke once again, bankrupt, on your uppers, that you realise another vision splendid has fallen apart and become a shower of rusty tinsel."

"I'm glad at least we agree on that."

"I'm not sure we do."

"No?"

"No, I'm still half inclined to believe the big show exists, even though it hasn't existed for me."

"And so if it did?"

"If it did I think it might make our present knowing talk sound like bright teenagers' prattle. I think it might make even a war-worn type like me, who'd always taken pride in being on the outside even of his own affairs, feel as if he was shooting the rapids in a leaky canoe. I think it might stop him from ever being patronising or superior about it again because he'd know it was something that was bigger and more important than he could ever personally hope to be or begin to be."

She looked at him then. "Are you employing the same technique as you used to get me to climb this mountain?"

"There's no technique that I know of that could make the difference. Either it is or it isn't, that's all."

"I distrust you and your arguments—profoundly," she said. "But I take it back that you are unsubtle. That was a mistake that I made."

"Well, it's healthy to revise one's judgments. I've recently revised a lot of mine."

The fire had gone down. It was cold in the hut, and he got cautiously up and began to replace the faggots. Outside a wind was stirring, moving through the mountains, lightly playing over the snow. They had turned the lamp down, but as the fire began to crackle a fresh light flickered about the room, and by it he went cautiously to look at her.

She was asleep. Her lips were slightly parted, her hair had curled round and was covering one ear; lashes black on cheeks; breathing hardly to be seen. She looked absurdly innocent; she had that faculty that children have of sloughing off the day's sins. An altar piece, an Andrea del Sarto madonna.

He stayed a long time watching her, content and able to study at his leisure a face that held magic for him either in movement or repose. When he had talked to her just now he had talked half to convince himself. Common sense told him that there could be, for him, only the rusty tinsel here over again.

The blanket had slipped and he lifted it to cover her shoulder. Then, thinking she would probably lose body heat in sleep, he took up his own blanket and put it over the other. She didn't stir. He squatted down before the fire, about three or four feet from her, shook a cigarette out of a packet and lit it from a flickering splinter of wood.

The wind was getting up. It was howling now like a distant wolf, out there among the crevasses and the lonely peaks. Perhaps tomorrow it would be too rough to go on. Perhaps it would be all they could do to get down. Down to Athens. What waited in Athens? The letter from Madrid? Not yet. But all the problems of the things he had set himself to do. They seemed to belong to a world that hadn't a great deal of relevance up here in the snow. He moved his head again and found that she was watching him.

She said: "What time is it?"

"Twelve thirty."

"Only that?"

"D'you want the night to go so quickly?"

"Don't you?"

"Not specially."

"Why don't you lie down?"

"I like it like this."

There was silence for a time, and he thought she had gone

off. Then she moved to put the palm of her hand behind her neck.

"I don't need your blanket."

"It's better there than not being used."

"Were you standing over me just now?"

"Yes."

Silence again. He flicked his cigarette into the heart of the fire.

She said: "Your face is like a ship's prow pushing forward all the time into choppy seas."

"Thanks."

"Your nature's like that too, isn't it. Pushing on, never letting up. Why do you not accept life as it is instead of trying to worry it with your teeth all the time, like a terrier with a bone."

"Is that how you see it?"

"I wish I could tell you something about George. It would prove you wrong about him, but alas it is secret."

"Something about General Telechos?"

She looked at him quickly. "Why do you say that?"

"I know about the possible link-up politically."

She said: "You know too much."

"Maybe."

"I think perhaps after tonight we shall both know too much of each other."

"Except the vital thing."

"What is that?"

"You tell me," he said.

Just before two he again built up the fire. It was the last of the wood, and when this went they would have to shiver for a while. He lit another cigarette.

She said: "Can I have one?"

"I thought you were asleep."

"I have been. Light it for me, will you?"

He lit it and passed it to here and for a bit they smoked without speaking.

"Have your blanket."

"No."

"Lean back on something."

He looked around and then moved back against her trestle, so that he was sitting with his shoulders near to her waist. He said: "I detect a mother instinct."

"You are the worst detector I have ever met."

Her hand was lying beside him and he took it. The fingers curved round his and then relaxed. They finished their cigarettes and threw them away. But he continued to hold her hand. So Menelaus found them when he came in at three-thirty. Only this time Gene was asleep and Anya was awake, staring with rather terrible eyes at the dying embers of the fire.

17

They drank the rest of the coffee and swallowed a few mouthfuls of bread and honey. The wind was still blowing but the night was clear. When they opened the door of the hut it was bitterly cold, but by the time they had been on the move for half an hour, the bite had gone out of the air. The going was dangerous because the snow was loose and treacherous and much of the ground underneath was rubble and loose stones. Then after a time they went down into a declivity between the two humps of the mountain which stood out on each side of them against the starlit sky. "That is Old Man Rock," muttered Menelaus, as if afraid of being overheard. "This is Wolf Mountain. It is a bad place to be caught in a storm."

They stopped for a few minutes and then attacked the Wolf, climbing round its side and up to its great white head.

When they got to the top after another hour the sky was paling slightly but it was still dark. Menelaus switched off his torch and ploughed across to where a wooden cross was half hidden in the snow. "This is the place to be. If you stand here you are out of the wind. . . ."

For a few minutes he stayed with them, talking at a great rate, then he went off and stood by himself staring out over the mountains, his tall, gaunt, short-coated figure outlined like an Evzone against the lightening sky.

Since they woke they had hardly talked together at all; Menelaus had been with them all the time and they had been strangers. They stood together now, staring and unspeaking. Then Anya said harshly:

"Without enmity—without bitterness—I think this is the last time we can ever meet."

He didn't look at her. "If you give me your reasons I shall probably agree with them."

"We are on opposite sides in all this. I am not a traitor to the people I care for. You are against them and therefore I am against you. Nothing we can do can alter that—even if we wished to do it."

"Is that your reason?"

"We come from different civilisations—what is the word?—irreconcilable. Everything we do and think is referred back to different principles, different sets of values. You cannot build a bridge across two thousand years."

"Is that your reason?"

She didn't say any more. The wind was dropping, as it so often does at dawn. The light came very quickly. One moment day was over the horizon, then it was in the sky, then suddenly it had fallen on them. One moment the land all about them was secret and unknown, then it was suddenly all in place, assembled, a crag here, a heap of boulders there, a ravine, a waste of snow.

And as the light came the view fled away from them for endless distances through the crystal air. Mountains and forests, land-locked bays, arid plains, tiny villages. Sea beyond land and land beyond the sea and sea beyond the land again; and then the sun came up a wild cadmium colour and the yellow feathers in the sky crimsoned and preened themselves and the washed green streaks faded and disappeared.

"You are lucky," said Menelaus, coming back to them and baring his broken teeth. "It is good today. It is very good. See over there Mount Timfristos. That is seventy kilometres away. Could you believe it! And over there to the north—see, that way and much further—is Pelion; and beyond and behind it—to the left—is Ossa. And more to the right, far beyond the sea, that grey mass, I don't know what it is but they say that is still Greece. Imagine it! And that, looking right into the sun, that is an island, I have forgotten its name. South, those are the mountains where you came from. And here, here in front of us is the Gulf of Corinth. And behind that the mountains of the Peloponnesus, see the peaks like teeth. It is good after all that we came this morning."

"It is good," said Gene. Anya didn't speak.

They stood in silence for a time. Menelaus went over and began energetically to kick away the snow from round the cross.

She said: "To find that cross on the top of a mountain dedicated to the Old Gods . . . One would say it would have been better to have left at least *this* little part of the earth to them."

"It could be that the old and the new gods are not so different."

She shook back her head as if there was a wisp of hair in her eyes. "Could that be Mount Athos—that Menelaus said was 'still Greece'? It is surely too far."

"Anyway, it's going. It's not as clear as five minutes ago. The miracle's nearly over."

She said: "Miracle? Yes, it is almost that. A pity, when the eyes can see so far . . ." She didn't finish.

He said: "Were those your real reasons why you felt we should not meet again?"

"Would they be yours?"

"Not altogether."

". . . But you agree that this should be the end?"

"Yes." After a minute he added: "We're running on rocks—at least, I am—so quickly that to miss total shipwreck . . ."

She said: "You want me?"

"It goes without saying, doesn't it?"

"But it is much more than that?"

"Much more."

"If it was only that."

"It can never be only that."

The sun was gaining warmth, but the day and the moment seemed very cold for them both.

She said: "Then go, Gene, go. Leave me as soon as we get down. Leave Greece and never come back. Promise you will go—at once—so that I shall never have the fear of meeting you again."

"I'll go," he said. "Write it out of your life. I'll go."

18

She got back to her flat about six on the Monday. When she put her key in the door she found it unlocked. It was late for Edda. Then she could smell his cigar smoke.

He was sitting turning the pages of a French novel, a glass with brandy in it by his side. His pince-nez glinted as he turned and nodded and half smiled. "You're late, Anya."

She went over and after a barely noticeable hesitation kissed him. "Late for what, darling?"

"I said I'd drop in for a drink about five today."

"Did you?" she said flatly. "Of course it's Monday! Have you been waiting long?"

"An hour. I'm usually punctual."

She went across and unstoppered the sherry decanter and took up a glass. "What a day! I need a drink."

He added: "But it appears I shall be unpunctual now. My next meeting is just due to start."

"I'm so sorry. I was quite mixed in the days of the week."

"Have you been out of town?"

"Yes. I'm dirty and lame. Can I fill your glass?"

"Have you been with Gene Vanbrugh?"

She sipped her drink before replying. "Yes."

"Where did you spend last night?"

"Why do you suppose I wasn't here?"

"I rang. But there are other reasons. Go on."

"I spent it in a hut in the mountains near Delphi."

"With Gene Vanbrugh?"

"Yes."

With his tidy fingers he put a book-mark in the pages of the novel and closed it.

"Did he make love to you?"

"He was not invited to."

"I shouldn't have thought a man of his type necessarily needed the invitation."

She said slowly: "For once it is not your place to think. Six years ago I made a bargain with you, George. When I break it I'll no longer take your money or your flat."

Lascou's ductile sensitive mind seemed to accept the statement and close around it and absorb it undigested, moving on all the time into prepared country. "Darling, it's strange, this sudden feeling for this man. I think you have even tried to disguise it from yourself. Perhaps it is the unfamiliarity of such a person as Vanbrugh. Please, I am not trying to blame you, I am interested, inquiring. I am on your side—though frankly I don't think he is worth it."

"Worth what?" she said, still with a queer tense politeness. "Three days of my time? I have given longer to the Earthquake Relief Fund."

He watched her attentively while she finished her drink. Then she sat down and began undoing one of her stockings through her skirt.

He said: "Where is he now?"

"I don't know."

"Did you go by car?"

"Yes. He hired one, but asked me to return it to the garage for him."

"Where did he leave you?"

"At Daphni."

632

"What are his plans?"

She slipped down her stocking and took off her shoe. "D'you suppose he discussed them with me, his enemy?"

"I imagine you had some conversation in thirty-six hours."

She flexed her ankle. "I borrowed shoes up there; but I see there's no blister after all. I shall not be lame for life. Talk? Oh, yes, we talked: God, what a bore it all was! What a silly little man he is! I shall take a bath and then go out to dinner somewhere and on to a night-club. The Little Jockey, probably."

He watched her foot for a moment, then his eyes travelled up her leg to her thigh and to the peculiar twisted angry grace of the way she was sitting.

"Anya."

"Yes?"

"Look at me."

She raised her head and gave him a smile as taut as a wire.

"In the last ten years I have lavished a great deal of money and attention on you."

"Yes, George. One of your less profitable investments."

"Far from it. Working admittedly on the finest material, I have turned you from a long-legged underfed waif into one of the most beautiful and sought-after women in Greece."

She slipped on her shoe and got up. "Dear me."

"And it's been worth it. Don't think you owe me anything. If it ended tomorrow I should regret nothing. But there may be one drawback from your point of view: I am not willing that it should end tomorrow."

"Don't forget your other audience is waiting."

"Anya!"

She turned on him like a flash. "Well, *what* do you want me to say? What do you want me to do? D'you want me to tell you that I've separated from this man and will never see him again? Well, I have! Today. This afternoon. Before coming here. When I left him that was good-bye! And d'you think I *care*!"

His eyes flickered. In the last year he had become much less tolerant of opposition from any quarter. "Yes, I think you care—in some rather perverse, unformulated way. Men like that appeal to something in women. If——"

"At this moment, George, you do not appeal to me! In my perverse unformulated way I find you very offensive."

They stared at each other. Like brother and sister quarrelling, they showed their tensions in the same way. Suddenly supple and pliant he said: "Don't let's fight over this, darling. I say that not because it's not important enough; but because it is too important. I'll go now."

"Whatever you say."

"But I put this to you to think over—if it ever came to the point, I should not be willing to lose you—to anyone. I put it to you both as an entreaty and as a threat."

"A threat? Oh, come. Isn't that a little heavy in the hand?"

"Life frequently is. It's only we would-be sophisticated ones who try to take the sting out of it with a laugh and a shrug and a few cigarette stubs and a cocktail shaker. Scratch the sophisticate and you will find the polish goes barely skin deep."

"You terrify me."

"No, my dear Anya, I don't terrify you. You lived too long in terror to be able to feel it any more. But you are a very honest person, within your limitations, as, within my limitations, I try to be. I was not trying to offend you when I said what I did—only honest. But I do hope if I threaten you—or him—or anyone else—you'll not think I'm merely bluffing."

She said: "I could never accuse you of that."

He picked up his white pigskin gloves. "Remember, preferably, that I have loved you since I first saw you. Nothing has happened since then to make me change my mind."

"Does your mind direct your love?" she asked desolately. "That must be very convenient. Or better still perhaps, can one direct oneself not to feel at all?"

19

The letter came at one o'clock on the Tuesday. Maria
had been on the look-out all day. Several times she had been
in to Philip, who lay on his back on his bed in a litter of
cigarette ends, but he wouldn't speak to her. For two days he
had spoken to nobody. Once each day he had been out of the
house to buy more cigarettes, but each time when he came
back he seemed worse. He was getting through nearly a
hundred and fifty a day.

Often there was no one in the shabby office-reception-desk
when the post came and it was slapped down on the shelf
which topped the half door into the office. Anyone was then
free to paw over the letters and maybe take what didn't
belong to them. She was down before eight and hung about
until the morning delivery came, but there was nothing for
her. Then just after twelve she went down again and stolidly
read the cinema advertisements for an hour. Mme Nicolou,
who ran the boarding house, was frying some fish, and the
smell and crackle of it came through to the lobby, but Maria
had no sensations of hunger or thirst. All normal feeling had
gone on the day of Juan's death, leaving nothing but
the one desire. She carried it with her like an ikon, in her
breast. For a week she had fasted like a saint before some
time of trial.

It was a strong envelope when it came but not very big,
being about seven inches by five, and not even registered.
But she knew her cousin's handwriting. She crept with it up
to her bedroom. Philip was useless. One person only she
could be sure of, and that was herself.

She slit the envelope up the side and took out a flat
stained waterproof wallet about the size of a tobacco pouch.
With it was a brief letter from her cousin which told
her nothing fresh. She opened the wallet. Inside this, behind

a mica screen, was a man's photograph and some details of his age, appearance, profession. In the pocket of the wallet were about ten letters. She opened the first letter.

Maria Tolosa's father had been a night club dancer too, and before something went wrong with his kidneys that killed him off prematurely they had travelled Europe together. So she had a smattering of all the western languages, Greek among them. But reading Greek was a different matter from speaking it, and to her anger she found she could not read these letters at all. Five of them were badly stained, but they were all quite clear. The dates ranged from 1947 to 1950.

She bit her thumb nail. Sufficient to see the pieces of the jig-saw? But she wanted the pattern. She had a belief in her own memory. A thing in her own mind was more indelible than any paper.

And although she trusted Gene Vanbrugh she knew she had nothing as yet stronger than instinct to go on. Here was one way of putting him to the test. Get the letters read by somebody else and then ask Gene Vanbrugh to read them. If he didn't know she knew what the letters contained and the two accounts tallied. . . .

But who? . . . Mme Nicolou? Mme Nicolou had not always kept a B-category lodging house. Before the war she had been an actress of promise, until the starvation of the German occupation had jogged her mind one groove out of true. She would be able to read the letters and, what was better, would soon forget them.

Maria slid the letters into their wallet. Afterwards, after they had been read, they would go next to her body in the top of her girdle, where temporarily they would be safe. . . .

She unlocked the door and found herself facing her brother-in-law.

In thirty-nine Spanish summers Philip Tolosa had never sweated so much as he had done in this one week of cool Athenian spring. He was sweating now.

"So it has come."

Caught with the thing in her hand she could not deny it.

"The letter? Yes. There are some papers. I am taking them to get them read."

"I shouldn't do that." He made a move to take the wallet but she held it away.

"Why not?"

"Let me see what it is."

"You wouldn't understand. You know less Greek than I do."

"Where are you taking them?"

"To Mme Nicolou."

"Don't do that. Give it to me. Let me see."

"No. See it later."

"Maria!"

She said: "I was his wife. What was his is now legally mine."

"You don't know what you're talking about! You don't know the danger we're in."

"Do you think I care for danger!"

"Well, *I* do. If this——"

"*You*," she said with contempt. "It is nothing to do with you if you don't want it to be. I can handle this quite alone."

"You young fool!" He grasped her arm, but feverishly, almost without strength. "Don't you know this house has been watched every minute since Juan died! What chance have you of doing anything on your own? What chance has *either* of us——"

"Then why did you press me to send for this, if you thought——"

"Because it was the only *hope*! Maria, I tell you I'd no choice! If Juan had taken heed of my warnings! I tried to persuade him. I threatened not to come to Greece. I wish to God I had broken up the act before we came."

"Get out of my way!"

"If you do anything with those letters except hand them over they'll kill us both!"

"They? They? Who are they?"

"Do you think I would choose this? Do you think I wanted it that way——"

637

"You—*betrayed* him," she said suddenly.

He stood with his back to the door, his face the colour of wet linen. He showed his teeth slightly each time he drew in his breath.

"You call it that. Of course you call it that. But d'you think I wanted to do it? D'you think I cared nothing for him? He was my brother as well as your husband. I tell you I tried to stop him—I quarrelled with him! I knew what he was up against. Besides, it was a betrayal on *his* part. When one ceases to be a Communist one does not cease to have some honour, some loyalty. . . . I do not know how they knew it was Juan, that he was responsible for the attempt to get money; for that was due to no move of mine. All I heard, all I got, was notice to report to the Party. I am still a member, you know. What was I to do? It was right to go from all points of view, to divert suspicion. But when I got to the meeting place, it was no party meeting at all—only thugs waiting for me. . . ."

She stared at him, but she said nothing at all.

"They beat me up—d'you remember I said I'd fallen in the street. . . . It was Juan's life or ours; they put it to me, one life or three. . . . When he was dead they came again—get the papers, they said, or it will be the end next for you. . . . Well, I've got the papers. Now they're going to have them!"

She moved carefully an inch or two forward and spat in his face.

Brushing the insult away as an irrelevance, he wiped his hand across his cheek. "What chance have you got? You couldn't even get out of the house. I tell you you're fighting the world."

She said: "You are an Andalusian. I am from Castile. When a man from Castile does what you have done there is only one thing left. He *destroys* himself."

"Maria——"

She thrust at him with both hands, thrust him aside and took the handle of the door, got it half open. He clutched her arm, tried to snatch the letter, and she swung round with her

638

clenched fist and all the weight of her body behind it. It took him off balance and he fell down. She pulled the door and was out.

Half down the stairs she stopped to gulp for breath and listened, but he wasn't yet following. She slid into the office, which as usual was empty, but the door beyond was open and she heard the clatter of plate and fork. Mme Nicolou was just finishing lunching alone, in a pink artificial-silk kimono and scarlet mules. She had dyed blonde hair, heavy and straight and drawn back in streaks so that the white tips of her ears showed through it. The two sides of her face didn't quite match; one side was wide-awake and confident, the other eye drooped as if it had just seen a sly joke.

"The laundry's been back an hour, dear. I specially asked them to be quick; it's two sisters who work for me; and they haven't charged extra for the bloodstains on the shirt; help yourself to it if you want it; over there; my, how I hate cooking for myself; one stinks of the food before one can put a knive to it." She picked up a piece of dark-coloured bread in her long pointed finger-nails and began to rub it round and round on her plate mopping up the grease.

Maria shut the door behind her and stood breathing thickly. "Can you read these letters for me, Mme Nicolou? They belonged to my husband and I can't read this Greek. You know."

Mme Nicolou twisted the crumbling bread into a ball and pushed it into her mouth. The grease smeared her lip-stick and ran down her chin. She wiped it off on the arm of her kimono, which was already black just there. "Men are always writing. Why I don't know. Why were they ever taught to write? It only leads to trouble, and don't we have enough trouble without that. I knew a man who——"

"Mme Nicolou, it is urgent."

The other woman stared. With her tongue she carefully explored her teeth. "That was what the man said. It's urgent, he said." Her drooping lid closed, showing more of the blue eye-shadow. "But you can't fool me. Urgency, I said, is for Germans and the other vandals, not for Greeks who know how to live. . . . Well, where are my glasses? Let me see."

She fumbled a pair of black evening spectacles out of her pocket and put them on. Maria thrust the first letter into the woman's long, thin hand. She stared at it.

"These are old letters? Was your husband in Greece in 1947?" she asked after a minute, fixing Maria with her wide-awake eye.

"Can you read it?"

"Of course. But it is not the official, it is the literary script. *Demotiki,* they call it. Mm-mm, people pretend to prefer one or the other. As if it mattered!"

As she was speaking Maria saw someone crossing the street towards the house. A stout man in a black alpaca coat who walked with a slightly anthropoid roll. He had a beard growing like a bonnet string under his chin. She heard his footsteps come into the hall but they did not go up the stairs.

"Not to *yourself*," said Maria sharply. "*Aloud* for me to hear!"

Mme Nicolou had been mouthing what she read. "But, dear, this doesn't sound like a love letter. Mm-mm. . . . Was your husband called Anton or George? I can't recollect."

"*Read.*"

"It says," began Mme Nicolou. "Mm-mm, it says, 'Dear Anton, the usual stuff is here. A purser from the Italian ship brought it. Five thousand. Via Paris. I can add to this one for one, but not in gold. With prices soaring that's too precious to me and I regret I can make what I consider better use of it. Well, it all comes to the same thing in the end. Don't tell your masters.' " Mme Nicolou raised her head. "Was that someone ringing the bell?"

"No. Go on."

"Where was I? 'Your masters. Mm-mm. . . . They expect a man to have not thought of self-advancement. Do you too? I believe no creed is above criticism or dogma too sacred to be submitted occasionally to the lights of common sense. I have too high a regard for your intellect to suppose you think otherwise. Regards.' And it is signed, 'George.' Does that

640

mean anything to you? Was he your lover? It doesn't sound so to me."

"Is there a key to this door?"

Mme Nicolou put her hand inside her kimono and scratched with great concentration and satisfaction. She scratched like a bitch after a flea. "No, dear. My husband lost both keys before he died. He was careless. But then nothing mattered to him but sex. It was his religion, his meat and drink. So I had a bolt fitted."

"A bolt? *Where?*"

"At the top there. Men have always followed me. At one time my dressing room was never less than two deep. Never less. In Sofia. I remember once in Sofia——But why have you bolted it now? I sleep lightly in the afternoon."

Maria stood with her back to the door. Her heart was beating. She knew now the extent of Philip's cowardice and betrayal. "There's—a man outside. He has been trying to make up to me and I don't want anything to do with him. Go on."

"Go on? What with? Oh, the letters. You look upset. Has this man been annoying you?"

"No. Go on."

"And your husband only dead a week. They have no decency, men. You may not believe it, Mme Tolosa, but I was brought up very strictly. My mother warned me when I was thirteen——"

"*This* is the second letter. *Read* it."

There was a gentle knock on the door.

"Shouldn't we open it?"

"No."

"Well. . . . This begins like the last. 'Dear Anton, Mmmm. . . . I hope you got everything as promised. Your rebuke might have come straight out of the party ink-pot. Oh, I know and agree with most of your arguments, but I claim the right to an independent voice now and again. Anyway, I'm sure you won't wish to dispense with my valuable assistance. D'you realise it amounted to eighteen thousand pounds sterling last year? Incidentally have a care

641

how you receive Mlle d'A. She may be all we wish her to be, but she's also a famous actress and expects to be treated as such. Let Manos meet her. He has the approach that women like. All that she brought is now delivered into your hands——'"

There was another, louder knock on the door.

" '—into your hands.' Mme Tolosa, do you think this man will soon go away? Perhaps I could speak to him? I shall have to go upstairs in a few minutes. It's a trouble I suffer from."

"I want you," said Maria, "to call the police."

Mme Nicolou put down the letter as if it was hot. Her face seemed to try to break up. "The *police*? What are you talking about? They were here last week! I couldn't stand another visit like last week: it reminded me of when the Germans were here. I can't *stand* it! Tramp, tramp, I can't stand the sound of the *boots*."

She put her hands up to her face and began to cry.

Maria gripped her shoulder. "Tell me, where is the telephone? You have one in here?"

"No. . . . There—there is only the one in the hall."

"Is there another way out?"

"There's a back door. But I don't want to be left a-alone. This man might rob me."

"He wants only me. Don't open the door to him until I'm gone."

She grabbed up the two letters and put them back in the wallet. Then she slid through into the little scullery with its bubbling stove and copper pans. Coffee was steaming in a pot on the side.

She opened the door to the street. A tall young man stood there. He had a long narrow nose, smiling eyes, and a pert girlish mouth.

He said: "Hullo, sweetheart," and smiled and put up a hand to her face and pushed her violently back into the scullery. He followed her as she fell and shut the door behind him.

20

Gene was there ten minutes before her, and as soon as he saw her he knew what her phone call had meant. She came stumbling into the cellar, half blind after the brilliant light outside, lurched against the stove, making the tin chimney sway and rattle, came up against a chair and clutched the back with both hands.

"I've lost it!" she said in a sobbing voice. "They took it from me! Philip had sold us to save his own skin! Now there's nothing left!"

He tried to make her sit down, and poured her a brandy, but she swept the glass off the table and it tinkled to pieces on the flag floor. Tears began to run down her face, over the bruises on her cheek and the cuts on her mouth and chin. But even now, though she had recently fought two men and been knocked down and kicked by them, they were not tears of weakness but of anger. She cried like a man, harshly and coughingly.

He heard the story through, while men brought in and arranged the furniture overhead ready for the evening auction. When she had finished he said:

"The letters were all signed?"

"I've told you. I saw only two. They were both written to Anton and signed George. I know no more than you about the last eight."

"There was also this identity card?"

"It is not an ordinary identity card but I think a Communist Party membership card. I am not sure; I turned at once to the letters."

"You saw the name on the card?"

"Yes, it was George Lascou."

Something was scratching among the waste paper in the cellar. The movements upstairs had stopped.

Gene said: "I hope nobody knows that you know that."

"I don't care what happens to me now. I have been cheated, robbed in every way. There is nothing more to lose!"

"Were you followed here?"

"I don't know."

He went across the cellar and slid a grating aside. "Yes. Zachari is outside."

"Zachari?"

"The young man with the nose. You've torn his suit. No wonder he kicked you."

"So I have led them to you."

"It doesn't matter. There are six ways out of this cellar."

He came back and lit a cigarette. "Maria, do you know who Lascou is?"

"Yes. I have not played quite fair with you. I think I have almost known that all along."

"How?"

"Juan mentioned Lascou's name twice in front of me. But it was then only a name. When he died I suspected but could not be sure. Then you put me off by saying Avra. But gradually this week-end I had come to the conclusion. Lascou was in the news. I have not wasted this week-end."

"What have you done?"

"That does not matter. What is there to do now?"

He frowned down at his cigarette. He was not a man who took defeat easily, but to go on now would be the act of a fool. For her sake as well as for his own, the right way was to cut losses and go.

But would *she* go? Even if he told her to, would she go? He looked at her and knew she would not; and a worm of satisfaction moved in him that he could find an excuse for not letting up.

He blew away a spiral of smoke. "The letters won't be destroyed yet. Lascou has been out of town all day. He's addressing a public meeting in Piraeus at six, so he's not likely to be home before eight. As these things you had are dangerous to him, he must want to see them and destroy them with his own hands. Otherwise he would never have any peace of mind."

She threw back her mane of hair: "Well?"

"He's likely to have them delivered to his flat, which is on the top floor of——"

"Yes, I know where it is. Well?"

"I think I could take a chance on getting them there."

"He has a secretary and others about him."

"The advantage is they'd not be expecting me."

"You would have a bullet in your back."

"Not in his flat, I think. For the next month at least he must be above scandal. If I failed I should be arrested. But that may happen anyhow."

She stared at him sombrely. "If you got these papers, now that you know what they are, what would you do with them?"

"Hand them to the Army Intelligence."

"Would he be shot?"

"I don't know. But it would finish him in the way that matters."

Her eyes hadn't moved from him. "It is very unlikely you could do this."

"But worth a try."

"Did you know that Lascou's wife lives in a separate flat on the opposite side of the top floor?"

"How do you?"

"I have not wasted my week. Between the flats there are communicating doors. It would be easier if you called on Mme Lascou first."

"It might be." He had been watching her. "Maria, don't take a hand in this yourself."

She said: "I went up on Sunday, carrying laundry. I got right to the door of her flat without being stopped and could have gone in. I did not go in. But I think you could get in that way."

21

Gene did not take Maria's advice. While a woman looking like a laundress might get into Mme Lascou's part of the building during the day, a man at night would need a better excuse. And his quarrel was with Lascou.

He left the cellars before Maria and slipped into the cinema next door. When his watch told him it would be dark he came out and took a devious back-street route for Constitution Square. He blamed himself bitterly for not having been more active in saving the letters, but his self-critical faculties, always alert, hadn't even the satisfaction of being wise after the event.

The Square was crowded. People were taking advantage of the first pleasant evening to sit out of doors, drinking coffee and gossiping. The tobacco and newspaper kiosks were doing good trade. The moon, shining between the trees, was only another streeet light hung too high for the best effect. The Parthenon was flood-lit. The windows of the penthouse of Heracles House were in semi-darkness.

Gene turned in at the swing doors past the concierge, walking like a man with a purpose. The lift was in use and he had to wait until the *libre* sign flashed on in green at the side. He opened the door and stepped in, noting that the concierge had not turned. He chose the sixth floor. The lift wafted him up.

Three concerns shared the sixth floor, a lawyer, a ships' broker, a tobacco exporter. The business day was over and there was no one about. At the end of the passage was the door leading to the fire escape. He looked about as he came up to it but there was no one to see him push it open and step out on the steel platform. He wedged the door with a bit of cardboard so that it would not lock behind him.

Up here the moon had more say in things. Midgets moved

irrationally about the chequered floor of the square, their lights hung at a uniform level a few feet above their heads. The gardens and the palaces beyond bloomed in the soft night air, and fashionable Athens twinkled discreetly as it climbed the slopes of Lycabettus.

Moving under the shadow of the platform above, he quietly climbed the fire-escape steps up to it. A smooth concrete ledge a foot or so wide ran a complete circuit of the building at this floor level. Gene didn't know whether there was any architectural reason for it or whether it merely existed to satisfy the architect's latent and otherwise care-fully suppressed urge for decoration; but when one came level with it one found it had the disadvantage of a slight slope downwards and outwards so as not to provide a lodgment for rain.

He lowered himself on to the ledge and his rubber soles landed comfortingly on solid concrete. Though it was a secure foothold, no handholds were provided, and it meant edging one's way along, face and hands pressed to the wall and body thrusting against the building to counteract the slope of the ledge and the subtle gravitational or psychologi-cal pull of empty space and a seven-storey drop.

The building was a great rectangular block of ferro-concrete and the angle of the corner he must get round to reach the balconies and the french windows of the penthouse was an exact right angle. To do it there had to be some moments when a man was delicately balanced. He leaned his face against the concrete and carefully wiped his hands down the sides of his trousers. Then he put one hand firmly on the wall he was leaving and stretched the other to lay it flat round the corner. Having gripped the angle so far as he could, he put out a foot and groped until he had a firm footing on the other side. Then he began to transfer his weight.

As he got his body half way round a button of his jacket caught on the edge of the corner. It seemed to upset his balance, and just for a few seconds the whole weight of the building appeared to lean forward upon the angle of concrete that bisected him. Then he withdrew an inch the way he had come and deflated his chest and curved it inward and the button got past. Soon he was round to the other side.

From here to the first balcony was about fifty feet, and this side he was less exposed to the lights from below. A sudden police whistle startled him once, but it was not blowing at him.

The balconies did not project but were recessed into the main structure, and the stone balustrade was within his reach, so he was able to pull himself up. This was one of the balconies attached to the large salon, and had a fountain in its courtyard. The windows were wide open. The room was lighted now, but in a subdued way. Two shaded lamps burned beside the fireplace, that was all. There was no one to be seen. He stepped in.

Considering its size, the room wasn't an easy one to hide in. There were places enough for a casual moment or two, behind a Louis XV settee or in the shadow of one of the statues, but nothing for a long wait.

Up here the sound of voices from the square was like the murmur of the sea. Four doors to the room. A light was burning under the door to the entrance lobby, but the others were in darkness. He chose the nearest, the one he had seen Lascou and Major Kolono come out of on Saturday night.

The door creaked noisily as it opened on a study. By the light coming in from the salon he could see a filing cabinet, beside it a cupboard, a telephone on a desk, a tape recorder. A black jacket was hanging over the back of a swivel chair. As he hesitated on the threshold, voices and footsteps came from the entrance lobby.

It happened so quickly that he had only seconds to make a choice. He stepped inside the study as the other door opened and more lights suddenly lit the big room.

Wisely he didn't try to shut the door behind him; there was no time; Lascou's voice and another, probably his secretary's. Gene slid behind the door, there was nowhere else; the bright lights from the salon showed a plain square

648

room, oddly workmanlike after the decorations of the others; some bookshelves, a safe, a radio.

". . . disposed of right away," George was saying. "How long has Mandraki been here?"

"Over an hour, sir."

"Well, I'll not keep him waiting any longer. Shut the windows, will you."

The light clicked on in the study and George came in.

He had not even waited to take off his coat. If he shut the door after him Gene would be standing like a dummy. But he didn't shut the door. He dropped his brief case and a package on the desk and then moved out of sight. Presently there was the noise of the opening of a heavy metal door, and he came into view again with two clips of new banknotes in his hands. They were 1000-drachma notes. He opened a drawer and took out a long thick envelope and put the notes in. They crackled as they disappeared and he licked the flap and sealed the envelope.

All this was done with his back half turned to the other half of the room.

"Otho."

"Sir?"

"Give this to him."

"Yes, sir."

The oiled head of his secretary came half into the room and a hand accepted the envelope. Lascou followed him out of the room as he withdrew, but then suddenly turned back and picked up the package he had put on the desk. He went out again but did not switch off the light.

"See that he leaves by the side entrance."

"I take it you don't want to give him any further instructions?"

"I don't want to see him again. And Otho."

"Sir?"

"I don't want to be disturbed for a quarter of an hour."

"Dinner is ordered for nine, sir."

"Then let it wait."

Gene did not hear the secretary go out, but after a while

he concluded he had gone. For some minutes he waited for Lascou's return to the study. But it didn't come. Then he heard the clink of a glass.

The French clock in the salon began to strike nine.

When it had finished Gene moved. As he did so he touched the door and it gave a loud creak. That finished it. He stepped into the salon.

George Lascou was rising from a chair to face him. In the empty fireplace ashes smouldered, and on a small occasional table were some faded letters a waterproof wallet and a glass of marc: Lascou had one hand in his pocket. When he saw Gene he withdrew it holding the smallest gun Gene had ever seen. It was about the size of a cigarette case.

Gene said: "I guess your doors need oiling."

Lascou's surprise drew at the corners of his mouth and eyes: the years of comfort and good-living had slipped away, he looked hungry and alert.

Gene said: "I came about those letters."

"How did you get in?"

"Through the window."

Another clock was striking nine. The little crow's feet on Lascou's face softened and smoothed themselves out as the normal secretions began to work again, the reassurances of thought and position; he sat back in his chair.

"What are you doing here?"

"I told you. I came about those letters."

"What letters?"

"The ones you wrote years ago to Anton Avra."

"These?" said George, pointing with his revolver to the faded papers on the table. "I was just reading them as I destroyed them. I didn't write badly in those days."

"They've caused a lot of trouble."

"Yes, I suppose they have. None that I looked for, I assure you, Vanbrugh."

"You should teach your subordinates not to keep such dangerous evidence."

"He wasn't my subordinate," Lascou said. "He was my brother."

650

Gene came slowly forward. "That's something I didn't know."

"Even the omniscient find gaps in their knowledge."

"I'm not omniscient and I'm not armed. D'you mind if I sit down?"

"I was going to suggest it."

Gene took a corner of a seat about ten feet from the Greek. The table was between them. They stared at each other, men from different worlds. Although violence was implicit in their meeting, the moment they confronted each other it was as if combat had to be on a rational plane.

"Which was the right name, yours or his?"

"Avra means nothing. Many Communists have pseudonyms. . . . Anton was fifteen years older, was trained and indoctrinated in Russia. Mine was a local culture."

"Which differs from the party line?"

"A little."

"Was that why Avra kept the letters?"

"For him they became the big stick which would keep me faithful. Seriously, how did you get in here?"

"Through the windows. I've told you."

Lascou shrugged. "You can read these letters when you want, but of course I shall burn them in a few minutes."

"Well, you might as well put your gun away. You wouldn't use it in here."

"I wouldn't *wish* to."

"Mind if I smoke?"

"Get one from the table, not out of your pocket."

Gene did as he was told. He offered one to Lascou but the Greek shook his head. They were still studying each other.

Lascou said: "I wish you'd be honest with me. What do you want out of all this? Is it just money?"

"No."

"Then what?"

Gene said: "You pretend to hope for some sort of a majority at this election, but you know the only way it could happen would be if you came to power with the help of the ten or more splinter parties you're at present tied up with.

651

That would be like driving a car with ten men holding the wheel. So either way, win or lose at the election, you need General Telechos and the army."

"Telechos is right wing, Vanbrugh. If you knew the slightest thing about him——"

"I know that he owes the Bank of Greece a million drachmae and that you're guaranteeing the loan. Not that Telechos, even to save his wife and family, would co-operate with a Communist. But I think it will persuade him to play along with a man he doesn't trust."

Gene lit his cigarette. He knew that time was on Lascou's side, but he was taking the chance.

"Telechos," he said, "is one of the last of the old guard. They're thrown up, his type, all over the world from time to time: the senior officer who has always been above politics, the man the army can trust, and the nation too. He's immensely popular just now with the army—you'd call him the last of the Papagos line."

"And in what way do you suppose he is going to co-operate with me?"

"A *coup d'état* after the elections. There hasn't been one since the war and it's time Greece was true to her traditions. You haven't the power to do it on your own, and if Telechos did it on his own he'd split NATO and lose the American loans. But you can give just the right democratic flavour to it all. You have the tongue, the easy diplomatic explanation, a parliamentary party which will have more seats by then if not a majority; you'll make the reassuring pronouncements, you'll go and see the ambassadors and the sentimental Grecophiles and explain apologetically how it is. *Then,* when you and Telechos are firmly settled in there'll be a gradual shifting of power. Once you get your fingers on things, Telechos will be squeezed out with the other officers who've helped him, and the right centre will edge further and further left."

Gene stopped. During his last words he thought he had caught a glimpse of something moving, reflected in the polished wood of a table halfway down the room. He

652

carefully hadn't turned his head; but now he shifted his position to put a leg over the arm of his chair and allowed his eyes to wander idly. There was nothing.

Lascou had not spoken. He had only moved once, to sip his glass of marc.

Gene said: "Were you ever a true Communist? I don't reconcile it. It seems to me that you covet power for its own sake."

"I covet power for the use I can make of it, as any honest man does. The fact that I want to build something on more ideal lines doesn't make it a worse undertaking."

"Can you ever build something good on murder and bloodshed and lies? Can you found an ideal state by seizing it and ruling it against the wishes of the majority?"

George's pince-nez suddenly caught the light: contact was cut off by a series of glints and refractions.

He said: "The majority often doesn't know what it wants—certainly it hasn't an idea in the world what is good for it;—and I mean *truly* good for it, economically, socially, culturally. Violence as an instrument of policy I dislike: it should always be the *last* and not the *first* resort. But when it has to be used, then I agree with Thrasymachus, that it can help to win all the power and the glory of the world."

"How many will die in the coup? And how many before and after? Tolosa was one. Am I next? And then, when he's served his purpose, General Telechos?"

"I assure you that in the end there will be far less bloodshed and corruption in my state than in Washington D.C. You accuse me of egoism. What of yours? You remind me of a Christian missionary who goes abroad to convert the natives to a creed nine tenths of his own parishioners don't practise. Why don't you clean out your own stables? There's plenty of room for proselytising in Washington D.C."

Something moved again in the reflection of the table. Perhaps it was Mandraki re-summoned by the pressing of a secret bell.

Gene said: "I've no particular creed. I'm not here to

653

spread any gospel. But you forget I was here in 1944 and 1945. That's why I've come back now. I've seen Communism at work. I've seen the cold mass slaughter, the children dying, the brutality to women, the absolute ruthless callousness in gaining one set objective. Above all I've seen the lies—so that no words have *any* meaning any more. *Nothing* that's worth living for has any meaning any more." He stopped and said quietly: "You asked me what I wanted out of all this. That's what I want. Just to stop you. Just to stop that ever happening in Greece again."

"Does it occur to you that that is my aim too?"

"You go a queer way——"

"Has it ever occurred to you that by trying to stop me you are trying to arrest the course of history?"

"Is that how you consider yourself?"

"I'm swimming with the stream. Face up to the facts, Vanbrugh; look at the truth. The present Greek state is a house of cards, kept in being by money from the West. Everyone who knows *anything* admits that. It can't go on for ever. Already the Americans are getting tired, as the English got tired. When the money stops, Greece will slip into its proper place in the new pattern of the Balkans, which is a Communist pattern. The *only* way to save it from the pogrom, the mass starvation, the kind of imposed brutality which has happened farther east is that before then it should possess its *own native* Communism well established and rooted in its own ancient traditions. As Jugo-Slavia has, but *much* better, more subtle in its workings. Only a man like myself who understands the *mystique* through and through can see how to wed the individualism of the Greek with the collectiveness of the modern state."

It was a hand and it had moved for a moment round the base of the Hermes statue.

Gene said: "You're being frank tonight."

"With a reason."

"Oh, I'm sure of that."

Lascou picked up one of the letters and crumpled it into a ball, flicked it into the fireplace. "That's where they're all going; but now that you're here, now that you've given yourself up of your own free will, I want to tell you *my* point of view. . . ."

In a mirror Gene saw a woman move behind the statue, a peasant woman in a black shapeless dress and with a black cloth covering her head. But you could not mistake her build or her eyes. It was Maria Tolosa.

". . . You presume to think that you're the only patriot," Lascou was saying. "You protest you love Greece. Well, so do I; I want to serve her too, and who's to say which of us knows best? You say Communism is bad. I know, good or bad, that it's inevitable in his part of the world. So did Tito. Stop me now and you lay up a far worse fate for Greece in the future."

"I can't stop you, it seems."

"Happily not."

Maria Tolosa had moved, was about as far from the Greek as Lascou was from Gene. Something glinted in the light. Gene's eyes, caught in a sort of magnetic field, could not stay on the Greek. On his last visit he had seen and admired the thing she held. The blade was of bronze, very ancient, with a lion hunt inlaid on it.

He fumbled with words, they knotted on his tongue. "N-now that I've—that I've failed—what d'you propose to do about it?"

"It must all wait until after the election—even later than that. There's no other way I can shut your mouth———"

"Drop it!" Gene said, the words spilling now, as if he had swallowed too many. "You—won't get anywhere . . . Revenge isn't . . . Maria! understand, you———"

"Sit down," George said. "If this is———"

"Maria!" shouted Gene, starting up.

Lascou didn't shoot him because he heard the movement behind him and half got up as the knife slid in. It went in as easily and as undramatically as a knife into a cake. It encountered no bone, no opposition. The small gun wavered away from Gene as he stretched up, but it still didn't fire. The trigger finger had slipped out of its hold. Lascou looked up in surprise at Maria, a strange woman he had never seen before.

Maria screamed: "*That* is for Juan!"

He was standing now, the knife handle sticking out of his back like a Christmas joke. There was a dreadful sense of unreality. He put the tiny gun on the table and fixed his pince-nez. Then he wobbled slightly, steadied himself with the back of his chair, straightened. "Get a doctor," he said to Gene.

"For Juan!" panted Maria, her hair and lips suddenly loose as if blowing in a wind. "For Juan! For Juan! For Juan!"

"Where's the phone?"

"No, not phone. A doctor—ground floor. Get Otho. *Bell!*"

Gene made a move and then stopped. Lascou had put a hand to his mouth and to his obvious surprise it came away slightly stained. Always neat, he fumbled to take out the folded handkerchief from his breast pocket, and while he did so a trickle of blood suddenly ran down his chin, leapt from chin to floor. His eyes flickered upwards as if reaching for something they couldn't find; he snatched at the table with the letters on. Gene jumped to hold him but the table went over and he slithered down dragging Gene with him. A new sign was written on his face. He said with terrible incredulity: "I mustn't *die*. . . ." And while he spoke he was already going, sliding over the edge of life, clinging and slipping at the same time while the world tilted against him.

He choked the blood out of his throat and said: "Burn the letters."

Gene nodded.

The pince-nez slipped. "Tell Anya . . ."

And then he was no longer with them. Only one finger flexed as if still groping for the trigger it would never find.

22

They were alone together in the great salon while the French clocks ticked and the traffic mumbled far below. The room had become very still: and thought had stopped with movement. Time went round them, passed them by.

Then Maria Tolosa fell on her knees. "*Santa Maria*, Mother of God, Holy Mary, Queen of Heaven, *Santa Maria*, Mother of God, Holy Mary, Queen of Heaven," and a jumble of Latin words slurred together, over and over again, like beads told in terror without thought or meaning, just a talisman to hold on to in the void her own act had created.

Some of Lascou's own incredulity still lingered after him: it couldn't happen so quickly. No noise; no blood; the human envelope, punctured in a single vulnerable spot, had deflated like a tyre. Gene bent over him; but during the civil war he had seen too many such. He straightened up, wiped his hands on his coat to quiet them. He went to the outer door. No sound outside. Another door, open, led into a sort of butler's pantry—this way Maria had come. He shut it, came back.

He scraped together the scattered letters, the membership card—a phrase caught his eye: '*so don't upset yourself; one stays, however reluctantly, faithful to the general scheme of things.*' The miniature revolver. That in his pocket too. It was ten past nine. They had three or four minutes. Maybe.

Lascou had stayed faithful to the general scheme of things. Gene went to the praying woman.

"Maria, where did you get in?"

"Holy Mary, Queen of Heaven, *Santa Maria*, Mother of God——"

"Maria, listen to me!"

She stopped, stared at him without recognition.

"*Maria!*"

657

Her eyes weren't even seeing him. He caught her shoulders and shook her.

"*Maria!*"

"Yes?"

"Where did you get in?"

"Through her flat. She was out."

"Did anyone see you?"

"There was a little boy."

"Did he see you?"

"No."

"Why not?"

"When I ring the bell he runs out into the passage and I am able to slip in without—without him seeing me."

"Listen," he said. "Can you listen?"

She wiped the back of her arm across her face. "Yes."

"There is a way out—not going back that way. No one must see you. Understand?"

"I saw the dagger as I came in. God gave it into my hand. Then I heard this man talking. I have to destroy him. . . . It is God's will."

"We must leave separately. Can you walk?"

". . . Yes."

"See that door? Go through the vestibule beyond it, to a passage outside this flat. Go past the lift to the end of the passage: at the end there's a door behind curtains. Understand?"

"I think so."

"It will be locked on *your* side. It leads to the fire escape. Go down that. The last flight, to the street level is weighted so that you have to stand on it to swing it down. Understand?"

"Yes." Her balance, her possession was returning. She kept filling her lungs with trembling air and blowing it out through her thick pouted lips.

"It will land you in a yard. The door into the street will be bolted on the inside. It's on the left of the fire-escape. Now then this is more difficult. You have to remember a street."

He paused and waited. He could not go too fast.

"Yes?" she said.

"Go to the kiosk at the end of the square—remember it?—Papa André. Ask for number 12, Eleuthera Street. Got that? Then do what you're told. Do exactly what you're told and ask no questions."

She was still on her knees. "You think I am wrong to do what I have done. I know you do! But it was God's will! God put it into my hand!"

"Leave that now. Do you want to get back to Spain?"

"What does it matter?"

"I can't help you unless you'll help yourself."

She tried to get up, swayed, stood with his help. "I will do what you say."

He took her firmly by the arm, led her to the door. She said: "It was he who killed Juan. He——"

"Yes. Now then...."

He opened the door into the vestibule. There was no one about. They crossed to the further door. As they did so, a boy's voice came, calling. "That is the boy," she said. "If he——"

"Now." He pushed her out.

She swayed across to the other wall of the corridor, glanced at him out of pain-dulled eyes. Then she put out her hands against the wall, set her jaw, stiffened and began to walk down the corridor, swaying as if she was drunk.

He could not wait to see if she remembered; he shut the door and slid back through the vestibule into the salon.

Quieter than ever now. The clocks said fourteen minutes past nine. Out with his handkerchief. Handle of the knife first. Sounded easy, but in practice not so: blood had oozed out round the hilt; a spot or two got on his handkerchief. Now the table he'd grasped. There was brandy spilt on it; he picked up the fallen glass, then had to wipe that. More haste etc. His own cigarette end. How many handles had she touched? The boy calling again. The door of the study. Up and down it. Difficult to be sure where one had had one's hands.

"Papa! Papa!" said a boy. "Are you there?"

The door from the pantry was opening. Gene flew across to it, got to it as a small dark boy came in.

"Otho said you were back——" He broke off. "Oh, I thought . . . Who are you?"

Gene said: "Your father isn't here. He's gone out again. Have you a——"

"But Otho said he was back. I want to show him——"

He made a move to go round but Gene barred his way. "Where is Otho now?"

"Back there. Do you want him? I'll fetch him. What if——"

"*No*." Gene caught the boy's arm. "Is dinner ready?"

"Dinner?"

"Yes. Your father said he wanted it when he came back. Will you go and see."

The boy's suspicious dark eyes were fixed on Gene. He was seeking and sensing something wrong. There was a contagion of tension.

"Why can't I go in?"

"You can, when you've seen about dinner."

"It's nothing to do with me—I had my supper an hour ago. Where has Papa gone?"

"I don't know. Hurry up, now." He gave the boy a push.

Michael turned to go; and then with the speed of a fish in a net, darted under Gene's hand into the room. Gene whirled round and grabbed his coat but could not hold him. He caught him in the centre of the room staring across at a man's body which lay islanded in a sea of white carpet.

Gene caught his arms as he began to scream. Kicking and wriggling he was dragged back towards the pantry door. His teeth nipped like a badger's as Gene tried to stop him shouting. Into the pantry he went, half fell as Gene released him, turned back to the attack, eyes glazing with fear and fight. Gene had opened his mouth to try and reason, to reassure, to smooth over the truth with gentle lies, but he saw it was no good. He slammed the pantry door in the boy's face. No key. He dragged across a chair and wedged it under the handle. The screaming stopped, and a kicking and a rattling and an animal panting took its place.

Gene flattened his hair, tried to get his breath, pushed up his tie into a tighter knot. She would be clear of the building now. Time to go.

The inner vestibule door now, one glance back. Forgotten anything? Anyway it was too late. A silent man speared like a dolphin. Otherwise the room was just as he had entered it half an hour age. Only the pattern of life had changed. The elaborate salon had become a pantheon for the man who had created it.

As he reached the outer door the assault on the pantry door suddenly changed, the kicking stopped and the door creaked and bulged under a sudden weight. Otho had come.

No one in the hall—yet. Out you go. Along the passage to the fire escape. As he neared the lift it suddenly glowed with light, and he slid rapidly past and gained the heavy curtains at the end which hid the escape door. The lift hissed and the door opened and Manos stepped out. He went straight to the door of Lascou's flat and pressed the bell. After a second he saw that it was ajar and pushed it and went in. Gene came quickly from behind the curtains and went to the lift. As he got in he heard shouting. He pressed a button; with agonising slowness the lift door closed; he began to go down.

Telephone messages travel faster than lifts. Might be someone at the bottom waiting. But he hadn't yet been seen, been recognised; the boy would hardly give a coherent description.

The lift stopped at the first floor. He got out, wedged the inner door with a packet of Gauloise cigarettes. To the curtained door on this floor: push the bar and go out on to the iron platform above the fire escape. Crowds, lights, traffic, people, noise were suddenly full size again, telescoped up to him. This was the way he had left the building on Saturday. He stood on the steps of the last flight, and as they swung down ran down them into the darkness of the yard.

The walls of the yard stood up all around him. It was deeply shadowed in here, a pool out of the sun. Only one light showed on the first floor; soon there would be others. As he moved towards the door of the yard someone tapped his arm.

Maria stood there in the dark. She looked dreadful. The brief shot of energy he had been able to pump into her had dissipated itself like adrenalin. She said: "The door is locked."

"I told you. But it will unlock."

"Not. I could not."

She swayed and he grasped her arm, pulled her across the yard. On Saturday there had been a bolt at the bottom of the wooden door, but when he bent to this he found it already pulled back. He tugged at the latch but it wouldn't move. He felt along the door with his fingers.

Someone had found it unbolted from the inside on Sunday morning. At the top there was another bolt. He could reach it with his fingers but couldn't get grasp enough to shift it. He looked at Maria but she was too far gone to help. Back across the yard, casting about, nose down like a rat, he grabbed up a bucket, ran back with it, stood on it, tugged at the rusty bolt. The bolt grunted and screeched back.

He took Maria by the arm and guided her out into the street. One or two people stared at them as they came out; Maria needed his support. Since Saturday the outer wall of the yard had been plastered with election slogans. They began to walk towards the square.

She said: "And I do not remember the name of the street."

"Maria, an eye for an eye isn't much of a philosophy these days."

"It was a repayment. He had got the letters. Look at my face from this afternoon. What else could I have done?"

They reached the busy rim of the square, crossed to the great space given over to cafés and promenading and talk. He stopped and looked back. Heracles House without its founder showed no distinguishable change. The top floor was lighted but no distress flares blazed. Nothing in nature's aspect intimated. . . .

She said: "And now the scores are even."

"Not if you're caught; they won't be even then."

"I don't care what happens to me now."

"There are other things to live for besides revenge."

"At least I can live with myself."

Circulation, you could tell, was coming back to her brain.

"Eleuthera Street you must ask for. Number twelve. But if you take this way out, you must promise me two things."

"Yes?"

"Do what you're told, no questions asked. No breaking down or breaking out. And if you're caught, no talk about the people who are helping you. Got that?"

"Yes, I understand."

"There is the kiosk. I am coming no further with you."

"I am not such a fool as I seem, but—I am shaken. You know? I have never killed a man before. God, it is much worse than I ever thought!"

Gene smiled wryly: "It usually is."

23

He pressed the button, the coins tinkled and he said: "This is Vanbrugh."

The tired voice of the old man at the other end said: "Well, my son?"

"I need your help. The way we once talked of it—remember—the last time I was here."

"Of course. When will you come?"

"It is not for me, it is for a woman. I want you to get her out. She's on her way now."

"A Greek? What has she done?"

"No, a Spaniard. Name, Maria Tolosa. You'll find her very upset, stunned, but she'll do as she's told. She must go."

"By the way we talked of? Yes. It may take a little time——"

"Get her as far as some port—Bari or Istanbul, where she can take a ship for Spain. If she needs money, give it her; see she has enough for her passage."

"And you? You are all right—safe?"

"If she's clear, when she's clear, I'll maybe take you up on that promise myself."

"She is wanted for something?"

"No. It's unlikely she ever will be. But there's the risk. You feel like taking the risk?"

"Of course. She will not talk?"

"She'll not talk. I'll phone you this time each night, if I can."

"You will like me to make arrangements for you? In two, three days? It's as you feel."

"In two or three days, maybe. But it wouldn't be safe—us travelling together. First things first."

"So long as you are sure, my son, that you are putting it the right way round."

He glanced through the glass at the crowded taverna half fogged in steam and smoke. A radio was blaring a local dance hit. Near the phone a fat man with a napkin tucked under his ear was gulping up dripping spoonfuls of *avgolemoui*. Two girls were drinking retsina out of blue mugs and shouting a conversation at the proprietor who stood behind a marble slab cooking something on a charcoal fire and working the bellows with his foot. Gene tried another number.

The ringing went on and on.

"*Pronto*," said a voice at last.

"Mlle Stonaris, please."

"Mlle Stonaris is out. Who is that who wants her?"

"Can you tell me where I can get in touch with her? It's a private matter and urgent."

"She has gone out for the evening but she did not say where. Can I leave a message?"

"Thank you, no," he said, and rang off.

664

It was not yet eleven. He pushed his way out of the taverna and then through the interwoven crowds in the street. He jumped on a trolley bus crawling up Venizelou Street but got off it again about a quarter of a mile beyond Ommonia Square and made in the direction of the main station. He turned into a mean street lined with stalls and the remnants of a market. Faded vegetable leaves and stalks crunched and slid under his feet; a boy with a tray of sweet almond cakes cried his wares. Someone caught Gene's arm.

"*Oktopadi*," said an old man. "Fat shrimps. A bargain price for these I have left. Don't go in. The police are there."

Gene stared at a wizened face. "Where?"

"They came this morning an hour after you left. They have questioned the old woman but she will tell them nothing. Can I be permitted to sell you half a kilo?"

Gene felt in his pocket and began to count out some dirty notes. "They have found my things?"

"That is so. I did not see them but that is the message."

"Old Agnes?"

"They can do nothing to her for taking a lodger in all innocence. She asked me to be on the watch for you. Thank you, *koubare*. Eighty drachmae change."

"Keep it. Was there any other message?"

"No, sir. Your health, sir. And *thank* you." The old man turned away.

After a moment Gene went along the street as far as the next turning, ducked into a narrow alley and walked quickly down it. At the corner was another small taverna; he went in and ordered beer.

It was quieter here and the proprietor, a lowering Boeotian with Slav cheek bones, did not encourage custom. Gene smoked a cigarette while he thought it out.

Agnes could tell the police nothing even if she would. Nor would his belongings: a change of clothes, some money, shaving tackle, letters of introduction to two Greek publishers. He had latitude, time to breathe, time to get out. But sooner or later—and it might not be more than a matter of hours—someone would bring his photograph to the little boy, and the boy would point and say '*yes!*' Then it would no longer be a little game, side-stepping a few policemen egged on by Kolono to question him about an accident he had not even witnessed or to harass him on some technical infringement of regulations.

He watched a lizard inching its way up the wall beside him. It paused now undecided and flicked an experimental tongue. He must get out of the city, if possible out of the country, before the real hunt began. Every hour counted.

But one thing counted more than hours, even if it meant missing the night plane out.

A customer's shadow touched the wall as he moved to a table and the lizard darted suddenly into a crack. By the time the shadow was gone the lizard had gone.

One other call had to be made now for different reasons.

He finished his drink and left. He walked back the way he had come, moving easily through the strident crowds, cutting across the main streets until he was in the quieter residential district. Mme Lindo's house was well lighted, more so than he had expected. He pressed the bell.

Louisa recognised him at once and let him in. "Good evening, sir. The others are all in the drawing-room. They've just finished dinner."

"Mme Lindos has visitors?"

"Oh, yes, sir, I thought . . ." She looked at him. "You—weren't coming to the party?"

"I wanted to see Mme Lindos privately. Is there a chance to do that?"

"Well, sir, I can't . . ."

A door opened on the landing above and Mme Lindos began to come down the stairs; with her was a tall dark woman; they were both in evening dress. Near the bottom Mme Lindos stopped, holding the banister and peering.

"Gene. So you have come after all."

"Yes," he said, making the best of it. "But I'm afraid I can't stay."

"Of course you must stay. I have a surprise for you which may help you to change your mind." She came awkwardly

666

down the rest of the stairs, looking at him keenly. His was a difficult face to read, but there was a casual-seeming alertness about it that reminded her of the first time they had met. "Gene, allow me to introduce you to Lady Camwell. She and Sir Giles are visiting this country and are naturally interested in our press. Mr. Vanbrugh is an American with a profound knowledge of Greece."

Gene bowed and murmured the usual things. His memory had come to him; Vyro and his fiftieth anniversary; he *had* been invited here tonight; a week ago only; a week ago he had come here in innocence, or it seemed like innocence now. He said in Greek to Mme Lindos: "Sophia, I'm in trouble."

Mme Lindos had been moving them towards the drawing-room. "Trouble? What sort?"

"I want to talk to you alone."

"Come in, then. How can I help?"

"Money. And some advice."

Mme Lindos said to Lady Camwell: "Forgive us, my friend likes to practise his Greek. It is a joke we have." To Gene: "Of course. Anything I have. Are you in a hurry?"

"I can stay a little while."

"I told you I have a surprise for you. Mlle Stonaris is here."

Gene stepped back as if he'd moved on to an unbolted trap-door. "I thought you didn't know her."

"She phoned and asked if she might come. She came before the others and asked me questions about you. I persuaded her to stay on. What is wrong, Gene? Tell me now."

"I'm on my way out. But it's not a thing to involve my friends in." He smiled at Lady Camwell. "Excuse me."

"Of course," said Lady Camwell vaguely. She was a tall absent-minded-looking woman in a long greenish dress that didn't fit her and didn't suit her.

They went into the warmth and chatter of the drawing-room. Coffee cups clicked and a dozen faces turned to look at him. Only *she* did not look up.

Leon de Trieste; two Americans called Regent, proprietors

of a Chicago magazine; Sir Giles Camwell looking like an elderly schoolmaster; the Greek Ambassador to Turkey, who was on home leave, had his sister with him; there was a scattering of other distinguished Greeks; Angelos Vyro, of course, and in a far corner his younger son, Paul Vyro, talking to Anya.

One or two of them looked at Gene's clothes. Anya's eyes at last came up to his. They were as cold and as hostile as he had ever seen them. All the same, for ten seconds he forgot murder and the people round him, and she didn't go on with what she was saying. Then she looked away and the thing was gone like a momentary shiver. The boy beside her was all eyes; to re-claim her attention he got up and brought her more coffee. She said something in her soft voice and he laughed.

"I keep the squares on the walls to remind me," said Mme Lindos. "In one's mind's eye one can still see . . . Left was the Utrillo; that went first and paid for wood and coal. Right was a Toulouse-Lautrec, the Moulin Rouge from the balcony, it was considered one of his best; above was an unfinished Cézanne. . . ."

"I don't know how you could bear to part with them, really I don't," said Mrs. Regent.

"When one has had no food for two days it is quite astonishing how weak one's artistic sensibilities become."

"The installation of modern printing presses," Regent was saying to Vyro, "is the aspect of modern journalism most frequently neglected. Nobody, I say, can carry up-to-the-moment ideas if he's using yesterday's tools. . . ."

Gene stood obstinately over them until Anya was forced to say: "You don't know M. Paul Vyro? Mr. Vanbrugh."

"I rang your flat," Gene said.

She looked at him again, blindly now, deliberately dropping a blankness between them. "Oh?"

"Your maid said she didn't know where you'd gone. Was that a diplomatic ignorance?"

"Does it matter?"

"In this instance, yes."

668

"Well, she didn't. I came here—quite on impulse."

So she would not be telephoned here.

"Maybe I can see you home? If——"

"Mlle Stonaris is coming to see over my father's news-paper," Paul Vyro said stiffly. "We shall be leaving in a few moments now."

Gene was given coffee and a glass of *raki*. On the tray also were cubes of Turkish delight and a dish of apricot jam.

". . . Istanbul," the Ambassador's sister was saying to Sir Giles Camwell in perfect over-precise English. "In those days one had lovely times. . . . And every summer swimming and boating on the Bosphorous. But it was difficult for a girl. One dared not venture out alone or some Turk would come up behind one and pinch one's bottom. . . ."

Cigars were being lighted, but there was a general move-ment as if people were ready to go.

"You are in *Aegis* yourself?" Gene asked the young Greek, since he could not get rid of him.

"No, in law. It is my elder brother who is editor. No doubt he will meet us at the paper."

A hand touched Gene's. Mme Lindos said: "Come and talk to me for a moment." As they moved off she said: "I have only about two thousand drachmae, and some of that is upstairs. As much as you want tomorrow."

"Thanks, what you have will be plenty."

"Why are you leaving Greece like this?"

"I can't explain here."

"I wonder if—Dear Count, thank you, but I never drink now. Alcohol, I think, is bad for one at either of the extreme ends of life. . . . You are coming to the newspaper with us, Gene?"

"You're going?"

"I don't want to, but fifty years of friendship demands it. Why don't you spend the night here? Perhaps I can help you in other ways."

"I can't. From now on the less you have to do with me the better."

She was spoken to by M. Vyro. Gene glanced back at Anya and Paul Vyro. He was bending towards her deferentially, she was smiling at him brilliantly, destroying him with her look.

Gene said to Mme Lindos: "I must come with you to the *Aegis* offices. I must see Anya alone."

"I'll get you the money. Go in the third taxi."

"Thanks."

"You look tired. What have you been doing?"

"What you told me not to."

Her wise eyes went over him again. "I was afraid you might."

"Lascou is dead."

Her expression did not change. "So. . . . When?"

"This evening."

"She does not know?"

"Not yet. I must be the first to tell her."

"I'll arrange it. Wait for me."

The company began to file out, Sir Giles bending his benign head to the confidences of the Ambassador's sister; Lady Camwell trailing tall and vague with the Comte de Trieste; Anya with Paul Vyro in close attendance; in the hall Gene waited with M. Vyro and Mrs. Regent. Temporarily a sense of inanition had come on him; he was a puppet caught up in these elderly formalities; for him it was a period of quiescence which he must make the most of, resting within himself while still on his feet. What news *Aegis* would have for its evening editions tomorrow!

Mme Lindos came down the stairs. "I'm sorry to have kept you, Angelos. I had forgotten my bag."

They went out to the taxi. M. Vyro handed Mme Lindos in with old world courtesy. Gene shared a seat with Mrs. Regent. They drove rapidly through the bright streets, which were still busy at midnight.

Mrs. Regent said: "Sam and I are making a comprehensive tour of the Balkans and the Near East—with our movie-camera. Our 16 mm. goes with us everywhere and later, properly edited, the film has nation-wide distribution in the States. My husband speaks the commentary."

Gene shifted in his seat.

"We have two days more in Athens, then we go on to Rome. Our Ambassador is planning a big programme for us there. We shall make no more than a whistle stop in Vienna, but shall study Istanbul extensively and then go through to the Arab countries. We plan to have three weeks over here altogether. I guess we felt this was too important a commission to entrust to anyone but ourselves. Do you know Greece well, Mr. Vanbrugh?"

"Pretty well," said Gene.

"Maybe you're not interested in the political scene. Sam and I have visited fifty-seven countries in the last two years with our 16mm. movie-camera. We have very efficient sub-editors who carry on in our absence. I may say we're very pleased indeed with the situation as we find it in Greece. We're very impressed with the way the political parties are presently handling the situation. When we return to the States we'll be able to interpret election events over here to our readers over there with up-to-the-minute freshness and understanding."

Gene didn't speak. The car had turned off the main streets. Mrs. Regent said: "Are you one of these Europeanised Americans, Mr. Vanbrugh?"

"Why?"

"You don't seem to me to have an American way of speaking."

"Oh, I have."

She looked at him. "To tell the truth I haven't much room for Europeanised Americans. Some of them talk like Englishmen, and in that case I say it's better to *be* English and the hell with it. Besides that, most of them live over here and by their behaviour are no credit to their country or their countrymen. They live loosely in Paris or London and pay no heed to world trends."

"Here is the letter you wanted," said Mme Lindos, opening her bag and handing him an envelope. "I will give it you before I forget."

671

They were slowing up. She said to Vyro: "I hope this visit will not entail a lot of walking, Angelos."

"Ten minutes will see us through. Then we will meet my son in his office and drink champagne. It is merely a little formality; but you may go straight to the office if you wish."

He spoke stiffly and she patted his hand. "No, no, I would like to come."

They drew up outside the offices of the *Aegis*, a squat white building with a polished mahogany hall. The rest of the party were in the hall waiting, and a number of others had joined. Among them were the French ambassador—the Vyro family had strong ties with Paris—several members of the Greek press, an Egyptian official, an American Gene didn't know.

At this point each member of the party was presented with a souvenir of the occasion. Each woman was given a silver propelling pencil, each man a penknife. They were all dated and inscribed: '*Presented with the proud compliments of Aegis on the 50th Anniversary of its foundation.*'

Gene edged away from Mrs. Regent, who was talking to the new American, and towards Anya, who was still being cavaliered by Paul Vyro.

"Anya, I have to see you. I'm sorry—after yesterday—but it's vitally important."

Gene glanced at young Vyro but he did not give way.

Anya said angrily: "What is it?"

"Come, mademoiselle," said young Vyro, "the others are moving off."

They went up in lifts and walked through a large editorial room. Gene found himself next to Lady Camwell, who looked at him vaguely as if she was not sure whether she had seen him before and then said: "Is this a daily paper?"

In a room full of Linotype machines, at which men sat setting up their columns, M. Vyro halted the party and began to explain.

". . . trouble?" said Lady Camwell.

"What? I'm sorry, I didn't hear."

"Are you in trouble?"

He stared at her. "Why?"

"I heard you saying so to Mme—what's her name."

"You speak Greek?"

"In my parents' house we all had to read and write it before we were ten. The modern is a little difficult at first. Can I help you?"

"Thank you. Thanks a lot. No. . . ."

They went downstairs. A member of the staff began to tell how a raised surface was etched for printing. The Greek-ambassador to Turkey and the French ambassador to Greece had their heads together in a corner, but the subject was clearly nothing to do with fish-glue emulsion.

Mme Lindos said to Gene: "If it is true, what you told me before we left. . . ."

"It's true."

"How did it happen?"

"Not naturally."

"Oh. . . ." After a minute she said: "You want to tell Anya Stonaris that?"

"I want to tell her it was not my doing."

"Is it likely it will be thought so?"

"Possibly—later on."

"You must leave at once. I have a cousin in Piraeus. I think he could help."

Gene patted her arm. "This is none of your business."

Vyro stepped forward beaming. "You are not too tired yet, Sophia?"

"Not too tired but tiring."

"A few more steps, that is all."

The group moved on to the foundry hall. Here moulds were coming in and being thrust into the giant casting box. Beside this the great metal-pot was bubbling with molten metal; and at a signal the metal ran down the pipe into the casting box, where it spread over the mould. An impression of fatality began to take hold of Gene, as if he was in the grip of foreseeable circumstances which left him no hope of escape. He saw a predictable end as one might if caught on a conveyor belt and moving towards the cogs of a great machine. The sweat kept starting from his body.

The casting box was open, and men with leather gloves picked out the semi-circular metal plates and carried them still warm towards a further door. At this door M. Vyro stopped and stood on a stool and made a short speech. Gene edged towards Anya.

As he did so Lady Camwell got in his way and he felt something pressed into his hand. It was a roll of 50-drachma notes. "You may need them," she said. "I've always believed in backing my fancy." She looked across absent-mindedly at her husband. "I'm not often wrong in a man."

M. Vyro was talking about the two new printing presses in the room beyond, how much they had cost and what they would do, and how they were now going to be set in motion for the first time. It was fitting that they should first come into use on the fiftieth anniversary of the paper's founding and still more that they should be switched on for the first time by his oldest and dearest friend Sophia Lindos. . . .

Gene said: "Thank you. But I . . ."

Lady Camwell had moved on, leaving him with the notes. He thrust them into his pocket as absent-mindedly as she had given them; money was for a future which now might never arise.

He looked for Anya and saw that she had moved with young Vyro towards the door and away from him. He changed his direction and edged nearer. He could not shirk the compulsion of the nightmare, but he bore like a load of guilt all the dreamer's anxiety to avert catastrophe.

Somebody led a little applause as Vyro stepped down and Mme Lindos limped forward to press down the switch. As she did so a low pitched hum began in the room beyond; it increased second by second as the party moved towards the little door, soon it over-rode the noises in the foundry.

Some had already passed in. Gene caught Anya's arm as she reached the door. "Anya, I *must* tell you. . . ."

She stopped and looked at him, her eyes wide and hurt. Then she shook her arm free. "*What* have you to tell me?

674

Nothing that I don't know. It was a weakness on my part, coming here; I know; but I'll get over it. I'll get over it. Leave me alone."

She turned and rejoined Paul Vyro who was waiting at the door. Gene followed them in.

The roar of the screaming machines inside was like the obverse side of sound. One had broken a new kind of barrier beyond which noise was the basic medium instead of silence.

There was not much room in the hall; the visitors grouped in casual spaces here and there to watch. Four men tended the presses, ant-brains ministering to the monsters, tiny dwarfs reaching a hand into the vitals with oil can or rag. Gene was right beside Anya again, but all communication was reduced to gesture. Once he shouted at her but she did not even turn her head.

Mme Lindos had drawn as far away as possible from the machinery, her quizzical eyebrows a sufficient expression of her views—tolerating and condoning her old friend's pride but disclaiming enthusiasm. By gestures Vyro himself was indicating exactly how the machines did their job, explaining how the paper raced round the plates at lightning speed, snatching at the print and whirring through the folders and cutters, to be magically transformed into a completed newspaper and flipped down upon the delivery platforms in quires.

After a time the noise took not only one's ears but one's breath. It was something for which one's body had only a limited absorption. As the first newspapers were delivered, men lifted them upon a moving platform which carried them away to the packing room, and Mme Lindos had already taken a step or two in this direction. As the party began to move M. Vyro took one of the papers out of the quire and opened it to demonstrate the completeness of the modern miracle.

It was there. The headline took up nearly half the front page. In black print of enormous size at the top of the page were the words LASCOU ASSASSINATED. Below them was a photo of George Lascou. What caught Gene entirely

675

by surprise was another word WANTED, and under it a quarter page photograph of himself.

24

The robots went on their screaming way, swallowing up bales of blank paper and spewing out an endless repetition of the same sensation, the same news, the same shock. The ant-brains were busy at their tending and took no notice; the papers were flopped endlessly upon the delivery platform and borne away. It went on without purpose and without sense, an automaton grinding uselessly through its routine.

Not all had seen the news. But enough to take in the first part. Vyro himself stared at the paper and then held it for others to see. Mme Lindos saw, and it was her first glance at Gene that gave Vyro the hint of recognition.

But none could speak. They were puppets jerked by invisible wires of surprise; gestures, expressions, became larger than life, grotesque and slightly inhuman. Vyro dropped the newspaper back upon the others, but the Greek ambassador to Turkey picked up another, and then Leon de Trieste. They mouthed at each other. Someone tugged at Gene's arm. It was Lady Camwell. She gave a jerk of her head towards the door they'd come in by. Gene looked at Anya; she had gone grey in the face.

Gene moved back towards the door. A hand caught him. Paul Vyro shouted something in his face, making his meaning clear; Gene shoved him hard and he went back against a bale of paper.

At the door two others were moving towards him. Through the door and slam.

In the foundry room deafness was beset by indistinct ordinary noises trying to come in. No lock on the door. A man came towards him carrying a newly-cast cylinder for the presses. He said something to Gene, can you get away from the door.

"Way out?" said Gene.

The man answered but Gene was still deaf; he leaned forward and the second time heard; "Over there. The green door."

Gene began to run down the foundry room. The others were out before he got to the green baize, but he was through it. A long dark passage dusty and cold ended in a small office with several time registers, but no one in charge. A door faced him in the semi-darkness; he fumbled for the handle, scraping fingers on the woodwork. Double back and push open the office door; voices and shouts down the passage.

Rough coats and heavy boots. Two doors. Wash-basins. If this was a dead end he was caught. But there was another door, a door with a push bar. He pushed.

Someone was coming through the office as the door opened and he fell down the two steps into a narrow alley. He ran along it, came to the end and an empty street. Down the street at full speed, the opposite direction from the main doors of the building; a wider street. But he'd gone wrong: it wasn't a street but a square for unloading lorries. It was ill-lit; two lorries were there backed against a wall, abandoned for the night.

No way out. Buildings cast rectangular moon-made shadows. He shinned up into the van of one of the lorries, but the ignition key was missing. Then through the rear window he saw that the lorries were backed against an alley which ran into the yard of a factory. As he slid round and down and disappeared behind the back wheels he heard footsteps running in the square.

The yard of the factory seemed just another cul-de-sac. Doors locked and bolted from the inside; empty packing cases from which two cats stared their disapproval, broken bottles, corrugated iron, steps. He took the steps four at a time. At the top was a locked door but beside it a concrete path ran round the corner. He stopped a few seconds for breath. All pursuit was a delicate balance between coolness and speed. As bad to be too hasty as too slow. But not many yards away from him someone had opened one of the doors of the lorry.

He went round the corner hardly hoping, found that the raised path went along the side of the building, and beyond the wall were steps leading down into the street at the factory entrance. This street was not empty but he got down and wriggled unobtrusively over the small gate at the bottom of the steps. Then he began to walk briskly but not too briskly away from the scene.

Lucky about the taverna; from it you could just see the steps leading up to her flat. An old yellow house, bland and bleached; two great palms stood before it like Corinthian pillars gone to seed; he had been in the taverna half an hour and while there two o'clock had struck. A meal swallowed as an excuse for occupying a table—also he had not eaten for twelve hours, and who knew when next?

This feeling of being hunted, really hunted again, was like a reminiscent pain, forgotten until it returned; not since early '44. A sensation to be dreaded: the beating pulse, the catch of the breath, the loneliness. Yet it carried savours. One had the freedom of the atheist denying God; there was nothing more to lose but one's life.

As a young man his nerves had lain too near the surface: he had fought them as well as the Germans, disciplined them so that a triumph over one became a triumph over the other. Contempt of his own nervous and physical stamina had often carried him past the breaking point; beyond it was a no-man's-land few knew and understood.

Tonight after leaving the newspaper offices he had spent half the Lindos-Camwell money on a change of clothing. Behind Pandrossou Street you can buy almost anything at almost any time. A second-hand suit of Greek cut, a pair of spectacles, a wide-brimmed hat, a bottle of dye, an old gladstone bag which now held his own clothes.

The murder of Lascou had been broadcast on the late news. The police, said the proprietor of the taverna, were seeking a noted foreign *agent provocateur* who had been seen committing the murder.

"What nationality?" Gene asked.

"They did not say—Bulgarian I would guess." The proprietor rubbed greasy fingers down his blue striped apron. "They are the trouble makers. Hairy perverts. . . . Oh, well, a politician more or less—but there are those one could spare more easily than Lascou. Not that he's of my party, d'you understand; I could not vote for a man like Manos. And Spintharos—well, I can tell you sometime about him—poo! you wouldn't believe. But Lascou—he was not a bad figure of a fellow."

She came in about half past two, and there was a man with her. Gene thought it was Manos but they were past too quickly to be sure. He dallied in the taverna drinking coffee, but the proprietor was waiting to close so he paid his bill and got up to go. As he did so Manos came down the steps and passed out of sight. Gene went to the door in time to see a pale blue saloon drive away.

Good night to the proprietor, and he pulled his hat over his eyes and stepped into the street. There wasn't anybody about and a light chill wind rustled a newspaper thrown in the gutter. Lights in her rooms now, but cagily he walked first to the end of the street and looked quickly back. Out of the corner of his eye he thought he saw something stir beside the trunk of a palm tree just beyond the house. He waited patiently but there was no other movement except a gently waving frond. The lights in the taverna had gone out. He came back and walked up the steps.

When she saw who it was she tried to slam the door in his face but he got his foot in the door.

"Anya, I must see you."

"I—don't want . . ." There was a sharp angry struggle and then the door gave. He was in a hall with double doors leading into a large sala, but she had gone from the door and

679

was inside lifting off the telephone. He stopped in the doorway, short of breath.

"Go on," he said. "Ring the police if you want to."

"Why shouldn't I?"

"Go ahead. There'll be time to talk to you before they come."

She had changed into a green jersey and narrow black velvet trousers. They stared at each other. He said: "D'you really think I killed him?"

"Didn't you?"

"D'you suppose I'd stab him in the back? Is that what you think?"

She put the telephone down. The hard certainties had gone from her eyes. He came into the room.

"You have a maid?"

"She goes home at night."

"So we're alone?"

She didn't answer but put up her hands to her face. "God, I think I'm going to faint."

He went to a corner cupboard and clattered among the glasses and bottles there, came back with half a glass of brandy. "Sit down. Drink this."

She said: "Michael said you were there."

"Michael?"

"George's son."

"How did he know who I was?"

"He'd seen you on Saturday. He always peeps in at his father's guests."

"I was there. But I didn't do it."

She burst into tears. "I loved him."

He got her to sit down. She tried hard to keep her hands steady to hold the drink, but they were shaking like someone with ague.

She said: "I have b-been holding on tight, tight. One can't go on for ever. . . ."

"Don't try. . . . Finish this."

She took the glass in her own hand again but could not steady it, and he took it back, holding it while she sipped.

He said quietly: "Anya, I had to come and see you. It was the only thing to do. The one absolutely necessary thing in my life now is to get this straight with you."

"I thought—you see what I thought."

"You wouldn't have, if you'd had time."

"But you were *there*. . . ."

"I was there."

After a few minutes she began to steady herself. It was with an anger directed against herself. She blew her nose, tucked the handkerchief into the waistband of her trousers, took the glass a second time, trying to claim self possession, like someone denying illness because it was shameful to be weak.

He said: "I also came to you for another reason. Because I'd promised George."

"You promised *him*?"

"When he was dying he said two things: 'Burn the letters' and 'Tell Anya'. I've come to do what he said."

"I don't understand. What letters?"

"The letters that came from Madrid."

"Some did? Today? . . ."

"That's what I have to tell."

When he'd finished she stared at the pile of letters he'd put on the table before her.

"So what you said, what you implied in the mountains—that was true."

"Yes. . . ."

She took up one of the letters, read a few lines, let it fall.

She said: "As men go I do not think George was a bad man."

She said it half challengingly, as if she expected him to disagree. But he said nothing and got up to re-fill her glass.

She said: "George made his money perhaps to begin with in shady ways, and he increased it tenfold by speculation during the inflation. But the money, once got, he used often in good ways. He was, within limits, kind and generous to his wife, *devoted* to his children, he gave money and time to the arts. He loved his country. He was a *thinker*. I thought, I always believed, that he was working for the future of Greece."

"So he was."

"These letters prove he was a Communist?"

"Communists are not necessarily bad men. They are only working for what we conceive to be a bad thing."

"With my background it is hard to see the difference."

"Yet you say that you loved him."

"When did I?"

"Just now."

She got up, went to the mantelpiece, subtly recovering herself every moment. "D'you suppose that I can take his death without feeling it? He did everything for me. He made me, kept me. I owe everything to him."

"Did you give him nothing in return?"

She made an impatient gesture. "He said so. But when someone who has been very close to you dies, you *feel* that loss here—you don't first weigh everything in a balance and think should I be sorry, should I grieve, should I be upset!"

"No. I know, my dear. I'm sorry."

"And where is this woman that you say did it? Where is she now?"

"Soon out of Greece, I hope. I had to give her the chance to escape."

"*Why*? If she did it, she is responsible, not you! Are you too making a mistake in your feelings?"

"She's nothing to me except that I have to take some of the responsibility."

"Why?"

"Without my help Juan Tolosa's widow would have gone back to Spain. Her brother-in-law would have given up the letters as the price of his freedom and they would never have been heard of again."

"And George would have been free to go on with his plans for a *coup*. Is that what you wanted?"

"*No*," he said, coming up against it hard like a wall. "*No*."

"Well, you've stopped him."

"I've stopped him and I'm glad—even if it meant his death—even if it means mine. But too many other people have got involved for me to have satisfaction out of it. I didn't expect it to lead to a woman committing murder and a child crying for his father and . . . you being hurt——"

"And you are wanted for that murder." She turned on him. "D'you realise what you've done? It's not just a question of getting out of Greece. Wherever you go you'll still be wanted—and when you're caught you'll be extradited wherever you are—and you'll have to stand your trial here in Athens! And who's to believe your story—except those who know and—and perhaps understand?"

He shrugged. "I'll worry when the time comes."

"You have taken such a risk in visiting me. Every minute counts now against you."

"I had to see you."

She would not look at him. "What am I to do with the letters?"

"What you please. He asked me to burn them."

"But you haven't."

"Not yet. I had to bring them to you in case you doubted what I told you."

"I can't now."

Gene said: "In a way, even doing this, I haven't played quite fair with him. 'Burn the letters. Tell Anya.' He didn't mean it this way."

"Does that worry you? You have such strange scruples."

"Well burn them now—now you've seen them. They've caused enough trouble."

"And what are *you* going to do?"

"Go," he said. "I can get out all right."

She considered for a second. "I don't believe that."

"Why?"

"It's—a hunch. When you came into Mme Lindos's. . ."

He held up his hand. "What's that?"

"What?"

683

"A car, I think. It may be nothing. . . ."

He went quickly to the window and moved the blind a fraction of an inch. A car had stopped at the door and men were getting out.

"Police," he said.

25

Gene said: "What way out is there?"

She'd gone that transparent white which sometimes follows fever. "No way but the front. This house stands with its back to another. Everything comes through the front."

He grabbed up his hat and bag. "Then I'll get out of here."

"*No*"

He stopped a second, his movements as high-strung as hers.

She said: "Let me think——"

"There's no time to think——"

"Stop!" She got between him and the door. "It's too late: you know what the staircase is like: they'd see you."

"Perhaps not leaving this flat; I can take care of myself." He tried to get past, she caught his arm, he wrenched it free but she snatched it again.

"Then maybe I can put you in the clear," he said, raising his hand.

"*No, no, no!*" she said. "I can hide you. Let me *think!*"

"The window?" he said.

"Wait."

She fled past him into the bathroom, turned on the bath taps, was back.

"This way."

She led him into a bedroom. It looked like a spare room or a maid's room. He said: "Which way does this window look?"

As he spoke there was a ring at the door. They had lost no time.

"Here. . . ." She beckoned him to a chest of drawers beside the bed. "Help me."

He helped her to lift the chest out. Behind in the wall was a panel about two feet square. She pressed some sort of a spring catch and the panel swung open.

"*In.*"

"If they catch me this will mean——"

"*In.*"

He crawled through into a mass of pipes, which were obviously behind the bathroom. The trap door was for getting at the plumbing, but it was not a man-hole as such because there was no room for a man. He had to force his way in and lie on a tangle of pipes, with his head bent against the sloped roof and his feet cramped at the other end. The panel would just shut and he was in complete darkness. He could hear her struggling to get the chest of drawers back in place. Then the door-bell went again.

For half a minute there were indistinct noises. He heard her calling something. The taps were shut off.

Silence fell, except for slight hurried movements in the bathroom. Something dropped on the floor. Then she must have opened the door to them for he could hear the growl of men's voices.

He could tell she was arguing and indignant; but after a minute she gave way. Heavy footsteps. The hot water pipe was burning his back. It was very close in the confined space and he could hardly move an inch any way. His shoulder was pressed hard against the door. The footsteps moved on.

Suddenly her voice came quite clearly: "Do please look in here if you wish!" They were in the bathroom.

"I'm sorry, madame. You realise it is solely a matter of duty. I personally should not wish to intrude on your grief."

Nevertheless their apologetic manner didn't seem to be preventing the police from having a thorough look round. He heard them moving about. His shoulder was cracking.

She said: "I think it a little strange that you should suppose *I* would conceal this murderer."

"I'm *very* sorry, madame. We thought perhaps he might have got into you flat unknown to you."

"And into my linen basket while I was in the bath?"

"Of course not. That's enough, Cassimi."

They went out, and for a time Gene could only hear movements further away. Then abruptly they were again within hearing. They had come into the spare bedroom.

She said: "But who was this man who reported that he had seen the murderer entering this building?"

"We received the information. We took it to be a reliable source."

"How do you know that this man even knows the murderer? How do you know it is not a hoax?"

"We can't be sure, madame. But it is our duty to check the information we receive."

A cupboard door opened very near Gene.

Any minute the pressure of his shoulder on the panel would make the spring catch fly open. Yet he could not move to take away the strain.

"There are other flats in the house, officer."

"It is what I was thinking myself, madame. This is a spare room?"

"My maid sleeps here when she sleeps in."

"She isn't sleeping in at present?"

"As you see."

There was a creak of the bed.

"If I may advise you, madame, I would suggest that you keep your door locked for the rest of the night."

"It's a custom I often follow."

"Yes—er—I beg your pardon. Is this the last room?"

"There's the kitchen."

"Of course. If you will——"

"It's this way."

A long wait in blackness and in heat. Sounds and movements for a time, and once Gene thought he caught some stirring in the bedroom still, as if perhaps one of the men had stayed behind in the room. Then there was a murmured conversation in the sala. Then silence.

Lack of air in the man-hole. Gradually the pipe, which had nearly burned through his coat, began to cool. The beginnings of cramp in both feet. Mustn't think of cramp. Or suffocation. A door banged somewhere in the distance but no footsteps followed it.

He began to count. It was a way he'd followed for years of getting through high discomfort. He had counted to beyond four hundred when someone turned on the water again in the bath. That went on for two or three minutes and the pipe behind him grew hot again. He began to wriggle his feet, fighting the cramp again and fairly sure that any slight noise he made now would be covered. He was soaked in sweat, and it was running off his forehead, down his face and trickling inside his collar. The water stopped. Then someone came into the room and he heard the chest of drawers being cautiously dragged back.

Light fell into the dark. She said: "I think they're searching the other flats. Are you all right?"

"Yes, fine."

"Can you stick it for a few minutes more until the car goes?"

"Yes, if you leave the panel open."

He watched her feet move away. She was wearing the same green pumps, but above four inches of bare ankle was a scarlet bathrobe. He stuck his head out and gulped at the air. Almost immediately she was back.

"They've just gone. Did you hear the car?"

"All of them?"

"I can't be sure. But it's safe to come out."

He began to wriggle through the opening and got to his feet. There was no feeling in either of them and he collapsed into her arms and thence to the bed.

She said: "I am sorry. I could have come earlier but I was expecting a trap; I thought they would come back."

He began clumsily to massage his feet, and she stood and

watched him. Presently she pulled off her bathcap and shook out her hair. He said: "Did you change into all that before they came?"

"Yes. I was terrified of two things. The bathroom was too—unused, too unsteamed. And that mark." She pointed to a scrape on the polished parquet floor. "I made it pushing the chest back. I was in too much haste."

He got up, first testing one leg, then the other. "I'll give them another ten minutes and then go."

"Go where? I was asking you when they came."

He limped back into the living-room, moved over to the blind, peered out. "It wasn't the police who saw me come in. I don't like that. This evening, when I went back to the place where I'd been staying, the police were there. I was warned just in time. I doubt if they would have found me on their own."

She tightened the cord of her bath robe. "There's the paper. The Lieutenant left it for me. Perhaps he thought I would recognise you better."

He picked *Aegis* up and stared at the two photos, at the glaring headline. The paragraph underneath was very brief—later editions would carry more. "No name or nationality."

"That's a government tactic, I should say. If possible they'll hush it up or try to call you British. But it won't stop them bringing you to trial. George had many friends."

"I'll get out."

"Which way can you go?"

"I shall make my way down to Piraeus and smuggle on board a ship, if possible one going to Venice. From there there's all Europe to choose."

"It will be impossible." When he looked at her she added: "Without help."

He offered her a cigarette. She shook her head. "Do you know, there is only one safe place for you, Gene, for the time being."

"Where?"

"Here."

He lit a cigarette for himself, broke the dead match, put it in an ash-tray. "No."

"Yes."

"Well, thanks, but I don't see it."

"It is obvious. Everyone will expect you to be on the run, to be trying to get out of Greece. The last place the police will look is here—*which has already been searched.*"

He thought round it carefully. "Maybe you have something. But even if that was so, I'm not willing to involve you any more."

She said: "Don't you know I am involved?"

"Not if I get out now."

"Whatever you do now—I am still involved."

He looked at her, his eyes going carefully, almost painfully over her face. "Yes ... in that ... but that's not the way I mean."

"I sent you away," she said. "It was your view too. But tonight you have come back. That is—just the way the cards have fallen. It does not mean I may not be permitted to help you."

"It does if your safety is concerned as well."

She said: "If you stay here tonight I think I can make arrangements. I have money and still some influence. Perhaps you could leave tomorrow night, but that will depend."

"And your maid?"

"I can telephone her. I will tell her not to come."

He shook his head. "If I stay tonight it may mean I'm stuck here for three or four."

"Does that matter?"

"Yes, yes, yes. Every hour increases your risk. D'you realise what being an accessory after the fact means?"

"Do you realise that I don't care?"

He came across slowly and put his hands on her elbows and smiled his crinkly smile at her. "You don't care?"

She looked at him directly for a moment, then glanced beyond him with a sort of removed matter-of-factness, a drawing back as if he were a stranger. "I must hide you here until I can make arrangements to get you out. What chance do you think you would have of slipping through tonight or tomorrow at any Greek port or station or air terminal?"

"I've slid out of difficult corners before."

"But this is not war. You have not got the population on your side. You have no passport except one which will get you instantly arrested. You have no disguise but a pair of spectacles. You admit you will not ask your friends to help you. Therefore it's essential you should stay here."

He released her and walked up and down once, thinking it over, knowing she was watching him.

He said: "Are you proposing I should spend another night with you in—in intimate celibacy?"

"I don't know what that means."

He explained.

"Yes," she said. "Yes. . . ."

He smiled at her again. "You think—that is going to answer with us now?"

"With things as they are, it cannot be any other way."

26

They slept for three hours. She had set a clock to wake them but before it went off he was stirring, moving round the sala, examining the grey empty street through the slats in the venetian blind. He made coffee, and a few minutes before the clock was due to go off he went into her bedroom with a tray and touched her hand.

She was instantly alert. "Yes?"

"Just before seven and all's well."

She slowly relaxed and yawned against her fingers. Her hair lay thick and black on one bare shoulder. Her face looked strangely naked and unguarded without make-up in the filtered morning light.

She said: "I had horrible dreams."

"Coffee?"

690

"Thank you."

They drank in silence.

He said: "I wouldn't have waked you so early but for calling your maid."

"Have you looked out?"

"Yes. There's someone watching the house."

"What? Who is it—the police?"

"No. A young man I first saw with Mandraki at The Little Jockey."

"So you were right."

"They may be watching only so they can follow you when you go out."

"I must telephone Edda."

He left her while she got up. Looking for a towel in the bathroom, he opened a drawer and found a razor and a tooth brush and some hair cream. In a small silver box were collar studs and cuff links, and clean handkerchiefs. For a moment they shocked him, and he was startled at being shocked. Sometimes common sense barely goes skin deep. A stain lay suddenly across his mind—like an overturned inkpot.

When he came out she said: "I've given her two days off. She knows about George's death, of course."

"I'll make breakfast while you have your bath."

"There's no new bread. Edda usually brings it."

"If it's old I'll toast it."

Over breakfast they didn't speak for a while. Presently she got up and switched the radio on. They listened to an advertisement and then the news came through.

"Progress is being made in the search for the international spy who is wanted for the murder of George Lascou, ex-minister and leader of the newly formed EMO party. All available police have been allocated to this task, and Major Kolono, who is in charge of the investigation, stated that an arrest could be expected shortly. The assassin is described as of medium height, fluent in Greek, about thirty years of age, brown hair, grey eyes, of thin build but muscular and athletic. All Athens is shocked and horrified by this dastardly

691

crime which robs the political scene of one of its most talented and popular figures.

"M. Stavrides, deputy leader of EMO, stated late last night that the death of George Lascou will not affect his party's plans for contesting the election. 'We shall go on,' he said, 'saddened but inspirited by the example of this good man. And we shall win.'

"In Salonika yesterday dock labourers——"

She switched it off and ran her hands up and down her arms as if to suppress a shiver.

When she sat down at the table again he touched her hand. "That's nothing fresh."

"I don't like to hear it."

"What are you going to do today?"

"Mme Lindos is entirely to be trusted?"

"She's an old woman. She mustn't be caught up in this. She lent me money; that's enough."

"Gene, give up for a little while denying to your friends the privilege of helping you!"

". . . Anya, what made you go to see her yesterday?"

"I thought you had gone. I thought I wanted to know more about you."

Thinking of the things he had found in the drawer, he said: "Perhaps we already know enough."

She looked at him. "What do you mean?"

"It was just a casual remark."

"But what did you mean by it?"

He hesitated and then said: "I was only thinking that for love you must have some degree of innocence. . . . Maybe we both know too much ever to achieve that innocence again."

She got up and went to the mantelpiece. It was a sudden almost defensive movement he had not seen her make before.

He tried to follow up the sentence, but he was struggling with feelings he didn't recognise in himself. Before he could add anything the front door bell rang.

"Oh, good day, Mlle Stonaris, I didn't know if your maid would be in yet. I'm glad to see I haven't disturbed you. I've only been stirring myself some few minutes but I had to come round at once to tell you about the water."

"Water, M. Voss?"

"Yes. I woke about twenty minutes ago and could hear the dripping. *Tap, tap, tap,* it went, and I thought it was raining and dripping on the window sill. Then when I got up I found a pool on my bathroom floor. It appears to be running along the beading of the ceiling and be coming from a corner by the hot water pipes, but the water is only just warm. Have you a leak in you bathroom?"

"No."

"I feel it must come from up here. There's nowhere else, is there. Could you make sure? It's leaking quite fast."

"Of course. Will you wait in here a moment?"

She showed her neighbour into the little vestibule but no further. Then she slipped quickly through the empty living-room into the bathroom. Gene was in there, having decided in the absence of a police car that there was no need to hide.

"You heard?"

"Yes. There's no leak here."

She glanced under the bath. He stayed her with fingers on her arm. "I may have damaged something last night in the man-hole."

She went out. "I'm very sorry, M. Voss. There seems to be nothing, but I'll look round."

"I'd be very glad. My bathroom floor is quite awash. Could I help you at all?"

"No, I'd prefer to do it myself. My maid will help when she comes."

"Well, if you can't find anything I'll have to send for a plumber. But perhaps you'll let me know when you've looked again."

"I'll phone you, M. Voss."

"Thank you. Thank you."

She showed him out and went back to the bathroom. Gene said: "There's nothing to see here."

They went into the maid's bedroom and pulled the chest away. He opened the man-hole and wriggled part way in.

"Yes, it's here."

"Much?"

"There's a split at the joint. I must have done it when I forced a way in."

She crouched beside him, said rather stiffly: "Can you stop it?"

"It's iron. You can't mend it without tools; there's a leak at the joint. I might try wrapping it with cloth."

He tried wrapping it with cloth.

"That's no good," he said. "It'll have to be a plumber."

"Can't you put something underneath it? A basin, a bowl?"

"It's pretty difficult because the water runs down the pipe instead of dripping direct to the floor. But if you get me something I'll try."

She got him a basin. When he'd put it down he said: "Have you a stop-cock?"

"Yes, I think so. Under one of the tiles in the bathroom."

"I thought for today maybe we could do without water. It would save a plumber."

"It won't work. It cuts off the water for the downstairs flat also."

He bit the end of his thumb. "Then a plumber it'll have to be."

"I don't like it." She squatted on her heels and frowned.

"It will be better than having the man downstairs complaining."

"I shall have to wait in until he comes."

"Maybe not. Go out and do what you want to do and phone the plumber when you come back. In the meantime if I can have a good supply of old rags I can keep it under control for an hour or two."

She phoned a soothing message to M. Voss, and changed into a black frock and went out. She said, still distantly: "Don't answer the door. Don't answer the phone. I don't think anyone will come."

"What are you going to do?"

"I don't know. I don't know yet at all."

When she had gone the flat was suddenly foreign and empty. He was not a man to whom inactivity was ever welcome, and inactivity at present was harder than usual to take. So long as Anya was with him he could forget it, but as soon as he was alone he began chafing at his own helplessness. To him movement was not just a means of escape, it was a way of defeating the enemy: the positive choice instead of the negative one.

Before she left Anya had opened the windows and pulled up the blinds. It was necessary to give any watchers the appearance of naturalness; but it restricted his movements to the far side of the rooms and even made these undesirable. When the sun came round this afternoon it would be right to let the jalousies down again.

It was a brilliant day and summer was falling on the city. One or two white clouds hung in the sky but their vapour was being absorbed by the sun. A bee droned lazily in and out of the open windows. People walked on the shady side of the street. A little puff of dust rose every now and then with the wind. In a corner on the opposite side a thin dark sneering young man with a drooping bow tie and a petulant mouth shifted from one elegant leg to the other and spat. Gene saw him and knew that he had not followed Anya.

The leak took most of his time. He tried tea towels and floor cloths to mop the water up, but the result didn't justify the effort. In the end he let it run and devised a series of basins and cups to catch most of the leak.

Once he cast about the flat for the Avra letters he had brought, but in the panic of last night Anya had either hidden them securely or burned them. Once the telephone rang. It went on insistently, and after a minute he crawled to the window and peered out. Zachari was gone. He waited there on his knees till the phone stopped; then presently the watcher opposite came back to his post.

The little Limoges clock with the blue and gilt face struck ten and then half past. With the windows open he did not dare switch on the radio. Opening the escritoire to put away a book he saw a roll of strong sellotape and thought that even yet there might be a chance of saving a plumber. He went back and pushed the basins aside to see if he could bind over the split.

With his head and part of his body inside the hole he had no chance of hearing someone come into the flat and then into the room behind him.

27

Nerves long trained will show their training in a crisis; like soldiers under ambush they answer by instinct, responding to the conventional call. When someone exclaimed behind him he didn't crack his head on the pipes but slid quickly out and sat up to stare at a short thick-set woman in a linen coat and white shoes.

"What is it you are doing here?"

"He swallowed saliva in his throat and coughed. "I didn't hear you come in."

"Who are you? What is it you are doing there?"

He said: "What business is it of yours?"

Her halting Greek had given him a lead. But he wanted to be quite sure.

"I'm Mlle Stonaris's maid. Where is she?"

"She's just gone out. D'you want her?"

"I come to pick something up. I do not expect . . . What is gone wrong?"

He was in his shirt sleeves, and even the old gladstone bag he had bought was on the floor behind him, lending the right colour to the idea. "There's a leak. The man downstairs called me in. Name of Voss. It's coming through in his bathroom."

"Is it you are from the builders?"

"No, I work on my own." He took out a packet of cigarettes and offered her one. "They're French."

"No, thank you." The surprise was leaving her and she was a little on her dignity. "I come for a dress. It so happens to be in here."

"All right." He lit his own cigarette.

Still sitting on the floor he watched her go to the wardrobe. If you watch someone, someone hasn't the same opportunity to watch you. His chief danger was lack of tools; but it was unlikely she'd stop and peer into the man-hole.

She took a black frock from the wardrobe, and then out of a drawer a few things she didn't let him see.

She said irritably: "What is the matter; can you not mend it?"

"Oh, yes, nearly done. Just taking a breather."

"When is Mlle Stonaris coming back?"

"She said she wouldn't be long. She said if I was finished before she got back I was to let down the catch."

The woman hesitated. Gene knew pretty well what was going on in her mind. He said:"I'll not be more than another hour."

"Another hour! ... Phoo! Be sure it is good work. Often one hole is stopped and another made."

She folded her frock on the bed and then laid it carefully over her arm. Gene opened his brown bag and pretended to look for something inside.

"Are you going on holiday?" he asked.

"Perhaps." She was on her dignity again. "Where did Mlle Stonaris say she is gone out?"

"She didn't tell me. Why should she?"

The woman moved to the door and went out. But she didn't leave the flat. He thought she was just slightly suspicious and uncertain and was perhaps looking round to see if anything had been disturbed. His mind flickered over the things in the flat. Nothing to tell her he had been here all night. Lucky he'd made this bed. His hat? No, that was in here. Coffee cups? Anya had stacked them in the kitchen. Cigarette ends? Unlikely she'd read anything from that.

He heard her moving about in Anya's bedroom, then in the kitchen. He picked up a piece of old piping left on the floor of the man-hole and began to tap one of the other pipes with it. Silence fell. He knew she had not gone. Was she sitting waiting for *him* to go? Anya might be out till one o'clock.

He picked up his piece of pipe and went out into the sala. She was not there, but the first thing he noticed was this morning's *Aegis* face upwards on the piano with his own photograph staring at the ceiling. He could not touch it, not even to turn it over.

He went into the kitchen but she wasn't there. She came quickly and suspiciously out of the bathroom as he opened the nearest drawer, bending his head over it.

"Yes?"

"Have you a small spanner?"

She hadn't yet recognised him. "Do you not have your own tools?"

"My spanner's too big."

"There are a few things in that cupboard."

He opened the door of it and rummaged about. He took out a pair of pliers. "These may do. Thanks."

She stood aside to let him pass. He wondered if he should make the move, his hand over her mouth, into the spare room. It was the act of despair, the final surrender to panic.

He went past. He went into the sala with the paper staring from the piano and thence to the spare room. As he did so he heard a key in the outer door of the flat.

He couldn't greet her as she came in, to warn her and explain, but he stood just within the door where she could see him as she went past, and clinked the pipe with pliers.

She came through the double doors and began to speak; but stopped in time.

"*Edda!* What are you doing here?"

"Ma'am, I thought already you had left for the hotel and I have the need for my black dress. So I came up for it."

"Oh. . . . Oh, I see." Anya had heard his hammer from the spare room.

"You do not mind? It is my best dress and I have the wish

to visit my brother. And then I find this plumber here." The voice was lowered. "I think perhaps it is best. . . ."

"Yes, of course. . . . ."

The voices mumbled on. Gene went back to the man-hole, breathing deeper. Edda had taken it on herself to make the situation clear.

Anya came to the door. "Have you nearly finished?"

He withdrew his head and they looked at each other. There was a glint of irony in his eye. "About ten minutes, I expect, ma'am. I've just to tighten the joint."

"I see. . . ." She put down her shopping basket. "All right, Edda, everything will be all right now."

The Italian woman still wanted to linger; she explained that she'd passed the time tidying up, and would Mlle Stonaris tell her which hotel it was to be? and she was desolated to hear the terrible news, and she hoped . . .

Anya got her to the door and out. When the door was shut she leaned back against it and stared at Gene.

They didn't speak. He slid across to the window watching. Edda came out and down the steps and walked off up the street. But Zachari from his corner, though he may have taken note of her leaving, did not try to intercept her.

". . . You were in there when she came?"

"Yes, I never heard her."

"She has her own key. It never occurred to me. . . ."

Gene watched the Italian until she was out of sight. "It's a chance we'll have to take. There wasn't any other choice except keeping her here by force."

Anya opened the paper she carried and put it beside *Aegis*. "They all have the photo. And you see now, there's a reward. . . ."

It was a copy of *Telmi*, the principal newspaper of the EMO party. Gene's photograph occupied three-quarters of the front page. Under it was a headline in red offering 25,000 drachmae for information which would lead to the discovery of the criminal.

He said: "The most I had on my head during the war was a hundred pounds in gold. Prices are rising everywhere."

"Manos is behind this," she said. "Manos and the party. It is enough to make every man look at his neighbour."

"What have you been doing?" he asked.

"I have seen Mme Lindos. Also I called in and ordered the plumber. He is coming round at once; that was another reason for getting rid of Edda quickly. I have bought some food. Also I went to Heracles House."

"You've done a lot."

She began to pull off her gloves. "The—funeral is this afternoon. You know of course to be quick like that is the custom in Greece."

"Yes."

"I must go."

"Of course."

"It will be a big one. EMO will try to make capital out of the loss of their leader. If they can bring you into court as a murderer—an American who at one time worked for the British—it would appeal to this—this stranger-hating emotion which has been creeping over Athens of late. . . ."

"And your arrangements?"

"Where will you hide while the plumber is here?"

"In your bedroom? He may want to go in the bathroom."

"Well, go in there now, will you? He may be here any minute."

Gene took his bag and slid along the inner wall to her room. He found her peering slant-wise through her blind.

"There is someone in the flat on the opposite side of the street. . . . Oh, I don't know; it may not be anybody; one comes to suspect. . . ." She lowered the blind a little. "It is reasonable now; the sun is coming round."

"You saw Sophia Lindos?"

"Yes. But I think you will have to stay here another thirty-six hours."

The telephone rang.

She went out, and came back after a minute. "A reporter. They tried to get me to talk at Heracles House. I hope they won't wait outside here. . . . Where was I? Oh, Mme Lindos. There is nothing yet settled. But I said I felt sure I could get you out of Athens if she could get you out of Greece. So for the moment it has been left that way."

"You're being very competent about it all."

She lifted an eyebrow. "Competence can be so dull."

"Where you're concerned?"

"Well, tarnished, then. Perhaps that is the word." She picked up a pair of nylons from the back of a chair and folded them and put them in a drawer. "Isn't it what we've both agreed?"

Before he could reply the door-bell rang.

"It will be the plumber," she said. "While he is here I will do some telephoning and try to get a meal ready. Then I shall be able to keep an eye on him. I'll tell you if he's going to be very long."

The sun was coming round to the bedroom windows, and Gene saw that it would soon be reasonable enough to lower the blinds completely. He heard Anya using the telephone, and a conversation she had with the plumber. At the taverna where he had eaten last night the proprietor was brushing the steps, which led down; he therefore appeared to be brushing all the dust into his room and not out of it. Behind the blinds of the room on the opposite side of the street someone moved; a hand reached through the slats to fumble with the cord and raise the blind a few inches. In the street below Zachari had apparently gone. The plumber began to knock.

Anya slipped into the bedroom and at once went to the jalousies and let them right down.

"Half an hour. I have spoken again to Jon Manos and also to Mme Lascou. It was necessary, you understand. Also I must have your passport when I go out."

"It's here."

"Put it in my bag, will you?"

They were talking in whispers, her face close to his but her expression very distant. Once her breath fanned his cheek.

He said rather quietly: "Anya, I want to talk to you."

"Not now. It is a silly time."

"I think we've both been deceiving ourselves."

"About what?"

"About this." He drew her against him and kissed her quietly on the mouth. She shook her head for a second or so after their lips touched. The plumber continued to hammer. Then she slid away, put the back of her hand up to her mouth and looked at him. "You don't suppose that solves anything?"

"Not on its own. It will in time."

"Don't be a fool."

"We've been deceiving ourselves, because that's the only thing that really matters between us."

"Is that what you think?"

"That's what I think."

"You know we both agreed it was impossible."

"I knew we agreed nothing of the sort. We agreed it was ill-advised, slightly crazy, unrealistic, likely to get right out of hand and so the more sure to come a crash in the end. But now——"

"This morning you said, just after breakfast you said——"

"Just then it was as if for a second Lascou had come between us. It was entirely my fault——"

"Has he ever stepped aside?"

"I don't think he's ever *been* between us. Not in the way that counts. . . . Anya, at least accept what you yourself said last night. We tried to write this off. By chance we haven't been able to. So we can no longer avoid what we tried to avoid. Isn't that it?"

"Is that it?"

"There isn't any escape for either of us." he said. "You know that now."

She turned her darkest glance on him, half smiled, half shrugged, her eyes slipping over him. Perhaps her attitude expressed exactly what she felt, a delicate but sensual disclaimer of responsibility. Her fingers closed round his and then she left the room.

Time passed. Zachari's replacement was Mandraki. Gene felt a prickling of the skin when he saw him. This was

702

something instinctive, something much more fundamental and less cerebral than his antagonism for Lascou. The plumber took longer than he had said, as plumbers always do. Anya did not come back.

Conflicting with his unease, with his impatience in inactivity, was a ripple of excitement coming up as it were against the current, a wave running up a river. The sunlight was broken in pieces on the floor where it came through the blinds. In his mind, in his heart, it was as if all the disparate pieces there had come together, as if all the hesitations and qualifications of experience had solidified and become a knowledge and a unification no less complete than would happen to the sunlight on the raising of the blind. The foreseeable future was short. he was content to let it be so.

At last there was more conversation in the sala, and at last Anya came back. She smiled at him with that rare brilliance she seldom gave to him, as if a little afraid of its effects on herself.

"He's gone. And our lunch is ready."

Going down the stairs the plumber fingered the pen-knife he'd found on the floor of the man-hole. He wasn't a thief, but it seemed a handy little thing and he'd lost his own a few weeks ago. He hadn't noticed anybody returning *that* to *him*. Besides there was nothing to prove that it belonged to the wonderful looking girl who had called him in. It might have lain on the floor for months and have belonged to some previous owner.

At least he thought that until he took it out of his pocket in the bright light of the street and read the inscription on it. It ran: *'Presented with the proud compliments of "Aegis" on the 50th Anniversary of its foundation.'* He had to stare twice at the date which followed, because it didn't seem to make sense that it should be today's date. But there it was.

He crossed the street and turned past a man lighting a cigarette. As he did so the man touched his arm.

"Been working in number four, brother?"

"What?" The plumber moved to go on but the hand held him. The man was all in black, fat, with a beard growing only under his several chins.

"You been working in Flat 4? I thought I saw you come to the window up there."

"What's it to you?"

"What was wrong with the plumbing, brother? What did you do in there?"

The plumber said: "A burst pipe. I mended it. That's the way I earn my living—not by standing on street corners."

The bearded man breathed in his face. "Be easy with your answers, brother. I'm not asking you this for love. Remember, I don't love you. What was the man like who let you in? Middle-sized, grey-eyed, bit of a foreigner?"

"Look," said the plumber. "You're chasing the wrong hare. There was no man. Only a girl. You've got the places mixed."

"Didn't you see a man in the flat at all?"

"What business is it of yours?"

"None, brother. I just like to know. Did you go in every room?"

"How do I know? I'm a plumber, not an architect. I tell you, I saw no one but the girl, the lady, whatever she is. Now move aside."

28

The funeral was at four. Anya left at three, in her deepest black and wearing a veil. She was gone until eight, and when she came home he saw at once that the distance was back, the defensive shell. Not only had she truly grieved for George, she had been in contact with the people and the world she understood and had known all her life. It was as if she had been re-injected with a familiar drug.

"You're in the dark. Has anyone called?"

"Someone rang the bell at four. And there were two phone calls."

She dragged off her hat and veil, threw them into a chair, went to the blinds to see that they were properly drawn, then switched on two of the table lamps. "Oh, I am so tired. It is—you know—the emotion."

"Let me get you a drink."

"Thank you. I will change out of these."

When she came back she was wearing the narrow black velvet trousers again and a scarlet tailored shirt with stiff cuffs. She smiled at him but not freely. He took her the drink and she curled up on the settee with her feet under her. He offered her a cigarette but she shook her head. He did not smoke himself but squatted on the piano stool and watched the expressions moving on her face.

"Do you want to hear about it?" she said.

"Only if you want to tell me."

"Then not. I would rather not."

"Did you go back afterwards? To Heracles House, I mean."

"Oh, yes, I had to; it was expected. In a way I wanted to. . . . I wanted to see it for the last time."

"You have come from there now?"

"No, I left at six. There was nothing more for me after that. . . . I have come now from Mme Lindos. And I have seen several other people."

He waited but didn't speak.

"Mme Lindos thinks she can fix it for Friday. Not before because her arrangements, you understand, have to be made at a distance, and she dare not use the phone. My part is easier."

"And what is your part?"

She shrugged deprecatingly. "It is not very clear and it is not very original, but I think it will work when the time comes."

"Friday, you mean?"

"Friday morning."

"I don't want you concerned in it."

"I am not. At seven every morning the milk comes here in a small van. The man leaves his van and delivers the milk outside each flat and then drives away. On Friday morning a milk van will come at fifteen minutes to seven. The man will bring the milk up, and when he reaches this flat he will come in and give you his coat and cap and you will walk out and drive the van away. You will drive the van out of Athens—I don't think you will be stopped—and as far as you can towards the destination that Mme Lindos is arranging for you; all the way if possible."

He looked at her with a little wry smile. "It is in the classic tradition."

She flushed slightly. "It is not very clever but it may do."

"You've found a man to take the risk?"

"I have friends. And I can pay more than the official reward. . . . You know Nafplion?"

"On the Peloponnese? I've been near it."

"It is a small harbour. There are fishing boats. Mme Lindos has a friend there. I shall have to go out again tomorrow morning."

"What for?"

"I have left your passport with a man. He is photographing the photograph. He has promised to make you into a French citizen. There is also the question of getting lire and francs."

Gene said: "If you can do all this for me in a day, I wonder what you could do in a lifetime."

She looked at him as if trying to see deeper than her gaze would penetrate. "I do not see the hope or the prospect of that."

"I think there's the hope."

She looked down abruptly at her glass, and appeared to meditate on that too. She did not reply.

They were about half-way through supper when Jon Manos called.

They had made the same preparations as at midday against a surprise. Nothing of Gene's was in the sala except

706

the plate from which he was eating, his wine glass, a slice of bread.

Manos came in, hair-oiled and plump-cheeked and smelling of Roman hyacinth. "My dear, I hoped you wouldn't have started—it's early yet and I've found a new place in Ekali—very quiet, we could dine privately. What do you say?"

"Thank you, Jon, but I've almost finished. In any case it is more fitting for me . . ."

"I understand how you feel. The formal rites this afternoon. EMO did very well at short notice. Mme Lascou, I thought, did not behave politely to you."

"I thought she was splendid. We met as mourners."

"Of course. Of course." He glanced once round the apartment, summing it up swiftly and in a different way from ever before, like a man suddenly being asked to bid at an auction. Then his eyes came back to the girl as she sat on the arm of the settee and summed her up too, missing absolutely nothing, from the curve of her breast under the scarlet shirt to the hand rubbing itself meditatively along her trousered leg. "Anya, this will make a difference to you."

"And to you, Jon."

"Naturally. Will you smoke?"

"No, thank you. But please smoke yourself."

"We have—a lot in common now, Anya. We both—attached ourselves, in very different ways, to a star. And now the star has fallen!"

"I hadn't looked at it that way."

"Of course I am putting it too bluntly. But many years ago . . . May I?" Manos slipped off his thin white overcoat and dropped it on a chair. ". . . many years ago, when I first met George Lascou, I saw him as a coming man in the biggest way. One had to be with him only a little while to appreciate his penetrating yet subtle mind, the great driving force behind that too quiet manner. I—made my choice. Sometime—I don't know when—you made your choice. That is what I mean by saying we had much in common. Of course, in our different ways, we had much to contribute in return."

"You're too kind."

Manos paced across the room lighting his cigarette. His white foulard tie contrasted with a navy blue shirt and a suit with a just visible pink stripe. He said: "My trained legal mind was of great value to him in his transactions. We helped each other. I learned much from him. I hope—to carry on in his tradition, as it were. All will not be lost, Anya, all will not be lost."

She remained perfectly quiet, holding her knee in her hand now, profile to him, ankle gently swinging.

He said: "It was my ambition to serve George faithfully until he reached the highest eminence. I would have been his second man. Stavrides is a nonentity who would have been swept away after the election. George was agreed on it."

"So?"

"Now that George has gone I serve Stavrides for the time being. He is the only figurehead we can rally behind. But he is too weak to survive permanently." Manos stopped in his pacing and made an expressive gesture with his hands. "He will go and the leadership will devolve on me. That's certain."

"So?"

"I cannot hope to bring to this position the gifts that George Lascou had. But my best will not be inconsiderable. It's not impossible that you're looking at a future Prime Minister of Greece."

Anya got up then and poured herself more wine. "Will the *coup* go on?"

He looked at her quickly. "You knew of it?"

"Of course."

"George did not tell me he had told you."

"George told me many things."

"Well, it cannot. General Telechos has already indicated that he will deal with no one else. I shall see him again in the morning, but I'm afraid the chance is lost."

"Then your chances of being Prime Minister of Greece . . ."

"Will depend—temporarily—on the outcome of the election. But we shall not lose votes through George's death." In his pacing Manos stopped before a mirror and tightened his tie. "Anyway, I'm not sure that it would be a good thing to win this election."

"Why not?"

"The country is too evenly split. With Telechos, yes, we could take over and hold what we took. Without him—and depending on parliament—it is better I think if the Government is returned, but with a very small majority. Then we can exploit their weaknesses, make capital out of the discontent that must come, and carry the day next time."

"Wine?" she said. "Or brandy? It is George's brandy, so you should like it."

He glanced at her, sensing the equivocal, poured himself a drink. She said: "Do you think the Communists have a chance?"

"The Communists?" He took time over putting back the brandy bottle. "They're finished—we could never stand them back in Greece, could we?" It was half a statement, half a question.

"George talked of it sometime. He said that there were many disguised Communist sympathisers."

"Some, I suppose. . . . Do you know any?"

She smiled. "They do not confide in me."

"No." He stepped uneasily away from the mirror. "The immediate point is not that at all—it is that EMO has a chance—and I with it."

"Which you intend to take."

"Which George would wish me to take—in the interests of Greece."

"And in your own."

"He would have wished me well, because, as I repeat, I have always subordinated my own interests to his. Even my interest—my very deep interest to his. Even my interest—my very deep interest in you."

It was out now. If she had not taken the point before, it was here plainly stated. Manos's take-over bid did not stop at political parties.

She sipped her wine and looked at him over the top of her glass.

"Don't you think, Jon, that it would be better to leave talking of that until a little time has gone by?"

"Naturally you're upset. Naturally you want time to adjust yourself. We all do. But I didn't wish you to be in any doubt as to the way I feel. My holding back has been entirely out of loyalty for George. . . ."

"Has anything been seen of the man who—did this thing?"

"Vanbrugh? He hasn't been caught yet, if that's what you mean. But he will be."

"It's twenty-four hours."

Manos's eyes had become smaller and colder. "You knew him well, didn't you?"

Anya shrugged. "I knew him. Because George asked me to, I made a friend of him."

"He regretted that later, didn't he?"

"Who, George? I don't think so."

Manos finished his drink and poured himself another. "I happened to be at Heracles House when he came back from visiting you the day before yesterday. He was very angry. He said little to me, but I gathered that he had quarrelled with you."

Anya leaned her elbow on the mantelshelf. "Dear Jon, between a man and a woman things like that can always happen. It's quite true he thought I'd gone too far in encouraging Gene Vanbrugh. So he was jealous. That did no harm. I should only have had more flowers, more presents when he came to his senses. But alas, that did not happen, cannot now ever happen."

Manos said: "I'm glad to know there was no foundation in it. Glad for myself, of course. And glad for you. I did not see how you could possibly betray all the things we have been working for these last ten years."

Anya said: "What exactly *have* we all been working for these last ten years?"

They stared at each other, and ultimately it was Manos

who made the little disclaiming gesture. "Need you ask? For the good of Greece. But this man Vanbrugh will be caught—I've no doubt at all."

"Why?"

He walked across the room, his shoes toeing in. "In politics, money and diplomacy will not always do everything. Political life is rough sometimes. I used to argue with George. He always preferred to exercise his power through money if he could. Sometimes he could not—and then he would leave it to me."

"And you?"

"In my legal career I have made contacts where contacts sometimes are invaluable. Little jobs can be done at a price—and no questions asked."

"You mean the Spaniard?"

"So George told you that. It seems——"

"Why did you take me to the Little Jockey the night before it happened?"

"How can one explain these impulses? Curiosity, bravado, a wish to see these people for myself. . . ." Manos made another of his gestures, dismissing it with his plump hands like a legal technicality. "What is important is that I have not left it entirely to the police to trace this Vanbrugh."

When he talked he moved like a dancer, a slow step here, a quick step there; it was a trait that had always amused her. Now it no longer amused her.

"And when did you—decide not to leave it entirely to the police?"

"Monday evening."

"Did George tell you to?"

"No. Sometimes he would hesitate too long. In this case *I* hesitated too long also."

"Is it without any doubt that this man killed him?"

"He was clever enough to remove his finger prints, but Michael's evidence alone will convict him."

"Michael saw the blow struck?"

"No, but everything else. Have no doubt, my dear. Vanbrugh will be found, alive or dead."

She came back to the supper table, picked up a plate and put it over another, slid her used knife and fork on to them. "Forgive me, Jon, I think I am going to bed soon. All this has greatly upset me. . . ."

"Of course." Smiling with his teeth and talking all the time, he allowed her to see him to the door. He took two little side steps and bent to kiss her hand. "Don't forget what I said, Anya."

"About what?"

"About ourselves."

"No. . . . No, I'll not forget."

His smile encompassed her breasts, her shoulders, her neck and face and eyes, and then slipped politely past her to take in again the handsome room he was leaving. "I suppose you haven't heard—you will not have heard yet how any of the money has been left?"

"To his children, I expect," she said. "In trust for his children."

"And in the meantime?"

"I don't know. I hope none of it has been left to me."

29

You heard?"

"A good deal of it." Gene moved away from the blind. "The man outside hasn't spoken to him. They're obviously not sure themselves."

"It was Jon Manos who did this—not George."

In silence they cleared away the things. Then she washed up and he wiped.

He said: "Do you care anything for Manos?"

"How could I? A man like that!"

"He has George's bad qualities without his good."

"He could *never* lead Greece. He can only buy the gangster and the bully."

"Which he appears to have done pretty efficiently of late. I don't think we should under-rate him."

"I don't under-rate him but he has no hopes of ever taking George's place!"

After a minute he said: "Was it true, what you told Manos, that you allowed me to make the running on instructions from George?"

"Not instructions. But he thought it a good thing."

"I see."

She said: "And did you first 'make the running with me,' as you call it, to find out more about him?"

"Yes."

She looked at him thoughtfully.

He put down a plate. "I think we've come rather a long way in a week."

"All your invitations to me were—part of this policy?"

"Of course. As all your acceptances were?"

"I didn't come to Delphi because of what George had told me to do! You heard. We quarrelled because of it."

He took up another plate. "I didn't ask you to Delphi to find out about George. By that time I was in love with you."

"But you—went on helping this Spanish girl?"

"It was something I'd promised her—and myself—before I even met you."

She stopped. "I asked that out of jealousy. It's a feeling I have never had before."

He put his hand on her arm and turned her gently round. Her eyes were warm.

She said against his mouth: "So I think I love you too."

When they separated it was as if they had run up five flights. His fingers were trembling. She leaned against the chromium sink.

She said: "And yet—can you understand it?—in spite of this and in spite of what we have said, I don't want—anything here tonight."

"You mean, this flat?"

"*His* flat. He is—to me he is still here. You said this

713

morning that he had come between us. He cannot *help* but be between us here. *Everything* reminds me. I am still part of his belonging. Are you superstitious?"

"No."

"Neither am I. But there are some things that one . . ."

She stopped and looked at him.

He said: "What's between us is too important to begin wrong. I've confidence enough in my chances of getting clear to let this opportunity by if you think it right we should, for the right reasons. But I make one condition."

"What?"

"That we stop talking as if this was something temporary. Whatever else, it isn't temporary. It's the big thing for me—like no other ever. I don't have to say it again, do I?"

She answered: "I think it is the first time you have ever said it."

The plumber had finished his evening meal, and although his children were still up and making a noise, his wife was out, so he enjoyed his daily paper in more detail than usual. It was the warmest evening of the year, and he was regretting he had not gone out for a glass of mastica with his friends, when something he read took his attention, not solely because it was in blacker type. (*Telmi* was a great paper for bigger and blacker type.)

"The murderer was last seen at a ceremony held to commemorate the 50th Anniversary of the founding of the newspaper *Aegis,* from whose offices he made his escape on being recognised. In the interests of fair play we forbear to comment on a situation in which a man such as this, a notorious criminal long wanted by the police, finds himself in the company of high-placed Government supporters, entertained by them, on the best of terms with them, while the blood is still wet on his hands from the commission of his latest and vilest crime."

The paragraph puzzled the plumber. He took out the penknife he had found and stared at it and then re-read the paragraph twice more. The man with the beard stopping him

714

on the street corner—did that mean anything? And—in spite of his denial—the voice he *had* heard in the flat?

"It's no good," said the constable, next morning. "The sergeant's busy. Tell me what you have to say and I will tell him."

"He is my cousin," said the plumber sadly. "It is a family affair."

"Family affairs can wait until the sergeant is off duty. That he will be at six o'clock. You can see him then."

"Certain family matters," said the plumber, "demand immediate discussion."

Flies hummed in the lazy sunbeams that fell through the shutters of the dusty police station. Nothing else stirred.

The plumber added: "I have come here specially to your station, neglecting my work, in the heat of the day. D'you suppose I would go to that trouble without cause?"

The policeman scratched his shirt sleeve. "What is it all about? Your wife? Your daughter? His? Tell me, then I will judge."

"I'm sorry, it is a private matter. But I will tell you it may be to do with the police also."

The plumber had been skilful in the way he had worded his argument. Affinity and consanguinity meant much.

"At four," the policeman said, but speculatively.

"Now," said the plumber.

The flies buzzed drearily and the policeman irritably flicked one away.

"Someone is dead," said the plumber, playing his last card. "It is a matter I must discuss with the sergeant as man to man. Then it may be for someone higher up still."

"Well, well," said the policeman. "Wait here. I will see."

Major Kolono was just beginning his lunch when the call came through.

"What? What? Who is it? Speak up! What information? Who gave it you? Yes, of course, if it is of value. But is it of value? Very well, I'm listening!"

He listened. He said: "Where was it found? Number what? Flat 4. This plumber found it? What was he doing there? . . . I see. Wait a minute, the address is familiar. I will just make sure about that. Hold the line."

He walked into his office and took up another phone. "Find out who lives at Flat 4, number 11, Baronou Street." He waited until the information came through, then stumped back to the other telephone.

"You fool!" he said with considerable pleasure into the receiver. "Don't you know who lives at that address? It is Mlle Stonaris, M. Lascou's mistress. She was at this Anniversary Reception on Tuesday night at the *Aegis* offices and would naturally receive any gift which was being presented on such an occasion. What does it matter where the plumber found it? In any case her lfat has already been searched. What? I say it has already been *searched!* Send your plumber about his business and attend to your own!"

He slammed the receiver down and poured himself another half glass of wine, to which he added iced water. Then he sat down to his interrupted *pepóni*. But towards the end of the meal certain thoughts began to stir in his mind, like frogs in a pool after the ripples of the stone have settled.

30

It was by far the hottest day of the year so far in Athens. For the first time the sun was a presence to be reckoned with, an injection into the blood-stream of the city. Pulses beat faster, blood flowed hotter and thinner, shadows developed substantial architectures to be sought before they shrank at noon. So now it would go on each day, iron hot in the morning, punitive almost until dark, changeless through the summer until the parched city was swept with the storms of autumn.

But in Anya's flat, with the windows open and the

jalousies down, it was only pleasantly warm. She went out early. He did not like her calling on Mme Lindos again, but there was no escape for it. To pass the time while she was gone he read the morning paper through to see if there was anything fresh relating to Lascou's death or to himself. There was nothing new, but on the back paper his eyes suddenly came on a paragraph headed 'Spaniard's Death.' 'Philip Tolosa, 39 year old Spanish dancer and harpist, was found gravely injured in the street outside his hotel window from which he had apparently jumped or fallen. He died on the way to hospital. Tolosa is the second of a troupe of Spanish dancers and entertainers to meet his death in an accident since the troupe arrived in Greece three weeks ago. His brother was knocked down and killed by a car, which failed to stop, in Galatea Street on the 12th. Mme Nicolou, proprietress of the boarding house, said that Tolosa had brooded a great deal over his brother's death and seemed to be unable to get it off his mind. An inquiry will be held tomorrow."

Gene folded the paper. A contrived accident? It seemed unlikely. No one now had anything to gain by his death. For ten days Philip Tolosa had been working himself into a frame of mind from which there was no return.

And Maria? Safe by now. She was the only one of the three that mattered.

It was noon when Anya returned, bringing his new passport. It was not a bad copy. He did not think it would satisfy the Deuxième Bureau, but it would pass the casual examination of a frontier officer. The photograph was no worse than the original.

"And Sophia?"

"She has had word from Nafplion that it is all right as far as there."

"So tomorrow morning I leave."

"Yes. I'm afraid so."

"I wish you could come with me."

She said: "When you are free let me know where you are, that you're alive and well. That is the first, all-important

717

thing. When that is so, then—maybe—we can begin to plan."

They had their mid-day meal near one of the shuttered windows. They ate and talked in a filtered, aquarium light, but more yellow, thicker, as if it was a world of sunfish. They ate a cold chicken which she had bought, and zucchinis and a mixed salad, and drank a white Tour la Reine.

They didn't talk much. There was still eighteen hours for planning. Just now it was a warm and friendly companionship that didn't need words. It was an astonishing advance in their relationship—of far greater import than the mere physical act of love would have been.

By the time they finshed, traffic in the street outside was drying up like a trickle of water in sand, pedestrians almost disappeared, more blinds came down, dogs and workmen curled up in the shade and slept.

They sat there exchanging a word or two, in their own quiet country, isolated now. They were protected not so much by indifferent walls and slanting jalousies and locked doors as by the sleeping town. For two hours nothing would stir. He came to sit beside her but made no move to touch her.

She said: "Do you want—now—to make love to me?"

"Only on your terms."

She said: "I know it is strange for me, a woman like me, still to have qualms. . . . It is pretentious perhaps a little." She smiled at him, considering her words. "It is very difficult. I am not just an animal desiring to be desired by you, but neither am I just a detached brain existing in a—a vacuum. My reason says to me: the fact that this has come in George's flat at a time when George has hardly gone from you, where everything, everything is reminiscent—and I grieve—you may not believe it but I grieve—for a friend. . . . All that is ill-tasting only because of a coincidence of time and place. My reason says, how can that really affect what is so separate from it in thought and feeling that it might be happening to someone else? If you refuse this now it will prove nothing except that you are turning away from what is

718

good, what is true, because you cannot rid your memory of what it tries to forget."

"Your reason has a lot of reason on its side."

"But there is another thing. We are in the very centre of danger. What we feel for each other should not be flawed by fear, by the heart jumping for the wrong causes, by a chance telephone call, by the ring at the door, by the siren down the street. It should not be flawed by being snatched at in haste and in dread."

He was a little while replying. In the centre of his mind was a truth that he now fully recognised but was afraid to grasp at and discipline too soon. It might even escape him in speech, in the effort to be completely honest both with her and with himself.

"Anya, I don't know what is true or not true about tomorrow. I can only be sure of today."

"And today?"

"Today I have absolute certainty. I don't need to say it or to think it any more."

"And you would begin this—now?"

". . . You must decide."

"Lift off the telephone," she said. "That way we can be sure it will not ring."

31

Major Kolono woke about ten past four. Sometimes baby octopus gave him acute indigestion and he was nervous about his stomach. He knew he should see a doctor but he was terrified of being told that there was something gravely wrong.

He got off his couch and went into the next room for the bismuth tablets, and while he was doing so that other discomfort, of the mind, returned. Memories of Saturday came to trouble him—he had seen the wanted man talking to

Anya Stonaris—and *why* had her flat been searched? There'd been some report, that . . . He swallowed the tablets and blew out his chest to let them go down; he persuaded himself he felt better. Then he sat in his chair and pressed the bell, and when it was not immediately answered he kept his finger on it until it was.

His second in command came bustling into the room fastening the top button of his tunic. "Sir?"

"Have you done anything more to check that plumber's report on Flat 4, Number 11, Baronou Street?"

"No, sir. I thought you were satisfied. You gave no instructions."

Kolono stared his subordinate down. "Everything in this department I have to do myself, it seems. No one has the initiative to stir a finger; I wonder how you live in your own houses; are you spoon-fed, dressed and washed? . . . Telephone to the offices of *Aegis* and ask if the penknives which were presented to guests on Tuesday night were given to everyone, especially if it is remembered whether Mlle Stonaris received one. And I want to see that plumber. Also get me Mr. Manos on the other line."

"Very good, sir."

The man went out, and Kolono rubbed his little black moustache and belched. A routine inquiry; but Manos would be able to tell him whether Mlle Stonaris still retained any power, whether it would be permissible to worry her a second time. It was a good policy while on the subject of Vanbrugh to ring the various branch stations for news. An inquiry would keep them up to scratch.

He had finished with two stations and was lecturing a third when his assistant came into the room. Kolono slapped the phone down and said: "Well?"

"Sir, penknives were given only to the gentlemen at the Anniversary Reception. The ladies received fountain pens."

Major Kolono felt a knot twist in his stomach, and it was not dyspepsia. "So."

His second in command waited patiently.

"Mr. Manos?"

"He is out of town, sir. He is expected back this evening."

Kolono said: "How did it come about that Mlle Stonaris's flat was searched in the first place? An anonymous report, wasn't it?"

"A phone call, sir. Late on Tuesday night."

"Nothing was found?"

"No, sir."

"Who was the lieutenant who searched the flat?"

"Andros, sir."

"Send for him at once."

Mme Lindos was a woman of resource. She had seen more wars through than she cared to remember, more civil upheavals and revolutions than she could count. She had suffered the loss of a husband and a son, weathered the storms, it seemed to her sometimes, of more than one lifetime. She could not have survived without great courage and resource and the constant exercise of them.

When her cousin's son-in-law, who happened to be Kolono's second-in-command, called her on the telephone just as she was about to sit down to tea and gave her an urgent but guarded message, she didn't get flustered or panic. She told Louisa to take the teapot back to the kitchen and to keep it warm, then she picked up the telephone. There was a certain risk attached to the use of the telephone, since the line might be tapped, but it was a risk that did not disturb her. She still had a few friends in exalted quarters.

She also had one or two friends in Athens in a lowlier sphere, people whom she could trust, and she decided that now was a time when she must make use of them. She first telephoned the proprietor of a small garage whom she had helped to start in business ten years ago. Having talked with him she rang Anya. The line was engaged.

This was the first point at which she showed some emotion. She lit a cigarette and got up from the telephone and limped across the room. Then she came back and tried again. Still the engaged note.

It was now a matter of timing and carefully calculated

risks. It might be that the line was being deliberately cut; or it might be that in five minutes she would still get through. Either event must be prepared for. She pulled across a pen and a piece of paper and tore off the address. Then she scribbled a few lines and put it in an envelope. She rang the bell.

"I want you to take this round to Baronou Street. Deliver it only to Mlle Stonaris, who you remember came here on Tuesday night. And Louisa...."

"Yes, ma'am?"

"Take a basket with some flowers in. Take these flowers from the vases. Just put them in the basket as if you were delivering them. It is a matter of appearing you are going on ordinary business, not delivering a message, d'you understand."

Anya said: "Darling, I am so afraid."

"What, now?"

"Now more than ever. I have so much more to lose."

"Yes.... I felt that this morning."

"Did you? I didn't know."

"Happiness is a maker of cowards. Who cares what you lose if you've nothing to lose? But maybe it also makes fighters who fight longer in the end."

"I feel over-burdened, frightened of the danger around us—now, at this moment."

"It's not likely to have changed in two hours."

"It has for me."

"I mean literally."

"I wish you'd put the telephone back."

"Soon."

In the flat on the opposite side of the street someone had switched the radio on, but the music came to them diffused by distance, disembodied, remote.

She stirred restlessly. "It is strange to be so happy and so unhappy at the same time. The heights are no higher for the existence of depths. I want no more than Parnassus."

"What's that thing of Flecker's? 'We stood at last beyond

the golden gate, Masters of Time and Fate, and knew the tune that Sun and Stars were singing.' ''

After a pause she said: "This afternoon several times, you have spoken to me in Greek. It was like something within yourself speaking, something deeper and more instinctive than your own tongue. That, I think, convinced me more than anything. . . .''

"Of what?"

"Of what I was most anxious to know. Gene."

"Yes?"

"How will you ever clear yourself even if you do get away? How *can* you? It is impossible without some help from this girl. Even then you would be guilty as an accessory. Will she be out of the country yet?"

"Today, I should think."

"I have this feeling, as if something terrible is going to happen, as if our happiness is already fated. It's a premonition. God, that one should be so morbid! It must stop." She raised herself on one elbow and kissed him. "Tell me this fear is not true.'''

Holding her, he said: "Darling, it's not true."

"I wish we could escape together."

"So do I."

"Do you know the Cyclades? I believe we might be forgotten there. They are hard and windy, but so beautiful. Hot with a lovely sea-heat in the summer, and shell-clear water, like Sounion. One can fish and swim and sit in the sun all day. I think there one could lose ambition, which destroys so much of the world."

"Do you like sailing?"

"I have never done as much as I would want to. And you?"

"We might try together."

"First we must get you out."

"And then you will join me."

She sighed. "It sounds so easy. But I think it will be safer in the South Seas."

"Yes, I might not need to wear a beard there."

She said: "Oh, Gene, there is *no* way, there is *no* way. . . ."

"There is, there is," he whispered. "We will find it."

After a while she murmured in his ear: "The telephone."

"Right, soon."

"Now."

"Right." The telephone by the bed did not work unless the other was connected, so he slid to his feet and padded out into the next room, put the telephone back on its rest, peered through the blind. The street was quiet but there were a few more people about, and cars moved up and down it. The sun was slanting, falling full upon the blinds, and the sala was warmer than the bedroom. The remains of the lunch they had eaten looked untidy and desolate. The little French clock said twenty-five minutes to five.

He went back into the bedroom and found Anya dressing. He interrupted her.

"So soon?"

"I—yes. I feel safer. Is there anyone in the street?"

"Not anyone who shouldn't be there."

He held his face against hers. Her hair touched his forehead and he blew it away. She laughed.

"We must have a wonderful dinner tonight, Gene."

"I'd like that."

"I will devise a menu. My mother taught me to cook, you'll be surprised to know."

"Give me the key to your wine cellar," he said. "Or have I already seen it?"

"What?"

"Your cellar. That's where I hid on Tuesday night? I thought the white wines were rather warm."

She said laughing: "I bought a lobster this morning. With pâté before it. Or is that too rich? A good soup. . . ."

"I'll risk the pâté. Darling, do you play that great piano in the next room?"

"Of course."

"Then will you do that?"

"Now?"

"Sometime soon. You see, I don't know you yet, and I want to get to know you."

She said: "And there are those things from the excavations at Sounion. I promised to show you them."

"We mustn't over-crowd the evening."

She put on high-heeled mules of fine kid. He watched her.

"Why not those bedroom slippers?"

"I cannot bear to be sloppy."

He laughed. "But *I* am sloppy."

"No, you're not. Not in the ways that matter. Your shirts, your shoes. . . ." She stopped. "Seriously, Gene. . . ."

He laughed again. "How often have you said 'seriously' to me already?"

"If you would speak Greek to me I should not have the habit. But Gene, this is really serious, really important. Last night, talking about the arrangements I had made for your escape, you said to me, 'if you can do all this for me in a day, I wonder what you could do in a lifetime.' "

"I meant it."

"But I want to say this now: if we have luck, if we have some life together even for a short time, I shall not try to organise it—not even with the help of Mme Lindos."

He said: "And in reply, seriously, if that happens, you can dictate your own terms. I shall be in no mood to bargain."

She stood up and buttoned the back of her dress. He went again to the window. The palm outside was rustling its leaves like a great elephantine fern; one huge frond almost brushed the window. On the other side of the street people were opening their shutters as the sun left them. The shutters immediately opposite were pale grey in a pink-washed house. A woman was brushing her hair, just seen as a pale arm moving regularly in the dark room.

He turned and found Anya smiling at him. She said: "You're wondering how I could live simply on an island if I can't bear to be sloppy?"

"I wasn't, but I can if you want me to."

She said: "It is not what one wears, darling, it is an

725

attitude of mind. I'm sure I should not disgrace you in Tahiti."

He said: "You have very quaint ideas of who is conferring the favour in all this. All I ask, when I write to you, is that you should come."

The telephone began to ring.

They looked at each other. She slid out of his arms and went into the other room. From the doorway as he dressed he watched her.

"Yes. . . . Who?. . . . Oh. . . . Yes, he is here. . . . What is it?" All the laughter had gone from her face. She held out the telephone. "It is Mme Lindos. For you."

He took the phone, his mind registering the incaution of these women. Then he heard that unmistakable dry voice, rather masculine over the phone.

"Gene?"

"Yes."

"You must go. The—the people who called for you on Tuesday night are coming for you again."

He felt what he had never felt before on his own behalf, a qualm of panic.

"When?"

"The message was a little indefinite—naturally. But I think immediately. I have been trying to telephone you for fifteen minutes. I think they will be round any moment. Now listen. Understand this carefully."

"Yes?"

"In five minutes—if these people who are coming for you are not there before then—a taxi will draw up at the door. I do not know what sort it will be, but the young man driving it will be looking for you. Be in the doorway ready. The taxi will not stop its engine. As it draws up go out and jump in. The driver will help you as best he can. Is that clear?"

"Yes. What are you——"

"It is the best I could do in an emergency. It may already be too late. If my maid comes with a note before then, tell her to come straight back to me. I——"

"Sophia, I cannot let you——"

"You must be there waiting, for my friend will not stop. That is asking too much. He will tell you the rest. God go with you."

He spoke again but she had rung off.

He put the phone back, turned to look at Anya who was standing tall and straight watching him.

"I'm on my way out," he said.

He dressed like lightning, fishing out the old gladstone bag with his own clothes still unjettisoned, put on his spectacles, hat, talking to her. . . .

"Don't worry about me. Clear these things. Wash the glasses or break them. If they——"

"*Gene*, what when you get in the car? Did she say nothing? . . ."

"It's up to me. And looking after yourself is up to *you*. If they find no traces of me here they can do *nothing* to you. Understand? Nothing. So don't come down with me. Cigarette ends, remember. The newspapers on the piano. Look round the bedroom——"

"What do I care about myself? How shall I hear from you? How shall I know you're safe?"

"No news, good news. But I warn you of one thing. If I get out you'll hear as soon as I can let you know. You'll *never* get clear of me now. *Never*. Understand?"

She said indistinctly: "Food, wine; take something with you in that bag. Here, give it to me. . . ."

While he unlocked the outer door and peered cautiously up and down the stairs she flew to the kitchen, found a small bottle of brandy—that and half the chicken and a piece of cheese and a stick of bread went in on top of the clothes. He was back at the window looking out. There was still no sign or sound of the police. But Mandraki was there now, leaning against a wall about thirty yards away on the opposite side.

He took the bag from her and they went to the door.

"No further. Wash those plates. Darling, darling, I must go."

"Remember me," she said.

727

They kissed. He said: "Anya. . . . Good-bye."

She kissed him, but couldn't speak. Then he was gone, pattering down the stone stairs.

32

Wait at the door. How long to wait at the door? Four minutes exact had passed since putting down the receiver. No taxi. Street empty. So it was a question of waiting. But which would come first, the taxi or the police car?

Every second made danger more extreme. If the police came first he was caught without a hope. Sophia Lindos's friend might not be as brave as she thought. Getting the request from her he would no doubt decide with a typical shrug: better have a breakdown, apologise to her afterwards, not really worth the risk of falling foul of the police. Perhaps he was smoking a cigarette now in his garage; pity, he'd think, I'd have liked to help the chap.

Anya's risk was increased too by this wait. They must accuse her if they found him here, on her doorstep. Better if Sophia hadn't made any plan, left it to him. At least now he would be on his own. He wasn't afraid of Mandraki. Shake him off. Or push him under a bus. He could fend for himself. Athens was his native ground. A dozen holes.

A gypsy was coming down the street leading a brown bear on a chain. When he stopped, people at once began to gather round to watch. The *romvia* was still an attraction when he ventured into the city.

Outside the taverna a lorry was delivering a barrel of resinated wine. A car came down the street, swerving round the lorry, and seemed about to stop. But it went on again, gears whining, turned a corner on its brakes. Someone in a hurry, but not for him.

The gypsy wore a leather waistcoat over a green shirt with old brown breeches. He beat on his tambourine and the bear hoisted itself on its hind legs and began to shuffle laboriously round its master. A crowd was the perfect cover; but this crowd was too far away. But for Mandraki, of course, he could have gone across, and waited with the watching people, inconspicuous and fairly safe. To stand a chance he *must* go; it was suicide to stay in this doorway——

... An elderly black taxi with yellow artillery wheels and yellow doors came purring up from the opposite direction. It slowed and almost stopped, moved on and came to a stop in front of the *romvia*. The driver was peering up at the numbers above the doors.

Gene slid across the pavement in one streak and got in. The young man driving had curly brown hair and was wearing a boiler suit.

"M. Vanbrugh?"

Gene nodded and slammed the door and fell into the back as the car jerked violently and screamed out into the centre of the street. He didn't look out of the back window but lay on the seat until the taxi had turned twice and was making downhill towards the centre of the town.

When he looked behind there was nothing following. He leaned forward and said to the driver in Greek: "Thank you."

The driver grinned and switched down the 'libre' flag. "Think nothing of it."

"Where are you taking me?"

"Where do you wish to go?"

"To Piraeus."

"Mme Lindos thought otherwise."

"What did she suggest?"

"Nafplion. She said ask for Constantinos Salamis in the square beside the cinema."

"We can't go all the way there in your taxi."

"It's not my taxi. I stole it from the rank while the driver had gone to ease himself."

"You're a man of resource."

"But naturally."

They were coming rapidly into the busy section of the town.

Gene said: "Then what are your plans?"

"Soon, when we have gone a little further, I will get out and leave the automobile to you. What you do with it then is your own concern; I am glad I shall not know. You are right that this taxi will be noticeable if you drive in it all the way to Nafplion."

"It will be noticeable before then," said Gene, thinking of Mandraki.

"There is a train leaves the station for Nafplion at six."

"And the station will be very carefully watched by the police."

"Maybe. But there are other stations. The train stops at Eleusis and at Megara. They are not so many miles out of Athens, and I do not suppose they will be picketed."

"I think Corinth will be watched."

"Maybe. But by then you should be on the train." The young man, having exhausted his ingenuity, was becoming slightly less interested.

Gene glanced behind. It was impossible to be absolutely sure in this busy street, but he could see nothing suspicious.

The young Greek mopped the back of his neck. "Do you know your way out of Athens?"

"Yes."

"Then I will turn down at this next corner and leave you. It is best to do it in the centre where it will not be conspicuous."

They swerved into a side street and stopped. The driver jumped out and made a pretence of going round and examining a rear wheel. Gene got out and joined the driver. They put their heads together a moment, and then Gene straightened up and in a leisurely manner strolled to the driver's seat and got in. The other man kicked the tyre a couple times and presently went into a shop for some cigarettes. Gene felt for the pedals, restarted the motor, glanced behind him, then drew out into the traffic and moved off.

A hunted man is like a man at the centre of a cyclone; there are periods of calm when it's impossible for him to assess the strength of the storm around him. Gene tried hard to take an impersonal view of his chances.

Police of course would keep a special watch at docks and stations and airports. What else? Road blocks? Trains stopped and searched? Special checks at appropriate places on identity cards and passports? Hardly likely unless he was reported on a particular route. For a man in his position it was almost as dangerous to take too few risks as too many.

The homicide rate in Athens was probably the highest of the European capitals. But this was a special murder, of a statesman and a millionaire. How far could EMO put pressure on for extra measures?

The taxi had to go early. Mandraki would soon let the police know how he had left. But again, to be too timid would be to lose an initial advantage.

This was the same road so far as they had taken to Delphi cutting across the peninsular through Daphni. He was well away from the railway line now but the two ways would converge at Eleusis, as the young Greek said. Already one or two people were staring at the old taxi. Not that this mattered much—people always did stare in Greece—but if one of them remembered. . . .

Short of Daphni he slowed to a crawl. Two or three kilometres beyond the little town he remembered there was a fork in the road: if he turned left there he would be doubling back to Piraeus. The police might expect him to do that.

Almost in sight of Daphni he saw a side-lane turning sharp to his left and climbing up into the narrow mountain range separating the road from the sea. He swung the car up it and changed down, grinding the unfamiliar gears. The old taxi began to lurch and grunt up the hill.

It was half a mile before he came to cover, and he beat the guts out of the engine getting there. Thin low scrub of laurel and myrtle grew beside what in wet weather might be a rushing stream but now was a rubble of small stones, white and smooth as skulls.

He drove the car off the road, bumping between two boulders, and grounded it hard in the middle of the river bed. When he got out he found it was hidden from the road. He tipped his own clothes out of his bag, dropping Anya's bread, rolled the clothing in a ball and hid it under a rock, retrieved the bread and shut his bag.

He ran back as far as the main road, then walked more slowly through Daphni. People in doorways stared at him, but unspeculatively, as they would have stared at any moving object that came into their line of vision. Once out of the town he went on more quickly. It was ten minutes to six and his chances of catching the train at Eleusis—even if he decided to take the risk—were small. Eight or ten kilometres yet.

The road here was downhill and uninteresting but in a little while would run beside the sea. A peasant cart turned out ahead but it was moving no quicker than he was walking, in fact he began to catch it up. Then he saw a little knot of people standing at the side of the road, two or three of them carrying baskets and one with a child in arms. He joined them. Several of them stared and two nodded a good evening, but everybody was talking too animatedly to notice him for long. Not that there was anything in their talk to get animated about, but it was their nature to make the best of indifferent material.

Roads were so few that no vehicle going in this direction could be making for anywhere but Eleusis; but when the bus came up five minutes later it was marked Megara, which was 20 kilometres beyond.

He crowded into it with the others. He stood near the back between two black-dressed women, one with a basket with live fowls. A man in a sombrero hemmed him in in front and a boy with a dog rubbed against his legs. Everything smelt of garlic and old sweat. The bus jolted into movement and the conductor fought his way through to get his fares. Everybody was talking, and somewhere at the front a young man was trying to play a mouth organ. Gene took a ticket to Megara. He worried for Anya, how she had faced the police when they came, what she was doing now.

At ten past six the bus lurched into the narrow streets of Eleusis. It stopped near the waterfront while sixteen people fought their way off and another twenty got on. There was a policeman at the stop watching the crowd but he took no special interest in them. Gene thought of the Greek phrases, 'It does not matter. Let us do it tomorrow.'

A hand touched his arm. "Are you from Argos, *patrioti*?"

He looked down at the man with the sombrero, who was peering up at him. "No, from Lavrion." It was his usual reply, to pick the opposite side of Greece.

"Well, well, I thought your cloth came from Argos. I am a tailor there." He looked more like a brigand with his fat body, a nose jutting like a scimitar from under his hat, a stubble of beard.

"It may be that it did," said Gene. "My own suit was damaged in an accident and I bought this second hand in Athens."

"Ah, that explains it, if you will pardon me. The *koukoulariko* comes of course from Kalamai, and I rather think . . . You'll pardon me." The Greek put out a black-nailed finger and thumb and felt the edge of the cloth "Yes, that's it. There was not much of this heavier type, and it was made up locally."

Everyone in the bus lurched as it began to move. A faint welcome air stirred the heat and the smell.

"Are you going to Argos tonight?" Gene said.

"I hope to. I have something to pick up at Megara and then I intend to catch the automotrice."

"That's the diesel train?"

"Yes." Swinging and lurching, the little man got out a watch. "One has to be hasty but I have caught it before. I am in Argos then by nine-thirty."

Gene said: "I too am going to Argos—or near there."

"By the train?"

"I had thought so. But I have never been before. That's the best way?"

"It's the only way if you wish to get there tonight. And the steam trains tomorrow morning—they barely crawl."

733

"I am a radio mechanic," said Gene. "I have business ultimately in Nafplion."

"Well, the train will take you there tonight. You will be there before ten. Permit me to introduce myself. My name is Diomedes Cos."

Gene gave a name he had used during the war, and the bus lurched on towards Megara. Everybody talked, and M. Cos was full of information. He was also full of curiosity about Gene—a common characteristic in the country districts; it was a candid, unassuming curiosity, giving and expecting to receive a free exchange of information as a way of enlarging one's acquaintance and passing the time. Gene was forced to keep his wits at stretch.

The sun was low in the sky, and the water of the bay had become a willow pattern blue, brimming so full it seemed as if it was going to over-spill and flood the land. Megara loomed up climbing its two low hills; they bumped and rattled through the squat white concrete hovels on the outskirts and then lurched through the town and came to a stop in the main square. The doors of the bus opened and people were spewed out upon the cobbled street. Children cried, dogs barked, street sellers offered sweetmeats in bags and grilled mutton on wooden sticks.

"The station is over there," said M. Cos. "I shall hope to join you in a few minutes." He went off across the square on fat purposive legs.

Soldiers here, talking in listless groups, squatting around some sort of a gambling game, sitting on the walls. Gene walked to the station. He was in time for the train. There were a few people on the platform and a number around the booking office. No evidence of police; but one couldn't be sure. He didn't go in.

There was a kiosk near, and he bought a bottle of wine, a *baclavá* cake, a magazine about radio. He was still reading when Diomedes Cos came hurrying back across the square with a big parcel under his arm. Gene followed the tailor into the station and caught him up at the booking office. They exchanged nods and Gene said: "I was hungry

734

but I was afraid there wasn't time before the train came in."

They bought tickets. There were two men in the booking office but neither had the interest to raise his eyes. They pulled tickets out of cubby holes, accepted money and shoved masses of dirty small notes back through the grill.

On the platform Cos said: "You see, there was just time. The train is signalled."

Two crones whispered together in the long slanting sunlight. A priest with a black beard paced up the platform ostentatiously reading his Bible. A small almost yellow-skinned boy clung to his mother's skirts waving a blue and white Greek flag. At the end of the platform an oleander tree gleamed, its leaves brilliant and undusty. There was a hoot in the distance, and a small diesel train slid into the station.

Only two carriages, and those connected with a continuous passage down the centre. Gene stuck close to the fat little tailor; a man on his own would be more to look at. There were a few seats and they got two with their backs to the engine near the middle of the train. Opposite were a young man and a girl.

The train moved off at a good speed, whining like a big vacuum cleaner. After a time Gene offered Cos wine from one of the two cardboard cups he had bought, and felt for the penknife he'd been presented with at the *Aegis* offices. But he couldn't find it.

"I'm sorry. I thought I had a corkscrew."

"No matter. We will ask the guard. He will have one."

The guard had not got one, but he said he would ask the driver who always carried one.

As they neared Corinth the sun dipped flaming behind the great Peloponnesian mountains. The light flared from behind them; rocks and cliffs and cypresses stood up with startling blackness against the glow; for a few minutes it was unearthly, as if the events of four thousand years were burning behind the hills—Hercules was hunting his lion and Agamemnon riding out to war. The train stopped at a squalid station and then moved slowly off and crawled across the viaduct spanning the Corinth canal. Almost every passenger in the train stood up to peer out of the windows at the long narrow slit of water. As they ran into Corinth station twilight was already clustering over the lower hills.

Bustle and movement. Gene saw two policemen walking slowly along the platform peering in the train. This was the testing point, the obvious place to come in, asking people for their papers.

The policemen came down, revolvers tap-tapping in holsters. The child with the Greek flag waved it at them. Gene poured more wine into the tailor's glass. Cos was a supporter of Karamanlis, and Gene asked him whether he thought the government would go back. That gave them conversation while the policemen went past.

The train began to moan again, and moved off. Gene leaned back and slowly allowed his grip to relax on the cardboard cup. 'It does not matter. Let us do it tomorrow.' He bit into the almond cake. It was very sweet and rather dry.

He wondered if Anya was all right. The loss of the penknife worried him. Already this afternoon seemed a week ago. Now the recollection of it came back like a floodlight on a dark day.

Everyone still talked in the train, talked in high voices above the whine of the diesel; but Gene found his eyes shutting. He tried hard to hear what the fat tailor was saying but the words began to blur. He nodded and came half awake to look through bleared eyelids and see Mandraki sitting opposite him.

He jerked his head up, fighting something stronger than sleep, drugged wine perhaps; shook his body, tried to get to his feet, was bound hand and foot, struggled, raised his hand to strike; and then the fat white face blurred again and became the bristly chin and hawk nose of the tailor.

Night had fallen while he dozed. The train ran along swaying gently, a ship on a dark sea. There was a feeling of ostracism, and of being exposed to peering faces that could not be seen.

Half asleep, half awake, he thought of Maria Tolosa. With a mixture of illusion and clairvoyance, he saw her on a small Turkish steamer, sitting in the steerage holding some bundle of clothes she had got together, lonely like himself and lost. The memory of her as a talented vulgar good humoured night club singer and dancer was overprinted by the memories of her since the bereavement, the tight dragged head shawl, the determination and the bruised face.

Through the rest of the journey he talked and dozed. They stopped two or three times at tiny wayside stations. The Greek tailor talked animatedly to the girl opposite him who, young and pretty though she was, already had the beginnings of a dark moustache. The train hooted and began to slow again.

"I leave you here, *patrioti*," said Cos, breaking off suddenly and speaking to Gene. "In a little while now you will be in Nafplion. Remember the restaurant where I recommended you. And when you want silkcloth like that again. . . ."

Gene shook hands with the tailor and also with the young man and the girl although he had hardly spoken to them. It was all very friendly and homely; the alarms and pursuits of Athens were far away. It had been a feeling he had often known before, as if Athens were a state within a state, having its own frontiers and its own aggressive tin-foil civilisation; outside the city and beyond its boundaries one came into the essential eternal land of Greece, slow moving, warm-hearted, hard, convivial, courteous, sincere. One was already beyond pursuit.

The train stopped and his friends got out. He waved to them through the window. Many people were leaving the train here, and the guard said there would be a ten minutes stop, so he got out and walked slowly along the platform stretching his legs and trying to blink the sleep from his eyes. Another train came muttering in on the opposite platform, a steam train going the other way. The engine had been built by Krupp's, probably for shunting work, seventy-three years ago. The carriages might have come from an old nineteenth-

737

century print. As it shuddered to a stop, doors opened and crowds streamed out, many young people laughing and joking, a few carrying blowers and wearing paper hats.

As they went past, Gene said to the guard of the steam train: "What is it? What has been happening?"

"The festival at Nafplion. It's held every year." He moved on, furling his flag.

"Those police on the platform," said a girl laughing as she went past. "Why were they there?"

"To look after us," said her boy friend, and blew his paper blower in her face.

Gene stood still. There were a lot of children on the train and they were taking a time to be got off. Police on what platform? he wanted to hurry after the girl and ask. But did he need to ask? Like a lump of heavy driftwood in a shallow stream, Gene began to move slowly with the crowd. As he did so he saw two men making for the waiting automotrice. They were not in uniform, but you couldn't mistake them. They stopped at the centre door of the train and one of them drew back and glanced up and down so that he could keep the whole train in view. He had his hand in his pocket. The other man got on the train.

The driftwood, as if it had come into deeper water, began to move more easily with the stream. At the barrier there was a cluster of people waiting to go through, children, black-clad women, boys laughing. It was a toss up—either that way or a dart across the railway lines. But always he had avoided the panic move.

The man at the barrier was snatching tickets as the people went through. There did not appear to be anyone with him, anyone watching. Gene went through squeezed between a fat woman with a basket of oranges and two short-trousered bare-legged boys. The ticket was taken from his hand. He glanced over his shoulder and saw that one of the men who had gone to the automotrice was walking back to the barrier.

Outside the station dim street-lights and a narrow rutted square. Walk in the same direction as most of the crowd. A man in a taxi, seeing him better dressed than most, called out to him but he hunched his shoulder and went by. It seemed a long walk but he did not look round again. Twenty steps to the corner, ten, five. A long street. People were spreading out, this way and that, giving him less chance of cover. A darker street to his right, leading back in the direction of the railway lines. He took it.

33

He got to Nafplion just after midnight. He had walked all the way. In the dark and along the country roads there was little danger; even if the police were sure he was in this area they would not have great forces at their disposal. No doubt the taxi had been found, and at once the police had been alerted along the various routes he might have taken, south towards Piraeus, north in the direction of Levadhia and the main railway line to the Balkans, west into the Peloponnese with obvious attention to the only train feeding the area that night. It was his luck that he had got so far.

He had left his bag on the train. It held nothing of value except the food and brandy that Anya had put in; but for the police, if they identified it with him, it was proof he was in the neighbourhood and only a step ahead of them.

The town of Nafplion was still lighted. He came in along the Tiryns road; cafés were open and music came from one or two. He passed the bus station, where two crowded buses were just leaving, and made into the centre of the town. He had never been here before and had to ask his way. He found the cinema, which had clearly changed its religion, having begun life as a mosque: a few tattered posters hung outside, three photographs of film stars fly-spotted and faded in the sun.

"Constantinos Salamis?" he said to a passer-by.

The first did not hear him, but the second pointed back to a lighted doorway and went on his way trying but failing to walk straight. It was a taverna, bigger than it looked, music came from it as well as stumbling men. He went in and groped a way among smoke and feet and talk and the braying of an accordion; found a seat, slumped into it, for once near the end of his tether. He needed a breathing space and food and rest.

In the middle of a group three men were prancing round one other who, middle aged and thin and bald, was twisting himself into wild contortions and leaping into the air while the audience roared and clapped in time. Everybody had had plenty to drink.

"Sir?" A slim dark young man had come to the table, clearing an empty mug and wiping a dry patch on the table.

"Have you food?"

"No, sir."

"Wine, then. And I want to see M. Constantinos Salamis."

"I am Constantinos Salamis."

Gene glanced at his neighbours. But they were all watching the dance and roaring witticisms and advice. "Mme Lindos has sent me."

The young man bent to wipe the table again. "I do not think we can serve you."

"Why not?"

"We were not expecting you until tomorrow, and—it is difficult."

"I can pay."

"So would we, if we were caught. It is not the money."

"Then I'll go."

"No, wait, I'll bring you the wine."

He went off and Gene stared at the dancers. At length one of them slipped and fell and there was a howl of laughter and applause.

Salamis came back. "If you are hungry there is this cold *katsiki*. It is all we have."

"Thanks."

"And stay a while. This is a bad night. We will see what we can do."

The man who had fallen had sprained his leg and they carried him to his chair laughing and cursing. Then two other men, without much urging from their friends, got up and began to sing an unaccompanied song which seemed to derive, as the cinema did, from the Turkish occupation. It was a love song hung with quavering trills and appoggiaturas, nasal, oriental and sad.

The cold kid, helped down with strong red retsina had a tonic effect. He began to recover, to look around. Salamis came back.

"When you go out," he muttered, "go to the back door. You will be let in."

As soon as he had finished Gene paid his bill and left. This taverna was just the sort of place the police would come to. The sooner he was out of sight the better.

Mme Salamis said: "He must stay here tonight. There is not much risk and we can do no less."

She was a pretty young woman except when she showed her teeth, which were decaying.

Salamis shook his head. "I have seen too much of this during the war to risk it all again—my business, my wife, my baby son, even for Mme Lindos whom we owe so much to."

Gene said: "There's still six hours of darkness. I can be miles away by morning."

"No, do not misunderstand me," the young Greek said. "I will take risks but not by keeping you here. That is too much. Let me think. There are better places to hide."

"It's not merely hiding," said Gene. "I want to get away."

"Oh, I think that is the lesser part. We had begun to make arrangements for that. Carlos has the better boat and he thinks nothing of being away a week. No, it is not that. It is keeping you until tomorrow night when one of the boats has the right excuse to go."

"Let me fend for myself till then. I can meet you by arrangement."

"Was that someone in the shop?" said Salamis. "Wait, I must see." He went out.

Gene looked around him, at the cradle beside the girl, at the low wattage unshaded electric light, at the triptych in the corner with a red-glassed oil lamp burning before it.

"Do not worry," said Mme Salamis. "He will look after you."

"I don't think I want to be looked after," said Gene.

She smiled and went on with her sewing.

Salamis put his head round the door. "It was no one. But wait, I have an idea and wish to telephone."

After a while Gene said to the girl: "Your husband speaks as if you were in the war. You look too young."

She smiled again. "We are Cretans. During the war my husband fought—and then he was captured. The Germans left him and his fellows in the prison starving. I and my friends used to go down and feed them. We met then and fell in love and promised that if we lived through the war we would marry. Afterwards he was taken from the island and then I did not see him for six years. I thought he was dead."

"You must have been very young."

"My husband was eighteen when we first met and I was thirteen."

For ten minutes or so Gene leaned with his head against the wall, half awake and half dozing. It was three o'clock and the lethargy and fatigue had come back to his limbs. He had had only broken and short sleep for the last four nights.

Sounds and memories adhered to his brain like strips torn from a complete pattern; the day's events had been blown to shreds and left only these defeated flags fluttering. The voices in the train, the grind of gears in the old taxi; Mme Lindos said: "You've got to go; the police are coming." And Anya: "Tell me, this fear is not true." "Those police on the platform," said a girl's voice. "My spanner's too big," he said. "I thought you might have a smaller one." He could not find his penknife; there should have been a corkscrew on that. And Anya said: "Take off the phone. Take off the phone, Gene. Take off the phone."

He started up as Salamis came back into the room, his pale sallow sad face expressionless.

"Do you know the town?"

Gene stared at him, then shook his head.

Salamis said: "There is an island in the bay. Bourtzi. You have heard of it?"

"No."

"There is a castle on it. Very small. The owner is away and there is no one there. The caretaker lives near here. I have been to see him. It would be a place to hide."

"You can trust him?"

"Angelos? Ye-es. It is not our way to sell our friends."

"I am not your friend."

"You are Mme Lindos's friend."

Gene said: "Do you know what the police want me for?"

"It's of no importance."

"Do you know that they are offering a reward of 25,000 drachmae for my capture?"

"Money is not everything."

"Thank you."

The Greek glanced at the cheap clock on the mantelpiece. "It is time to go. The moon has set. You will need food and drink for at least twenty-four hours. I will arrange that with Angelos in the morning. There is danger tonight: first the risk of being seen in the streets now, which are empty; second of being seen going out to the island."

"How far is the island from the shore?"

"Oh, no distance. Six hundred metres."

"Then I can swim."

"I hoped you would suggest it."

The girl made a movement. "You should take him by boat, Tinos."

"It was partly of his own safety I was thinking," said her husband. "This is a small town, monsieur, and very little can happen without others knowing of it. The quay will be empty and dark, but I know from experience that we should be lucky if we were not seen using a boat."

"I'll swim," said Gene.

Salamis took a heavy key out of his pocket. "This will let you into the castle. Inside you'll find a bed. Angelos will

743

come in the morning. Now I'll take you as far as the quay."

"There's no need. I'm used to finding my way in strange towns."

"That may be, but it is necessary to know which parts of the quay to avoid. Also, in this case, two men are less noticeable than one."

The girl got up and went to the door and opened it to put an empty tin out. "There is no one about."

Gene got up and held out his hand to Mme Salamis. "I have a feeling that your husband won't allow me to pay him for his help."

"Your feeling is right," said Salamis.

"But you have a child?"

She looked up at her husband who frowned and then shrugged. Gene said: "No parent would deny his son. . . ."

The girl said: "Thank you. If Tinos will allow." She accepted money and folded the notes slowly into a small bundle.

"Thank you," said Salamis. "Now come. . . ."

"It is quite safe from here if you can swim well. Do not lose the key."

"You'd better burn the suit."

"No, no. Angelos will bring it over to you in the morning. He will also bring you word of arrangements for tomorrow night."

"We shall not meet again?"

"I hope not." Salamis's teeth gleamed briefly in the dark. "For our own sakes, I mean."

"Then good-bye. And thank you."

"Down these steps. There should be nothing to run foul of between here and the island. God go with you."

"And with you," said Gene.

He found water at the eighth step, slipped slowly into it and began to swim. The water was quite cold but refreshing. There was no risk of missing his mark: boats and the harbour end stood out clearly in the starlight, and right ahead of him a black hump shaped like a coconut cake showed up between the jaws of the bay. Apart from the harbour light some lights still showed in the town, and there were evidently high cliffs to the east.

A few minutes brought him to the edge of the rocks. He had no difficulty in finding the landing quay, which was just a concrete step running out into the sea; but as he climbed up, a sharp pain went through his stockinged foot and he knew he had cut himself on something.

Twenty yards across a flat sanded surface took him to the door of the keep. He limped up the steps, took the key from his belt and pushed it into the door.

He had little enough energy to look round the place. There was a courtyard and various other doors, one of which he found unlocked. It led into kitchens and then downstairs into queer cell-like rooms with the sound of water lapping close under the windows. In one of the rooms was a bed. He stripped off and lay down on the bed. In a few minutes he was asleep.

34

He woke to the sound of someone whistling. It wasn't a jolly tune but three or four notes repeated over and over again in a monotonous and depressing way. He got up, knowing at once where he was but not realising it was full daylight. He pulled on the clothes he had, which had lost some of their wetness in five hours.

A man was coming down the steps carrying a bag. He was short, square shouldered, red haired and walked with a limp. He didn't seem to notice the eye at the door, but when he got to the bottom step he put his bag down and said:

"Your health. There's clothes here and food. And Carlos will be here for you tonight."

Gene came slowly out. "Your health. What time is it? My watch has stopped."

"Nine o'clock. I'm later than usual, but last night was the Festival, so one is up later today."

The man had a queer neck as well as a limp; the bones were deformed and he held his head as if looking round a corner. Gene bent to the bag and pulled open the string.

His suit and his shoes were inside.

"The food will cost you eighty-four drachmae. Meat is not cheap in Greece today. And there is bread and fruit and wine."

Gene gave him two hundred. "I should not have heard you but your whistle woke me. . . ."

"You slept well?"

"Like a log."

"Just so. Just so." Angelos gave him a peculiar smile. "You a foreigner?"

"Why d'you ask?"

"It says so in the paper."

"I have some Greek blood."

"Ah. But your eyes are too light."

"What about your own?"

Angelos laughed. He laughed silently with his head on one side and his mouth open. It was like a man having a fit.

"The police are looking for you, *koubare*. They've not found you yet. You were last seen at Argos. That true?"

Gene nodded as he got into his suit. He was used to summing people up quickly. Young Salamis had been as clear as day. Not so this man. One was in muddy water from the first word and the first glance.

"Have you looked around the castle?"

"No. I came straight in here."

"Instinct—that's what it was—instinct." Angelos had his convulsion again. "Well, there's nothing to the castle. But I warn you if you move about keep off the skyline, for someone will be sure to notice you, and the police don't believe in ghosts even if we do."

Gene followed the man up the stone steps. Outside the sun was blinding. They were not on view in this enclosed courtyard.

746

Gene said: "Someone is coming for me tonight?"

Angelos looked at him round the corner of his shoulder. "Tomorrow morning. Carlos will pick you up, and I shall be glad to see the back of you, I can tell you; but he cannot do so till the moon has set, which will be at four. You'll see his boat leaving the harbour at sundown. A handsome boat. I wish I had one like it."

"You do?"

"Yes. It's a blue one, and if there's a breeze 'twill carry a red sail. In the night 'twill come back for you. You'd best be ready on the little quay. There'll be no light but you'll hear the engine. Once you're off you'll be in their hands."

Gene walked with the man across the courtyard and found himself limping in company. Angelos looked at him suspiciously and Gene had to say: "I caught my foot on the rocks when I landed." He slipped his shoe off again and looked at his heel.

Angelos twisted himself with laughter. "Sea urchins. They're all over these rocks. They'll give you trouble. Once in they'll never come out. They'll fester and weep. Only way is to cauterise 'em. Red hot needle. Something for you to do this afternoon."

"I can't wait to try," Gene said.

As they came to the outer door Angelos stopped again and looked at Gene over his shoulder like something he'd forgotten. "I'll have to have the key, mind. Leave the door unlocked when you go. I'll come early tomorrow morning and lock up."

"It's a queer place to live."

"Think so? Oh, some people like it. My uncle liked it."

"Was he the owner?"

"He lived here. He was called Angelos too. On the side of the angels, eh? That's what I always say."

"Have you ever lived here?"

This amused Angelos. "No. It was all finished before I grew up."

"What was?"

"This place. You know what it was?"

747

"No."

"I thought not. Some people don't mind. Some people do. Hundreds of years ago it began. This part belonged to the Italians. Venice, you know. Up there, on the cliff, that's the prison, see? They had a hangman, of course, ready when needed. But we Greeks didn't like a hangman in our midst—and a foreigner at that—in the town, hobnobbing. Wasn't nice. And dangerous for him. He'd get his throat slit. See? So he lived here. Lived here for centuries. And even when there was independence, when Greece belonged to the Greeks, they still kept the hangman here. This was his house. And this was where they did the dirty work. That was where the gallows used to be—up there. My uncle was the last executioner. They've moved it away from here now. Pity, for by rights the job would have been mine."

"Pity," said Gene.

"Yes. Comical you being here really, considering what you're wanted for. Very apt when you think of that room you slept in. I suppose you went there just as if you'd been guided."

"Guided to what?" said Gene.

Angelos opened his mouth and laughed silently sideways. "That used to be the condemned cell."

Gene lay in the hot sun, his damp shirt steaming, and watched Angelos row away across the pale water of the bay. Gene was no surer of him than after the first word. He had gone off limping, sly, peering, gusty, lustful, full of slightly obscene laughter, leaving his prisoner where he could get at him any time. There were eighteen hours yet during which Angelos might call at the police station and earn the reward. A sobering thought.

As the heat of the day grew, the prickles in his foot began to throb and he tried to dig them out. The sea urchins clustered all round this island like a second line of defence, evil black pincushions showing through the glass-green water. Perhaps one had grown for every man hanged. Difficulty about getting the prickles out was that they

748

constantly broke, and he gave it up half done to eat some of the food Angelos had brought.

After he had eaten, and with a rag round his foot, he looked over the castle. The island was tiny, no more than a rock jutting out of the bay, the castle a round keep with a central tower, a few dungeons, an enclosed parade yard. He went down again to the room where he had spent the night. It was only six or seven feet above the sea. There were still the marks to be seen where the window bars had been removed. The walls had been re-plastered, and he wondered what scrawls and last messages the new plaster covered up.

It was cool here after the heat upstairs and he felt sleepy again. The bed still bore the impression of where he had lain almost unmoving through the night. He lay down in the same place and allowed his mind to slip back into its preoccupying groove. Everything in his life and future seemed now to be coloured by thoughts of Anya.

Presently he fell asleep.

He got the last prickles out of his foot just before the sun set. He bathed his swollen heel in cold water, wrapped it in a strip of handkerchief and then limped to a point of vantage to watch for his boat. He saw it leave just as dusk was falling; there was a little wind and the red sail was set aslant. As it went out, its engine chugging, it came quite near the island and Gene saw two men aboard. They didn't glance at the island. He watched the boat until it was out of sight round the south headland, then he crouched where he was for another half hour watching the lights winking on all over the town. Some broken cloud had drifted up just before dark, but the moon, now three quarters full, was brilliant.

Dry clothed and rested, he went back to the kitchens and ate some supper. He saved some of the wine for later. He had slept so well that there was now no sleep in him; in any case, although there was still seven hours to wait he could not take the risk of lying down again. This especially so because of the onset of cloud and an increase in wind. If the night grew dark enough they might come for him before his time.

749

Or if the wind grew strong enough they might not come for him at all.

By midnight there was no moon and a light drizzle was falling. The wind had veered and freshened but was still nothing more than a strong breeze. The water slapped against the rocks in little spiteful wavelets as if the castle were a ship pushing against the tide. He wandered occasionally about the place, but after sitting for an hour in darkness in an easy chair in one of the two living-rooms he found the moon cast disturbing shadows, so he went quietly down to the kitchens and thence into the condemned cell. He had six cigarettes left but he would not light a match in case some reflection showed.

Then when lying on his bed in the cell he heard what sounded like a footstep outside. In a quick but silent movement he was up and had opened the door, and for a moment thought he glimpsed some shadow of a figure at the top of the stone stairs. He went after it, but when he got to the enclosed courtyard there was nothing to be seen. Then the door of the cell below creaked as the wind pushed it to behind him.

Thereafter he began a systematic search of the place. Through shadowed rooms constantly lit and darkened by cloud and moonlight he made his way, backwards and forwards, backwards and forwards, watching and listening.

Eventually satisfied there was nothing inside at all, he began a tour of the few battlements, crouching whenever the moon shone, moving again at the next cloud. The drizzle had stopped and shadows were lengthening; he looked at his watch. If they were prompt only another seventy minutes. But they might not be prompt. They might be hours late.

He squatted beside the place where the gallows had been, a cigarette between his lips for company, though unlighted. Maybe the footsteps he had heard were echoes of an earlier time, someone leaving the cell and climbing the stone steps. Through the generations, through the centuries, this island had borne its one-way freight. All had come here for the axe or the hangman's rope: the patriot, the criminal, the fanatic.

Walking courageously, dragged here fainting or screaming, head on block or head in noose. If anything lingered here, an ambience, a flavour. . . .

The moon went slowly down, swelling as it neared the mountains. A great black canopy of cloud stretched almost across the sky, and it was from under this that the moon flung its last light slantwise across the bay and town. The houses climbing the hill on one side were white as if caught in a car's headlights. As one watched, the reflected light faded as the moon was misted by the vapours from the land and turned yellow and then orange.

Gene stirred his cramped limbs and moved to go down. As he did so somebody whistled faintly, a flat two notes, cautious, inquiring.

Not only were they prompt, they were a few minutes early. A Chinese lantern shaped like a deflated football was still showing between two humps of the land. Gene moistened his lips and whistled back.

The boat had come in under sail, gliding undetected across the bay, making use of the breeze and the slap of the sea to come alongside the jetty without even Gene noticing it, though he had been on the alert.

He slipped his heel in his shoe, fastened it, and then padded down the steps to the stone courtyard, opened the great door and stepped through on to the rough gravel approach to the tiny quay. The boat was there and the two men were standing beside it. Gene walked up to them. As he got near he saw the vessel had a short stubby mast, and his eyes, acute beyond ordinary because of the long hours in the dark, saw two other men crouching in the shadow of the jetty.

So Angelos had earned his new boat.

Gene turned to run, to jump off the low rocks into the sea, but one of the policemen, nervous in the dark, stood up quickly and shot him in the back.

35

The small whitewashed room had tumbled down upon him in irregular intervals of consciousness throughout the first thirty hours. Walls moved in landslides over continual precipices that hurt his eyes and his back and left him glad to return to the darkness of the pit. Only in the daylight of the second day did he recognise his identity again and the separateness of movement about him. A woman was with him, an old woman and sometimes a man, inside the cage that the whitewashed room periodically became, a wire fence woven between castle turrets; attention reaching him through it like messages passed into a concentration camp.

At the foot of his bed was a slip of paper that the man sometimes wrote on and then put back, some record of progress or betrayal. The woman washed him and gave him liquid to drink; even her hair was like wire, rusted with streaks of grey. Once he heard what the bearded man said. It sounded like 'he'll do' or 'we'll do.'

Thereafter a period of sleep, and it was waking fully conscious and completely aware of his position for the first time that he saw the bars across his window as the cause of the illusion of the cage. . . .

After that it was dark for a long time, and the unshaded electric bulb hurt his eyes when someone switched it on. The nurse came in, and with her were the doctor and Major Kolono.

The doctor said: "I'll give him another transfusion in the morning. It will strengthen him for the journey. More than anything it's a matter of rest and recuperation now."

"Can he walk?" said Kolono.

"I suppose he could, well strapped up. It's chiefly weakness now from loss of blood. But the obvious thing is an ambulance if you intend to take him tomorrow."

"He's got to go tomorrow," said Kolono, fingering his moustache. "We want him for interrogation."

"I shouldn't advise interrogation for a day or two. It might cause a relapse."

"We want him for interrogation," said Kolono. "It makes very little difference to us whether he has a relapse or not."

"That's just as you say," said the doctor, looking annoyed. "It's my duty to point out these things."

He left the room, but Major Kolono went to the window staring out with his hands clasped behind his back. The nurse gave Gene a milk drink in which some drug was rather unsuccessfully disguised. Then she asked him if he could eat anything and he said he could. When the nurse left the room to get him food Kolono came and stood by the bed. He watched Gene for a while in silence.

"So you are still alive, eh?"

Gene didn't answer. His strength needed conserving.

"The bullet missed all vital parts," said Kolono. "Pity. It might have saved us the trouble of taking you back for trial."

Gene said: "I thought—you would enjoy that."

Kolono took out a cigar and fitted it into a short yellow holder. "It is my duty to tell you that the woman calling herself Maria Tolosa has been arrested in Thessaloniki."

"What? . . ." He was too weak even to pretend. "What are you talking about?"

"She was taken on Saturday as she was trying to board a ship. We have been on the look-out for her, you know. She was seen leaving Heracles House on the night of the murder."

There seemed to be grit in Gene's teeth. He tried to speak but could not. Kolono's words carried conviction, and they carried defeat too, ultimate defeat, turning to mockery all his efforts of the last five days. After this nothing was left, not even credit, not even a justifiable memory.

Kolono said: "Of course it will make no difference. Whatever her testimony may be, we shall make specially sure of convicting you. Whichever of you actually used the knife does not matter. You will be charged jointly. Our taking her won't have helped your case at all."

Through the day that followed Gene gained strength, but it was slow, and in a way it was like the recovery of a very old man: one climbed laboriously back to life only to find that life had nothing left. He had never felt so down. There was a gap in his usually purposive mind, like a rift caused by an earth tremor, across which as yet the usual communications did not reach.

The nurse, who was under orders not to talk to him, told him only that it was Monday, that he was still in Nafplion, in the prison on the hill, and that so far as she knew he would be leaving that evening for Athens. At noon he was able to sit up and eat the meal that she brought him, and from then, almost in spite of himself, his strength came back quickly. During the afternoon he slept a little and dreamed of Lascou's death and the gallows at Bourtzi and of Anya calling to him from far off.

The doctor came in at four and inspected the two wounds in his side. He prodded them a good deal too much and then injected Gene in the thigh. From the feel of things it wasn't the first injection he'd had there. Another official came in and they talked in low tones in a corner of the room while the nurse re-dressed his side.

The slanting sun was falling in through the window, and the bars were shadowed like a prophecy across the floor. The nurse's sunken eyes followed the movement of her hands, which were gnarled and whitened with work, as if they had spent long years over a scrubbing board. She was not good at her job and fumbled and let the bandage slip.

The official was signing something. Signature, gaol delivery, passing of custody, of responsibility from one official to the next; the death penalty still existed in Greece, but life imprisonment was probably as likely; strange if he came back here to serve it; he'd already seen the inside of the gaols of Athens; the Germans had crowded them with offenders; so had the revolutionaries, so had the counter-revolutionaries; it was Mr. Wet—Mrs. Fine during the years after the war. Would they allow him to choose his own defence lawyer? Anya must keep out of this. Contact with him now would ruin her. He must get her word, through Mme Lindos perhaps, warn her she could not help now and must not try.

Major Kolono came into the room and the conference continued in the corner. Presently the two other men left and Kolono waited until the nurse had done. When she too had gone he stayed by the window for a while, hands behind his back in his favourite attitude, the sun glinting on the bristles of his moustache.

Gene waited. Several minutes passed in complete silence. Kolono turned, his face half-lit now, the other half shadowed. He said: "You will leave at seven this evening for Athens."

"Whatever you say."

"Can you walk?"

"I haven't tried."

"I will drive with you personally. Then there will be no chance of escape."

"I couldn't get far at present."

Gene watched the man's regular false teeth gripping the cigar holder. He badly wanted to smoke.

He said: "I don't know if it's any good appealing to your sense of chivalry, Major Kolono."

"What d'you mean?"

"Well, why don't you drop this charge against Maria Tolosa and let her go? She's not much more than a girl and it's me you want really, isn't it."

"It is you we want really," Kolono agreed.

"She saw her own husband killed. She was half crazy with grief. She didn't know what she was doing. Why can't you be lenient with her and concentrate on me? I came to Greece to get Lascou and I got him. Isn't that enough for you?"

"What is enough for me, Vanbrugh, is beside the point. The law of the land must now take its course."

"But you're not without influence. The prosecution might even refuse to believe her story, turn her off without bothering about her. I'm quite willing to make a full confession."

"That you did it?"

"That I did it."

Kolono's eyes were like dark olives freshly moistened. "I wish I could make use of that."

"Can't you?"

"Unfortunately, no."

The spiral of smoke was going straight up. Kolono did not seem to be drawing on the cigar.

Gene said: "Put it to your superiors. It would save time, trouble, publicity. On the one hand you'd have two people in the box fighting all the way; you'd have us both making accusations—it wouldn't help. On the other you have one man with a full confession, trial over in a day, and the Spanish woman shipped off without being allowed to become a nuisance. Don't you think that's worth considering?"

Silence fell.

Kolono said: "Unfortunately I may not consider it. I have another proposition altogether to put to you."

"What is that?"

"What would you say if we offered you your freedom?"

. . . .

Dressed in the now frayed and stained suit he had bought in the Plaka, Gene was helped to the door of the ambulance and got in. He was glad enough to lie on one of the bunks after the effort of getting there; but on the whole his strength was not bad. Major Kolono climbed in and sat on the opposite bunk, and the ambulance drove out of the gates of the prison. It was not quite dark yet but the sun had set.

Gene said for the fourth time: "What's the catch in all this?"

Kolono lit another cigar. "In a few minutes from now this ambulance will stop with engine trouble. While we are stopped you will leave the ambulance and go."

"D'you like it better that I should be shot again while trying to hobble away?"

"It would give me great pleasure to be able to do that personally."

"And that's the arrangement?"

"I am here to tell you the arrangement. Where we stop will be at an inlet on the coast between—well, no matter—at an inlet. A boat is waiting there to take you to Brindisi. Once you reach Italy it will be your personal concern to return to Paris."

"I don't understand."

"Maria Tolosa has not yet been publicly interrogated. But she was privately interrogated by me this morning. She is prepared, under pressure from us, to swear that the man who was seen leaving Heracles House with her on Tuesday night was her brother-in-law, Philip Tolosa."

"Philip To . . . But he's . . ." Gene stopped.

"He is dead."

There was a pause. Gene said: "Do you mean you intend . . ."

"I can promise you nothing absolutely—except your freedom tonight. And that on conditions."

Gene said: "The boy——"

"I am not Chief of Police. I am not the Public Prosecutor. I cannot influence them. But I am in charge of this case, and I will do what I can. On conditions, we are prepared to prove that Philip Tolosa, not you, killed Lascou. It can be done. You are alike in build, figure, colouring. Manos, who was in the flat within three minutes of the murder, and M. Lascou's secretary, are prepared to identify Philip Tolosa as the man who committed the crime. It is a case of mistaken identity by a boy of eight. From there on you will be free."

After a time Gene said: "That may be; it may be possible, what you propose; but I don't begin to understand why you're proposing it. Who is behind this?"

"There are two conditions, as I have said. One is absolute secrecy. You return to Paris and keep your mouth shut. No reporters. No interviews. No idle talk with friends. In no circumstances do you say anything about your visit to Greece."

"And the second?"

"The second is that in no circumstances do you ever return here."

"That's more difficult."

"Murderers can't be choosers."

They jogged along for some way in silence. Gene felt glad for a moment that the conversation had stopped; it gave him time to relate it to common sense, to breathe.

"And Maria Tolosa?" he said.

"That is for the law to decide. If this proposition is carried through, she will appear rather as a witness than as a collaborator. That is not because we care what happens to her but because it is necessary to our case. She might get off; she might at worst go to prison for a few months. Again I cannot promise anything."

"And if I refuse to go?"

"It will be very much worse for Maria Tolosa if you stay, since the need for us to use her mainly as a witness will have disappeared. Just as I have pointed out to her that it will be much worse for you if she insists on telling the truth."

The ambulance lurched and rattled over the rough road.

"Why am I so dangerous to keep?"

"Perhaps you will learn that before you leave."

"From you?"

"Not from me."

"We are meeting someone?"

"It may be."

"Who?"

"You will see now," said Kolono, stubbing out his cigar and putting away the end in his case.

36

The ambulance came to a stop. The driver got down and opened the doors. It was clear that he was a party to the arrangement. Gene pushed himself into a sitting position and allowed himself to be helped out. Kolono followed.

The moon was full. They had stopped in a side road. A low wall bordered it, with pine trees on one side and on the other the sea. Low jagged rocks hemmed in the narrow mouth of the bay. Every now and then in the distance a lighthouse winked. A flock of dark sea-birds was winging silently across the sky.

In the lane a few yards ahead of them an old Buick was parked. Two people were standing beside it. Gene recognised them at once as Jon Manos and Anya.

Getting to her he almost forgot the pain in his side. She did not come to meet him. Kolono followed close behind, and in a minute the four were grouped together out of earshot of the soldier standing beside the ambulance. No one seemed to want to be the first to speak.

Then Kolono said: "Well, here he is."

Manos said: "Do you agree that our part of the bargain is now fulfilled?"

Anya said: "It will be when he reaches Paris."

"Anya," Gene said.

"Is your—wound bad?"

"No, nothing. Why are you here? What is this arrangement?"

Anya's voice sounded tired and hoarse. The colours and tones of their last two days together had quite gone from it.

She said: "I want five minutes with him alone."

Manos said: "Be hanged to that. Get him on the boat."

She said; "I want five minutes with him alone."

"*No!*" said Kolono. "Anything you say must be said in front of us."

After a minute Anya said: "I have made a bargain with these gentlemen, Gene. For a certain consideration they are prepared to see you out of the country. That is all. It is as simple as that."

"I don't understand you," Gene said.

"You did not finish reading the letters from Anton Avra to George Lascou?"

"No, I thought you'd burned them."

"In the haste that first evening I put them between the music inside the piano. After you left I couldn't remember at first—then I found them. In the last two letters there were other names mentioned besides his own. Six names in all. Two are here with us tonight. . . ."

"And?"

"I realised the letters were still not quite useless. I took them to the Bank of Greece. They are now in its vaults with instructions that in the event of my death—or yours—they are to be delivered personally to the editor of *Aegis*."

Gene leaned against the wall. In the reaction and in his weakness the importance of what she said kept escaping him. He would grasp it and then it would slip away from him.

"Anya—"

"Come, we've wasted long enough," said Manos coldly. "The boat is waiting."

Gene did not move. Some machinery of warmth had begun to work, but surrounding it was a block of ice in which all his ordinary feelings were still congealed. He tried to shake himself free of it.

"And what happens to the letters when I reach Paris?"

"They stay where they are," said Anya.

"And you?"

"I too stay where I am."

The birds were winging overhead again, wheeling round as if disturbed in their privacy.

"So that's it," Gene said. "Then I'm not going."

For the first time Anya moved and he saw her expression:

there had been hard bargaining and a hard fight and it had left its mark; in the moonlight her face looked drained of blood but not of feeling.

She said: "It is a fair arrangement, Gene. Otherwise they will not play their part."

"What difference would it make?"

"They do not trust you, my dear. I will stay as their security."

"Come if you are coming," said Manos impatiently. "We are not on a deserted island."

Gene said: "Is there more behind the bargain than this?" He looked at Manos.

Anya took his arm. "There is nothing more. I promise you. Can you not believe that?"

"Normally. But in this this case I . . ."

Manos turned on him. "Listen, man; you're lucky to have had this woman to fight for you! Well, now we *have* fought it out, round a table for five hours, while you were lying in your bed in Nafplion. You were not consulted in this and you are not being consulted now!"

"That's what you may think——" Gene stopped because Anya was pulling at his arm.

Manos said: "For a certain consideration we are prepared to pay. We are prepared to pay by misrepresenting the evidence in this case to make it appear that George Lascou was murdered by Philip Tolosa, who committed suicide on the following day. In doing this we are taking a considerable risk. In particular Major Kolono is risking his whole career. If this goes through you will be free, completely free. But we do not trust you. Once this case is closed we shall have no further hold on you. Well, you have your hostage, these letters. We shall have our hostage, this woman, who has worked in our midst all these years."

"And d'you think I'm willing to get out on those terms?"

"You've no choice."

"If Anya joins me in Paris——"

"If she were to join you in Paris, what guarantee would we have that you would not at once give an interview to the reporters? Your word? It's not worth a spit. *But* if Anya stays here, then if you have any care for her safety, as she says you have, you dare not talk because of what we would do to her. The bargain has been struck. Now get out and never come back."

Quietly but insistently Anya began to move him towards a break in the wall where a path led down to the beach. Koló́no turned to speak to the soldier, and Manos momentarily turned with him.

She said: "Gene, it's the only way. . . ."

"But it's impossible——"

"I tell you it's the *only* way! Later——"

"What other conditions are there? You—Manos?"

"No. I am quite free so long as I stay here——"

Just before the others caught up with them he felt her slip a small package into his pocket. They went on. The moon was still low and the moonlight only caught one edge of the bay like a bar sinister on a crusader's shield. A fishing boat moved quietly at a jetty even smaller than the one on Bourtzi. A man swung along the deck, strap-hanging by various ropes attached to the mast. The sea was quiet.

Anya's hand was on his arm. He held it to him, his mind tingling from the impact of her last action—groping, trying to see its way.

To gain time he said: "And how long has this—bargain to last?"

"Five years, ten years," said Manos venomously. "What does it matter?"

"It matters everything——"

"Listen, Gene," said Anya, squeezing his arm warningly. "We have fought this out and fought this out. You must see their position. Talk from you in Paris would still damage even with no proof. Accusations from me would be much worse. After all I was George Lascou's mistress. Until the election's over they *must* keep us quiet. After that, each month that passes will slightly reduce the harm we can do by talking. As George is—is forgotten, so anything connected with him will have less news value. The letters will always remain just as dangerous for them, but our unsupported word will carry less and less weight. In time—"

"But how much time?"

"We cannot decide that now. But perhaps—though I don't want it—some interval is the right answer for us. In that way we can prove something to ourselves." She stopped. "But that is for the future. I believe, if it is everybody's wish, a settlement can be arranged. They cannot feel safe with the Avra letters still in existence. I might die accidentally and then exposure and ruin would come for them. Sooner or later we can make some arrangement for the exchange of the letters. And part of that arrangement could be that we can come together again—if you are still of the same mind."

"I haven't any other. Believe that."

She said: "It will be for you to choose. . . ."

"If you are going," said Manos, "get on that boat. Otherwise the bargain ends here and now."

Anya said: "Jon, *our* bargain stands. But he must reach Paris in safety. These men will look after him?"

"Of course they'll look after him——"

"I promise you," she said, "if this man dies, you and your friends will go before a military court on charges of treason within a week."

"Here!" called Manos angrily to the boat. "Here's your passenger."

One of the two figures on the boat stepped on to the jetty and came down to meet them.

Anya said: "Gene, write. . . ."

"Writing won't be enough."

"But it will help—for a time. And remember—I have done what I can. It is now for you to choose as you think best."

She had said it twice. He had to answer. Picking every word with care, for every word must carry its message to her and not to them, Gene said: "You must realise that if it comes to me to choose, I am not interested in these men and what their past histories were. They are small fry. George

763

Lascou was the only real threat to Greece, and that threat is gone."

She said; "Yet I have tried to—what is the expression you would use?—to put the ball back at your feet. That is how it should be. Never forget that you have freedom to change your mind."

"Never forget," he answered, "that I shall never change it. There will be no conflict over that. I am not interested in these men."

Manos was listening suspiciously. The sailor took Gene's arm. Gene made a pretence of trying to free himself. But his next words were not spoken in pretence. "To leave you here like this with such men——"

"I have been in the company of such men all my life."

"I know. But there must be some other way——"

Anya said: "If you refuse to go you will be taken on board. This far I am quite prepared to—arrange your life."

The sailor's grip tightened. So did Anya's for a moment and her cold soft lips brushed his cheek. Then her fingers sharply relaxed as if quick now to have done with the moment of parting. He let her fingers fall one by one. Then she was a foot away. Then she was standing between the two men, the moon shining on her face. Then she was one of three figures in the distance.

Gene sat crouched over the gunnel in the stern of the boat. He fingered the Avra letters she had given him but did not take them out. The strong smell of petrol came up to him as the old four-cylinder motor began to chug its way out to sea. A sail flapped above him but as yet caught no wind. They'd gone, the two men, but she still stood there. He raised a hand, hardly capable of the gesture because, whatever the promise for the future, however much through her great courage it might now lie again in his hands, this was for the present a gesture of good-bye. He did not expect her to see it, but she saw it and waved back. Then after a few minutes he could no longer see her figure but only a mark on the beach which would have moved had she moved. He persuaded himself of this long after his eyes could see nothing against the dark land.

They reached the entrance of the bay. The opening was only thirty feet. They slipped through like some slow-moving aquatic animal avoiding the claws of a crab. The sail flapped above his head and the boat listed gently, quivering with a different and more sensitive life. On the port beam a lighthouse winked. A few lights showed here and there round the ancient coast, but ahead it was quite dark.

A hand touched his shoulder.

"Come below, sir," said the sailor. "We've orders to see you come to no ill."